THE BEST OF MEN

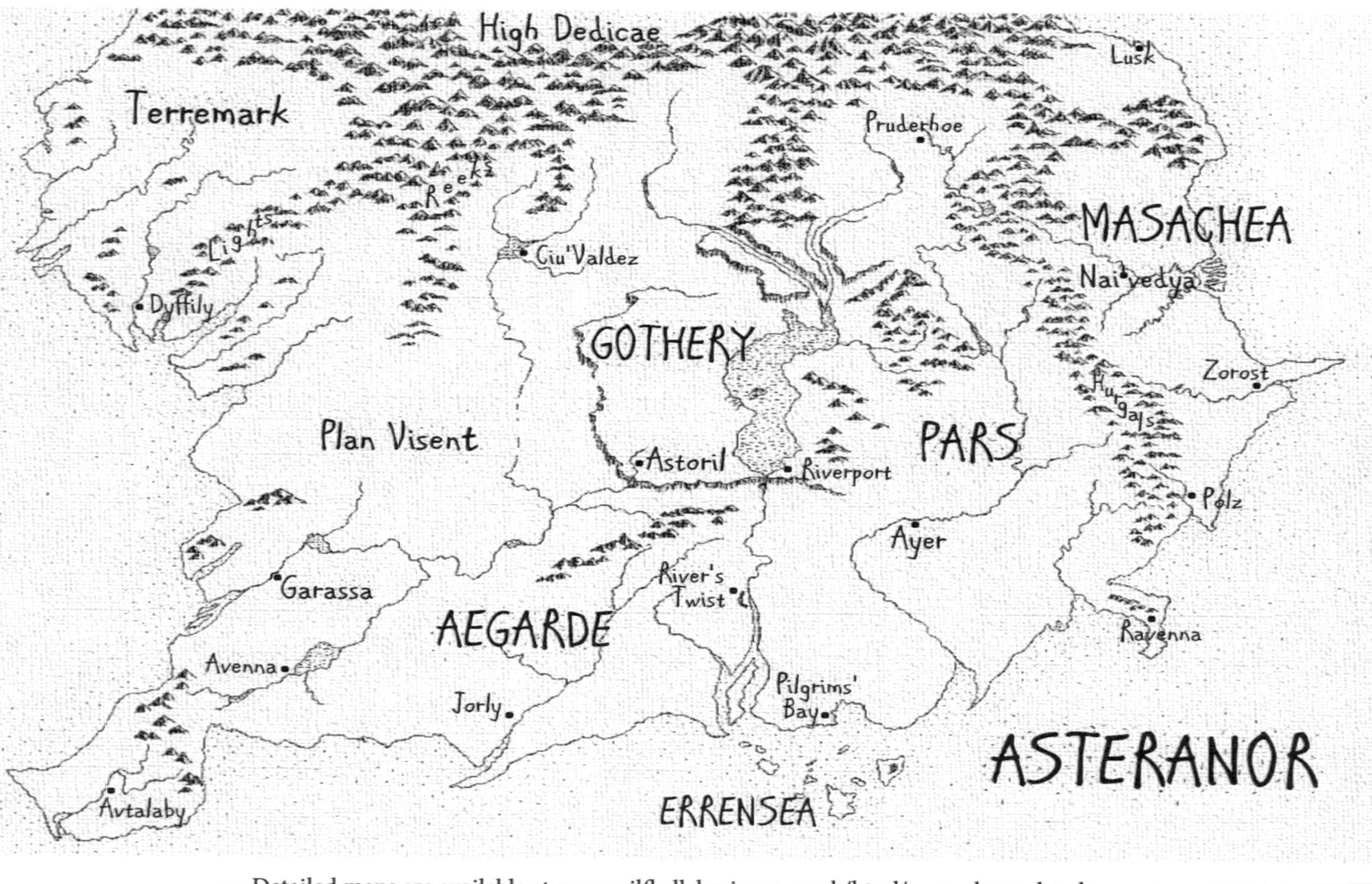

Detailed maps are available at www.wilfkelleherjones.co.uk/html/...

A SONG OF AGES

VOLUME I

THE BEST OF MEN

WILF JONES

Kindle edition 2014 by Sorcerer's Ship Press
First print edition 2016

For permission to reprint or broadcast write to:

Sorcerer's Ship Press*
14 Hambrook Close, Gt Whelnetham,
Bury St Edmunds,
Suffolk IP30 0UX

ISBN-13: 978-0-9570202-4-5

Typeset by Inverse
Cover Illustration by Rowanvale Books

*Detailed maps are available at
www.wilfkelleherjones.co.uk/html/maps_home.html*

*Sorcerer's Ship Press is an imprint of Write Now! Publications

ACKNOWLEDGEMENTS

Mary, Robert and Isaac keep my feet on the ground. Without them I'd have spun off into space and ended up lost and lonely. Fantasy worlds are a fine thing so long as you don't end up living in one.

My thanks also to Write Now! The Bury St Edmunds Writers' Group. Writing a novel is a solitary endeavour but getting it right only happens when other people are involved. If you're lucky an editor who understands your work will cast an unblinking eye over your manuscript, point out the flaws and help you iron out the wrinkles. That option is not open to every writer. Instead, I've been lucky enough to join a community of writers determined to put up their work for rigorous critique. At each meeting comment, analysis, query and corrections come in from all sides, careful as scalpels. With every piece we dissect we learn better how to be critical of our own efforts, our writing improves and the flaws and wrinkles become easier to identify and to fix.

But it's not just surgery. Sometimes, when you get it just right, that audible intake of breath, the stunned silence, the explosions of laughter, the excited babble after you've finished your reading are all the encouragement you'll ever need to keep going, to keep writing, and to aim at perfection.

Thanks especially to George Wicker, who got me singing again.

CONTENTS

Acknowledgements

'The Preface' 1

I

COINCIDENT

'An enquiry into the true geography of Earnor'............................ 8
The Burning Book...11
Visionary 19
Black Company 33
Heartland 45
Disorderly Behaviour...56
Children of the Ruins 67
Blood, Blight and Ballistics..72
Feeding the Fishes..93
Living Legend 98
Living Myth... 111
Kentreth's Grave 125
Isolde 128
Booty..139
Trouble in the Marketplace.. 147
An Extraction 153
A Trip Upriver...157
An Island in the Sun 171
The Kingdom of Halfi..181
Passage 192
Demonography..208

II

INTRUSIONS

The Creation And The Beginning Of Strife.....................226
Tea and Toasted Rabbit.....................228
Found and Lost.....................241
Mixed Reception.....................258
Ancient History.....................272
Baked it Black.....................282
The Siege of Eternity.....................299
Sortie.....................308
Bangers and Mash.....................318
The Sword of Ages.....................326

III

THE EVIL THAT MEN DO

The Gift of Ah'remmon.....................342
Ablutions.....................344
Doctoring Philosophy.....................359
Shopping.....................373
Passing Through.....................382
The Empire of Whojit.....................398
Landmarks.....................416
Miracle.....................429
New Paths, Ancient Landscapes.....................447
Abduction.....................465
'Die, Foul Seed of Demons!'.....................474
Moreda.....................486
Miss Travers and the Sorceror.....................495
Queen of Tempest.....................509
Swords and Sorcery.....................519

Loose Ends..541
Liberation...551
Missing...561
Tumultuous Flight 566

IV
LESSONS IN CONFLICT

Jaganatha 584
Manouevres..586
A Welcome of Sorts 600
Current Affairs...................................... 616
The Ages of the Earth 630
Monsters...646
The Best of Men 656
The End to a Busy Morning.................666
Brink of War 672
First Blood 680
Points of View 690
The Conqueror 700
The Farewell...709

EPILOGUE

Audience 722

'THE PREFACE'

College of Errensea, 3027.2.06

'And there you are, my dearest, only waiting for the touch to bring you to life.'

The bulky figure, silhouetted by the light of the lantern he carried, reached into the opened cabinet. His cautious hand withdrew the slim, calfskin-bound grimoire. He caressed the oiled cover, traced the embossed lettering with a smooth fingertip. The words spelled out in Middle Parsee: *'Majiks Mayoris'*. He tapped the spine with a long, strong fingernail and giggled. 'Such an original and imaginative title! Still, interesting enough I think.' He slipped the book into a pocket deep inside his midnight-blue robe with a profound sigh of satisfaction. It had been so easy. The locks on the library doors had not tested him; the guardian spells were put aside as quick as thinking. He was impatient with their stupidity. To keep such books, so rare and so powerful, in this measly box, and so poorly protected? It was beyond belief. He moved to close the doors of the cabinet but then stopped, listening.

Though all was silent in Holander's Crypt, the intruder, for so he was and a thief too, had become convinced he could hear a noise. It was a small, murmuring, jangle of a noise that shivered his shoulders. He turned to view the narrow corridor behind him. The lantern's glow crept out into the gloom, but there was nothing to see other than the cold marble floor, the towering racks and the tightly-packed books they housed.

He stepped along the aisle. Despite the silence all around the jangling continued. He realised then that the noise was in his mind. *Most peculiar,* he thought. The revelation brought him to a standstill. He looked all around. Nothing seemed out of place. He considered the sensation. If it had been a real sound there would have been a clear direction for him to follow. What about this not-sound? It had begun in the back of his head as he faced the cabinet and then rattled in his temples as he turned to walk the aisle. Now? He spun on his heel, eyes searching the shadows along the way he had come. And there it was: something odd on that lowest shelf a few yards back. He approached and lowered the lantern. There, hemmed-in by lesser peers, stood an ancient volume of enormous proportions.

He cocked an ear. Was this it? Would it call out to him, acknowledge his presence? He gave the game a few moments, and then a few moments more. Apparently it would not. The murmuring, ringing not-sound continued but if somehow the book was involved there was no obvious sign. It stood there, nothing more than one volume among thousands, mute, unmoving, lifeless as a gravestone. *Ha! And silent as a tome! Enough of this nonsense,* he decided, *there is business to be done!*

Seconds passed and became minutes. He did not move a single step. Striving to be beyond distraction, he found himself held by the sheer size and weight and mass of the thing. It was a curiosity. He liked curiosities, and he might never see this one again – what would be the harm in a quick look? Without warning his resistance crumbled. All his attention, all his thought fell towards the book as a body would fall to the earth. Hardly managing to keep to his feet, he bent to examine this fateful attraction. With a fold of his sleeve he rubbed away the grime obscuring the titles. In gold lettering on cracked brown leather ran the promising legend:

Cantaro Aetaticum
En Haslem

'What are you then, a history book?'

He placed his lantern on the floor and knelt, the better to grip and to lever the mighty work off the shelf. It was impossibly heavy and slipped out of his grasp, thudding onto the stone floor and spraying dust everywhere. He tut-tutted his distaste. With two hands he hauled open the cover. The flyleaf had a preface inscribed with green ink:

The intruder chuckled. 'Some people do not know when to stop. What is he going on about this time, I wonder?' He turned some pages and began to read. His Middle Parsee was a little slow and the majority of the names and places mentioned were unknown to him but the words he read tickled his imagination. 'How very interesting, dear Haslem. *The Song of Ages!* Splendid, but did you really mean to write this out for everyone to read?' He shook his head. *So foolish!* He frowned. The jangling was giving him a headache. *And what is the point of this? Surely you didn't want us all deafened?* He wondered how to stop it. Perhaps the ringing would lessen if he moved away from the book. He walked to the end of the aisle but if anything the noise was getting worse. He returned and addressed the book directly:

'Well then, what shall we do with you? Steal you as well?' He sized it up. 'No. Too noisy, too weighty. We were made for each other, this is true, but I would need a donkey to carry you. For now, back on the shelf, I think. If all goes well, and it will, there will be plenty of time later for us to get better acquainted.'

It was a struggle. A fat belly did not lend itself to bending double and lifting heavy weights, and getting the book back where it should be left him red in the face. Too much wine and too much food: it could well be the death of him, but not just yet awhile he hoped – he had far too many plots and plans on the boil. As he straightened he put out an arm to steady himself but his hand pulled too heavily on a loose shelf and several books tumbled to the floor.

'Who's there?' a voice called out.

The intruder's heart lurched in his chest. That damn ringing in his head must have deafened him to everything else. He did not pause to recover his lantern but ran-off as fast as he could manage. Within seconds he had crashed through the grille door of the Crypt and scurried out into the maze of corridors beyond. The flapping of his feet marked his course this way and that but he did not once hesitate. Even in the dark he knew the way fine well. He was making for the exit and the chance of escape. It would be a close thing though, for this was certainly a chase: some way back, and catching up, other footsteps were pounding away.

His breathing was ragged by the time he had dashed up the staircase to the ground floor. At a teeter he clattered through the Great Hall, in the darkness colliding with chairs and misplaced stools, the library itself slowing his pace. As he barged through the main door into the Library Walk his pursuer shouted out for him to *Stop*. The word fell upon him; the command yanked at the muscles in his calves. A lesser man would have fallen to his knees but with only a few muttered words the intruder rebuffed the command and plunged onwards.

A tree-lined avenue crossed the end of the Library Walk. With his lungs fit to burst, and utterly exhausted, he played a last card. He stopped at the first tree he came to, leaned up against it and, just as the other bowled into view, he disappeared.

The other was a tall man wearing a dressing gown and slippers. The intruder observed this interloper through invisible eyes and knew him at once: it was the Wizard Beltomé. How could he have known to leave his bed and come to the library? The man trotted a few yards in one direction and then a few in the other and then stopped to catch his breath. There was only a sliver of moon and low in the sky: he would make-out very little by its light, and yet he stood motionless for a good three minutes. The intruder struggled to maintain his position, willing his enemy to move on, to admit defeat. Instead Beltomé cupped his hands and spoke soft words and a glow that shone red through his fingers became white and bright as the palms spread wide. Almost the intruder moved, quailing from the seeking light. But if he moved he'd be found. He held on to his posture though the rigour of it cramped his muscles.

The wizard, holding his palms before him, searched left and right, at one point passing barely an arm's length from his target, and yet still he did not see. He moved away along the walk, ten yards, twenty and then stopped. The intruder heard him curse softly: there was nothing to be discerned, nothing to be found. Dismissing the light Beltomé thrust his hands into his pockets, and then marched-off at pace over to the faculty house, intent no doubt on raising the alarm.

His quarry waited until he was well out of sight before easing away from the tree to become visible once more. He staggered – to say nothing of the chase, the spell that had made him part of the tree had been unpleasant and painful – but his face was thunderous.

Damn you, Seama Beltomé, he raged inside. *Well, you have had your chance and failed. And you will fail again—*

A pair of blackbirds, roused from sleep, twittered and flapped in the branches above him. Their movement gave him pause and focus. He looked up and smiled, a quick and broad smile to encourage, and he reached out a friendly hand to beckon. The hen squabbled and held back but the cock, with images of worms and grubs filling its thoughts, was seduced by the promise. Dropping onto his benefactor's palm the blackbird tipped his head.

Hah! So eager to come to me, an endearing attitude. Ah, and a fine creature you are, so handsome, so young, with so much to learn.

The bird chattered a little, still trusting but impatient for the food.

It is unfortunate, bird, that you have not yet learnt when best to stay silent!

And then he clutched the poor thing tight in his fist, crushing until he squeezed the life out of it. Dropping the wreckage of bone and blood to the pavement at his feet, he picked the small clinging feathers from his hands. Bereft, the mate, without a chirrup or final song, flew away as quickly as she might.

Assuaged by blood, the intruder, thief, or whatever else he was, master of all he assailed, patted the book in its secret pocket to make sure it was still there, took a deep breath and began to smile once more.

Very soon, Seama, I will be Tap-Rod and your interference will end.

I

COINCIDENT

'An enquiry into the true geography of Earnor'

(an extract from the 'New Introduction to Edison's Geografia' by
SARAYAN, Philemon; Gombret Publications, Astoril 3069)

'*Whatever the world may have been in Ages past we are left now
with four major landmasses and two great oceans.*

'*Sullinor is the greatest continent stretching from the ice lands – the
Adiathemos of the North – down through many changes of topography
and usage into the steamy forests of the lower tropics. It is wide too:
four thousand miles from furthest east to furthest west. It is a land of
great contrast but for all its size and variability the entire continent
is subject to the rule of a single polity: the ar'Andálan Empire. The
Andálans have held sway over Sullinor for so many years that,
outside the Great Collegia, common knowledge of anything preceding
the Empire has sunken into the grass.*

'*Asteranor[1] strays to the east of Sullinor across the Sea of Birds[2].
A less sprawling land, on the whole more temperate and protected
from the Sea of Ice by the High Dedicae: the world's mightiest range
of mountains. The Sea of Ice, a terrifying place of grinding floes and
precarious existence, denies all passage to the northern coastline making
of this an unknown land. Below the Dedicae, Asteranor is home to
the four countries of Aegarde, Pars, Gothery and Masachea. The loose
arrangement of The Holy Isles, independent of the four countries,
rides the currents of the Errensea to the south of the continent.*

'*Oxitor and Oxitor'ulta are named clearly enough for West and
Far West but these continents are largely unexplored by the people of
the Middle and East, the only exception being those four city states of*

---

1 A cautionary note: it is often explained on Asteranor that "Sullinor has the
sun but we have the stars!" however it is worth saying that in Parsee while
Aster may mean star, Aste can mean East; and even more confusingly, Sul
may well mean Sun but Sule indicates southerly and sullin may be translated
as middle. Things are not always as they seem; explanations given within,
whether popular or scholarly, are not necessarily always true.

2 An inadequate name. To give him his due Edison said as much to the
residents of the Kelling Isles, masters of this stretch of sea, but they were
insistent – to the north was barren ice, they said, and to the south the wider
ocean had skies unhindered by the beating of wings. While this was not
wholly true Edison wisely decided that further argument was unnecessary,
the Kellings renowned for their strong opinions and fierce disposition.

the north, recently allied in the face of renewed 'Andálan aggression, and named in their own terms the Tetra-Ka Republic.

'The two oceans are great opposites.

'The Pelagos is navigable in her kinder months, she abounds with fish and bird and mammal, she is decorated by many chains of islands, the chief of these being the Arco Sulli, and is seen by all as the great provider.

'Vastos, covering three-fifths of this world, as far as it can be known, is utterly empty of land, of life or hope of life. The few brave souls who have made adventure on this sea and yet returned have described the waters as corrosive and sterile.[3]

'This then is the object of our attention: Earnor, a world blue-green and full of life on the one side, but grey and dead on the other. Edison's Geografia is concerned exclusively with the living and offers no conjecture as to the nature, origin or purpose of the waste or the contrast between the two. Given the significance of recent events and raised interest in such questions I have made suggestion of further reading alongside the bibliography and index in the latter part of this volume.'

---

3 Their return was invariably a desperate ordeal with the acid waves cutting into the timbers, the spray shredding the sails and the crew dying of thirst, starvation and need of good air. Their ships were so damaged by the trial they were left unfit for further voyage; and the same could be said of the mariners.

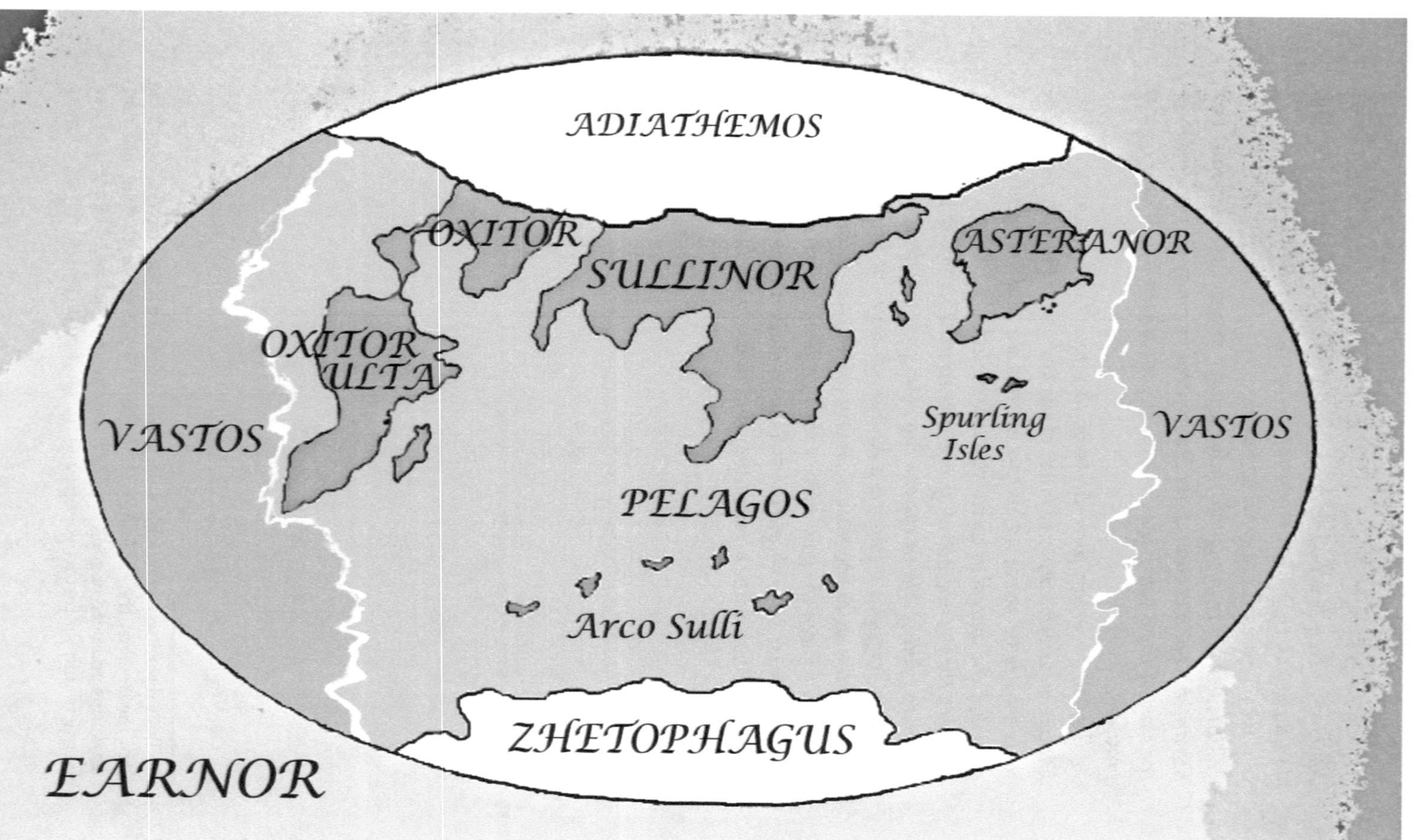

ADIATHEMOS
OXITOR
SULLINOR
ASTERANOR
OXITOR ULTA
VASTOS
Spurling Isles
VASTOS
PELAGOS
Arco Sulli
ZHETOPHAGUS
EARNOR

THE BURNING BOOK

College of Errensea, 3057.6.02

For Seama Beltomé even the beginning was traumatic.

It was a muggy day in June. The students were four weeks away from term end and many were suffering still the annual examinations. Bad tempers, a crowded library, grumpy teachers desperate for the summer break, and now a dreadful, sultry, storm-threatening wind rolling in from the Spurling Sea: this was his least favourite time of year. Thank the stars he wasn't a teacher. The knowledge, the books, the dedication to learning was all fine; the thought of having to cope with whole classrooms of panicking young men and women, completely terrifying. It was hard enough trying to get to grips with his own capabilities. Today the palpable nervousness that filled the corridors and common rooms was so oppressive Seama decided he would be best out of it. He put away his papers, changed out of his gown in favour of more sporting clothes, picked up a duelling sword and made his way over to the lists.

It wasn't far. The College occupied several acres of the land between the City of Errensea and The Quays, the ancient river harbour of the island now made redundant by the more substantial docks of the Eastern Bay. The lists lay alongside The Quays, just behind the Escartine Library.

Lance-work was taught still, though the fashion of war was changing in the world outside, and mounted archery had become popular among the more adventurous students, and so in most months of the year the lists were a groaning place of straining horses, struggling youths and, inevitably, a regular stream of injuries. For the month of June, however, the lists were deserted: a concession to those more modern-thinking educators who insisted that the real work of the College was more to do with the mind than the body, and that martial arts should not be encouraged. Much to Seama's disgust there were now no examinations offered in the art of war.

In the half-covered practice yard was a space given over

to swordplay and that was where Seama found a morose Fox Garner, chewing hard on his sliver of mint twig and crudely, with hammer and nails, fixing new limbs to the battered wooden stroke-stocks.

'Glad to see them gone, Gaz?'

Fox looked up, pleased to be distracted. 'No. I hate this job – bores me to death. Rather be shouting at the kids any day.'

'Better you than me. On either job.'

Fox shrugged. 'Those who *can* do – the rest of us get saddled with all this. Oh I can't wait to retire. Just one more year, Seama, and I'll be out that front gate dancing and singing and I won't look back.'

Seama didn't know whether to believe him. Fox Garner had always seemed so pleased with his work. 'Oh come on Gaz, it can't be as bad as all that. Or can it?'

'Depends on what you mean by bad. You know me. I do things my own way. It's a rough job, a rough study. People get bruises.'

'And the odd broken limb?'

'Only six this year – ha! Pathetic isn't it.' Fox spat out his stick in disgust, clearly disappointed the tally was not worse. Life, it seemed, like his mint wood, had lost its flavour. He whacked hard with his hammer at a protruding nail on the nearest frame.

Seama thought he recognized the signs. 'What is it this time?'

'Waldin's a bloody old woman, Seama, and he's driving me mad! Look, it's my job to make sure they can use a sword properly, not wave it about like a three year old. Make sure they can fight their corner. That's what we're about isn't it? To make them the best they can be? Now how the jiggery can I do that without the odd accident, every now and then? Not as if we can't fix 'em. But every flaming week, down he comes from his fancy office, stands there watching 'em with that snivelly look on his face, and then starts badgering on at me about how reckless I am. And with the kids watching, an'all! I tell you, one more brainless letter from some pansy of a parent about his poor little Algernon and his stupid black eye and that's it, I'm gone. '*Why*

12

can't you just use the stocks to teach them?' he says. I'll give 'im stocks – and not this sort, neither. As if I was hurting 'em for no reason. As if I *liked* it!'

Seama raised his brows at that one. 'Times change, Gaz, people expect us to be a bit more careful.'

'People are getting soft.'

'Maybe,' Seama conceded. 'Things are not so bad these days. We're making progress, Gaz. Well, that's what they say.'

'And who are *'they'* then?'

'Well, all those people who don't have my job to do for a start. And all those people living in the cities who've never seen a sword, still less used one. In fact, all those people we've been spending all these years trying to protect.'

Garner decided to bash at another nail. 'Things get quiet for a bit,' he said, between blows, 'and everybody thinks – *bash* – the world's changed – *bash* – and all the bad things – *bash* – have gone away – *BASH* – it's *pathetic!*'

Seama couldn't help smiling. Fox never changed.

'What're you grinning about?'

'They can't help it, Gaz. They want to live quiet lives; they can't see why it shouldn't be possible.'

'They'll learn.'

'I hope not.'

For all his faults at least Garner's pessimism had nothing malicious about it: he nodded sincerely enough. 'Well I *hope not* too, Seama, but you know I'm right.' He gave a great sigh. 'No, forget it,' he said, 'not worth the bother. Anyway, did you come down here just to lecture me or is that blade of yours going to get some use?'

'I'm hoping. Seems like an age since I last did anything. I need to loosen up, Gaz.'

'Loosen up or sharpen up?'

'Both. Sometimes this place is too straight and too dull for words. I need to get out and about. Things've been far too quiet for far too long.'

'Well come on then,' Fox said, tossing his hammer into a tool-box, 'let's get it sorted.'

It was hot, and the yard dusty, and the pair of them needed pints of water to get through, but at least it was action. They were playing best of nine – hits on the breast-plate that was. Both were skilled enough to make sure the hit was a knock-back without being heavy enough to cause damage. Most of Garner's students would have been terrified by the apparent ferocity and speed of attack. Three – two to Garner and a clever feint and twist gave him a fourth but when the point of his sword snaked through and caught Seama low on the right, his opponent swung away as if he'd been pole-axed. Garner backed off expecting some sneaky ploy.

'You'll not catch me like that Seama,' he said.

But it was no ploy. Seama dropped his sword and clutched at his temples.

'Gods above,' he cried, 'That damn well hurts!'

'But I hardly touched you.'

Seama stood erect. He shook his head as if trying to get rid of water in his ears. The most peculiar sensation had gripped him. A sudden knowledge of danger mixed with a calling impossible to ignore. And he knew the source immediately. He had been called once before and the memory of the compulsion had not left him. But so strong was the summons this time, so strident, it rattled in his head.

'You alright, Seama?'

'Yes, I… uhm… Oh, not again! Look Gaz, I have to…' He bent to scoop for his sword but changed his mind. 'I have to go!' he yelled and took-off at a sprint, leaving his weapon lying in the dust of the yard and his friend utterly bewildered.

People swung out of his way as he pounded along the pavements aware that if they did not move life would not seem so good. He was projecting a warning even as he ran. He took the steps of the library entrance three at a time, charged through the vestibule and as he reached the Great Floor he was shouting out for Holander and Grek to follow. Hurtling down the ancient steps to the lower stack he collided with a couple of dawdling students, their papers spewing everywhere – he didn't stop to apologise.

By the time he reached the grille door of the secure area he could hear Holander clattering along behind, a predictable stream of unpleasant oaths tumbling from the chronicler's lips as he ran.

By now the summons was shrieking inside Seama's head. The problem was close and critical. And yet this time there was no one there: Holander's Crypt was locked. Seama used his key, crashed open the door and raced through the aisles, desperate for release. At an intersection indistinguishable from all the rest he flung himself to the floor and kneeling, passed his hands over the cold marble in two wide arcs, drawing a circle about him. The stridor filled his head and made it difficult to concentrate but he knew the formula well. As he spoke the words of the spell, rather loudly, he bent forward and touched the floor with his forehead.

'They're safe!' he announced. Holander and Grek had caught up with him. 'No one has touched them.' The Great Books were no longer kept in a cabinet visible to the naked eye. The Council had learned a lesson some time ago and now the key works were held in a place both within the library and yet removed from it. The mystery of how to gain access to these perilous volumes was a fiercely guarded secret.

Seama staggered to his feet, head in hands. Those few words were as much as he could manage. The shrieking sound was now intolerable.

'So what's going on then?' Holander demanded, 'What's happening Seama? Seama?'

The wizard had begun to sway. He knew it must be here somewhere. He lifted an arm and pointed back the way they had come. The other two turned to look and then staggered as one of the shelves just beyond them exploded into flames. The shrieking stopped. Free at last, Seama plunged forwards into the billowing smoke. Reckless of the danger he sank his hands into the fire to reach for the book that was burning. He tried to block out the heat, repel the fierce flames, restrict the damage, but his calm had been shattered by the racket in his head and he didn't get it right. The flames were fierce, rapacious, grasping. The sleeves of Seama's shirt bloomed in a ball of fire, the pain hit him like a hammer. He collapsed. Holander and Grek wasted no time. As they hauled him away, Grek produced a spell that drenched the wizard's clothes, she doused too the huge book that lay beside him. Holander gripped Seama by his shoulders.

'Are you alive, Seama? Speak to me!'

Seama coughed and spat. Ashes from the reeking fire hung in the air.

'Yes, yes,' he gasped, 'I just… ahh… just fainted. I think. I'm fine; fine.'

'Well you don't look fine.'

He did not. The practice breastplate had been some protection but the chemical flames had ripped through his sleeves and collar reducing them to clinging cinders; his neck and shoulders were blistered but it was the state of his left arm that shocked them.

'Gods Seama! It's unnatural. How could it burn so hot? That'll never heal.'

Seama looked at the blackened and mutilated limb in some alarm, appalled by the scale of the damage. He tried joking about it.

'My technique must be better than I thought: I can barely feel a thing.'

'Never mind the technique, you've burnt the nerves. You wait till you start growing them back, then you'll feel it.'

'You have a splendid bedside manner, Holander.'

'Look at this,' Grek interrupted. She was examining the book. Most of the pages had burned to ash, the remnant a soggy mess. With delicate skill she had begun already the task of ex-spelling the water and had managed to peel apart the first few pages without causing damage. 'It's something of Haslem's.'

Seama looked up making his vision swim and roll. He was very nearly sick and yet…

'Let me guess: something called The Song of Ages?'

'Can't tell you just now, Seama, the cover boards are wrecked and the title page is half gone but it's Haslem's hand, no question.'

'It must be the Song.' Seama had no doubt. 'Don't you remember, Hol? When the 'Randálan tried to become Taprod?'

'That was quite some time ago, Seama, thirty years or more.'

'Was it?' Seama was surprised. Sitting on the floor, struggling to kill the nausea that threatened to overwhelm, he glanced up at the concerned face above him. Wrinkles were deep around Holander's eyes, his hair was white and only a hint of black stayed in his beard. Thirty years indeed. Seama grimaced as a wave of pain from the better arm rolled over the numbing spell that was meant to contain it.

'We're going to have to get you to the infirmary Seama. I've called the Master. Let's forget about the book.'

'That's what we did last time, now look at it.'

'We were a little busy weren't we? He stole the Mayoris if you recall.'

'Of course I do!' Seama couldn't help snapping as the pain got the better of him once more. 'I've burnt my arms not my head!'

Holander grinned. 'You are human then?'

Seama smiled ruefully. 'Yes, Holander: as human as the rest of you, and just as easily distracted. If I'd gotten round to reading the book the last time it called—'

'But I thought it was the Mayoris summoned you.'

'So did I then, but now I'm not so sure. You remember how we found The Song?'

'Not sure I do, Seama.'

'It was sticking out too far, the dust had been knocked off it. That's what I thought. It just seemed out of place. But what if I was meant to find it? It was definitely The Song calling me today.'

'Well it won't be calling you again,' said Grek, 'Best part of it's completely destroyed. I'll get started on rescuing what I can, no doubt of that, but you won't get much. What ah… what was it about?'

What was it about? Seama hadn't found time to read it. The distraction had been a serious challenge to the power of Errensea. The Song of Ages had been re-shelved and then forgotten once more. It didn't seem so important at the time.

Greteth
Coldharbour
Hannayford S.C.
SKIRT
Dreffield
Altiparedo
Slaney
SADDLE
Fletton
Tumboll
SEGYLLIN PART
Banya's Harbour
Astoril
Riverport
Ripon
Moreda
Mulhacen
HUECCA
Ayer
MISIN PART
River's Twist
Barrasford
MATAGORDA
Misinmouth
KNOT ISLAND
Pilgrims' Bay
Brist
Lindis
Errensea

VISIONARY

Escartine Library, College of Errensea 3057.6.29

'Senile tommy-rot!'

That was Holander's considered opinion. Statement made, he continued on his way with Seama skipping to keep up.

'Tommy-rot?'

'That's what I said. Nothing more than that.'

'This is Haslem we're talking about, you know.'

'Yes, yes, you're right, I'm sorry: senile tommy-rot and no style.'

Seama couldn't quite work out whether Holander was being serious or not. Of course, anyone might read The Song of Ages and count it as *tommy-rot* very easily. Over the course of the last few weeks, in-between sessions with the healers, Seama had set himself the task of reading and re-reading every page, half-page or scrap Grek managed to recover. After drying, most of the sheets had been too brittle to hold and so Grek had her scribes indexing and copying till their heads ached and their wrists were sore. Grek would eventually have done as much for any damaged text in her precious library, but Seama's obsession inspired her. Luckily for the scribes, of what was once a mighty volume less than one hundred pages remained. Seama carried a copy with him now, clutched to his chest with his bandaged left arm.

Struggling through a great deal of pain, the wizard had found his chosen task frustrating. With the conclusion and biggest part of the argument gone what he had left to work with seemed confused and nonsensical. The main body of the text left to them was in the form of a narrative history but clearly owed more to myth and legend than recorded fact. Taken at face value the words he read told the story of a Constant War, the curse of mankind, as it was in the beginning and how it progressed through time. The most recent events described were remote and strange and unknown. There were peoples, races and civilisations with names Seama had never heard. He was not completely sure the events described had occurred on this world he knew. He was not completely sure this was anything more than a tale written to amuse the author and confuse the reader. And it failed to delight. The structure was ungainly, the prose unremittingly dull. If the Book had not called to him so insistently, Haslem the Great or no, Seama would have left it to the ministrations of Grek and her students.

The only part that had any impact was the introduction. For all its confusion something in the words held him. Little of the discussion was specific. It spoke of old gods, of good and evil, of the never-ending strife between the two; it talked about The Ages of the Earth as though there were more than just the one; it pointed out key events of each of these Ages but in such a haphazard fashion it was difficult to be sure what came before and what came after. And yet there was something in it. There were names given that made him feel uneasy; there was a truth implied he could not quite grasp.

Holander couldn't see it at all, he couldn't feel it.

'Not only bonkers,' he continued gleefully, as he pushed past a knot of students congregating inconveniently at the rear exit to the Great Hall, 'but dull as last year's accounts. Honestly, Haslem could be writing about mayhem, murder and the end of the world and I'd still rather boil my head than read him. In fact, according to you, he is talking about the end of the world and how it already happened! I must have been busy or something and missed it.' Holander shook his head in utter denial. 'And you wonder I think it rubbish!'

Seama found it difficult to argue with Holander on either point. The dullness was indisputable – mostly based in the confusion – and the complex jumble of themes and facts was maddening. But it couldn't have been *tommy-rot* or anything like it. Haslem was the greatest scholar and wizard Asteranor had ever known: powerful, dedicated, astute and unfailingly serious. Well, according to his biographers anyway, but then they were a dour bunch themselves. And it was a thousand years ago at that. Fashion, style and literature had moved on. The biographers close to the events of his life, contemporaries or near-contemporaries, were themselves now lost in the past, with only their words about Haslem remaining to prove they had ever drawn breath. And they were men who knew their place, respectful and careful, mindful of their duty to conserve and glorify the Great Wizard's achievements, to record his legacy for the generations to come – not very likely then to have concentrated on Haslem the man, on his drinking, his jokes, his womanizing. If, in fact, he ever indulged in any of those habits.

'Can you see Haslem as a boozer, Hol?'

'What are you talking about?'

'You know, 'just as human as the rest of us.' Prone to bad jokes and heavy nights.'

'What, you mean like you?'

Seama laughed. 'Bang on the nail! No, I could never be like that but I know plenty who can. Take my friend Angren—'

'I'd rather not. Anyway, the answer is no. I suspect Haslem was a lot like you really are – and that's not flattery by the way.'

'Hm. That's probably what I think too. So the thing is, do you think I would write down anything *you* would call 'senile tommy-rot.'

'Well, no; but you're not senile yet.'

'I don't think Haslem ever became senile. I think this little book here might well be the worst piece he ever put together but that's only because his subject is incredibly complicated. Trust me, Hol, he was deadly serious; I just wish I could understand what he was getting at. After you.'

With his good arm Seama pushed open the swing door leading off the first landing of the main stair. They had come down to the Upper Stack, a mezzanine floor installed several hundred years back, between the Lower Stack and the Great Hall of the Escartine Library. That was one of things Seama liked about libraries: they couldn't help but grow and grow and that meant learning went on and on and there was no ending to it. An invigorating thought. But this continued accretion, accumulation, aggregation of the academic bricks and mortar of the College was hard to control and difficult to house. Even now there were plans in hand to build out behind the library back towards The Quays, using up a portion of the land given over to the lists – another cause of dispute between Fox Garner and the Master.

'I hate this floor.'

'Is that why you always keep to your Crypt?'

'Could be, Seama. But then again, I don't like it groaning away over my head either. When I'm up here I always think I'm going to fall through the boards, and when I'm in the Crypt I'm worried the whole lot will come crashing down on me.' Holander eyed the aisle ahead. The mezzanine quivered before them. It would be impossible to advance without ancient joists moaning a protest, creaking a complaint. 'I'll be glad when we can move the collection and rebuild the whole thing.'

'Don't hold your breath, Hol. I think Waldin's got other things on his mind just at the minute.'

Holander's head snapped round. 'What makes you say that?'

Seama tried to hide his surprise at Holander's reaction.

'Oh, nothing specific. I found him this morning worrying that the whole College was falling apart. Muttered something about the drains, I think.'

'Oh. Yes. There's always something. You coming through or are you just going to stand there?'

'Well, fine, yes.' Seama stepped through the doorway, letting the heavy door swing shut behind him, but then stopped, realizing he didn't know where to go next. 'Holander, you won't mind my asking but what are we doing here?'

'Ah now, seeing as you're so determined to have me think there's something in this damn book, I thought it about time we found ourselves some proof. And I figured that if Haslem's discovered some hidden history of the world we've somehow forgotten about, then probably someone else discovered it before him; perhaps even lots of people. He'll need to have found the information somewhere. And so, Seama, my lad, we're off to the *antiquities* and you're going to be doing an awful lot of reading. How's your Ancient Medean?'

Seama pulled a face. His Ancient Medean was rusty to say the least.

'Are you punishing me for something, Hol?'

'Not at all, Seama – I'm trying to cure you.'

'By locking me up with the Classics? Well if it doesn't cure me at least it'll bore me to death and that'll be an end to it. Couldn't we get a few students down here instead?'

'Would you trust them to find what we need?'

'And what do we need exactly?'

'Corroboration.'

'You make it sound like a crime's been committed.'

'Now then, Seama, we've already had words about Haslem's style…'

Oddly enough Seama found his task more rewarding than he expected. Once his brain accustomed itself not only to the grammar and lettering of the ancient Medeans but to the rhythm of their syntax and the style of their story-telling he actually began to enjoy himself. Better than that, Seama quickly discovered details in some of the older texts that he'd already seen referenced in The Song. Perhaps Haslem's much derided style had emerged from over-long exposure to these same classics. Seama couldn't help picturing Haslem sitting at his desk, one thousand years ago, in the library of Banya's Palace in the new city of Astoril, struggling with his translations just as Seama struggled now. How many weeks and months had he given to his task; how many blind alleys had he been led along; how many incomplete passages had driven him into a rage? And yet at last Haslem must have found what he was looking for: something to give order to his thoughts and body to his theory – but what? There were elements from disparate texts Haslem seemed to think important, but in sum the picture they gave of a history unknown to modern times was fragmented and frankly unbelievable. It was nowhere near enough to satisfy Holander's quest for proof. It wasn't enough even for Seama. What were they expecting, one key text to give them all the corroboration they needed? There was little chance of that. But as the days passed, while the Chronicler became yet more sceptical, and indeed scornful, the wizard became convinced the fault lay not in the absence of proof but merely in their lack of comprehension. The quest consumed him – he ploughed on undeterred.

When Grek ushered the poor man into his work room, the audible grumble of disapproval Seama produced was not really intended for Waldin's secretary. The gripe was simply a measure of his sudden frustration. Seama was aware of the irony even before the secretary began to speak but it had nothing to amuse him. For months now Seama had been desperate for Waldin to find him something useful to do, something that could relieve the boredom, something that would get him off the island for a while. And here it was at last, Waldin calling him to an executive meeting ordered by The Council, no doubt with some mission in mind. But why did it have to be now?

The frustration was still evident when he reached Waldin's office.

'You wanted me?'

Waldin was far too experienced an administrator to let bad behaviour put him off whatever he wanted to say. He sat behind his, to Seama's mind, overly large desk, in his large but only just large enough chair, and greeted Seama with a careful smile.

'Welcome, Lord Seama. Good of you to come so promptly. Very helpful, indeed.' Sometimes Seama found the Master's clipped tones rather irritating. 'How is your arm now? Septuagem has been telling me your recovery has been nothing less than astonishing – for which we are all, most certainly, grateful.'

The healing had gone well. Exceptionally well, in fact. There was general amazement. Seama's unprecedented ability to accelerate the growth of new tissue had all the professors in the school of medicine jumping in excitement. They were less than happy when he refused to let them investigate the process, and simply would not believe Seama was as confused by the phenomenon as they were. He could only suggest that the power within him had recognised a need to be ready for action. *Something* surged through his veins, obliterating the dead tissue and setting a fire in the cells of each nerve, muscle and tendon; the heat of it could be felt by anyone passing nearby, and in a darkened room his arm seemed to throw off a nimbus of blue light that no one could explain. It was all hugely uncomfortable yet somehow felt right and good. In a few short weeks his arm was whole again, the skin unblemished though still hairless.

'It works well enough, Waldin. Thanks for your concern. I take it you need me fit.'

Waldin looked offended.

'Genuine concern, Seama. But yes you are right, we have a problem. Marat, could you ask them to come through?'

The secretary, now on the other side of a thick door, acknowledged he had *heard* by ringing a small bell vigorously. He had none of Waldin's finer abilities. It was only a minute or two, during which Waldin got up and started to pull chairs closer to the desk, before the secretary led them in.

Sight was pasty-faced and blind to his surroundings, moving slowly under Holander's guidance. Holander shook his head slightly at Seama's unspoken question and favoured Waldin with a disapproving look.

'He shouldn't be out of his room, Waldin' he growled, 'You know that. Not when he's working. To ask him to come down for a meeting—'

'Actually, I asked if he might attend.'

Two others had entered the room, the foremost of these smooth-voiced Aiden Peveril, current Leader of The Council, cool and collected as ever but at least apologetic.

'We needed to know what he has seen but I was not aware he was still in contact. Will this cause him pain?'

'Distress, at the least, to be moved. Just now he doesn't know he's here.' Holander gently eased his friend into the security of a big leather armchair. 'It is not a comfortable thing to be so far away from yourself for so long. This has been going on for hours now.'

Waldin gave them all a somewhat sheepish look. 'We will look after him when he returns to us, but meanwhile we have matters to consider. Seama, may I introduce Gosbert Lanvers. He is our—'

'Our man in Astoril. Yes, we met a few years back.'

The fourth delegate was a lanky sort, clothes bespattered by recent travel and still sporting great riding boots as though he was ready for the off as soon as the meeting was over. Seama thought he looked a little uneasy.

'Gosbert. Good to see you. You're not often in Errensea.'

'Thank you, Lord Seama. No, this is only my second visit. It's a… a wonderful place.'

'But full of strange and scary people.'

Gosbert managed a laugh. 'I suppose I should get used to it. We don't see much in the way of magic back in Astoril. We're more to do with machines and engines than enchantments and… Well I don't know what.'

Seama smiled sympathetically.

'Unknown territory for you, I understand. But our 'magic' is not so different from your science and mechanics. There's room for both approaches.'

'And need for both too,' Waldin wanted to get things moving. 'Gosbert brings us news of one sort but it has taken him a long journey to bring it; Sight can give us detail with less delay. Aiden, will you begin?'

Peveril took his seat and indicated that others should do the same.

'Some of the time I think the issue rather clouded and complicated but actually it is all really very simple. Late last night a final piece of information was brought to us by Gosbert here. There was an emergency meeting of the Council. Whether because we were all tired and wanting our beds, or because the answer to our debate was very clear we came to a quick conclusion. We need to act and we need to act now.

'You will all know that Mador is fighting battles out in the East of Pars, has been since March. We consider the situation under control. Five of the King's armies are more than enough to contain the problem. Why the Sirdar should want to continue his attack is hard to fathom. The garrison at Aristeth was overrun more competently than ever his troops have managed before, and that's strange enough in itself, but in the general run of things after such success he'd surely have withdrawn, point made. We know he uses the dispute as an exercise to blood new recruits: when they are decimated he brings the remainder back – he believes it gives Masachea an army of battle-hardened warriors – but there has never been any suggestion he might want to go further than that.'

Seama stirred in his seat.

'You didn't bring us down here to talk about the Sirdar's brutalities. What has this to do with Astoril?'

'Well, you would think with Mador so busy in the East he wouldn't be much interested in the West and yet two weeks past the King ordered the armies of Anparas and Temor to barracks just north of Riverport. Rumour was abroad that Jemenser had begun to requisition ships and supplies for an expedition. Up until last night we did not know why.'

'And how is it I didn't get to hear about this?' Seama directed the question at the keeper of the Chronicle, who gave him a wry grin.

'Apparently you had too much on your plate already, Seama, what with your injuries and your studies. That right Master?'

'Yes it is.' Waldin seemed peeved that Holander felt the need to confront him. 'Seama's health is much more important to me than you suggest. Until we knew more there was no need to trouble him.'

Seama considered Waldin's face for a moment and then decided they were being unkind. Waldin carried a great deal of responsibility both as Master of the College and Chief Officer of the Council, and to be fair he handled both of his jobs better than anyone else could have managed one, Seama included. He nodded briefly.

'Good point. I was, and am very busy at the moment. So, Gosbert, what news did you bring?'

'I got the information from Fel Awdrey,' Gosbert began, 'But to be honest the situation wasn't a secret anyway. Ever since King Sirl fell ill the Prime Minister's been trying to promote this ah… 'Open Government' thing – basically it requires the Cabinet to put everything before the Assembly before they can make any sort of decision. As far as I can tell, all it means is that nothing gets done very quickly.'

Seama nodded. 'You'll find Sirl's keen on the idea too. He insists it goes back to the Founding but somehow got lost along the way. Not everyone's so enthusiastic though. Some people think all this fairness and openness will lead to disorder.'

'Well I'm thankful for it – it's a lot easier gathering information.'

'And the information *is*…?'

'Aegarde is threatening war.'

'War? With *Gothery*? Has Agwis gone mad?'

Waldin intervened. 'As it happens, Seama, yes he has. Or at least that's the story his odious son's been putting about. Sight believes it's a lie and actually Agwis is under house arrest. We suspect drugs were used. The Aegardean Senate seems to have accepted that Agwis is demented, dangerous even. They made Athoff regent and Athoff, now exactly where he wants to be, has sent an ultimatum to Sirl and is currently busy raising an army.'

'But the regions won't go for it, will they? Not for a war with Gothery, there's too much trade at stake. What does this ultimatum have to say?'

'Well Seama,' Gosbert leapt back in, keen to tell the story himself given he had travelled such along way to tell it, 'It's all to do with The Black Company. They're criminals, a hundred or more – almost a small army – and led by four *sorcerers*, if you can believe such a thing. Past month or so they've been raiding villages in the Skirt – over on the Aegardean side of the border, just north of the Saddle if you know it?'

Seama smiled and nodded. 'I think we're all familiar with the geography.'

'Well I'm not sure Athoff is. He's decided these raiders are based in Gothery.'

'Ridiculous. What do they do: swing down the cliffs on ropes? Utter nonsense.'

'Exactly. But Athoff's looking for an excuse. He says that if Gothery won't do anything about this Black Company, then Aegarde will. Either Gothery pays reparation and executes the ringleaders, or Athoff'll bring an army into Gothery and see to them himself. It's all a ruse. He's been making a case for claiming-back the plateau for months now – keeps bashing on about how Banya stole the land from Aegarde to start with.'

'But that was more than a thousand years ago – and it's not true anyway. Banya bought the land with The Oath.'

'Well you may know your history, Seama, but there won't be too many who'll care to remember it. Not on the Aegardean side anyway. 'A thousand years of insult' he calls it. What with all this new violence and terror, he reckons now's the time for Aegarde to put things right. He's been making speeches about it up and down the country. Not that he's any real interest in history of course. What he's after is Gothery industry and know-how and the wealth that comes of it. He's had enough of Aegarde being the poor neighbour.'

'For national pride he threatens war? There you have a measure of the man. But does he really think he could win?'

'Well that depends on the size of his army and how Gothery can respond. Sorry, a bit obvious. What I mean is Gothery's in a bit of a state just at present. It's hard to explain why, but people aren't happy, not with their bosses, not with the authorities. We're having real trouble just trying to keep order. There were riots in Dreffield last week, machinery wrecked, looting. Of course they sent the army in and it may be they were a little heavy-handed. I'm ashamed to say there were some deaths – I'll not say murder, as nothing's been proven.'

'But this is terrible, Gosbert,' Waldin put in, clearly upset, 'One cannot deny Gothery has a history of public dispute – the remonstrations, the rallies, all common enough. But riots Gosbert? How has it come to this?'

'Well that's the mystery isn't it? Everywhere you look there's something going on. All sorts of different complaints to start off with but all leading to the same result: trouble on the streets. It's become the fashion of the day.'

'What's the government to say about this?'

'Not very much, Seama. The general idea seems to be that if they ignore it for long enough, things'll eventually settle down.'

'Great plan. And what are they doing about this ultimatum? Ignoring that too?'

'Mostly they're just arguing among themselves. And that was the point I was trying to make. With the country in such a mess, and the government all but paralysed, well, it's all good news for Athoff's chance of success. He'll be reckoning up just now how few soldiers he's going to need. Ten thousand? Five thousand? He must think he can win quite easily.'

Seama took a moment to think it through. Athoff's end of it could wait a while. In Aegarde building an army was a long process. Nothing could happen very quickly. In the East, however, Mador Bhadrada was not so handicapped. The King of Pars had standing armies to command and he wasn't the sort of man to ponder his options for too long. He would not be happy with the thought of Athoff Ringsøyr some day soon sitting on Sirl's throne in the Palace of Astoril; and he'd not be at all happy with the thought of ten thousand Aegardean soldiers sitting easy on ground only the breadth of the Hypodedicus away from the Medean Part. It seemed very obvious to Seama what the Partain King would do.

'To secure his own borders against a possible threat from Aegarde, Mador's going to invade Gothery first.'

'That is how the Council see it,' Peveril agreed, 'We expect there to be movement before the end of the month.'

'Now look, I don't want to sound overly dramatic,' Waldin said, 'but we are on the brink of disaster. Unless we do something, and soon, the whole continent will be at war: Masachea on the Partain border, Athoff threatening everyone from the west, and Mador, no doubt reluctantly, planning to take Astoril before the month is out. And right at the centre of it all Gothery: fine, innocent and vulnerable Gothery, likely to suffer most. We cannot have it gentlemen. Gothery is the future we need; Gothery is the progress we have been nurturing for a thousand years. We need her intact and independent and strong, and not some plaything of chaos.'

Seama was both surprised and impressed by the passion in Waldin's words but he wasn't so sure of the analysis. 'Chaos?' he said, 'You use the word as if it could explain everything. I don't believe it. This is no coincidence. It is strategy, from one end of the continent to the other. Though for what, or for why or by whom, I cannot think.'

'Coincidence or strategy,' said Peveril, 'it makes little difference. The Council has decided it will take action. And the start of it is keeping Mador within his own borders. That achieved we may then turn our attention upon Athoff and the Aegardean succession.'

Holander, who had been listening silently, more concerned with Sight's seeming agitation as he twitched and shivered in the armchair, spoke up at last.

'That's just the way The Council always thinks. It's all politics: how to keep things stable; go in at the head of government, control the state and the state will control the people.'

'You speak as if we do these things for our own benefit.' Peveril was annoyed. 'What should we do? The people of Asteranor need peace first and foremost – it is our job to provide for that.'

'That's not what I mean. What are you going to do about this Black Company? Leave them to get on with it while our lot are ponceing about in Garassa and Ayer? Chattering with Kings and ministers isn't going to get anything sorted. We need to get our hands dirty.'

Aiden looked as if the notion of 'getting his hands dirty' was something deeply unpleasant and to be avoided at all cost. 'We cannot solve all the ills of the world but we will give thought to the Black Company when Sight has spoken. Help can be sent. For now what is important is setting Seama on his way—'

'But what about the book?' It burst out of him. As Holander and Aiden crossed swords Seama had become distracted. There was a feeling building in him much like the head-spinning, gut-wrenching urgency the summons had provoked a few weeks ago, but all of it hung upon the word *strategy*. In that moment Seama understood they were missing something vital, that there was something critically important he had to do. He had no idea what it might be but was strangely convinced The Song of Ages held the key.

Waldin pounced as though he had been waiting for the

objection. 'The book is a book, Seama, nothing more than that.' Waldin looked around the room, challenging them all, 'Does anyone here think Seama's book more important than acting to prevent a war and all the despair and agony that will bring?'

'It's not my book, Waldin, it's Haslem's. The same Haslem who created Gothery in the first place. The same Haslem who more or less invented this notion of progress you hold to. The same Haslem, just in case you've forgotten, who gave us our greatest spells. From what I've read so far, Waldin, the Song of Ages may well look to the past but Haslem's message is all about that future you've been looking for. Our future. We need to find out what it means.'

'Really Seama, the book has been sitting on a shelf in the library for nearly a thousand years – what makes it so important today rather than yesterday or five years from now? We have work to do. Mysteries can wait.'

It was so annoying. Seama felt as if he might explode like a Besma Ball. Obviously there was sense in what Waldin had to say but he just knew it was all wrong. Something about the Song screamed out for attention and nothing the Master could say would quiet it. 'Look Waldin, the book wasn't burned a thousand years ago, the book didn't summon me five years from n...'

'NO!'

It was Sight. He had thrust forwards, his hands gripping the arms of the chair white-knuckled. 'You cannot!' he cried, 'You must not!' He stood abruptly, quivering in outrage, his eyes fixed on a horror they could not see, sudden tears pouring down his cheeks. 'No!' he demanded; 'No, no,' he sobbed. He pushed blindly away from Holander's reaching arms, staggered across the room as if trying to run away from the pictures in his mind, and then with a final wordless cry he collapsed. What Sight had seen had been too much. Far too much.

BLACK COMPANY

Huaresh, Eastern Valdesia (The Skirt) 3057.7.18

'You must keep them quiet. You must! I can't do anything about the noise you're all making.' Signoren Bassalo tried hard to keep the panic from his voice but there was so little time. Another baby began to skrike and several of the smaller children were whimpering. 'Andras, I'll have to start now or they'll be on us before I get a word spoken. You'll have to do something about the noise. Get the babies under the stage at least.'

'I'll try, Signoren, but won't it make them cry all the more?'

'It's what can be heard outside that counts, not in. I have to go.'

Andras nodded. 'It's the only way. Do it right for us, Signoren, we know you can.'

The Signoren could think of no reply. He shrugged, took one last look at the women and children and the old men all crowded into the spaces between the tables and benches, cast his eyes over the children's pictures that covered the walls and then quickly hurried out through the front door.

Outside the schoolhouse everything seemed as normal. It was a pleasant summers' day of blue sky and high, white cloud. His newly painted cottage over by the brook looked prettier than ever: pink walls, climbing honeysuckle, a multitude of flowers bright in his garden. Further on was Claudia Bera's tiny white house with its weedy vegetable patch. He'd been meaning to get the children to help her tidy up a bit: she was at least eighty now and marvellous for her age but some things were beyond her. Not that she'd admit it. They more or less had to frog-march her to the schoolhouse. 'No black devil's having me out of my home,' she declared and would have stayed put if they'd let her.

Of course there was no one in the village street that curved away beyond the white house. Up past the smithy at the top end a handful of young men had been set to let fly some arrows and then run off into the trees as fast as they could. Deeper into the village the others were hidden up between the houses on the forest side, behind sheds and water-butts, or crouching in the long grass along the brook's edge; maybe forty all told. According to Serrio and his brother, the Black Company had left Ardache on the road for Huaresh more than two hours past. The brothers had ridden hard while the Company had dallied but still they could not have gained more than an hour. The last report that came in only five minutes ago said at least thirty frighteningly well-armed men were barely a mile away, looting the Gunez farm. When they tired of doing that they would come. Old man Gunez' face when he heard the news was black with fury, his sons were cursing.

Time to get on with it. He couldn't start the spell too soon: every minute he could fool them before his strength ran out would be important. He could manage three hours or maybe a little more. All of the wealth of the village had been spirited off into the woods with the able-bodied or was hidden here in the schoolhouse. It would be hard to find. The cottages and houses, emptied of anything worth stealing, deserted by their owners, would be no use to them. They might set fires but surely they would leave.

The Signoren walked briskly to the rear of the schoolhouse and climbed rather less briskly up the rickety bell tower he'd had built twenty years before. Of his fifty years a full twenty-five had been spent as teacher to the children of the village and of the woods and fields for miles around. He helped out with some healing along the way whenever old Carva's herbs wouldn't do the trick but he hardly ever had cause to use his power. The schooling of Errensea had made him half a wizard but he was never comfortable with magic and had mostly abandoned the art. There was something about wizardry that made him feel isolated when all he had ever wanted was to be a part of everything.

And now the 'everything' he so treasured was under immense threat. A gang of cutthroats had been terrorising the region for almost a month now and today their path of violence and destruction would lead to his beloved Huaresh. From the top of the tower Bassalo could view the whole village. He could make out the young archers standing in the shadow of Rudy's workshop, could see the white, chalky road disappearing under the cool arches of the Twelve Oaks Inn. The beer barrels had been broken less than half an hour before at Andras' insistence. They must give the Black Company *nothing* to stay for. Some had argued they should let the Company have all the loot it could find while the people hid safe in the forest – but that had been tried before. In Reno, in Perdesh, according to reports, the Company had not been distracted by the lure of property. Their first intention and delight was all in killing and torture and destruction; the blood-hunt had merely fired their enthusiasm and ferocity. And that lust gave Andras the basis of his plan. They would give the Company someone to chase and they would try to make it seem the village had been abandoned. The men who would be doing the running were mostly confident their woodcraft would see them clear and safe. The women and children and the infirm could not run and so they would have to disappear from sight. And that disappearance would be down to the skills and strength of a fifty year-old half-wizard who had not tried anything so difficult for more than quarter of a century.

It was an uncomfortable perch, squeezed in beside the bell, but he had to put discomfort to one side. He began with an exercise to clear his mind. There was no room for doubt or fear; he must box up his memories, his emotions, the distractions of his body, all of his hopes for the future. All he wanted inside his head was the schoolhouse, the field alongside and the words of the spell he intended to use.

The schoolhouse was at the edge of the village, the road curved away from it, the brook circled behind. If the schoolhouse had not been built on this field no one bar the farmer would ever walk there. If he could hide the schoolhouse from common sight they would all be saved.

The noise of cheering or jeering from the other end of the village reached him. He began the chant.

It was so important to keep it going, to make sure the words never varied, to release his power into the spell in a steady trickle. Too much too soon and they would be lost. And at the same time he mustn't let the boundaries wander: a shimmering in the air would draw attention; the edges must be clear and exact. He knew the schoolhouse and the path to it so well after twenty-five years, he knew the field beside it. He would overlay the one with the other.

'*Em'moreth il faro, an faro en dahar,*
Ancul le'avo en tra'are, io'tra'are en dahar.
Em'moreth il faro, an faro en dahar...'

Power and the direction of that power was the basis of this deception. There were simple tricks that could be done with mirrors and with hidden doors. The fairs were full of them. Such trickery could not work here. Bassalo created this illusion from within himself. He had to use the Language of Command to bend the power he held inside; it was the power within him that bent the light others would see.

Em'moreth il faro, an faro en dahar,
Ancul le'avo en tra'are, io'tra'are en dahar.
Em'moreth il faro, an faro en dahar,
Ancul le'avo en tra'are, io'tra'are en dahar.
Em'moreth il faro, an faro en dahar,
Ancul le'avo en tra'are...'

He stumbled over some of the words at first and found it difficult to establish the rhythm. Rhythm would be his friend, rhythm would give him the spell word perfect for as long as it would take. After the tenth pass it was there: the spell established, his concentration absolute. All he knew was the spell and the image of the field. His eyes were closed to anything that might be beyond the image. His ears were dead to the sounds below. There was only the spell and the image.

If he'd been able to see he would have seen the young lads let loose their flurry of arrows and miss their targets because of the fear that took them. He would have seen one of the lads stumble as he ran for the woods. He would have seen that young man hacked to death and then beheaded. If he had heard the screaming and then the laughter of the man who carried the boy's head on a pike, terror would have consumed him and whatever hope the village still had would be on a pike too.

The Black Company had come to Huaresh.

'Hold back, you nancies! Hold back I say! You can get those pretty boys later. Let's see what else we've got here first.'

Morgan Trant pulled himself up in his saddle. He wasn't a big man and the extra few inches and the straight back helped them to ignore the fact. They were a rabble of mercenaries, robbers, murderers and rapists all very handy with their swords and fists and dicks and there was not a single one of them he'd trust not to stick him one if he lost control. But they were his for now. They were having the time of their lives and they knew Morgan was the one who kept it all coming. Semmento and the other three gave them their chance, that was fair enough, but sorcerers were not captains or generals. Without Morgan to martial them the Black Company would fight like the rabble they were and, soon as you like, they'd all be dead.

'Right lads. A bit of order! Hoggy! Get rid of the head, you'll be needing that stick-knife soon. If I've got it right there'll be more of them. Could be on either side. I want you to take your lot down the brook there. Mart and his'll foot it house to house. They'll come running Hoggy, so try not to miss any this time.'

Hoggy grinned a leery grin and gave him the finger.

'And you, you tosser! Rest of you stay up just in case they've a surprise for us. Well, get on then!'

Morgan liked to watch. He was good with his sword, imaginative when it came to hurting people and free enough with his own dick when there was something sweet on offer and he had a bit of privacy. But he liked to watch. The taking of a village was a scene that never galled him. The brutality on the one side, the pain and despair on the other was a drama that filled his dreams. It was a drug to him, he wanted excess of it. And yet the watching, the need to witness the perversity of others, a perverse act in itself, gave him an excuse. It wasn't *Morgan Trant* committing the atrocities the Company revelled in, he was merely the professional general tasked to deal with a group of men who were exceptionally vile. He had more than half-convinced himself he was a decent man in a difficult situation. This ability to deceive himself helped in the deception of others.

Duke Torgrim had liked him, saw him as hard but fair, loyal and keen to please, a 'foreigner' whose allegiance to the Kellinghalles was to be celebrated and rewarded. The problem Morgan Trant had was that the reward he'd been given for betraying his own people – the so-called 'foreigners', the Cymrais, who had held the land of the Terremark for thousands of years before the corsairs of the Kelling Isles had decided to settle there – had been a position he liked well enough, but there was little in the way of the wealth he so desired.

He had been made Torgrim's gaoler. It was his job to drill the bad men and turn them into tough but expendable foot-soldiers, another weapon in the Kellinghalle's never-ending war with the self-styled Men of Oak. The fact that most of his prisoners were Dyffili Dross, 'foreigners' themselves, distinguished from the Men of Oak only in that they had no higher purpose to their villainy than blood lust or the hope of monetary gain, was not seen as a problem: these men would butcher their mothers and rape their sisters if they were allowed. Indeed some of them already had by the time they came under Trant's control.

Without doubt he was he eager to please but the loyalty was all a sham. It seemed to Morgan Trant he'd been given a golden opportunity to progress, though not in the way the Duke intended. Trant certainly trained them well enough, taught them to fight as a unit, taught them to obey commands, but from the outset the commands were his alone. This gang of cutthroats would be Morgan Trant's personal army and the Duke would live to regret the day he had promoted a Cymrain.

The King in Garassa had a warrant out for Trant and his army. They had a warrant out for Gaspar Semmento too. The irony of the situation made Trant spit with frustration. Originally he had been Semmento's employer. He had needed a major distraction. The Duke's army was busy in the north of Terremark but the Dyffili Militia were still on hand and a good seventy of them were set to guard the Duke's treasure-house.

The demon Semmento had called, crashing about in the central market place, was just the distraction Trant needed. Half the militia took off to fight the thing, leaving the way clear for him and his lads to walk in, spill a lot of blood and take as much gold as they could carry. Five years later on with half the men hunted down and dead, most of the gold either taken back or spent, and with Trant still on the run, Semmento had found him again with a tasty proposition and a fresh heap of gold to get them started.

He built himself a new army. A few of the Dyffili Dross were still free and worth finding again but the major part of his new force came from the sinks of Garassa: a place that attracted the lowest of the low, condemned by their poverty, and the highest of the high, happy to abuse the former, and those who stood between committed to exploiting both.

It was a good company he had by now, well drilled and vastly more experienced in the fight than any force they might meet. Unless Duke Valdez got off his bony arse there'd be no one to stop them. And he couldn't see that happening so long as they kept to the plan. These small villages and towns of the border country were virtually independent communities with little connection to the horse breeders of the Valdesian plain, even though the collectors of Garassa had parcelled them together. They were good, decent, hard working people who paid their taxes without a fuss but saw no need to offer allegiance to the Valdesian Duke. Allegiance is a two-way thing. They were proud of their prosperity and proud to be free but they had no army to defend them. For the Black Company they were easy meat.

Mart was having a feast. They'd flushed out a dozen already. Five or so had got past Mart's men and one of those had managed to give Hoggy the slip, and there would be words about it later, but otherwise the killing was routine and functional. The brutality displayed was not so far as vicious or inventive as it would become when they had a little more time but everyone knew there was a job to do first. The lads were becoming quite professional. Either that or they still had bad heads from the night before.

There was a shout from Hoggy. All of a sudden three of his riders were down and a good fifteen village-men had legged it into the trees. This lot were obviously not as stupid as some they had come across. Armed only with half-bows, rabbiting knives and pig-sticks they had fought their way through sword, mace and spear and hurt the Company in the process. There would be punishment for that.

'Trant!'

Just then the sorcerer Chaldonie and his so-called guard came trotting up past the smithy. Good, that was another ten for him to play with. He ordered the twelve he had with him off to join Hoggy's troop making them seventeen on horse to chase fifteen on foot. Mart could carry on checking out the rest of the village while Morgan himself would stay with the new arrivals. Chaldonie expected a certain amount of attention and Morgan Trant was wise enough to make sure he got some.

Chaldonie refused to travel without a guard to keep him safe. He rode between two columns of five as befitted a man of his stature. Trant laughed at the thought. Chaldonie's physical stature was the weediest, most pox-ridden in all Aegarde. And he was certainly insane. The problem was he had *power*, wizard's *power*, and he was devilish quick with the demons too. Many were afraid of what he might do and even Trant was a little wary.

'How are we in this... *place*, Trant?'

'This *place* is Huaresh. *We* are very well. Well, I am! How are you? Bum still sore?'

Chaldonie spoke no words in response to the captain's irreverent jibe but his eyes flared. They were pink in the pupil and very bloodshot eyes, and utterly alarming to anyone not used to them. They did not alarm Trant but after a moment's thought he decided to play the game.

'It seems the villagers have all gone apart from some stout lads who are trying their best to slow us down. I can't imagine we'll have too much trouble catching up with the rest of the village. Then the boys can have their fun.'

Chaldonie grimaced in disgust. 'They are so bestial,' he said.

With a shrug Trant tried to give the impression he was equally disdainful and completely detached from the worst excesses of his men, but Chaldonie was too caught up in his own concerns to notice.

'There's nothing for me here then?'

'No, I think—'

Just at that moment a volley of arrows sang between them, and although they missed both Chaldonie and Trant one of the guards was pierced through the neck. A party of the villagers had turned back, emboldened perhaps by their escape, and were trying a little more shoot-and-run. It was a mistake everyone might regret. Chaldonie was not to be attacked.

As the horse bucked beneath him the sorcerer screamed out words of a hideous tongue and the spell he made was like a knife through canvas. The air before them shook as though exploding and then ripped apart, the colours of the world severed by a vast and menacing blackness. The edges of this wound in space throbbed as a hollow roaring surged through the gap, and then, blundering out of darkness into the light of day, came the most extraordinary demon Trant had yet seen. This one appeared to have no head or eyes. Instead it had five limbs, each of equal length, joined together with little in the way of a torso between. It reminded him of a starfish except that the limbs did not taper but were more like the legs of a giant elephant, and that the legs seemed to be made of jelly, and that this creature was something like twenty-five feet high or wide from toe to toe. As it cart-wheeled down the high street, in a spray of who knew what, the awful lesion hanging in the air shivered shut, leaving the world whole once more. Trant heaved a sigh of relief. The opened door always unnerved him. One demon displaced was bad enough!

'Couldn't you get a better one?' he snapped at Chaldonie. 'In fact why did you bother?'

Chaldonie glared at him once more. 'I was under attack.'

Meanwhile the monster, seemingly oblivious to its location, continued to whirl about leaving a trail of destruction in its wake. The limbs battered and smashed through wood and brick and stone. Mart's men ran for their lives.

'What use is this?' Trant demanded.

'I think you will find the demons scare people,' said Chaldonie.

'Damn right they do; they scare me too. We were doing just fine without this one.'

'And yet I was nearly killed!'

Morgan screamed in fury and frustration. 'Mart! Get your men back on their horses and get after those bowmen! And you, Chaldonie, I want you to sort out that demon before there's nothing left for us to take. Look at it!'

They looked. The creature had reached the end of the village and there was no saying where it would go next but as they watched something very odd happened. As it crossed the field boundary it completely disappeared, as though it had ploughed into a river and sunk beneath the surface. A disappearance in itself was nothing unusual and Trant presumed Chaldonie had merely found a new way to send it back to wherever it had come from. But no, somehow there was an almighty crash and lots of screaming and there it was again, inexplicably battering through a large white building Trant would have sworn wasn't there half a minute before. In panic people emerged from the wreckage: women and children, women with babes in arms, and old men trying their best to save them.

'The buggers!' Trant cried. 'That's a new one. Chaldonie, get rid, we don't need it anymore. You've found us what we came for. And here come the boys, right on cue.'

Chaldonie, smirking in triumph, glanced back along the road. The clattering of hooves under the arches of the inn confirmed that the main body of the Black Company was here at last. The demon, splashing about in the brook by now, affecting neither villain nor victim, had done its unwitting work and so Chaldonie, with a casual gesture, sent it back into the darkness.

Morgan Trant meanwhile looked on with satisfaction as the boys with many a whoop and a cheer began to run down and take whatever size or shape of quarry took their fancy. All tastes would be catered for. With Morgan, the trick was in choosing which assault would be the most exciting to watch.

Bassalo could not close his eyes.

His body was transfixed twenty feet above it all on a splintered shaft of wood but his sight was transfixed by the horror unfolding below. He was not in pain as a remnant of his trance stayed with him blocking out most every feeling, dulling any expression of emotion. The trance would fade over the next hour or so, the feeling would return and the agonies would begin – if he had not bled to death by then. Death would be something to hope for. He knew this was true. He knew this because his eyes were obliged to see everything. He saw Andras punished by amputation for having dared to attack the attackers, his torso strapped to a post in the middle of it all so that he could watch the rape of the village. The Signoren saw all his little girls and boys abused, children he had taught to read and write and draw, to value nature and understand the seasons, to run and to play as though the world were a normal place. He saw their mothers tortured. Through the years he had taught them all, helped them to be happy, given them the confidence to face the world and enjoy their lives. The world was now a different place: a land of torment and cruelty and terror. In the field, in the gardens and commons, and on the village highroad that had brought to them this day only villainy and disaster, the savagery continued without remorse. What was once ordinary had become hell.

His eyelids refused to function. Try as he might to gain some respite from this appalling scene the muscles failed him, they would not shut. His eyes were doomed to shift from one thrashing nightmare to the next until the rest of his body failed completely. Finally, hopelessly, he let his gaze rest upon the chaos just beneath him: the ruined schoolhouse, a desecration much less painful to witness even though it represented the destruction of his entire life's work. Gone were the desks, the settles, the chalkboard, all were in shards and splinters. Gone was the creaking stage that had supported a thousand nascent performances for mums and dads, aunts and uncles through all the generations. The platform had collapsed in on itself and...

And what was that?

Another crime to torture him?

On her side, lying still, a young woman and, nestled close at her breast, bloodied yet, the cord cut and tied but still trailing, a naked new born babe. Amelia Verdasso it must be. She had been overdue, the women had been fussing about her as the Signoren had left them to climb his tower.

His eyes watered. Unable to blink away the tears he found it difficult to focus. One arm, the lower arm, had curled around the infant but the other was twisted and broken behind her back; her neck was bent at an impossible angle. She must be dead. Surely she was and yet, barely registered through the blur of his tears, had he not just seen the briefest movement?

Uncontrollable hope surged through him, battering aside the paralysis of the trance. No matter his position, skewered at the top of this shattered tower, no matter the whooping violence all around, no matter the utter despair that sought to drag him to his grave, amid the ruins something moved. Down there, shielded by the devastation of all he had once been, a heart was beating. The understanding of what that could mean flooded his thoughts. If there was life then there was a chance that not everything on this desperate, evil day was lost. Deep inside him this wild knowledge of hope brought with it sudden, unlooked for strength.

Without a blink he wished away the tears; without a blink he made sure of what it was he had seen; without a blink his eyes witnessed a miracle.

Amelia's lower arm had fallen away, *pushed* away by the infant's thrusting limbs. The child had lost her nipple. He was determined to have it back. Instinctually, arms and legs and body working together, he inched across her chest and would not be denied. Down there, hidden from the view of all but the gods of the sky and one ruined man, a newly-dead mother gave suck, and her newly-born child clung fiercely to the life she was giving him, and he would not let it go. How he struggled!

Bassalo could not close his eyes but, for all the torment they had endured, he knew that now for a blessing.

HEARTLAND

Proud steps, echoing deeply, set the woodland flowers a-shiver; her whinny quivered the tall trees. She was a bay warhorse of remarkable weight and strength, livery of green and gold hung with tiny bells and tassels, her bridle and empty saddle wrought of chased leather. Dressed for a pageant she was power incarnate prettied to be less frightening.

On a whim she cantered; for a lark she ran fast, bells shrilling. Abruptly she charged off the greenway, clattered through the trees, splashed through a brook and burst onto the road again. Like a foal she frolicked among the woody paths of Pars' heartland, far from danger, far from evil. She was safe and free and her heart was full.

Almost free: a tender slavery ruled her. Even now she heard his call. It was like a whisper, it was like a kiss. He was ready.

The glitter deep in the forget-me-nots gave him away. Armour aflame in the high sun he struggled with the pans and bags and other gear, all to be hidden up for the onward journey. Seama was now less than a mile from Ayer; noon would see them climbing the river bluffs to the ancient castle: there seemed little point in taking the bedding.

The wizard looked up as the charger neighed her approach.

'Rested then?' he asked and she nodded in agreement. He grinned. 'Now who's a pretty Bellus?' The tease provoked a snort of disapproval. She did not like the decoration and didn't care who knew it. 'What can we do, Bellus? The Court will have its way.' Seama was sure Mador wouldn't care if he turned up in night-clothes but there was etiquette to be observed, and even the King had to bow to that. Ayer was an ancient citadel, a seat of great power on this continent, demanding of respect; should Ayer require a degree of pomp and pageant then a degree of pomp and pageant is what she would get. Even if that did mean dressing up in armour elsewhere considered old-fashioned.

'Heavy arms, Bellus, and a breastplate and greaves too – I'm a beast of burden. And speaking of such, what shall we do with The Mule? Leave him here?' Bellus snorted again. Seama laughed. 'Yes let's. Safer that way, he'll only cause trouble. You should have seen him when he got rid of the packs! You should have *heard* him! No, we'll let him wander. He's far too noisy for the Palace.'

As though in response to his words a raucous braying arose from a beech thicket close-by, but the owner of the voice came no nearer.

'Stay then!' he called. 'Come on Bellus, we'll get no better.'

It was a habit of the wizard to talk to his animals as though they understood him.

His road to Ayer followed a route through the calm woods and farmsteads of the Misin Part, a beautiful if un-dramatic country. Seama was a son of the wind-blasted Isle of Athel in the Errensea, more at home with a raging ocean and tall cliffs than this carefully maintained and utterly predictable parkland, and yet there was something irresistible about the place. This was the home of the Partians; they had fought to protect it through sixteen hundred years of trauma and conflict. The desire of generations had carved the landscape into something comfortable, green and fat, inviolable as a matron, immune to change. Seama's home with its salt-stinging winds and craggy littoral was so far removed from these surroundings that he felt suddenly, achingly out of place.

Seama's role in life was all to do with protection. Whenever the Council saw fit, which meant often, he was sent out to solve problems, to offer support, to protect the vulnerable. So what was the point of sending him here? If anybody *needed* his help right now it was the villagers on the Aegardean border. Mador certainly didn't need help, just a kick up the backside and a stern warning, and anyone from the Council could have done that.

'It has to be you, Seama.' Peveril had insisted, 'Sabresten and Melchiot are in Polz by now, making for Nai'vedya – we *have* to know what the Sirdar is planning next.' Gow Sabresten and Otrom Melchiot were key agents for The Council, men of authority, easy to trust and powerful too. 'What with that and the group still up at Aristeth we are a little thin on the ground. And besides, Seama, *who else* would Mador listen to if not you?'

Seama had not taken it lying down.

'Look, Aiden, the question that really needs answering is who else should be sorting out this Black Company? You heard what Sight had to say about them. They are an abomination. Packing me off to Ayer adds five days to my journey. A lot of people could die in that time. Waldin, tell him.'

Waldin had been uncomfortable with all of this ever since Sight's outburst and subsequent report. He wasn't the cold fish some thought him. And yet he did not hesitate.

'We all share your impatience, Seama. If I had the power… if *we* had the power, if *you* had become Tap-Rod then, perhaps, we could have done something immediately. As it stands we don't even know where they are. Whether it is shock or something else, the fact is Sight has lost the ability to track them. So, I have sent messages to Roar McAndre and Colm Peveril. They are already at River's Twist, much closer to the problem than we–'

'Roar and Colm? No disrespect meant to you, Leader, but your son isn't twenty. Waldin, you must know he's far too young for a mission like this. And Roar McAndre, he was a great force in his time but–'

'Seama, to you everyone is either too young or too old: it colours your perception. The rest of us are not so well blessed in our governance of age. A blend of experience and youthful power, rarely available in one man, is what we need in your stead.'

Waldin strayed between compliment and criticism in his argument and though niggled Seama took his point, 'And that's why you think the pair will work well together.'

'It is.'

'Well I think it's asking for trouble.'

'We'll see. However I'm not sending them out to *fight* the Black Company – that will be your job. Their job will be to locate this foul crew and gather information. Knowing where to find them will more than make up for your days lost in Ayer.'

Seama let his shoulders fall. He knew he had lost the argument pretty much as soon as it started.

'How will they let me know?'

Waldin cleared his throat. 'Roar has his bird,' he said.

'Not the eagle? Not again. You know it nearly had my hand last time we used it.' Seama shook his head. 'Bad tempered, foul mouthed and vicious, and those are its good points. It should never be let out of its cage, never mind sending it off as a messenger.'

Aiden Peveril looked up from some papers he had been taking the opportunity to sign. 'An animal that hasn't fallen under your spell, my lord? Surely not?'

Seama returned him a tight smile.

'I am better with creatures that walk upon the earth, Aiden. Though there's a spell or two I'd like to try on that damn creature if I get the chance.'

Waldin shrugged. 'It's always perfectly fine with me. There must be something about you it dislikes.'

'Well the feeling is mutual.'

'What I always wonder,' Peveril mused, 'is just *how* it manages to find people?'

'I don't think even Roar could tell us that. But Seama, there is an easy answer. I will have him contact De Vere instead. You will be meeting up after your trip to Ayer, I take it?'

'I haven't sent word yet, but yes. There's plenty of groundwork to be done and he's far the best man for it.'

'There we are then, problem solved.'

And so it had gone: arguments bypassed, wrinkles ironed out. Seama's route had been made up for him: the fast clipper from Errensea to Pilgrim's Bay, Pilgrim's Bay to Ayer, Ayer to Riverport, a ship to cross the River-Sea, a canter through Gothery's midlands and finally off to find The Black Company somewhere in eastern Aegarde. He just hoped he could make good time. Seama needed a quick solution to this: to defeat the sorcerers, dismay the villains, to lift the spirits of their victims and arm the people to their own defence. And all this, of course, to succour the suffering, to bring hope, yes, and all this, of course, was very important… but deep down, shamefully acknowledged, Seama knew full well the real reason he wanted it finished. However cold and brutal the deeds of the Black Company, they were nothing more than a distraction. The sheer ferocity of their attacks was designed to create outrage, the outrage provoked reaction and dispute, and the dispute was made critical all to draw the eye of the Council. For Seama, if no one else, that fact was plain as a pikestaff. The thought of it made him feel queasy. How breathtakingly callous to cause so much pain and anguish and horror simply to create a diversion. How evil the mind behind such a design. But what deed, what event, what plan was that dispassionate mind so keen to keep hidden?

Seama had no doubt where the answer lay. The burning book burned through all he knew. His interest had turned to obsession, his obsession had become need: need to understand, need to connect, a need to… something, he knew not what. The book dominated his waking thoughts and unsettled his dreams; it both disturbed and thrilled him. For all the confusion, for all of its ramblings through dubious history and spurious chronicle and incomprehensible commentary, Seama had finally developed a clear notion of what this Song of Ages was all about. It was quite simple: the burning book was a warning.

He had brought it with him, tucked into his saddle bag, a facsimile of all they had left. Every morning and every night he read as much as he could. Some of it was maddening, full of words he didn't and couldn't understand; some of it was laboured and boring to him, the author shovelling out information in the hope that some of it would stick and mean something; but increasingly Seama's eyes and thoughts were drawn to passages describing, far too briefly, the early days of this age of the world. Eight thousand years ago, an epoch lost to common knowledge, a presumption of an age when mankind, scattered and homeless, struggled to find a future; a time when whatever had gone before was slipping away into fancy and myth. But deep in the heart of that fancy and myth, as cold and hard as stone, stood a truth, a monument of the past, a reality that was once so important the whole of creation had to bow before it. It was there in the Song, obscured by time and Haslem's ageing brain, but there nonetheless. A menace lay upon the borders of this new existence of man, an angry and a jealous menace, waiting only upon the slightest chance to return.

Seama's notion had spawned a theory that carried at heart an easy proposition: whatever it was waiting then, all those years ago, it waited still; a force standing in the wings of the daily drama of the people of Earnor, watching and yearning as the pages turned, cloaked in deception, armed with fear and ever poised to make an entrance.

War was coming, that was it: the essence of Haslem's warning. A mighty war! And all the disputes and the squabbles and the wicked deeds of this year were merely the opening scenes of a much greater tragedy. Seama knew this to be true. He just did not know how, or where, or when or why.

Small meadows and strip fields sloped away from the left hand side of the road down to the winding River Misium. Cattle and sheep browsed the lush grazing by the river; farmsteads and hamlets dotted the valley. The 'city' of Ayer, set fair amid this pastoral scene, was a cluster of streets grown up around the market yards beneath the castle hill. Most of the buildings here were houses for rent, inns or hotels. Ayer was a bustling place. A weekly fair brought merchants from all over the continent; the King's court brought in petitioners and emissaries and no doubt any number of spies but the permanent population was relatively small. Many of those with work in the town came in every day from the surrounding countryside. Pars had true cities of course: Riverport on the Hypodedicus, the city of Pilgrim's Bay, Pulonia and many large towns but the country was essentially rural and it was considered right that Ayer, with its feet in the good earth, was capital of Pars and King's Residence.

The road up to the castle bypassed the town. There were not

many visitors though who would have dared approach the castle directly. Protocol would force most people seeking an audience with the King, or indeed with any of the Lords of the eight Houses, first of all to attend the bailiff's office down at the town hall. There a request might well be considered over several days before being accepted or denied. But Seama was not most people. Seama was a friend of the King.

It had been many years ago at the time of Mador's marriage to Jehanne that their friendship had begun. Even now this familiar path brought back the most bittersweet of memories.

The wedding of the King of Pars to the daughter of Maximilliam Meladre, Convener of the Apian Part, was so important an event that the then Leader of the High Council of Errensea, Astrig Beladaer, had journeyed to Ayer in a great company. With him the Governors of Lindis and Brist, their wives and children in tow, and Waldin Omroot, newly appointed Master of the College, and, just to round things out, the several grand masters of commerce who were key to the thriving trade between Pars and the Holy Isles. At the Leader's request Seama Beltomé accompanied the Master. His official role was to stay behind after the festivities for long discussions with Mador and his ministers on the political and economic challenges that lay before them all. Unofficially he was there to make sure Waldin did not overstep himself: a wise old head to counter the new Master's youthful arrogance.

The wedding itself had been a joyous affair due almost entirely to the great beauty and goodness of the bride. Jehanne Meladre was not a woman of mystery or guile or anything at all calculated. She was simply the most attractive person Seama had ever met. She drew people in with no greater enchantment than the power of natural grace and honesty. Sitting at Mador's side she seemed to make him greater than he could ever have been without her. She took up his blazing spirit, without any sort of apprehension, and made of it something solid and wholesome. Everyone at court was in love with their new Queen, and Seama no exception, but Jehanne kept her heart for the King. It was a sight so rare to see people of such great power so much at ease and so much in love; and their love made them a generous couple. In the weeks following the wedding Seama was given all the time he needed not only to do his work, but time to relax and time to think and time to become friends. Wizard, warrior, ambassador of the Council, Seama's world was all restless activity, constant event. These few months of quiet and kindness and simple pleasure were perhaps the happiest of his life. For several years after, Seama's face became well known in the Partian capital. He visited at the least excuse and his visits were inevitably a cause of celebration. Pars was a lively place in those days. Hope and vigour seemed to imbue the whole country and Seama had no doubt of the source. The birth of the King's first child should have been a moment of the greatest joy for the whole nation.

Seama could feel the pain of it still. How could so shining a soul could be taken from them in the glorious act of giving birth? It seemed utterly wrong. Jehanne's death hurt everyone. A pall of grief descended upon the country, from the smallest cottage to the greatest of houses. Everyone was stricken. Seama could only imagine the pain Mador must have suffered. The King's refuge was in his love for his daughter. The Partians were a strong race. They knew that all life sooner or later meets death; those left behind can do nothing more than get up in the morning, take a good deep breath, and remember to treasure each and every love they have left. And who would blame Mador Bhadrada, after the death of his precious Jehanne, if he treasured his tiny Xandra a little too much.

Bellus made that warm noise Seama loved. Was it from her throat, her mouth, her chest? She meant comfort; she was nudging him back into the present. That was the thing about riding: it was all too easy to drift off into reminiscence and sentiment. Affectionately he ran his hand along her mane but Bellus nickered at him.

Gently rebuked, Seama looked above and there she was, Castle Ayer, gazing imperiously from her prominence, taking in a view of the countryside for miles around, vast, impregnable and utterly assured of her place. Eight sides of honey coloured stone with a turret topped by a spire at each corner: each of

these turrets a stronghold and armoury for one of the eight
Royal Houses of Pars, their banners flying bright to mark them.
The curtain wall was seventy feet high; the turrets another
thirty feet above that. Within the curtain was a wide concourse
surrounding the palace, through the years kept clear for games
or ceremony or muster. The palace itself, octagonal to match
the outer walls, was home to the King of Pars and all his court
from Chancellor to pan-scrubber. At the very centre was the
King's Tower rising definitively over the rooftops, beneath it
the Throne-room and Presence and flying proud above all the
Partain Short, standard of the Partian Union.

It took him only a few moments to see that something was
wrong.

The flags fluttered in what should have been gay colours; the
sun still managed to find the odd sparkle on the gilt roofing of
the King's Tower but the normally yellow walls appeared grey.
Close-up Seama could see that weeds grew everywhere, tall
and bitter, and in many of the fenestrations glass was cracked
or shattered. The flags seemed sullied whenever a cloud hid the
sun and rust grew thick and red on the lowered portcullis.

Seama's heart fell. No one walked the walls to enjoy the day,
windows were closed, not a voice was heard. The castle seemed
desolate. Seama didn't know what to make of it. He urged Bellus
onwards. They came to halt on the ever lowered drawbridge and
waited.

Nothing happened for some minutes. Seama declined to
call out. Then abruptly there was movement, there were voices.
Seama listened more carefully than the owners of those voices
could have expected.

'Come on Cam, wake up, you've got company.'

'Wa.. whadya say?'

'Come on, get with it. Alaric'll have you on latrines if he
catches you sleeping. It's him. Get it sorted while I get over to
the Palace. Come on, move it!'

'All right, all right, keep your hair on.'

More noises: chair legs scraping on a stone floor, a leathern
cup knocked off a table and bouncing on the flags, the drawing

of bolts on a door.

Cam's voice called out from the shadows on the right of the gateway.

'Over here, please, Lord… er Seama.'

He looked like a ruffian. His clothes were worn, torn, unwashed; he had not shaved for days, and despite the 'please' his words were spoken with such laziness and disregard Seama was angry.

'Why?'

'Why what?'

Seama decided that Cam was a dullard. He was about to explain what he meant, as simply as possible, when the man walked out of the shadows. The shabby clothes were familiar.

'The King's Colours?'

'Sorry, My Lord?'

'You are wearing the Colours of 'Mador's Guard.'

'I am a Guardsman, I wear the Colours.'

'Really?' Seama couldn't believe him. Mador was very particular about his personal guard and this man was not fit to clean the stables. 'I asked why I should enter by the postern gate.'

'Because the iron's down.'

'I can see that. Can it not be lifted?'

'Not without the order.'

'Who's order?'

'Captain Goss, I suppose.'

'And where is Alaric?'

'I uh… not sure. Saw him at breakfast but er–'

'Enough! We''ll use the gate.'

'This way then. Oh, you'd better dismount, the door isn't very tall.'

'You surprise me.'

Through the gate, Seama clanking and Bellus snorting at the indignity of being squeezed through a passage designed only for men, the pair parted company for a while. The wizard let them lead Bellus away to stabling but only after clear warnings about the consequences of neglect, and then strode off, ahead of his own escort, towards a drab, untidy palace.

This was not the reception he had expected.

55

DISORDERLY BEHAVIOUR

Castle Ayer 3057.7.18

Mador had all his retainers down in the central courtyard; he was itching to give them a roasting.

'Well hurry up, damn you!' he yelled at the latecomers. He paced starkly before them as they hurried into line. Why, they had gone too far! He would not accept such… *mutiny*. Yes, mutiny indeed to ignore the upkeep of this castle, a castle that was so much more than stones and mortar, that was the emblem of all that Pars and the monarchy stood for.

'Well, what have you to say for yourselves?' he demanded, thrusting the question like a gaff into their midst. Some of the servants actually backed away from it. The King did not wait for an answer. 'I have *never* seen Ayer in such a *disgusting* condition. Just look at it!' he raged, prodding a pointing finger at the roof where tiles had slipped, 'And that!' at the broken windows, 'And that!' at the refuse wind-blown into the corners of the yard.

Aghast, Mador's servants gazed at the decay thus revealed.

'And it's not just outside, it's even *worse* indoors. Have you no pride? Are you all blind? Wherever I look, wherever I have not been this past month, it looks as though a storm has passed through! What's the meaning of it? Well? Are you dumb?'

Though their eyes were open they seemed half asleep. Mador had to shout just to get through to them. He couldn't understand it, these were his best, most trusted servants. In the past they had run the castle with energy and pride and skill; now look at them: all they could do was fidget and stare at the cracks in the flagstones and the weeds that grew in them as though they were seeing these things for the first time.

Arianna Foxton, Mador's chief butler, oppressed by the collective silence and goaded by duty began to stammer her way towards some sort of mitigation. She wanted to explain all the difficulties of the last month. She told him of how busy they had been, how they could find no time for all the mundane repairs. She told him how when anything was broken they would have to put off the mending till the day after and by then it was forgotten. The strange thing was she could not recall what it was they had all been so busy doing. The worst problem, she said, was that all sorts of things seemed to break with the least provocation: a plate or two would crack in the washing bowl; a flagstone would crumble underfoot; the new paint would peel from the walls if you just leaned against it. The castle seemed deep in dust and every day there was more no matter how hard they tried to clear it up. She supposed that in the end they had ceased to bother. With no one to draw attention to the mess, she said, they hadn't realized the extent of the problem. She concluded by suggesting that with the King in his chambers and the armies all gone 'there seemed little cause to keep the castle tidy.' A foolish thing to say.

'Little cause!' Mador bawled. 'I'll give you little cause! In some places, 'Rian, your *head* might depend upon such 'little cause' – I cannot believe you would ever say such a thing. What has happened to you all?'

'I do not know, Majesty,' she replied, 'I really do not know.'

At a loss for words Mador looked about him at the squalor. As if he didn't have enough troubles! And as he allowed his eyes to wander, he saw a door open and there was the wizard, Seama Beltomé, looking cross and ill at ease with his cumbersome armour, and that was something at least, wholly expected but not completely welcome.

'It's about time *you* turned up!' Mador more or less shouted at him.

Perhaps a little startled at the King's aggressive tone, the wizard's escort accidentally slammed the door behind them. The percussion produced a rattling, skithering noise. From up above one of the loose slates slid off the edge of the half-roof and smashed into a hundred pieces at Seama's feet. Mador's reaction and cry of warning came far too late.

'Seama, are you hurt?' Mador turned to his butler with a snarl. 'Cause enough 'Rian?'

As the butler bowed her head in shame, the wizard, unperturbed, bent to study the many slivers and shards on the ground before him. He grunted in a dissatisfied and yet satisfied manner and then stepped forward to meet Mador in the bright sunshine bathing the centre of the yard. His armour glowed in the sun.

'Well Mador, I agree, it *is* about time I turned up. You were expecting me?'

'I've been waiting all morning. I came down to get this lot organised to give you a proper greeting, a bit of entertainment, a feast, that sort of thing… well, things got in the way. But yes, you were expected.'

'How is that? I sent no word.'

Mador snorted, incredulous. 'I make it my *business* to know what is going on in the world, Seama, and most especially on my doorstep. One of my men rode day and night to say he'd seen you in a couch house at Barrasford. I presumed you were headed this way.'

It was small consolation, maybe, to gain the upper hand but the irritation on Seama's face made Mador feel so much better. Mador was very much aware that Seama preferred to keep his comings and goings to himself.

'You shouldn't be so famous, Seama,' Mador advised, and cheerfully enough, but the wizard's reply was uncharacteristically cold.

'No Mador, I am perfectly happy you knew I was coming. I'm just annoyed I didn't mark your man.'

Mador wondered what Seama would have done if he had 'marked his man' – kept him quiet somehow? 'Perhaps you're out of practice. Anyway, as you can see, I'm a little busy right now. You won't mind wait–'

Seama didn't give him time to finish.

'Mador Bhadrada! I have travelled two hundred and seventy miles, sixty of those out of my way, just to see you. I arrive to find your castle in disarray, your guard insolent, your servants incompetent, and you labouring under some strange delusion that shouting at people till your lungs burst will somehow make things better. And on top of all that you're threatening to invade Gothery! I have to ask Mador, are you in your right senses?'

There was a pause of only a few seconds but in that time many of the servants ducked away, hands on heads as though they expected bricks to rain from the sky. And in that time Mador's anger finally came to the boil.

'*Right senses?*'

'That's what I said. Your actions seem incredible to me.

'My *actions?*' Mador wanted to strike the face before him, wanted to rid it of that look of unforgiveable superiority. 'How dare you question me!'

'I dare,' the wizard threw back with danger flaring in his eyes, 'Just Like That!' And at the snap of his fingers the ground beneath their feet quivered and in windows nearby diamonds of glass fell from their leads. The captive servants moaned in terror, wanting to run, fearing to move. But the King, on his own ground, was undaunted.

'Do you think to threaten me, wizard?'

'Hah! I have no need of threats.'

'You have need of respect! You have need of humility! You have need to remember *where you are!*'

'What?' the wizard scoffed, 'face to face with a fool? A potentate blessed with no more sense than farmboy?'

Mador felt himself quivering with rage.

'You, wizard,' he bawled, 'are in *my* country, in *my* castle. *I* am the King around here and you are *subject* to my word!'

Seama took a step back, but not because Mador's face was so close up and menacing. It was the sudden realization that hit him, that staggered him: it wasn't only the *material* of the castle that was affected but the people inside it too! And even he, the great Lord Wizard Seama Beltomé, was not immune. An astonishing thought! An incredible spell! He wondered what he should say next. Mador was very close to calling up his guard. It could all become very ugly. But should he try to explain? Or was it best to postpone? The King would have to know sometime soon.

'Mador,' he said, as calmly as he could he could manage, twitching with the struggle of it, 'I must beg your pardon. That was… not what I intended. I… *we* need to talk. Quietly and reasonably.'

Mador was glaring at him still, weighing up no doubt how easy or difficult it might be to have his guest thrown into prison.

'Really Mador, there is much more here than me being grumpy and you defensive. Has Tregar said nothing about this? Mador?'

Tregar MacNabaer was Mador's court wizard. The King looked away as if embarrassed. He began to walk and gestured for Seama to follow. The fight it seemed was over, for now.

'Mador, what have you done?'

'He's not here,' the King said, sure they were now out of earshot, 'Not in the castle anyway. Look Seama, we had an argument, quite a shouting match in fact. It was unseemly. He went too far and well…' the King sighed, plainly regretful, 'I told him to leave.'

'Leave?'

'I do not employ a wizard to shout at me, Seama – *or* to make my decisions for me. Much like you, he overstepped the mark. I told him he was dismissed. He left.'

Seama was not actually surprised. Tregar's relationship with the King was fiery at the quietest of times.

'So where is he now?'

'How should *I* know?'

Seama couldn't help smiling at the petulance. And oddly enough that brief smile seemed to push some of the ill feeling further away. Perhaps that would be part of the solution. 'But Mador,' he said, 'I thought you made it your business to know everything.'

Mador looked at him, and the sulkiness shifted to a sheepish grin.

'Ha! You're right, yes I do. Always.'

'And Tregar?'

The grin fell away. 'I'm told he's been making a nuisance of himself in the old Dog's Breath. Taken up residency; drinking himself into a stupor.'

Seama pursed his lips. That was bad news. 'It's been a while now, hasn't it?'

'Three years, Seama. I did not mean to be so… I never thought he'd go down that path again, but he was blazing when he left. Looks like he took it all to heart.'

'So what did you argue about? Gothery?'

By now they were a good twenty yards from the assembled servants and facing away from them. And that was just as well for the question provoked an incredible change in the King. What had been a moment before a man of strength and decision, a man of confidence and courage, was transformed in an instant into something wretched and cowering and defeated. Mador's face crumpled like a frightened two-year-old's.

'She's gone, Seama,' he whimpered, 'Gone. And I don't know what to do.'

It was coming at them in waves. That must be it. Overrunning diligence, bludgeoning self control and destroying courage quite as easily as it wore away at the physical integrity of the castle. Seama, shocked and swayed himself by the power of the spell, struggled to keep his voice level and matter of fact.

'You're talking about Xandra?'

'Yes, yes. My daughter is missing. I don't know…'

The King could not continue and reached out a hand to find some support on the nearest wall, causing a cascade of yellow dust to drift to the floor. Seama could hardly believe it. Bereft of the anger, the fight, and the fire that ruled him, King Mador Bhadrada was all uncertainty and impotent fear. Seama shook his head furiously. They couldn't let this happen.

'Mador, we are better than this,' he insisted, '*You* are better than this. I know you are not a coward. You must be calm. Whatever may have happened, there will be an answer. Now, what do you mean? Has she been taken?'

'She's with Sands, with Jaspar but… I don't know what's happened, Seama, I just don't know. They've disappeared: the whole damned army! That's why we argued, Tregar and me. I am King of Pars, Seama, *King of Pars!* Not just a father. My *duty* is to the people, the biggest threat they face is from the West. Well, isn't it? Isn't it? But Tregar told me I was a fool. Said I should look after my own, forget the rest.' Wavering as he stood, Mador bowed his head, putting his palms together before his face as if in prayer. 'Oh, I wish to the Gods I had listened to him.'

Seama scowled. He was filled with sudden frustration and even anger at the King's weakness. 'I still don't understand, Mador. This is ridiculous. *Where* have they gone? Sands was the only house left at Ayer – where've you sent them?'

Mador took deep breaths. Seama wondered if the King might faint. He fought hard to control his rising irritation but it must have shown in his face.

'Look, Seama,' the King said, raising his palms as if to push away the wizard's temper, his voice gruff but broken, 'This is all too much for me now. I am not myself.' The King looked over at Arianna and the others all doing their best to study the earth at their feet. 'Look at them,' he said, 'Wilting as they stand. But they should not be seeing me like this. They deserve better.'

Seama, clawing his own way through the clouds of confusion that enveloped them, found he could agree on that at least and the anger began to abate once more. 'Yes Mador. We need to end it for now. You do know this is all wrong? Yes? Good; and I will have an explanation for you, but, as you say, it must wait – at least until I have spoken to Tregar.'

The King nodded grimly.

'Find him for me, Seama. Tell him… if you can, explain that I did not want this. I'll… well, I'll just finish up here. When he's sober, Seama, I'll see you both in the Presence. Do you understand?'

'The Presence? Oh, of course,' Seama nodded, 'Good idea.'

'Yes it is. Ha! Apparently I am not yet *completely* useless. I'll be more able. We all will. And then we can decide what to do.'

Seama wondered whether it wouldn't be better to act immediately, he had never seen the King in such a state; he himself had never been in such a state. But Mador it seemed had decided their course and that was that. And what would he have done anyway? They both needed respite; Seama knew he needed to be free of the spell to even begin to think clearly. In some respects Mador was proving the more resilient.

A brief touch on Seama's shoulder, a nod of sympathy, and then the King, determinedly, pulled himself erect.

'There's work to do Seama,' he said. 'So let's get on, shall we?'

'Seen him? Course I've bloody seen him. He's got his arse parked in my parlour, fartin' an' drinkin' an' swearin' an' I'm just about fed up with it!'

Seama didn't know Aldo Rodber particularly well but he could tell the man was at the end of his tether. Landlord of The Dog's Last Breath, Aldo generally tried to maintain an air of propriety and the words *arse* and *bloody* were reserved for his most unruly guests. He had his standards.

'I take it you've been letting him drink too much?'

The landlord was quick to his own defence.

'*Letting him*? Think I'd say no to him in that mood, do you?'

Seama nodded in sympathy.

'He's a little hard to handle sometimes, I suppose.'

'Well you suppose right. He came in last Tuesday afternoon with a face like thunder; din't tell no-one what he was so het up about and none dared ask. Most just got out of his way, to tell the truth. Settles himself in a big chair next the fire, yells at me to bring him two quart of beer and a bottle of that whisky he's so fond of; drank 'em down until they ran out, ordered up the same again and carried on until he *passed* out. Slept until noon next day and then started all over again. Been the same routine ever'day since. I think he's only been out of the chair t'have a pee – a decency for which I suppose we must be grateful.'

'Why didn't you give him a room?'

The landlord puffed out his ample cheeks. 'You might have other ways about you than I can credit, mister wizard, but can you see a normal bloke like me shifting that great lump? I did try. Near put my back out. Oh I wish you'd do something about him; if you could only get him out of the parlour it'd be a start. Bad for trade, he is, stinks to high heaven and he's forever bothering my customers.'

'He can get a little argumentative–'

'Argumentative I can handle, it's all the silly jokes that's causing the trouble. He spent yesterday evening making frogs fetch up in people's drinks, then he turned my best gravy green and no one'd touch it. One daft bloke gave 'im a talking to. Well you've never seen anything like it: made a cloud hang over his head and it rained and rained on him, right there in my parlour, till the floor was a lake and this stupid bugger soggy as a drowned dog. Upped and left at a ruddy trot, I can tell you, and I don't blame him but that's another regular gone and I can't see him coming back. Not until that joker's long gone.'

Seama couldn't help grinning at the absurdity.

'Well you might think it's funny but 'at's money to me.'

Seama tried for contrite. 'I do beg your pardon, Mr Rodber, honestly I do. I can see this has been something of a trial for you. It's just that he's normally so reluctant to use magic – I think I can see why now, but I didn't realise drink could make him so… well, ridiculous.'

'And I still don't see why that should be funny.'

'Perhaps you're right. Well then, I suppose I'd better do something.'

Just then the door to the back parlour burst open and a young woman ran out, half in tears and half in a rage.

'That's it,' she cried, 'That's definitely it! He can get his own food and sodding drink!'

'Language, Sally!'

'You want to tell *him* that, Mr Rodber.'

'What did he do?' asked Seama.

Sally looked up at him ready with a sharp word but then blushed, realizing who he was. 'Never you mind, sir!' she said, then turned on her heel and more or less ran for the kitchen.

Seama took a good deep breath before he plunged into the room. Visibility was poor: none of the lamps were lit and though the fire seemed to be drawing well enough the atmosphere was very smoky. But sight was not the most offended of Seama's senses.

The unwashed, inaccurate pissing, drink-reeking stench of the man filled the room, that and the uncontrolled wheezy laughter of someone in hysterics who's been laughing for far too long. The high backed chair by the fire was rocking with both. If only the fire had not been lit; if only he didn't insist on wearing woollens and fur even in the height of summer; if only he wasn't six feet tall and three feet broad; if only it hadn't been Tregar MacNabaer it might not have been so bad.

'Tregar?' he called out cautiously, 'Tregar Mac?'

The laughter faltered. Seama made his way towards the hearth. The laughter ceased. As he rounded his quarry's den a leg shot out, took him down by the ankles and sent him tumbling head first into the chair opposite. The laughter rang out with renewed vigour and the only words to emerge between the gasps and guffaws were:

'Go' ter wetch… ye feet en her' laddie.'

Seama, furious, struggled to right himself, getting his cloak all tangled in the process.

'That was *not funny*, Tregar.'

Tregar did not agree and continued to giggle like some huge, idiotic bear. Seama glared at him, trying to regain a little dignity, and yet leapt to his feet in alarm when a loud voice shouted out just behind him: 'Whoopsadaisy!' The rug he landed on promptly jerked from beneath his feet and dumped him back in the chair.

From the empty bar in the corner by the door a deep brogue rumbled out: 'Make yoursel' cumf't'ble, zurr' quickly followed by a much sweeter tone, in a passable imitation of the departed serving girl, piping up close to his ear: 'Now my love, what's your fancy?'

Seama's annoyance reached a critical level.

'For Gods' sakes, Tregar, get a hold of yourself.' But Tregar was far beyond the ability to take his advice, and far beyond any ability to see the danger signs.

'Ay, just what I said to the wee lassie,' he giggled, 'Well, somethin' like that.'

Enough was enough. Tregar didn't seem to care what he did or said and Seama decided to respond likewise. He stood up, aimed a sharp kick at one of Tregar's shins, and then, without any further physical contact, he flipped the armchair backwards sending Tregar arse over tip, crashing through an occasional table, to belly-flop painfully on the Old Dog's polished boards.

A lesser man might have given up but the bloody-mindedness in him forced Tregar to bounce up onto hands and knees before he succumbed to the vomiting. The vomiting knocked the stuffing out of him, and Seama relented in his invisible grip on the man's stomach.

As the pool of mess spread before them, Seama called out to Aldo, who had been waiting anxiously outside in the corridor.

'Landlord,' he commanded, 'A room and a bath, if you please, and *lots* of cold water.'

CHILDREN OF THE RUINS

Huaresh, Eastern Valdesia ('The Skirt), 3057.7.18

Carla lies motionless. Like a dead thing. Dark is coming on. Their work finished for the day, the crows with caw and croak are leaving.

She sits bolt upright. She cannot look to her left – her mother was on the left. She dare not look to the right for something sticky is making a pool there, a pool she had put her hand into only a moment before. She will not look at her hand.

Instead she stares stiffly straight ahead into the ruins of the schoolhouse.

A new sound has roused her.

A call or cry. At first she thought it was a cat but now she understands that it's the squalling of a baby. A baby of the ruins.

Her legs are sore. Her arms growing bruises. Her back tender. Everything hurts. She considers squalling herself. Not crying like a baby demanding attention, but because she should. Because. Instead she sets her face hard, pushes to her feet and begins to step carefully through the scatter of bodies, making sure not to stumble. She makes her way, not as a terrified and abused seven year old might, but as her mother would whenever something needed to be done.

Mr. Gjultera's house is on the right, and Old Ma Bera's little cottage. Both of them are smashed at either end as though a great big hammer had swung through the gap between. Floor boards jutting out from half way up wobble and creak as though someone is walking on them. But no one is there. Not even a ghost.

And then Ma Bera's front door swings open.

Carla wants to run but cannot. She is fixed in place mid-stride, back heel up, front toes curling into the dirt. Not able to look and see who or what is coming because she cannot turn her head. She senses a dark shadow: a suggestion of someone, bending to retrieve something from the road, and then bringing it to her. The suggestion stops some yards to her side.

'It's a coat. A coat for you.'

He moves close, holding it out for her to take. Only now does Carla realise she is half-naked and shivering.

'It's for you – you're cold.'

Released by sudden anger screaming in her head, she snatches the coat from him, swirling it around her shoulders; she drags it in at her middle with two fists, and then sinks to her knees to gather in the warmth.

Benito had heard the baby too. He'd been lying still. Still and quiet for an age. Long after the noises in the village had finished. Down in the cellar. The cellar that belonged to Mrs Bera. Where his cat had gone. He wondered where the cat was now.

But he heard the baby start to skrike – wanting someone to come. So he got up and climbed the dark stair into the back kitchen, past the larder into the parlour and through to the front door.

And there was the girl – Carla, a classmate of his little sister – standing still in the road, though it looked like she was walking. On the floor in front of him was a coat – one of those jacket things Mrs Bera always wore. He decided it would be best to give it to Carla, then maybe the cold wouldn't keep her frozen in one place.

As they climbed through the planks and boards and broken furniture, the baby began to cry non-stop. *A good job too,* thought Benito. The crying made him easy to find. Carla rolled up her coat sleeves and picked him up, took him from the cold stiff body of his mother. Benito took off his jumper for Carla to snuggle him in. The baby boy cried and cried. Benito didn't mind that.

'You need to give...'

The voice came out of the air. Carla crouched to the ground, shielding the baby with her own body.

'He wants... milk'

The voice was cracked and weak.

Benito looked up, and there, silhouetted against the dusk sky, doubled over a shaft of wood at the top of the old school bell-tower, like a worm on a stick-pin, was the shape of a broken man.

Oswaldo Bassalo was surprised that any of it still mattered. He should be dead already. Most likely he would be dead in just a little while. But for as long as he was living he'd try to help them. Whatever the cost. The pain from his wounds bound him tight, making it hard to breathe, still less to speak. The children were silent, both looking up at him as though he was an impossibility.

'Must … help me … down.'

His words came in bursts. He wondered if they could understand him. The baby had stopped crying now, perhaps warmed into an exhausted sleep. Carla gently laid him on the ground, making sure he was well wrapped, and then got to her feet. *One thing at a time* – he'd told them a thousand times. She stepped over to Benito and pushed lightly at his back. The boy did as he was told and stepped closer to the tower.

'Signoren,' he said.

It was an acknowledgement at least, but there was no certainty in the boy's stance. Carla came to stand next to him. Oswaldo concentrated on trying to make his words strong and clear.

'Benito … find an axe.'

The boy didn't move. Oswaldo smiled inside, despite the pain. Benito at fifteen, apprentice to his father now, hadn't changed much from the schoolboy the Signoren had taught. Benito was kind and tolerant and sensitive, so good in many ways, but he was rarely quick to action. He needed to consider everything he heard and saw for a good long while before coming to a decision. Oswaldo realised he should have explained *why* he wanted an axe.

Carla wasn't so slow. She would do Benito's thinking for him. The girl took his hand and after a quick glance to reassure herself that the baby was safe, she led him over to his father's house. Oswaldo could not see what was happening as they clambered through the ruins to the back but he imagined the girl struggling to lift the big axe and then Benito stepping-in to help.

A new scene swam into his view. Minutes had passed. Below him now Carla was angry with the boy. He stood motionless, looking as though he might cry but the girl was dragging at his shirt, urging him to the base of the tower, and thumping his chest when he wouldn't move. The boy shook his head.

'No, can't,' he said. 'It'll hurt the Signoren bad.'

Carla relented in her attack. Then she put a hand upon his forearm, and looked him in the eye. She nodded her head, giving him permission, releasing him from fault. The seven year old was taking responsibility on herself.

Oswaldo wouldn't have it.

'You must!' he spat out. '*I* tell you to.' Speaking so forcefully tensed the torn muscles in his stomach – his words came out as a howl of pain but he wouldn't let up. 'You must Benito – good lad – chop me down or I will die. Your father would be proud of you. So proud. Can you do this Benito? For me? For the baby? Carla is right – you must do this – for us all.'

In the village scores of Bassalo's people knew pain no more: not the women battered or skewered, not the children beheaded, not Andras amputated till the blood drained out of him. For Oswaldo every axe-stroke was agony, but agony is not death. He clung to every jolting, jag of pain as though pain could empower him; it would designate him among the living.

This had been a day of horror but also a day of miracles. The biggest spar that impaled the Signoren had torn through the fat on the right of his belly, scraped the surface of the muscles beneath, and come out again through the left hand side. Who would have thought that being fat could be a good thing? Not an organ injured. And the pain in his back was awful but he was sure his spine was undamaged. Most likely though, he would never use his left arm again: another shaft had pierced his shoulder and in the trauma of the fall, the impact had forced it deeper, pushing his shoulder-blade out at right angles to his back. The biggest part of the bleeding came from this wound. Carla launched herself at it with a wad of cloth, and pressed to stop the flow, and pushed to stop the shoulder blade looking so bad. Bassalo screamed all the while and then passed out.

When he came-to she was still there, still pressing but weaker now. The shaft had been drawn – Benito sat to one side looking at the bloody end of it on the ground before him. Carla kept looking back at him, needing help, but the boy didn't notice. Bassalo wondered that she didn't call out to him.

'Benito, good lad,' he said, and the boy looked round, startled perhaps that the Signoren could yet speak. 'Do you know where your mother keeps her needles? Her sewing box?'

Benito frowned. 'It's under her bed,' he said. 'She always sews in bed. Where it's warm. She says it's *a grand job!* Always sewing and knitting. Dad says it's a pity you can't knit money.'

Carla had known what the Signoren intended. He thought she might have done it anyway, whether he'd asked or not. She kept up the pressure on the wound until Benito returned and wouldn't relent until the boy knelt to take her place. She was so white-faced when she stood that Oswaldo thought she might faint. He should have known better. Carla wouldn't allow herself a moment's rest or weakness. She rummaged through the sewing box, scattering the contents all around, until she found what she needed. She took out a bobbin of the best silk yarn and a curved needle.

Oswaldo could see her poor arms shaking as she tried to thread it.

BLOOD, BLIGHT AND BALLISTICS

Ayer Town 3057.7.18

In an upstairs room of The Dog's Last Breath, a public house now emptied of the public by all the screaming, swearing and roaring of the past couple of hours, Tregar, inadequately wrapped in an under-sized bath robe, was propped up against a bolster in a decent bed, sniffing suspiciously at a pungent pot of a black liquid he did not recognize.

'What a reek!' he said, 'And I have to *drink* this?'

'Yes you do,' Seama insisted, 'I'm told it's very good for these situations. They've been using it in Garassa for quite a while now.'

Tregar was not impressed. 'They're strange people in Garassa.'

'That may well be, but given they've taken to drinking gin like it's some sort of profession, maybe they have some idea of what they're talking about.'

Tregar shrugged. He wasn't up to arguing. 'Aye well, mebbee,' he said. 'Here goes then. Slante!'

He tipped the pot and took a quick sup, and spat it out again in the same second.

'Great Spurl's Tits! That's bladdie hot!'

Seama laughed. 'They say it's no good unless it's hot as a furnace. You're supposed to blow on it and take a sip at a time. '

'Thanks for letting on.'

A more cautious approach yielded better results and after only a few of the recommended sips Tregar eased himself back against the bolster pleased with this new discovery.

'Ye know,' he admitted, 'It's not so bad. I could get used to that. What d'ye call it?'

'Rahi – they ship it into Garassa from Sulle' Sullinor. Aldo tells me his merchant picks it up in the Stralli Market every six months or so. Astoril's gone mad for it apparently. It's making good business for Aegarde.'

Tregar chinned the air. 'It's a damn pity Aegarde can't just stick to business then, instead of all this nonsense Athoff's been getting up to. Have ye spoken to Mador about it yet?'

'We've had a few words but no not really. He told me you had a disagreement.'

'Aye, that's one way of putting it! More like a fight. Right there in front of the whole Privy Council. It is just possible I went a little too far – I think I called him dim-witted. Somethin' like that. But he was just as bad, ye know. You should have seen him, Seama, prancing about the room like a lunatic, ranting on about invasions and tactics and what have ye. I was seriously beginning to think he was losing his marbles. Talk about wrong-headed. He just kept going on and on about his 'duty to the nation' and how Jaspar'd have to look out for himself.'

'He must have had his reasons.'

'There was not a scrap of *reason* involved in it, Seama. Look, you don't go invading another country when you're under attack at home. That's what I told him. Mebbee I should have tried harder, tried to calm things down but, and I don't know why, it all just came out yelling and swearing.' Tregar took another sip at his Rahi, trying to think back to the origins of the argument, feeling sure he was missing something important. 'It was odd ye know. I'd seen him earlier, up in his snug. He was upset o'course, who wouldn't be, but honestly there wasn't any shouting or anything like it. He was just thinking things through, weighing up the risks, making plans – the way he usually is. I was sure he'd settled on sending the armies north. What changed his mind I don't know. It was like it was the argument itself, if that makes any sort of sense. I don't know, Seama, it's all madness. Let's face it, straight as a skooger what he *should* be doing. He just seemed to take against me saying so. Did he tell ye about Sands?'

'He said only they'd disappeared. What's happened?'

Tregar shook his head. 'Good question, Seama. If only we knew. There were reports, about three or four weeks past, from up Norberry way – just about as far from the capital as could be—'

'I'm pretty good at geography, Tregar.'

'Aye well, but it's worth bearing in mind it takes a good few days to get messages through. We should be thinkin' of extending the Fast Post further into the North, though just now most of the riders are still caught up running the road to Aristeth and back. But we could train a few more. They're not that expensive. Getting the ponies now, that might be a bit diff—'

'And the news from the North, *however late*?'

Tregar couldn't help chuckling. 'Always gets t'ye, doesn't it?'

'Always. It's *maddening* when people don't stick to the point.'

'Right then, let's see if I can do a little better. The news from the North was confused: raiders, an army, trouble-makers. Vague as that. Villages set to fire; refugees heading anyway they could. The stories came in not long after Mador got to hear about this trouble in Aegarde with these sorcerers and cuthroats or whatever. He'd already sent Anparas and Temor over to Salthall barracks just in case Sirl… er… how shall I put it? Just in case *he needed some help*. So, them gone, all Mador had left at Ayer were Sands and the King's Guard. Didn't have much of an option.

'More reports were coming in all the time, panicky now, odd stories about *outlanders* scaring people from their homes.'

'Outlanders?'

'That was one of the words used, no real explanation. You got the impression the tale was getting worse by the telling. 'The White Men', that was another name, though given for some or all wasn't too clear. Well I guess it 'minded Mador of this Black Company. What if there was another gang Norberry way up to the same sort of shenanigans? And if they were connected, would that mean the Aergardeans were involved? What if Athoff was attacking on two fronts? Sands was sent to find out – the full army, nearly eleven hundred all told.'

'A robust response. And Xandra with them?'

'Sands *is* nominally her House.'

'And, of course, Xandra, being Xandra, was tired of kicking her heels here in Ayer when everyone else was out having fun.'

'Aye well. She's been getting worse recently. Mador wouldn't let her go east back in March – didn't want the Masachees given a fresh target – she was hopping mad then and she's been trouble ever since.'

'So they went. What happened when they got there?'

'They went by Segeston and Gull Lake and through the Skelldane. Not much sign of trouble in the south of the Part but by the time they'd crossed the Oswynne they started to run across some of these emptied villages. No sign of war – the folk had just gone and left their living behind them. According to Jaspar's reports the problem seemed worse the further east you went. But it's a big area we're talking about. There was no point in having the army traipsing back and forth till they found something, so Jaspar turned round and headed for Greteth. He made a base at the castle and sent out scouting parties instead.'

'Very sensible. Sound man, Jaspar.'

'Well, you'll not get *everyone* at court to agree with ye. Some think he's lacking experience. And they may be right, but he's intelligent enough and his judgement is usually up to the mark.'

'We're wandering again. What next?'

'Nothing. Jaspar'd been sending out dispatches daily but we've had nothing at all after that one report from Greteth. We gave it four days and then Mador had some fast riders diverted from Aristeth. None o'them came back. It's a bad business, Seama. Course, we don't actually *know* anything but King's messengers don't go astray by accident. I have a very bad feeling about it. What if Sands has found more trouble than he could handle?'

'A bit fanciful, Tregar. He has a whole army with him. What do you think is up there?'

'Ach! You're right, daft idea. I don't know. What I do know is Mador should get his head back together and send reinforcements. He needs to find out what is going on in Norberry and forget all this Gothery nonsense.'

'Completely agree with you. We ought to go to Mador and tell him just that. I did ask Aldo to bring you some food but if you can drink up quick I think we ought to be moving right away.'

Tregar nodded an 'aye' and then gave his attention to the rahi. Seama sat in a chair and pondered upon the situation. He didn't like any of it. Not this trouble in the North, not the ongoing problems with Masachea in the East, and especially not Athoff's warmongering in the West. Each new event made him more convinced there was some hideous plan at work underpinning the whole sorry mess. And if that was the case then he wondered what he should do about it. Like Mador, he was worried he might make a bad decision and head off in the wrong direction entirely. Where was the heart of it all? Who was at the bottom of it? Could he do anything more than fight the fire directly before him? He certainly couldn't ignore it.

'Seama? What are you thinking?'

'What I'm thinking, Tregar, is it's about time we were doing something positive. We need to see Mador and get this all sorted, that's clear – make sure he has his priorities straight, make sure he sends the troops where they're needed. But there are enemies everywhere you look and they all need facing. First and foremost we need to counter this attack on the castle.'

Tregar looked a little muddled but he took another sup at his drink to give himself time to get it all in order. 'Aye. Right enough. All a matter of priorities, as ye say.' He was reviewing the options. 'This trouble in the North certainly needs sorting. We need te get Anparas and Temor deployed, quick as we can. Two whole armies ought to do the trick and then…' He looked up from his mug in some puzzlement. '*Whit* did you say just? About the castle. *Which* castle?'

'Castle Ayer, Tregar. It is under attack, right now, and we – that is you and me – we need to do something before the whole place collapses.'

Tregar was no longer in the bed but fighting his way out of the bath robe. The rahi was decorating the wallpaper.

'Spurl's tits, Seama, what are we doing jawing here if Ayer's under attack?'

'Well, sobering you up, actually.'

Tregar gave him a fierce look. 'You mean, I've been sitting in this stupid place drinking myself into oblivion and all the while…' A revelation hit him. 'What sort of attack? You're talking about a spell of some sort?'

Seama nodded.

'Aye well. Just let me get these revolting clothes back on and ye can tell me about it as we go.' He paused in his struggles, a rueful look coming over his rugged features, 'Mador *is* expecting me back, I take it?'

'Yes, in The Presence, soon as can be.'

His face lightened in relief. 'Well that's alright then. Good, good. Presence eh? Right then, if he wants us there quick, let's go for his Back Passage.'

Aldo Rodber picked up the tray, wondering whether bread and cheese would do the trick, or perhaps he should do a fried egg to go with it, and maybe some bacon, but then decided he couldn't be bothered. Tregar always had to take things too far. Fair enough it was three years since the last one but this time was definitely the worst. He'd been totally out of control. What it had done for The Dog's reputation he didn't like to think. Tregar was just lucky Aldo hadn't given up on him and called the constables to turf him out. No, after all the support he'd had already, and the credit he'd squandered, Tregar'd just have to make do with what he got. And he was getting no more either until he'd had the decency to apologise and had damn well paid his bills. Thank gods Seama had come along.

He pushed open the kitchen door and stepped through into the corridor, still musing, only to be bowled over in an instant by his erstwhile and continuing tormentor, reckless in progress, followed a little more cautiously by his supposed saviour.

'Sorry Aldo, didn't see you there,' Seama threw over his shoulder as they charged off towards the cellars.

Aldo shook his head wearily. He stooped to pick up the bread and cheese but then, realizing what was happening, dropped it once more and ran after them yelling:

'You can't Tregar. You can't. It's all locked up!'

Tregar, waiting for him at the bottom of the cellar steps, grabbed him by an arm rather than his throat, for which Aldo was thankful if surprised. Tregar was showing restraint.

'What d'ye mean?' he growled. 'Why's it locked?'

Aldo half regretted following after them. He pointed at the grille gate to their left. Sure enough the bolt from the mortise lock was shot 'Be… Been locked up since the last time you used it,' he explained.

'Well, *bring* me the key then.'

'Mador said I wasn't to let you.'

'I don't care *whit* Mador said. We need to get up to the castle. You need to bring me *the bladdie key*. Right now!'

Aldo squirmed out of Tregar's grip and backed away. 'Honest, Tregar, I just can't. Said he'd take my licence if I let you through again – so I… er…'

'So you… er… what?'

'I gave the key to Arianna Foxton.'

Tregar slapped the heel of his fist against the wall in frustration. Aldo had moved away at the right time. 'So the little bladdie butler's got it. Just *bladdie* fine!' Aldo sidled around to put Seama between them. The court wizard eyed him angrily. 'Ye're useless, ye know that, don't ye,' There was still an edge of menace in his tone, but then, as abruptly as a candle snuffed out, the fire of Tregar's anger was extinguished and he relented. 'Ah *whit's* the use!' Knowing he was defeated and there was nothing anyone could do about it, Tregar seemed to relax a little, resigned no doubt to the inevitable slow cart up the hill by way of the main road. 'Looks like it's going to be the *long* way round, then.'

Aldo, relieved to be let off the hook, grimaced sympathetically. 'Sorry,' he said, 'but it *was* the King's orders.'

Seama, assessing the gate that was causing the trouble, glanced back at his colleague. 'Sounds like you annoyed him, somehow,' he observed.

'Aye well, I wiz a little bit drunk I suppose.'

'A little bit?' Aldo almost laughed. 'We heard you scared the kitchenmaids half to death.'

'Aye, that's what they said, anyway. Hardly my fault they'd startet using the room for stores though.'

Aldo shrugged but Tregar chose to ignore him. Instead, he looked over Seama's shoulder.

'What d'ye think?'

'I think it's a pity my friend Terrance isn't with us – he's good with locks. But perhaps a little brute force might just do the trick. Just the one bolt after all.'

Seama unsheathed his sword.

Aldo gasped. 'Where did that come from – I didn't see it before.'

The wizard smiled. 'You weren't supposed to. A small charm that stops you looking at the scabbard. Anyway, let's see what we can do.'

Seama slid the tip of his sword into the gap between the grille door and the iron frame that retained it, pressing up against the bolt as if he thought the bolt was made of tallow and he could slice right through it. And then he sliced right through it.

Aldo was amazed and bent in close to see.

'Careful!' Seama cautioned. He reached for a broom and used it to pull open the gate. The part that touched the gate charred black in an instant and began to smoulder. 'It'll be hot for a good half hour. Best not touch any part of it.'

Aldo nodded vigorously, grateful for the warning. 'Tell you what,' he said, 'If you make sure to tell Mador I tried my best to stop you, I'll go up and get you some decent lanterns.'

As Aldo climbed the steps back up to the kitchen he heard Tregar say with no small degree of wonder in his voice: 'How did you do that, Seama? I've never seen the like.'

Obviously not all wizards were the same and didn't have the same abilities. All of them, however, were at the least intimidating and at worst downright impossible. Mador might well get annoyed that Aldo had offered the pair any help at all, but anything to hasten their departure even by a minute was fine by him.

'So what's the story behind the passage?' Seama managed a conversational tone as they plodded along by the light of Aldo's lanterns but actually he wasn't much in the mood for idle chatter. There was something about their journey that made him feel ill at ease. He wasn't at all sure whether it was to do with tunnels in general – he had never liked them – or to do with this one in particular. 'It's been here some time by the look of it. You'd have thought I would've heard about it somewhere along the line.'

Tregar grunted. He was making heavy weather of the steep incline with the poison of the alcohol still doing unpleasant things to his insides and to his head.

'Aye, ye'd have thought so.' He belched. 'I feel sick.'

'Well make sure you keep it in,' Seama warned him. 'Bad enough being down here in the dark without you making a mess to tread in.'

Tregar grunted again and plodded on.

Seama plodded after.

'So, the tunnel then?'

'Look alright. But if I am sick it's your fault.' Tregar stopped plodding and took a few deep breaths. 'It was made by Iskandar, second and last. Heard of him?'

'I've seen his name in lists. Wasn't he something to do with the Landsman's Charter?'

'Er, don't know. I'm not really too good on proper history – I just remember the stories. The human stuff, ye know. I think it was something like five or six hundred years ago if that tallies.'

'It does. Fairly significant piece of legal history but probably not that memorable. What's the story?'

'Well this Iskandar was quite popular as king's go, known affectionately as 'The Old Dog' but not because he was a faithful sort. Fact was, he was a bit of a hound and everyone knew it. His one weakness – ha! one weakness: whenever have they had just the one? Anyway, his weakness was for the young ladies. There was a constant stream o' them even when he was in his teens – a regular philanderer, you'd call him. His wife on the other hand was a one man woman, utterly devoted, beautiful as a summer night, but most importantly, scary as hell.'

'Why scary?'

'Well, it might have been a bit of prejudice coming out but as she was some sort of Masachee, and from Lusk of all places, naturally the scandal mongers decided she must be a witch. While Iskandar was always the nation's favourite his wife was hated by everyone, whether she deserved it or not. Ye've got to wonder why he married her – except for the looks, of course.

'Now, early days of the marriage Iskandar behaved himself

pretty well, but as the years passed by, as ye might guess, the young lassies again began to catch his eye. His big problem was the Queen – Layala was her name – she had a jealous streak wide as the Misium and a lot more powerful. And because everyone else knew about his affairs, very soon so did she. Story has it the queen's maids were disloyal little minxes, to both parties. It was no surprise at all they got to hear about it whenever the King made his little trips into town, where he'd been and who he'd been seen with: the servants always do. And this lot were devilish quick to make sure the Queen heard the bad news too. Wanted to see her embarrassed, I guess. Of course that led to real trouble. Layala, in a tearsome rage, out and threatened Iskandar, right in front of the Privy Council, to have done with his wicked ways or she would end them herself. No one could say why he was so weak – perhaps he knew her for the witch rumour made her, and was just plain scared – fact was, he jumped to her demands like a whelp te its master. The poor lass who'd last erhm... *benefitted* from the King's attentions was taken down into the market square, flogged till she bled and then sent on her way with not so much as a penny to buy a day's peace. Iskandar the while, in some sort of terror of his wife, pledged himself to mend his ways.

'All well and good, but, as ye ken, the pledging and the doing are mostly different things. There's never been a lack of young lassies in the world and always plenty with a fancy to bedding the rich and the powerful. So, the temptation was always there that might cause an old dog to stray, and the danger was there too. That's when he came up with his brilliant plan.

'There was work going on to make the palace kitchens bigger and to dig another well shaft. So, while they were at it, he commissioned the builders to do a bit extra for him. In the case of *direst* need, he told them, to ensure the safety of the royal family, he needed an escape route. Whether they believed that or not, I cannot say. I don't suppose they were particularly loyal but I daresay all the extra money he promised got the tunnel dug pretty quick and more or less kept secret.

'Of course all that money was spent for the one purpose

only: to get Iskandar into town and to his trysts without anyone getting to hear of it. The house at the end of the tunnel wasn't an inn in those days, more like a close house for the King's agents and he reckoned they'd be the last people to betray him.'

Seama snorted at that. 'I don't suppose they had anyone coming in to do the cooking and the laundry then?'

'Aye, you see the flaw, Seama. Of course the servants were sworn to secrecy too but it takes just the one. However, things seemed to move along in the King's favour for a few years at least and there's four or five dalliances to keep him amused. That three of these girls disappeared unexpectedly should have given him a warning but mebbee he wasn't too worried what was happening to them if only he was allowed to continue.

'Naturally enough Layala had gotten to know all about it. I guess the whole nation was waiting for her to do as she'd threatened, and common rumour about the missing girls was rife. Question was, did she pay these lassies off and send them away, or did something much nastier happen to them? No one knew but, as long as naught was said, the King felt free to carry on his career.

'The end of it came when the latest young lass got ideas above her station. Some people said she was the image of the Queen in the first days of their marriage, some said she made herself up that way quite deliberately. Whatever the case, the King fast became besotted with the wee hussy, couldn't deny her a thing and couldn't countenance the thought of the Queen doing something against her. Eventually the girl was daft enough to go that one step too far: she wanted the King to divorce his wife and marry her instead.

'I guess he havered and hawed at first. Even if the Queen had been your average sort of woman, it was a drastic step to think o' taking. Fact is she wasn't anything like average and not at all normal. But the young lass kept up her campaign, and our Iskandar got to dreaming of a new wife, and finally the lure of the girl proved just too much. Almost as if she'd put a glamour on him hersel' the King found he had no will left to resist. One evening he sends his girl a message saying he's made a decision, and if only she'd wait for him he'd come along later that night to give her the news.

'Back in the Palace Iskandar has dinner with his wife, completes his evening's duties and then trots off to his bed in the normal way. I guess he was in a *graether* of anticipation waiting for the servants to finish their tasks and go off to their rooms, but soon as he may, away he goes, down to the cellars, quick through his contraption, and then off along the Old Dog's Back Passage, where we are now.

'Sometime after midnight the Captain of the King's Guard and twenty o' his men, warned by an anonymous message that the King was in danger and where he might be, turn up at the close house ready to fight a battle if need be. But all they find, just come through the doorway out onto the street, is Queen Layala, hair draggled, clothes covered in blood and in a terrible state of anguish, screaming and sobbing.

'"Where is the King?" the Captain demands and lays hands upon the woman to shake the truth out of her. "What have you done?"

'Well the Queen wasn't having any o'that. With the strength o' a man she threw him off and stood there, straight and still, defying them all. And her deadly gaze fell upon them one by one, as if she wanted to be sure they would all mark what she said.

'"What have I done, you ask," says she, "Nothing but love him. Nothing but try to give him the prize ever he sought. He was *my* husband, King of Pars – the reason for my life. And you, his *loyal subjects*, you call him the Old Dog and you laugh at his foolish ways and revel in my misery. Well no more! If you want the Old Dog you will find him within. Do not expect too much. I have given him all I could and yet it was never enough. Never enough. And now it is over."

'In rush the guards, in rushes the Captain, all to find the King seated at a table, head dipped to examine whatever lay on the board before him. But they were too late. His life-blood, in a pool all around him, poured from a dozen wounds in his chest and his neck. On the table lay a leathern bag with the contents all spilling out: a pigs liver, an emptied flask, sticky to the touch and the severed hand of a young woman. You can imagine the horror of the Captain but he was a strong man and not to be deflected from his duty. He was quick to understand that the Queen had been practising the blackest of all arts. She'd destroyed the girl and the King was mortally wounded. Ignoring the blood he came in close to see if anything could be done. "My King," he begged, "What crime is here?" And sure enough the King was not dead but clinging on to his ruined life as though there was something more he had left to do. There was barely a twitch of the hand to beckon but the Captain understood and he stooped to listen for the King seemed to have something to say before the end. With his one, final, ragged breath, Iskandar, King of Pars, made certain his wicked wife would be condemned by all and reviled throughout history. "She promised me love and life," he said, "she gave me only blood."

'The story goes that at her trial Layala cursed the court for its blindness. The King's brother, Rúhandar, she said, was at the root of the all the rumours that dogged their marriage and made a mockery of the truth; she would gladly face even the ugliest death, she said, rather than drag out her days among such fools and villains. They hung her in the market place and the people brought wood and oil and rosemary and burned her corpse to drive out the evil she had brought. Rúhandar took the throne, as was his right, and set a law that never after, for shame or otherwise, could a King of Pars be named for Iskandar. It is a fact also, with or without a law, that never after did a king of Pars even think to marry a Masachee.

'Now that, my friend, is the story o'the King's Back Passage.'

'And the reason for the pub's name, to boot.'

'Aye, nice to get it all sorted isn't it?'

'Quite a horrible tale really. You wonder what was the truth behind it.'

'Do ye? Seems pretty straightforward te me.'

'Nothing to do with men and women and witchcraft, if that's what it was, could possibly be straightforward. And nothing in history ever happened exactly as we remember it.

Misremembered detail, unreliable witness, the problem of interpretation: history is very much what we make it.'

'Ye're no fun.'

'Maybe. Contraption?'

'Ha! Thought you'd come back to it. Weel, if we can get going again – and oddly enough I do feel a little better after all that – we should come to the contraption in ten minutes or so. Let's say it'll be a surprise fer ye. Meanwhile, now I've done with *my* story-telling, I think it's your turn. So what's the news on this spell and what it's doing to the castle? Feel no pressure but just make sure ye tell me *everything*, then mebbee I won't sound so stupet when Mador starts quizzing me.'

Seama's tale was much less dramatic. Someone had set a spell of dissolution upon the castle. He explained as they forged ahead.

'Do you remember how to cast a blight?'

'Am I supposed to?'

'Standard teaching for the fifth years – I'm sure you'll have had it when you were a student. Perhaps you'll remember being taken to the beach and making up sandcastles?'

'Sandcastles?' Tregar, walking ahead of Seama said nothing for a few moments but his shoulders lifted into a shrug. 'I can remember building sandcastles in my younger years but I don't remember… Ah, now wait a minute. This'll be the one where you're to build the castle and then knock it down without touching it, that right?'

'Well nearly. The students who fail the test are the ones who give it *the push*. Other more subtle students fill the castle with water and pull at a few grains here and there. They fail too. A pass is given only to the students who understand that all things eventually decay, decompose, come apart, and they have to understand why.'

Tregar grunted in derision. 'Well, it's easy isn't it? Erosion, the weight of the earth, the work of the elements.'

'You pass. Nearly. It is a matter of other attractions. The castle is put in place by our own force, using the weak cement of sand in water. Our will, we could say, is what makes and holds the castle together for a period of time. But other forces will assert themselves. Left to itself, through the drying power of the sun, the pull of the earth, the scouring of the wind, the weight of the tide, our sandcastle is doomed before the day is out. Of course everything we build, everything we create is subject to the same problem: other forces continue on their set course just as we continue on ours.'

'So,' said Tregar happily, 'I'm right then. In effect what you're saying is it's all to do with external forces. In that case what's so wrong with giving it *the push*?'

'Sorry, you fail. A two year old can knock down a sandcastle. But what if you could influence the action of other forces and you could do that without the use of kinetics? What if your will could cause all of the forces of decay to increase their natural activity, to work faster together? And that you could localize the effect? A *word of dissolution* supports the forces of decay, lends them greater power, enables them and drives them into greater action.'

'All sounds a bit pointless, Seama, direct action's the way with me. You know, I do remember now. It took me so long to figure out what the teachers were talking about that my sandcastle dried out and fell apart anyway. I'm not sure I got any further. But drying out now, that's one of the processes ye say?'

Seama groaned. 'Yes it is, but you're supposed to bring the thing down in four minutes not four hours.'

'Oh well. It's not the only thing I failed at. But anyway, the key point you're trying to get into my noddle is that someone has set a *word of dissolution* upon Castle Ayer.'

'Exactly.'

'Well,' Tregar said, the weight of his thought bringing him to a halt, 'It occurs to me that Ayer's a good bit bigger than a sandcastle.' He turned to face Seama. 'Wouldn't it take a lot of power to bring it down – a hell of a lot?'

Seama mirrored Tregar's frown. He didn't much like the notion.

'Yes. Yes it would,' he agreed. 'Obvious really.' He pushed past his companion and strode on with a renewed urgency. 'I couldn't do it,' he said, 'I might manage a wall but not a house. To bring down a castle, especially this castle, it should be impossible; but trust me Tregar, that's what's happening.'

Tregar had to trot to keep up.

'So how are they doing it then? How could anyone be more powerful than you are? Oh right, right. I see: they're *borrowing* the power.'

'That's what I think. And if they are borrowing power then I doubt the donor is anything benign.'

'Dangerous business, Seama, messing with dark powers. You'd have to be mad to try it, or desperate.'

'Or supremely confident.'

'Any idea who?'

'None at all. Come on, let's get the journey done. The key thing is to stop the spell. We can worry later about who set it.'

'But I thought… Oh!'

Tregar's note of surprise echoed oddly. Seama realized the big Spurladian had stopped again, but not it seemed because he was weary. The light of the lanterns cast deep furrows upon the court wizard's face, making his expression even darker than normal, but Tregar looked worried. He signalled that Seama should step back a few paces.

'Look,' he said pointing back the way they had come.

Seama was surprised to see that, easy to miss walking up but in plain sight from where he stood, the tunnel had a spur. An unpleasant, tight looking thing.

'Where does that go?'

'Oh not far. Just to a room. I guess it's a cave the builders used to keep their gear in – lots of rusted metal in there, other stuff. But look at this.'

A few feet in was a door-frame but the lintel and posts had given way, and the heavy door had fallen down and together with the rubble it half blocked the entrance.

'There's a bad smell to the place,' Seama said, his dislike of the Back Passage increasing by the minute. 'I wonder *why* they put a door in there?'

'No idea. Keep out a draft? Keep the smell in? Who knows,

but that's not what bathers me. Last time I was here that door was in its place, sturdy as ye like.'

'So? It's hundreds of years old by your reckoning – as we were saying everything falls down eventually.'

'But what if it's this cantrip?'

'What, so far down? Seems unlikely.' Seama rubbed his hand across a patch of the wall nearby. 'Up above, if you rub at the walls the surface is loose, friable; the grains come apart. Solid rock down here though. I think we'll be fine.'

Tregar grimaced. He wasn't so certain. 'Well let's hope so. I wouldn't much like to get stuck down here. Luckily the contraption's not far now: we'll soon be out.'

It was when Tregar admitted he didn't know which bolt to pull that Seama began to think he had made a mistake. They could by now have been rumbling up the Castle hill in a cart, slowly and steadily. And safely. He had presumed Tregar knew what he was up to.

'What's the worry, Seama? If I pull the wrong one, we'll just never get moving. And then I'll know.'

'You sure?'

The contraption was a stone platform with three walls around it – making it seem as though the tunnel had come to a dead end – and no roof above, just a shaft: an empty, vertiginous ascent into the dark. The platform quivered as they stepped onto it. On either side, on identical metal poles fixed into the platform, were the main release handles, full rings of iron the size of a large fist and above them, in series, three bolts with simple cross pieces. The ballast bolts and the release handles slid into a slot lined with greased iron made in the side walls. The middle ballast bolts on either side had been pulled back out of the slot.

'Look, the middle bolts are set for two normal people or one heavy person like me; the others make the platform lighter, or heavier. It's that simple.'

'Right.'

'Ah, away with ye. It'll be fine.'

And with that assurance Tregar pulled simultaneously at

both of the lowest bolts. There was a squeal of metal on metal and then a shudder. But that was all.

'See what did I tell ye. There's another weight released. Now then...'

He laid his paws on the handles.

'Always a bit better if you can pull both at the same time or it wobbles a bit when it starts.'

He pulled.

The platform stayed where it was.

'A bit stiff,' he growled. 'Don't think I pulled them out enough. Will we do one each, d'ye think?'

Seama, feeling very uncertain about the whole thing, nodded reluctant agreement, planted his feet eighteen inches apart for better balance and grasped the left hand release.

'Here goes then. One, two, three, PULL!'

The bars grated against their holes but then came free, and in a stately, pleasing fashion the platform began to rise, though with increasing speed.

'See,' Tregar said with a grin, 'Easy as pie. Don't worry about the speed, there are dampers to slow us down at the t—'

It was at this moment of comforting vindication that the remaining ballast fell off completely.

They hurtled up the shaft as if shot from a catapult, the platform bashing at the sides, knocking the pair of them off their feet. Seama had time only to scream: 'You said there'd be—' before they smashed through the rotten timbers of a trap door, launched up at a ceiling of powdery plaster, now with less momentum, and finally came tumbling to a halt upon a cracked slate-stone floor.

Seama allowed himself a few moments to establish that he was still a single piece before completing his earlier thought in an accusatory tone:

'You said there were dampers!'

He glared at Tregar who looked as if he might like to reply but all that came out of his mouth was vomit once more.

'Charming.'

Exhausted by the motion, Tregar rolled onto his back, wiping his mouth with an already disgusting sleeve.

'You just going to lie there?'

'S'ms like goo'idea,' Tregar managed, but then moved slightly, shifting his body off one of the larger pieces of wood making up his sick bed.

'Bit of a surprise,' he grunted, 'The trap. Wasn't there b'fore. More like a cabinet thing. Ye slowed te a halt and then just opened the doors.'

'How long ago was that?'

'Three years, mebbee.'

The rotten planks of the trapdoor had disintegrated into a shower of spars and splinters and dust all around them. Seama swept his hands over the floor and gathered up two handfuls of the detritus.

'Three years only and the timber's as bad as this?' he said as he let the stuff trickle through his fingers.

'Dry rot?'

'Decay, Tregar – and I don't think it took three years. More like three weeks. Thank gods the kitchen girls never stood on it.'

He pushed himself to his feet.

'C'mon Tregar. By the look of it the blight is getting worse – by the hour.'

They passed along ill lit corridors and up narrow bare staircases to reach the public levels of the Palace, and all the while Tregar grumbled away about the filthy floors and the grimy doors. Seama became excessively irritable.

'It's the spell, Tregar, not the domestics,' he snapped, 'Just save your grumbles for the enemy – if we can ever find him.' He bashed through the final servant's door separating them from the Throneway, the ceremonial approach to The Presence, but then stopped in his tracks. 'Tregar,' he said without turning, 'I think you'd better you prepare yourself for a shock.'

Once bright with the light of a hundred lanterns but now gloomier than the worst winter's day, the Throneway troubled their eyes and sapped their spirits. Tregar was dumbfounded. Only one lantern in ten was lit but even in the poor light they could see hangings crumpled to the floor, tables on a kilter, suits of armour – the physical history of a strong and proud people – collapsed in pieces and turned red with rust; the carpets looked as if they'd been dragged through a farmyard, the chairs were rickety and the crumbling paint on the walls carried great dark patches that spoke of water getting in somewhere high above: it was as if the castle was diseased.

'Neath's Sake, Seama, ye could've told me it'd be so... so bladdie awful.'

'Actually I couldn't Tregar. It's ten times worse now than earlier. Now watch yourself. It's not just the castle it attacks: this thing gets at your head too. That's why we're so irritable.'

Tregar scowled. 'Ye think so? And I thought that was how you were normally.' He rummaged about in his trouser pocket. 'Anyway, let me tell ye, this spell's not getting at me – not this time.' He pulled out an amber coloured crystal the size of a duck egg and proceeded to wave it in a pattern before his heart and before his forehead. 'There ye go: that's me protected for a little while at least.'

'Lucky you. Don't suppose it would help the rest of us?'

'No, you're right; sorry about that. It was given to me by our Seer before I left Spurl for Errensea, years ago. Only works for me, I'm afraid. So, the question is: what else can we do – for the castle and for everyone in it? Is there a cure to be had? Ye know it'd take days to trace the root of the spell and even then...'

Seama smiled wryly.

'And even then we might not have the ability to kill it. What we need, Tregar, is a different approach. It all depends on the Presence and the Throne but I do have the makings of a plan. C'mon, let's see what we can do.'

The Door-ward of the Presence was still in his place, his black garb and silver regalia as smart as it should be. The orbed staff he carried was of polished ebony, shod with steel. The heel of it hammered into the brass foot-plate three times and then once more as the Presence doors swung inwards. Seama sighed with profound relief.

In contrast to the Throneway, the Presence had lost none of its glory. It was as if the doors had opened upon a raging fire, the red and gold blaze of it bursting out into the darkling corridor as if it could re-ignite the torches and bring vigour to the mordant stone. Seama could feel the energy and the desire rushing past him. This was much more than he could have expected.

He glanced at Tregar, standing red-faced in the glow of it. Mador's wizard was equally impressed.

'Gods'o'Number, Seama. I've been in the Presence a thousand times – two thousand – but this? I've never known anything like it.'

Seama nodded enthusiastically. It was like standing free in strong sunlight after an age of wandering lost in darkness and misery. Doubts that clung to him like shadows as they had passed along the Throneway dissolved into nothing and hope bloomed in every thought.

'It is just amazing,' he breathed, 'Do you feel her Tregar? Ayer – she's beginning the fight back!'

FEEDING THE FISHES

Riverport 3057.7.19

The man in the broad brimmed hat and dark cloak leaned closer in to the sidewall of the building. Just around the corner the front door slammed shut, a key was turned in the lock producing a nerve-raking shriek for want of oil. He heard the steel bar drawn across the face of the door, slammed home and then padlocked. There would be no entry that way. A moment's panic came over him when he heard heavy steps approaching but then Rixbur shouted 'No! Not down there, Dog. We're heading into town tonight. The cock-fight, remember?' Dog grunted in reply and the others laughed for some reason – perhaps the Dog had made a gesture behind Rixbur's back. How often had he seen that over the last couple of months? Nothing else was said.

He waited until the sound of the iron-shod boots of the hill-men disappeared into the general murmur of Low Docks Street and when he was sure they had all gone he slid out of the shadows and peered down the length of Red-dock Passage. Empty. There was nothing here but warehousing: no shops, no houses and consequently no one around to spy him out. The only merchant at all worried about theft in this generally safe City of Riverport had just left and taken his guards with him.

Angren smirked his 'got you' smirk for a few seconds, savouring the victory even before it was achieved.

'Right Rixbur, you asked for it.'

On the left-hand side of the house was a narrow cobbled alleyway sloping down to the river. This particular storehouse was one of the more mouldered affairs that stood with their feet in the water with no pier between to keep out the damp. Towards the bottom end of the alley the cobbles were slimed from years of regular flooding and Angren found he had to step very carefully indeed. It would be ludicrous to sprain an ankle at this stage. Close up against the water the battered remains of a wooden jetty were more of a liability than a help and he decided not to trust the rotting timbers: the waters of the Hypodedicus here were cold and fast flowing and while Angren was a good swimmer he didn't want to lose either his cloak or his hat as he'd only just bought them and rather liked the style. The harbour beacons lit up the main docks away to his left but they were not bright enough to be of much use at this remove and so Angren had to wait a few minutes until there was a largish gap in the cloud cover. Luckily for Angren the moon was at slightly more than a half.

When the light came he purred in satisfaction. A single glance told him he'd remembered it all aright. A few days before he had leant out of that door high up, the one with the derrick and pulley above it, and seen down below what seemed to be a course of bricks standing proud of the wall: a ledge just about the line of the first floor windows. He'd marked it because he couldn't understand why it was there. Not for decoration surely? Now with the same course at the level of his waist he could see that the whole building below the line was by way of being a sturdy foundation, an extra support against the force of the river. And it had been well thought on, Angren decided, as he studied the hollowed bricks down around the watermark.

Angren was well aware that the first floor windows were shuttered and bolted from the inside. The door on the second floor was not. He had made sure of it. The curious thing was he had pulled the bolt free from its housing and tossed it into the river at least two days before he'd seen any real need to do so. He'd still been working for Rixbur then.

He had with him a bail hook with a cross-piece handle. Driven into the mortar it gave him just enough leverage to haul himself up onto the ledge. Carefully he sidled along until he reached the first inset window embrasure and there he rested. The second section was less easy: the bricks were in places crumbled away and he was lucky that none of them broke beneath his weight. The hardest part was when he realised the wall he was clinging to had begun to slope outwards as it bowed with age. His fingertips were soon raw from having to dig them into the mortar layers above him. He reached the safety of the second window just as clouds hid the moon once more. He bided his time, sitting on the sill with his feet dangling over the waters. Presently he began to rummage in the bag he had slung under his cloak. What came out was a coil of rope. Angren was very handy with rope. It took only three attempts to loop the line over the derrick just in the correct place. He took the precaution of tying together the lower ends in three large knots to the handles on the shutters. It would mean leaving the rope behind but it made the ascent so much easier. He virtually walked up the wall to reach the door.

Things were going well. The bolt had not been replaced, the door pulled open nice and easy, he swung himself inside. Then he tripped over something in the dark, fell with a thud, crashed through the poorly fastened trapdoor, plummeted twelve feet and landed shoulders first on a table covered with lots of hard metallic things. The thickness of his cloak saved him many a cut from the daggers he had now scattered all over the floor.

The clangour woke something up. Two somethings. As he gasped for breath, wondering whether he had broken anything, a clattering of paws and a snarling, vicious barking came hurtling through the building to greet him. If the lanterns had not been lit he'd have been no better than dead meat. Two wolfhounds bounded onto the table as he rolled off it. The first weapon to hand was a small knife that he threw at the nearest dog but missed. He ducked under the table as they came for him, kicked at their heads and missed, rolled out on the other side and came up holding one of the pikes that had been laid beneath the table. At last he had an advantage. With his first swing he managed to whack the nearest dog with the pointy end, lopping off an ear. The dog howled in pain but the other snatched at the heel end of the pike and nearly pulled it out of Angren's grip. The wounded hound came on again as he struggled to wrestle the pike free. It went for his throat. Angren ducked beneath the dog as it leapt, thrust hard with the pike at the other and then pushed upwards all in one flowing movement sending the wounded hound tumbling through the air. The audible snap as it crashed into the corner of the table gave Angren some hope. He looked for the second hound. It was rolling on the floor clawing at the pikestaff Angren had forced down its throat. The gurgling noise was horrible to hear. With as much kindness as he could muster, Angren used one of the daggers at hand to break the dog's neck before removing the shaft. The other dog was already dead.

'Well you two beauties were a bit of a surprise. Wonder where he got you.' He gave the dog's mane a rough stroke. '*Fine* dogs you were too. Pity you were his.'

The next hour or so was the hard work he'd come for. The store of weapons in the place was considerable. Rixbur had everything: halberd, pike, lance, pig-stick; swords of every style and size; mace and hammer and spike, bows and crossbows and several very unorthodox weapons. Angren had a plan for them all. He opened the two shuttered windows overlooking the bay, peered out briefly at the full and roiling waters below and then began the laborious task of consigning the stock to the bottom of the river. He kept only a few pieces for himself: a couple of secret affairs for emergencies and a beautiful diamond and ruby hilted stiletto because it was far too pretty a toy to decorate a fish's gullet.

In the course of his labours Angren found the safe. He thought about it for a while and then went back to test its weight. There was no way he would be able to open it. The lock was a two key affair, probably Slaney made, very complicated and Angren was no lock-pick. But could he shift it? A straight lift? Not four hundred pounds of Dreffield cast iron. Could he tip it? He pushed hard at the back end and after a lot of effort he rocked it forwards and it fell and smashed the slate floor beneath. That was as much as he could do: try as he might he couldn't shift it any more. Still, Rixbur would have the devil of a job righting it and with luck the lock would be damaged and hard to break through.

Rixbur's desk was nearby. When he'd done all he could, Angren returned to the desk, took a quill pen and a sheet of Rixbur's best Rivelline writing paper, wrote a few words and left it there for Rixbur to find next day. It read: 'Payment in full; received with thanks!' He didn't indicate what the payment was for; he didn't sign it. There was no point in leaving any proof he'd been there but he knew Rixbur would understand.

LIVING LEGEND

A racket of crashing and snapping and plunging through years of mounded leaves gave away his chaotic approach. The wizards were standing on a bank at the edge of a beech-wood. There was a solid looking path through the wood over to the left that would have made for much easier progress. Tregar shook his head, annoyed by the idiocy.

'Ye'd have thought he'd go round.'

Seama grinned. 'Easy to tell you've never met. Mule doesn't 'go round' anything. It's not his style.'

'Good gods, a beast with style now is it?'

'Well, *a* style anyway. Look out!'

Erupting from a catastrophe of twigs and broken branches at reckless speed the Mule charged at them. Tregar jumped to one side but Seama stood his ground. It was a game they had played before. Mule stopped short inches from Seama's nose and then began to spin in circles like a dog trying to catch his tail. It needed catching too: not much more than a stump it whirled like a sling, only faster. He wasn't as tall as Bellus but had a straight, strong back and broad shoulders. His ears were huge; his white-whiskered face grinned incessantly; his mane was bristly as a scrubbing brush. A ludicrously comical appearance, people chuckled at the sight of him. He was a jester on four legs, his braying uproarious laughter.

'So, *this* is the Mule,' said Tregar, dizzied by the antics, 'A formidable companion though I wouldn't think he was much use if he carries on like that.'

The braying and spinning stopped abruptly. The grin seemed sinister as the Mule stalked towards him.

'Whoa, boy. Steady now. Gods Seama, can he understand me? Is he safe?'

Seama laughed at Tregar's discomfort. 'Now Mule, let's leave the nice wizard alone, shall we? I'm sure he meant no disrespect.' He walked between them, ruffled the scruffy mane, and the

Mule backed off, braying a few times as if excusing himself. 'Honestly Tregar, I don't exactly know what he understands. He's an unusual creature. I can get into the minds of most animals, not that it's normally worth it given how little most of them think, but Mule's different. Trying to read him is like trying to read a boulder; probably to do with how stubborn he is. But I'll warn you now, he really does not like criticism. I'd apologize if I were you.'

'Apologize? Te a Mule?'

'*The* Mule. I would.'

Tregar shrugged at Seama and then bowed to the Mule. 'I'm sorry if my comment offended, Sir Mule; I ask your forgiveness.' He foraged in his pockets, 'Can I give ye a carrot? I'm sure Sirrah can spare one.'

Mule took the carrot more or less graciously. Such apologies were most acceptable.

It didn't take long to sort out the packing with the Mule helpfully content to chew grass and stand still. Bellus stood a little way off, watching the proceedings. Tregar tried to help things along, passing up packages, holding things steady while the straps were tightened.

'Looks like he's a fine addition to the team,' he said, picking his words to avoid any possible offence, 'Quite the personality. How did ye meet up?'

'Just plain luck. I got him at the Stralli market. I wasn't looking for an animal – just there with a friend of mine – but he started braying like a mad thing whenever I walked past. Just about destroyed the corral trying to follow after me and wouldn't let up. To be honest, I think the dealer was desperate to get rid of him. He gave me such a good price I couldn't resist. It was all a bit odd really. The man said Mule'd walked into his camp the night before they got to Astoril, no harness, no ostler's mark, no way of knowing where he belonged.'

'You're lucky no one's tried to claim him then. How long ago was this?'

'Two years, or thereabout.'

'Never! It can't be so long since ye were last in Ayer.'

'Longer, it's more like three years. They keep me busy, Tregar.'
'Aye, I ken, sorting out the world's woes no doubt.'
'Well…'
'No need to deny it. There's never an end to the troubles of man, Seama, and I for one am thankful you're always around to help out.'
'It's a job, Tregar.'
'But one you're very good at. Always have been.' Tregar paused for a moment, his forehead wrinkling as he tried to nail down a new thought, or an old one. 'When was it we first met, Seama? That was all to do with some kerfuffle out eastaways, was it not?'
Seama had no trouble remembering.
'It was. Cenophon, the Masachean from Polz. He decided the Footings were inside Masachea, demanded rent from the farmers. Mador disagreed. Fifteen years ago I think, not long after you were taken on. No, I'm wrong, it was fourteen: Bellus was a seven-year-old at the start of it.'
Tregar was amazed at the notion. 'Fourteen years?' The frown returned to his face. He looked over at the powerful charger patiently waiting for them to finish their preparations and looking as though she could have carried all the packs herself and both wizards too. 'She's doing affey well for a twenty-one year old, Seama,' he said, 'I reckon it must be rubbing-off.'
'What must?'
'Braw health. Ye know ye've weathered pretty well yoursel'.'
Seama made no comment.

Soon they were back on the road, travelling briskly, Tregar on his hunter Sirrah, a horse not much used to long journeys but strong enough, Seama on Bellus towering over them, and Mule trotting along, often some way behind owing to his habit of stopping frequently to sniff a little here, grab a little grass there and mooching about as he pleased. Tregar thought he behaved more like a dog out for a walk than a pack animal. Still, Mule seemed happy in his work and he made sure he never lost too much ground, his packs bouncing and clattering whenever he ran to catch up.

At first the wizards didn't talk much, both easing themselves in, letting their limbs and their thoughts fall into the rhythm of their ride. It was Tregar, inevitably, whose thoughts felt they needed an airing.

'Didn't take much to persuade him then?'

'Mador you mean? No. All he needed was to get free of the spell for him to get back to normal and start thinking straight. That's the wonder of the Presence for you.'

'And the wonder of good sense. I'm glad he saw it my way in the end.'

'Your way? You didn't notice he had the orders written before we got there then?'

'Ah weel, mebbee. But he wouldn't have sent us on if we hadn't managed to do something about the spell.' Tregar secretly felt a little put out that Mador had recovered himself before they'd ever had a chance to help. After his temporary desertion he'd wanted to prove his worth and his loyalty. Haslem the Great had beaten him to it.

They entered The Presence, literally staggered by the rush of determination and defiance. It buffeted them like a strong wind, it invigorated, it renewed. It was like walking into an explosion and the source of all this raw energy was thrillingly clear.

The Presence of Ayer was more than just a room, more than simply architecture. It had been built *in power* by Haslem. Yes the stone masons had done their work, labourers had carried, bursars costed but the true glory of the room lay in the magic that underpinned each layer of stone and gave unparalleled rigidity to each marble column. And there was a focus, a fulcrum to that energy. Without it, those lacking any sense of magic might see only the gaudiness of the room: the use of coloured marble in the pillars, the multi-coloured lanterns, the richness of tapestry and ornament and statuary that Edison had made so much of in his famous *Geografi*, was evident in every yard of the Approach. And yet even the most blockish of men would put all that aside when assailed by the crowning glory: the Partain Throne itself.

Four mighty columns of greenstone rose to the heights, octagonal in shape, banded with strips of gold and silver. High above great arms stretched from one to the other forming arches that were the main support for the Kings Tower. Below, set on a dais of white marble, stood the Throne. Made of the same jade as the columns, strengthened by the same spells, the Throne seemed to radiate power just as the sun gave off heat and light. And as the sun is sometimes dulled by the passing clouds or cooled by the change in seasons, the power of the Throne both waxed and waned. There were days when men bowed their heads, averted their eyes because something that penetrated sang out from the silver tracery in the surface of the jade, shone from the diamond and sapphire clusters, erupted from the golden diadem mounted above. Many people had come to that throne with untruths to tell, with treachery in their hearts, only for the lies and treason to be laid bare. It was almost impossible to tell a falsehood before it. The spells laid by Haslem required allegiance and truth and brooked no dissent.

But never had there been any day like this day; never had the Throne responded to threat in such a forceful manner. It was as though the Presence had declared war, its forces ready and resolute and needing only a word of direction to set all in motion.

And Ayer's general in all this, King Mador Bhadrada, sat upon his throne in glory, unperturbed by event, and utterly assured that victory would be his.

'He had never a doubt Tregar. As soon as he took to the throne. I think Mador can feel the power of it even more clearly than we can. The Throne was made to protect the King, after all. He could feel the strength coursing through him and he knew there was enough in that strength to defeat any force of magic.'

'Aye, I'll not deny that. But it's not just about the power, is it. A sword is a grand weapon, Seama, but you still need a hand to wield it. The throne had all the power and the intention but it wanted direction. Without our guidance all that fizz and sparkle would've come to diddlyfart.'

'Diddlyfart?'

'Just a word ma fæther used. But d'ye not agree?'

'The first step had been made and that was enabled by Haslem. Without the first step we'd have got nowhere. But yes we had to be there to push it to another level.'

Working together the wizards had invoked the Power of Ayer. Their spell had called upon the castle's True Purpose – it wasn't easy, stone is not quickly impressed – and they married that purpose to the raw energy of the Throne and the Presence; and they issued a Word of Growth, and a Word of Renewal to set against the Spell of Dissolution. They had done nothing to try and trace the spell. Mador and Ayer and Pars were a great threat to any enemy, they were the greatest defence against any invader. That their combined power was made safe was enough for now.

'Neat trick that, getting the castle to save itself.'

'I thought so. Anyway, it's done now and we're free to get on with everything else. And Mador's free to be the King we know. It was painful to see him so affected. But I think he'd have held on a lot better if Xandra could have stayed with him. Not like your Iskandar, Tregar, Mador is seriously a King with just the one weakness, and anyone could forgive him for that.'

Tregar nodded. 'We surely can. As ye know, I've any number of weaknesses mysel', but that wee lass is certainly one o'them.'

'Really?'

'Ach, get away wi'ye. She calls me uncle and that's good enough for me. She's got a soft spot for you though.'

'And now you're being silly. It's just she's known me all her life – I'm a constant, like the castle walls or the sun coming up.'

'Heap of stone with a sunny disposition eh? No, you're right. Actually she doesn't seem much onto men. Too much to do, I suppose. She's still young, though. How many years now have ye been a friend o' the family?'

'Oh, since the marriage, I guess. Twenty-eight years?'

'Twenty-eight years? More than quarter of a century.'

'I can do the maths, Tregar.'

'Aye well, it's just, what with ye looking so young an' all – my maths must be a bit off.'

Seama didn't like the way the converstion was turning but there seemed no way of stopping it. In the end he was surprised only at the roundabout route Tregar took in getting to the question that so clearly troubled him.

'Y'know, there's a tale in my family,' he began, 'In everyone's family, I should say, back in the Spurling Isles. A lifetime away it seems now, but tales were bread to us then. I remember them all, right down to the last word. But this one was about a wizard who came to our shores, once upon a time; he came to our rescue, saved us from a monster o' the seas. Now then, this is how they'd tell it – translated for ye. It may seem a little odd in places: we have a few words in Spurlese you lot don't seem to have bathered with.'

'I'm sure it'll sound fine.'

'Mebbee. Well, here goes.' Tregar began the tale in the style of his fathers and Seama remembered it well.

'A deep-swimming Kræken, an'eldvildret monster,
crawlt forth upon the slakit lånd,
defiled the shore and the shoreline,
and a'the fields beyond the shore,
and a'the hames beyond the fields.
The Kræken spoilt the food in its spite,
poisoned the clean wæter;
and the people could nothing but hide.

No wåpon had they to pierce that hideous skin,
no power of magic had they to dismay.
When a'then seemed lost,
and the monster devouring e'en the childer o' men,
then he came to them:
then the mighty wiezart,
come for their succour,
alone and unbidden
when a'had seemed lost.
Come to the Spurl, he did,

come to the sunnert Spurl.
Dreight o'er the Miedden,
he came to the heart and the soul of the Spurl.

Warrh–Mester they calt him:
he faro'emed a'ff the seas of the world,
and where he wish'e'at the seas wud not hinder him,
and a'the winds ran for him:
his sail nea'loost
in the seas of the world

'The Elders begged handr'o'him
and clear did he answer then:
'I'm come t'dreither this fiend, naught an'less.'
On an evil day darkling, alone he set onward,
striding to meet then his foe in the dale,
and none dared come near then for fear of his ean'.
Some watchet from a distance, lang i'the lea,
and after described the battle so grim:
They saw the dun shadow,
fell shape o'the monster,
one full quarter filling the far Westring vale,
and små'there below him,
the små'shape o'a man,
hard to be seen in the deep dackle dale.
This man he cried out then:
a voice that rent clouds then,
and a'the folk watching a'feared for his ean'.
Again he cried out, and as he cried out
the Mester o' Warrh took fire in the dale.

Then through the reeking
watchers in wonder
saw now the wiezart with flame at his hand.
Held he a fiery wånd,
star-bright to blind them,
star-bright and dinning

in the darkness of the vale.
Fierce as a beacon
advanced on the Kræken,
and ever he came,
and the Kræken wud'wane,
wary and feared o'the terrible flame.
And then wi' a rush
the Mester he caught him;
the fiend was frozen wi' fear and misdoubt.
He thrust then his brand,
his fiery, keen brand sharp
into that cold and aughlit maw.

Watchers saw then a terrible sight:
like rags tæken oil,
the sluhlik beast took flame.
In vain the beast sought,
in pain the beast havered,
but ne'er could regain
his hame in the warrh.
The heat of the blazing
reached those in their hiding,
found them in wonder,
and fear of an eand;
but the wiezart undaunted, ran clear of the fiend,
and left him to fate in that dra'briht dale.
With the flame fierce and death to him
the Kræken was strackert:
and the Wiezart's draht rran'flam'
had lendert his ean'.

'Told!' Seama was impressed. 'You've done that one before.'

'Aye, in ma heed anyways. Ye ken we have this saying, a request really: 'Tell me the story, and please lie!' A good tale should never be hampered by the truth. But I've to tell ye, Seama, there's not much o'a lie about that one. Or so I'm told. Fact is, it was a favourite tale of my growing years. A wiezart alone against all the odds: setting out for the good o' common folk. Not just a warrior, but protector and healer too. He fought the evil, he watchet it die, and when the fight was finished he set about curing the ills that evil had brought. He doctored the people and the fields, made the waeter clean again. It was a tale to stir my youthful heart. Since I was wee I'd carried just a little o'the *power* but I'd not known what it was for. Now I wanted to be just like this *Warrh-mester*, travelling the world, fighting monsters and righting wrongs. Ye know: a boyhood fantasy, I suppose. And so I set mysel' for the College, and I worked as hard as I could, and eventually I got part of the way to where I had wanted to be. And luckily that proved to be far enough, and now I am easy with what I am. Never a doubt, though, I owe a deal o'thanks to that tale, and as the tale was true, Seama, the debt is owed to the hero.

'So, to come to the point,' he said, looking to find something in Seama's expression, 'While I took pilgrimage and suffered training for vocation's sake, I had always the idea of seeking out this great wiezart. I wanted to know just who he was, and where he'd come from; I wanted to hear all about his adventures, I wanted to learn all there was to know. Not that I hoped to meet him: I expected to find him in the books, in the stories of the masters. But no matter how often I tried I was always disappointet and not a word of the tale did I find; there was never even a mention o'that name we'd given him.' Tregar rolled his eyes and shook his head. 'Honestly, I cannot believe I was so *stupet*. D'ye know, it was only in this last year I finally got it straight. Mador was after showing-off his favourite landscapes, yet again, and there was one canvas I came across that was new to me: a view of the Old Docks on Errensea. 'This by Dossena?' I asked him – of course I'd seen some of the series back in the College gallery when I was a student. 'Yes,' he says, 'Had it in store. A jubilee present for my father, from the Council.' Well that seemed fair enough and it was all I needed to know but then: 'I was only nine or ten,' he says, 'I remember being so excited, it was such a grand occasion. They all came up for it: Ordolan from Aegarde, and Erling – Sirl's uncle, Beladaer of course, and a whole lot of people from the Isles. *Beltomé*,' he says, 'made the presentation.' Well that's natural enough I thought. 'That'll have been Seama's fæther, then?' says I, not doubting I was right for a second. But Mador just looked at me as if I was dim-witted. And that's when it finally clicked. Honestly, Wave-Master! I ask ye! I know I was a *sumphety* lad, but growen up you'd've thought I could've got there by mysel'.' Tregar twisted about in his saddle, the better to peer intently at his companion's face, the better to challenge him. 'Come on now, Seama, tell me the truth,' he demanded, 'Back on Spurl: that *was* you, was it not?'

Seama couldn't easily reply. He knew what the answer should be, but it all seemed so long ago, as though it was just a story he had heard. But yes, he was the wizard of the tale. And also he was not. Then he was a young man eager to prove himself against the mightiest. It was his first campaign, the first of the many times he would risk his life to conquer death. But when it was over and done the glory he had sought didn't seem to matter so much to him and actually he had felt humbled by the experience. It was the children who had died despite all he could do and the courage of their parents that changed him. Seama Beltomé was now a man of wisdom, of experience, a man of strength and decision: a different man. But the answer Tregar sought was more straightforward than that.

'Yes, Tregar, I was the Warrh-Mester. It was quite a name; I was proud of it. But I have gained in perspective over the years. Seama's a better name. It's very popular in the Isles, given for sailors' sons and fishing men. A name with humility and that's how it should be. It's no wonder you couldn't trace the story, though. By the time I came back to the College I'd had enough of the *all the blaether,* as you'd say. It didn't seem right. Don't tell Holander but I laid a spell on the Chronicle: the entry's there but no one's going to find it. And that's what I want. Never let yourself be fooled by pride, Tregar Mac. Don't be a seeker after glory or honour or fame. Life has a way of finding out your true worth. Oh yes, and try to avoid lecturing people, it is a form of pomposity! You'll have to forgive me, but after a while you get to thinking yourself wiser than you really are.'

'Ach, nae mind that. You may feel free to lecture me whenever ye like. But Seama, how old *are* ye? I'm hardly a stripling but that tale I told was told to my fæther afore me.'

'Do you really want to know?' Seama hated this; he wanted Tregar to drop it. People became uncomfortable when they discovered his age or even guessed at it. They were always looking for signs that said his features were mere illusion. They weren't. For that matter, Seama himself became uncomfortable at the thought of it: he felt guilty to possess a gift he could not share with others. And he had learned that endless youth made old men jealous. 'You know yourself,' he said, 'how to keep off old age to a limited extent? Yes, and you will use that knowledge more as the years pass. I have no superior wisdom to lend you. I'm just better at it. There is something in me, in how my body is made, in the *power inherent* I possess, that allows me the skill. I can't explain it. Let's leave numbers aside, Tregar. Honestly, I try my best to forget the years, to live a day at a time. I see little point in keeping a tally.'

There were people in the wide world who were as old as Seama: he was only one hundred and eight years of age. But their bodies knew the cruelties of time. Seama, however, seemed no more than thirty years old and no illusion was involved. Since the age of sixteen his body had aged only one year for every seven winters. The episode on Great Spurl was ninety years ago when Seama was eighteen years old. He didn't normally care to look that far back. He began now to think of those frantic days when he had so much to learn, and lost in memories said no more. Tregar decided not to press the point and he too found thoughts enough to keep him quiet.

Seama wished he could just sit down and talk with this bear of a man. Talk as he had never talked to anyone before about his life, about what it was to be Lord Seama Beltomé, the renowned wizard; what it was to be one hundred and eight years old. He never spoke about the loneliness. It was true he had many friends still living, and many more were now dead, but there was and had been, he felt, something lacking in his friendships. Jealousy about age and health was not the only stumbling block. Without exception his friends considered him something greater than themselves: they held him in reverence. And because of this he didn't seem eligible for the normal relationships enjoyed by others. He had never married. Though there had been several opportunities he had always found an excuse and backed away. He couldn't do it. It wouldn't be fair on any woman, he decided, to see him ever young as she grew old. Not fair at all.

They cantered on, and Seama kept his thoughts to himself. His life was a burden not for the sharing.

LIVING MYTH

Medean Part 3057.7.19

It was a westerly route they took through some of the most populous parts of Pars. They passed through villages where people waved and wondered to see two such proud and strong men riding through, but the travellers never stopped except to water their horses.

For some time they made no conversation as they concentrated on their road and their own thoughts, but Tregar never could stay silent for long. Leaving other matters behind them, they fell into tales of past days. It was hard not to laugh at Tregar's amorous and often ludicrous adventures. Seama was reminded that Tregar had been a troublemaker in his youth, having an eye for the girls and a good fight. Often in the wrong place at the wrong time he had been in as many prisons as bedrooms but never for as long: holding a wizard is by no means easy, especially when you think him a drunken lout with no more sense than manners.

Tregar rarely revealed his profession. He used magic only as a last resort. He had found that mystical powers got in the way, particularly with women. And so he had taught himself to use a sword well. He was proud of his duels up and down the three continents, of his victories and even his defeats. And though all this had happened when he was younger there was little doubt, even after fifteen relaxed years at Ayer, that Tregar wasn't someone to pick a fight with.

And yet he was a warm-hearted man. He seemed to have more friends than he could easily count and though he saw these friends rarely he spoke of them with great affection. He had never married but this was no tale of missed opportunity or unrequited love: he'd just never found anyone he needed to be with. He had no regrets. He didn't need to have children to make him feel complete.

Seama sighed a little too loudly for Tregar not to notice.

'You'll've made a lot of friends yoursel' over the years,' he prompted. 'Was there never—'

'I have friends, Tregar. But it's hard for them. When you're on the road as much as I am – well sometimes I make it difficult for them to keep up. Most people need a place to be. It means that sometimes they have to stay and I have to go. And then life seems to tie them down: wives and children come along and get in the way. It's hard being an adventurer forever.'

'And maybe it's hard, too, seeing other people settling down? Do you never feel the need—'

'I have my family with me. Bellus and the Mule keep me going.'

'Ah, weel, I'm sure ye love them well enough but—'

'I do, Tregar. They're all I need.'

Within three hours of the descent from Ayer, they rode steadily into Torhead Bottom. Torhead was a hamlet of seven houses with an inn and hordes of children: escapees from the nearby school. The inn looked promising. Both of them tired, hungry and thirsty, they agreed to stop for a while.

Still close to Ayer the famous wizards were recognized quickly enough and the publican was eager to refuse payment for the food and drink he supplied. Pressed to name some other reward he settled for a few tales of adventure for the gathering crowd, 'and perhaps a bit of magic for the kids'. So Tregar handled the tall tales and, after a little prodding by the audience, Seama produced some sleight of hand to delight them. In terms of ale sold the innkeeper was well paid for his food, and when it was time for them to leave no one was sorrier than he, and the cry of 'come back soon' was most sincere.

A mile on, before the foot of a large drumlin, the road split two ways, and here the wizards paused. It was time to part company.

'Well, Seama,' Tregar said, 'I'd wish you good luck but I don't expect you'll need it: a bunch of sorcerers shouldn't trouble ye too much.'

'I'm glad you're so confident. I suspect they'll be trouble enough. But, no, I'm not too worried about my end of it.

Sorcerers are only men after all. What you'll have to face may be another matter.'

'That's rather a strange thing to say, Seama.'

'Is it? You know, all day long we've talked about this and that but never a word about the task in hand. Why do you suppose that is?'

'What's there to talk about? Where's the point in speculating about some mysterious enemy no one's actually seen; where's the point in trying to make connections, one group with another? You saw what it did to Mador. If you hadn't promised that the Council would take care of this Black Company, and all the trouble with Athoff too, Jade Throne or no he'd still be panicking.'

'Oh I don't think so. You don't give him enough credit. It was the spell that got to him. But never mind that, I'm more concerned with what's to come. You may see no point in it, Tregar, but speculation is my stock in trade. It's the basis of theories and the theories are sometimes close enough to the truth to be important. Take a look at all the problems we're facing, Tregar; do you see no pattern there?'

'Er, no, not really.'

'Well I can. And it makes me think that our biggest problem may well be in Norberry, where you're headed.'

'Well, thanks for that.'

'I'm serious, Tregar. You say we don't know what's going on in the north, so there's no point even thinking about it. You'll just go along and face whatever there is to face and there's nothing more to it than that. But I think these *outlanders* are important, Tregar. It's important who they are.'

'Go on then. Ye've obviously got some theory or other, so spit it out.'

Seama laughed. 'Always the direct way, eh Tregar ? But you took your time with The Kræken of Great Spurl so you might give me a minute or two to get to it.'

'Not as if we're in any hurry.'

Seama chose to ignore the sarcasm.

'For a start, they're no army of Athoff's whatever Mador

might think. Have you ever been to the Dedicae?'

'Not much,' said Tregar, 'I went to look at the Coldwater Gorge once, from the Kellestan end, and that was pretty impressive; and when I was younger I spent some time in Terremark and got to know some mountaineering types. They were forever trying to get me to go with them but I didn't much like the climbing when I did. Too much hard work getting to where ye're going and then too much hanging on by your fingertips in the pouring rain, thinking ye're about to die. Not what I would call fun. And what's the point to it, anyway? A lot of effort just for a good view.'

'It's the challenge, Tregar. Some folk need the risk to remind them they're alive. The mountains are dangerous: climbing suits them. But it doesn't suit everybody. Even if Athoff gathered all the mountaineers together there'd be less than a hundred and I doubt they'd agree to go to war for him, whatever he promised. And anyway even if he could get them to climb the Table, how could they possibly get across the Coldwater? No, it's not Aegardeans. The whole idea's absurd.'

Seama had thought long and hard about it, he was absolutely sure of himself, but still he looked for support.

'Do you agree so far?' he asked.

'Agree? Why not? I will admit it seems unlikely.'

'You say unlikely, I say impossible. Whatever, if not Aegarde, and Gothery we can discount as allies, then it must be Masachea. That's what I thought at first. In the normal way of things it's easy enough to cross the Hurgals. But then Mador insists he has the crossings under his control and I believe him. You'd hardly get a haywain through never mind a small army. Fair?'

'Almost. What if they came in after the attack on Aristeth? Everything was coming apart then. I remember in Ayer we had opposite reports every other hour. Nothing was secure 'til the four Houses reached the border.'

'You're saying an army has been roaming around northern Pars for four months and nobody noticed until a few weeks ago?'

'Well—'

'Of course not. Now there is *one* path over the border that wouldn't be guarded. The Masacheans know it well enough and it could put them quickly into the east end of the Norberry Part. The pass that divides the Hurgals from the Eastern massif.'

'Now you're being ridiculous. Kentreth's Grave? Your Masacheans, Seama: they're no' gods.'

'You don't need to be a god to walk that path, Tregar. I've done it. I made the crossing.' It was hard not to pause for effect. Tregar was visibly shocked. It was a remarkable claim to make. Seama almost enjoyed the look of incredulity, but at the same time he couldn't help feeling oddly uncomfortable to talk about it. 'Only once, of course, a long time ago.'

'But… You couldn't! For gods' sakes, Seama, it's against The Rule.'

'Perhaps that's why I did it.'

'Then you've all the makings of a fool. Waldin'd throw a fit if he knew.'

'He does know, but he wasn't so high up in those days so it wasn't his place to say anything. Actually Waldin and Holander nursed me after I got free of it.'

Tregar's habitual grimace softened slightly. 'What happened? How did ye survive?'

'I don't know. I think I nearly died. It took a long time for me to recover.'

Seama shook his head at the memory of it. What on Ea' had possessed him to think of taking on such a trial, when everything they were taught warned against it?

'Kentreth's Grave. So few escape and those who do are damaged. I knew that, but I couldn't help myself. Perhaps the lure was just too strong. *Power*, Tregar, that's the promise. That one line in the Texts: 'If thou desireth the *Greater Power*, seek then Kentreth's Grave.' No explanation, no advice, just that one teasing sentence. It's driven hundreds to try it. And hundreds have been lost.

'Yet the promise is so vague. You go into it still guessing: what is this 'Greater Power'; how can you claim it, make it your own? Nothing is clear. It's all down to interpretation and you know how easy it is to misread the Texts. Oh, I survived, Tregar, and I can tell you my power is stronger as a result but I don't know whether it was worth the pain. It was… as if a fire raged inside me, destroying everything I was and everything I knew; it over-filled me. There was nothing I could do to let it all out.

'I was lucky: a farmer found me lying in the dirt, raving and delirious I guess, twenty miles or so from the Stone. I could so easily have fallen over a cliff or drowned in a pool. He was a good man. Watched me through my madness and when I was able to tell him my name he sent messages to Errensea. By the time Waldin came for me the fever had gone but left me a weakling. Even though I could feel the power coursing in my veins I couldn't use it for months after.' Seama winced as though the mere memory galled him. 'Never be tempted, Tregar: the path to power is a dangerous one. If I had my time over I would not take it.'

Tregar looked at Seama, half in wonder, half in disbelief at the madness of the endeavour. 'Well,' he said, 'I think I'll give it a miss then.'

Seama smiled wanly. 'Good choice. Anyway, to get back to the point of all this, even if some group of Masacheans did manage to enter the valley there's little chance they'd have come out on the other side. Common soldiers could not endure.'

Tregar was frowning and twisting at the reins he held as he tried to encompass the meaning of Seama's revelation. His horse, Sirrah, snorted and stamped restlessly. 'What happens to them, Seama?' he asked, 'The people who try it? You say hundreds have perished. Did they die after they got out or…?'

'They did not get out.'

'That's why it's called a grave then?'

'Not what I meant. They did not come out but neither did they stay. There were no corpses or skeletons. Not that I could see.' Seama sighed. How could he explain if he didn't himself understand? Having introduced the topic, Seama was now oddly desperate to leave the mystery of Kentreth's Grave out of the reckoning. And yet he knew that he shouldn't. It was only as he spoke of that terrible place and what it did to him that he understood a connection to The Song of Ages; he realised there and then, and not before, where those echoes came from, those memories given life by the words he had read. He shied away from the notion. It was too much to think about here and now. 'No Tregar, I'd rather not describe it; I probably couldn't find the words if I tried. Let's keep to the job in hand. The tale is this: if Masacheans cannot use Kentreth's Grave, and all other passes are guarded, then this lot in the Norberry Part must be someone else.'

'It doesn't leave many alternatives, Seama.'

'There weren't many to start with.'

'So, what then? Mad Mountain-men of Jinsa?'

'This is no children's story, Tregar.'

'What sort of story is it then?'

Seama nibbled at his top lip, reluctant to continue. Why was it so hard to tell? He had been all around the houses but now that he came to it, 'the theory' building in him, he was reluctant to continue. Was it because he was scared he might be proved wrong and look foolish? What if Tregar laughed? Holander had laughed. He had called the Song 'senile tommy-rot' and couldn't understand why Seama was drawn to it. All Holander wanted was to get to grips with the pair of villains who had set a fire in 'his' library and wanted no truck with 'half-wit theorising.' Seama was still smarting from that one. The last thing he wanted was Tregar adding insult to the injury. The problem was that, if the theory was right – and given what he'd been told about Jaspar and his mysterious Outlanders, it could well be – then Tregar would very likely be the first to meet them. It. Whatever they or it might be.

'Two guesses left,' he told Tregar at last, 'The first that these Outlanders are criminals, robbers gathered together over the course of a few months. They've seen their chance with all the armies tied up on the borders, and encouraged by stories of the Black Company in Aegarde.'

'To my mind, Seama, that explanation's been on the cards since the beginning and ye've taken a deal of time to come to it.'

'That's because it is the most likely and one I cannot satisfactorily fault.'

'Though obviously ye don't believe it. Ye still haven't explained what ye meant by wondering whether it was *men* I faced. Give me your guess.'

Seama took a good, deep breath and began.

'There's a book, Tregar, by Haslem. It's called The Song of Ages. The reason I know anything about it is because it called me.'

'Called you?'

'Summoned me. Very powerfully. Twice. The second time it happened was just a couple of months ago.' Seama went on to give Tregar a short version of the events surrounding the fire in the Library. Tregar was outraged.

'They could have killed hundreds of people if you hadn't been there! Setting a fire in a library! For Neath's sake, were they mad?'

'It was just the one book, Tregar. They used naphtha: all over the inside covers, fired at a distance by a fairly simple spell. But you're right, the consequences could have been terrible.'

'Aye, and no mistake. They could have had the entire collection in ashes. Have we any idea why they did this?'

'To stop *me* reading it, I presume.'

'Is it a book of spells?'

'No. Well not the bit we saved anyway. It's more of a history.'

Tregar's frown deepened. 'I've never much cared for History books. By Haslem too. Some people would say it was asking to be burnt, but I don't understand, why didn't they just steal it?'

'Not easy, Tregar. It was a huge thing, heavy as a paving slab. They'd never have got it past Grek. What *I* don't understand is why now? The book's been in the Library for a thousand years: all the world could have read it twice over.'

'That was going to be *my* question, Seama. That and why are we bathering with this? It doesn't seem to be getting us anywhere.'

'Well, part of the 'why now', I would guess, is because the book is important now and wasn't before, though that's not much of answer. And why are we bothering? Because I think it's a part of everything that has been going on.'

'You'd better explain that. What *is* going on?'

'Well, it's clear someone, or some group of people, is at the root of all the madness of the last few months: Gothery in chaos, Sirl ill; the Masacheans attacking Pars as though they've found a new purpose in life; Ayer itself under attack; and then to top it all this mystery in the North.'

'Ye're determined it's all apiece?'

'Yes, I'd stake my power on it. We have an enemy, a single enemy. I don't know who and I don't like to think I know why, but he's been pushing the pieces around the board and plotting our destruction for months now. To say he has us on the back foot is understating it. We're in deep trouble. How close we are to the end game we just don't know. What we need, and fast, is information and that's why you have to go north to delay them, while I go to Astoril.'

'What about the Black Company? You promised Mador—'

'Yes, yes. I did, I will. But do you see what's happening? We're being pulled here there and everywhere. But the answer's in a library somewhere, not out on the road. The answer's in what I *haven't* read.'

Tregar wouldn't have it.

'Oh come on now Seama. Is that not going a bit too far?' At last his impatience was beginning to show. 'How could a history book have anything to do with what's going on now, today?'

Seama could feel the argument slipping away from him. Tregar sounded almost offended. Not knowing what else to do he reached down into his saddlebags and produced the sheaf of papers that had so enthralled him. He held it out.

'Here, take a look at this. Then you'll see. It's a copy of everything we could save from the fire.'

Tregar looked doubtfully at the wad of paper in Seama's hand.

'Ye don't think I've time to read that lot, surely?'

Seama was disappointed by the reaction. He riffled through the pages and selected two. 'At least read this part,' he said, handing them over.

Tregar sighed theatrically. 'Neath's Sake. You couldn't have had it translated then? My Mid' Parsee's not all that good y'know…' he glanced over at Seama looking for some give but got none. 'Ah weel, I suppose I'll manage.'

Seama waited. After about five minutes of puffing and blowing from Tregar as he struggled with his grammar, the Court Wizard slapped the pages with the back of one hand.

'This, Seama Beltomé, is a piece of fiction!'

'That's what Grek said.'

'So why are ye wasting *my* time with it?'

'I think it's true. You haven't read enough. Yes there's a creation myth in there but the rest is all names and dates and places—'

'Which *I've* never heard of.'

'Of which most people have never heard, true. But, if you read the introduction – the piece I gave you was a part of it – and you learn that 'the reign of Ah'remmon ended when the Greats of Earnor joined themselves with Glorious Ohr'maz and with He that is Time' and that 'Ah'remmon is cast out' you have to realize it's a style of story-telling. It's a metaphor of the truth. Men do the deeds in this world, not Gods. I talked about this with Grek. She was convinced Ah'remmon simply means 'The Enemy' or 'Evil Enemy.' Whenever was there an enemy *not* considered evil? All it's saying is there was a massive war and the Enemy was thrown out. Now, if you go to the relevant bit of the narrative, it's there you get the real events with the names of the kings involved, the dates of their reigns, the names of their kingdoms, their allegiances, the battles, the victories, defeats and so on. It's very complex. I don't think anyone could have *invented* such detail. Haslem couldn't have done it and he wouldn't: for someone like Haslem fiction was far too petty to bother with. This is a real history, Tregar, a history of *all* the ages of Earnor.'

Tregar looked unconvinced. *'All* the Ages? Well, silly me, but I thought there was only the one. None of the histories I've ever seen goes any further back than the Wandering. Even if there was something before then, how could we know anything about it. Are there texts you've read that us lesser mortals aren't allowed to see? No, of course not, not histories anyway. So if it isn't fiction, where did Haslem get to hear of it? Have you thought about that?'

'Yes I have.'

'And?'

'I don't know.' Holander's thought that the information might be found in the antiquities had, by the look of things, come to nothing. There were hints and speculations but they'd found nothing that could really be called a source. Not so far, anyway. 'Look, what I do know is that no one had more knowledge or power or skill with that power than Haslem. Somewhere in his writing, either here in The Song, or maybe in another work, Haslem will have left us a clue as to how he did it. 'Till we find it we will just have to stick with what we have in hand and try to work out what he's trying to tell us.'

'So the bit you gave me: what's that supposed to tell us? If I'm reading it right it's all about banishing *The Followers from the Land of the Just.*'

'The *Followers* are also called the *Children of Ah'remmon.* And sometimes it says *Creatures of Ah'remmon.*'

'Creatures, eh? And these creatures are the same as followers?'

'Possibly; probably. It might just mean they're bad men.'

'You don't believe that, do you?'

'No.' Seama had visited King Sirl's museum in Astoril. There were ancient bones there, large and monstrous remains that did not seem to have anything at all to do with man or any beast yet walking this world they knew. 'I don't know what it might mean.'

'So, where are we now? These *Followers* are, banished from *The Land of the Just* – which I take to be Earnor –and they're cast into *The Wilderness,* somewhere called *Kyzylkum.* That right?'

'Your M'Pars isn't so bad after all.'

'Bad enough. What's this bit about Kyzylkum being *the land beyond The Heights* then? Which heights? Or is this another of those metaphors?'

Seama took another deep breath. 'That's the point, Tregar: I don't think it is. I asked Grek what she thought about that bit and she said it depends on who originated the story. If it all came from Haslem's head then it was impossible to say: Haslem should have said what he meant. But if Haslem was merely reporting the story, say from one of the Classics, it might be easier to understand. If you go back to the very earliest texts we know – that is anything Medean, up to four thousand years old – it can mean just one thing. In all the ancient stories each range of mountains is given the name we know now, all bar one. One range is known simply as 'The Heights', more important than all the rest. The Wandering People revered The Heights as the home of the gods.'

'And The Heights were?'

'The Dedicae.'

'Kyyzylkum lies beyond the Dedicae?'

'Well possibly. More likely 'through' the Dedicae.'

'Neath's sake!' Tregar wasn't grinning. He had guessed at "The Theory" and just like Holander he rejected it out of hand. Seama felt a keen sense of failure. Tregar continued: 'Let's get this straight, what you're saying is that north of the Dedicae there's a land – this Kyzylkum place – and it's full of people or creatures or some such, all descended from these 'Children of Ah'remmon', who by the way happens to be the personification of Evil. And *you think* they're coming to get us, and that's what's waiting for me up beyond the Francon! Honestly Seama, it isn't even a *good* children's story.'

'I'm serious, Tregar. Tell me, how long is it since a book last summoned you? When was the last time someone set fire to a book just so you couldn't read it? This is a warning, Tregar, and I think we'd be foolish to ignore it. What more can I say?'

'Not a lot. *I* think there's a brigand army to fight and *you* think it's monsters.'

'Not monsters, well, maybe. The fact is I don't know what to expect.'

'Seama!' Tregar had had enough, '*Something* is going on. That I can accept. But all this nonsense is stretching my patience. Look it doesn't matter to me that your book was written a thousand years ago and you only have a bit of it anyway. If it spoke sense I would have not a problem with it. But a land *beyond the Dedicae?* We all know the Dedicae marches all the way to the sea. It's on the maps! There's nothing up there but cliffs and rocks and a very rough ocean. Your monsters would have to breathe underwaeter.'

'But Tregar, we know only what we have learned. How can we really know what lies beyond the Dedicae unless we go there?'

'Am I te believe nothing I've been taught?' This time Tregar was plain angry, the underlying growl in his voice by now almost menacing. 'No Seama, I'll always trust Errensea. They made me a wiezart; I'll not reject their teaching. Now never fear: I'll think about whit ye said, but I suggest you do the same. Meanwhile we're wasting time. Sirrah's impatient to be running and I want to be getting this journey startet, so we'll be off now. Right now. Goodbye, Seama.'

And that was that. With a twitch of the reins and a click of his tongue he turned his hunter toward the right hand fork of the road and made him trot. Tregar had listened to too many words, words he had no intention of accepting; now he was off to look for some good straightforward action. Seama didn't try to call him back.

Mule, who had been remarkably silent and attentive throughout the discussion, for some reason decided to punctuate this scene by braying a sort of farewell. It came out perhaps closer to a barracking. Bellus snorted in protest and Seama covered his ears.

'For Gods' sakes, Mule! Can you not be quiet!' he shouted.

Mule could not, or would not.

Tregar, hearing the racket break out behind him, came to a halt and looked back. Mule relented.

'Fare-ye-well, Seama,' the wizard yelled out in a gargantuan voice, 'Be sure to send me my soldiers, quick as ye can. And good luck with that *family* of yourn. Farewell!'

And this time Tregar kicked Sirrah up into a gallop, and rounding a spur they were gone.

'Well, thank you Mule. I'm glad he didn't go away still angry with us.'

Mule snickered and then fell silent.

Seama sat motionless in his saddle for a good ten minutes after Tregar's departure. His family waited patiently for him to have done. He was not idle. With all the power he could muster he was looking ahead, along Tregar's lonely path, past wood and water, over the hills and through the deep valleys that marked this road into the far north of Pars. He had no distinction in the art but such was his *power* that, in most circumstances, his *sight* was good and could range two hundred miles or more. And yet today it failed him. The Carrig fells, Greteth, the Francon Valley and all the lands beyond were hidden from Seama's view. A strange mist clouded his thoughts whenever he tried to cast further and deeper. He sighed. There was nothing he could do but hope: hope that Tregar could manage, and hope beyond hope that his own ludicrous theory was wrong.

'Come on, Bellus,' he said at last, 'Come on, Mule. Let's get him his soldiers: I think he's going to need them.'

KENTRETH'S GRAVE

Norberry Part 3026.4.10

Kentreth's Grave was the name given by men to the pass of land between the Hurgals and the Dedicae. It was a place without explanation. Long ago, when the Wandering People had not yet explored all the lands of Asteranor, one of the Noble Tribes, whose chiefs were the ancestors of Sandar and called by history the Medes, had amongst them a chieftain named Kentreth'hal. He was a brave man, though History makes him seem foolish. His story was twisted by millennia before it came to be written down for future generations but, no doubt, remained true to the events even if the words actually spoken were lost. It was a tale of jealousy and rejection, an angry, love torn oath and a wilful, fateful journey into the darkness of a haunted vale. Kentreth'hal, the man, never returned to his love-lost or his family and emerged from the vale only as a broken spirit to bring one last warning to the living. The ghost came to the elders of the Medes saying:

> *Heed well my words,*
> *O Chiefs of men!*
> *Let not thy children,*
> *Strong or frail,*
> *Seek out my grave.*
>
> *It is forbidden*
> *To mortal men.*
> *Death or damnation*
> *Be their course*
> *If my words are forgotten.*
>
> *This is no curse,*
> *Take heed of my warning:*
> *Only the Sayoshant*
> *Will pass unscathed*
> *To say a prayer at my grave.*

The elders who had never seen a ghost before were duly impressed and made sure the words were heard and understood by men of all tribes. They placed a stone at the western end of the valley inscribed with the verse.

Naturally, the warning had been challenged by young men through the ages and it is true that some of them emerged from the valley alive but they were not unscathed. Even Seama would not claim to have been unchanged. Though he suffered both physical and mental injury Seama did recover. Unlike other survivors he kept his sanity, but he was affected more subtly.

Sayoshant had been translated as 'the Best of Men' and Seama Beltomé, sure of his *power*, thought he had a right to that title, as had many before him. Why would he attempt the crossing? Not to test himself, that much he was sure of. The fact that a feat may be achieved is no real reason for trying to achieve it. Did he simply lust after The *Greater Power* spoken of in the Texts? There was something in that, but it didn't explain all. Another force was driving him, a force more potent than lust. It was something to do with the *power inherent*. Something to do with that oddest feeling he had, every now and then, that everything he did was on one side of a bargain: a bargain he had made somehow in his dreams, that remained tantalisingly over the edge of memory and yet it ruled all of his thoughts. There was an obligation involved. The power he enjoyed *required* him to walk that path and Seama was happy to comply.

The stone was there, the marks on it clear though indecipherable to common men, yet still it had the power to turn them away. It made Seama pause and wonder at his peril. Ignoring peril he strode on into what seemed an ordinary pass. It was noon when he entered but within minutes of leaving the stone the sky above him seemed to grow dark. He stumbled on in a thickening gloom. Soon it was blacker than night, he could not see. Blind, he pushed onwards.

And then the nightmare began. Visions assailed him of men and women in torment, demons devouring, Gods raping the world. The temptation of immeasurable power pulled him from the path. Knowledge of final, inescapable despair dragged him to his knees. Lust and hatred ground him into the dirt. He was drowning in unfamiliar emotions but all the while a redeeming promise hung in the air above him. All he need do was grasp it and he would immediately have the power to control and to indulge in these new feelings. And he would have grasped it but for another force that buoyed him up. Every thought of evil the world has ever known was challenged by everything good there has ever been. Visions of peace and beauty and art and music vied with the heady fury of battle and the eager delights of cruelty and destruction. A battle raged within him: unsullied love fought unquenchable desire; there seemed to be no ending.

That was how he remembered it but no words he knew could really tell the horror and… and the *grandeur* of his experience. His soul was ripped apart. The two great opposing forces of existence examined him, tested him, right down to the last shred of whatever it was that was himself and none other. And finally, before he could remember no more, the Great Glory of being passed, admitted, accepted, approved by all that was Good and True; of being rejected, reviled and feared by all that was not. He truly was the Sayoshant.

He awoke, or came to his senses, on the Partian side of the pass. He had little recollection of the place itself but the memory of the horror and glory stayed with him. The trauma left him ill for nearly a year but the knowledge of Errensea had warned there would be a price to pay and this year of illness seemed only due. And after that year the power at his command increased significantly. He often wondered what had happened to those men and women before him who had given their sanity as payment. He presumed their fault was in rejecting Good and they were being punished, or perhaps they had rightly rejected Evil but hadn't the strength to survive the subsequent onslaught. It never occurred to him that they might not have chosen any particular side at all, that they couldn't, and the dilemma had cost them their senses. And the reason it didn't occur to him was because he *had* chosen and now he paid the real price. Irrevocably his allegiance was given to the one, his hatred to the other, and the world in his eyes was soon divided into two camps.

ISOLDE

Nether Makerfield 3057.7.20

'So what does it say then?'

She had to smile. The look in his eyes was all mischief. Gerald Robarn just loved secrets, and delighted in being 'the man in the know.' His retirement from Mador's service had not changed him.

'Father, you should know better. This is a public place.'

'Yes, dearest daughter, I am well aware that this very fine drinking house, which I happen to own, is a very public place; that is after all what it is for. However I note there are only three other people present: one is my innkeeper and the other two are Stam and Rona, a young couple I've known all their lives, so totally caught up in gazing into each other's eyes they would not notice if I stood on this table and danced for them. I am also aware that we are presently secluded in a nice corner far enough away for our speech to be inaudible to them all. Unless there is some invisible presence with a magical power of hearing far beyond the skill of cats and bats, then, daughter dear, we are safe to discuss whatsoever we will whether it be the disposition of forces or the extraordinary size of King Mador's underwear.'

'I don't think he will ever forgive that clothier.'

'It is one thing to make ludicrous clothes for your King and yet another to tell the world about it. But that is a long way from being beside the point. What about the letter? I know I'm just an old fool—'

'Rubbish father! We both know you're not an old fool but I really should not be talking about this. I know you're curious but this *is* the King's mail!'

'Yes, I am curious, Isolde, but more than that I am concerned. You have such confidence, you think you can take on anything and mostly you can, but Asteranor is a dangerous place just now. When all comes to all, my little Izzy, you are my darling daughter and without you I'd be lost. I want to make sure you will be safe.'

Isolde sat back with a sigh. She knew that this was as much simple manipulation as plain truth but ever since her mother died, nearly eight years past, her father had somehow lost the strength he was known for. She was indeed his mainstay and it was a role she accepted happily enough providing, of course, her father understood that it would work according to her rules and not his. She gave him her time, half of the time. Whenever she wasn't on some mission or other for Mador she returned to the Lyndons and enjoyed her life there. But it was becoming more difficult, her work more demanding, her personal needs not addressed. Between Mador and her father, between work and home there was precious little time for anything that was just for Isolde. Her parents had shared a wonderful relationship for forty-two years. They had first met at a party for her mother's seventeenth birthday and neither had looked at another since. There was an aching sadness in her father's eyes these days but at least they had found each other and shared a good life together. Where would Isolde find such a relationship? When would she ever get the chance to look? Not yet a while. She reached across the table and took her father's hand.

'I love you daddy but I need to go my own way. I am so like you: can you not remember yourself at my age? You would never have taken the safe road. Only mum could have held you back and she never did; she never wanted to: she loved you for what you were.'

'Hmm. For what I was, eh. Not what I am now. Oh, I am changed; I know it. I never knew love until I met Louise. My mother died when I was too young to understand anything and my father was always rather remote from us children. It was only in your mother and in you that I found my true place in the world. Losing her has hit me hard but for now I still have you. And you still have me, but I will not be around forever. Before I depart this world my darling I would like to see you find your own place.'

'Father, you are as strong as an ox. You'll be ninety before you die.'

'You could have said a hundred.'

'Let's not get carried away.'

Her father grinned. 'It's being carried away I'm worried about. But we're getting off the point. The original point, mind you: I still want to know what Mador is asking you to do. You know there's a rumour that Xandra has gone missing? Yes, well I'll not have him losing my daughter too.'

'Oh really father, you can hardly blame Mador.'

'Yes I can. Very easily. What fool sends his daughter to war?'

'Any man with a daughter like Xandra, I should say. Do you think he could deny her anything she'd set her mind on? She wanted to join her House and that was that. How did you hear about this anyway?'

'I have my contacts. As do you. Now, about this letter?'

'You can be quite maddening at times, do you know that?' The words were cranky but she was smiling: there was something of the old Robarn tenacity about him this morning and it was a pleasure to see. 'Well, why not. It's not as if I can't trust you to keep a secret. To be frank, father, there's not much to tell. Anparas and Temor are in Riverport—'

'Yes, I know.'

Isolde raised her eyebrows and Gerald allowed himself a small smile.

'And do you know why they have left their barracks?'

'No, not really. Oh I did hear a rumour that Mador was intent on invading Gothery.'

'Gods, is nothing safe?'

'Not very, but don't forget I had a position at Ayer for many years. I have many friends and I'm bound to hear things that others do not.'

'Not that you go fishing for it then?'

'I've been casting my nets for half a century, Isolde: it's hard to break the habit. Now it's more of an amusement than a job. The invasion is on, then?'

'I don't know that I would use the word 'invasion'. I've been told to report to Lomal for further instruction on my role in Gothery. I would imagine, as he knows me well, that I'll be asked to liaise with the King.'

'*Liaise* with Sirl?'

'Well, 'pacify' might be a better word. Reassure him that it's for his own good we've overrun his country and taken control. That kind of thing.'

Gerald laughed. 'Good luck to you. Of course this is all dependent on finding Sirl still in charge. I heard tell he was ill and that his doctor seemed to be running things.'

'One I've not heard. Who is this doctor?'

'I didn't get a name. But you'll find out soon enough, I daresay. When do you leave?'

'Tomorrow morning. I'll take the carriage, if you don't mind. I'll be needing my trunk if I'm to dress for the King of Gothery. Lord Anparas expects me, and some others, at Riverport docks by noon at the latest. It's thirteen miles. I need only set off at nine. Time for a good breakfast with my dear old dad before I go.'

'That will be very nice. I'll ask Jeffers to make sure the carriage is ready for eight. It won't hurt us to have breakfast a little earlier and you're more likely to be there on time. And Roddy can come with you too: Cook wants him to do some shopping for her. Now then, I've finished my sup and you never do, so shall we go?'

'Only two pints today, father?'

'One for the gut and one for the head. There was a poem I was working on and I don't want to get too cloudy for it.'

'Let's go then. Perhaps you can give it to me before I leave.'

'Perhaps. You're so kind to your old dad, anyone would think you liked to read my poems.'

'Some of them.' She linked his arm and they made their way out into the bright sunlight.

On a bench up against the wall of the drinking house away to the right of the main door sat a young woman. Isolde and her father did not register she was there. The homespun garb she wore was almost the same colour as the grey stone she leaned against and she was completely still. Only her eyes moved, strangely violet eyes that followed the pair down the lane. She listened to their conversation all the way back to the manse, heard the lock of the door rattle with keys, she heard the cook tell them supper would be ready in half an hour, she heard the gurgle of water as Isolde filled a bowl to wash her face.

Satisfied she drew herself up and took the path to the main road where she caused a farmer to stop his cart and offer her a ride.

The ability to hear through walls and over distances was only one of her skills.

Isolde kissed her father goodbye once more and hugged him tight. She was leaving him once again. For some reason the parting seemed more difficult this time. She found it hard to let go.

'Are we off then, Miss Iz?' Jeffers opened the carriage door for her. Thank the stars he still had Cook and Jeffers, both of them just young enough to see him through to the end of his days and both happy to do so. 'Best to get on, he'll be miserable when you've gone however many kisses you leave him with.'

There were tears standing in her father's eyes. She gave him one final squeeze.

'It's me that needs the kisses, Jeb,' she said. 'But you're right: it's time I got going. 'Bye Dad. It'll not be long this one before I'll be heading back to Ayer with some message or other. I'll call in on the way. Why don't you come up to Ayer with me?'

'Oh, they don't want an old codger like me up at court.'

'Nonsense father. You think about it. You've been hiding up at the Lyndons far too long now.'

He shrugged dismissively and then reached out a hand to help her into the carriage. Jeffers leapt up beside Roddy and with no more words and no more fuss they set off. She looked back once to see her father staring after the carriage, a forlorn look about him. She waved but he didn't wave back: his eyesight was none too good these days. She settled back in the cushions and tried to stop worrying about him.

Off on the road again! This was her life; had been these five years. She had grown up at court. Her father's work in Mador's service had kept the family away from the Lyndons, the family home, for the best part of every year until her mother died. As such she was perfectly placed to make an impression and as she matured Mador was quick to recognise her best qualities. She was good at engaging people. When she spoke people listened; when she listened they spoke. She had a cool head in an argument and she rarely lost one. She understood politics and commerce. In short she was the perfect ambassador for Pars and the King. Much of her talent came from her father of course but in one regard she had the edge on her dear old dad: she was quite lovely, and sensible enough to realise that without it being a matter of vanity. Beauty was a great weapon if used carefully. Men, and indeed some women, became positively stupid whenever she turned on the charm.

She allowed herself the girlish giggle she kept for her most private moments. Last year she'd been sent to mediate between rival fleet-masters down in Pulonia. The two aggrieved parties were each claiming exclusive fishing rights over the same stretch of water. Both sides were represented by equally pig-headed, slightly more than middle-aged men determined never to sign up to anything that did not give them complete victory in the argument. Straightforward arbitration would have got them nowhere. There was only one solution and within only a week Isolde had them weak in the knees and weak in the head. They were each so desperate to impress the ravishing creature so captivating their attention, that the original dispute between them became a minor consideration. They awoke from their dreams of romantic pursuit to find that not only had they done a deal and signed on the line, but they had agreed to be bound by the contract 'at the risk of the King's Law.' And then, worse still, they had then to suffer her 'best wishes' and departure for Ayer.

Sometimes she felt a little guilty. Her cheeks blushed fetchingly at the thought. But sometimes her charms got her in trouble.

Mador had insisted she must always travel with a guard or two to discourage any foolishness. Just at the moment, however, she was taking a rest from such support. Long hours on the road in close company with a beautiful woman could lead to misunderstandings: some men could think there may be a connection or a promise when there was none. Her 'relationship' with Redlan Ibbold had been particularly fraught. He was not a bad man, it was just that he couldn't cope with the feelings she unintentionally provoked. The man wandered a perilous path between professing undying love and displaying an aggressive jealousy that threatened to explode into real violence. He had been sent away with House Imperan to do battle on the slopes of the Hurgals as much for his own safety as for hers. Isolde had retreated to the Lyndons frightened and confused.

'What you want, girlie, is a man between your legs,' he'd yelled at her as they parted, '*You* know you do and *I* know you do. So what's wrong with me?'

It was a brutal way of putting it but she could sense the underlying pain in his words. So life goes: few people get exactly what they want when it comes down to love. He was right of course. She most certainly did want a man but it was not him. Not by a long way. She sighed the sigh that had been perplexing her father this past month. At least that was one secret he wasn't party to.

She shook her head but there was no one to see it. Where was this getting her? 'Why bother yourself Izzy' she said out loud, 'there's always work. And there's always friends too. And another thing, life is too short for talking to yourself.' And with that she stuck her head out of the window and yelled 'Move over Roddy, I'm coming up.' Long and delicate blue silk robe notwithstanding, she hauled herself out of the window, up onto the roof and plumped herself down on the box seat. Soon Roddy and Jeb and Isolde were exchanging jokes and laughter and her journey away from the Lyndons and her father began to seem not so bad.

It was just about nine o'clock when it happened. The carriage was rumbling on, young, flame-haired Roddy was rumbling on too about what he could buy for his lass, and Isolde was contentedly taking in the warm sun and the lovely scenery when with a squalling cry a young girl broke cover.

'Help! Please help me!' she pleaded, casting herself dangerously onto the road before the horses. Jeb had the devil of a job reining in but as soon as they came to a halt Isolde jumped down.

'Up you get, little one,' she said, hauling the waif to her feet. A comely child she was, a well made twelve or thirteen year old with a pretty face but the face was streaked with tears. 'What's happened to you then?'

The girl twisted away from Isolde as soon as she was on her feet as though she had been scalded by her touch.

'Not me, Miss, it's me mam. She's sick; it's bad and I don't know what to do. Can you come Miss? It's just back there.' She pointed to a track through the trees edging the road.

Isolde saw no reason to be wary but Jeb said: 'I'd better come with you.' The effect of those words on the girl was alarming.

'No! No you can't,' she yelped. 'You mustn't. You won't let him Miss will you?'

'Whatever's wrong?' Jeb asked, an aggrieved edge to his voice. 'I'll not harm you.'

The girl was shaking with fright. 'It's my mam, see...' she tried to explain, 'Some men came... and they... they hurt her a lot. Last night. They've all gone now.'

Isolde shared a look with Jeb. 'You stay here Jeb. She won't want to be seeing men just now. I'll be fine.' She reached into the pocket of her gown and pulled out a thin brass cylinder. 'If I need you I'll whistle.'

Jeb wasn't happy about it but he'd learned not to argue with Miss Iz whenever she had made up her mind.

'Right then. We'll wait. Just make sure you do whistle if anything seems not right.'

'None of this is going to be right, Jeb.'

The track led to a white painted, one storey, one roomed cottage. The young girl ran through the open gate but came to a halt before she reached the door, terrified to go any further. She looked back as Isolde caught up.

'She's in here, Miss. It... it smells bad.'

Isolde felt nervous but she put the feeling aside, stepped

past the girl and lifted the latch. When the door swung open the stench hit her like a blow. It was the acrid smell of ordure overlain by the unmistakable flyblown smell of a summer death. A hideous buzzing filled the air.

This was no place for a child. 'Wait for me on the other side of the fence,' she said to the girl, 'I'll be out again soon.' The girl did as she was told without question. She didn't want to go into the house and no one would blame her. Isolde stepped through the doorway.

There was no light other than from the door and it was difficult to make out the lay of the room in the gloom. She stumbled over to one of the windows, pulled open the casement and pushed at the creaking shutters. The stench was making her gag and she took in three lungs-full of clean air before turning back to survey the room.

Isolde was by nature self possessed whatever the situation but she almost screamed.

Over by the range were the savaged remains of what was once a grown woman. Her face was untouched but her body had been ripped apart. Her bowels were spilled everywhere, lumps of flesh were scattered round about: on the range, on the table, on the floor, a liver, a kidney, a womb.

Isolde couldn't hold it back any longer: she bent double and vomited.

'You alright, miss?' came the girl's voice through the doorway, 'What's happened?'

'Stay out, girl!' Isolde spat out the last of her breakfast. 'Go and get my friends, will you? Now!'

She heard the girl running away, sobbing again. Stock still, she closed her eyes and forced herself to calm down. Whatever had happened here it was over now. She had seen corpses before and been able to cope. A dead body is a dead body, nothing more or less, and it cannot possibly hurt you. *One more look,* she told herself, *just to see if there's anything more and then you can leave.* Bargain made, Isolde opened her eyes to the horror once more and set about her task.

She walked around the table, determined not to step on

anything that was not the floor itself, and examined the destruction at close hand. The woman's eyes were still open in a look suggesting surprise rather than terror. Isolde contemplated trying to close them but decided against: she would have had to wade through too much blood and flesh. It was an incredible sight. Surely, she thought, not even the most brutal of men would have gone this far. She bent closer to peer at the wreck of the woman's torso. The edges of the wounds were not clean cut as with a knife but torn and ragged. It was the work of claws. Was there some savage animal on the loose? But that wouldn't tally with what the girl said about men hurting her mother. Did they bring an animal with them?

Something moved. She heard it: a small something. Just past the range was a niche in the wall. Isolde was convinced that was where the noise had come from. A small, terrified part of her mind screamed at her to leave at once, to go no further, to not look. But Isolde looked.

And she could not bear the sight. Propped up against a small door like some discarded doll, was another child, her legs tucked under as though she had been trying to hide; her head dipped so that her long brown hair curtained her face. Her chest was bloody, she was dead. Isolde's eyes filled with tears. Had they no shame?

The noise came again. Just there in her lap was a white mouse: the sort young children keep as pets. It seemed unconcerned by Isolde's approach and continued to nibble at the piece of meat it had found and brought back.

By her size the girl looked to be about the same age as the girl who had brought her to this place. She wore the same style of clothes, had the same colour of hair. A sister perhaps. Isolde crouched and gently lifted the face by the chin to see if there was a resemblance.

'No!' she gasped.

The face was not similar, but identical. Just then a shadow fell across the scene. Someone was standing in the doorway.

'Jeb? Is that—'

She sprang to her feet and whirled round in the same

movement. The silhouetted form in the doorway was motionless.

'She was a pretty young thing,' it said. 'Ever so sweet.'

Stepping forward into the light from the opened window came a woman of Isolde's age, of Isolde's height and weight; she had the same long, golden hair and she wore the same face. The only points of difference between Isolde and this shocking apparition were in the cat-like claws and the bared fangs.

The whistle shrilled and had Jeb and Roddy running like fury. They met Isolde staggering back down the path with the whistle in her mouth. Her clothes were torn and bloody, her hair was in a tangle and her face was battered. She fell to the ground just as they reached her but immediately pulled herself to her feet and carried on.

'What's happened?' Jeb cried as he ran alongside, his arms desperate to hold her.

'I was attacked! Don't fret so. It'll be right, Jeb, but we have to go – right now. I fought her off and she went, but the Gods help us if she comes back. I'll explain when we're gone.'

'But what about the lass and her mother?'

'They're a long way beyond our help. Now let's go.'

When they reached the carriage Isolde clambered inside while Roddy and Jeb leapt up top. Roddy groped about under the seat for the crossbow as Jeb whipped up the horses. Hopefully whoever had attacked Miss Iz wouldn't be able to catch them but if they did Roddy wanted an argument in his hands.

BOOTY

Riverport 3057.7.21

At the top of a dark hill they stood, a great horse and a warrior figured against the grey light of the coming day. They had journeyed with little rest for two days, riding through the night, spurred on by an overpowering sense of urgency. Seama feared for the House of Sands, not knowing what it was he feared. He had tried frequently to gain some remote vision of the enemy in the North but all was shrouded by a yellow, evil fog he could not penetrate. Dark shadows prowled within, menacing but indistinct, nothing was clear. If only he could be there to help but his duty lay to the west. Tregar would have to cope and Seama could only make sure he got his soldiers without delay.

They waited, breathing hard, sending long streams of condensing air into the predawn cold. The dew was heavy on them in grey beads that picked out the spreading light. They waited to see what the dawn would reveal below. The horse whinnied as a stirring of the air brought with it the smell of the river that was like a sea and far away a gull cried.

Momently the light grew broader and the plain beneath, beyond the shadows of the Esterdales, awoke to the colours of the day, the dark fields becoming summer green and here and there ablaze with ripening gold. The sun was rising in glory behind them but Seama had eyes only for what lay below, down where the meadows came to an end.

There mists from the river rose with the sun, as though she were boiling the waters of some vast cauldron, and because of the mists Seama was denied sight of the river itself; but at the rim of the bowl, yet vague to the eye, was red-walled Riverport. Like a ragged tor thrust above the fields, the city was a haphazard pile of brick and stone, all packed tight within the guardian walls, so dense it was hard to believe people could live there. From a distance it was impossible to see the many streets and alleys awaiting silently the morning rush and clamour. The sun now glinted on a multitude of windows, dancing in bright colours as she showed off the stained-glass houses of the rich, and the gulls, flashing in and out of her rays, called mockingly for all of the townspeople to awake.

The houses were of all shapes and sizes and many stood dwarfed and dark in the shadows of grander neighbours. Near the docks and near the gates it would be seen that the houses were smallest and even more crowded together, while further away from the bustle rose imposing mansions, the monuments of families long rich from trade, and here too were palaces of the nobility, and the barracks of the militia.

Seama raised his eyes to take in a view of the docks that were the main artery of this heart of commerce and saw a crazy forest of masts and network of rigging standing proud of the tall warehouses surrounding the quays. The masts bobbed up and down and seemed to tangle themselves and then a topsail was unfurled, like a flag heralding the sunrise. The new day was truly begun as the earliest sailors prepared to take to the water, bound for Gothery.

Seama took a deep breath of the fresh, dew bound air and, without waiting to see whether the Mule had caught up, he urged Bellus on to descend the hills. It was a good road and he expected to be in Riverport in time for the morning meal.

Minutes later the Mule appeared on top of the hill, breathing heavily, disinclined to go further without rest but, after braying in complaint a few times, he noticed the acres and acres of sweet pasturage below and decided things could be worse. Not at all tired, he charged down the slope with all the packs on his back bumping and clanging and before long he overtook his master.

Behind dirty, red velvet curtains that like the hotel had seen better days, Angren was hiding and looking out surreptitiously through the chinks he had made. He was a weathered man of about forty years, his chin bore a scar from an old fight, his eye was bruised from a recent one. He was careful to lean only on his left arm, as the right one still hurt, and beneath his sleeve there was the mark of a steel-clad boot. Angren felt better today and to celebrate had bathed all over. Cleanliness made his wispy blond hair impossible to keep down and, though he preferred it slicked close to his head to disguise the increasing baldness, today he was beyond caring. He had shaved his six-month beard not simply to make him less easy to recognise but also it amused him to abuse the knife he had stolen. A diamond hilted dagger, made for a prince, was hardly designed for barbering.

He sighed over his half-empty pint mug. It was good beer and, much to his disgust, what he had left had to last him for the next hour. He was down to his last shilling, he had no job and, most importantly, he couldn't afford to get drunk for the sake of his life.

Rixbur Draven, 'The Armourer' as he liked to be known, 'Rixbur the Knife' as he was known, a man of substantial wealth according to the standards of the travelling merchants of his day, was a man with few friends but many enemies. And that was how he wanted it to be. Cheating people was one of his many skills, he delighted in treachery, and the suffering of others, preferably a suffering inflicted by him, was by far his chief amusement.

Unfortunately Angren had known nothing about Rixbur when they first met. The weapon merchant had offered him temporary employment as a demonstrator and extra guard for the perilous journey across the Dragon Plains of Aegarde – not for fighting dragons, of course, but because of rumours about brigands and sorcerers terrorizing Gothery's border. Even Angren had heard of the Black Company. Rixbur had offered him a small payment in advance (which Angren drank very quickly) and explained that, though his expenses would be paid on the way, his final wages were to be paid on their safe arrival in the Holy Isles.

It was fair to say Angren was well pleased with the job for the first few weeks and that, in turn, Rixbur was well pleased with his demonstrator. Angren was an expert weaponsman. The short sword was his favourite – he preferred to get in close to his enemy – but he was at the least competent with a wide range of other weapons, devastating with many. And Rixbur had them all from slings to staffs, arrows to spears, and he knew they sold better when people could see how to use them properly. As for bodyguards, Rixbur had them aplenty though normally he needed only four. Loyal as hounds, he had four mountain men from the far north of central Aegarde: they were huge men and not quite sane, especially when drunk, which they often were.

But, after the crossing of the plains and entry into wealthy Gothery, Angren found the expenses allowed him were far below his expectation and need. Rixbur seemed to delight in denying him any improvement, almost goading Angren into rebellion. Angren argued his case vigorously, and with increasing venom, but in the end it wasn't The Knife's wilful niggardliness that caused him to consider leaving. The big difficulty Angren had was with Rixbur's young wife, Sorella. To put it simply, Rixbur was as cruel to her as he was to everyone else. Angren could barely restrain himself when each day brought fresh bruises for the girl and, when every night brought sharp cries to his ears, beer and oblivion became the only solution. He did try to help her. In a mood of romantic heroism he made plans for her escape. It was to his lasting astonishment that she rejected his offer of elopement. She wanted, actually *wanted*, to stay with her lawful husband. 'It's not his fault,' she told him, 'He just needs to hurt people.'

Of all the things in life that confused him, and there were many, women were definitely the worst.

All things considered he had seen enough by the time he reached Riverport and he told Rixbur, to his face, why he was leaving. Rixbur took it very well. Indeed, he had expected, and possibly even engineered Angren's resignation, intending all the while to refuse fair payment. Rixbur claimed that, as the employ*ee* would not be fulfilling his part of the contract, the employ*er* was no longer bound to pay. A blazing row developed, with Angren doing most of the blazing, but Rixbur ended it by having the hill men throw him out. That was how he got the black eye. The bruised arm was the result of a more recent encounter.

A deeply satisfying evening of consigning Rixbur's entire stock, and therefore livelihood, to the bottom of the river had left Angren with a problem: Rixbur was going to kill him. Angren knew this because yesterday they had nearly caught him. He realised now that swaggering around the streets of Riverport as though he had not a care or an enemy in the world had been a little foolish. With Rixbur screaming threats and the hill men at his heels Angren had escaped only because he'd run into a troop of soldiers marching towards the docks. They didn't intervene as he brawled with Dog but by the time Angren had managed to pull free, leaving Dog rolling on the floor and spitting teeth, the roiling medley of shopkeepers and shoppers, artisans and apprentices, innkeepers and drinkers, all come out to gawp at and chatter about these Kingsmen and what might be going on, had so bunged up the narrow street that pursuit became impossible and Angren simply slipped away through the crowds.

Since then Angren had felt very uncomfortable indeed. Rixbur was not the sort to let it go. For one thing Rixbur knew nothing about his stock gathering silt in the harbour and must have presumed that Angren had stolen the gear and probably still had it; for another, vindictiveness was Rixbur's second nature. It wouldn't go well for Angren if they caught up with him again and so there he sat, hidden, waiting for some chance to gain passage out of the city but expecting every minute that passed to bring with it the four hill men, or some dark assassin, and a great deal of pain.

A tall man, haggard, dirty, walked into the dull light of the inn's common room, stumbling on an unexpected step, his eyes not yet adjusted from the bright daylight outside. Angren was immediately interested. The man carried a small, secure, leather bag close to his body. The sort of bag fat jewellers carried. But jewellers travelled nowhere without guards, they were soft and pampered, never lean and strong. Angren decided the man was a robber, come down from the Dragon Plains and, though never a villain himself, Angren wondered whether it might be useful to pal up with him until he made his escape. It would be less degrading, he thought, than taking a menial job on board a riverboat. But how would he get the man to trust him? Besides the man might not be all he seemed. Robbers rarely walk around with their loot all day without selling it. It was safer to take the money and enjoy yourself than run the risk of meeting the man you robbed. Perhaps he'd come to do business at the inn.

The man sat down at an empty table and shouted his order at the waiting girl and she scurried off, a little frightened by him. While he waited, impatiently, he scratched at his greasy whiskers and stared hard at everyone in the room as if to warn them off. Or was he looking for someone? Someone he knew only by description. Angren jerked back into the shadows, horribly convinced the man was looking for him. He gripped the hilt of his sword.

But the stranger made no move except to devour the meat and bread the girl had brought. When he finished he wiped his gravy-stained fingers on his trousers, drank his pint in only three draughts and then took himself out into the street again. Angren was so relieved he tipped back the last of his own beer – and then groaned, realizing what he'd done. That did it! No money to buy beer! It was ridiculous. Grabbing his floppy, now battered, broad-brimmed hat, he left the house by the back door and, choosing crowded alleyways, he made his way to the docks.

The docks were buzzing with activity. Boats were being loaded or offloaded, men shouted in wharf-side barter for goods wholesale and nearby a market for fresh fish and fruit from Down-River added to the hubbub. But it didn't take long for Angren to discover something extraordinary was going on in the docks that day. There stood the evidence before him: twelve riverboats. Cargo boats normally but now packed full of soldiers, and they flew amongst their flags the King of Par's Standard. It was an army of Pars taking on provisions, and nobody was told for what or why.

There was rumour and discussion all along the waterfront and, no doubt, some of it was closer to the point than the rest. The most credible tale was that Gothery had been invaded and Pars was mobilized to help. It was a reasonable scenario for the citizens of Riverport, but Angren guessed better, as did anyone who had lately come from Gothery. There had been no sign when he passed through that war was expected, and no sign in Aegarde they were prepared to attack. Two Royal Houses had been garrisoned for the past month in Salthall, a barracks town just north of Riverport, and Angren suspected they were being readied for war in Pars itself, somewhere Up-River.

That must be the answer, he thought, because the only other possibility was that Pars was itself intending to *invade* Gothery, and that was unthinkable.

All of this extra activity made problems for Angren. He was too poor to buy passage anywhere but had decided to swallow his pride and secure work as a crewhand on any ship travelling north or back into Gothery. The Holy Isles would be out of bounds for a while. But who wanted new men if the ships were dock bound? By royal decree no ship was allowed to leave the dead-water. Failure to obey would lead to incarceration. News of the embarkation was not to leave port. Angren knew that if he went to the city gates he would find them closed.

He hung around. For one thing, there was nothing better to do and, for another, he was curious. He managed to get himself close to the centre of activity. What appeared to be the flagship of the River Fleet was being provisioned while the rest of the ships, already loaded, were lining-up in the dead-water ready to go. He looked closely at the people on the quay, hoping for clues, and he saw, in the middle of a courteous cluster, two very important people. Surely they were the Lords Anparas and Temor, together masters of four thousand men at arms.

The courteous cluster, an assortment of men and women not in uniform but some of them well armed, were listening to whatever Anparas had to say. Occasionally one member of the party would step up to receive a roll of parchment. One woman in particular caught his eye and indeed caught the eye of every man lucky enough to be close by. Her hair was a mane of pure gold that shimmered and dazzled in the bright sunlight; she moved with the grace and poise of a dancer; the blue purple robe she wore clung to a lithe yet full shape he positively ached to explore. Though she had her back to him Angren just knew her face would be quite as beautiful. Both Anparas and Temor seemed to know her well; by his stance it was apparent that Temor wanted to get to know her better. Her sudden laughter was a delight to hear. Angren could have watched the woman all day long but he was released from her spell when a small commotion began towards the rear of the group. Someone was trying to barge through to the front and tussling with anyone who got in his way.

Angren moved closer for a better view. When he saw the man's face he gasped aloud. Angren was astounded. Without a doubt it was the stranger he had seen earlier, back at the hotel. Aides rushed to intercept him before he could reach the two lords but the man was insistent. He pushed forward and they struggled to keep him back until Anparas intervened. Soldiers held the man secure while the Lord began to question him and, though Angren couldn't hear the conversation from where he stood, it was evident the man had some information to sell. The guards relaxed their hold and allowed him to remove a scroll from his bag. His booty was more precious than jewels. Immediately they saw the scroll the two Lords waved away the guards and had the man accompany them onto the flagship.

Angren was baffled. A Partian noble would never deal publicly with such a villain. Angren couldn't shake the idea of the man being a highway robber, but there was obviously more to him than that. After a while of wondering Angren decided he could learn no more. He looked for the beautiful woman but she must have left the quayside. He toyed with the idea of trying to find her, disappointed he hadn't seen her face, but he decided that on balance he had more important things to think about. There was nothing for him here and so he left the docks determined to try the cloth markets. They were always busy and always short of labour. If he was lucky he'd be taken on by a traveller who could give him passport into central Pars as soon as the order was lifted. If he was lucky.

TROUBLE IN THE MARKET PLACE

Riverport 3057.7.21

In the cabin the situation was tense. The two Lords, Admiral Jemenser and the stranger either stood or sat, or propped themselves against the knobby bulkhead, staring at each other. Anparas broke the silence.

'Who are you?' he asked, eyeing the tall ruffian with more curiosity than suspicion.

'Does it matter who I am?' the ruffian demanded, 'I bear the King's dispatches, they bear his seal. Is it not enough?'

'No it damn well is not,' Temor's intrusion was terse, 'Not by a long chalk. Look at him! King's Messenger? I don't think so. And the orders? Simply incredible. Who's to say that both you and your message aren't false, meant to trick us into the wrong move?'

'None apart from myself. But you do not like the look of me. What can I say? I've worked for Mador many times. He has reason to trust me. What does it matter if my clothes are not as fancy as yours?'

He shrugged. It was up to them.

Lord Anparas frowned more deeply. He found it difficult to reconcile the way the man spoke with the way he looked. And when he thought about it, he could almost swear the fellow's accent wasn't the same now as it was on the quay. He was about to comment on the change but the stranger raised his hands.

'Enough!' he said, 'This is no time for games. I ask your pardon, but I just couldn't resist testing the disguise. You know me well, friends.'

Turning his back upon them, he ran his hands over his face, perhaps to further obscure what was happening as he spoke the words of what was, apparently, a spell. There was a silence. When the stranger turned to face them they were amazed. They knew him very well. Anparas struggled for the presence of mind to greet him; Temor still gripped the hilt of his sword, his comfort in uncertainty; Jemenser did the honours:

'Welcome to Riverport, Lord Seama. It's worrying you feel the need to resort to disguise in any town of Pars. Things must be serious indeed.'

'Serious enough, but disguise is always useful. I'm heading for Gothery and I'd rather my arrival was a surprise. But let's forget my plans for the moment, we've others to deal with and I haven't much time. Sorry to be abrupt, gentlemen, but really I shouldn't stay long: people might not believe me an ignorant messenger. Do you mind if I read the orders? I haven't seen them yet.'

Together the wizard and the loyal soldiers read and discussed Mador's directions. Seama emphasized the urgent situation in the North and the three Lords all revealed their great relief that the invasion of Gothery had been cancelled. They trusted the wizard's ability to handle the problems in the west without question. The King's orders were as Seama expected. Anparas and Temor were to go north immediately leaving Jemenser to organize the shipping of supplies to Coldharbour and from there on towards the Francon and Greteth. It would take a deal of fine planning. Seama, sure they didn't need his help, announced it was time for him to leave. Anparas was not satisfied.

'This is all very well, Seama,' he said, 'but what exactly is going on? We're told to rescue Sands but not what to rescue them from. Who is it: Aegarde, Masachea?'

'It's a vexed question. There's no easy answer and I haven't the time to go into all the ins and outs. I won't do it justice if I try.' Seama was still smarting from Tregar's rejection and didn't need another. 'Leave it for now. Tregar knows what I think. When you reach the rendezvous, discuss it with him before you go on. He'll have some ideas of his own. But now, I really must be going.'

They found it disturbing to see Seama twist his features once more but couldn't help watching. Anparas had the guards throw him out onto the quay and, to add authenticity, tossed him a very small bag of coins. Picking himself up, without dusting the dirt from his already grimy clothes, Seama walked away from the ships and, by devious routes, made his way towards a guesthouse, deep in the slums off the back end of Ragmarket Street.

Above him the sky darkened. A great pall of dense cloud had mounted up in the heat of the day and, as Seama and the generals discussed the frightening onset of war, the horns of the storm had encircled the city. It rumbled like an angry beast, exhaled a fetid breath over the rooftops. The breeze that ran ahead, desperate for escape, snapped the flags on top of the traders' warehouses but got no further than the waterfront. In the maze of streets the heat was oppressive, the thick air tense, expectant. From the alleys, between tall buildings the sky seemed black.

What with the news of the activity on the river and the stifling heat and the overbearing clouds, a sense of unease descended upon Riverport. Her citizens lost their normal vigour and stood, or wandered about, not knowing what to do. They stole nervous glances at the sky, muttering about the weather spoiling trade, and all the time they were really worried at the prospect of war and all it could lead to. It wasn't that they were cowardly but their lives were so bound up with commerce that if they lost their opportunity to trade, they lost their purpose. A war would disrupt communications and relations that had taken years, generations to build up. They might even be called upon to leave their stalls and workshops and warehouses and go to war themselves. It would be dreadful.

Seama walked through the crowds of despondent marketeers, too preoccupied to notice their lack of enthusiasm. Tempers were frayed; the moody silence was broken only by argument, and argument was brief and frowned upon by others. Seama heard none of it.

He was thinking of a village five hundred miles and fifteen years away from this day in Riverport. It was no great event he remembered, just a happy day spent in the company of a good friend. They had relaxed in the safety of a small village in the south of Aegarde after a hectic month among sailors threatened by piracy, over in the Sea of Birds. Through the morning they had rested on the banks of the River Lune, fishing to while away the hours. Actually, Seama didn't care for the sport and only pretended to fish, keeping himself amused by quietly creating convincing illusions of pike to scare-off the carp straying too close to his friend's hook. Frustrated, the friend gave up and led the way to an inn he knew that served a fine dish of smoked salmon. There was, Seama remembered with a grin, a very fine pint of beer to be had as well. Predictably, a good deal more beer than salmon was consumed.

The memory gave him quite a thirst and made him smile. And he must have seemed strange to those he passed by, as he cast about, looking for the hostelry: strange because he seemed to be the only person smiling in the whole of Riverport.

It became even darker, even hotter. Shutters were put up along the length of Ragmarket Street to protect the precious cottons and silks. People began to disappear indoors. They didn't want to watch the coming storm. Within ten minutes, apart from Seama himself, the streets were deserted.

And then, as if it had waited till all was ready, the rain came pounding down. Seama was drenched in just a few seconds and so decided to continue his journey rather than seek shelter too late. He welcomed the downpour: it was cool and cleared away the sweat of the city.

Strolling, unconcerned, through great sheets of rain, Seama had thought he was the only person foolish enough to be abroad and was surprised to hear the sound of feet on cobbles. People running for cover, he guessed. Because of the gloom he could hardly see a few yards around him, and the shout he heard was indistinct as the downpour drummed on the wooden roofs, but he knew something was very wrong. He ran. In the first tremendous flash of lightning five figures were outlined ahead of him. Fighting figures. One man attacked by four others; the four were the biggest men Seama had ever seen. The defender used a short sword to parry blows from two longswords and two, very cruel looking, metal-studded clubs. He was doing remarkably well but it would be only a matter of time before he tired.

Drawing his own blade, Seama leapt into the fray. He took one of them from behind before they were aware of him, dealing the man a savage blow to the head with the flat of his sword. The roughneck dropped, stunned, but immediately two of his accomplices turned to give Seama more serious attention.

They came at him with clubs raised and Seama backed into a niche between two stalls. The gap was too small but one berserker scorned the danger and charged in, hacking as best he could. Not quite prepared for the violence of the attack Seama was caught off-balance. His stumble saved him. The club whistled over his head and smashed into the timbers of the stall to his left. As his attacker struggled to right himself the wizard thrust his blade deep into the man's shoulder. He howled in pain. A vicious kick at his standing leg, dislocating the kneecap and tearing sinews, brought the big man crashing to the ground.

Seama trod on him to get at the third. Twisting away, this one was just quick enough to dodge Seama's first cut. Not the second. A thunder flash blinded him for an instant and Seama's eager blade bit into his wrist. The thug wanted no more of it and took to his heels, clutching at his streaming arm. Seama didn't spare him another thought but whirled about to go for the last of them.

'Nice work! Glad you were on my side. Four against one was pretty bad odds.' Distorted by the noise of the drumming rain the voice was still familiar. And so was the swaggering pose as the man stood, arms folded, shoulders well back, over the prone form of the fourth attacker. Seama stepped forward grinning. Another stroke of lightning illuminated their faces and Angren, the Weapon-Master, gasped and fell back a pace or two.

'You!' he accused. 'What is this? You're following me. Why? Did Rixbur send you?' Angren seemed confused. 'No. No, you wouldn't have helped... Look, I'm sorry if I don't sound all that grateful but, it's just I've seen you twice already today and I can't really believe it's a coincidence. So who the buggering hell are you?'

'You know me, Angren,' Seama said, 'This disguise has to be my best: first Anparas, now you. I wonder what Burgil'd think of it.'

'Burgil? But he... Seama? Well, you bugger, it *is* you! Seama

Beltomé, as I live and speak!'

They were overjoyed and embraced, both amazed at their meeting.

'I was only just thinking of you,' Seama told him, 'I was remembering Tyndaldale just before the rain started.'

'Gods, but that was a long time ago. Tyndaldale eh? I remember it well enough. Many's the cold night I've thought of the fair Andrena.'

'Trust you. I was thinking of the day, not the night. Hmm. I do seem to recall she was pretty, not that I saw as much of her as you did.'

'Stuff the prettiness, Seama, it's not what you have, it's what you do with it that counts.'

'I think you've told me that before.'

'Because it's true. Anyway, you old conjuror, how are you? And what's with the disguise, and what was all that with Anparas and Temor? What are you up to?'

'Steady on, Angren. You want me to discuss it in the street? Besides, you're injured and I'm soaked, so let's get out of this mess; I'll give it to you over a good jar. I daresay you've some sort of tale to tell yourself?'

'Oh, just the usual. I seem to have upset someone.'

'I'll bet you have!'

They were both laughing as, ignoring the injured, they walked off in search of the house where Seama had stabled his scrawny looking animals.

AN EXTRACTION

Dreffield 3057.7.16

'Shall we wake him up again,' said the fat man. He wasn't the sort of person to *ask* questions: he merely indicated there was a question half worth asking and then carried on as he pleased. His face was so heavily jowled that his small lips hardly seemed to move when he spoke; they certainly never smiled. He was tall enough to reach up to the bloodied face above him, grip the chin and waggle the head to see if there was any response to be had. There was none.

The thin man wasn't surprised. For a start the owner of the face had been hung by his armpits over those pegs for two hours now, his elbows pinned to the wall by iron cuffs to prevent him from falling. And before that he'd been sealed in a dirt barrel for more than a day and rolled around every hour or so to make sure he didn't sleep much. The fat man and the thin man and two other cronies had worked shifts. But the owner of the face wasn't sleeping now either: the shock of the pain had caused complete collapse. His hands were a mangle of stripped flesh, broken bone and shredded tendon. Even though he despised the fat man, the thin man couldn't help admiring the sheer callousness with which he executed his task.

'I'll get m..mo..more water,' said the thin man. He was annoyed his stammering had got worse since they had met each other and met Zaras.

The floor beneath their suspended victim was already wet and some of that wetness was the icy water they'd used to wake him twice before. The thin man was very sure their victim would rather not be woken again to the agony of his popping muscles and dislocating joints and whatever new torments they had in store for him.

'Shall we start on his feet this time,' the fat man stated.

'Nah, g..go for 'is back. Peel the ssskin off – seen it done in 'Dini.'

'There anything you din't see in fuckin' 'Dini?'

'N.. no, not really.'

'Piss off and get the water.'

The thin man did as he was told. There was a water-butt over by the door into this cellar room. He took off the lid and plunged a bucket into it still amazed there could be ice in there this far into summer. But that was wizards for you. He wasn't sure which one did it but couldn't help thinking it must have been the one who was like a block of ice himself.

'Hurry up with the water,' yelled the fat man, 'Boss said he wants answers and quick.'

'Which one: S..ssmiler or the s..ss..sspook? He—'

He had stopped talking because a hand gripped him by the throat.

'This one!' The hand wore a glove with spiky nails in the fingertips which were already drawing blood. 'The spook! Does that make you happy, Creel?'

The thin man just about managed a gurgle.

'I'll take that as a yes.' The hand was removed and Creel breathed again. 'Smiler, as you call him, has returned to Astoril. He is not smiling as much as usual. You are wasting our time, Creel. We need someone who was close to him. Ekstrom *cannot* have disappeared completely.'

Creel was scared to speak. Zaras stood before him, bejewelled and masked as usual, but the gaudy clothes he wore were cloaked for now. The mask, black and silver covering the whole of Zaras' face, did not hide the malevolence beneath and Creel wondered for a thousandth time why he'd ever agreed to work for this nightmare. Oh, he paid well but it was impossible to keep him happy. Just now he was very unhappy indeed. Creel's job was to find and bring in people who might 'provide information' but so far they'd learned nothing at all, or at least nothing of what was really wanted.

'This one r..ra..ran the man..ufactory. He's got to kn..kn.. know something.'

'Creel's right,' said the fat man, 'Let's twist him some more.'

'You really do take pleasure in your work, don't you Franner? Well I'm sorry to disappoint you but I'm going to do it differently this time. The Smiler has been teaching me a new trick.'

Franner grunted assent and stepped aside but Zaras didn't move.

'Take him down.'

Creel allowed himself a secret smile: Franno might have been able to reach up to the factory manager's face but Zaras, at only five and a half feet, could not. He was strong enough though, he remembered as he massaged his aching neck.

'Tie him to the bench. I don't want him moving.'

Creel helped Franner drag their victim over to a crude backless bench and then tied him tight while the fat man held him in place. Creel was practiced at this sort of thing. He'd learned a great deal in the City of Ar'al'dini far, far away on the bay coast of Sullinor where the Emp Radis had his most feared prisons. He knew the fat man was jealous of his time there, and naturally enough he reminded him of it on a daily basis.

Zaras indicated they should move aside but didn't speak. Creel sensed apprehension in the spook's stance, in the way he approached the victim only hesitantly. Perhaps there was something risky in what he was about to do. Zaras removed his glove. Creel was shocked. In all of the months he'd been working for Zaras he was certain he hadn't seen an inch of the man's flesh: the gloves, the mask were ever in place. It had gone on for so long he'd given up wondering about it. And now the glove was off. The hand beneath looked like any normal hand though in the light of the cellar it appeared grey and bloodless.

The hand reached out and took hold of the factory manager's head by the temples, the thumb and little finger tight on either side. There were muttered words Creel could hardly hear and did not understand, and then everything froze. There was no movement from Zaras, complete rigidity in his subject. For ten minutes nothing happened and then with a long sigh Zaras withdrew his hand.

He drew himself up. His head turned to face the pair of them.

'Nothing! Nothing at all!' he spat out. Creel feared for his life but the spook turned away. 'Get me,' he said, 'Get me someone who *does know*, and get him soon or I shall show you both the real meaning of the word *torment*. Do you understand?'

Even Franner nodded vigorously.

'What shall we do with this one?' he *asked.*

Zaras contemplated the wretched creature before him. 'I'll see to him,' he said.

The two looked at each other knowingly and made for the door. On the other side of it they paused.

'I'll bet he will,' said Franner. Creel stole a glance through a gap in the ill-fitting timbers and saw Zaras take out the needle-like knife that always made him shiver.

'I wish he wouldn't d..do that,' he said.

'Didn't think he went in for the older ones,' Franner commented. 'Thought he preferred them a lot sweeter.'

Creel felt queasy.

'Do you know something?' he said, 'I r..r.. really don't want to know.'

A TRIP UPRIVER

River Sea 3057.7.22

Aboard the creaking ship Angren and the wizard, undisguised, leaned side by side on a rail at the bow and watched the river seals skimming ahead. It was a delight to watch them: playful, carefree, ecstatic. Arcs of droplets hung in the air like rainbows in the wake of their high leaping. Who could ever think of war in the face of such innocent beauty? Who could think of death?

Seama sighed. Who indeed? Deep within him Seama knew that life was not intended to suffer war. Life was supposed to be joy, innocent joy, untrammelled by violence and tunes of glory. And it was by some perversity in nature, or in man, that this purpose, this divine intention was ruined. Too often there was hatred, pride, fear and lust; too often did those feelings lead to evil deeds, horror and death. Seama was himself a dealer in death, he doled it out like a bitter medicine. He had learned to fight fire with fire, but it hadn't escaped him that no matter how many times he turned the tables, applied the medication, no matter what power of magic he brought against it, somehow evil always survived, always thrived. He felt sometimes he was approaching the problem from the wrong direction: what he wanted was to eradicate the disease but all he could do was address the symptoms. The answer eluded him. As the years rolled by Seama came no nearer to ridding the world of evil and, in a mood that played with defeatism, he had come to worry that his gut feeling was wrong, that joy was not attainable, that life was meant to be perpetual struggle.

'A penny for them,' said Angren, seeing his friend with a frown on his face.

'More than enough!' Seama replied. 'I was philosophising when I should have been thinking. You could have my thoughts for nothing if I could make room for better ones. It's more than a war, Angren, more than politics. Evil is the root of it. There are enemies everywhere you look. Pars, Aegarde, Gothery, Masachea: they're all at odds with one another and if I'm right it's no accident. I think some terrible plan underpins every stupid event that's happened for the past six months. Someone out there is sowing seeds of ruin and if we don't act quickly we'll reap a disaster.'

'We're after some farmer then.'

'Do you have to make a joke of everything?'

'No, I just enjoy it. Seriously though, I always thought that when a tree's diseased you chop it down, and you burn it so the seeds won't grow again.'

'That's what I want Angren, but first we have to find the tree.' He looked out over the waters. Far ahead, beyond the bounds of the River-Sea, on the edge of sight was a hazy blue line that marked the beginning of the Dedicae massif. The distance was nothing. 'And when we do,' he continued briskly, 'Let's hope our axe is sharp enough, and that we don't get caught underneath when it goes.'

Angren spat over the side. 'We're warriors, aren't we? We find a way. No point worrying about failure and death – well not much. We just do what we can. The good'll win in the end.'

'You think so? Sounds like wishful thinking to me; you've been listening to the priests.'

'You've got to believe in something.'

'Well I wish I could be as sure. Perhaps I've been in too many fights – it makes you cynical after a while.'

They fell silent and opened their eyes and ears to what was about them: the wind, the gulls, the seals and, dispassionately working against their progress, the cold grey flood of the Hypodedicus, mightiest of waterways.

It would be misleading to call the Hypodedicus a river at this point. Here they sailed an inland sea, still powerful in its current, at its extremities one hundred and twenty miles wide and two hundred and fifty long, yet rarely deeper than fifty feet. Eight thousand years before Seama was born the bedrocks turned over deep below Asteranor and threw up solidifying lines of molten basalt, like glowing worms on the green surface of the lands now called Pars, Gothery and Aegarde. One of these thrust lines crossed and dammed the great river. Gathering up the melts of many winters the river pooled outwards and backwards, filling the shallow valley, drowning whatever could not move. The trees rotted, the crude dwellings of an ancient, now forgotten race were ground into the lake bed. Eventually the lake swelled to the lip of the cliff that contained it and forced a ragged, bouncing path down into the soft earth below the fault.

Now in Seama's day the river was settled in its course and, to those who peopled its banks, the Hypodedicus seemed eternal in its long journey from the High Dedicae to Knot Island and the Errensea. The River was the unchanging bastion of their lives. And it was no great divider as a sea. Men had rowed across the waters between Pars and Gothery, though sailing was the more obvious and less exhausting method. Nevertheless, whenever the wind dropped, it was wise to down anchor against the still driving flood. From Riverport to the nearest Gotherian landing the mariner must first journey north and then ride the current down into the saving dead-water on the western shore.

And here they were, tacking slowly upriver, but Banya's Harbour was not Seama's destination. Banya's first landfall in Gothery was dictated by geographical considerations: the cliffs in the south and the salt marshes in the north. In later times the same reasons were the cause of continued traffic through Banya's Harbour, which in turn was responsible for the great prosperity of the residents. But traffic and wealth make for a busy town where watching eyes may not be distinguished from thousands of others. It was not only Seama who wanted to avoid those eyes: Mador had thirty of his favoured agents on board, all set on their various missions by the orders the wizard had carried. They could have gained entry severally into Gothery but it would have been remarkable if their passing could have gone unnoticed. It was decided that they should together take a lonely route through the northern marshlands, keeping clear of the three or four villages and the main town of Fletton, until they were well settled on their different paths. Some would meet up with other agents, some would travel alone; dependent on their purpose some would travel by night while others could travel openly by day, taking on one guise or another or none at all as became necessary.

They sailed northward ten miles out from the coast of Pars for the length of two days' journey and then, at nightfall, the Captain turned their ship westward. As the thin moon came out to look at their passage, those still awake smiled to see that the seals continued to follow them, indefatigable in their play. It was a good sign. Many sailors believed the seals warded off the Spirit of the Waters, a spirit that could be benign or terrible at a whim and was never to be trusted. The more cynical recognized that the river seals were intelligent enough to keep well clear of danger. The River-Sea was a perilous environment. Common were the ever-shifting sand bars making navigation near the coast a nightmare for the inexperienced, and there were ancient boulders just below the surface that made life treacherous for those who strayed off the main routes. And to lose your boat on the River Sea could be fatal. The water was cold, the current frighteningly strong, and creatures other than the friendly seals scoured the depths. There were tiny fish with sharp teeth that travelled in shoals of agonizing death: the Schiff. There were large snake-like reptiles, the pangalori, with paddles instead of legs that made them incredibly fast, and some of these reached tremendous lengths of over one hundred feet. But the floating jellies, so transparent as to be invisible, were most to be feared. Some as large as five feet across, they had a poison that paralysed while the inverted gut enveloped its victim. As it began to digest the membrane turned a hideous red – popular lore said it was better to meet a red jelly than a clear one.

Few children of Pars or Gothery learned to swim in the River-Sea. Taking it for what it was the sailors learned to ride the currents in tense safety. The seals swimming alongside truly were a welcome sight.

On the third day Seama and Angren were woken with a welcome gift of rahi. Though the nights were cool they had preferred to sleep above deck as the quarters had a muggy, salty atmosphere. The 'Cottle' was a requisitioned fishing barque and smelled like it. It was one of Mador's agents who sought them out, a big strong man with an easy and open manner; his name was Garaid Barbossa, of House Anparas.

Angren groggily raised himself to his elbows.

'Thanks, Garaid,' he said with a voice full of gravel. He hated mornings. 'I shall savour every last drop. You never know when you'll get another in this business.'

'Don't say that. I'm not sure I can function properly without rahi first thing.'

'Or beer later, eh?'

'I am quite partial to a drop, now as you mention it. Saddens me to say that moderation is in order from now on, but I suppose I'll get used. Besides I get too fat on ale.'

'Rubbish! Good ballast I call it. Anyway, with all the women and the warring a young man like you shouldn't be getting fat.'

Both Seama and Garaid laughed at that. No one could fail to notice that Garaid already carried a lot of reserve flesh.

'Not everyone's like you, Angren,' said Seama, 'I'm continually astounded at your great ability to drink the house dry and still fight well, but how do you stay so slim?'

Angren put on a confident smile and, smoothing back his sparse hair, said: 'Well, I'm no wizard, I claim no miracle cures but, in all honesty, may I point out that I am the perfect example of the human male.' And just to prove it he flexed his biceps for them.

'Even if your head is a little swollen.' Angren gave Seama a sunny smile in response and then sank back into his blankets. "More beauty sleep? Well, I'm getting up. How far have we come, Garaid?'

'How far? Not sure. I couldn't count it in miles but Bibron says nine hours should see us across the River, if that helps. He's a bit worried about the marshes though. He can't understand how he's supposed to get through them.'

'Oh, you can tell Bibron not to worry. We'll get through; take my word for it. We're making good time. If you could stir yourself, Angren, we have a few things to sort out with the good Captain. Meanwhile, I'm off to feed the fishes.'

'Lucky fishes. Have one for me while you're at it.' As the

wizard headed off Angren closed his eyes. He wanted to get back to a dream he had been enjoying. He couldn't remember exactly what it was about but he knew there were women in it.

When he did get up it was past midday. Seama was bound to have said all he needed to say to Bibron and Angren had decided instead to pay his respects to the horses, but a commotion of laughter and jeering in behind the wheelhouse pulled him off-course.

With over sixty aboard, if you included Bibron's sailors, it was surprising only that things had been so quiet up until now. At last the natural reserve between folk all prone to keeping secrets and obeying orders had given way to an even more natural banter and jest and, by the sound of it, gambling too. Angren couldn't help but approve. And better still, while Bibron had the beer barrels well guarded and strict rations enforced for the sake of good order, the sheer level of noise raised gave Angren a campaigner's hope that all this foolery might well be fuelled by something a little stronger.

He was right to think so, but not as he suspected.

The women on board, each agents of the King, had mercilessly taken advantage of Captain Bibron's more gentlemanly instincts by accepting the Captain's quarters as their own, while the poor Captain had to sleep in the hammocks with his men. Only two of them had so far mixed with the others, a rough spoken giantess and a shortish, sharp tongued, black haired minx Angren had quite deliberately shied away from. Up till now Angren had presumed they were the only women present but today a third had emerged from the cabin. She was causing quite a stir among the men.

It was an arm-wrestling competition. At a table liberated from the galley sat a burly tattooed sailor with forearms wider than pork shanks and opposite him sat the giantess, dressed in brown leather, hair close-cropped, eyes fixed on her opponent with an intensity that must have made him nervous.

'C'mon, Berta, he's just a baby.' Her supporters cheered; the sailors jeered.

Garaid stood behind Berta's chair waving a clutch of white

and green paper, Gotherian tally notes, exchangeable for real money at any of the King's banks.

'Any more?' He yelled above the din. 'Ten to one on the bosun, fives on the lady.'

Angren cursed his lack of funds. This Berta looked too good a prospect. A few more wagers were laid and then the *referee* stepped in to start the match. She moved into Angren's line of sight, laughing at something said, and shaking that mane of gold in denial. It was the beauty he had seen on the quays back in Riverport and this time, as she counted-in the bout, he could see her face.

The black-eye was shading to red, the scratches on her right cheek were fading. It must have been quite a fight, or a beating. Angren, leaping to conclusions in typical fashion, promptly decided some man had done this. The memory of Rixbur's young and daily battered wife surfaced and left him with a strong feeling of anger that must have showed in his face. It must have showed because at that moment, as though she could feel his gaze upon her, she looked up, caught his eye and then instantly looked away.

The revellers roared. Berta had picked her moment, forced down hard and fast and smashed the bosun's hand into the table. Amid the cheers and the scramble for winnings and the picking of the next pair of contestants, Angren's golden haired girl slipped from his view. He considered moving closer. He could talk to her, perhaps – easy enough to pick some topic of conversation. But then it occurred to him he wasn't exactly the only man trying to gain her attention. The injuries didn't disguise the beauty of her face, the clingy dress she wore didn't obscure the desirability of her body. She was surrounded by a score of men made silly by her presence. For most of them this arm-wrestling contest was simply an excuse to impress. Angren decided not to bother.

Well, he thought, *I may as well see to my nags, and leave this filly to her fanciers.* It was a sort of bravado. Tearing himself away was a bit of a wrench.

Seama had brought both Bellus and the Mule with him, and Lord Anparas had presented Angren with a fine warhorse named Bayling, a strong, clean-limbed chestnut. The weapon-master had promised to take turns with the wizard at the grooming.

Angren was a fair horseman and, though he preferred to fight on his own two feet, a good horse beneath him did wonders for his confidence. For one thing a horse could be a lethal weapon and for another it could run away a lot quicker than a man could. In one way or another, horses had played an important part in keeping Angren alive for the past thirty years. In recognition he made it a firm rule that before he went to sleep and as soon as he woke he would give his horse all the attention it needed. What a pity for the many horses he'd owned that he so often failed to rouse himself before noon.

The horses were hobbled in the open hold of the barque and, to judge by their testiness, they were not pleased about it. Here the stench of fish was offensive. Bellus bore this ordeal with fortitude typical of her breed, and made no complaint. The same couldn't be said of the Mule. As soon as anyone came near he would break into the foulest braying that ever the son of a donkey could manage. It was as though he was swearing.

'Pack it in!' Angren said, 'I already have a headache from sleeping on this smelly heap. It doesn't need you to worsen it. You're wasting your time anyway: there's no alternative unless you can swim.'

And as though the Mule understood the sense of this argument, after only a few more desultory grunts, he shut up.

'Seama has you well trained, hasn't he?' the swordsman smirked, and then backed off as Mule tried to butt him. Luckily for Angren the tethers held.

Bayling was hobbled alongside and Mule's discontent seemed to be catching: the horse snickered and stamped as Angren stepped between the two. Stroking its flank, Angren was surprised to feel that Bayling was sweating and trembling.

'Don't like the water, young fella? Well neither do I, but don't worry, we won't be out here much longer.'

The animal wasn't comforted no matter how much he was

groomed and fed and so Angren went to ask Seama if he could do anything. Seama checked on all the horses and, after saying soothing and powerful words to several of them, he took Angren to one side.

'I know we're aship,' he said, 'and horses never like the motion, but these poor beasts are terrified. Your Bayling's not the only one. I don't know what's scaring them but horses are often more sensitive than men, so keep your eyes open. The trouble may be on the water or we may have brought it with us, but trouble there is, and it worries me.'

Angren wandered forward to the bows. He was pleased to see the seals racing and skipping ahead of the boat, but apart from the seals, and occasionally a few birds, nothing could be seen on the hazy waters. Settling himself on folded canvasses he took out his sword and a stone and began the daily ritual of keeping his weapons in good order. He was put in such a good humour by the sun and the seals and the task in hand it was hard for him to believe in any of Seama's dark warnings. Surely their enemy was miles away on the other side of Gothery? At least, Seama had yet to tell him any different. 'Angren,' he'd said, 'how would you like to help me put down a gang of villains?' And, after some negotiation about recompense, Angren decided that it would be safer to tag along with Seama than stay in Riverport. Seama had been vague about what Anparas and Temor were doing but, seeing as whatever the two Lords were up to was a long way from where he was headed, he decided to let it pass. He was not incurious, but Seama seemed reluctant to disclose anything more than the army's destination and Angren wouldn't presume to press him. Where on Ea' was Greteth anyway?

It was Angren who first noticed the fog bank rolling towards them. He had finished his task and, with a cool breeze making him shiver, he stood alone in the bows looking out. The seals had gone! Unaware though he was of sailors' lore, he realized that something was wrong. And while nothing broke the surface of the fast flowing waters near the ship, as his eyes lifted to look ahead he was astonished to see a white wall laid east to west across the River Sea. There were slow seconds before he worked out what he was looking at, and before he could find the words the ship's lookout cried:

'Ware! Ware! Fog blows ahead. Fog Cap'n. Fog ahead!'

The Captain had gone to speak with Seama. Just as Angren reached the bridge he was saying: 'This is a mighty strange fog, sir. I've sailed the River for twenty years and fog I've seen plenty out on the open water, but never anything like that. It's too thick. Sort of fog you generally see near land. Now, far as I remember, there's no island in this part of the sea: nearest is twenty mile north of here, unless my bearings are out completely. I'll tell you now, I hope they aren't, 'cause that bit of land would be Tumboll, the prisoners' keep. None has sailed within ten mile of the place in three hundred years. Leastway, none has been able to tell that they have.'

'What's so bad about this… erm… Timbol, or whatever you called it?'

'Really Angren,' said Seama, 'Didn't your mother tell you about Tumboll when you were a boy. No? I am surprised. It's a tale used to frighten bad children into being good – I suppose it makes sense you haven't heard of it. Let's go and have a look at this fog and maybe when we've decided what's to be done I'll give you the full story. You never know, it may still do the trick.'

By the time they had reached the bows, the fog was nearly on them. The Captain looked worried.

'If we were on the open sea I'd be happier, trouble is we're on the River. There're just too many great lumps of rock in this water, and besides I reckon there's land not far away, and we can't see it. Can you not make the fog go away, sir wizard?'

Seama laughed. 'Do you know, I think I could. But it would cost me too much. We'll find another way of getting round this problem. If there is land ahead, your navigation has gone wrong, right?'

'Well, I'd have to say yes, but I don't see how I *could* have gone wrong. Though I know some don't trust 'em, I always use a Karrel Clock, and it's never let me down yet.'

'Maybe so, nevertheless we're not where we should be. Either your compass has been tampered with or there's some power working against us. I must know what that power is before I make a move. Let's wait and see what happens. Meanwhile I'll help you navigate. The fog is on us, gentlemen.'

They all looked up, as if to catch the last rays of proper sunlight before they were enveloped. In a moment everything was hushed, the waters in quiet motion and the deckhands motionless, apprehensive. All trace of a breeze vanished and the sails hung lank and useless. The fog was so thick they couldn't see half the length of the ship, and it was deathly cold. The Captain gave the order for men to take up oars and, grumbling, they went to it.

'I suppose,' said Seama, 'we'd better make a start. Come and stand next to me, Bibron; you can instruct the men.'

Bibron nodded an aye but, before he could move, the ship was shaken by a sudden impact.

'Gods a'plenty, we're aground already!' Yelling out orders, and blaspheming by turn, the Captain threw himself across the rolling deck, making for the helm. He didn't reach it.

A bone jarring roar rent the air, a huge head ripped through the gloom and terror thrilled through every man and woman aboard. The pangalorum was of monstrous size. Its serpent coils encircled the ship in seconds, crushing men, horses and timbers alike; the scales rasping against the hull. Its mighty head lunged at the crewmen as they scattered in horror. The frantic horses, unable to run away, not even able to kick because of the hobbles, were an easier target.

Angren had never seen a pangalorum before. Faced with the unknown and with almost certain death he decided attack was the best policy. He grabbed a harpoon. Other brave men struggled with their swords, trying to defend the horses, but the pangalorum was too fast and caught at one of them with snapping jaws. The screams were terrible as he was dragged off his feet, but silenced when the monster tipped back its head, working its throat, and swallowed him whole like a heron taking in a fish. Now was the moment: Angren swarmed up some of the rigging to give him height, launched himself at the pangalorum's head and stabbed ferociously at an eye. The eye burst sending a jet of blood and humour into the air while Angren fell to the deck. The creature bellowed and in shock spewed out the half mangled sailor over the backs of the shying horses – but it was in no way defeated. With deadly intent it twisted right and left to seek out its attacker. Even half-blind the pangalorum found him easily. Angren's fall had knocked the breath out of him, and knocked him sick, and there he lay in full view, spread-eagled upon the deck, incapable of movement and waiting for the end. The grisly, ravaged head reared above him and blood from the pangalorum's wound rained down, spattering his face. He rolled, grasped at his harpoon and made one last effort to attack. The monster was unimpressed: a casual nudge from its snout flipped Angren onto his back once again and all the fight went out of him. It stooped to tear at his belly, but in that instant a dazzling, sparking white bolt, like lightning, shot from the bows of the ship and hit the pangalorum between gaping jaws.

It was a mortal blow. The monster began to writhe, smashing through mast and rigging in its agony.

Coughing and retching Angren struggled to his feet and staggered away. He could hardly believe he was still alive. Garaid caught up with him.

'Angren! Angren! You okay?'

Angren spat out a quart of bile. 'Grand thanks,' he said. The deck lurched and they both fell over as the pangalorum, still clutching the Cottle in iron coils rolled back into the river, its dying cries splitting the air around them.

'It'll have us over,' Garaid yelled at him, 'We have to get it off.'

He wasn't wrong: the Cottle started to tip and roll. Angren retched again but Garaid grabbed him by an arm.

'No time for that,' he said, 'Get your sword out.'

Without waiting for Angren to understand what he was about, Garaid laid into the nearest section of the pangalorum, hacking like fury. It was no easy task: the pangalorum was at least five feet thick. Others seeing the same danger followed his lead and soon the deck and the air above it were full of blood and flesh. Slabs and gobbets of dark meat slithered away into the river but there seemed no end to the creature. The ship continued to list and the stern began to dip beneath the surface. It was hopeless.

There was nothing for it. Bibron shouted out the order to abandon ship and his sailors ran to free the stays on the boats. There were only two, inadequate for the sixty aboard but at least some of them might survive. Angren, still woozy, doubted he'd be one of them. He sat back on the steps to the quarterdeck and put his head between his knees.

And then another terrifying roar shook the air.

The mate of the first monster, even greater than he, had come to take her revenge. A dark shape in the thinning fog she first circled the ship, her body undulating to drive her through the water ever faster, but then she turned in to attack. She would crush the Cottle in one mighty blow. What could they do? In thirty seconds they'd be as good as dead. Angren looked up to see but it made him feel too dizzy and so he dipped his head once more. It was odd, he thought, and perhaps his vision was blurred, but the planks between his feet looked wrong. And then he realized they were smouldering, and then, in a few seconds more, burning. Leaping up he saw the flames roll out and spread rapidly across the deck. Before he had the chance even to contemplate jumping ship he was engulfed.

There was no smell, no heat, no pain. It was all illusion, and the purpose was clear. The second pangalorum veered away unnerved by the flames and then began to circle again, enraged but frustrated. Unfortunately not only the pangalorum was fooled. Fear of those flames proved too much for one of Bibron's sailors. Gibbering in his confusion and pushing past the hands that sought to hold him back, he threw himself over the rail and plunged deep into the dangerous waters.

Those nearest, still desperate to keep their feet and stay on deck, looked down at the man floundering. This conflict with terrifying monsters and now the devilment of the cold flames must have turned his mind: he was screaming as his head broke the surface. Angren, clinging to the ratlines as the deck yawed, lost his footing and for a minute he dangled overboard before swinging back to safety. Below him the water was churning in a curious fashion, an underwater commotion that was nothing to do with the sailor kicking and struggling to stay afloat. A glittering shoal of tiny, silver fish swirled all around him. The water turned red.

Voices cried out in terror: 'Schiff, the schiff. Gods help us!' and efforts to free the lifeboats became frantic. The barque rolled again and as one of the boats was released it slid across the bloody deck, crushing one man against the main mast and bowling others overboard. Angren ducked in behind the galley house to save himself as the boat flipped over the side to land keel up on the water. Just then Seama emerged in a rush from the galley hatch carrying a large ball of what seemed to be white lard.

'Out of the way,' he yelled.

With agony written on his face, the wizard stumbled over to the portside and pushed his burden over the rail. The illusion of the flames onboard died as Seama drew himself up, squeezing his hands into fists as though the palms pained him. Angren, close behind now, saw the ball sink into the waves.

'*Anabo*!' the wizard roared.

Angren had no idea what the word meant but down in the water an incredible, bright blue fire bloomed and swelled. Impossibly, these new flames were real. They burned fiercely, beneath the tide, consuming both men and the Schiff indiscriminately.

Angren saw no more of Seama in this battle. As the fish burned black, the second pangalorum resumed its attack and the ship received one final, destroying blow. The ship was wrecked, all was lost. Men and horses were cast into the sea. Angren, attempted to jump clear but as he fought to climb onto some shattered decking a falling spar struck him a blow to the head and he lost consciousness.

AN ISLAND IN THE SUN

Tumboll 3057.7.23

The insolent waters of the inlet slapped his face and tugged at his sodden clothes. He spat out dirty water and pulled his exhausted body a few feet higher up the muddy shore. It was a strain to raise his head but he needed to see. More foul water, caught in his sinuses, came snorting back into his mouth as he moved, causing him to retch. Again. His insides were raw.

When he managed to look about him he could see nothing of importance: dawn was hours away and the dark trees made patterns against a starlit sky; the water glinted malevolently. That was all. At ground level everything was black.

He decided to lie still for a while, to let his head clear, to let some strength return. His battle with the river had left him a weakling; he cursed his weakness. Shortly he rolled over onto his back, snorted again and spat to one side. There was a taste in his mouth like burnt fish. He listened. There was little to hear above the lapping of the water, only a quiet breeze rustling the grasses along the forest edge and giving him a fit of the shivers. Testing his strength again, he had decided to seek for warmth beneath the trees but before he could move a different, less natural noise came to him: a significant noise.

It came from the near distance, not close enough to pose an immediate threat, but near enough to worry him. Many people were moving through the forest and they didn't try to hide their movements. They yelled, chattered, screamed, whistled and beat at the undergrowth. A shout went up and the clamour increased and people were running.

Terrible screams rang out: the screams of one man in agony. Then there was silence, and then a cheer, and then the dreadful beating began again as the hunt resumed.

Despite the chill of the night Angren was sweating. It was certainly a hunt and Angren was sure he was one of the hunted. He strained to hear correctly: which direction? There was little doubt. The beaters were drawing closer. Angren presumed that the woods near the beach were being scoured for his shipwrecked companions; they were being forced out onto the open beach, or herded perhaps onto some last spit of land where, cornered and weary, they would provide good sport.

It was time for action, and the sea frozen muscles, now charged by need, wrenched him staggering to his feet. He knew about hunts. The beater's job was to scare the quarry into making a desperate dash for freedom but the quarry that succumbed to fear and bolted was the quarry most quickly caught. If the line of beaters was thinly spread the best bet was to lie still and hope to be missed. Angren's advantage was the dark: even if stumbled upon the beater would be startled and Angren would have the chance to do something about him. Better still not to be seen at all. Having weighed the options, Angren found himself a suitable tree, climbed as high as he could and waited.

As luck would have it, another hunted man was Angren's downfall. He had laid up quiet in his tree and listened with relief to the hunt passing by beneath, not looking out for fear of being seen. Feeling pleased with himself, he was contemplating striking off into the depths of the forest, if fatigue would allow it, when he heard the clamour increase again and then continue to rise as the hunters came back towards him. One of his companions had bolted but surprised the hunt by running through the line instead of away from it. Angren saw him coming: it was one of the sailors. He limped as he ran. Catching up came wild looking men with hair done up into spikes and paint on their faces. They carried boar sticks and long knives. The sailor was done for. He had no chance of getting away.

Angren was in a quandary. Should he go down and try to fight alongside the man, both in such poor condition they would lose, or should he try to avoid attention and save himself? He was inclined to the latter course but the decision was taken out of his hands. Incredibly, the sailor was leading his pursuers directly towards Angren's tree and just before they could reach him the man leaped with amazing strength into its lower branches.

That was the end of course. As the sailor climbed higher the huntsmen swarmed the tree behind him and Angren came down slowly to meet them. Without words the two turned to fend off their many attackers. Armed only with knives, other weapons lost to the river, they did their best to delay the inevitable but although they managed to dislodge several wild-men from the branches they received too many cuts and were soon overwhelmed and dragged down to earth, in Angren's case still kicking.

He expected nothing less than a tormented death but instead they produced waxed twine and trussed up his arms behind him. And then they made him watch as his co-prisoner was disembowelled. Hardened though he was from years of sometimes brutal action, Angren closed his eyes as the creature that was once a man tried his best to save the guts that were falling from his gaping belly. He was all reaction: in too much pain and shock to think. The huntsmen were cheering him in his work. Two of them brought out more rope, grabbed at those frantic hands and tied them together. Whatever was left in the sailor tried to run, and his captors let the rope pay out maybe twenty yards before they pulled him back, staggering, crawling, slithering and trailing his innards through the dirt. They strung him from a strong branch high up in Angren's tree and there they left him: a live dangling feast for anything that could fly or jump, or could make its way along the branch and down the rope. The huntsmen seemed satisfied with their work.

Soon Angren was made to stumble through the scrub toward some unknowable destination, fearing the result of the journey but unable to do anything about it. The exhaustion began to tell as the march dragged on and, though he continued mechanically, one foot then the next, and then the next and on and on for what seemed an eternity, he was virtually senseless before they reached the journey's end.

He awoke in the heat of the day and was at once assailed by the sun burning his face where a coverlet had slipped, and by an appalling stink. He felt dreadful. Someone had thoughtfully covered over any bare skin with assorted scraps of cloth but he must have moved in his sleep. Looking around him, through narrowed eyes, he could spy little in the way of shade. The sun was ferociously hot and it looked down into a compound high walled by ancient and ruinous masonry. On three sides a line of columns parallel to the walls, with crumbling arches between them, suggested there had once been covered walkways to offer some respite but these were now open to the sky. Huge nettles grew up in the corners, and in the thin shadows of the perimeter, but the rest was all bare earth and, gods help them, several centuries worth of rotted pig shit. Angren gagged: the ordure was mercifully dry and hard but the accumulated smell was almost more than he could bear. The sun may have been damnably fierce but Angren could not bring himself to wish for rain.

He was not alone here. More than thirty Partians were imprisoned with him. They sat with their backs against the nearest wall where two inches of shadow and fewer nettles made for the most desirable residence; all had covered whatever they could of their bodies against the heat of the midday sun and Angren found it hard to tell who was who. He presumed correctly that all the prisoners were his companions of the wreck.

One of them noticed his movement and, nudging another who lay alongside, he picked himself up and walked over. The other man followed. The first, a swarthy, thick set man, was Bibron Farber, the ship's captain, and the second, stepping gingerly on the hot earth with bare feet, and massaging a sore left arm, was Garaid.

'Well, my lad,' said Bibron, 'should I ask how you're feeling, or is that a bad question?'

With his tongue thick from the heat and the lack of water, Angren replied with difficulty, though he tried to raise a smile: 'I should say I'm feeling with every nerve in my body, and none of it's good. Ouch!' A sharp pain in his hand made him jump. Hastily he pressed it into the clay and then flapped at his clothes. 'Flaming ants!' he cried: his clothes were crawling with them.

Bibron chuckled as Angren wriggled and slapped at himself. 'They give up after an hour or so.'

'Very comforting, I don't think.' Luckily, not many had

penetrated too far and after a minute more he stopped flapping. It was too hot for the effort required. 'I don't suppose there's any water around?'

'Sorry, you're out of luck, and so's everyone else. Those swine won't bring no water till they're good and ready. And they ain't ready yet, scumbags that they are.'

'Steady on, Bibron,' said Garaid, his voice slightly slurred, no doubt from his attempt to speak without moving his lips: he had a painful looking cut across his chin and lower lip. 'This lot seem to dislike bad language. I did try them with some last night, and they're not as liberal as you might think.' His attempt at a grin looked hideous but it made Angren smile.

'Where are your shoes, Garra? You seem to be bobbing about a bit without them.'

'Now that is not a funny subject. Some smart lad out there took a fancy to them. Little sod. This clay's baking.'

Angren nodded towards the furthest wall where a gate made of rough hewn logs provided the only visible means of entry, or of escape. 'Why not cut a piece of bark from that and strap it on your feet? It'll look odd, but it's better than burning your toes.' Angren was often impressed by his own intelligence and didn't mind sharing it.

'What an original and brilliant idea, Angren.' Garaid wasn't impressed. 'Perhaps you could lend me your knife, I'll see to it right now.'

Angren grimaced. 'Hmm. Not really with it yet, am I. Suppose they've taken all the weapons? Obviously. Pity about my dagger.' Regretful but not concerned, Angren was busy feeling at his collar and belt. Satisfied he grinned broadly.

'Well, Garaid, I can't help you now but I do have a few pieces you could try later.'

'I don't see no weapons,' said Bibron.

'They're well hidden, Captain. I have a nice long coil of wire in this band about my throat and if I use two toggles from my jacket it can be very nasty. Better still, there's a thin length of metal in my belt. It's sharp along one side and the belt buckle is the handle. It's a bit wobbly but it makes a reasonable sword

in an emergency. And...' he bent to examine his leg, 'Yes! *And*
I have a dirk hidden in the side of my boot. I'm surprised they
didn't notice that. Good job they didn't take a fancy to *my* shoes!
Mind you, I can't see a couple of blades getting us out of here.'

'No, but it all helps,' said the Captain.

Garaid was amazed by the hidden weapons. Partians in
general found it hard to be devious. 'Where did you find them?
I've never seen the like.'

'You'd be surprised what you can get. Even in Pars you can
find most things if you know where to look. No, it's a hobby of
mine. I collect weapons; use them too. Mind you, the sword's
pretty new: my last boss was a dealer, and a sharp one. He did a
lot of trade with all sorts of treacherous scum.'

'Can you walk, Angren?' Garaid asked, seeming to lose
interest in Angren's toys, 'because, if you can, I'd appreciate it
if we could get back to our spot by the wall before my feet are
singed.'

'That's nice. I appreciate your concern,' Angren replied with
a grin, 'for yourself that is. Anyway, I'll never know unless I
try.' He pulled himself, wincing a little, to his feet and wasn't
pleased to discover the many cuts and bruises that made each
step painful. Luckily none of the cuts were deep enough to cause
a real problem, they just hurt.

They had nothing to do but talk and keep as still as possible.
Gradually they became used to the revolting pig-pen smell and
that was some relief, but in a very short time the sun reached
its height and talking with shrivelled, parched tongues became
uncomfortable. They all took the best course and settled back to
wait for the cool of the evening. The hours stretched. The sun
glared at them as though angered by their presence while the
baked surface of the compound bounced back and intensified
the heat. The only things that moved were the ants and,
occasionally, the flicking fingers that crushed them. Evening
was a long time coming.

Their captors left them alone all day, and the captives had
no idea what was happening outside the compound. Nobody

could be seen through the various odd chinks in the gate and it occurred to Angren, as he lay, that the natives themselves must have retired to somewhere shady. He eyed the walls that hemmed them in. Ruined though the building was, the remaining close-set stonework made for a difficult climb, but if they were imprisoned for another day he might just risk it. Of course his thoughts were not precise, he had no plans as yet, but already Angren was thinking about the inevitable escape and, despite Seama's reproving lectures on the subject, already he was contemplating revenge.

As the sun began to fall westward the prisoners were pleased to feel a cooling breeze climb over the walls, though not so pleased at the dust it blew into their faces. With no word of warning, two men appeared above and a little to one side of the gateway. They lowered a large bucket of water to the dusty floor, taking little care to prevent spillage. From where Angren lay the men seemed to be suspended in mid-air but they must have been standing on some sort of raised platform, or perhaps it was the remnant of a stair or tower. The prisoners could be viewed safely without the risk of opening the gate.

Angren and Bibron were slow from the heat and couldn't prevent those nearest the bucket from drinking more than their share but they were in time, at least, to make sure everyone got some. Bibron was the last to drink and the men respected him for it. Some time later another bucket was lowered and this contained a mushy, millet-like porridge. Partians were mostly meat eaters and proud of it and they looked upon this grey stuff with disgust. But no one refused a portion: it might just keep them alive for a little while longer.

Evening came on and moving about, under the watchfull eyes of three of their captors up on their perch, became more bearable. Garaid, Angren and the Captain circulated among the prisoners, gathering whatever information they could. The first obvious point, quickly confirmed, was a tragedy for Bibron. Everyone had gruesome tales of the night before and everyone had heard the screams of unknown victims; apparently all the victims were members of the ship's crew. There were no sailors in the compound: all were spies and soldiers with their private missions in jeopardy. Most of them had been picked up out of the water as they came ashore by the same strange men that Angren had met. Others had been caught during the hunt, after they had escaped to the trees. A few of them banded together with six of the sailors and, with only a few weapons between them, they'd fought a desperate battle as they tried to leave the beach. When captured, all the sailors were mutilated or murdered before the rest were herded away. Bibron cursed the day he decided the crew would wear uniform for this trip.

'Why only my men? Bastards!' he shouted at the men on their tower. They were unmoved and said nothing.

Bibron cursed the savages to damnation; and he cursed the gods for their lack of protection; and he cursed the King for having set them on their journey; and he cursed himself for having brought them to this place. He stopped when he heard himself curse even the wizard for having left them.

'Bibron, don't think your men had the worst of it.' The quiet words came from Garaid. 'If we're still alive it's because we're at war and you must know why we're wanted. We all know something of the King's plans and I don't imagine we'll benefit by it. Brutality and our friends up there seem like old partners.'

Angren hadn't thought it through but it was clearly the truth. Some time soon the screaming would begin. But was all this planned? Had their enemies been expecting the Cottle? Had they engineered its destruction? Not the savages who had hunted them down of course: someone else, someone more intelligent and more powerful. But who? Angren had no clue, because, as yet, Seama hadn't told him anything about this lot. The Black Company was on the other side of Gothery, wasn't it? His worst thought was that the whole episode had been an attempt to take Seama himself. He sought news of the wizard, but no one had seen him, not since they were all cast into the water. Was he to believe Seama had drowned? Wizards were only men after all. But then, Seama was Seama, not just any old wizard. The thought that he might be dead was incredible to him.

The situation was not good. By the look of it they were securely penned in, overlooked by cautious guards, they were mostly weaponless, and more than half of them horror struck. Angren, even though he struggled with his own worries, didn't really understand the plain terror that held some of his gaol mates in thrall. Deep in shock from what they had already seen, they were all but immobilised by the fear of what would happen next. Angren ignored them. There were others, less affected, he could work with. Despite the seeming hopelessness of the situation there were options. There were always options, and together with Garaid and Bibron, the weapon-master began the debate, appraising their strengths, sizing up the height of the wall and making speculation on what lay beyond it. Their first task seemed clear: before they attempted any escape they would need some very basic information about their enemy. Reconnaissance was the key.

Angren studied the face of the wall furthest from the gate. Most of the climb was open to view.

'You'll never do it,' said Garaid, 'Face it, if you tried the climb now they'll see what you're up to, and if you wait until dark you won't be able to find your footing. And you wouldn't find out much in the dark either.'

'There'll be some moon.'

'A thumbnail. You'd need the eyes of Queen Bethel.'

'Who?'

Garaid shook his head in amazement. 'Did you have no stories at all when you were young?'

'Never mind the cat queen,' put in another voice, 'The pointing is too fine, you would need the Lizard's Toes.' The speaker was a small man Garaid had identified as Ruspa. This was the first time Angren had heard him speak. The weapon master looked him up and down: a thin, rat of a man, but obviously as fit as the rest of them; not handsome, his sharp features and the hard look in his eyes told against him.

'Any particular lizard?'

Ruspa almost answered and then changed his mind. 'Try it if you want to. That lot out there will no doubt find a use for your broken bones.'

'So what do *you* suggest?'

'Perhaps that you learn to listen more and talk less.'

Angren's smile became rather thin. Bibron stepped up between them.

'The man has a point, Angren.'

'Has he?'

'Well, I reckon the stories we have as kids are a lesson to us, and—'

'And if only I'd listened up when I was a lad I'd be a better man now? Or maybe I'd have a better idea of how to get out of here?'

Now it was Bibron's turn to bridle. 'Think you're clever don't you. Some stories are worth remembering. How is it, d'you think, that everyone here *except you* knows exactly where they are, and who those bastards are, and has a good idea of the kind of trouble we're in? You tell me that.'

Angren pursed his lips but found nothing to say. Bibron continued:

'We all know what sort of jackals our gaolers are. We all had the tale of The Halfi when we were children. Not you seemingly. But I dare say none of us here ever thought they'd find out any more, and I *know* none of us ever wanted to. It's not a nice story.'

Several people around them nodded or gave the 'aye' to that. Angren considered for a few seconds. 'Alright, alright! So I never listened. Well, I don't suppose we're going anywhere now a while, so why don't you tell me all about it? Then maybe I'll understand what you're all gassing on about. That do you?'

Bibron grinned. 'I reckon. Never too late to learn, as they say!' He planted himself on top of a low remnant of the inner wall and settled himself with a deep breath. 'Right then, this is the Story of the Kingdom of Halfi, and it's Bibron Farber as is doing the talking, so shut up and listen!'

THE KINGDOM OF HALFI

Tumboll 3057.7.24

'It all began years ago. Some say four hundred, some say it was more like five; but no one knows for sure, leastways nobody I know knows. And it all happened in Riverport, strangely enough, where they had a run in with some tinkers. They were a people like the travellers we know today 'cept that, as the story goes, this lot were originally from Masachea. Now they'd moved to Pars because of some trouble they'd been having as a separate tribe in Northern Masachee, and they came over the Hurgals all together and settled down wherever they could. For some reason people didn't like 'em: wherever they settled they weren't welcome. So, eventually, after a lot of what we'd call criminal doings, they set up as travelling traders and seasonal workers. Anyone, strong enough or daft enough to trust 'em, would give 'em whatever rough work they had and pay them a pittance.

'I don't suppose they had a good life. We weren't any kinder to them than the Masachee were, and nat'rally enough they'd no thought of being kind in return. And they certainly didn't see why they should follow our laws, given as they had their own. You see, though they didn't all travel together much, they counted themselves as part of one kingdom, and that not Pars but the Kingdom of Halfi.'

'This all seems tame doings to me, Bibron,' Angren protested. He was not a good listener, nor ever had been or he would already have known the story as told by his father many years ago. 'What's the Kingdom of Halfi to do with Tumboll?'

'Well, I'll be coming to that. I always think a tale makes best sense if you listen to all of it.'

'I'll do my best.'

'Well then. The reason they were unpop'lar may have been because they were very good at cheating, and they were very bad at losing face. By cheating I mean for example, they'd sell a man a horse with its fetlocks darkened up, but the horse would run right back to the Halfi and they'd have the darkening off before the idiot who bought it could come round to demand his horse back. 'Lost your horse mate? Run away has it? You ought to be more careful.' You know the kind of thing. Maybe they'd deal in gems but, because they were quick with their hands, they'd be selling glass for the price of diamonds. That's how they lived: each deal was a game, but they had to be the winners.

'Now, their downfall was because of this way they had. I don't know if you know but at that time the Masachee had only but a few pigs, and, as a result, pigs were worth gold to 'em. The Halfi shared that passion, though they'd rather get the pigs for nuthin'. Now, Pars isn't the place for pigs neither, not like The Fat Thousands. We've plenty of cattle and sheep so we've never bothered that much about 'em, but in Riverport all sorts of people come and go and this story's mostly about an Aegardean merchant who stopped there reg'lar on his journey to Masachea. And his trade, a'course, was in pigs.

'What all the fuss was for I don't know. I've had a good bit of pork in my life and I say it's nothing special. But these Halfi were crazy for it. Their problem was they were crazy anyway, worse than the average Masachee. And if they were *normally* crazy, they were *twice* as crazy about pigs, and *four times* as wicked in their plans for getting hold a' some.

'Now, this trader's name was Porlick and he was the biggest man in pigs there ever was. He made a stay in Riverport because that was the route, but he made it longer than most so's his wife could do her shoppin'. Rillia was her name, and she ruled him like a man rules a cur. He was no more than her fool, clever though he was at making money.

'She had this habit of setting herself up in a big house where she could have all the traders come to her, rather than the other way 'bout. Make no mistake, this pigman was one of the richest men who came through the city, and his wife was known for spending his money like water. Nat'rally, the Halfi got to hear about this Rillia and it weren't long before they came up with a scheme that would gain 'em the pigs they so treasured.

'Well, they acted like sweet innocents at first. They went along to one of her buying sessions, not to sell her anything mind, but to sing her a song or two. They had a minstrel with 'em. He was Halfi too but the thing was, this fella, well there was something magical about him. He could sing you songs that made you forget where you were or what you were doing, that thrilled you and frightened you, that made you happy and made you sad, as though everything sung was more important to you than anything else in the world. You wouldn't call him a wizard but he had some strange power that's never been heard since. Rillia was most taken with him and his songs and she had him come to see her every day. The fee he demanded was modest and she didn't hesitate to pay it. Every day he walked away with a pig, he did, but always had to promise to come back one more time.

'Old Porlick wanted to be getting a move on, and he complained and moaned about how long she was taking in Riverport, but she just tut-tutted him and told him to keep his peace. And stay they did.

'Rillia must have fallen for this songster and she made every opportunity to speak to him, and in all their talking he managed to let slip, gradual like, that the Halfi were a rich folk of strange powers, and that, though they'd never think of sellin' em, they had in their keepin' such wonders as you could not imagine their like. A'course Rillia then demands to see these treasures. She says that if they're so wonderful she'd have 'em at any price.

'And so we come to the cheatin'. Rillia must have been coming on into her fifties, and a lot of what she spent old Porlick's money on was unctions, and pastes, and washes, all to make her look younger. She knew Porlick couldn't love her if she became ugly, and he might leave her. She was vain, and rightly proud of her looks for her age, but she knew all about the wrinkles that were set to cover her face in just a few years, and that made her a soft touch.

'The next time this bard turns up he tells her he's brought with him the greatest treasure in the world. He spins her a yarn claiming that some of the Halfi, and the King included, had found the secret of *eternal life!* There was a drug, a potion, a precious water given only to a few, that if you had but one sip of it you'd never die. He said that their king was the very same man as set them to wandering a thousand years before; that he was almost a god to 'em. And all that came of this water of life. Now, Rillia's not as stupid as all that, and neither is Porlick, who'd come along to see what these wondrous treasures might be. Porlick calls the man a liar and the man acts all offended. Rillia agrees with her husband, this once, but she can't help thinking how wonderful it would be if it were true. The minstrel pushes it a bit further now: taking a flask from out of his purse and placing it on the table before them, he lets 'em look at it in silence for tense moment or two. "There it stands before you," he says at last, "The true elixir of life, drawn of the eternal font, lifeblood of the gods. Whatever is in you that grows old can become new, whatever is broken will be healed, whatever is weak will become strong. How would it be if you both could regain your youth and keep it forever? This is the great treasure of the Halfi."

'Well you can imagine what Rillia thought of that. And maybe you can imagine what Porlick thought too. So when this minstrel offers to demonstrate the true powers of the drug they decide to let him try. He calls forward one of the Halfi as'd come along with him, an old biddy he explains is his old Grandma or some such, and all together up they go into Rillia's private chamber.

'I don't know exactly how they did it but when the old girl took the drug, before their eyes apparently, the wrinkles disappeared from her face, and her hair grew long and new. It's up to you to decide what was goin' on – disguise and sleight of hand, illusion or whatever – but the point is that Porlick and his wife were taken in. It was all too excitin' a prospect for them to go thinking of trickery and deceit. The promise was too much for them and it made 'em stupid. A'course the wife wants to take the drug straight'way she lays hands on it and even Porlick, with visions of himself and his wife as young as they were when they'd first made love, well, he was more than ready and willing to do the deal. The Halfi minstrel drove a hard bargain, and Porlick ended up paying out a great portion of his stock for just one small bottle o' the stuff.

'Had it been me, I think I'd have taken the drug before I gave up my pigs to 'em, but somehow this Halfi managed to persuade him different. Porlick agreed it'd be common sense to tell people before he took it, just in case they didn't recognize him after, and so he decided to wait until the morning. But, after the Halfi had gone, both the merchant and his wife thought it'd be a fine entertainment if she took her dose before they went off to bed. And so that's what she did.'

Bibron paused for a moment to let the situation sink in. He looked around at those listening and smiled.

'Well then,' he continued, 'Here's old Porlick sitting on his bed waiting for his beautiful young wife to come along and share it with him, and there's Rillia looking at her face in the mirror waiting for the lines around her eyes to drop away and leave her pretty as a sixteen year old. Well, the drug changed her alright. But she never lost any of those wrinkles and she never lost any years. All her life she had hair black as a raven's feathers and never a grey: it was her pride and joy. But now, even as she watched, first one strand and then another, and then a handful, and then all of it, every last hair on her head fell away and there was nothing to do to save it. And it didn't stop there, oh no: away came her eyebrows, away came the hair on her arms, and under her arms, away came the hair on her legs. None of it was spared, not even right down to her... Well, as there's ladies present, let's just say there was one part as looked just that little bit younger after all.'

Some of his audience sniggered on cue though not all. Captain Farber was unconcerned. He always enjoyed his story telling whatever the reaction. But his primary target rolled his eyes. Angren could admit that the story was slightly more entertaining than crushing ants but, given the circumstances, he was growing impatient and had no time for jokes.

'Look Bibron, is this getting us anywhere? From what I've heard so far these Halfi seem alright. So, they cheated people, it doesn't make them crazy.'

'No it don't. But I've only told you about the cheatin' so far and nothing much more, so hold your horses. You'll see how mad they can be.

'Where was I? The hair! Well, Rillia flew into a rage about her lovely locks, but Porlick was more concerned with being cheated out of his stock. He cursed her as a stupid woman, cursed her for making him look such a fool. Did he have a thought for his wife and how she must feel? He did not. Porlick was in such a rage he took it into his head that Rillia was just as much party to the crime as the Halfi. "Get you gone to them, hag!" he cried, and he threw her out onto the streets in the cold of the night, "Go find your minstrel and see if he's a song for you now." And he slammed the door in her face and vowed there and then he never would take her back.

'Well, you might think that the end of the tale, and a cruel end too, but, sad to say, that was just the beginning. Porlick wanted his pigs and he wanted his vengeance.

'On the very next day, our trader went out and he hired himself some swords. Their job to chase after these thieves and, however they chose to do it, with as much blood spilled as they liked, return his stock to Riverport. Now who knows the ins and outs of it, but to cut it short, Porlicks's men were not the brightest nor were they the kindest. They bashed about the Part searching here and there, mistreating any of the Halfi they came across, and yet not one pig did they find. Looking like fools themselves they took a different tack. Against the law of the land, and against decency, they laid hands on a Halfi girl, a young woman and an important one too: almost a princess to them, her father being head man about those parts. Well, they took her in Coldharbour market and carried the girl, her screaming curses at them the while, all the way back to Riverport, looking to use her as hostage for fair payment, and a little more on top for their trouble. It was a mistake. The Halfi didn't like that at all and they came howling after them with never a thought of paying up, only murder in their hearts.

'Picture it: all the Halfi standing outside the gates of Riverport demanding their girl is given up, and Porlick up on the walls calling for the militia to pour oil on them if they came too close. Well, there's plenty of words spoken with both parties feeling aggrieved, and the hired swords stirring it up to their own advantage. I can't say whose idea it was but Porlick's men drag this girl up onto the battlements for all the Halfi to see; and then Porlick brings out, to show to the militia, the so-called wonder that started it all, that small bottle of elixir that'd cheated him of his stock. With the girl struggling but held fast, and the mercenaries all jeering, and the Halfi below screaming out threats, one of those bad men snatches the elixir out of Porlick's shaking hand, brandishes it high for all the Halfi to see, and then sets to forcing the whole lot down the poor girl's throat.

'Well, that was it. That's where the madness came in. You might think a young girl losing her hair is a shame, but it's not anything to go to war over. These Halfi didn't see it like that. They went wild: acted as though he had downright killed her by giving her the drug – not that they'd seemed so bothered about the effect on Rillia. Anyway, parley was now out of the question; paying up never a thought. As I said before, they were just about sane when they were winning but losing, they lost any shred of sense or decency they might have had. First of all they tried to fight their way into Riverport to get at Porlick and his men, and they'd have ripped 'em to pieces if they'd caught up with 'em, but the town militia was having none of it. They defended the walls and defended Porlick, though not through any liking for the man. They had a duty to keep Riverport safe and the way those Halfi were… well no one would've been safe if they'd a got in. But in the eyes of those mad devils it was like the city was taking sides against them. Luckily for Riverport there weren't enough o' these Halfi there and then to break-in through the gates. A few of them ended up dead and any number were injured from arrow fire and so after sunfall they gave it up and disappeared into the night. Everyone waited, for that day and for the next, expecting every hour that the Halfi would come back. Nothing happened. Not for a day, not for three. After a week had passed everyone began to breathe just that bit more easy and things in the city got back to normal. The people of Riverport had no allegiance to this 'Gardean trader and they thought nothin' of this mess was anything at all to do with them, that the Halfi's argument was only with Porlick and the sell-swords. And with the days going by without a murmur or hint that the Halfi were still around, they mostly began to think the problem had just up and gone away.

'Fools to think that way. The Halfi weren't forgetting any of it. It started with reports of people disappearing. Women disappearing, youngish girls – daughters of traders, of officers, of craftsmen. And not just a few. They couldn't credit it but within the month they realised that more than forty girls had gone and no one could find out where to. Even the most stupid must have worked out it was the Halfi and the parents of the missing girls feared the worst, thinking they'd never see their loved ones again.' Bibron shook his head. 'Do you know, I reckon it would've been better if they never had.

'Here's how it was: one morning as the Gate-watch were setting out to open up the town for the day – a good bit before dawn as they do still today – they found a sheet of parchment fixed to the inside of the Kingsgate. It read something like: 'Two for every year – the price you pay.' That's all there was but I guess they must've known what it was about, the Halfi girl being about twenty-one years, and they must have known it was gonna be bad, but they opened up the gates anyway.

'Naked, hairless and mutilated the poor girls were laid there on the road for anyone to see, anyone as had the heart and stomach for it that is. And there, standing just beyond, massed in the road and in the fields to left and right, hundreds of the Halfi. Stood there silent, watching as by lantern light the bodies were discovered, silent as the cries rang through the streets of the town, silent as more people came carrying torches, some to gawp in horror, some to weep, some to search desperate and hopeless. How could they find their lovely girls in amongst all that tortured flesh? The sun came up. The Halfi broke silence. They began to jeer, to curse, to scream, to shout; and they didn't let up until the militia and many of the townsmen, aye and quite a few of the townswomen too, took up their weapons and came out to meet them.

'There was a mighty battle. Porlick, finally realizing where his rage and his desire for revenge had led 'em, felt nothing but ashamed to have caused the death of all those young women. Taking up whatever courage he had left to him, out he went himself to try and stop it all. He took the Halfi girl with him; disgusted at what he had done to her, wantin' to make amends. But it was too late for that, it had all gone too far and they both got caught up in the fighting and both were killed. To cut it short, the militia won the day at last and very few of the Halfi escaped the field. They buried their girls together in a great mound which you can still see today outside the Kingsgate, but the Halfi dead, Porlick and that poor girl included, they burned on a great pyre that blazed for a week and cursed the streets of Riverport with a foul reek that lingered for months on end – a daily reminder of the tragedy that comes of revenge.

'And there once again, you'd have thought it'd ended but, as a fact, well the very worst was yet to come. I think I said that the Halfi didn't get together much as a tribe but spread themselves far and wide. So those who were killed in Riverport were only a portion of the full number. One of those who escaped went to their 'King', and it was him that made all the rest happen. They'd had enough, I reckon, done with running, done with all the casual persecution, done with being treated as freaks.

'I won't go into the hows, the wheres and the whens, but what they did is an abomination to stand forever. Halfi from all places took out into the night and whenever they could they'd steal a child. They took hundreds of 'em. And they didn't kill 'em straight. Oh no! By all accounts they took to *cannibalism*. The story ripped through all of Pars that the Halfi were stealing children and cooking 'em alive. Whether that was true or not the children were gone and that was a certainty. It was madness, cruel and wicked madness.

'Well, that was the final crime. The King of Pars, Rúhandar by name, sent out his armies. The Halfi were hunted through every last corner of the country and mostly killed. A few hundred survived, whenever the generals could hold back their men from their anger, and these few were held to trial and they were found guilty. Now, there'd been so much killing by then that people were sick of it; over the border the Masachee were making such a noise about this so-called 'massacre of *their people*' – not that they'd ever owned the Halfi before then; and so the King knew he couldn't have done with it and just execute 'em all. Eventually he decided, with his advisors and with the justices, that it would be best all round to exile the Halfi, to set 'em apart from normal folk. And so they put 'em on Tumboll. It was the Partian wizards as arranged it. Don't ask me how, but they set up spells to keep the exiles bound to the island, spells that would set a fire in 'em if ever they tried to escape. And so it was done and that at last was the end.

'Every few years the army would go over to Tumboll to make sure everything was secure, that the Halfi were prisoners still; but as the years went by they noticed the Halfi were becoming more and more savage, and madder than ever. Eventually it 'came too dangerous to visit and from then on, through all the generations, they've been on their own. And Tumboll has become a place of horror, a place to avoid for any as'd like to stay alive and whole. Worse than a land of demons! And Tumboll, Angren my lad, is just exactly where we are right now.'

And that was the tale as Bibron gave it. Without a doubt more could have been said but what he had heard was easily enough for the swordsman.

'So, let me get this straight,' he said calmly, 'What you're saying is we're on an island seething with maniacs who'd like nothing better than to torture us all to death, just for the fun of it.'

'That's about the sum. The story is probably exaggerated but it's more or less right. Fact we're alive now shouldn't encourage you too much neither: even in Pars they were accused of sacrificing people to their gods, so they're likely keeping us for some festival or other. They were said to have kept to cannibalism too, which is a bit odd if you think about it.'

'Why's that?'

'Well, this island may not have everything but it's not short of pigs. Place is supposed to be ridden with 'em. Apparently, and you'll like this, it was *Rillia* as brought 'em here. Too ashamed to live with good folk, they say, but still she had a right to Porlick's estate. So she gathered up all she had left, stock included, and asked for to be exiled to Tumboll along with the Halfi. Strange woman. The story don't say what happened when she arrived but, 'part from the pigs, I shouldn't think the Halfi were all that pleased to see her.'

PASSAGE

Tumboll 3057.7.24

'Well, whatever the story, we still need to know what's on the other side of that wall. Any offers?'

Angren looked around with a grin on his face: he wasn't being serious. He had been reasonably shocked by the cruelties of Bibron's tale but he decided nothing was altered. From the start it was clear they were held captive by brutal savages. That they were the descendants of maniacs was relatively unimportant. But while Angren found it easy to dismiss the tale as ancient history it was clear that many others could not. Childhood nightmares were not supposed to become real. He wasn't expecting any response.

'Easy job: spy out the land, find out what these lads have got planned for us. Someone with a good bit of strength and a steady nerve. No? Well then, we'd better see what old Angren can do.'

There was snort of laughter behind him. 'Praise to the Many for sending us a hero! Tortured by his injuries but ready and eager to risk his life. It makes me feel quite faint.'

She was just over five-and-a-half feet, slim enough and curvy enough. Her long black hair was plaited in a pigtail. She was dressed in a shirt and tight trousers, both black, and she carried a leather jacket over one shoulder. Angren, against all the evidence, inevitably expected women to be dependent creatures, physically weak and emotional. That description did not apply. Her poise hinted at an impressive strength, the mockery was confident and the look of amusement she wore, whenever she caught his eye, carried with it a warning. This one looked like trouble. He glanced past her. The other two women from the Cottle were backing her up: the big arm wrestler, huge and scary as a bear, and the woman with golden hair who seemed able to control the men around her with nothing more than a smile and a soft word. The blonde woman, Isolde, had been more or less silent since the wreck and the hunt but Berta had been swapping gruesome stories with the rest of them. She gave the impression that she was just about ready to start breaking some heads. It was all very unsettling. The little minx continued:

'But are you sure you're up to it? It's quite a climb you know. We wouldn't want you to fall off now would we?' Abruptly her manner changed and the mocking tone was dropped. 'My name is Sigrid, House Althoné. I work for the King. Who are you and why should we follow your lead?'

So far no one had bothered to ask, his friendship with Seama taken as a mark of allegiance, if not of authority. 'I'm a friend of... of the King,' he said, aware that without Seama around his credibility was possibly in doubt, 'and I expect we have the same sort of jobs to do.'

'Shouldn't think so: not unless you were intending to seduce your way through Aegarde. I don't always dress like this, *Old Angren*. But then, you wouldn't need seduction, would you, being Aegardean yourself.'

It was an accusation he could not deny and she knew it. Angren had wondered how long it would take for someone to question his nationality, but he hadn't yet thought of a way to explain his position. Bibron came to his rescue.

'So what if he is? You think it puts him on their side? Look, this man's a friend of the Lord Seama and if Seama wanted him with us, that's good enough for me. I don't think you should be questioning him. And as to following his lead, I'm willing to bet he's twice as capable of getting us out of here than you are, so why don't you just back off and let him get on with it?'

She laughed. 'Only teasing, Captain Farber. Hard to resist, it's so easy. Actually I never really doubted him. Any friend of Seama's is a friend of mine, no matter how *big-headed* he might be. But I thought it better to ask the question, and get an honest answer, than not. We all have to trust each other, Captain, and if Old Angren's going to lead us out then I don't want anyone doubting him.'

'Right,' said Bibron, 'I see. Well then, *does* anyone have a problem with this feller being Aegardean? Cause if they do, they can come and talk to me.'

Nobody said a word. Which was just as well as Angren was beginning to feel needled.

'Look, can we get on?'

'Well—'

'Well what?' he snarled as he turned to confront his new tormentor. It was Isolde. She jumped a little at his response.

'I er... it's just that, well, I wondered whether climbing the wall—'

'Gods save us! Look, goldilocks, I can climb it, alright? Let's just cut the cackle. Bloody women.'

He didn't exactly mean to say the last bit out loud. Isolde dropped the hesitancy.

'Now listen, you ungracious oaf, with your ears, and lets hope you have something in-between them. What I was going to say was that I don't think you need to climb anything. Actually, I think there is probably another way out – we just need to explore a little.'

Angren could have apologised but instead, hands on hips, he peered around in the manner of a mummer at pantomime, leaning to one side and then another, looking past her and all about, and then he shrugged massively.

'Four walls, a gate and lots of pig shit. What's to explore?'

Isolde shook her head in quiet amazement. Sigrid stepped up to him and planted her hands on her hips.

'Are you going to carry on like this? Because if you are we might just as well call in the Halfi and ask them to murder us right now. Because that's what's going to happen anyway if we can't figure out how to work with each other. Now, just because you have an idea that seems good, and appeals to your childish sense of adventure, it really doesn't mean it's the right one to go with. Now, as it happens I think Isolde is right. We've only looked around so far but we haven't looked closely enough. And we certainly haven't considered properly what this building might have—' She stopped. 'What?'

Angren was staring at her. 'Oh, er nothing' he mumbled, 'Er... What do you mean about the building? It's just ruins isn't it?' Actually the ruins were the last thing on his mind. What he was thinking was that she looked damn fine when she was angry.

She smiled. 'Ruins, Old Angren, are not built as ruins. This was a Oncer's temple at some point. That right, Isolde?'

'Not exactly, but something similar. The Church of the One Making is rather exact when it comes to their buildings. They supposedly believe in simplicity. So that arch above the gate should be a 'simple' arch – a semi circle and unadorned. As you can see, it is quite the opposite.'

They all looked. The arch seemed angular: no curves, only straight lines which disturbingly met at odd angles. There was no real symmetry beyond the parallel posts supporting it. Jarring, geometrical patterns were cut into the face of the stone.

'Now, how in hell does that stay up?' said the Captain speaking for nearly all of them. But Ruspa somehow knew the answer.

'It is a hidden arch,' he said, 'and what you see is only a form of decoration. A solid regular structure has been dressed to confuse the eye and your common sensibilities on the order of things. Most unusual.'

'Why the *bloody hell* are we rattling on about hidden bloody arches? Isn't there anything better to talk about? I'd've thought—'

'I imagine, Angren,' said Ruspa, 'the ladies believe we are in a close walk such as you would find in a Oncer monastery, even though, as the blonde one has explained, this is not exactly a Oncer building.'

'Shall I tell you what? I haven't a clue what you're going on about, I have no idea what a Oncer is and I'm getting really fed up with all the chat. For gods'sake can't we *do* something?'

Garaid laughed. 'Don't you know anything at all, Angren?'

'Not you too.'

'No. Actually I am on your side: it's time we did something. Look, a Oncer is someone who believes God made the world once and then sat back and let us get on with worshipping him. Unlike the Twoers who reckon he watched what we got up to, thought we'd made a mess of it, and remade the world again to see if we could get it right second time round. I may possibly be doing a disservice to both but all you really need to know is that they all build temples and some of them look like this. Perhaps when we get out you should take yourself off to Lindis and ask for a proper explanation.'

'Anyone else?'

Isolde looked at Sigrid to see if she had anything more to put in, but she just smiled sarcastically, and so Isolde explained:

'If this is a close walk around a courtyard, or cloister as they might say, then it's extremely unlikely there is only the one entrance. There should be three. One in each corner except the one that's left as a 'perfect angle'. So, if we check the corners, behind all those nettles, we might find a door.'

'And no doubt it'll be open and unguarded.'

'I don't know about you, but I would think a few generations have gone by since anyone did any exploring here. They may have forgotten all about it.'

Angren shrugged. 'Fair enough. Let's get on with it then.'

It could very well have been forgotten. There was a door, all rotten timbers, but it was set lower than the current level of the compound, possibly at the foot of stone steps now completely submerged by the dirt of centuries. All they could see was the top two feet of it. Prising away a sliver of wood Angren found compacted earth behind. The way must have been blocked for hundreds of years.

He emerged from behind the screen of nettles as casually as possible, readjusting his clothes as though he had been to relieve himself.

'Doesn't look too promising.'

Some of the others had been to look at the door already and were despondent to say the least. There had been nothing in the other two corners, or nothing they could find, but everyone was excited when Ruspa gave them the news that he'd struck wood after only a little work in clearing away loose rubble. Now the excitement was changing to despair. Angren looked at them with pity. There were some good people here and he didn't want to see them suffer.

'However,' he continued, 'we won't really know until we put in some elbow grease. The ground falls away towards that back wall so at least we shouldn't have a problem with the spoil. The nettles are dense enough – I don't think they'll see through. What we need is to make sure those lads up there don't suss what we're up to. We need a diversion.'

So a party was made up to start digging a latrine, some way away from the corner they were interested in, using their boots and a few broken slates they had found. Their captors were concerned at first that the prisoners were trying to dig their way out but when Bibron took down his trousers and mimed having a crap they understood and let the diggers get on with it.

And at the same time, one at a time, several others worked at clearing away the rotten wood and then scraping away at the compacted soil behind it. After an hour or so, after slow progress and no sign of anything other than clay and more clay, most of them had wanted to give up. The noise generated by digging the latrine had comfortably covered the sound of the other excavation but that job was now done and digging any deeper would seem ridiculous. So what to do? Angren wouldn't let them stop, not while they had daylight. At any time their captors could come for them, at any moment the torturing and killing might begin. He organised the prisoners to chatter, squabble, wander about, piss or whatever they could think of that would make noise without arousing suspicion, while one at a time a few of them, prone and much stung among the nettles, continued to scrape at the earth with Angren's dirk.

He finally gave in when he saw more guards arrive, up above the walls, all carrying lanterns. The light was fading fast. He was suggesting, in a defeated sort of way, that perhaps they should break for the night just as Berta emerged from her most recent stint.

'Good idea,' she said, 'It'll be a lot more comfortable in the tunnel I've just found if there's a bit of light to come back to.'

Dawn brought forth a sluggish day. The guards once again mounted their tower and observed dispassionately the feeding, the ablutions and the pacing of the caged men and women. They were not surprised when the prisoners scraped soil into the latrines to cover the smelly faeces, and they were easily distracted by a raucous dice game the captain got started – indeed they seemed fascinated by it. Nothing remarkable happened.

Hidden from sight the excavation continued. They had to be careful to disguise the disappearance of whoever was digging and they changed over quite often in case someone was missed. At first the task was hard: there was not much room to work in and the soil was full of stone debris. The tunnel Berta had discovered amounted to a space twelve inches high, an arm's length in, but after two hours of persistent digging the gap was much wider and deeper and progress became quicker. Ruspa made the break-through. He squirmed in to find that the mound of soil blocking the passage became a gradual slope down into darkness. He slithered down the slope and within a minute whispered back that he had found a bare stone pavement. It was difficult to keep the excitement hidden as they hauled him out of the tunnel. At a signal from Angren, Bibron managed to start an argument over the throw of a die which more or less explained the sudden hubbub.

'So what now,' Garaid asked Angren.

'Well, after we have had a little breather to calm down a bit, we need to talk it through.'

Sigrid exchanged a grin with Berta. 'And I thought he'd just charge off down the tunnel and expect us to follow,' she said, 'He's learning.'

Angren was not very keen on tight places. He had no idea why this might be, no memory of a frightening experience in his youth, no real belief in the idea of premonition – he just liked the open air. When it came down to someone having to explore the tunnel he was brave enough to put himself forward, but more than happy to let Ruspa and Sigrid take it on instead. Ruspa had already taken the first steps and seemed keen to go further; Sigrid, Angren decided, was simply trying to impress. He had no notion that she might have noticed his hesitancy.

But he wouldn't let them go immediately. Ruspa was not the problem: he was fairly nondescript from a distance but Sigrid was one of only three women and the guards might easily notice her absence if the exploration took too long. This day was even hotter than the first. They would wait until midday in the hope the Halfi would once again retire in the face of the sun.

The hours dragged intolerably. The prisoners frightened themselves with insubstantial rumours of torture and sacrifice, or theories of darker designs. These Halfi were unnatural, and not just in looks. Midmorning brought with it an unwelcome and unsettling development. From a distance, but clear as clear, came the sound of hammering and sawing. The Halfi were preparing something.

Noon came, the meal was delivered, the guards left the tower and the game was on. Ruspa went first and Sigrid followed with some difficulty. It was a tight squeeze in places and she was amazed Ruspa had managed to get through. He didn't look thinner than she was. If they were all to escape this way there was more earth to shift first. As she wriggled her way in, she reasoned it would be easier and less noisy to dig on the tunnel side of the mound, and that meant a lot more work for skinnies like her.

The darkness grew the further they went and soon touch was the only sense left to her, and that didn't help too much when she came to the drop-off. Suddenly she tumbled down a short slope and landed fair and square on Ruspa's back.

'Thank you indeed,' he gasped as he tried to get his breath back. The sound of his voice sibilant as the echoes slipped away into the unknown.

'Sorry.'

'Well let's just be a bit more careful, shall we.'

Sigrid was annoyed. 'You should have warned me – I can't see in the dark even if you can.'

'It *is* quite dark. I suggest we face away from the mound and reach out for the left hand wall and then move on really very slowly – I wouldn't want us falling down any more slopes.'

Sigrid took pleasure in making a rude gesture in the direction of Ruspa's voice but she understood the sense of the plan and did as he suggested. Rubbing away a smear of unseen growths she could feel that the wall beneath was very smooth as though made of tile rather than stone. An expensive option. They hadn't scrimped, these monks of whatever denomination.

'Are you ready, Sigrid.'

'Yes. I'm with you. Let's go.'

For a slow but sure hundred yards everything went well. There were occasional mounds of earth fallen through cracks in the roof but nothing that proved to be any major hindrance. The floor was as smooth as the walls, made up of oblong flags and grooved by the passage of many feet over many years. The incline was slightly downwards. But then Sigrid, close behind her partner, heard him hiss in surprise before she too touched the void with her left hand.

Sigrid crouched and ran her hands outwards.

'It's just another tunnel I think. I can feel the floor of it: the flags are laid at right angles to these in the main corridor. So which way now?'

'Perhaps some light would help us decide.'

Sigrid snorted in disbelief. 'You're not telling me you have matches?'

'Not exactly. It's an oilcan lighter I picked up in Dreffield. Made by a man called Besma, I believe – something to do with the cannons he makes.'

'Cannons?'

'Not really time for a discussion. Point is, only a small amount of oil left, so I thought I'd save it till needed.'

Sigrid heard a scratching noise and light flared in Ruspa's hand. In truth the flame was quite small but to their hungry eyes it seemed lantern bright. At last they could view their surroundings. Criss-crossing arcs of stone vaulted the roof of the main tunnel at least five feet above Ruspa's head, the walls seemed to be made of red or brown ceramic tile, and the flooring was grey marble. It was an impressive structure: less of a tunnel than a processional corridor.

The other passageway was lower and narrower and fell away steeply into darkness.

'I don't like the look of that.'

Ruspa nodded. 'And I don't like the smell of it – the air is… well, dead. Also I do not think we should be going downhill if we are trying to get out of here. We started at ground level and I don't remember climbing a hill to the compound.'

'No, we didn't, but does that make it the wrong choice? By the angle, I think this tunnel would take us in the opposite direction to the main gate. And, I don't know why exactly, but I feel as though this one is longer – much longer. Shouldn't we try it?'

'You're wrong,' said Ruspa.

'Well thanks for considering it.'

Ruspa clicked his tongue in annoyance. 'You are wrong, Sigrid, in that as yet we have no idea of what lies beyond the walls of the compound. We stopped Angren from making the climb if you recall. Any direction may be a disaster for all we know. And besides, even if it did lead us away that'd be of little use if we died of the poisoned air half way in. Can you not smell it?'

Sigrid, chastened, took a few hesitant steps down the slope and breathed in deeply. 'It smells damp but—' She stopped. The darkness drew her and repelled her at the same time. She was scared. Hardly realising what she was doing Sigrid backed out of the tunnel so heedlessly she thumped into Ruspa's chest and knocked the lighter out of his hand. The flame went out.

'Well done. Again.'

'Sorry,' she yelped. This time she felt like a fool. 'It was just so unpleasant in there, something was… I don't know.'

Together they fumbled around in the dark searching the floor for the lighter. Sigrid's hand closed upon something.

'Found it,' she said, but almost in the same instant Ruspa said the same.

'No,' she said, 'Not your lighter but something. Why don't you light up, then I can see?'

This time Sigrid heard only a clicking noise and a soft curse.

'Lost the damn flint. I have another but I'll never get it fitted in the dark. Unfortunate. A pity you panicked.'

'A pity you didn't hold on to it a bit tighter.'

Sigrid was beginning to dislike this little man. Did he never make a mistake? He was silent for a few seconds but then carried on as if Sigrid had said nothing.

'So our best course is to continue along this main corridor. It looked to me as though it was beginning to incline slightly upwards. An encouraging sign, I think. But we must remember on our return to keep to the left to avoid the other way.'

'Suits me.'

They moved on. Sigrid was glad to leave the argument behind. He was in the right: she *had* panicked but what worried her most was that she had no idea *why*. There were no eyes in the dark, no slithering creatures at her feet, there was no scrape of a drawn sword echoing in the depths. It was just a tunnel. But so cold, and so silent, and the way the light from Ruspa's oilcan had sunk into the darkness as if good honest light had no power there made her feel that, unheard and unseen, something of truly ill intent lay in wait. Down there, just beyond the reach of common senses, something evil had been willing her to take just one more step. As she moved slowly forward, close in Ruspa's wake, even though nothing could possibly be seen, she kept looking back over her shoulder. She could discern no movement, the echoes of steps were all their own. Nothing followed. The object she had found at the entrance to that dark way nestled in her pocket, disregarded for now.

Ahead, not only did the corridor begin to incline upwards but after only another twenty yards or so it turned sharply right. Here the blackness that fettered their senses became less complete, a greyness developed with each step and after another turn, this time to the left, they could see soft beams of light filtering into the passage from high up on the right hand wall. They hurried forward.

This time not a tunnel but an opening into free air, clogged by dirt and broken rock as at the other end. Some scrabbling at the detritus of several centuries found them no rotten wooden door this time: instead the daylight crept in between the bars of a rusted iron gate.

Ruspa gave them a tug. There was some movement but not enough for a quick exit.

'Berta could shift them,' Sigrid told him, 'Or that Garaid lad.'

Ruspa slid back into the passage. 'Or perhaps there's some better opening further on. We may find an escape not so dependent upon muscles.'

But no: further ahead the light waned and they reached an impenetrable wall of fallen stone and mortar. It was the end of their exploration.

'We'd better get back to Berta then,' Sigrid suggested.

'Yes, let's get back into proper daylight. Twenty minutes of this gloom and darkness is more than enough. And let's make sure we keep to the left and well away from that hell hole.'

Sigrid was surprised. It hadn't occurred to her that Ruspa felt as bad about the place as she did. He seemed such a cold person, she hadn't considered he might have feelings of any sort.

All through the night the furtive digging down in the tunnel continued. Blind the prisoners had to rely on touch alone but eventually their labour gave reward. The gap into the tunnel was widened and was now sufficient for the mightiest of girths; at the other end the bars that yet denied them freedom had been loosened to Berta's satisfaction, ready for one final effort. They waited only for the heat of noon once more. It was an uncomfortable wait.

General disappointment greeted the unmistakable sound of more Halfi arriving and the continuance of construction work. There was renewed hope when in the late morning they heard many of the Halfi joking and laughing as they left their work and by the sound of it left the village too. Things seemed to be moving in their favour. Angren spread the word that they all should be ready to go at his signal. Not one prisoner dissented, not one thought the chances any better to wait and see.

They welcomed a gusty wind that blew up shortly before noon. It took away some of the heat and encouraged the guards to leave their buffeted tower sooner than normal. They were startled by sudden, sporadic explosions and by a frightening roaring noise in the distance. A glance up at the sky revealed the source. A great pall of smoke billowed above the trees. Thankfully downwind of their camp, the forest was burning.

It was time. There were no guards to watch as one by one the prisoners crawled into the tunnel. Ruspa went first with Berta and Angren just behind, and the rest following in no particular order. Bibron Farber saw the last of them through. As Garaid disappeared into the darkness the Captain stepped back into the compound to take a last look at their prison. The walls seemed higher than before, the earth more bare and the eerie silence uncomfortable. He snorted, spat his good riddance into the dust and then, with grim satisfaction, made a rude gesture with his right arm in the direction of the main gate.

'Up yours, you bastards!'

He would have liked to yell it out but common sense prevailed and the curse came out as little more than a whisper. As he plunged through the hole that would take him to freedom the thought occurred to him that the silence they left behind might just be a problem.

A few moments later two of the Halfi climbed back up to their viewing point.

They had all been warned about that *other* passageway. Most of the prisoners clung to the right hand wall of the passage unwilling to learn any more about it. Angren, on the other hand, despite his discomfort at being underground, decided he had a duty to perform. Walking just behind Ruspa and his lighter, the weapon-master peered ahead. After only a few minutes in he thought he could make out a dark patch on the left hand wall. Bizarrely, in the uncertain light it seemed as though the darkness of the tunnel was seeping into the passageway before them. This was probably an illusion but it added to his sense of unease. But Angren had a solution for nervousness: his much practiced method was to ignore the feeling and carry on anyway. This attitude often made others think him brave.

At the opening Angren asked to borrow Ruspa's lighter

and holding it high above his head he stepped boldly over the threshold. Nothing much happened. He took twenty paces down the slope, his foot slipping only once on the slimy floor. Surprised to be out of breath, he stopped to take a rest. All he could see was the worn smooth grey stone flags at his feet and the muddy brown walls. Both the way ahead and the way back to his friends were equally shrouded from his sight. He took another five or ten steps without bettering the situation, and then without any warning the lighter went out. The suddenness made him yelp.

Back in the passageway Sigrid who had been the foremost of those tracking his progress shouted out 'Angren! Angren!' but by the time the noise of her cry had diminished they all could hear his steps toiling back up the slope. They couldn't see him but recognised his chuckle as he came close.

'Something up, Sig? I thought I heard you shouting.'

'Well I thought I heard *you* screaming.'

'Just a little surprised when the lighter thingy went out. Couldn't see any reason for it, though I did think the air was a little tight.'

'Tight?' said Ruspa.

'You know, hard to breath. To be honest I was just thinking of turning round when the light went. Here, can you get it lit again?'

They fumbled around in the dark trying to locate each other's hand.

'As I said to Sigrid,' Ruspa reminded them as he flicked the lever causing green sparks that caught the oily wick and gave them sight once more, 'It is very likely the air down there is poisoned.'

Angren frowned. That didn't quite explain it. 'Actually, it was more as if the air was getting less, thinner, as though the goodness was being sucked out of it.'

'Amounts to the same thing.'

'Does it? Well anyway, I think that's why the tunnel seems so unpleasant. I don't think there's anything down there to give us any trouble.'

'No demons or monsters waiting to attack then?'

'I shouldn't think so Berta,' said Angren, but then added with a laugh, 'Mind you, I don't always get it right. So, just in case, let's get out of here and find some better air.'

No one objected to that and Ruspa set off again at an increased pace, seemingly keen to put some distance between himself and the mysterious tunnel.

They all crowded round when they reached the bars, so much so that Angren had to urge them back to give Berta and Garaid some room to work. There was a little grumbling about this, and the echoes of so many people together bounced off the walls like the growling of some angry old dragon. More than one of them looked back into the gloom towards that other tunnel wondering whether the echoes might have a different source.

'Shush, you lot,' Berta whispered so loudly that everyone heard. 'I want to listen.'

The light of honest day illuminated her face but long grass and weeds screened the world beyond from view. The wind was still blustering and the roaring sound of the fire in the distance continued. Birds in a panic flew high in the sky calling in many voices. But there was no sound of human activity. They all listened for a good five minutes but there was nothing to be heard and they began to breathe a little more easily.

'Right Berta, Garaid, lets have those bars down,' said the Captain. 'I've had enough of being a captive.'

There was a general 'aye' to that and so the two of them put their backs into it. It didn't take long. Angren, not a weakling himself, couldn't help admiring the pair of them. Garaid grunted a bit with the effort of pushing and then pulling as they struggled to loosen the bars from the earth that had encased this gate for so many years, but Berta took it all in her stride and gave the impression she wasn't much challenged. The joints where the three cross bars met the five verticals, well enough rusted to be brittle, soon gave way to their combined strength, and, with something of a clang and clatter, the uprights were free.

Angren stepped up. 'Good work men.'

Berta gave him a black look.

Angren shrugged and then grinned. 'You know what I mean. The pair of you make a good team. Right, now for a little less power and a bit more stealth. Get everyone through while Ruspa and me take a good look around. C'mon, while it's still quiet.'

And without waiting for assent or dissent, Angren and Ruspa scrambled through the open gateway and disappeared into the scenery.

'Well,' said the Captain, 'You heard the man. Let's get out of here.'

And so they did.

DEMONOGRAPHY

Tumboll 3057.7.26

Berta took a few moments rest after her efforts. She took a few deep breaths of the promised free air and thought it pleasantly smoky. She watched the others emerge from the tunnel squinting in the strong light. It took a little while to get everyone out and Berta couldn't help wondering exactly how much time they would have before their escape was discovered. Clearly Bibron was equally worried. He posted lookouts at once but then returned to the hole to help the rest. So far the noise of their egress didn't seem to have attracted attention.

Of those already free most of them followed Berta's lead and took the opportunity to get their breath and calm down a little after the perceived threat of the passageway and the tunnel; but there were a few among them who were all for getting away immediately. A big man called Scortha was their leader.

'What are we waiting for? Let's go. We've got to get out of here before they notice we're gone. We should make for those hills in the eastern end.'

Garaid was scandalised. 'Just hang on a minute. Not everyone's out yet,' he growled, 'and don't you think we should wait for Angren?'

'What the hell for? I didn't ask him to go scouting. It's his look out if we're gone when he gets back.'

'Listen here, you scumbag, it's down to Angren and a few others that we're out of there. I didn't notice you volunteering to help.'

'Why bother volunteering when the arrogant bastard wanted to do it all by himself?'

Berta decided it would be a good idea to stop resting and take a stroll. She took a stroll towards Scortha and Garaid, wondering whether she'd be in time to prevent the fight.

'Arrogant bastard, you reckon,' snarled Garaid.

'On the nail. He might be a friend of yours but I'm not wasting time waiting for that Aegardean shit.'

Bibron had sidled up alongside Garaid. Berta wondered which of the three of them would start it.

'Tell me, Scortha,' Bibron said in a steady voice, 'Let's say we go now and don't wait for Angren. How far do you think you're going to get before the Halfi realise we're gone? Not far I guess. And where exactly are you going to? So far we haven't a clue which way's up and which way's down. So how long do you think it's going take 'em to track us down if we're wandering around like witless fools?'

Berta grinned. If Bibron really was trying to act the peacemaker he might have left out the 'witless fools' bit. Scortha didn't seem too impressed.

'What's *witless*, Farber, is hanging around here waiting to get caught again. We just need to get away from here as fast as possible, head for somewhere we can defend ourselves.'

'Oh and then what?'

'Figure out a way of getting off the Island.'

'You gormless clod,' said Bibron, now somehow forgetting that he was trying to calm things down, 'what were you thinking of: hitching a lift on a cloud? What we need is weapons, food and a boat in that order. And what we don't need is an idiot like you telling us what to do. So why don't you just shut it?'

Scortha was not easily cowed.

'Shut it yourself. I don't know who you think you are. You might have been the Captain when we were on the River but now you're just a fat bastard I don't have to listen to, alright?'

It took the efforts of both Garaid and Berta to keep them apart but the furious argument that followed only came to an end when Angren and Ruspa came rushing back to see what was going on.

'What the *buggering hell* are you lot trying to do? We could hear you squabbling half a mile away. You might be interested to know that there's a village just on the other side of those trees, and right next to that the gates to the compound we've just escaped from. Anyone'd think you lot want to get back in there. Now listen—'

He stopped, looking over their heads at the mound behind

them that covered over the roof of the passageway. The quickest of them spun to look just as the two young boys Angren had spotted whisked off into the undergrowth.

'After them,' yelled one of Scortha's supporters and some were ready to go but Angren shouted them down.

'Stay where you are.' He was incensed. 'For Gods' sakes! They're just children.'

'But they'll give us away.'

'It doesn't matter: we're off anyway. Right now! We're going to attack the village – don't worry, it's nearly deserted by the look of it. There's about twenty huts, big moot house in the middle. Now we'll need weapons if we're going to get out of here—

'As I was saying,' put in the Captain, 'An' food an'all.'

'And the only way we're going to get either is if we go in and take them. I reckon we go in fast, and we go in hard.'

Garaid at this moment clambered out of the passage with the iron bars of the gate gathered in his brawny arms.

'Here then,' he said to Angren, 'Reckon you might need one of these.'

'No thanks, give it to Berta' Angren replied, fumbling with the belt to his trousers, 'I already have something to scare them with.'

Berta guffawed and Sigrid squawked with laughter. 'What, down your trousers?' she said, 'Well it certainly scares me.'

'That I will remember. Actually I was thinking of this.' And out came the whippy sword he had described to Garaid back in the compound. Berta was amazed but others, she could tell, were envious. It was going to be difficult for them all but worse for some. A quick weapon count found them a few more hidden daggers but nothing much else.

As they got themselves ready for the off Berta took a moment to look at them all. They were an odd crew: men and women already bloodied and bruised, some of them experienced warriors, some plainly not. She saw faces set in grim determination and faces pale with terror. Few of them, she guessed, had any real hope of survival. A good job they had people like Angren and Bibron and herself then. Angren looked at her as though guessing her thoughts.

'So,' he said, 'Time to be doing. Those with the iron bars in the lead with me, knifemen second up and the rest of you get anything you can: belts, rope, wooden staves, anything you can pick up on the way, even if it's just a pocketful of pebbles. Let's go.'

They were expected. The two lads had given the Halfi warning enough for some hasty preparation. A line of eight young strong men armed with swords were strung out across the path into the village, but to back them up only another ten or so old gaffers carrying pig sticks. Angren was true to his word. He didn't stop to wonder at the inadequate defence their enemy had thrown together or spare a thought to pity them. He led the attack like a berserker and their opponents' line disintegrated in the mad rush. It was a massacre. The Halfi didn't seem to know how to use the arms they wielded. None of them were a match for Berta with an iron bar and Angren's sword slid through their guard as quick and deadly as a snake. Only the pig stick men caused the Partians any difficulty, killing two men and injuring several more before Garaid, Scortha and a few others hacked them into submission, using swords taken from the hands of those already fallen. The three Halfi still standing threw down their sticks and knelt on the ground before them.

Garaid went to find Angren and greeted him with a big grin on his face.

'Well that wasn't so bad, was it?'

'No, not too bad. But I didn't expect it would be: most of the men have gone somewhere else – this lot weren't much more than a bunch of lads.'

Garaid nodded agreement. 'The oldies gave us some trouble, though. We captured three—' He gestured towards the prisoners but at that moment there was a scream. The look of horror and anger on his face said it all. Angren turned. One of the old men was writhing on the floor with a pig stick in his guts; another was struggling to get free of the two men holding him as Scortha readied a second pig stick. Angren didn't hesitate. He barged past Garaid and hurtled up behind Scortha, flooring him in one quick movement.

'What the hell do you think you're doing, you bastard?' he roared. Scortha rolled over in the dust and lay on his back too winded for the moment to speak. 'They'd yielded! Hadn't they?'

Scortha sat up and spat. 'Just tidying up,' he said, 'I thought it'd be a good idea. We don't want enemies at our backs.'

'What are you going to do next: kill everyone in the village? The women, the children?'

'Well *they* would.'

Angren turned away, his face dark with anger. Garaid decided to step in. 'Much more of this, Scortha,' he said 'And I'll start to wonder which side you're actually on.'

Scortha's look was scornful. 'You're a pair of nancies,' he told them, 'This is *war* you know. Bad things have to happen.'

That was too much for Angren.

'Now look you, Scortha is it? You need to have a bit of a think about things. It's the Halfi supposed to be the murdering bastards round here, not us. Just now we don't have time for a discussion but when we get somewhere safe, me and you are going to have a little talk, alright? About what is right and what is not. Till then you just watch yourself or you'll find bad things happening to you. And that's a promise. Now, let's get on with searching this village shall we.'

Angren had the other two prisoners bound and left a couple of men to guard them but the rest of the Partians began the search. The first thing they verified was that the settlement *was* mostly deserted. Some women and children were found in one of the huts. The two young lads who had given them away were there, standing in front of the others, bravely brandishing knives. There was fear in every face. Angren wondered whether they had seen Scortha killing the old man. He stepped up, laid down his sword and raised his hands palm outwards.

'Take it easy. There'll be no more killing. We just need food.'

He wasn't sure they understood. He mimed putting food into his mouth.

An old woman moved forwards. She spoke in an accent strange to him but the words were common Partian as spoken throughout much of Asteranor.

'You are bad men,' she said simply, 'We do not trust you. We will not help.'

The memory of Bibron's sailor clutching at his guts as they spewed out of his belly filled his mind.

'Bad men? *We* are bad men? Do you not know what your men did to mine? They have murdered and mutilated more than twenty innocent men already. And *we* are bad men?'

She wasn't interested. 'That is men's work. Men are all the same. We will not help you. There is food, you find it, go away.'

There was no point in arguing. Angren was truly stung by the accusation. The women had witnessed Scortha's crime and there was no hope of changing their minds. It was a pity: they could have done with some help. He wondered how much time they had left.

'Right, let's get on with it. Bibron watch this lot. Garra, take ten and search these lower huts – weapons, food, nothing else. Scortha, you come with me.'

He made for the large building in the centre of the settlement. He had thought, when he first saw it, that it must be the moot house for the village but as they drew close he realised it was actually some sort of temple. What made that obvious were the ten priestesses standing guard at the entrance. They were all dressed in long but scant turquoise robes, which would have made for a pleasing outlook but for the fact that each of them screamed unintelligible imprecations at Angren and his men as they tried to gain entrance. Angren realised that the women were of various ages, the youngest less than twelve and the oldest at least seventy, each wielding a nasty looking curved knife clearly designed for blood-letting. Angren contemplated without relish the possibility that they'd have to battle their way past. Scortha no doubt would be delighted. Luckily the defiance put up by these fine ladies was confined to verbal abuse and they fell back inside as Angren drew his sword. Angren and his crew followed.

It was a peculiar place. The hall wasn't impressive. Wooden walls, low roof, the only decorations were pig's heads, a couple of ceremonial swords and some rude homespun hangings. There was an altar, as expected, and on it several bowls and more of those knives the priestesses used laid ready beside them. But behind the altar was an empty stone chair. Angren surveyed the chair, greatly intrigued. It was an item of greater quality than anything else in the temple, carved from a single block of dense black stone, of a scale and weight far beyond sense in such a small wooden hall. He wondered whether it might have been liberated from the ruins. A remarkable artefact, but even this was not what he found most bizarre. Another sight captured his eye.

Arranged on a raised dais beyond the altar and throne were five ancients, grey in the face, their skin dry and the flesh beneath it wasted. Angren thought them quite dead, and he wondered if they had disturbed some element of a funeral rite. But then one of the 'corpses' moved an arm slightly. Angren was hardened when it came to death and blood but that movement had his heart thumping and his skin crawling. And he wasn't the only one.

'He did move, didn't he?' said one of the others, with a noticeable shake in his voice.

Scortha laughed. 'Make you jump did he, Kris?'

'Made you jump too, I saw you.'

'Suppose I did. What do you reckon, Angren, they drugged up somehow?'

Angren had not a clue. 'You know what, I don't know and I don't care. We're running out of time. Grab those swords over there and the knives on the altar, and let's get out of here.'

Scortha laughed again but made for the altar. As he laid hands upon two of the ceremonial daggers the Priestesses screamed at him. Two of them even made to attack but were cowed when Scortha pointed at the knife in his hand and made a disgusting gesture with it towards a part of their anatomies. At this the oldest of the priestesses stepped forward and spoke something vile in a language they did not know.

'I think you've just been cursed, Sco,' said Kris, obviously amused by the notion. Scortha seemed less amused but wouldn't admit it.

'Think I give a fuck? Screw them.' And just to emphasise the point he hawked up a mighty gob of phlegm and spat on the altar.

Angren shook his head. 'You just don't know when to stop, do you?' Scortha leered at him. Angren was somehow glad Scortha was the target rather than anyone else. 'Come on,' he said, 'Let's go before they curse the lot of us.'

He cursed himself as they came out of the temple: the sound of shouting and screaming and the clash of swords greeted them. The main part of the Halfi had returned. The search had taken too long and now they had another battle on their hands.

'Nothing for it, lads,' he yelled, 'let's get stuck in.' And he ran back towards the edge of the village and the clatter of skirmish presuming that the others were following.

What they found was a fifty strong enemy besieging Bibron and the rest of the Partians holed up in the space between two of the huts. Angren approved. The position gave them only two fronts to defend rather than four. Angren and the ten with him piled into the smallest group of the Halfi and the suddenness of the move gave them a brief advantage. More Halfi came but Angren managed to cut his way through to Bibron and the others.

It was a rolling dispute. With the sheer weight of the Halfi attack pushing them back, they struggled to keep their position. Impetuously some of the Halfi ran in amongst them, at great disadvantage, and Angren gained two more swords. Seeing this, whoever marshalled the villagers was quick to change his tactics. So single minded was he that he ordered up archers to set flaming arrows in their own homes. The wood and thatch went up faster than a bonfire. The sudden smoke and heat forced the fugitives out onto flying spears and in the fury of the moment Angren lost ten men. He could see nothing for it but to attack and led the remainder of his force hard against the enemy line. The surprise of the move gained them ground but didn't materially change anything.

Many blows were struck, yards were gained and lost, but Angren's party took few lives. The Halfi had no reason to fight so close as time and the weight of numbers was with them. The struggle became nauseatingly futile. Whenever one of the Halfi grew tired, or suffered a minor injury, he would retire to lounge on the edge of the fight while a fresher man took his place. It was much like torture. Every five minutes one of Angren's men would receive one blow too many and crumple to the earth.

Fewer than fifteen now they were being forced back toward the compound. So confident was the Halfi commander that unexpectedly he brought a temporary halt to the proceedings, causing his men to withdraw to a safe distance. The Partians paused, wondering what would happen next and soon found out. In their leisure the Halfi had found the time to put on a show for them.

A struggling man was brought forward. His arms were bound behind his back, his legs were hobbled; there was a sack over his head. Angren couldn't remember having seen anyone captured during the fight and wondered who it might be. Three of the priestesses from the temple stepped out of the crowd of Halfi and marched up to face the prisoner. The oldest priestess took the lead. Gripped in two hands and held high above her head she brandished one of the curved daggers. Behind her the youngest of them held an empty copper bowl, while the third carried a glass phial filled with a dark amber liquid that seemed to soak-up the bright sunlight.

Two strong men, grasping one arm each of their unfortunate victim, made him stand erect and one of them pulled the sack from his head. It was Scortha. On seeing the dagger, and the bowl and the old priestess who had cursed him, his face crumpled in terror and blind panic.

'No, no, no,' he screamed, writhing in much the same way as the man he had skewered.

Angren considered an attack but the Halfi commander anticipated some response and ten archers stepped forward, aiming their arrows at the most warrior-like of the Partians still standing, Angren included.

The priestess addressed Angren directly. Her voice was clear, her words carefully pronounced.

'He defiled the temple. This is punishment.'

Scortha's shirt was ripped down to reveal his brawny chest and shoulders. The tendons and muscles strained and twitched as he fought in vain to free himself.

'Don't let them!' he screamed, 'Help me!' But it was all too late. A third strong man came to bend back Scortha's head. The chief priestess reached up and with the point of her dagger nicked a vein in his neck. Blood spurted out, splashing the priestess' robes before the young one came forward with the bowl to catch and keep whatever she could. Scortha's life was flowing out of him, but that was not their aim. The man holding back Scortha's head released it slightly and tried to force open his mouth. Scortha with the strength left to him clamped shut his jaw as tight as he could. The man pulled a knife and cut through Scortha's cheek, pushing the blade between his teeth to prise them apart. Scortha's resistance was over. His body slumped as though he had fainted.

Quickly now the old woman took the phial from her acolyte, removed the stopper and poured the dark fluid down Scortha's throat.

The Partians watched this scene in complete horror. None of them knew what had just happened, nor what the bleeding and the phial of liquid signified, but not a few of them grasped around at the edges of Bibron's Tale of the Halfi, and knew there must be a connection.

The show was over. They laid Scortha, still alive for now, on a stretcher with his neck turned so that the girl could continue to catch any blood that flowed from the vein, and they carried him away back up to the temple he had dishonoured.

It was a grim decision. Angren had never surrendered a fight he couldn't run away from, but the bleeding of Scortha had knocked the stuffing out of most of those still alive. Perhaps the incident should have made them even more desperate to escape but they could all see there was no hope of breaking free. There seemed little point in continuing the agony. He looked into the eyes of those nearest him. They each nodded, grim faced indeed. There was nothing for it. He stepped forwards to meet the Halfi and lowered his sword to the ground.

There was a sudden babble of concern and confusion among those facing him. Every one of them was looking over Angren's head. Turning to find out why he was struck dumb by what he saw and his words of surrender remained unsaid.

The ground shook with the tramp of colossal feet, trees swayed and toppled in the approach and it was the Halfi's turn to scream. As tall as a tree, a grotesque figure, a man's body bearing the head of a lizard, stalked into the clearing, tongue lashing, arms reaching, talons grasping. A Halfi demon, if Angren only knew. In an instant the fight between the Halfi and their captives was forgotten as friend and foe alike were scattered by fear. Here was a chance not to be missed: Angren tried to gather Mador's people together.

Berta and Sigrid were about to make a dash for it by themselves but they obeyed his command, and Ruspa scooted up to join them. In the clearing some of the Halfi had picked up burning brands from the enflamed huts and tried to attack, thinking that flames would scare the creature. As far as Angren could see the strange beast had yet to harm anyone and it stood, seemingly unconcerned by this puny onslaught, as though undecided about its next move. The attackers, emboldened by the lack of response, came in close. The monster bellowed and then spat a ball of flame at them. The Halfi nearest caught fire, the rest ran, except those who knelt to pray. There were more fireballs.

But still the beast made no move to chase, to pummel, to pulverize as it might have. Instead it peered about myopically as though it had lost something. Soon all the Halfi in the area had been killed by clinging flame, or were running hysterically through the woods. As far as Angren could tell, only the two women, Ruspa and himself remained, hiding behind an ancient wall.

The ground shook again as the beast took uncertain steps towards one of the few undamaged huts, and then again halted as though confused. Angren looked closely at the towering figure. It was naked, sallow skinned, lacking any trace of hair. The head and neck were scaly green and the eyes a wicked red. Angren could see each of these details in turn but a strange thing happened as his eyes moved from one to the other. Whatever he ceased to examine closely became indistinct, out of focus and more. It was as if his concentration on each detail lent firmness to what otherwise would be wavering and blurred. It didn't seem real, or was only real when Angren encouraged it to be so.

And then it collapsed. Not that it pitched forward and crashed to the floor, but rather it collapsed into itself, into nothing. Or was there something? Now Angren could see a figure of more normal proportions lying motionless on the charred ground.

Sigrid, Berta and Angren walked warily towards it. They nearly bolted when the figure groaned and rolled over. They did not because they realized that what lay on the ground was just a man, naked and barely conscious. Movement from within the hut beyond halted them but it wasn't the Halfi: Garaid emerged from the door, waving his arm in brief greeting, and he was followed by Bibron and Isolde, who was looking very shaky indeed. All of them converged on the erstwhile monster.

It was, of course, Seama.

They had a trouble-free if wearisome trek to where Seama had made his base. There were no Halfi to be seen and sadly no trace along the way of the three other survivors of the battle: most likely they had been recaptured. With Seama so exhausted, Angren realized that any hope of rescuing them was past. Seama could barely walk and needed both Berta and Garaid to support him along the way. The weapon master was shocked by his friend's condition and wanted an explanation.

He learned that Seama had been busy.

The wizard had been spilled from the Cottle with the rest of them and forced by the current onto the land. He was uninjured. Wanting to see what was happening to everyone else he climbed the nearby headland as the fog began to disperse. The Cottle had gone down already and a mast, like a finger pointed at the sky, was all that could be seen. He had to presume that others had also come ashore and so he went looking. He found two of Bibron's men injured on the rocks below and recognized them as the near-identical twins, Edro and Piedoro. They were easy to remember: though reliable enough they plagued their crewmates with practical jokes and were never content unless they were bickering with each other. When Seama caught up with them there was no mood or time for either. Edro, the darker, stronger man, was attempting to climb the rocks and carry his unconscious brother, Piedoro, both at the same time, and this despite a long jagged gash embedded with splinters all along his left arm.

With Seama's help, Piedoro was brought to more comfortable ground and revived. The wizard was attending to Edro's splinters when they heard the hunt begin. His strategy to cope with that was simple: with a little magic and a lot of common sense they hid up until it was finished.

When the first morning had come he set out to explore, leaving the recovering twins to make a start at building a raft. Before evening he knew all about the compound and about the slaughter of the animals that had come ashore.

'You mean the horses?' Angren demanded. 'Slaughtered?'

'Yes, the horses.' Seama spoke quietly, but Angren shouted, furious and anguished:

'They survive the sea to be murdered by madmen! It's disgusting. Why? Why should they kill horses?' His anger would have cut their throats; his anger was for his friend, for what they had done to him with their wanton violence. In himself he felt guilty. This was the first time he'd thought of the horses since the shipwreck. He had found little time to develop a relationship with Bayling but that didn't make him feel any better about it; but what about Bellus and the Mule? Angren thought of Bellus as an old friend, what must she have been to Seama?

'They're bored with pig meat,' Seama told them, his voice flat, emotionless, 'and consider horse-flesh something of a delicacy. I don't know which animals drowned and which were killed, but I found no survivors. I didn't see Bellus but by the time I arrived there was already a pile of hide and bones; I couldn't get close enough to see properly.'

Angren could think of nothing to say. Seama was holding himself in check and now was not the time to push him. Bibron too seemed to understand both Seama's anguish and also his need to put it by for now.

'Did you see what they were building, Seama?'

Seama looked up at him, confused. His thoughts had been elsewhere.

'Building? Oh, the stand, you mean. Yes they were preparing for a visit I think. There's a place less than a mile from the village, an open bowl of land. They had made a platform… there were tables and racks.'

'Racks?'

'Yes, Angren, by the look of it you were all to be questioned. Publicly. There was a throne too which I presumed was for their overlord, whoever that might be. The horse meat was most likely for a feast to greet him. He was on his way here earlier today, with a large company of men, but I managed to put him off.'

Seama explained that throughout the second day on the island he had used his skills to keep the twins hidden as they struggled with their task. So complete was his spell that it was possible to continue their raft building heedless of the noise. But for some reason he could not fathom this simple work drained him, and when the day was done he had found it difficult to sleep for a second night in succession. Early on this morning, as the prisoners in the compound were waiting for their chance to escape, despite the exhaustion that threatened to overwhelm him, Seama once again drew upon his *power* to finish off the raft with binding spells. Then, leaving the twins on guard, he set out upon his mission to free the captives.

His first job had been to raise a fire. Using *sight* he was soon aware of the procession from the north of the island. If the extra men had reached the village there would have been no possibility of escape. The obvious answer was an 'uncontrollable' forest fire to block their path. The Halfi were terrified: the fire charged after them as they ran away as though it had a mind of its own. Seama was an adept at harnessing the wind to his own advantage, but the effort cost him dearly, and that cost him time. It was after noon before he reached the open bowl. Here the majority of the villagers were making the final preparations for the day's entertainments. Seama had begun to make his way around the clearing when he saw the two guards come running to bring news of the prisoner's escape. Most of the men picked up their weapons and ran off quickly in the direction of the village. Try as he might Seama couldn't catch up with them. By the time he arrived the houses had already been fired. Where he had hoped to use a little magic and a lot of stealth, the Partians were already fighting a losing battle. Time was short and a demon from Halfi myth was all he could think of.

'Was it real, Mr. Wizard?' asked Bibron, 'I don't fancy the idea of them things wandering around as they please.'

'It was real to the Halfi, they're a religious folk, but it just was me. Or to be more precise, it was an illusion that used me as the base and reference point. What is more, it was unbelievably hard work.'

'I've never seen you like this Seama,' Angren said. He didn't like it one bit: Seama was supposed to be invincible. 'Are you ill? Can we do—'

'All I need is rest, Angren. I have been using the *power* for three days solid without an hour of proper sleep. It was too much. When we get to the raft, Bibron, I expect you and your men to get us off this damned island and over to Gothery. I won't be able to help you.'

'If you've saved my boys, Seama, then I owe you. We'll get us across.'

There was little more to tell about Tumboll at this time. Seama took them to the raft and they put to sea immediately. This time there were no monsters to contend with, no fogs to obscure their way and, happily, a small natural breeze took them under its gentle wing, making the oars redundant. As they sailed away from the island they were gladdened somehow to see the raging fire and the black smoke. It was some payment for the lives lost.

Though nothing could gladden Seama he was determined at least to prevent himself from grieving openly. Constant action had allowed him no time to think over the past few days but here on the cradling River he was in danger of surrendering to emotion. He would not allow it: his companions depended upon him. There was work to do. Something about this whole affair was very wrong. This episode was no accident. And if there was purpose to their capture he'd like to know what it was. He plunged his mind into working out the possibilities. He considered it one way, he considered it another. His thoughts, hampered by weariness, tumbled over themselves dizzily. When he realized he was getting nowhere he shifted his attention to memory exercises, essential regular work for any professional wizard, and he found them easier to manage. He recited to himself the great list of True Names that filled the Books of Lore: he sought solace in repetition. Whatever happened, he could not, would not allow his brain to idle.

He avoided conversation: someone was bound to bring the talk round to… At one point he even started to run through his multiplication tables. He didn't want to fall asleep but it was inevitable. Eventually his head, full of irrelevancies, fell forward upon his chest and his eyes closed.

He was vulnerable when he awoke. Confused by sleep, he had no time to return to the mental disciplines that had sustained him, and without warning the tears began to flow. He cried silently but so grievously he thought the pain would never stop. His thoughts slid back to that wondrous day when Bellus was foaled. Great-hearted Bellus! She had been the mainstay of his love for twenty years, and now she was gone.

II

INTRUSIONS

The Creation And The Beginning Of Strife

An extract from 'The Song of Ages' attributed to The Keepers of the Truth, published Astoril 3069 by Gombret and Son.

Time, called Zurvan, was God all alone, and so he created Man; and he created the world and the stars that Man might have a home. But because he could not both create and then Rule, for that would deny his Divine Purpose, God could not share the world and stars with Man and must dwell apart.

And yet Zurvan would not leave Man alone and Fatherless with no hand to guide him. Of himself he made a son. The Son would rule the world and the stars and he would be as a Father to Man. Everything That Could Be was in The Son as he dwelled in the Womb of Time but that whole became divided into a spirit and person of Good, and a spirit and person of Evil. That Good Child of Zurvan was called Ohr'mazd, and the foul opposite Ah'remmon. Aware of both as they dwelled in the Womb of Time and knowing his plan was spoiled, Zurvan vowed that whichever of The Twain, whose names and nature were yet hidden from him, would present himself as first born, he would be King of All That Is. Now Ohr'mazd was Understanding and Ah'remmon was Ignorance. That Good One of Knowledge, whose brightness reveals, told the words of the Father to the Evil One, whose darkness encloses. And hearing those words the Spirit of All Lusts ripped himself untimely from Time's Womb.

Zurvan beheld a mean and black and noisome creature and was dismayed for the child of his womb was not the child of his present thought. Where was the child generous, bright and clean smelling? At last Ohr'mazd came forth in his glory!

Loathsome Ah'remmon, seeing the other, was in doubt, knowing his own power to be less. Quickly he said: 'Have you not made this vow: that whichever of my two sons shall first come before me, him shall I make King?' And Zurvan, that is Time, meaning not to violate his oath said to Ah'remmon: 'Oh False One! Yes, Kingship shall be granted you for nine thousand years, but over Ohr'mazd you shall have no dominion. And after nine thousand years Ohr'mazd shall reign and do whatsoever pleases him, for his shall be the time of Long Dominion.'

At Zurvan's word Ah'remmon grew feared and angry and said: 'The Kingship is mine according to your vow; this world you have made is mine according to your gift; and Men, created for your purpose, will serve me as their God. Is this not all of your making?'

Zurvan was wrath with Ah'remmon. 'Deceiver you are by your lust deceived,' he said. 'My purpose cannot be denied. Thy brother, Ohr'mazd, does know my mind. In your despite he will see my creation to its end. Have you your Kingship but know this, False One: thy reign cannot last.'

Now Ah'remmon's fear had come to fury at these words. 'Father,' cried the Master of Lies, 'Am I nothing to thee? You have made us both, my brother and I, and yet you have love for one only and would see the other destroyed. And so I make this vow that will last through all the ages of the world: *My Brother will be my enemy and I will not suffer his rule; If I die he will die and all your hope is lost.*' Ah'Remmon's face shone with triumph at this oath, for having spoken he knew it must become true, but that radiance was as fire to burn all it might touch and yet it gave off no light. 'What say'st my brother to this?' said he, 'Have you no words to comfort our Father?'

Ohr'mazd in his wisdom spoke then nothing but turned his bright countenance upon Ah'remmon and smiled. At that smile all of Creation sang with hope, for the Light of Ohr'mazd banished all the darkness that Ah'remmon sought to wreath about the world. And The Spirit of all Lusts could not endure that smile and must turn and flee, seeking darkness to hide his shame. Never again would he look upon the face of Ohr'mazd.

TEA AND TOASTED RABBIT

Black Hills, Segyllin Part 3057.7.24

Tregar had all but done with the first leg of his journey. For five days he had ridden hard after the kindness of Torhead, taking little rest, knowing that Seama was very likely taking less.

He was a strange man, the Wizard Beltomé, a man of terrible power and enviable skill but that surely was only a part of it. Though he counted Seama a good friend there was a barrier between them that Tregar found hard to fathom, a barrier indeed that seemed to stand between Seama and the rest of humanity. Seama went his own way whatever friendship or society or authority might seek to demand. Even in his dealings with the Council, Seama maintained an uncommon degree of independence. Yes, he worked tirelessly in the Council's name but only because the work suited his purpose. Luckily for all, Seama's intentions were benevolent. There was no politicking or machination here, no desire to order things according to his will. In fact Seama consistently rejected all attempts to draw him into any position of governance, and though the Council had asked, more than once, for him to have-done with his wanderings and to take up The Staff of Power, Seama always refused. 'There has been no Tap-Rod for over a hundred years,' he'd said, 'and we have managed very well without one.' He'd caused quite a furore, just a few years back, by insisting, in Parleyment, that the appointment would be a waste of his best qualities. There were hard words all round. Some members said it was an insult to the office for Seama to suggest he had 'better things to do'. The story of the confrontation had taken wing all over the continent and opinions on the matter were given breath from Garassa to Nai'vedya. There was debate about the viability of Errensea's pre-eminence over a continent of four proper and equal nations; doubts were spoken about the justifiability of giving ultimate power into to one hand alone; in sceptical Gothery there were parties, revitalized by the issue, dedicated to denying even the basis of the dispute, braying out their call to clear reason over occult powers. It was all to little point. Lots of huffing and puffing for weeks on end but nothing was changed: Errensea stood resolute and Seama wouldn't move an inch.

All ridiculous of course. People rarely listened to what was actually spoken. Tregar was convinced there was nothing flippant in Seama's response: he was being honest. The problem Tregar had was in deciding what those 'better things' Seama had to do might be, and what it was that made him so determined to do them. The clue, he decided, was in the eyes. There was a look of yearning there, a look of terrible need sometimes that Tregar thought disturbing. Seama was looking for something not to be found in Errensea and the search for it controlled his every thought and deed. Tregar's interpretation was that the Wizard Beltomé was the victim of a life-spell: a geas.

A life-spell is an attempt to infect the 'nature' of the victim; commonly invoked at birth it would attempt to alter the whole course of the victim's life. The geas controlled behaviour. A naturally quiet man would rage when faced with authority; a blithe man would find himself plotting to betray his friends. The geas was very often used by those wishing to curse and bring destruction upon the children of their enemies. Very often. But there were other circumstances, other uses. Tregar held to the belief that the spell could be used to good purpose. In fact he believed it need have nothing to do with an external force at all and that it could be self-imposed.

Tregar hadn't discussed this notion with others and it could easily have been wrong, but it seemed clear to him that Seama Beltomé had quite deliberately given himself a geas. It took the form of a quest, but a quest with no obvious end, that drove him on and on through the years, that drew him away from anything that might be considered an easy option and pushed him towards toil and danger. Tregar wondered if Seama was still aware of this spell or whether he believed the decisions he made and the actions he performed were quite normal. He wondered if Seama knew where his life was leading him. Perhaps this nonsense about the Dedicae was something to do with it. And this book of Haslem's too. Tregar wondered if it was all linked. Seama's unstoppable need to conquer evil was almost legendary and it gained him respect. Was it now beginning to have undesirable effects? Was the man so concerned with a final victory over evil he had come to invent a final enemy? The more Tregar considered Seama's theory in this light, the more ridiculous it seemed. What if it was completely wrong? How would Seama react? A life-spell is a hard spell to break, and hard on the victim when broken.

Or so said the Books of Lore! Tregar had never been driven by anything more than average ambition. This is not to say that Tregar was a poor wizard. Far from it, but it was true that after the ventures of youth he was content to sit back and fall into the settled life of Mador's court. His duties, mainly to do with healing, were not dull as such, but they were infinitely less demanding than the problems regularly confronted by Seama Beltomé. Tregar did not envy him those problems: healing was honour enough for a boy from Great Spurl. He had found much satisfaction in his life.

And now this!

He had shaken out his old fur cloak and oiled his favourite boots. Back on the road he wanted the comforts of familiarity and his cloak and boots had been with him through many an escapade. He'd found the old breeches too but decided to leave them at home this time as they seemed to have shrunken around the waist.

What a pity his old horse, Wanderer, was gone. Fine hunter though he was, Sirrah wasn't much used to long journeys that didn't lead home. No doubt this campaign would improve his character: he was far too proud of himself.

'What did ye think of Bellus then? I saw you! Trying to show off like that. I doubt she was impressed, my young bucko. You're a wee bit short on experience for that one I'd think. Still, we'll see what you're made of. There's a way to travel, Sirrah, and battles to fight when we get there maybe. I hope you're looking forward to it. Now then, I've a sore backside and you're getting to stumbling, so what say we have a break?'

The horse did not reply. He was too tired to think straight

and the pictures in his mind were of nothing but food and water and rest.

They had fairly flown along the earlier stretches of the road into the north, passing through dozens of villages at a gallop, but within two days the landscape had changed. No longer could the road weave a path through the valleys: long escarpments that stretched for miles, east to west, replaced the drumlins. One wearisome, winding climb after another slackened their pace. They shared this road with sheep drovers and with slow moving ox-carts that travelled from market to market across the region; they stayed for the first three nights at inns along the way, each full of the noise and bustle of the travellers and their livestock. With all this activity around him Tregar found it hard to believe that anything in the country could be wrong. It was only as the miles lengthened and the villages and markets and inns became fewer that the reality of his journey began to sink in. He was leaving behind the mild airs, the quiet beauty and the comfort of Par's heartland, leaving behind the commerce and the energy and the feeling of being at the centre of things while ahead lay only days of toil, the promise of harder times to come and inevitable peril. The populous south was a blessed land, impregnable without the need for walls, sovereign without any need for caution or fear; the far-flung north with its sparse population, harsh weather and unforgiving terrain seemed anything but. The juxtaposition began to eat away at his sense of adventure. He saw little hope of it recovering.

By the sixth day Tregar was having to rely on what food he carried with him as the fields gave way to a high acid moorland. He travelled the Black Hills, a lonely landscape given over to the shrill of the grasshopper and the eerie call of the curlew, an awkward and often dangerous land. Sirrah struggled on through impossibly springy tussock grass and half-dry peat bogs; Tregar struggled with his route, confused by the twisting, ill-defined track. In a wetter season a wise man would have avoided the area entirely.

Marked by the maps, not far into this inhospitable country was a small valley, and in the valley a solitary farm called

Small Cuttings. It stood close to where a little used road from Riverport joined up with Tregar's route, offering a range of options for the onward journey. Mador had made it the point of rendezvous with Anparas and Temor. According to Ayer's Hall of Records, one Owen Cookson owned the farm. Tregar hoped he was a patriotic sort: the arrival of three thousand soldiers, even with the best of intentions, was bound to create havoc and the requisitioning of food to feed them was likely to test any man's loyalty. The more Tregar thought about it, the less he liked the idea of bringing him the news. Still, that was the least of his worries: by rights he should have reached the farm by early evening on this sixth day and so far there was not a sign of it.

Tregar, or rather Sirrah, plodded on. It was too treacherous underfoot to risk any great speed – the last thing he wanted was a lame horse. The wizard grinned wryly as he considered how maps tended to make things look so straightforward. The 'roads' marked as crossing the Black Hills were nothing other than slightly more trodden earth than the ground surrounding them. On the maps the gradual curve of the road suggested an easy journey but close up the path was so convoluted he suspected he was going round in circles. He couldn't count the times he had lost the track completely.

At least it was a fine evening. The clouds were out only for decoration in the reddening west. The breeze that seemed to increase moment by moment was warm after travelling over leagues of summer-kissed grassland and added music to the closing day as it whistled, hummed and plucked its way through the dry clattering stems. It blew up blizzards of fluffy grass seeds that sparkled in the sun's last rays. It rummaged in Tregar's swept back cloak, tickling life into his weary muscles. And the scent it carried of wild flowers, warm earth and distant trees almost entranced him out of his saddle. How pleasant it would be to snuggle down for the night, deep in the grass: to give himself up to the nature around him.

'Blast!' he swore aloud as he realized that once again he had lost his way. 'I don't know, Sirrah. Why do I bother? I'd probably do better with my eyes closed. Come on, laddie, let's try one more time. We're bound to get there eventually. I'm almost positive we are.'

The light was nearly gone by the time he saw the farm ahead. He could only vaguely make out that there were three buildings and, at this distance, it was hard to tell which was for living in, as the lights had not yet been lit. Nevertheless he took the liberty of promising his horse good stabling and something to chew on as a reward for the day's efforts. To say he was relieved to be somewhere, anywhere at last was the least of it.

It was twilight when he reached the outfields, the young moon had yet to rise. Finding the gate in the prickle fence was not easy and when found it took a lot of opening. Still no light shone, no dog barked warning.

'Hello', Tregar yelled, and the wind that grew ever stronger took the word from his lips and carried it off into the hills. 'Hello, is anybody at home?'

There was no reply.

Tregar dismounted to leave Sirrah in the yard while he walked over to the nearest building. Opening the door he decided it was a barn. He created a light with his crystal to make sure, and in doing so found a torch in a bracket just inside the door. Returning to his horse, he searched his bags for the tinderbox and used that to light the torch.

'Well, Sirrah, there's no need for ye to stand about in this wind. Let's get ye settled in here, then I can have a good look round. You never know, ye might find me sharin' with you tonight.'

Inside, Tregar did not bother to tether the horse but allowed him free range. There were a number of green sheaves scattered about, as though they had been tossed in out of the rain, and so he broke open a couple of them. Sirrah was duly thankful. The wizard, not long out of feather beds, was pleased to note the large quantity of straw strewn about. Though it was old and probably full of mice it might well be the nearest thing to comfort he would find. He found a stack of cut turves, dry and ready to burn, in one corner of the barn but what he could not find was water. There seemed to be neither well nor tank. Sirrah, at this stage, was too tired to bother much but Tregar had been looking forward to hot tea and was niggled that he might not get any. Leaving the horse and saddle bags where they were, and taking the torch with him, he went to explore the other buildings.

The second he tried was an open ended shed with nothing inside bar a few rusty rakes and spades and what may once have been a plough, though it was so collapsed it was hard to be sure.

The third building was much smaller than the others and Tregar was right to presume it had once served as a dwelling. The badly fitting door needed to be forced but when closed again its swollen timbers kept out much of the draught. The windows were shuttered and, considering the general dilapidation of the farm, they were still surprisingly sturdy, though one rattled in the wind. There was only one room with a fireplace and chimney at one end, a low roof and a few odd bits of furniture: namely a table, three chairs and a pallet bed with no mattress. The floor was made of wooden planks that groaned with every step.

Next to the fire was a kettle, blackened and battered but still whole and next to that, as if in answer to Tregar's unspoken prayer, a bucket of water. It did not smell badly. The scowl he had been scowling became a grin and he went to retrieve his bags in a happier mood. Gathering up the straw for his bed, he wondered who could possibly be responsible for leaving the water. Perhaps some sheep farmer caught away from home.

His good mood didn't last long.

The wind, a robust friend earlier in the evening, was now beginning to outstay its welcome. It whined in the chimney as if to emphasise how lonely and uncomfortable the place was. It steadfastly refused to make way for the fire he was trying to make. The peat proved difficult to light after all and he ended up using some straw and the broken seat of one of the chairs before he could get the flame to take. He had no bellows and they would have had little effect anyway as the wind was determined to go the wrong way. Just as the turves were beginning to catch a great gust threw itself down the chimney, scattering burning straw around the room. At this rate he was more likely to burn down the house than achieve anything more useful. Nevertheless, he tried again and eventually managed to produce a pathetic excuse for a fire that smoked heavily, as peat fires should not, and created little heat. And then the chimney had a coughing fit and the smoke started to puff and billow into the room.

Tregar choked and had to put his head outside the door for fresh air. He was surprised that the wind didn't seem half as strong in the yard as it did in the chimney. Inside the smoke gasped and sputtered and giggled into the rafters. Somewhere there was a blockage. Suddenly Tregar was very annoyed and he marched back to confront his tormentor. Poised to summon the power necessary to blast through the blockage, he was surprised by a loud knocking. Someone was hammering at the door!

With his eyes streaming from the smoke he turned to look at the door in amazement. He could have been no more stupefied if the door had spoken to him. Who could possibly have turned up at such a desolate place; and where had they been a few moments ago when Tregar had looked out into the yard? The knocker knocked again very insistently and so Tregar called out:

'Come on in. The door is not locked.'

The door flew open.

A strange man entered. Somehow he managed to give the impression that he had nothing to do with the way the door had opened. He was such a small, frail old man with something of a limp, rather stooped and he had, as far as Tregar could make out in the smoke hazed torchlight, a withered arm. He wore a voluminous cloak, which he held back with the better appendage, and a broad-brimmed floppy hat with a starling's feather in the band. It was hard to see his face but a grey beard straggled down his chest.

'Tut, tut,' he muttered, or something similar, 'A little less violent next time, if you please.'

He looked up and transfixed Tregar with a single piercing eye. The left eye wore a patch, a black one patched itself with a piece of red check where it pressed against his nose. He looked faintly ludicrous. Tregar would not let himself be fooled by that. He wondered how the old man had come here and who he might have been talking to, as there was patently no one else with him.

Here was a person of some power.

'So Master Tregar, and how are you?' His voice was high pitched and cracked but there was nothing frail in the challenge of the question. Tregar could think of nothing to say beyond the obvious and decided not to bother.

'C'mon. I am there somewhere in that poor memory of yours. But anyway, let's not concern ourselves over whoever I might be or why I know you. Master Tregar, I am here to find out who or what *you* are. You seem to have become quite important.'

'I don't understand,' Tregar ventured, 'How do—'

The old man cackled. 'What you are at the moment, I think, is a child moving from rage to fear. Why let a little smoke upset you? Are you so afraid to use magic that it becomes an angry last resort?' He paused and looked harshly at the fireplace. 'Up! Up and out the chimney Boggart. You have played your tricks too long in this place. Get out before I blow you to the Leagues of Utter Death, out! Before I send you to the Wastes of Time, out I say!'

A nervous chittering came from the black hole and then with a mighty rush and wail something was gone. Then the fire glowed red and the room emptied of smoke.

Tregar laughed aloud. Whether in amusement or embarrassment he wouldn't have liked to say.

'A Boggart? Is that all it was? Not even as argumentative as some I've dealt with.'

'No? Oh I think he was, but he was not stupet. Few creatures would argue with me, Mester Wiezart.' Tregar thought the old man's tone haughty and would have commented on it but the old man didn't give him the chance. 'Right! It's you and it is magic I have come to talk about, but before that we need some supper. Put on the kettle and make us some tea; I shall see to these.'

Like a conjuror he produced from under his cloak a pair of fat rabbits. Saying no more he set to skinning and cleaning them as expertly as a butcher. Tregar shrugged and went to see to the kettle.

As they chewed on sizzling pieces of tender flesh and shared tea from Tregar's tin mug the wizard studied his companion. He struggled to identify him from any part of his past life. He was of such startling appearance and overbearing personality that Tregar was certain they had never met. No one could forget such a misfit. And yet the old man had insisted that Tregar knew him. Was he from Errensea perhaps, an old tutor, an elder of the Collegium? It seemed impossible.

And why was he here? Why seek him out in these dreary northlands? Why come to him in the dark of night? The greybeard, for his part, seemed content to eat and drink, warm his feet and chatter but Tregar had to suspect a deep purpose to this meeting.

And yet the old man was full of trivialities. He talked about the weather and compared it to the climate in other parts of the World. He talked about places the much-travelled Tregar had never even heard of. He would not explain, though Tregar asked, how he had known about the boggart, or anything at all about his powers; instead he began to talk about food and drink. But as he talked, the old man's gaze never wandered from Tregar's face. It was most uncomfortable. The wizard felt as if all his secrets were laid bare and that nothing he thought could be kept hidden.

As soon as he had finished his meal the greybeard said:

'Now. It is time we got us down to business. I brought you here because—'

'You brought me here?'

'Why yes. Don't be surprised. That's part of what I wanted to tell you. There are many more beings in this world that have much more power than you. Or, to say it right, they have much different sorts of power than your own. Oh, I don't just mean people like Beltomé, though they are worth remembering; there are other powers – like me.'

'Like you?'

'Why do you repeat me? You're a wiezart aren't you? You have been taught your Powers. All these idle years have done you no good: you have lost memory and you have lost respect. You have forgotten even me! How can you expect to fight the evil ahead if you can't remember your allies? Eh?'

Tregar was nettled by the criticism. So what if he did have a lazy memory? It was no great problem and even if it was, no stranger had any right to chide him for it. And the man definitely was a stranger. Hackles raised he said:

'I'm not going to remember allies I've never met. And I count on my allies for truth but everything ye've said for all I know could be lies.'

'Lies is it?' said One Eye, and he seemed angry, 'Well perhaps that brings me to my second point: I don't like your attitude to all this. And I didn't like the way you spoke to Seama either. Is there no one you believe?'

'What's it to you *whit* I believe or not?'

'It is everything to me. What do you think this war is all about? This is not your average squabble, you know. Now, just you shut up your mouth and listen to me for a bit. I will put it as simple as I can.'

Tregar harrumphed: he wasn't much used to being told to shut up. However he decided to listen first and quarrel after. The old man waited for his attention and then continued.

'To make a start,' he said, 'I am not supposed to be here. It is not allowed. In the Middle Order we have obligations both ways. We are not humankind and cannot fight as humans do. Talking and advice are human ways. There is a limit to what I can tell you. You are in a war of good against evil and though that is a description fitting many a war it is none the less true for that. Some will say that this war is extraordinarily so and many will believe it and it may be true. But I say to you, Tregar MacNabaer, the enemy you fight has many minds and not all are all bad. That is the key. That is the key to the whole sorry mess. Remember, though you will scarce believe me when you see them, evil's warriors are human with souls the same as yours. You will ever see things in black or white despite the evidence all around you. You must learn to see grey. And with mankind most greys are closer to white than black. Understand why that is true and it will save us all a lot of trouble.

'You are in a war of strange power. You will be Earnor's

answer to that power, you and some others. Yes you! It seems an unsuitable choice to me: a so-called wiezart who's scared to use magic. Let the *warriors* fight, Tregar, you must learn to use your skill – and not only when you lose your temper. If you are a wiezart, behave like one!

'I cannot tell you how to fight them. I cannot tell you their weapons or even their names. There is much you have to discover for yourself but if you think about what I have said you may find your way to victory. A victory that armies cannot win, that rejects dour deeds and glory. You may even understand what that victory means. There are no prophecies to tell us who will prevail in this dispute or indeed whether it is possible to prevail and so you must generate your own reasons to hope.'

What thoughts were in his mind Tregar could not guess but the old man gave a long and weary sigh. 'Ay, ay. Maybe it has gone on too long. We must end it. You must do your best and know, before I go, that the fate of the gods is, most surprisingly, in your hands.' He shrugged to indicate his confusion and then got to his feet and walked toward the door.

Tregar was bemused. What was all the nonsense about the Middle Order and obligations? What did he mean by claiming not to be human? He certainly looked human. And his message: what did that mean? Had this funny old greybeard told him anything at all? Some of what he said about magic Tregar surely recognized in himself but he had always thought that restraint in the use of his *power* a good thing. The rest of it meant nothing to him. And yet, the old man had spoken with such authority and such knowledge. How could he have known what Tregar had said to Seama? How could have known that Tregar would find his way to this ruin? And how could he know anything about the coming conflict?

'Why cannot ye tell me more?'

'I have told you enough, and that is more than I should. There is a balance, you know, and I have disturbed it. Others like me actually oppose our design, but they are similarly forbidden to act. My talking to you allows a response. Who knows what trouble this has caused. Now I shall take my leave of you.' He looked at the door and it opened gently for him. 'That is better, well done.' he said. Tregar could restrain himself no longer:

'Who are ye?' he demanded, thinking it would be his last chance. The old man was gleeful.

'Heh, heh,' he cackled, 'you still have no idea, have you? Eh? I'd spend a while working on that memory if I were you! Must have been all those parties in Ayer: addled your brains. Ah me. Well now, I hate to see a creature suffer, so I'll tell you this: I have been called a God, Tregar. They called me wild and furious and said I was the god of battle and victory. Quite ironic really. To others I have been inspiration and that is better, though I started out as the god of wind. You could call me Greybeard and in fact you have already.'

Tregar flushed red at his own stupidity but he was determined to stand his ground. 'It is a poor god to be half blind,' he said, looking for confirmation. The god smiled.

'I gave my eye to gain wisdom and wisdom can see more clearly than any eye.' Tregar had guessed right. 'Now, I bid you keep to luck and common sense. Just remember what I said to you. It may not have sounded important but I hope the meaning comes clear. Goodbye Wiezart. I shall leave the paths bent but you'll find a way with a little skill. Farewell!'

He was gone and the door pulled shut sharply behind him. Tregar rushed to the door and wrenching it open was not surprised to find the yard empty.

Though not a religious man, Tregar found himself offering up a prayer of thanks to Imvar, the god of his childhood. How else was he to respond to divine intervention? He could hardly pray to the same god he had shared a supper with. But pray he must for the first time in twenty years. It did not matter that he understood very little of what had been said, he just knew that with this visitation he was blessed and his cause just, whatever that cause might prove to be.

'Uovin!' he cried to the empty room, 'Uovin Himself has spoken to me!' and such a mood of exhilaration took him that he danced across the yard and told Sirrah all about it.

FOUND AND LOST

The Saddle, Aegarde 3057.7.24

The villagers of the Skirt and the Saddle were running before the storm. It was amazing to Roar that one small company of villains could create such chaos. The impromptu refugee camp on the Gotherian border was swelling by the hour. The border guards were outnumbered by two hundred to one already and it was only down to the placid nature of the refugees that they had not been overwhelmed. Inevitably enough, the more determined, more adventurous types had bypassed this crossing completely. The Saddle, so called because here the cliffs fell away like a seat between pommel and cantle, had just the one major road crossing the border but on either side acres of farmsteads and woodlands and small tracks provided no obstacle for anyone travelling light. The fifty guards had enough on their hands to even think of policing a border ten miles wide. Here on the main road they held back the greater tide. The villages of the Skirt, a fertile scoop of land nestling under the tall cliffs to the north of the Saddle, had been quiet and prosperous places far removed from criminality, disturbance or the threat of war for years out of mind, and quiet places made for quiet but prosperous people. Desperate to avoid the Black Company but, doing their best to salvage some hope for a future, they were decidedly unwilling to relinquish their worldly goods. It was as though they had attempted to relocate their lives. All around him were carts laden with furniture and ornament, baskets of hard pressed chickens, dogs up on the bench seats growling people off as their owners struggled with the tents and bedding. The earliest birds had quickly taken up all the best pitches and now sat comfortable in roped-off enclaves, their relatives all around them, sitting in their best chairs, drinking their hot rahi or cold tea, shooing off the neighbours' goats from nibbling round their tents and tending their cooking fires. A regular parade of children, laden with skins and pans, ran, skipped and chattered their way down the path to the Gate Water with the warnings to 'come back soon' flying unheeded over their heads. Donkeys, still in harness, tired from their labours, surveyed the scene with utter disdain. Roar McAndre looked on with mixed feelings. He didn't know whether to admire these people or despise them. It was only as he looked at the children, faces open, busy with children's things, that he understood. Normality in the face of disturbance: that was their aim; denial of the oncoming storm, the determination to seem 'in control'. But not for themselves: it was all for the sake of their children. This was courage.

Roar, now feeling very humbled, walked alongside those children, leading-on the two horses, his own Calliope and Colm's Gyrax, and listening-in to the piping voices and all the reckless clatter. It was really very wholesome. And looking around him, the day was warm if promising showers, the fields were green though uncut and the hedgerows still were full of promise. A good place to be in the normal way of things. Roar trawled through his memories of twenty years gone. As he recalled, the way of things hereabouts was that twice a year, Spring's End and Autumn's Crack, these very meadows were home to a popular and famous three day fair. Crowds came down or up from either side of the border to trade goods and news and to share the entertainments. For these lads and lasses, moved by their mum's orders or dad's warnings, or more likely their own overwhelming indifference to both, this ground was actually a place of holiday; for their parents of course, it was a place of commerce. The familiarity with this ground was for all a matter of some comfort.

Roar stopped to allow this new, more accurate understanding get a view of the proceedings. The familiarity was perhaps what made the atmosphere of the camp, increasingly, more like a fair or market than anything more desperate. In fact, now that he looked at it in the right light, forgetting his own petty grumbles, it became obvious to him that this familiarity had so shifted the perceptions and attitude of the refugees that the whole affair had become less like an escape from horror, and more like a straight and inviting opportunity for open trade and serious business. From somewhere behind the line of trees to his right, he could hear a lot of neighing and snorting and the tell-tale cadence of an auction in full swing. *Ha! There's the human race for you*, he thought crossly, *never let a chance for gain pass you by.* Sometimes he despaired. His new born admiration for these people, quite unfairly, collapsed in an instant.

If only he wasn't so tired he knew it'd be easier to take heart from all this, but the fact was his backside was sore from too much riding, his thigh muscles were cramping more and more often as their journey progressed, and, dear gods, today even his bones seemed to hurt. It was all getting to be a bit too much. At his age. And everything seemed so much the worse from having to travel with young Colm Peveril. He found just trying to keep up with the lad truly draining, and the brashness and the fitness and the cheerfulness Colm seemed to delight in just made the old man want to spit. Waldin interfering again, that was the root of it. He seemed to have some bizarre notion that Colm would be Roar's perfect apprentice, and all because he was good with his hunting dogs. Hunting dogs! All they ever needed or wanted was occasional praise and the odd bite on the ear. Colm, of course, rounded that out with his dog whip for good measure. And Waldin, of course, thought that sort of thing demonstrated 'an affinity for animals much like your own.' Waldin could be very annoying sometimes. Ear biting! How vile.

And, of course, it was for the cause of him getting a break from that irritating young man, rather than for any reason of efficiency, that Roar McAndre was leading their horses to water while Colm had been sent off to gather information. Roar had a plan, a simple plan for his next few hours on this earth: he'd picket the horses next to some decent little pool, tell them to relax and enjoy it, and stay where they were, and then find himself a nice sunny spot somewhere nearby where he could put up his feet and catch up on some sleep. With that in mind he glanced skywards and watched the sun disappear behind a think bank of cloud. *Typical!* he thought.

'Nice horses Mister.'

Roar looked around. Dipping his head to see under Calliope's neck he saw a cheeky looking lad, in rough clothes and without shoes, no more than thirteen, peering back at him.

'They are; well spotted. Do you like horses?'

The boy grinned. 'I'm like to: m'dad's a trader. Teaching me the business, ent he.'

'You're a bit young for business, son. Shouldn't you be at school?'

The boy pulled a face. 'School? No thanks, mister. M'dad says s'long as I can read a contract an' do me sums I'll be alright. Don't need none o'those teachers yammerin' on at me 'bout kings and stuff.'

Roar, with seventy years of experience under his belt, could not honestly disagree with the lad. This one would find his way in life whatever happened.

'So, you don't belong with this lot then,' Roar said, indicating the mass of humanity washing about them, 'All these townies and villagers?'

The boy looked all around and then shook his head slowly, the look on his face indicating quiet amazement at the way others seemed to live their lives.

'A travelling family?'

'Ar, we travel alright. Buy the horses cheap over by Valdez, drive 'em up into Gothery and then down into Sullin Part – we get best prices down there.'

Roar nodded. 'But now you're all caught up in this and it's not good for business I suppose?'

'Longer we keep 'em, more we have to feed 'em. Border guard won't let none o' that lot through an' they won't let us through neither. M'dad reckoned a bit of offloadin' 'ud be best. You can hear'm over there,' the boy nodded in the direction of the auction. 'Fair old voice 'e got on him.'

'And do you know why all this is happening?'

The lad wrinkled his nose, thinking back on it.

'Not much,' he said, 'We were down in Altiparedo, just passing through, when this great fuss set up in the market place. There was this man, all messed up and bothered, an' shoutin' 'bout somethin' or other; an' all the people round were shoutin' back and gettin' all aeriated. It was all upsettin' to 'em. I don't know what exactly – you'd have to ask m'dad. He just said 'Time we were gone from here!' and away we went. But I reckon it must be to do with these bad'uns they got up north of here.'

'And how long ago was this?'

'Couple or three days? 'S'only thirty mile round the Hammerhand.'

'This Altiparedo, is it a big place?'

'Big place? Well, I reckon; more like a town than village. What I saw of it. Big market anyway. If you go there you'll find out won't you? But look Mister... I... er... Can I... er...'

The lad seemed to have lost interest in Roar's concerns.

'Something wrong?'

'Wrong? Sorry?'

'You're a little distracted. Is there a problem?'

The boy was looking up at Calliope with a strange look in his eyes.

'Oh. No. No problem. Well, yeah; look Mister, can I ask you a question, given I've been answerin' all yours?'

Roar snorted in disbelief. 'The answer is No! I won't be selling you either this horse or the other.'

The boy laughed.

'Tell truth, Mister, I did think o' makin' an offer – m'dad'd expect it – but no: you di'nt look like the sort for tradin'. But that there: what's that perch for, up on your pommer? Ent never seen one as big as that. You a falconer or somin'?'

'Well, not exactly. It's for a friend of mine.'

The boy raised his eyebrows, trying to imagine what sort of friend.

'So,' said Roar, 'you're interested in birds as well as in horses.'

The boy wrinkled his nose again.

'No, not really. Just saw you goin' past and... well, I just thought I'd ask...'

The boy seemed puzzled somehow. Roar wondered about that.

'Would you like to see him?'

'He'll come for you, just like that?'

'If I call. But let's move over a bit. We need somewhere

quiet. Wouldn't want him to scare the animals hereabouts; or the people for that matter. My name's Roar, by the way; what's yours'?'

'Sammy. Sammy Tozer.'

'Well Sammy Tozer, today you will meet someone truly remarkable.'

Sammy looked at him in appraising sort of way.

'You know, Mister, thought I already 'ad.'

Sammy followed Roar without any qualms. They left the river path for a small field banked all round by hedges and tall poplars and so far free of settlers. There was something here Sammy didn't understand, but none of it seemed wrong and whatever might happen the boy knew he could always take care of himself. Besides, the old guy was still grinning away. Normally Sammy would have counted that grin a bit of a victory: his line an easy manipulation to make the mark feel good – but no, not this time. He'd said what he meant.

He looked up above him. What with the limited space and the high hedges, the heavy grey-blue clouds looked like some giant tent roof rucking in the wind. A storm was closing in on them. Roar's black cloak whipped up behind him but the man himself was unmoved; in the gathering gloom the light in his eyes seemed brighter than was possible. Sammy felt almost giddy with excitement.

The old man threw him a look, an eager and a challenging look, and then turning his face to the ragged sky he let out a tremendous cry. Sammy nearly staggered at the power of it. With no sort of word in the cry, or at least not one Sammy could understand, the old man's voice soared and roared and wavered and cracked and pierced the clouds. It was thrilling…

And yet Sammy had an idea that it didn't really mean anything at all, that it was just for show, to give him something to remember, or to give him something to explain. Somehow Sammy knew that the real call was more in Roar's head and more in the head of whatever he was calling to. And that was an idea that completely enthralled him. Over such a distance!

Watching the old man's face carefully Sammy saw clearly the moment when Roar realized his call had been answered.

'He's comin' then, Mister?'

'Yes, he's coming; very soon.'

'You're a wizard, ent you Mister.'

Roar took a deep breath and then turned to look at him.

'Yes, Sammy: that's what they call us. Though I feel no wiser than anyone else.'

'But you're not like anyone else. You've a power.'

'Some power. But there's nothing to be scared of in it. It's merely a skill, like any other. Just like you're good with horses.'

'Some horses.'

'Only *some* horses?'

'Well, yeah.' The nose wrinkled yet again but this time there was a smile in there too. 'Some are that dozy there's no dealin' with 'em. But there's others… well, you can talk to 'em.' Sammy wouldn't normally have said as much to anyone, not his dad, nor his brother, but somehow he reckoned that such a notion would hardly bother a wizard, especially not this one.

The old man's eyes widened.

'That was a more surprising answer than I was looking for, young Tozer. Are you telling me you can talk to horses?'

Sammy laughed freely, released from a tension that had bound him all his life. 'Anyone can talk to horses, Mister. Just that most people ent understood by 'em. An' they don't reck the answers they get neither.'

The old man laughed with him.

'Do you know, Sammy, I think you and me need to get better acquainted, and soon, but look over there, down by the river. My friend is coming.'

Sammy held his breath. Up above the trees, in bright splashes against the purpling sky, white barred pigeons burst into the air in sudden fear and then dropped hastily into the canopy looking for cover. A chorus of children's voices whooped in delight and then, like a lightning bolt given freedom, a huge golden eagle hurtled into the sky, climbing higher and higher, without any need for a current of air, so powerful was each beat of his tremendous wings; and then, as he reached an apogee directly above where they stood he dropped like damnation upon them.

Sammy actually threw himself to the ground, covering his head with his arms, not knowing any way to escape. There was a great thump as something hit the ground not five feet behind and Sammy rolled away in terror. Nothing happenend. Sammy sat up and suddenly realized how silly he must have looked. The eagle, if eagle was a word that could properly describe the creature, was already perched upon Roar's saddle pommel casually ripping the head off a fat rabbit. But the rabbit looked tiny in its talons.

Roar pulled Sammy to his feet.

'Come along young 'un, and be polite: rabbits are starters not main course. Sammy Tozer, this is Cuahtemoc, my very powerful friend.'

Roar thought it amazing that the boy, after his initial panic – and who wouldn't panic – didn't seem at all scared. Cuahtemoc regarded him mercilessly and continued to rend his catch. But then again, Roar got no better. Cuahtemoc was a friend who took a lot of getting used to. Respect came before loyalty. Weakness did not gain respect. The boy seemed to know that. He stepped forward, without wavering, to introduce himself. No matter the words he spoke, now it was as if he were a King talking to a King.

'I'm Sammy Tozer, horse trader,' he said, 'You will always be welcome in any place I call my home.'

Cuahtemoc paused at his meat and as he looked the boy squarely in the eyes the rabbit dropped to the floor. Roar was astonished. That never happened – food was too serious a business. The eagle shifted on his perch and then, with exact symmetry, slowly extended his wings to their full span.

Sammy returned the gaze, stood erect and raised his arms, palms out, fingers splayed.

Roar felt shut out. There was pain in that, but it was fleeting. This was so unbelievable, so unexpected, so *important*: how could he be petty about it? Cuahtemoc was still his—

'He loves you.'

Roar felt warmth bloom deep inside him.

'Does he?'

'He does; you know it.'

Cuahtemoc gave out a mighty cry then, a cry that put the wizard's effort to shame, and for the first time in many years Roar could not understand the full meaning of it. Fields away that cry made hundreds of people start in wonder.

'Messing about with that bird of yours again?'

Both Roar and Sammy turned, shocked to be wrenched from a moment so intense, and both completely offended. Colm Peveril didn't care, he rarely noticed the effect of his words on others. He failed to notice the eagle's steely gaze.

'Time to be off, Roar: I've found them.'

Roar shook his head in annoyance.

'You really are the limit sometimes. I suppose you mean Altiparedo?'

'Well if you knew already, you should've said. Good news, eh? Now we know where they are, or where they'll soon be anyway, we can go and sort them out.'

'Sort them out?'

Roar looked at him in disbelief. The bare muscular arms emphasized by the sleeveless vest, the neck thick from hours of throwing weights around, the picture of self-confidence that was his broad face, none of this did anything to make Roar feel any better about him. Colm was all conspicuous power, a natural athlete and arrogant as they come.

'Well there's no point waiting around for Seama to turn up is there? They're only a bunch of sorcerers.'

'So that makes them an easy mark does it?'

In answer Colm smiled, lifted both hands, clenched them in fists and gestured at the white five bar gate at the field entrance. The whole thing exploded into flames, hot and final; burning spars flew through the air.

Roar pursed his lips.

'Let's hope you didn't hurt anyone. Look Colm, I know you're confident and powerful and eager and all of that. I was a bit like that myself once upon a time. But the simple fact is we are charged with a mission: to find this Black Company, find out how they operate and then get the news to Seama. We are instructed to do no more. It's his job to *sort them out*. You need to remember that.'

Colm wasn't happy.

'Look Old-Father-Time, what you need is a bit of umph; a bit of energy. That's why I'm here. You know that don't you? But you go on like I need a nursemaid or a… a chaperone or something.'

'The word you are looking for is *mentor*. Part of my job is to be just that. Gods above know you need one. You're with me to learn the meaning of the word *restraint*. An alien notion, I understand. You need to learn that in some circumstances a bit of umph is the last thing you'll need. A bit of umph could get us in trouble. So, let me say it one more time: we have our mission and we will stick to it – whatever heroisms you may have had in mind.'

Colm didn't bother to hide the anger and dissent in his face. Roar often thought he behaved more like an adolescent than a young adult. He wondered momentarily whether that was a matter of upbringing rather than nature. He came down on the side of the latter.

'Have I made myself clear?'

'Clear enough.' The normally smiling face became sulky. 'But we're still heading for this Altiparedo place?'

'Yes we are.'

'Right then,' the sulk shifted as quickly as it had come, 'That's enough for now – but when we get there, well, we'll see what this Black Company's like. You might change your mind.'

'Not likely. I promised Waldin and your father—'

'So who's the pikey, then?'

'The what?'

'The gyppo lad. You want to watch that bird of yours, Roar: they'll take anything not nailed down.'

Cuahtemoc took to the air in a wing-beat and clipped Colm squarely round the back of his head with a clenched talon in the process.

It was a dangerous moment. Colm let out a cry that was more to do with embarrassment than pain, and raised his hand to strike. Roar's sword rang as it left the scabbard…

But Colm backed off.

Cuahtemoc, unconcerned, had swivelled in flight and was miraculously back on his perch only moments after he had left it, attending to his recovered rabbit.

'If it comes near me again, I'll kill it.'

'And I will kill you. But we'll not let it come to that.'

Colm and Roar faced each other in tense silence for a good minute before Sammy ended it by saying:

'Suppose I'd best be gettin' back to m'pikey dad, then.'

Roar shook his head as he put up his sword.

'Don't take such a name to yourself. It's a name given in disrespect, and in prejudice, and in ignorance.'

'Na. Reckon I've heard it an 'undred times before, Mister, and it ent never done me any harm yet.'

'Nevertheless.' Roar turned to his so-called apprentice again. 'Tell you what, Colm Peveril: why don't *you* take care of these horses for an hour or so; get them settled and watered while I go with the lad and buy him a pie or something – by way of apology. Cuahtemoc'll stay with you if you need company. And *if* I've calmed down before I find a baker I might just buy you a pie too.

'Come on then Sammy, you can talk to our friend later.'

Black Hills, Segyllin Part 3057.7.25

The paths were so bent as to be annoying. Tregar had slept well after his night vision and waking early had set out with purpose. Sirrah was happy enough after they found the stream that curved around the back of the yard and Tregar hoped to get his journey done the quicker for it. He took his directions from the sun and chose the most obvious route and for some time was pleased with his progress. Soon the farmhouse was miles behind and though the path wiggled this way and that it was not a worry to him.

It was not a worry until two hours later when he decided to rest his horse. He looked about and seeing a hummock of sorts just to one side he scampered to the top for a better view.

'Damnation!' he shouted aloud, causing Sirrah to start. The horse went back to picking at the acid grass when he realized that nothing was out of the ordinary: the master was merely giving vent to frustration in his typical manner. What had caused this sudden and continuing outburst he neither knew nor cared.

Just on the other side of the hill, hardly half a mile away, was a cluster of ancient farm buildings. A small stream curled around the back of the yard. It was the very same farm Tregar had started from. He cursed and raged for a good five minutes before common sense and some semblance of calm returned.

'Well, Tregar laddie,' he growled at himself as there was no-one else to say it for him, '*Whit* is the point, ye stupet twerp, in having a god share your tea if ye can't listen to what he says? *Use magic*, he said! And not just when you're angry. So you cool down a bit and have a think!'

And that is what he did. He sat down on top of the hill and allowed his thoughts to slip inside his mind and search for memories of the training he had taken so long ago.

The Collegium Magi on Errensea was the only school of magic that Tregar knew. He presumed it was the only such school in the wide-world and that thought made him feel special. The magic taught was determinedly eclectic: while one day might be spent in the alchemical laboratories, on another the students would concentrate their efforts on the Texts of Power. There were Names to learn, languages to master; there were minds to read, there was matter to move; there were lessons in destruction, lessons in healing; the education was broad, the knowledge was deep. Tregar was always better at the physical certainties of magic, the sleights of hand, explosions, intercessions and the knowledge of True Nature; he was worse at using his own *power inherent*. They had told him from the outset that *power* such as Seama possessed could never be his. He could accept that. He was disappointed to learn that there could be no artificial increase of his initial strength through training. Either you had the *power* or you did not. They could help him to improve his ability to direct the *power*, of course, but it wasn't the same and he remained unimpressed by the whole subject. It was only in healing that he did well, where his use of the *power* seemed to come naturally.

The Texts of Power explained the whys and wherefores but it was doubtful that even the greatest of scholars could understand it fully. Tregar couldn't understand at all. Why should one person have *power* and another not? Why should the gods have greater *power* – was that why they were gods in the first place? Why should all creatures so differ in the type of ability they had that a boggart may have the *power* to become invisible and control the airs, and yet be susceptible to the right words spoken by a weakling who could do neither? As far as he could remember the maxim, *Power is the consequence of the Struggle; the Struggle is the constant war between Good and Evil.* But how could the *Struggle* come before the *Power*? It didn't make any sort of sense to Tregar and he deliberately ignored as much of the theory as he could possibly get away with. After the words of Uovin he now wished he'd paid more attention. If the God was to be believed, and how could he dare disbelieve, the *Struggle* and the *Power* were central to what was happening. He had to admit that it all lent some credence to Seama's ideas.

Tregar shook his head as if to shake up his thoughts. These musings were getting him nowhere. Literally. What he needed now were some specific techniques to get him out of this boggy labyrinth. He found, on reflection, that there were certain questions to be answered before he could progress. Firstly, and all inclusively, why was he lost? It was not such an easy question. Was it because the road was in reality complex and maze-like? He knew of a solution for that. When faced with a maze use a maze-boy, a quicksilver.

They are not rare. His teacher had taken the class out walking one summer's day and had them compete to see who could find and then control the greatest number. The idea was to gather them in a whirling halo about your head and the student with the brightest halo was the winner. Finding them was the easy part. They came to life in the Sun's rays and you could see them in all sorts of places, stray sparkles, flashes and glimmers that dart from pond to tree, roof to pavement with the speed of light. Some maintained they were simply *reflections* of light, and maybe that was so in some manner of understanding, but they behaved in a most unpredictable fashion, leaping from glassless buildings to the fields of grass hardly bothering to follow the rules reflections are bound by. It was easiest to see them for a long time if you lay on your back and let your gaze reach up into the shimmering blue of a hot day. They so luxuriate in the Sun that they play a game of trying to reach it. Tregar watched them shoot up into the sky and climb, and climb. It looked from below as if they were weaving erratic dances as they rose. When one got so high as to pop out of sight there was always another ready to take its place.

That was a long time ago. Grown men rarely have the time or enthusiasm for sky-gazing. Tregar remembered that he had not won the competition. It was the *control* aspect that let him down. A quicksilver moved with the speed of light, it could explore any maze in a second and show you the way out. So long as you could make it obey you. Sadly, Tregar's memory of the event did not include any recollection of the spells he would need. They must have been somewhere in his memory but he realised it would take a mazeboy to find them.

He decided to follow another tack.

What if the road was straight and Tregar was just seeing it bent? He could be following an illusion. Tregar decided that was the most likely explanation, but really he just hoped so. He knew very well how to break this level of illusion. He recalled the spell that would give him true sight and, rocking on his heels slightly, he voiced it three times with his eyes closed. It was as simple as that if you knew the right words.

Looking down he saw that Sirrah was nowhere near the road though he'd not moved as he waited. There it lay away to the West and, though it weaved through bog and hummock, it was essentially a straight road into the North. Tregar's grin broke into a laugh. 'The Old Goat!' he said. As the god had intended,

Tregar could see that it was often easy to succeed if only he put his mind *and* his *power* into it. Almost childishly pleased with himself, he chuckled as he went to mount up.

Sirrah was never surprised by his master's changing moods but he was more than confused when asked to walk through a bog, he was reluctant. Laying a hand on the horse's head the wizard, with a few words, cleared Sirrah's view of things.

'Happy now, are we?' The horse snorted. He didn't sound too happy. 'Aye, there's still a way's to go, Sirrah, I can't deny it, and go we must; but take heart: there'll be a welcome for us when we get there, with a warm stable, a nice brush down and some proper food. And, if you're very good, maybe the same for you too.'

The day was warming, the air was clean and fresh and their path was clear before them. Confident they would soon reach their journey's end and a well-deserved rest from their labours, Tregar felt brighter and happier than he had for several days. It was not so bad a thing after all, Tregar thought, to be a messenger of the King.

Francon 3057.7.25

With her back to the high cwm and unseen before her the deep Francon vale, black Greteth stands alone. This morning, clammy fingers of air probe dark corners and closed doors. The sun that warms a wizard's path in more southerly fields has no power here. Above, below and all around, a besiegement of smothering fog.

Holman Cator peered into the mists from the open gate of the castle and pursed his lips. There was nothing to see but the fifteen yards of metalled road disappearing into the gloom. He was thankful at least that as yet there was nothing to hear. No threat to perceive greater than the blinding fog itself. With a good road to follow and a good horse to carry him what was there to fear?

He weighed the tightly rolled sheet of vellum in his gloved hand as if to test its importance. There was almost nothing to it. A few sentences perhaps. What price could be laid on each word written? What was the worth to those left behind, what benefit to the hand that received? He would never know. His duty did not extend to content or discussion. His task being the mechanical act of transportation, there was one question only that should concern him, and a fine question it was too: looking out into the unknown once more, he couldn't help but wonder what exactly would be the cost of delivery?

Hard shoes ringing on the cobbles of the gateway roused him from his misgivings. His doubts must have been catching. The dapple grey mare was snorting in protest, eyes rolling and biting at the bit as the ostler dragged her through, as unwilling as a beast could be. Holman raised a wry grin.

'Jaspar said I'd have the fastest not the daftest.'

The ostler shrugged. 'Never seen Zara so vexed. But don't you worry, Holman, she'll run all right, all the way to Ayer if you let her. Strongest girl I got.'

'Well I hope you're right, Robert, but if she just gets me out of the valley and this damn fog that'll be good enough for me.'

Robert nodded, a grim set to his features. He found nothing to say. Or rather there was no point in saying anything. They both understood the situation.

Holman glanced at the scroll once more, checking that the seal was properly intact before sliding it into the hard leather dispatch case hung from his belt and securing the lid. Nothing for it now, he thought, no chance of turning back.

'Those girth straps tight enough Rob?'

The ostler gave him a look.

'Just checking – I'd look a fool falling off before I get out the gate. I'll have the stirrups a bit higher though.'

As Robert sorted the left Holman sorted the right. The difference they made was a matter of an inch and no more. Robert wasn't fooled and nor was Holman: he was simply delaying the inevitable.

'Right then,' he said, 'let's do it.' With a surge of energy he grabbed at the reins and launched himself into the saddle. Zara bucked just the once but then calmed as Holman settled in his seat.

He looked down at Robert. Just the two of them and the horse; just as he'd wanted it, his friends banished from this leaving. One grim face was bad enough.

'Cheer up Rob. I'm off to get help I reckon, and I'll make sure I do. Wish me luck.'

Rob grimaced as he tried to keep his face straight.

'We'll all be thinking of you Holman. Min guide you and guard you. Ride fast and arrive safe.'

Holman shrugged.

'I'll do my best.'

And with that he pressed Zara forward a few reluctant steps beyond the protection of the gate arch. The crack and scrape of her shoes on the compacted stones bounced off the walls, but louder to his ears was the powerful thumping of blood in his own veins. Zara paused as if readying herself and then moved on a few more yards without prompting, head high, scenting the road before them.

'Good girl, good girl,' Holman said feeling the quiver of her strength through his thighs, 'now for it!'

The slightest touch of his heels was all she needed. Without a cry or a whinny she bolted forward, attacking the uncertain fog.

High on the castle walls, those banished friends lean out to watch Zara's first challenging steps. Their hearts lift to witness her power and poise, her coat gleaming white against the darkness of the road as though she were some creature of the gods, shining in the dark; their hearts fall as in the space of a heartbeat both horse and rider are taken by the consuming mists.

Deprived of sight, each of them follow the sound of hoof-beats descending the winding path to the valley head. They strain for clarity. Did those hoof-beats falter and stop before, down in the valley, a thousand invisible drums began again their hideous boom and rattle? Was that only the cry of an eagle echoing in the cwm high above?

MIXED RECEPTION

Magic could not make the terrain any easier to cross and so it was late afternoon before Tregar reached Small Cuttings. Today there was no wind to accompany the last hours of his journey, only a sticky, oppressive heat. Tregar was relieved. He had learned that even a breeze could be a treacherous friend. Yesterday's wind had been no common force of nature. Uovin had used it as part of an intricate spell to mislead and ensnare him. Uovin, after all, was the God of Winds. Of course Tregar felt honoured by the visitation but, from now on, he wanted no more delays.

Lacking all movement the air was very close and the sweaty heat made Tregar itch in all sorts of places. Neither was Sirrah very pleased as he had more surface to itch than his master. In fact the horse was having by far the worst of it as the unyielding tussock grass sapped his strength and the mosquitoes, preferring horse to man, tapped his blood. In the depths of Sirrah's mind was an idea that his master could and should do something about the flies but he had no means of communicating this thought other than by twitching his ears and flanks in irritation. Tregar, engrossed in his own grumblings, didn't get the message.

'I don't know, Sirrah,' he said to the horse, 'maybe I'm too long in the tooth for all this. Ye just wouldn't believe how tired I am.'

The horse snorted.

'It's time we found this here farm. I don't know about you but I could do with a long cool drink and an even longer snooze. And what about a bath eh? That'd be nice.'

He crested a small hillock as he was gabbling on but, preoccupied with wants and desires, he failed to notice the group of four men toiling on the slope below. They were not slow to see him. Their startled cries made Tregar sit up. His sudden appearance seemed to have surprised them and so to allay their apparent fears he held up his hand in the familiar

Partian greeting.

An old gaffer was the first to reply but the others followed his lead. Taking the reply as permission to carry on, Tregar rode down to meet them.

'Go round! Go round!' they cried warning. Tregar hadn't recognized the furze bushes that lay between them. The plant bore thorns the size of sewing needles and grew in dense banks over most of the slope. The men, wearing thick leather gloves, jackets and leggings, had been busy cutting away at the edges of one these banks. Though he may have known in the past, Tregar couldn't now remember why men should go to so much trouble to cut down bushes. If they had to clear the land why not simply burn it off?

'Good day to ye,' Tregar began cheerfully as they looked him up and down, suspicion evident in their eyes. 'Thanks for the warning. Vicious looking stuff that.'

'Ay. It is if tha doesn't look out for it,' said the old gaffer, 'Travelled far then?'

'Oh, quite a ways. I wonder could ye help me? I'm hoping to find a Mr. Cookson of Small Cuttings. Do ye know if I'm still on the right road?'

'And what would thy be wanting with Owen Cookson then? He don't get many visitors; not from overt' moors anyroad.'

Tregar had no intention of telling his business to all and sundry. 'Are ye from Small Cuttings yourselves?' he asked.

'Some of us. I live in one of th'ome farms thereabouts. My name's Skillern, what's thine?'

He was a shrewd old bird, Tregar thought: he would have to tell them something.

'Let's just say I carry an urgent message for your Mr. Cookson, a message from Ayer.'

'From the King, he says,' piped up one of the younger men, 'Hadn't we best take him wi' us Will?'

'Oh well, happen you're right, Gest,' Skillern conceded glumly. He seemed disappointed that the stranger was not more villainous. 'But you mind he goes straight to Owen. Time we were packing up anyroad.'

Without a word of explanation the men set about stacking the last cuttings they had made. From the strain of their labours old Will turned a sharp, though amused eye upon Tregar.

'Tell thee what, Mister: tha didn't half give us a scare, popping up like that overt' rise. We thought tha'd appeared out of nowhere. Nobody uses that way, no one proper anyroad. Thought tha must be some sort of fairie, but then fairies are supposed to be beautiful so I reckon we were wrong there.'

It was Tregar's grin that won out. He laughed with the rest of them. What would they think, he wondered, when they found out exactly who and what he was. He would have to tell them eventually.

He dismounted, despite his weariness, so that he could talk to the men as they walked. They appreciated the gesture. Now they'd decided he was no demon they were keen to talk. Most of all they wanted to ask him about Ayer. The three younger men were not much travelled but Will had been to the capital several times though not for many years, the last not long after Mador had attained the throne. He had gone with Owen Cookson's father to argue some point about taxes: 'not that we were trying to avoid them,' Will explained seriously, 'but something were not right clear and it's best to know where you stand.'

For his part, Tregar asked questions about Small Cuttings. He learned that the settlement was bigger than the maps made it. Will described it as having become 'almost what you'd call a village.' Set in a stony valley it was sheltered from the worst of the weather; houses were stone built, slate roofed. The land was not the most fertile you could find but generations of hard labour had improved the chances of worthwhile farming. It was a matter of pride to these people that they managed to produce enough grain and root crops to sell at market. As he studied the harsh landscape, Tregar couldn't help being impressed. To manage a surplus from such an environment must not have been easy. Stirrings of guilt at the thought of the requisitions to come were hard to keep down.

The workers also told him all he could ever want to know about furze, and Tregar was suitably amazed at the many uses that could be made of it. Primarily it was a fuel, a fast burning kindling. He should have guessed that much. The pleasing yellow flowers that disguised the plant's thorny nature were boiled and distilled to provide the main constituent of home-made textile dyes. The thin bark was rich in tannin, essential for the curing of skins. And of course you could use the whippy branches woven together as a fencing material prickly enough to keep the sheep off lettuce. A wondrous plant in all respects: Tregar complimented the men on their skill with it. He wished he'd never asked. He was intrigued by one claim, however, concerning the plant's medical potency. The tangled roots, dried, shredded and boiled for many hours produced an oily liquid variously called Deathsbane or Pinchflesh. The people of the high moors used it as a tonic for fevers; they claimed it brought colour to pallid cheeks, banished aching heads, quickened the blood. And there was one tale that, used by the wise in a manner undefined, the liquor had the power to bring the dead back to life. A disturbing idea. Tregar was a medical man who did his best to cheat death but the thought of bringing someone back once death had won made him shudder. Some things, he was sure, were best left alone.

As they talked they descended into a small valley and before long they could see the buildings that made up the hamlet of Small Cuttings. It was a delightful valley in the summer warmth, a pleasant contrast to the windswept and barren moor that hemmed it in. Here were tended fields of vegetables and wheat and barley; there was a good road and sturdy houses with bright flowers in the gardens.

'What is your man like then, this Mr. Cookson? I mean, is he likeable enough?' An innocent question, Tregar thought.

'Well then, stranger, I think I'm not int' best position t'answer that one,' said Will with a wry grin, 'I think tha should wait till tha sees 'im. Mek up thee own mind. Alright?'

One of the younger men laughed at this exchange but nobody said anything to explain and so Tregar left it alone.

As they reached the outskirts of the houses they met other men and women returning from their various tasks away in the

fields, all ready for their supper. Tregar was surprised to see
so many. Once on the main road Will Skillern gave them all
a 'Good Evening' and made off down a small path towards a
cottage set in a copse of stunted rowan trees.

'You mustn't mind owd William. He can be a grumpy
beggar at times,' said one of the young men. He had introduced
himself as Seth and was a good looking, hazel haired lad of
eighteen or so and cheerful enough to be good company. Seth
had been the most avid questioner and listener of the group.
'You'll find that Will and me dad don't really see eye to eye
just at'minute, about all sorts of things. Not that he'd say owt
against him to a stranger.'

'And not with Owen Cookson's son standing next to him,
eh? Why didn't ye say before?'

'Didn't make any difference really. I'm only one of his sons,
an't' youngest at that. Anyroad, here we are and I think we'd
best do as Will says and find my father before we do owt else.
It's this way. He should be wi' our Gordon about now. I'll see
you two later: Tom, Gest.'

The main house was a surprisingly large and rambling
affair more like a country manor than a farm but, no matter
the size, it seemed full to bursting with Seth's kith and kin.
Tregar had to apologize at least six times as he bumped into
bustling women or dark eyed children busy running errands.
The women smiled and said a polite 'Good Evening' before
hurrying on but the children were openly curious at Tregar's
unexpected appearance, and they watched him carefully until
he was out of sight.

Mr. Cookson was 'wi' our Gordon', his eldest son, in a
conservatory attached to the south wall of the house, busy
disagreeing about some facet of crop management. Tregar's
arrival brought them to their feet.

'This gentleman's from Ayer, father,' Seth said, clearly
embarrassed he couldn't introduce the man by name as he
didn't know it. The father was more direct than his son.

'My name is Owen Cookson,' he said, 'and you are?'

'My name is Tregar MacNabaer. I am Mador's court wizard.'

'Your name was enough. I think there's just the one Tregar in the Kingdom and you fit the description. I have heard only good about you but, and I mean no discourtesy, should I be pleased to meet you?' A look of practised suspicion was graven on his face; he came to the point quickly. 'The Crown rarely has news that is to our benefit. Why has Mador sent a wizard to speak with a farmer?'

Tregar was taken aback by Mr. Cookson's blunt approach and couldn't think of a suitable and safe reply. The farmer, to give him his due, noticed Tregar's indisposition and seemed sorry to have caused discomfort. 'No,' he relented, 'This isn't right. I beg your pardon. That was not mannerly. My questions will wait till you're rested and fed. Seth here will take you to his house. He has room. If you have spare clothes we'll get those you are wearing washed. If not I'm sure we can find a shirt and trousers for you.'

'Thank you, Mr. Cookson,' Tregar said, relieved he could put off the bad news a while longer, 'I did indeed travel light and these are all the outer clothes I have. It'd be good to change out of them, but what I really need is a bath, if that's possible? Oh, and my horse needs some attention. I made him work hard to get me here.'

'Seth'll see to it. Come to the hall for dinner and we'll talk then. I'll want some answers mind. Now Gordon, do you think this rotation will...'

Tregar and Seth took themselves off as quickly as Owen changed his conversation. The wizard wasn't looking forward to the evening ahead. So plainly cynical about the aims and demands of kings, Owen Cookson would not be a happy man.

Seth wasn't married but engaged to a girl who lived in a town some way north of Small Cuttings. As a wedding present he was building a house. The kitchen was still a building site and the yard was full of stone, sand and cement, but further in several of the rooms were quite serviceable. Seth apologized for the mess as he showed Tregar through to a pleasant bedroom he had already fitted with a divan, a chest of drawers and a huge feather bed. Handing Tregar a warm robe he told the wizard to make himself comfortable and then ran off to organize the hot water.

It wasn't long before Tregar was dozing in a steaming bath where all his aches and his worries seemed to drift away. He was a strong man, no one could deny it, but after six days of hard riding he was so tired, more tired than he could readily remember. There was a time when this escapade would have seemed no more than a jaunt but the years at court had made him soft. He luxuriated in his well-earned bath knowing there would be hard labour to come. Diplomacy didn't come naturally to Tregar and the prospect of having to beard this farmer *without* losing his temper along the way did not appeal. He dipped his body deeper beneath the surface and sighed in pleasure. For now, Tregar decided, the diplomacy could wait.

It was a good thing Seth came to wake him or he would have snoozed there all night. The lad had brought with him towels and a bundle of clothes. He seemed delighted to have the wizard as his charge and his first intention was to make sure his guest was well-dressed for dinner.

'It weren't easy trying to find clothes for thi,' he said as Tregar dried himself, 'there's not many round here as big and as tall as you. Even me dad's a bit ont' skinny side but he does have quite a collection of stuff in his attic. Now he doesn't use it much but look here at what he's found f'thi. They've given it a bit of an airing.'

'Good grief,' Tregar muttered. Seth showed him garments too rich by far. There couldn't have been such silks on anyone between there and Riverport. A snow white linen shirt with lace frilled sleeves, an exotically brocaded green slub-silk tunic; the black satin trousers put him in mind of the fleet masters of Pilgrim's Bay, rich men all and proud as peacocks. Tregar thought them ridiculous.

'I'm sorry,' said Seth as he forced Tregar into his party dress, 'but we couldn't find as good a pair of shoes to match. Roads are mucky anyway so we'll all be in boots. Right fine is that,' he finished admiringly.

'But I've never worn clothes like these,' Tregar protested, 'I feel stupet.'

'Don't worry we all have t'have our best on tonight. We don't often have a wizard staying wi'us, and when he's the King's messenger, well! Anyway, it's either those or nowt because your own are in the wash.'

Tregar winced as he caught sight of himself in a burnished copper mirror. Even in Ayer he'd hidden himself in woollens and furs, scornful of the foppish style common at court. This was altogether embarrassing.

Of course nobody in the hall was dressed half so well as he was, despite the holiday best, and so he was pleased that neither his arrival nor attire created much of a stir. There were more important things to do than gawp at visitors. Seth, at his side, explained the scene as men and women cleared a messy oak table. It was a huge table that could probably seat more than thirty, very long and narrow and rounded at the ends.

'My grandfather bought that over forty year ago way down in Coldharbour. We think it came from Aegardean wood but we don't really know. You'll like t'have noticed we don't have a great deal of wood round here, well not like that anyroad.'

'It's very impressive,' Tregar managed, 'How many people use it?'

'Oh, it varies, but usually over twenty.'

'It seems we've arrived too late, though.' The wistful tone in his voice was very obvious. He was damnably hungry.

'Oh, don't worry thesel': that were onlyt' first sitting. There's too many to eat at once. Kitchens say they can't do it. No, the children eat first but they'll all be off to bed now, unless they've housework to do.'

'Not out playing?'

'Oh no,' Seth told him in a serious tone, 'There's time enough for playing,' and then added when he saw Tregar frown, 'Don't fret, it's not hard on them. As me dad says: "a bit of discipline never hurt anyone".'

Tregar and discipline hadn't seen eye to eye when he was a child. For some reason the thought of it made him ill at ease. He had no chance to consider this feeling. They had idled by the door as the table was re-laid by some of the older children but now Seth nudged him with an elbow.

'Ne'then,' he said, 'Here they come. Let's get you introduced to everybody.'

Tregar first of all shook hands again with Mr. Cookson but was then greeted by at least another twenty-five members of his family. With a memory like his he stood no chance of remembering the majority, but he did manage to fix a few:

There was Marjorie, Cookson's wife. She was a jolly soul, very different in mood from her husband, but some intuition told Tregar there was a clever mind at work behind the blithe facade. She had a number of daughters and daughters-in-law of whom Tregar remembered Kate, Sally and Rosemary by reason of their attractiveness, and Elaine by reason of her humour. Sally and Elaine were not married being only seventeen and nineteen respectively.

Of the men, besides Gordon and Seth, Tregar noted only the husbands of Kate and Rosemary – namely Harry and Robert, both taciturn men who hardly spoke to the wizard all evening – and Cal who was Owen Cookson's middle son. He was slightly smaller than average and had a wayward eye which made conversation with him an odd experience as the right eye looked in all directions save forward. This handicap, however, seemed not to worry him and Tregar ended up thinking him the most pleasant natured of the whole company. He found it merely curious at this stage that Seth consistently avoided conversation with his brother.

A courteous girl of fourteen or so asked them to take their seats while soup was served and Owen had Tregar sit at his right hand. There were no delicacies, just good homely food: soup, roasted lamb, potatoes and green vegetables, or as a treat lettuce and tomatoes. Owen Cookson's conversation was as straightforward as the victuals.

'So Master Tregar, you're here for the King?' His shrewd eyes fixed upon the wizard making him feel uncomfortable. The man had already guessed that Tregar's news wouldn't be good news, and Tregar couldn't help feeling guilty about it. He finished the bite of bread he had taken after his soup and, after a sip of water, began reluctantly to tell his tale.

'I bear more than the King's greetings, Mr. Cookson. I carry his instructions. May I ask, before I continue, have ye had any news of the North lately?'

'Not many farmers travel at this time of year. Too much to do. And we don't get many visitors apart from traders out of Coldharbour or Riverport.'

'But you've had some news, surely?'

'Yes, we've heard a few things. From Coldharbour mostly. There were stories of strange goings on up beyond the Francon. I didn't reckon much to them.'

'But what did they say?'

'Oh, something about armies or villains or something, and if you'll believe it some nonsense or other about ghosts.' He said the word 'ghosts' as if it left a foul taste. He took some water. 'There's nothing more stupid, if you ask me.'

'Well then. Let me tell ye what I know, nonsense or not. We've had positive reports that someways north of here there's a marauding army destroying villages and towns as it goes. Outlanders or The White Men they've been called, but we haven't a clue who they are or where they're from.'

'And this is for definite, Tregar?' Seth asked, the look on his face and the tone of voice almost copying his father, surprising the wizard who had initially thought them quite dissimilar, 'So how far North are we talking about?'

'We don't know. The Army of the House of Sands has gone to face them but we've heard nothing since they reached Greteth, the fortress at the end of the Francon. They'd seen 'nothing substantial' according to their last message.'

'Is it not just rumour then?' This a steady, reliable sort of voice.

'I'm afraid it isn't, Gordon, it's something more than rumour if it can stop the King's Messengers. Besides all this seems part of one strategy. Have you heard of our problem with Masachea?'

Cookson snorted. 'We're not as cut off as all that, Tregar.'

'Aye, well, of course not. Anyway the situation is unchanged.

More than half of our force is held up on the Eastern border. What you won't know about is the trouble in Gothery.'

'There's never war in Gothery!' The farmer seemed shocked. There was general upset around the table as Tregar explained what he knew of the situation. Gotherians were a peaceful, hardworking race much like themselves, good neighbours and, if you went far enough back, many of them kinsmen to the people of the Segyllin Part. War in the east and north and now in Gothery: it began to seem to some of them that everything good and decent was under attack in some way.

Tregar tried to allay their fears by playing down the threat of war in the west but Cookson at least wasn't taken in.

'You say this Black Company is not but a small band of trouble makers, yet by the sound of things they'll be ruin to Gothery and us too if this goes on. What will Mador do about it?'

'There is a plan though I'm not sure I can tell you all about it, good folk though you are.'

'We need no secrets, Tregar. Words and stories go astray even in the most friendly places.'

'Aye. Thank you for not pressing me. I think I might lighten your hearts a little though, without too much risk. The Lord Seama has taken on the troubles in Gothery and that should be a comfort to us all.'

There were nods and murmur of approval. Seama was the foremost wizard in all of Asteranor, renowned for righting injustices of any scale. News of his involvement was taken as reassurance that all would soon be well. The idea that Seama might be shipwrecked on the island of Tumboll was far from any mind at that table. Curiously Tregar had to fight with his own complacency to realize that nothing was certain.

The diners were only half aware of where all this was leading and Tregar decided to be more direct.

'Mador and Seama have decided that our Northern mystery needs resolving and that if there is an army to fight, then we must fight it. Sands cannot be considered in our plans: it's as though they have vanished.'

'So,' the farmer ventured, 'we're to send another army. Are you recruiting, Tregar? It would seem to be a waste of better talents.'

'No, you're right Mr. Cookson, this is no attempt to commission men. I am here because Anparas and Temor will arrive at this farm within the next four days. I'm to prepare their way and help guide the campaign.'

'Two armies coming here?' Cookson asked incredulous.

'Yes.'

'What, two thousand men in my small stead!'

'Three thousand.'

'What the bloody hell am I going to do with three thousand men? How will we feed them? How will we feed ourselves this winter if they eat us out now? Life's not so easy on these moors, Master Wizard.'

'They will bring food and supplies with them, of course, but yes, even if they have enough for a long journey, they'll need your surplus anyway. There is no way of knowing—'

'I won't do it,' Cookson wasn't quite shouting but it was a close thing. 'My job's to look after these people here, keep them fed, keep them warm. I can't just give their food and their fuel away, whatever you or Mador might think.'

'Father!' Seth broke in, 'You can't do nothing if Pars has to fight.'

'If Pars has to fight? What do you know about war lad? Nowt, and neither do I. It's all very well for our rulers to have their quarrels but they always expect us common folk to do the work and then lose our lives. How can I give away food for my hundred to over three thousand just so they can go and get themselves killed? It's just not sense.'

'Mr. Cookson!' Tregar felt his temperature rising. He had to take a deep breath before he continued. 'You may have a hundred to look after but cannot ye see, the King has the whole nation to protect. We're not talking about a quarrel here but the defence of Pars, and you have a duty to help. Now wait! Before ye say any more I have a letter written to you in person by King Mador. I don't know what it says but I think ye should read it now, before one of us says something we might regret.'

Tregar took out the letter and passed it, seal uppermost, into Cookson's snatching hand. The farmer left the table to read it, walking about the back of the hall, and as he read a thoughtful frown grew upon his face. With a shrug of his shoulders he returned to the table.

'I still don't like it, but,' he said waving the letter at the wizard, 'given this I suppose… Aye, well, there's no choice anyroad. I'll give you what I have, but you'll need more. How many days will you be here?'

Tregar was astonished at the sudden change in the man's attitude. Completely astonished.

'Er, well, I'm happy ye seem to appreciate the matter a wee bit better now, Mr. Cookson. As to the number of days, again I don't yet know. Anparas'll have a lot to say about our strategy before we set off. The soldiers will arrive in four days, as I said, and I'll need to do some scouting meanwhile. We'll have a better idea when I've seen what's ahead. I've two days out and two days back so maybe I'll find a better base for our start.'

'Fair enough. You'll probably find it best to head towards th'Hannay. I'll get my people sorted before your return. Are you travelling alone, Tregar? Why not take a guide? I know a man who knows the area well and he has an interest in that direction.'

'Well, I'd be grateful for the company. Six days alone is enough for a man like me. When can I meet this guide?'

'You have already. It's young Seth here.'

Seth had been watching and listening intently and now, for some reason blushing as he spoke, he said: 'Thank you, Sir, if you agree to take me. I had a mind to travel that way anyroad but the journey'd be better in company. I'm like to be a help an' all: I know all the quickest paths.'

'He does that. Seth has been on those roads often enough. He was just waiting on my permission to travel them again. The time seems right.'

Seth grinned broadly, made up by the turn of events. 'Thanks dad,' he said and then added in a mock aside to Tregar:

'I've been getting on his nerves lately. I reckon he just wants rid of me for a bit.'

The meal ended in much better humour than Tregar had reason to expect. He could scarcely believe the change in Cookson's response. Mador was the fount of all authority in Pars and one might expect his words to carry weight, but for his letter to provoke such a transformation was nothing short of incredible. Not a grumble had escaped the farmer's lips since he'd finished reading it. Tregar was more impressed by Mador now than he had been for some time. What had he written? Tregar didn't have the gall to ask.

ANCIENT HISTORY

The Necromancer made a sign and the guards of the chamber closed and locked the door. They seemed relieved to have it shut.

'Do you think she feels anything now?'

The Necromancer was surprised by the General's question.

'What do *you* feel? Now that you share her blood, will it not be the same?'

The General grimaced. In the dancing flare of torchlight his features were hideous, his voice like stones in a tin funnel. 'I am not strung up like game to be bled and bled again.'

'You sound as though you have some sympathy for her plight.'

'Maybe I do. In different degrees we all here suffer the same affliction. Fellow feeling is to be expected. Even among us exiles the 'blood' does not govern all our thought.'

'Free will is still alive then in the court of the Banished God?'

The General coughed up a laugh. 'He can't seem to get rid of it.'

The Necromancer was surprised once again. These Kumites were not supposed to have a sense of humour. He would have to reassess his preconceptions. What did he really know about them after all? It was true that the Halfi and the Kumites were linked by the nature of their curse, but at least the Halfi lived a true life under the sun, felt the rain fall upon their heads, walked in the snow; they knew about death, they saw babies born, they understood both sadness and joy. What was life for the Exiles? It was too easy, given the way the Kumites looked, to presume that they knew only pain and fear, envy and hatred. The General's dry wit and his pity were a revelation.

What *did* Rillia feel? Nothing? Perhaps he ought to reassess that presumption too. Now that all the emotion had gone he could afford to be more objective. And yet it was hard for him now to think of her as anything more than a carcass. Too many years had passed as she hung from her web, too much blood had been taken. He had witnessed the slow destruction of everything she was to him, year following year following year. By now he was no longer sure the creature she had become deserved the same name. Such a time had passed that he no longer cared. Her obsession had long since killed the love of Dulsibot for his darling Rilliana.

The Necromancer turned his back upon the chamber.

'It's this way,' he said indicating a modest round arched doorway of the Tolmarck period. The castle had been built long before the Halfi had arrived on Tumboll. The Necromancer took pleasure in explaining as they walked through it.

'This is the oldest part of the Palace. It was largely ruinous when we came here, we had precious few tools allowed us and so the stonework for the most part is makeshift and rough. But here and there you can see some of the good, older work. Bagran's great-grandfather had it built on the remains of the old temple. You'll remember the Wizard talking about Bagran and the Sword, I think? Yes, this was the seat of the Anparites. They had it for more than six hundred years but just about the time Banya finally abandoned Pars blight fell upon the place. Or so I read! I haven't come across any explanation of what the blight was or why it began just then, but certainly it lead to the downfall of the family on Tumboll. Their wealth, their abilities, their renown just seemed to dissolve into nothing. It was only when Cativaro Anparas took a bride from the House of Sands, Jessica, and moved his seat to Arbreston to the south of Gull Lake, that the family-line and fortunes revived. It was under his rule that Anparas finally became a Royal House. Now *he* was a strange one, Cativaro: the seventh son of the then Lord Canto Anparas who was himself—'

'Necromancer, your story-telling does not have the potency of your singing.'

'Ah,' the Necromancer cringed slightly, 'Yes, you are right, it does not carry the same power of compulsion. Forgive me, this tale is not really old enough for you. It must seem dull. For me the history of my enemy is a lively study.'

The General snorted at that. 'Lively? They are all dead and gone. Really Necromancer, to know your enemy is one thing but to analyse the small doings of his forebears smacks of unhealthy fascination, does it not?'

The Necromancer shrugged. He was not offended. 'I read a great deal and I forget little; and though it may seem nothing to you I have walked the confines of this house and this Isle for nearly five hundred years. Reading is my only release. As for subject matter, I must read whatever I can lay my hands upon. With Gothery and Pars being my nearest neighbours, what there is rarely strays beyond their own present concerns or their heroic past.'

He stopped talking and stopped walking: they had come to another arched door. It was not locked and opened easily as though the hinges had been well oiled. Beyond it lay a steep flight of stairs, descending into darkness. There was a faint sound of chanting emanating from the depths.

'But anyway, I will not apologise for my reading. It is ever *illuminating* to study the past. You never know what you might discover: this for example.' He made a slow gesture, uncurling his fingers from the fist he had made with his right hand, and as they uncurled the walls of the stairwell began to glow softly. 'Not my magic: I found the secret to this stair and the hall below in a book. And I found the book in a hidden library set within the walls of the palace, completely intact and undisturbed for many centuries.'

'Lucky for you. Shall we go down?'

The Necromancer smiled and led the way. 'Luck? I am not so sure. It was almost as if I *remembered* how to find it and that was very strange given that I had never laid foot on the island until then. And it was an interesting find, to say the least. From its contents the library seemed to have nothing to do with the Anparites though it was hidden within a house they had built. I would hazard that in all the centuries they lived here no more than a handful of people came to know anything about it. In fact the walls seem to carry the memory of only one man. His name was Lamuel and he too was a historian but of far greater resource than I can claim. Let me tell you General, there are texts in that place that even you would be happy to read. Texts that speak of the time before the Choosing.'

The General stopped in his tracks.

'The Choosing is known? But the Wizard assured us—'

'What would it matter? They'll know all about you soon enough.'

'I am concerned they may already know too much. I am concerned there may be some knowledge here that could help them. I am concerned that we are expected.'

'I wouldn't worry about Lamuel's books, General. As I said, the library was well hidden and its use is exclusive to me. What you need to worry about is whether the Smiling One has managed to locate all the copies made of Haslem's version of things. I say version because I think that Lamuel was his source. There is a book of Haslem's letters, written to Lamuel that—'

'Wait, wait, wait!' the General butted in, 'There is something missing here: who, precisely, is *Haslem?*'

The Necromancer was incredulous. 'He did tell you about The Song of Ages, didn't he?'

The General was not pleased. 'Neither the Wizard, nor My Lord Master thought to mention it.' He attempted to clear his throat without success, anger seemed to clog it up. 'What is this thing so unimportant that I, who have command of the entire expedition, should not be told of it?'

The Necromancer took a deep breath. 'The Song of Ages is a book giving a history of, well, everything. Its discovery is what initiated all of this. Haslem wrote it down and you might thank him as our benefactor but I think the information came originally from Lamuel. We have destroyed one copy of the book but we know there were several made and sent to who knows where. It would not, I think, be a disaster if the book were found by members of The Council but it is hard to say what they might take from it. Certainly this work is what gave our friend the means of making the passage.'

'I had thought his coming a scheme of my Master. Are you telling me that this is all the design of the Wizard?'

'General, you know your Master better than I. As I understood it the Angra Mainyu was banished. You must decide whether his reach is yet long enough to overcome the distance put between our worlds. For most of my life the Halfi have prayed to an *absent* God with little hope, or fear, of his intervention.'

'Even when close-by My Lord is not given to answering prayer and supplication. That is not his nature.'

The Necromancer pulled a face. 'What a fine god we hold to. We will talk more about Haslem later, and about the Wizard. For now, no more! His creature spies upon me quite as much as she aids our cause. Here we are.'

The stairs came to an end and a short corridor beyond opened onto a wonder. It was a vast subterranean hall, weirdly aglow in the same greenish phosphorescence that had lit the stairway. The light shone down and up and all around. Clusters of stalactites decorated the high ceiling but the floor had been cleared and smoothed. At the centre was an altar built to reflect the natural architecture above, carved by the look of it from the mightiest of stalagmites, but prodigious above that stood an ancient stone-hewn throne. The altar was made to serve the occupant of that throne and the throne was made for a God.

The Necromancer witnessed a gleam of recognition in the General's eye. The throne and the altar claimed all his attention. It was hard, even for the Necromancer who had visited the hall on hundreds of occasions, to gaze upon that empty seat and not imagine what it might be when occupied.

The General from habit bowed deeply and was silent for some minutes. When he drew himself up he glanced at the Necromancer and seemed to smile. 'I think that my Master's reach is as long as ever it was – whatever his brother might think.'

The Necromancer shrugged. 'All I know is that it is our task to be his hand in this realm.'

He gestured at the hall and the work that was done there.

The General pulled his eyes from the Throne and opened them to another wonder. In the obscuring gloom this was a scene of carnage. A thousand corpses lay on the cold stone floor, each laid out as if this was some vast mausoleum. The dead lay awaiting final services before entombment. The faces, of men and women and yes, even some that we would call children, seemed grey and rotten in that ill light; but their eyes were open.

Presently near the altar, a restless figure, a young woman in a plain blue robe, flit from one body to the next touching those faces, each in turn and as she moved she intoned the same words in a litany of command over and again:

'Coro'Sueve,
Manu all iber,
Forosch tra'ore,
Conn ple revenn,
In terrat Hannay!'

Her chanting echoed through the hall.

'So many, General. Can it be done?'

'Why not? She has a limitless power to draw upon. Can you not feel it, Necromancer? *My Master is here.* This hall was worth all your reading.'

The Necromancer controlled an involuntary shudder. He wasn't at all sure he would relish being in the true presence of the God and chose to understand the General's claim as metaphor. The General seemed excited, if that were an emotion available to a Kumite.

'It *will* be done: tonight they will defeat a whole town without a weapon drawn!'

'An interesting tactic.'

'And necessary. We are not yet great enough to have done with this. But soon, and then these thousand souls can rest. They are almost completely drained, you can see it. It is a hard task but each was more than willing. It is such a… a *delight* to them.'

'Delight?'

'I use a word that you would understand. Look at their faces more closely.'

The Necromancer knelt beside the body of a young looking man. He did not breathe, or at least not in the same way that the Necromancer breathed, and blood did not pulse at the temple or the wrist as it pulsed for him. And yet the face he studied was not at rest. To the Necromancer it seemed as if the boy wandered abroad in some wide-eyed dream. Expressions of wonder, surprise, amusement and even lust governed his features. Some of what he was seeing did indeed seem a very delight to him.

'What does he see?'

'Oh, commonalities for someone such as you, Necromancer. I was one of the first to attempt it. You know what normal life may be but we have forgotten mostly everything we once were. I do not mean so in an intellectual way but in terms of the emotional remembrance of what life is. Simple matters. We watch them being alive: eating, working, sleeping. We watch the children especially. You may think it strange but bodily functions fascinate us. And our fascination serves to make them more uncomfortable. We give them no peace, not at their toilet, not in their beds. Have you any idea what it must be like for us to watch them engaged in sex? 'Making love' is a phrase lost to us.'

The Necromancer laughed grimly. 'And an activity lost to me even though I walk the paths of Earnor and see common life all about. Nepenthe and that web have taken away both the ability and the desire. I had not thought that observing the same might provide vicarious pleasure.'

'It is not some vicarious pleasure that affects us, Necromancer. It is the promise. This is the first taste of what we have had denied us: it is a first taste of what we will have again'

The general spoke with a passion. The Necromancer heard it in the words even if it could not be discerned in the voice. The Kumites shared a terrible yearning fully to realise just exactly what *yearning* was. Perhaps the treatment would work and Rillia's blood would be the medium of relief; perhaps the Wizard would find his chemist and find another way. Perhaps, perhaps.

'There is a long way to go before that can happen, General. To say nothing of Pars and Gothery and the Council of Errensea, there remains the small problem of Nepenthe. What can be done with Rillia will work for me and mine. It has worked for me this long while. And we had the pigs too. The curse of Nepenthe *we* carry in the blood but how is it with you? It is in your blood and your flesh, muscle and bone and has been for an age with no amelioration. The Smiling One insists that it cannot work for The Exiled, though it may seem to help a little. Until he finds the chemist your hope will be denied.'

The General made a sound that was almost like a growl. 'We were told he had this man in the palm of his hand! It is as well the Wizard stays on this side of the divide. Our Master would not be forgiving—'

'Your Master, as far as I can tell, does not even know that word. And neither does the Wizard. It will go badly with this man when he is found.' The Necromancer paused to look around him once more. The witch was out of sight, presumably beyond the Throne but he could still hear the words of her spell bouncing off the walls. The voice was beginning to sound a little strained. 'Will this do? I doubt she can manage any more than this for now.'

'She must. Greteth is in the balance. I admire the Wizard's spells and admire the witch's skill but all must continue until we are ready: all of this, and at Greteth *and Ayer*. There must be no respite until we have the strength.' The General gripped the pommel of his sword. The Necromancer could see that a mighty frustration was building in him. 'The way we have is too slow! Did he not tell us we would be rid of the Guardians by now? They are still there. They seem as little charmed by that smiling face as I am.'

The Necromancer felt no sense of allegiance but still thought the General unfair in his criticism.

'As I understand it, without him there would have been no passage at all, no one to bring us together, no promise of a future: nothing but *continuation* unto the end of all things. Is that how you would have it?'

'Another chance would have come. It has been so long now. We have learned to wait.'

'And each day a *delight* I suppose?'

'A hell, as you know well enough.'

'Oh I cannot know, I only surmise. What a fine and painful irony it must be: in life they chose to deny the existence of God and sought a life eternal; now, condemned by God for their lack of humility, they are given eternity but must live each day in service to his foul son. It is almost poetic.'

'*Poetic?* I would call it a tragedy, Necromancer. You really have spent too long with your books. Writers make fanciful what is hard and cold and real. Tell me, why *do* they call you The Necromancer?'

'Though those I try to help are not strictly dead neither are they wholly alive. To the un-afflicted my activities must seem bizarre. A useful title: it helps me govern. Who would be so foolish as to argue with the Master of the Dead? They seem to have forgotten that I was once merely Dulsibot.'

'That is the difference, Necromancer: I *am* The General. Not only is that the name I am known by, but it is the only name I have for myself. In exile we have not merely lost the world but we have lost ourselves too along the way. Few of us now retain any sense of identity. And that is not anything to do with poetry: it is damnation.'

Dulsibot, the Necromancer, decided not to respond. Loss of personality seemed to him more a blessing than a curse. Personality kept a tight hold on hopes and dreams and desires. Very often in normal life dreams remained unfulfilled and a great many people went to their graves unhappy. What must it be to suffer an eternity of denied hope? Perhaps it would be better to forget everything, name included. Dulsibot was not one to dwell on his lot in the world but sometimes he couldn't help thinking that he had himself *outlived* this life. It was a wearying business, immortality. There were days when he found himself wishing for a good honest death, and wishing that his race had never heard of, or listened to the Black God Ah'remmon, and most fervently wishing that the Blood of the God had never been spilled. But he knew that nothing that had been done could be undone and so, whatever he might wish, he carried on.

'By the way,' said the General, breaking the Necromancer's train of thought, 'My lieutenant has told me that you had a little trouble here a few days ago, somewhere in the south of the island?'

He was wondering when it would be mentioned. 'Do you remember the spell I told you about? Using the Wizard's mirror? We have used it a number of times now. Three ships in the past six months and we latched onto another three nights past. The image it gives isn't very detailed but it's sufficient to get an idea of what you're dealing with. Well, everything was working smoothly and I had the southern tribes ready to take them when they landed. But then the oddest thing happened: I felt that something was wrong. I have never known it before but I could sense the presence of *someone*. The last thing I wanted was some Power coming to the Island, so I decided to sink them. I sang up a pair of pangalori to break the ship. Somehow the male got killed but its mate finished the job. My plan was to feed them to the Schiff but nothing happened as I expected. Apparently, most of the crew and passengers escaped and managed to swim to shore. Luckily the Pigmen were ready for them and they captured most—'

'What of this Power you spoke of?'

'That is a little unsettling: there was no trace. I cannot believe that whatever or whoever it was would have been destroyed in the wreck. But if it reached the Island then it did a very fine job of staying hidden. I just don't know.'

'Not good news. But what have you done with the captives? I am sure they'll be willing to help. More than willing if persuaded properly.'

The Necromancer smiled a wry smile. 'I allow the tribes a tithe of the 'takings' – some of them still have a taste for it so long as they're gutted and hung – so the crew wouldn't have been telling us much. But the remainder, the passengers, had been put in a compound for safekeeping.'

'You say 'had been.' Has something happened to them?'

'Well...'

BAKED IT BLACK

The soggy moors came to an end. After nearly twelve miles as the crow flies, or sixteen as the horse stumbles, they reached the broad valley of the River Hannay. It was a fertile valley well marked out with fenced or walled fields – fields now heavy with barley, oats and wheat waiting to be harvested.

'These cereals have come on early, Seth,' said Tregar.

'They always do in this cut. Nobody's sure why but they're a month earlier here than they are down ont' Plain, and we're always a few weeks behind. Though we don't do much cereal at Cuttings so I'm no expert. Dare say there's somat int' soil though most folk reckon it's because o't' river. Dost' know about th' Hannay then?'

'What's there to know? Is it not like other rivers, wet and running?'

'No. I mean: yes it's wet, but most rivers I've come across are like to be cold.'

'But this one isn't?'

Seth laughed: 'So they don't know everything then, folk in Ayer?'

'Put it this way, I don't know everything; but believe you me, whatever you're babbling on about there's bound to be someone in Ayer who knows all about it, most likely some bod from His Majesty's Chartroom. However, no one thought it important enough to mention, so tell me about it.'

'Well you'd not want to drink from it, not straight. The water's warm and there's a taste to it. Grand for bathing in though. They've a great tank int' centre o' town, and people come from all over to swim in it.'

'Ah. Right now, I remember something about that. The Hannayford Spa isn't it? Supposed to be good for people with the shingles.'

'People say it cures all sorts o'things, but it is good for aches and pains. Tried it mysel' and it worked a treat.'

'So what makes it so warm?'

'God's Kitchen.'

'What, boils it up in a pan, does he?'

'Somat like that. No, it's a part o't' moor up away east of here. It's a strange place, right warm underfoot as though there were a great fire burning underground. Becks fair boil up at top.'

'I'd like te see that.'

'Aye, tha should visit some time. We all go up to t' Stewpot every winter – that's th' highest fell, and th'ottest. It's right peculiar, you can climb up to t'cairn at top and i'the distance there'd be snow all around, but thy'd be standing there in thi shirt sleeves.'

'What makes you go there in winter? I'm inclined to stay by the fire at that end of the year.'

'Oh, we go there to thank the Gods, and to meet up wi' folk from all around. We've a chapel up there. On days we've all agreed to we go up and do our duties. If there's owt that needs sorting between us we do that too. Not business mind: no trading. It's not our place, you see.'

'I do indeed. And who do you pray to?'

'There's lots of gods, they say, but we thank Tamaz the Grower, and we ask a lot of Uovin of the Winds as he brings the weather we get an't' courage to face it.'

Tregar was absurdly thrilled to hear the name spoken. What would Seth think of him having shared a supper with the god himself? He decided it would be best to keep quiet about it. But thinking about the God and his visitation brought Tregar back to the task in hand: there was work to do. With never a glance at the moor behind him, he spurred on over the firmer ground.

They made for a town of dark slate-roofed houses that straddled the river. On either side, as they rode, in all the fields there was no sign at all of the men or women needed to work them. Tregar was puzzled and worried.

'I don't understand,' said Seth, 'I've not seen anybody, have you? There's always plenty of people around. Where've they all gone?'

'Would they be in town? Is there no carnival or the like they could be at?'

'Not when there's barley to cut. Look at it. They're well off, Hannay folk, but they can't leave good grain like this to rot. It's not right.' He seemed upset but Tregar wasn't sure why. Seth was shading his eyes against the sun and looking down at Hannayford.

'Look,' he said, 'all the chimneys: there's not a bit o' smoke in any o' them. I know it's not cold but you'd think there'd be cooking. Do you see that pottery?'

Tregar could see the startlingly red, thirty-foot-high brick construction down at the western edge of the town. It was oddly shaped: round and wide at the bottom but tapering to four blackened chimneys at the top. It looked something like a cows dugs turned upside down. Tregar wasn't well up on potting but he had seen many similar buildings, after all there were no small towns of Pars and few villages that didn't make their own crockery. Not many were as large as this one.

'I see it: a big place too.'

'Aye, Mr. Richard makes pots to sell 'up and down't' River' as well as round Hannayford,' Seth explained, and Tregar took him to mean the Hypodedicus River in this context, 'But d'you see, there's no smoke even there. There's nearly always somat being fired.'

'Ye seem to know an affle lot about that pottery lad, but tell me when we get there. Come on then, let's see what the devils are doing in Hannayford.'

It was a peculiar feeling riding into a town built for bustle, the crowded buildings eager for activity, when in all of its roads and alleys, yards and corners there was no living soul and the houses were separated by a cavernous silence. The people had gone; the cats and dogs had gone. Back yards were full of empty chicken runs and short posts with ropes trailing that had lost their goats. Even the birds had abandoned the streets, away with the rats plundering the fields of grain.

Only the flies remained. In their shortage they tried to make feast on the two men and their horses. The flies swarmed thicker with every yard they progressed. The horses began to kick and buck and the men flapped their arms frantically. It was intolerable.

With a grunt of disgust Tregar moved his hands to mark out an ancient pattern and spoke words in a language that Seth could not have understood. His command killed thousands of flies in a second and made the remainder depart in search of easier pickings. The ground beneath them was now brown and black and crackling. Though relieved, Tregar wasn't certain he had done the right thing. He had used magic as the God had advised but it had seemed too easy an option; and was it right to destroy so many creatures simply because they were an inconvenience. There was an arrogance implied by the action that Tregar didn't like at all.

'Whatever you did, I'm glad you did it,' Seth said. 'We've too much to bother about wi'out being plagued with flies. I don't like it, Tregar: there's not a body about.' The youth's brow was furrowed. He peered uncertainly along the length of the deserted High Street.

'Can ye see any monsters down there, Seth?'

The farmer's lad took a few seconds to realize that the wizard wasn't being serious.

'It's not right to mock, Mister Wizard. Monsters or not, something bad's happened here. I'm off to Mr. Richard's, are you comin'?'

Tregar felt slightly sheepish.

'If that's where ye need to be, then why not?'

They clattered through the town raising a racket but there was no one left to hear or to make complaint. Seth galloped on and Tregar struggled to keep up but at the pottery gates the lad pulled up sharp. The gates were open, as was usual, nothing threatening or odd was in view but Seth seemed reluctant to pass through.

'Whatever's waiting for us, Seth, it won't change for us dithering out here.' Tregar had some sympathy for the lad, frightened of what he might find. 'Look, why don't you show me the way?'

Seth pursed his lips and then nodded. 'You're right,' he said 'Best to get it done. Let's go.'

Passing through into the yard Seth began to call out.

'Hello! Hello! Ro? Rowie! Where are you?'

There was no reply. His voice was plaintive.

'Mr.Richard? Jez? Is there anyone?'

'Give it up lad,' Tregar puffed out as he dismounted, 'There's no one here; but let's have a look inside shall we?'

Seth led the way down around the kilns, in among the stacks of fired pots, through the wheel sheds and finally up to the tall house. Tregar had an idea of what they might find. The lad, of course, expected the worst, but Tregar wouldn't offer him comfort until he was sure. Inside the open and half-empty cupboards and drawers, the pale squares on the walls where paintings used to hang and the general lack of clothes told them half a story. The inhabitants had packed up quick and gone. Tregar wanted to know the where and the why.

'Ye know the people of this house well?'

'You might say,' the youth replied with a tremulous voice half way between the fear of what might have happened and the relief that so far it had not. 'My intended, Ro – Rowena that is – she lives here with her father and brothers. I thought they'd been murdered in their beds. I thought… Where've they gone, Mr. Wizard? I've got to find her.'

'Calm yourself lad! There's been no murdering. There is no death here. I'd guess that they carefully packed up their valuables and left the house and town in an orderly fashion. And I don't think anyone has been here since they left, or at least no villains anyway.'

'How do you know?' Seth demanded, his intuition clouded by emotion, 'Perhaps that's where all the clothes and jewels and paintings went int' first place.'

'No, no, no! Look here: the kitchen, tidy, clean as a whistle. Ransackers don't regularly do the dishes before they leave.'

'I suppose. Aye, that'd be Rowie, she's very house-proud.'

'Well c'mon then,' said the wizard, ushering Seth out of the house, 'A lot of people on the road must leave tracks. They'll all have gone together, if I'm right. So where would you go from here if an army threatened from the North?'

'I'd go to t' Stewpot,' Seth said without hesitation, 'if I were by myself, that is. If I were travelling wit' kids and all, though, I reckon I'd go down onto t' River Plain. There's lots of roads to choose from down there.'

'Right then, let's check the West Road.'

Altiparedo, Aegarde 3057.7.25

It was a short man dressed in black directing the proceedings. He sat on his horse yelling out orders and, by the way he kept flinging his arms around, Colm guessed he was also swearing a lot. None of the words yelled or sworn were audible at this distance but it seemed obvious that his efforts were dedicated to getting his lazy rabble of a force to stand in some sort of battle array.

'He doesn't look too happy.'

'He's finding it hard to get them to jump to. What you are seeing, Colm, is the arrogance that comes from having things your own way for far too long. They think it's going to be easy.'

'A good time to attack then.'

'What, the two of us against a hundred?'

'Mmm. A bit one sided you think? Well just me then, that'll be fairer.'

Roar lowered his spyglass and turned to remonstrate. 'You know you really are the—'

But Colm was grinning. 'Just getting you going, Roar.' Colm couldn't help it. The old man was so easy to rile and taking the rise was Colm's favourite sport. 'Face it, before we go in I'd need to know more about these sorcerer types. Can you make them out?'

'Look Colm, there will not be a point when I sanction 'going in'. We're here to observe and that's that. Now pipe down while I try to figure out what they're up to.'

He went back to his close reconnaissance and Colm decided to leave it a while. Without the benefit of Roar's spyglass Colm gazed all around trying to take in the scene as a whole. They lay beneath a bush up on a slight swelling of the land some quarter of a mile away from the action. The action was a cluster of men on horseback gathered just out of bowshot of the wooden walls of a small town, milling about as if they had nothing better to do on this sunny summer's day. Up on the town's walls, presumably upon some walkway, hundreds of the townsfolk watched nervously. But Colm could see the sunlight glinting on dozens of arrow-tips. They were scared but determined to make a fight of it.

'Not enough of this Black Company to lay siege.'

'No,' Roar agreed, 'and they don't seem inclined to even try. Look they're pulling into shape at last. Just a line of what? Say thirty on each side of the main group. No ladders, no rams. I don't know what they think they can do with a formation like that. Not exactly set out to make an attack… oh.'

'What is it?'

Roar gritted his teeth.

'Can you see the group in the middle.'

'Well I can see them, but not clearly.'

'They have prisoners. I can see women and children and some men, all tied together, surrounded by some of this Black Company on foot.'

'They're going to bargain for them. Look there's a horseman headed out towards the gates. With any luck they'll shoot him.'

Roar was outraged. 'It's parley. We just don't do that. And what do you think they'd do to the prisoners after? You just don't think do you.'

'Oh, I think alright, I just don't think the same as you.'

Roar returned his attention to the parley.

'Doesn't look much like bargaining. More like an ultimatum. You should see their faces. One or two defiant as you'd like but most look plain terrified. That's it. He's done and heading back.'

'Short and sweet.'

'Short anyway. There's a lot of arguing up on the walls.'

'What are they doing now? The Black Company I mean, with the prisoners… Are those stakes they're setting up?'

Roar swung back to see. And then he was silent for a minute

or so.

'Here,' he said finally, passing over the spyglass, 'take a look. They mean to torture them. One family at a time. Teach the townsfolk a lesson.'

Colm's face turned red with fury.

'The bastards,' he exploded, 'He's going to bleed them. That child… If he touches her I'll kill him. I knew we should have attacked.'

'No. We shouldn't. The odds are against us achieving anything.'

'Not if we got the townies on our side. We go in, I do a lot of damage to the soldiers, you take care of the sorcerers. We can give them something to fight for. Come on Roar. We have to.'

Roar pursed his lips, reluctant to say anything.

'Don't do this, Roar. They've already started on the mother… stripped her down… and…' Colm threw the spyglass away from him in despair. 'Listen to her, Roar. Just listen.'

They were not far enough away for this to be just some mute show. The mother's yelps and screams of pain, the husband's impotent shouts of threat and fear, and the squalling of their young daughter all carried through to their unwilling ears.

Roar clenched his jaw as if the action could hold him still and banish the rage. Now was not the time to be weak.

'We *stay here*. And we watch.'

Colm beat the earth before him with the heels of both fists.

'You're a coward, a stinking little coward. This how you've lived so long: running away from fights? Hiding behind orders? Well, answer me you bastard.'

Roar could have reacted badly to Colm's accusation. It was a ridiculous insult. But Roar was determined to do his job, and do it properly. Trying to cut out the hideous sounds of torture he retrieved the spyglass and trained it upon the scene once more. But there was more to see than the agonies of the victims. He had already marked out three of the sorcerers. One was the skinny, almost orgasmic torturer, another was the huge man wearing some sort of hood or mask standing nearby – by his poise, the man in control of events – and the last, a grossly fat man, sitting some way off upon a padded chair, apparently busied with eating jellied sweets or something similar.

'Right. So what are you looking at now? Enjoying the view?'

'I am looking, Colm, to see what these sorcerers are doing. They're supposed to be the key to all this. And there were supposed to be four of them but I can see only three.'

'Who cares what they do. Not as if you're going to fight them is it.'

'It's our job to find out how they operate. Ah, there he is. Over by the stream.'

Colm, still in a rage, managed just about enough self-control to take a look.

'Man on the horse? He looks odd somehow... white?'

'An albino by the look of it. But... what is he doing?'

'You tell me, you've got the glass.'

The albino was gesturing at the water below him. The stream ran past him towards a grilled culvert in the wooden palisade and then on through to feed the town. Looking closely Roar could see that the surface of the water was frothing with movement but even with his spyglass he couldn't make out why.

'I'm going to have to try the *sight*.'

Colm sneered.

'Sure you can manage?'

'Can *you* do it?'

'Well no, but it's a bit of a lame trick when those bastards are out there killing people.'

Roar shook his head. 'Just shut up and let me get on with it.'

He had to concentrate hard. Some people could use the *sight* as easy as breathing but of the two of them young Colm hadn't even begun to understand the beginnings of the skill, and old Roar still found it a tremendous struggle. At least the distance was short and need was pressing. With his eyes closed, the better to focus, he homed in on the water rather than the albino. For a few moments water was all he could see, churned into a froth, but then...

'Ugh.'

'What? What d'you see?'

Roar slumped as he stood, his shoulders dropping as though utterly defeated.

'It was all a distraction. All of it: the ill-discipline, the captain ranting, the parley, the torture. All just to keep the townies looking out, instead of running away.'

'I don't understand. What's he doing?'

'Rats. He's filling the place with rats.'

Colm pulled a face but he was unimpressed.

'Can't stand 'em myself but a few rats eating the supplies won't—'

'Did I say 'a few'? There are thousands of them. And they're not normal rats. Too big. Teeth are wrong. I don't think they belong in this world. You remember we thought they didn't look set up to attack? They weren't. They're set up to finish off any that get out alive.'

Colm was confused.

'But why would they come out…' And then the truth of it hit him. 'No. You're joking.'

'I am not. Listen: it's begun.'

Sure enough, something new to assail their senses tore through the air: frenzied, agonised screams of pure terror that grew in number with every passing second. It was appalling to hear.

Roar took a deep breath. 'It's a massacre— Colm. Colm stop! What are you doing?'

Colm had launched himself onto Gyrax.

'Don't you dare, Colm. Come back, for Gods' Sakes come back!'

But it was too late. Colm had kicked up Gyrax into a mad gallop and was charging down on the albino with murderous intent.

Roar shook his head in despair. So this was it. He pulled himself up onto Calliope's back, paused a moment to fondly ruffle her mane and sighed.

'I'm so sorry my Calliope. He will be the death of us – I know it. But I must try.'

The mare tossed her head in response just once. And then she walked on proud and defiant.

High above them all, riding a current, almost out of common site, Cuahtemoc heard the call and changed his stance and picked out his first target.

Hannaydale 3057.7.26

There was a trail for all to see and to follow if they had a mind. The moisture from the nearby river kept the road softer than was usual in Summer and so the ruts made by hundreds of carts, the hoof prints of horse, goat and cow, and the tracks of two thousand people had written clearly the story of an evacuation. In haste the refugees had taken what they could and were heading for the Hypodedicus and maybe, eventually, the city of Riverport.

What worried Tregar was not that the people had left their homes but that he couldn't understand why. Using his little practised but competent *sight* he failed to identify anything malevolent, or even dangerous, within thirty miles. That distance was the approximate limit of his ability. Neither was there any physical evidence of any enemy to be found: the town was untouched and the un-trampled crops were firm testimony to the absence of armies. Tregar mused upon the food that lay there un-harvested and the people forced to leave their livelihood.

'I wonder if we will have to fire these fields,' he said aloud, 'The grain could benefit our mysterious enemy.'

'It could,' said Seth, who was now more manly, reassured about the whereabouts of his loved one, 'It could if we left them time to cut it. What we should lay hands on, and burn if we can't take it, is the grain that's already been taken in. And the milled flour, and any o'the salted meat. That's what they'll be after if they've any sense. Mind you, if the wind were right, burning fields'd be hard to cross. We must remember that if we get the chance.'

Tregar was pleased with the lad's common sense and told him so: 'Seeing as ye have all the answers,' he continued, 'what do you think we should do now?'

'That's not so easy,' said Seth and Tregar was pleased to see him grin, 'Not for me at any rate. You'll guess I want to follow the track and catch up wi' em. They can't have been gone more than a day and they can't go fast wi' cattle. But I'm supposed to be guiding thee, not running after women.'

'Ye must do as you see best, Seth. I wouldn't stop ye from going off to find your Rowena and I certainly wouldn'a criticize ye for it.'

'Aye, thy mightn't but me dad and me brothers'd give us some stick alright.' Seth laughed ruefully at the thought. 'I reckon she'll be alright wi' her dad. Best out of it. Don't worry, I'll get thee home before I tek me own way.'

'Good for you. And good for me. My confidence at route finding has taken quite a battering recently. For now though, I think we'd best get back to town before night comes.' He nodded toward the sinking sun. Though they had set out reasonably early the moors had been difficult to cross and it had been six o'clock by the time they reached Hannayford. They were at present a straight mile out of town. Tregar was doubtful about their safety, not trusting his 'Sight' more than he had to, and he wanted to hole up for the night. Seth, however, was not easy about going back to Hannayford.

'It gives me the creeps, all those empty houses; but there's a house over there. Can't we try that?'

He pointed out a slate roof, not a quarter of a mile away, thrusting up over the tended trees of an apple orchard. Tregar agreed and so they rode on till they came to the drive leading to it. As they turned onto the cinder track Seth shouted out, making the wizard jump.

'Smoke! Look: must be someone home.'

He was so eager for news he nudged his reluctant horse to a canter. Sirrah wearily matched them.

'Steady on Seth,' Tregar called, 'There is someone home but we don't know who. Let's be a bit more careful, eh?'

'Sorry Tregar, 'appen your right. Shall we go through t' trees: it'll be harder to see us coming.'

Though there was smoke billowing from the chimney, black and evil smelling, there was no sign outside of man or beast. The building was of grey flint much like the houses in town though this was only a single storey. The black painted front door was locked and very solid and so they took a little path around the side of the house to reach the back door. It was ajar. They halted, hesitating.

'I've baked it black, he he he,' came a deranged and possibly female voice from inside the kitchen. 'I 'ave: 'ssoverdone. What d'you say to that, ragamuffin? Nice and crunchy?'

'Whaaaat?' said another voice, 'Th'art mad. It's bad enough I tell thee… Never liked it anyroad. Sticks to yer teeth. What d'yer say: black? Black? Tsch, never liked it.'

'Mad? Y'cheeky bugger. I'll say I'm mad: mad as a pancake. A black pancake; he he!' Racking coughs followed, presumably after an attempt to eat whatever she had cooked. 'Could be alright wi' a bit o' salt. And tea! Yes, a nice cup o'tea. It would.'

'Oh you're proper mad you. What d'yer think yer doin', baking it black like that? You'd never eat it, not now.'

Tregar and Seth stood amazed and uncertain by the open door. Trying not to be seen, Tregar peeped inside and saw a man and a woman of middle age. The man sat at the table and the woman was peeling potatoes at the sink. There was a foul, charred smell in the room. As she peeled, the woman carefully dropped the peelings into a cooking pot but allowed the potatoes to fall on the floor. Whatever had burned lay in cindered remains on the table and the man was poking it about with a grubby finger.

'Who're you?' the woman said, pointing at Tregar. 'You can't go anywhere without 'em poppin' up. Snooping here, snooping there. Every night! Like they owned it! Pasty faces the lot o'them. Go on, go away. How many times 'ave I to tell you?"

She didn't want a reply. Tregar was about to speak but the woman picked up a potato and threw it at him, fetching him a quite a whack on the ear. He ducked out of the door quick.

'Gone again,' she yelled after him, 'popping in, popping out. If they'd just keep still. Bloody spooks, slavering over my cooking.'

Tregar had seen and heard enough. Rubbing at his ear, he walked back again to the front of the house. Seth followed.

'What do you make o' them then, Tregar?' he said.

'Well, she nearly made mincemeat out of me,' Tregar answered with a grin, 'Madness. Mad as – as pancakes, the both of them. If I had more time I'd try to help. Maybe in a few weeks. But I'd like to know just what she meant by 'spooks'. Who do ye think she was talking about? Something very strange is happening hereabouts, though I can't see those two making any sense of it. Well Seth, do ye prefer this to town?'

'Not likely, but then I can't say I'm keen on either.'

In the end they spent the night in a barn, both wary of empty houses, and as a result they didn't discover the answer to the riddle. For the past week the people of Hannaydale had been plagued by strange manifestations. They began shortly after nightfall: ghostly visions that took the shapes of men and women. There was a smell of death about them, their faces were pallid, and yet they were quite animated. Dozens of them simply walked through the walls and through the furniture of people's homes to confront anyone they found within. They clustered in kitchens to terrify the cooks, they invaded living rooms to scare the children, they made a racket in bedrooms to wake those sleeping. They spied on everything and everyone, taking especial delight in embarrassing their victims at moments of defecation or lovemaking. They gathered in numbers to laugh and to giggle at young boys and girls surprised naked as they prepared for bed.

They were a strange and evil crew and no one in Hannaydale could abide them. The teachers and the doctors and the aldermen and the priests all struggled to give them a name, fought over definitions and floundered when called to explain or reassure.

Some tried to make the case that these invaders were real living creatures. They couldn't be ghosts, they said. Ghosts were remembrances given form, memories caught up in the trauma of the past, spirits that populate the spaces once occupied by lives long since over, all unaware that the world had moved on and had forsaken them. Ghosts, they insisted, were a sad and insubstantial portion of mankind condemned to a status that allowed for no change and no redemption. Some of the protagonists had become quite philosophical in their argument. These spectres now plaguing the town were far from being sad or forsaken. They had intelligence and will and a determination to interact with each other and with their victims; they were entities alive in all respects bar a physical presence in the world. They had wicked intent. It was obvious, the debate concluded, that these visions were most certainly not ghosts.

But for all the discussion, argument and conclusion not one side or the other could think of anything to do about them. So far nobody had suffered any physical hurt but the Hannay folk, allowed no peace, were in a fractious state and tempers ran high. Some people had been scared witless by the apparitions and the elders were worried about the sanity of many more. Eventually a meeting held in broad daylight on the steps of the Hannayford Town Hall ended with the sad decision to evacuate the town and villages immediately and to send messages to the King. They could only hope that the plague was temporary, and that soon they could return to take up their lives once more.

The spooks were pleased to help them on their way. On the first night of the massed march sleep was disturbed by many appearances. Just before dawn they culminated in spectacular form as hundreds of spectres, dressed for battle, charged at the camp. The 'ghost' army struck terror into the hearts and minds of the refugees. Hysteria settled upon them like a swarm of bees and in frantic haste many upped and fled leaving their possessions behind. Those men and women of stronger will staunchly held their ground and were relieved by the timely arrival of the sun whose rays dissolved the visions as though they were a morning mist.

As Tregar and Seth settled in for a good night's sleep, at the cottage in the orchard the 'pasty faces' returned. The couple, far too proud to be driven from their home, determined to weather this storm, played unwilling hosts to at least twenty of the creatures. The wife determined to oust them.

In a frenzy of rage she ran about her house waving a carving knife at the intruders. Time and again she tried to stab the vile things not understanding that the steel could not hurt them. Her efforts and her ranting served only to amuse. They led her a merry dance, screaming in mock terror, shouting out warnings and shrieking with fits of the giggles. It was a scene from the madhouse. The husband, unable to respond to the onslaught but adamant that he would stay his ground, sat in his chair, eyes tight shut with his fingers thrust into his ears.

The noise built to a peak when one of the spectres had the marvellous idea of standing directly in front of the husband's chair, enticing the wife's attack. She stabbed and stabbed as the leering ghost laughed in her face and was pleased to see blood at last. Her torment continued all night and would every night until she was there no more.

Ignorant of her plight, in the wholesome light of day, Tregar and Seth set out on a journey to a place known as Moorsend, the intended limit of their reconnaissance. Here the moors turned to craggy fells, precursors of the Francon Heights which themselves were a minor outthrust of the mighty Dedicae massif.

The journey discovered only more of the same lack of life though in truth the population was ever thin in these severe uplands. They stayed the night in a summer hut built by shepherds whose sheep were now scattered, and in the morning Tregar again tried his 'Sight' to see what it would reveal. He cast out all his memory of recent days and concentrating on the road at his feet urged his mind along it, ever northward. He saw the land rise and fall, brooks and rivers running, heather and fern growing, rocks like frowning brows on the foreheads of hills. He saw no men or women, nor many creatures other than the crows floating on the air like charred smuts of paper as they searched for scarce carrion. At his distant limit the mountains piled up as high as four or five thousand feet and beyond those he could see no more. Halted by distance he widened his search but nothing of importance was revealed. This sinister lack of an enemy seemed worse to him than any sighting could have been, but at least there was nothing to fear for another thirty miles, and that was something. He just hoped that a long journey to the fight, wherever it was, wouldn't overtire the soldiers before the fighting began.

Having seen all they could Tregar decided to return at once to Small Cuttings. Seth brought them back a different and even more desolate route and still they saw no one. After two wearying days, made so much worse by the gloom that fell upon their spirits, they descended thankfully into the home valley.

It was a changed place that greeted them. No longer a hamlet of sturdy grey houses upon green and yellow fields but rather a city of white and khaki canvas and hardly a blade of grass to be seen. The armies had arrived.

'Well Seth,' said Tregar, 'What do ye think your father will say now that the dreaded three thousand are eating his food and trampling his meadows?'

'Oh, don't worry about me dad. He keeps his word and he won't gi'thi any bother. He'll likely be a great help if he can. Let's face it, the King has offered him a lot of compensation.'

'Compensation?'

'Aye, didn't tha know? He's paying well over t' odds for any food you take and some more besides if he can help the army get on. The way you told him about the armies just takin' food had him right upset. He didn't understand. But wi' compensation, and promise of a fair deal in Ayer, and some transport, well, he comes out of it very well.'

'I might have guessed.' Tregar was not best pleased. Was it right that Mador should have to pay to feed armies that protected them all? Where was the patriotism? Tregar was saddened by the King's acquiescence but at least it showed that Mador knew his man. What was the sense in appealing to higher values when monetary gain carried more weight?

THE SIEGE OF ETERNITY

The tall, broad-shouldered man climbed the worn steps to the high battlement. He was cloaked and hooded with heavy black wool and in such surroundings his facelessness made him a mysterious figure. All about him, like an extra cloak, swirled a dirty grey fog: a fog that held the early daylight at bay; a cold fog that somehow weeviled its way into a man's body, into his head; a fog that distorted perception, that made even the most innocent seem menacing.

The man paused to huddle the folds of his cloak closer to him and to look out into the heavy air. He stood at an angle of the stair where, by some fault of design, the parapet ran lowest, a dangerous place exposing head and shoulders above the protecting stonework but an excellent viewing point. Comfortable even, on a peaceful, sunny day, with the spectacular vista of a perfect U-shaped valley all decked with hanging streams and fertile fans. Today there was no sun and no view. It was not simply that the fog fettered sight. It was as if the mist was an acid that had so eaten away at the landscape that it was hard to believe anything was left.

Suppressing a shudder he continued on his way. He shook off his burden of gloom quite deliberately, picked up his step and even practised a smile. He couldn't quite stretch to a jaunty stride but he did try. First tour of duty this day and he had important work to do: to raise spirits, a smile perhaps among the men and women of the watch. They were in a dire situation, sitting on the edge of untold disaster, faced by an unseen, unknown enemy and every last one of them suffering from a creeping despair. The reason for that all around them: the castle, the fog, the fear. What could he possibly do to rid them of fear? How was he to give them hope? Soon now they would be called upon to prove their worth in battle and it was his duty to see that they were ready for the challenge. *His* duty because they were the stalwarts of the House of Sands and he was Jaspar, their Lord.

It was the thought of the responsibility that made him nervous, the apprehension hardly surprising considering how little time he had been given to prepare for such a command. That's what he told himself. Not that it could be said that Lord Ammel had neglected his son's training: when young, Jaspar had the best tutors in the country. What Ammel had done was to follow custom. Amongst the nobility of Pars it was normal for future leaders to be given an academic education until adulthood, another fifteen years after that to come to terms with public life, people, work and commerce, and then at the sensible age of thirty-five the responsibility of power as Lord's Deputy. After that higher office would depend upon the health and energy of the present incumbent. Jaspar was five years short of becoming Deputy when his father died.

It was unusual in those times for a man to die at only fifty-three years and in Ammel's case completely unexpected. He had hunted all day, feasted all night and, as he walked to his bed in the Palace of Ayer that winter morning, barely six months past, he collapsed and was dead. Tregar, walking by his side, found that he could do nothing and though the wizard later explained to Jaspar all he knew about weaknesses of the heart, Jaspar could never really comprehend it. Ammel had been a man renowned for a strength and stamina far exceeding his peers. It was commonly believed, though not properly tested, that his skill with the broad blade was unmatched in all of Pars. This legend gave him an enviable aura of power independent of his position. Jaspar had no such skill and no such aura to help him through and his father's unexpected death left him wanting.

The Lords of the other seven Houses did their best in the short time left to them at that Winter Court to give Jaspar some clue as to what was expected of him. Mador himself had determined to take him under his wing after the thaw but it wasn't to be. Disaster struck in the shape of Masachean hordes charging through the melting snow at Aristeth and soon the King had much more to worry about than Jaspar's lack of training.

It was this lack of training that Mador cited in his decision to keep Sands at Ayer during those earlier troubles: how could the

King be certain the army would follow so inexperienced a young man? Mador wouldn't risk it. Jaspar grimaced at the bitter irony. His inexperience had saved them from a straight fight only to land them in something far worse.

In reality Jaspar was very well equipped for formal warfare. Though he may have lacked certain graces of court, and his skills as a leader were untested, when it came to strategy and tactics he was, without question, a genius. When others were playing at politics Jaspar was playing either the boards or the lists. He was a fine horseman and expert with a lance and often went an hour at the joust before being dumped and trounced, but beside the lists were the Generals' Boards, miniature fields of battle with soldiers of lead, and there he ruled supreme. A sign of a misspent youth said some, a tiresome fascination said others. His skills certainly earned him the respect of the sergeants and men-at-arms he vanquished and the praise of the grey-haired Masters he bamboozled, but they failed to impress more widely. There were certain courtiers who never failed to point up his deficiencies in other areas. They liked to talk about the problem of his immaturity and indeed of his lack of age: there were no lieutenants and hardly a sergeant younger than Jaspar in the whole of Sands' army. And while willing to admit to his abilities on the boards they would always make the point that boards were not true terrain and toy soldiers were not real men and women.

Whether these comments were made through jealousy of his position or through simple concern about the House of Sands Jaspar was never sure, but he was inclined to believe them completely fair. War games always presumed that opposing pawns had equal powers, would always obey commands and the conflict would be won or lost according to the skills of the general. In real life an army of children might do well by their genius strategist, but would they always do as they were told, and how would they fare in a battle with grown men?

Jaspar looked around him at the wet stone and the gloom and hope seemed to drain away. Governed by fear his army was no better now than an army of children. What could he do to give them strength? Not enough. And how strong was this force hidden by the mists that he must ask them to face? Too strong. Here was his first chance to order a real battle and he knew before he began that already he was on the losing side.

'Good morning, Sergeant Stretter,' said Jaspar, raising a somewhat strained smile for the first statue of a man he met, 'Or am I being overly optimistic?'

"Good' is not the word I would have chosen, Jas… My Lord. There's been no change. Not a whisper of a breeze and by crikey it was a cold one last night.'

'Well, never mind, your watch is nearly done. Have a good breakfast then get your head down. It'll all seem a bit more bearable when you've rested.'

'Maybe.'

They were both in some doubt about that.

'It'll not be long now before they start again.'

'No, sergeant.'

They were talking about the drums. For almost a week now whatever it was that hemmed them in, hidden up, un-assailable in the mists, had been making its presence clear. At first the drums were used only to greet movement within, to threaten any who sought to leave the castle. There were no voices, no whoops or cries or whistles to accompany the percussions that echoed through the deathly air and clamoured in their ears, only the drums. There were drums that were not quite snare drums as they had a nasty ringing metallic note to them. There were drums that were like bass drums, but they had a turn to the note as if the skin had started slack and become tight. There was something that sounded very like a child's rattle or the clattering of bones. And there was no music to the way these instruments were used, merely a regular pounding of the bass overlain by the others as and when the players pleased. It was a spasmodic cacophony beat out with malice.

How to explain that noise as it affected those listening? This unseen crew hammered nails into the strong hearts of those within the castle, they battered out any clear thoughts and deafened the reason of all who were forced to listen. The drums said: 'We are here' and 'There is no escape' and 'You all will die' in a language that all could understand. Without the need of words this infernal orchestra shouted out derision and contempt for anything that was decent or honest or indeed human.

And it rang out every day, sometimes only for a few minutes or sometimes for hours at a time. The soldiers of Sands never knew when it would start or when it would finish. They came to hate the silences between. Even now both Stretter and his Lord were in a state of high tension, waiting for the first maddening thump or rattle. If only they could be seen, if only their tormentors would come into the open none of it would seem so bad, but the blinding fog was the drummer's friend and Sands' enemy.

'You wonder whether it'll ever go away,' Stretter said trying to cast out with simple conversation the present and promised fear, 'I've never known fog like it. Must've been at least two weeks. And it's... well, I don't know: putting us apart, you know, as though we were in another world and everything we ever knew before has gone.'

Jaspar struggled to disagree with him but he couldn't afford to let the men think like this, nor allow himself to speculate or fantasise. His task would be made no easier for it.

'Was there nothing to report from your watch, Sergeant?' he asked.

'There was.'

'The same as before?'

'Quite a few more than last time, My Lord, quite a few.' While the day had the drumming to unsettle the army the nights offered a greater terror. 'Some of the men can't cope with it, you know. There were some ready for running 'til the Heir came and put a stop to it.'

'She was up all night again?'

'Seemed like it. And I'm glad she was, Lord Jaspar. Oh, she wasn't having any of it. Stood up to them, she did, cursed 'em all to hell and even took a blade to a few. All to show us cowards just how powerless they were. Walked straight through 'em at one point.'

'Good grief!'

'I know. Never have dared it myself.'

'What happened then?'

'Oh, nothing much to Xandra. Shades were none too happy about it though. They made a big show of not being set back but she'd shown 'em up for what they were, so they gave it up for the night.'

'Few living men can abide her mettle, Stretter, is it any wonder that the soulless cannot endure?' Jaspar favoured the sergeant with a sly wink and the man chuckled despite himself.

'No surprise to me. But, you know, we needed her last night and I'm not ashamed to say it. Never have thought it possible, her being such an argumentative, pushy little cuss, but she's a real hero to Sands now, and no doubt.'

'Gerald Stretter! I'm not sure how to take that: The Heir of Pars 'a pushy little cuss'? Are you complaining or praising?'

'A bit of both, I suppose. Not that I should be opening my big mouth about it. Mind, if I'd been speaking to any other noble I probably wouldn't. Sorry if I spoke out of turn.'

'Nonsense, everyone is entitled to an opinion. For myself, I think she's a lovely, good-natured, placid young woman.'

'Ha! You'd better pack up your sarcasm and stow it, Lord Jaspar: the Lady in question is heading this way.'

Burning torches had thinned the mist within the keep and Jaspar identified the stocky figure of Mador's Heir as she walked the opposite battlement. She had donned a steel helmet and carried, as ever, her long sword naked in her hand. It was a quality blade fresh from the armouries of Ayer and she was eager to have it taste blood. Jaspar looked upon her muscular form with approval. He particularly liked the brown, well-worn leather trousers and jerkin she preferred: a style fashionable among the more able ladies of Pars. He could tell by their sudden changes of posture as she approached that the rest of the watch were equally impressed. She spoke to each and every one of them, doing more for morale in a few words than Jaspar felt he could achieve in a week of speeches.

'She'll be a while getting here at that rate,' he noted, 'but, my word, I wish I could look as sprightly after being up all night.'

'She do put her all into it, don't she.'

'Well, what do you expect? She's found a cause at last after all those years of court nonsense. She's bound to want to make the most of it.'

'My Lord Jaspar,' said Stretter, his voice begging his pardon, 'whilst we've a minute or two, do you mind if I ask whether there's been any news? The lads were wondering, you see, as it's been quite a few days since you sent your last messenger. None have come back, have they.'

It was not a question.

'You may ask. It's only fair, but I have nothing to tell you.'

It was not a real question, there was no good reply to make. When the fog first descended upon them they had thought nothing of it and Jaspar, despite the long lack of replies, persisted in sending out messengers as though nothing was changed. But then the drums began and doubt assailed him. How could he continue to think that his men were getting through. Six days past the drums had been accompanied by screams: the screams of man and horse too near and too clear for him to stomach any more of it. It had been a hard decision to make. His duty required him to keep open the lines of communication but if that meant sending his men almost certainly to their deaths, where was the sense or honour in that? It was immoral to waste their lives. He had decided he must end it. One last volunteer was called for; one final despatch was written explaining that there would be no more. The volunteer, Holmon Cator was one of his best: a huge man of great strength and a fine horseman too. He was given the fastest horse they had. If anyone could win through then he could. And he went so willing, and so brave. His heroism made Jaspar feel ashamed.

Today, five days on and not any change in their circumstances, he had risen earlier than was usual for him, earlier than was necessary. He was preparing to make a decision. It was ridiculous, he told himself after that last attempt to draft the despatch, to be immured by nothing more substantial than fog. Even the ghosts that prowled the night with increasing regularity proved no tangible threat. Not to their bodies at least. But this waiting, these ghosts and drums and the awful silences were eating into the men's souls, eating into his soul like a cancer. He couldn't let it continue: it was time to take the initiative.

'I am glad to see you out so *early*, Jaspar! Bed is no cure for this one,' she said. Xandra's bright, strident voice hailed him loudly though they were only yards apart.

'And I'm glad to see you so fresh,' he returned, 'considering your nightly labours. I hear you have been chasing phantoms.'

'And why not? Paltry things when you come down to it, but still the ghost of fear stays with the watch I think. Ask Stretter.' Her grin was sarcastic but as neither of the men wished to pursue the issue she let it rest. 'I'm fresh,' she told them, 'because I'm battle keen. I tell you Jaspar, the prospect of a fight is what we all need to buck us up. What do you say? Have you decided?'

'Not yet. But—'

'But soon, I hope?' Her question sounded more like an order, though Jaspar knew she wouldn't attempt to assume his command. Not unless dared. Jaspar would not be so rushed.

'What do you think it is that surrounds us, Xandra? Just the fog? Or maybe a ghost army behind it as weak as those you vanquished last night?'

'I am not so naive or insensitive as that, Jaspar.' She chided him with a dip of her head. 'I know there's some sort of power there, something to fear, but in my view, even in the face of fear, we must act! I thought you were the gamer. You must realize you're playing by their rules. The longer you wait, the more discontent and cowardly your army becomes. At least if we attacked we could force some response. We might learn something about whatever's out there. For now, we know nothing.'

Jaspar shook his head. 'Not nothing, Xandra. I can't tell you how I know this, but there is one thing of which I am certain: our enemy is here and is numbered in thousands. It fills the valley below us; it has bypassed the castle and gained a foothold in the cwm at our backs. We are besieged. That is the only certainty we face.'

'Then let us face it now. This siege has lasted forever already.'

Jaspar shivered. She was right on that at least.

'It seems like that,' he agreed, 'I find it hard to remember anything else. The fog is in my brain.' He looked out as he spoke and the others followed his gaze. The blankness held their eyes for a few moments, but only after what seemed like hours to Jaspar could he blink it away. 'It is very strange but I had a dream last night that this siege was eternal. Evil bringing constant war to the gates of the righteous. I suppose that's merely a description of life. Strife never-ending, Evil against Good, in a siege of eternity, and we all play our part on either side as chance decrees.'

Far down in the Francon the first drum roll of the day sang out a confirmation. Xandra chose to disagree.

'Chance has nothing to do with it, Jaspar. It is choice. And besides, this siege is none of our doing. They are evil enough though. You can hear it and you can smell it.'

It seemed to them all that the fog had an unusual foul odour: the smell of putrefaction. Jaspar spat out the vile taste of it and made his decision.

'Well then,' he said, 'we shall play our part. We shall sally forth against malice and see what happens.'

'It will lift our hearts, Jaspar.'

'I do hope so.'

SORTIE

Francon 3057.7.30

Jaspar's plan was to send out a sortie of one hundred horsemen. They would ride out fifty yards into the cwm, carrying torches and kindling, and there make a watch fire that would be visible from the walls. Leaving a company to guard it, the remainder would describe an arc about the rear face of the castle, building more fires in a semi-circle at its extremities. The manoeuvre was designed to bring them closer to the enemy without provoking immediate retaliation, and to push back at the blind fog that walled them in.

The Lord of Sands called a meeting of his senior officers to explain this plan. There was uproar. As a man the older officers condemned the idea as disgraceful. A hundred to face an army? If the enemy but raised its finger only a handful would survive.

'A handful is sufficient,' Jaspar told them. 'Our aim is to gain information, very basic information it is true, but crucial. At present we don't know whether we are fighting men or baboons. We know nothing about them. If there is battle and only five of ours return we will at last have some information that may help us survive this war.'

'At the cost of all that is decent!' cried one of the hecklers, his face a furious red. 'How will you pick the lambs for the slaughter? Will you tell them they're being sent to their deaths?'

'I shall tell them why the sortie is necessary.'

"Sortie'? Shouldn't you be honest and call it a sacrifice.'

'With respect, My Lord, and you, Commander Selby, may I speak?' This was one Lieutenant Biethal, one of the younger officers present, only a few years older than Jaspar and a shrewd gamer who had often taken points from his Lord. 'It is simply this: we have no workable alternative to Lord Jaspar's plan. By the sound of the drumming their numbers are less in the cwm than in the valley. If we send a hundred, a good force, we might just get somewhere. Less and we couldn't cover a useful area; more and I would worry about committing too great a part of our force too early, before we know anything. We need to know *something* before we do anything more than this. I see no other way for now.'

'Rubbish,' Selby growled, 'We could send out a handful of the best scouts. They'd do a far better job at a fraction of the risk.'

Jaspar was becoming impatient.

'Commander, do you really think anyone could leave the castle unmarked by the enemy? Do you believe that this 'handful of scouts' would be allowed to return?' He turned to challenge with a look all the gathered malcontents. 'Does anyone? No! Biethal has summarised correctly; there is nothing to be added. I am decided, gentlemen. What I need now are volunteers, not grumblers.'

Selby's face blazed redder and his mouth opened to express his anger at being silenced by a man who had barely started shaving, but one of his peers laid a quietening hand on his arm. Sense prevailed and the Commander contented himself with a gesture of disgusted resignation before sitting himself down at the back of the room, no longer willing to take a part in the proceedings.

Jaspar did his best to ignore him, realising that the man's lack of respect would deepen whatever he said. A soft chuckle from nearby reminded him that the Princess was present though she had remained uncharacteristically silent till now. He couldn't understand her amusement and so decided to ignore her too. Biethal, his only real ally so far, stood up to speak again and Jaspar let him.

'Yes, Biethal?'

'I will take my company, My Lord. If I may?'

What the devil was he playing at? Jaspar needed all the allies he could get: Biethal was the last person he wanted on this expedition. 'A noble offer,' he said, hiding his panic well as he searched for a way out, 'but I had thought to ask for volunteers from each company and then choose by lot.'

'I beg pardon, My Lord. I know it would be selfish of me to advance my name unfairly in this but I've already spoken with my people about the possibility of some action and they're keen to try it, whatever the risk.'

'Brave people. However, we'll draw lots between the volunteers here, so who else will stand forward?'

Jaspar waited. He wouldn't look at their eyes, considering it unfair to shame a man into acting against his wishes. He waited and still there was no response.

'Not one of you?' he demanded, suddenly angry with them.

'Let Biethal go if he thinks this is such a good idea,' Selby called from the back of the room, 'Everyone else knows how stupid it is. If the Lieutenant thinks he can bring it off, why not let him try?'

'Commander Selby!' Jaspar barked back, 'This surly behaviour must not continue. No matter what you think of me, the rank I hold demands respect. It is neither right nor wise for you to attempt to coerce the Lord of Sands. Do you understand me?'

Selby was startled by the force of Jaspar's reaction but he was a proud man and wouldn't back down. 'My Lord Sands,' he said, emphasising the title, 'I merely advise you of my opinion. I would counsel the King himself if this step were his. This whole idea is wrong and I'm loath to see any man forced into suicide. Let the young fool do it if he wants: he's the only volunteer you'll get.'

'Not the *only* volunteer!' her voice boomed at last. 'Your words smack of cowardice, Commander. Were I you, I'd say no more. I will myself accompany Biethal and his command on this mission and, I give you fair warning, we shall return to shame you.'

Selby couldn't answer her, though he looked fit to try strangulation. Alternate expressions of fury and uncertainty played upon his face.

'Go then!' he shouted finally and stormed out of the room slamming the doors behind him.

Whatever could Jaspar say or do now? Selby would always be a problem but hopefully a successful sortie would bring the others round. For the first time in this whole affair he was truly glad of Xandra's presence, though it was debatable whether her words had actually strengthened or weakened his authority. And the mission? Biethal must go: there was no other choice, and so must Xandra. He couldn't refuse her in such circumstances, could not deny her in front of the others. What more was there to say? It had all been decided for him.

He dismissed the gathering after only a few more words and then took himself off to speak to Biethal's company. In essence the message would be: take care, be brave and come back, because I need you. He tried to tell himself they had a chance.

Xandra rode out at Biethal's side, her sword out and swinging. Jaspar stood on the battlements to watch whatever he could of the action through the cloudy air. He ordered a fanfare as the gates opened, and the trumpeted challenge was blown with vigour, but the Lord of Sands squirmed at the sound they made: it was discordant and flat.

She was excited! No, that was too weak a word for what she felt. The thrill of the mission was exciting but there was much more to think about than that. What a week this had been! It was in times of great need that heroes stood forth and so it was at Greteth where Xandra Bhadrada had shown the world why she was heir to Mador's throne. It was Xandra who had taken the lead, Xandra who had shown courage in the face of prevailing fears. As one the army sang her praises. Xandra had never been popular before. Back in Ayer she'd behaved like a brat and knew it. Too fond of her own way; too bored. While her peers were out in the world a-doing, Xandra had been stuck in the palace condemned to study. No doubt she was to be Queen of Pars one day, but she felt that day would be so long in coming she would die of learning first. What was the point in studying dusty old politics in dusty old books when outside there were real battles to be fought? Her only solace had been legends of past heroism. She wanted nothing less than to emulate the mighty victories or even, if fate decreed, the glorious defeats of Partian history; the only fear was that her time would never come. Frustration was vented on those around her: servants, tutors, suitors or comrades.

Her father, the King himself, was wary of her temper. Xandra considered it fair on the rest that she should make no exception.

How things had changed. Here she was, the hero of the hour, ready to embark upon a dangerous mission, and simply adored by her people. Her people!

That was another reason for euphoria. She was at last the victor in her rivalry with Jaspar. Of course it was still the case that he was Lord of Sands and her Commander on this expedition, but what did all that matter if the soldiers of Sands looked to her and not to him for leadership? She'd never understood why she, the King's Heir, should have to defer to Jaspar in the first place, after all he was hardly a proper Lord. Not even Xandra would have considered crossing Ammel, his father, but Jaspar was only a little older than she was, and surely no wiser. As children they had shared classrooms where she had always been his better in all the finer skills. What had he been any good at? Playing games! It was ludicrous that he should be considered her superior.

She joined the expedition determined to have her way and expected no opposition: he had always deferred in the past. It came as both a surprise and an annoyance that Jaspar proved to have a mind of his own and was not prepared to bow to her dictate. In fact he seemed to delight in contradicting her. She found his attitude insulting.

Now none of that mattered. It was Xandra the men trusted not Jaspar. What had he done for them? Locked them in this jail of a castle. It was the Heir who had saved them from the spooks; it was the Heir who agitated for a sortie. At last he had bowed to better judgement and agreed to play it her way.

She was elated; that was a better word, she decided. She showed it in her bearing: the way she leapt into the saddle, armour gleaming, blade unsheathed; the lance scorned as a coward's tool. She showed majestic courtesy in the way she allowed Biethal the command, but rode at his side lest he forget she was present. She saluted Lord Jaspar as they paced the horses toward the opening gateway, but yet managed somehow to convey the idea that she was taking the salute from him.

They passed through the guardian wall and the trumpets blared, Xandra moved by the defiant flourish that spoke of brave deeds to follow. Noble and proud her bold soldiers. Ten yards, fifteen, and the trumpets still rang in her ears; twenty yards, thirty, and her mind was galloping to vanquish the retreating mists though her horse, in fact, could manage only a trembling walk.

In the space of a heartbeat the drumming broke out all around them, the fog fell thick, smothering sight and hope, and horses, men and women were screaming their sudden fear.

Xandra whirled about in the saddle. The castle had disappeared as if someone had taken it away. All she could see were snatches of horse and human tearing blindly through the packed air. Frightened as much by the sudden movement as by the fog, her own horse took off, ignoring any attempt to turn him. Her clothes were sodden with the foul vapour that rushed by. What in the name of Pidra was happening? She would not believe it was just the fog and the drums that started the panic. An attack on the rear of the column perhaps? Whatever it was, she understood immediately that her glorious mission, her first battle had failed before it had begun. Horses buffeted against her, bruising her legs, as she tugged at the reins to no avail. The pain of it seemed to make her poor beast worse than before and he plunged on in torment. The end came when horse and rider smashed into the midst of a confused snarl up. Limbs and leather tangled as horses collided and many riders were thrown.

Xandra landed face flat in the marshy ground and curled into a ball for fear of being trampled. Hooves pounded the earth only inches away and she sprang to her feet to clutch desperately at rein or halter, but the horse ran too fast and her fingers caught only air.

She was alone in a world of grey. The turmoil of cries and movement died in the unseen distance, the drumming diminished and ceased and a silence covered her like a shroud. The fog, drawing in ever closer, became a cell, became a tomb. She found herself crying. Was it fear? She was oddly more frightened of being afraid than of the present danger. Her prison of grey was welcome in those few minutes of tears. She was a proud woman, and strong, and needed others to know it. No unseen ears would hear her sob, she could not permit such weakness: hidden tears were bad enough.

'Help. Help, please. Can anybody hear me?' A voice from the left. 'Please, can anyone hear me?' The voice a frightened whisper, the owner not bold enough to shout. 'Help me please, my leg is broken.' Xandra heard him try to move, winced as he cried in pain.

'Hold still man,' she said, her voice devil may care, full of its customary bossiness. The tears were gone in a blinking. She was afraid no more. 'Keep talking until I find you. What's your name?'

'Kershall, My Lady.'

'Not so far gone you don't recognize my voice, then. Well, keep talking man, you can't be far aw— Oh!'

'Aaaah!'

'Sorry, didn't see you, thought you were a rock. Can you believe how thick this fog has become. Going to be hard seeing what to do. Let me have a feel down—'

'Aaarh!'

'Sorry again, but it can't be helped man. Going to hurt a lot more before I get you back to the castle.'

'Perhaps you ought to leave me, My Lady; get yourself—'

'Almost an insult, Kershall.'

She had meant to say it lightly but it came out as a threat. Sometimes she disgusted herself.

Xandra splinted Kershall's leg with his scabbard; a plucky soul he tried to talk his way through the ordeal. They discussed what had happened and were not surprised to learn they were both equally confused by the turn of events. Half way through her task Xandra was tempted away by the sound of horses nearby. Her first thought was to catch one but she knew she'd stand a great chance of getting lost in the chase. Kershall deserved better. Her second thought decided her: what if the horses belonged to the enemy? It was much safer to stay hid. She continued with her work, cautioning Kershall to be as quiet as possible.

As she finished off she began to wonder just where the enemy had disappeared to? Wasn't it strange that she had seen nothing of them at all?

Which way should she walk? There was no way of knowing where the castle might be. Out of habit she put her hands on her hips and looked about. It was useless. She could barely make out the shape of Kershall as he lay before her. How on earth was she to—

'By all the stars in heaven,' she boomed, 'that is a beautiful sound!'

Trumpeters on the castle walls were blowing a retreat.

'Listen to that Kershall,' she cried in glee, 'Jaspar has them blowing for us. We *must* get home now. Put your arm around my shoulder, man, and keep your weight off that leg. Ready? Let's try it.'

Very, very slowly, in a weird parody of a three-legged race where the winner is last in, the King's heir and her charge hobbled off in the direction of the trumpets.

They heard voices.

'Biethal! Xandra! Japheth! Sorren!'

Men on the parapets were shouting the roll call of the lost troop. Xandra tried to move on faster. How many would find their way back?

Then, even as hope danced in her heart, trumpets blared behind them.

Jaspar's stomach pitched as the fog wall fell. 'By Gods! It's alive' he cried. Every man on the battlements could hear the drumming and the screaming and the running of horses. *Uovin! Ten seconds and they're gone.* The Lord of Sands concentrated on the sounds, trying to sort out the meaning of all he could hear. He expected the sound of metal on metal, sword on shield but it never came.

They all waited, breathless, a good ten minutes before anyone moved. The drumming had abated; various sounds of horses splashing about, the cries of frightened men and screams were their only news of the sortie until one man, clutching a broken arm to his side, stumbled through the fog wall, twenty feet from the gates. He appeared not to notice the castle but continued to stagger onwards, across the face of the building. Jaspar ordered his rescue and two men dashed from the gates to get him.

The Lord of Sands ran down to meet them, but as he cleared the first flight of stairs he charged into one of his trumpeters, knocking the woman's instrument to the floor. The clatter drew his eye and in a sudden rage he snatched it up and thrust it into the soldier's hands.

'Blow it woman. Blow the thing 'till you burst! A retreat! We must give them a chance.'

An instinct for survival told Xandra to stand absolutely still as the sound of trumpets now broke out all around her. They all blew, note perfect, the Partain retreat. The purpose was clear: *there was to be no escape.* This lost troop of Sands was doomed to wander in the dark until… until what? She was sure there would be no battle. They would be picked off, one at a time. The enemy would gain victory at no risk. *Damn their wizards!* It was the fog that defeated them. 'Don't turn!' she barked at Kershall. The trumpets rang and rang but she knew which direction was right: it must be the first. They couldn't have known a Partain retreat! Determinedly she pulled Kershall onwards, a groan at every step.

After five minutes of madness the trumpets fell silent. Jaspar must have recognised the problem, but he wouldn't abandon them, and the roll call continued. The King's heir discovered by this that she was heading too far to the left. She changed course just in time. Within less than a minute the enemy's mimics were calling too. It was maddening. She did her best to ignore everything, to close her mind to the torment.

Ignoring, she couldn't understand Kershall's sudden reluctance to continue. He was tugging her back, wanting to go back the way they had come.

'Biethal!' he yelled at her, 'It's Biethal!'

Sure enough, she could hear the lieutenant's voice: 'To me!

To me, men of Pars. To me!' But it sounded as though he was calling from the bottom of a well, and the voice grew less clear with every cry.

Biethal was a strong man of sound judgement, admirable in every way, but still she wouldn't follow. He was wrong, confused by the enemy.

'Biethal, Biethal,' she cried, 'Not that way: this way. This way!' Her powerful voice rang clear but it seemed the lieutenant couldn't hear. The distance between them increased. 'Biethal, Biethal, come back!' she called, but the lieutenant was lost to them. She was never sure afterwards but at the time it seemed the last she heard of him was a long and shuddering scream.

She was firm with Kershall, who was whimpering with pain and fear, and they continued on their course. Sure of herself when nothing else was certain she would not be side-tracked. Ahead a red glow bloomed amid the deathly grey. Diffused as it was, Xandra could see that it was the light of a great fire and, to judge by its height, one built on the castle walls. And near. Jaspar had done it: a beacon that could not be imitated. He had thrown out a lifeline to draw them in.

Twenty yards out and she was praying to the gods she scarcely believed in. Ten yards out, with people rushing to her aid, she was so thankful and relieved she was in danger of crying again. Finally, safe within the guardian walls, she was so proud of her efforts in returning to the castle, lost to many, that her fear disappeared from memory. Despite the absolute collapse of her designs she was positively triumphant as her people, as her house cheered their hero's return. What glory!

BANGERS AND MASH

The clattering of billycans and clamour of male voices sounded like a battle and made the yard a seething place. The cooks had set up an open-air kitchen where the high fence sheltered the fires from the wind and the fracas of lunchtime had just begun. There was a constant stream of soldiers flooding into the yard at one end, eddying around the serveries and rushing out at the other. The day was hot and many of the soldiers went bare-chested to keep cool or, in some cases, to show off their muscles, tattoos and battle-scars. The language of these seasoned warriors was indelicate and the air was ripe with crudity. The armies of Anparas and Temor were all-male.

For the women and children of Small Cuttings the yard was out of bounds, but several of the young farmers had gathered to talk to the soldiers or listen to their tales of heroism and adventure. They longed to be soldiers themselves, strong and brave and honoured, not plodding ploughboys. Cookson watched with some distaste the bragging and posturing. Those young farmers, *his* young men, had asked for Owen's permission to join the army. They didn't exactly need his permission, of course, but throughout their lives they had accepted his authority and would even now respect his decision on the matter. They wanted him to say yes but he said nothing at all. Owen could understand the attractions of camaraderie, of glamorous tales, but he knew well that soldiers played down the bad times: the betrayals, the defeats, injury and death. He couldn't decide what to do for the best, but he was determined his lads would have the full story before this fancy went any further. He had called at the yard to ask for Lord Anparas' help, whenever the generals came out for their meal.

The two Lords, Anparas and Temor, all of their captains and Tregar were in council in one of Cookson's rooms on the other side of the house, away from the noise. They had invited Owen to join them but he'd refused. 'Strategy is for generals not farmers,' he told them and explained that there were besides a number of problems he had to see to. He made it plain that these problems were entirely to do with the arrival of the dreaded three thousand. But it was all a sham. The real reason he didn't want to attend their meeting was because he was frightened. Frightened of becoming any more involved. He couldn't become a part of this war, he had to keep it at a distance. And that was not because he was cowardly. Normally he was a brave man but just now, and he didn't understand why or how, just now he had the most awful feeling that this war, this campaign in particular, held in it complete disaster for him and for his family. The feeling wasn't specific but however vague in terms of events it left him with a persistent, over-ruling fear of some intolerable personal tragedy. The intensity of the feeling shocked him.

As he stood there, on his own ground, contemplating this strange emotion, the Lords and the wizard and Cookson's own sons came into the yard to claim their share of the food. Cookson was surprised to see his sons in such company. Seeing the Master of Small Cuttings standing alone the small group put their hunger aside for the moment and came to greet him.

Lomal, the Lord Anparas, was first to speak. He was a man of fifty years or more, spare of frame and quick on his feet; he had greying hair that once was black and wore a quiet smile forever on his lips. Owen liked the man: he seemed kind though serious, fair minded and intelligent.

'Mr. Cookson, Good Afternoon. Will you have lunch with us?'

'I don't often eat at this time of day but I'll take a bite, My Lord, to keep you company. Your meeting was worthwhile, I hope?'

'Long and weary!' This from Lord Temor, breaking in on the conversation. His name was Shaf but Cookson had noted that few people used it, unsure perhaps of the man's quick temper. He was younger than Anparas, maybe forty-five and at his peak. Though short of stature he was stocky and clearly a man of great strength and poise. He wasn't the sort of man Owen could take to: too brash for the farmer's taste, too fond of his own opinion.

'It was dawn when you sat down,' Cookson reminded him, 'So you've had at least six hours hard labour. Long enough to make your plan?'

'It was and I'd wager it'll be to your liking. I think Tregar would be the best to tell it, but after we eat I hope: my breakfast seems a long time gone.'

For politeness' sake Owen nodded assent but he was annoyed. Why couldn't they tell him now and have done instead of wasting his time? He realized though that it was his own fault: he should have attended the meeting. With a shrug he walked with them to the canteen.

'And have my sons been helping your work, Mr Wizard?' he asked as the burly man fell into step beside him.

'They have, Owen, and I can tell ye their help has been invaluable. Really, they know their way around these parts so well. I'm sure they've saved us days on our journey. Especially your Gordon. He must have been quite a wanderer in his youth.'

'He's not exactly old now, but yes, before he married he was always after new places and faces; especially fond of the mountains. I remember we had a few arguments about that but I daresay it was the making of him.' Owen Cookson was proud of all his sons but Gordon, his first, he had learned to admire as a man. He was solid and dependable without being stick at home and narrow minded.

'Ah yes, the mountains, not very safe, but that was what helped the most. I may as well tell ye, we've decided we'd be best approaching from two sides. Anparas will take a route across the River Plain to meet supplies we're having shipped to Coldharbour. He'll make a base there and then carry on up to the Francon. Temor, the while, and I'll be with him, will work a path through the mountains. Ye probably know about Greteth and the Francon?'

'I know a bit of geography but I've never been there.'

'Well, taking all your force up the Francon against the end wall wouldn't be so good if an enemy holds the head. So half our force must come from the South, straight into the cwm behind the castle. I wasn't too keen: didn't think we could do the climb and fight after, but your Gordon's given us a good route and he's sure we can do it. I'll show ye on the maps after lunch.'

'Thank you. But for now – and please don't take me wrong: your plan of action does interest me – but what I'm really bothered about at the moment is the when not the where. How many more days will all this continue?' He indicated the roiling crowd. 'I need to work out how much food I'll be left with.'

'It's an imposition, I know, but the reasons could not be more urgent. Anyway, messengers will go ahead to Coldharbour today; tomorrow the first of the Anparas foot will leave, the cavalry a day later; Temor the other way about. Give us three days and ye'll have your fields back again.'

'And in a right state they'll be, but at least that's one problem sorted.'

'Ye have others?'

'Always,' Owen grimaced, 'but one in particular comes to mind. D'you see those younger lads who've just come into the square, all sorts of odd weapons between them?'

'Aye.' Tregar had asked Lomal about them already. They were greenhorns, joined the army on the road from Riverport. As the army travelled Anparas had ordered a recruitment and many youths were keen to prove themselves.

'Well the recruitment didn't stop when it reached Small Cuttings and I've now fourteen of my best wanting to be part of it. I've our future to look after, Tregar. Small Cuttings will be short of hands and short of husbands too without them. They've asked for my agreement but how can I say yes? I cannot decide.'

'I don't know what you should say, Owen, but there really isn't much time left for debate. Why not talk to Lomal? I'm sure he'll be happy to advise ye. Forgive me, but my thoughts are too full of strategy and magic at present to give the matter proper attention.'

Magic? Tregar's comment took Owen by surprise. Of course he knew what wizards were about but, as far as he knew, Owen had never experienced any form of magic, and he couldn't really understand what it meant. That a wizard should be standing beside him with a head full of spells and whatever, ready to use at a whim, was, now that he thought about it, a bit of a worry. And the thought that *magic* had something to do with the war was worse.

'Those sausages look good,' he said, 'Could you pass us some of that salt, Tregar?'

The sudden change of subject was accepted without query. The wizard's eyes were already full of gluttony. Soon they were both hurrying to catch up with the others, each carrying a plateful of sausage, onion and potato in one hand, and a steaming mug of tea in the other.

They all sat on a garden wall to eat their meal. They talked of mundane things at first, of flowers and crops, of clothes and schools, but it couldn't be sustained and before they had finished eating weapons were mentioned, and then war and soon they were well into the crisis at hand. It was impossible to pretend that all was normal when all around them sprawled the armies of two Royal Houses.

'What I don't understand is who it is we're fighting,' said Seth, voicing a common complaint. 'Here we are, mekkin armies, marching north and still no one'll say what there is to meet.'

'That's because we don't know,' said Lomal, 'Our mission is to find out what is happening in the north of Pars: why are people leaving their homes; where is the House of Sands? We may have an army to fight, or we may not – we simply do not know.'

'Even I have narry a clue, Seth,' said Tregar, 'or rather, nothing more than an idea of Seama's, but that was so vague it's not worth repeating.'

'Oh come on, Tregar! You can't do that. What idea?'

'Seth Cookson! How dare you?' Owen was outraged. 'A son of mine so insolent to his betters? I'll not have it. What were you thinking of?'

Seth reddened. They'd treated him as an equal but of course he was nothing of the sort.

'I'm sorry. I am. It's just, well, it's all so frustrating.'

'No Seth, I'm sorry,' Tregar said kindly, 'My fault. I should either speak or be silent.' Turning to Owen the wizard said: 'Maybe your boy is right to press. How could we expect you to commit your people on such scanty information?'

'But we must!' Temor wore a look of irritation. He'd finished his meat and drink and now stood on the path before them, hands on hips. 'Look, there's no worthwhile information to be had. That's what we're off to get. Better be told nothing than be misled by speculation. Just think of it: you go looking to scare a few bandits but find yourself attacked by dragons. Where's the good in that?'

'Dragons? Do you think it could—'

'I think,' said the wizard quickly, before Seth could say any more, 'that we can stop that rumour from spreading *right now*. It's most unlikely, so don't go gabbling it.'

Seth was silenced but Owen, unable to believe in the wizard's reassurance, said pointedly: '*Something* up there's frightening people. Or they'd have stayed put.'

'Yes. But the only way we can find out is by going north ourselves. That is unless your men have caught up with the Hannayford people?'

Owen had sent some of his own men to intercept the refugees at Lomal's request.

'If you're after starting tomorrow they won't have time to get back here before you go, even if they've found them. Anyway, th'Hannay folk have run before the storm. Do you really think they'll know what's behind the clouds? My lads'll come back with news but I wouldn't expect too much.'

Tregar nodded an 'Aye', Lomal sipped his tea and Temor threw himself down amid the buttercups beneath the wall.

'Do you reckon,' he said, finding speculation easier from a prone position, 'they're Aegardean or Masachee?'

Lomal laughed. 'I thought you didn't want to know.'

'No. I said we shouldn't allow *others* to worry about it. Besides, I was only asking which was favourite.'

'How could it be either? The Aegardeans could never cross the Table and the Gorge, and the Masacheans we know about. You know yourself, Shaf, how difficult it is to hide troop movements over short distances, never mind five hundred miles. It's not on. I know that Seama's theory sounds implausible and vague but it does seem to fit the facts.'

Owen had had enough.

'I give up! This is maddening. What is this idea Lord Seama's given you? I've lads in my charge who want to become soldiers, but I'm damned if I'll let them, unless I know what the hell is going on.'

'You tell 'em, dad,' said Seth. His father glared at him.

'*Vairy well,*' Tregar submitted with a heavy sigh. 'Here it is: Seama has found some ancient texts in the Library on Errensea. They refer te a land called Kyzylkum, a land that lies north of the Dedicae and yet south of the Sea of Ice. It's explained that the people of this land want nothing more or less than to rule Asteranor; all they need do is discover a pass through the mountains for the invasion to begin. Seama suggests they may now have found the pass. There ye are. Can ye understand my reticence?'

'But I thought the mountains ran into the sea?'

'I did make that point te Seama but he more or less asked whether I'd actually been there to find out. Which of course I haven't, and more t'the point, neither has anyone else.'

'Then why's it taught?'

'Beats me. Most of our knowledge is handed down: we cannot discover everything afresh for ourselves. Sailors sometimes stray into the Sea of Ice; few come back. Even when they do they still cannot give us news concerning the whole length of the range. I did think the Geography of Asteranor came from Haslem's day, and maybe even from Haslem himself, but the odd thing is, that key text Seama found, The Song of Ages he called it, was in the scholar's own hand.'

'So it may be true?'

'Yes, Owen, I suppose it may.'

'And the people of this Kizzil place, what sort of people are they.'

'That I can't say. There wasn't much time for Seama to give me the full tale. I do recall one thing: the text called them 'the Creatures of Ah'remmon' and Ah'remmon is supposed to mean 'Evil'. What that actually means is anybody's guess.'

'It's all guesswork! Well isn't it?' Temor looked for support. 'Haslem may well've been the greatest wizard we've ever known but it doesn't say he knew everything. Did he ever meet this Ah'remmon? Supposed to be a God you tell us, but I've never heard of him. Did Haslem ever go to this wilderness place? I doubt it. It's all speculation but even if it were true that's not the real point anyway. How can any of it help us? We still have to march north, still have to face them whoever they are.'

Owen didn't like the sound of any of this. Ancient texts, the threat of war, a forgotten God? Was that the root of the premonition that stalked him? Reality: the reality of Winter, Spring, Summer and Autumn, of crops and weather, of birth and death, that reality was drifting away from him. Ever since the wizard had come everything had seemed so strange, so threatening; or had it all started earlier when… He shook his head. Anparas was speaking.

'Yes, we still have to face them,' he said, 'but may be if this text was studied, we'd get a better idea of what to expect. It's an ancient maxim: to defeat your enemy, you must know him first.'

'You've fallen for all this weird talk, Lomal. There's nothing mysterious in warfare. One group wants something the other group has and they try to take it. What's the point of talking about how evil they might be? I say defence is bettered by counting heads with a sword and not by heeding ancient songs.'

'I'd like to believe ye, Lord Temor,' said Tregar, 'My inclination would make a match, but over that I respect the Lord Seama – how could I not – and he was deadly serious.'

Owen too felt he would like to side with Temor, but that horrible feeling of imminent disaster kept growing and growing within him and got in the way. This Song of Ages must mean something. This hidden land, these creatures of Evil must be more than a story. The threat sang out to him, sang through him. There was nothing anyone could do to stop it: they were coming. With violence and destruction and hatred in their hearts, they were coming. He just knew it.

THE SWORD OF AGES

Small Cuttings 3057.7.31

Morning arrived and Owen's premonition had grown into an almost palpable presence. It went everywhere with him. It was an angel of doom that whispered of defeat. It threatened indescribable torment and everlasting shame. He tried to shake it off but it clung to him like a leech.

He had half decided to tell Tregar about it and was walking out to find him when he was approached by three of the young men who wanted to join the army. At Owen's request Lomal himself and one of his officers had spoken to the lads about the reality of warfare but, despite the gruesome nature of the discourse, Owen was saddened to hear that not one of them had changed his mind. Owen had to agree with their request. He had expected some opposition from the parents but they seemed more proud than anxious. Why was he the only one against it? He told the three, who were acting for the rest, that they would go with his blessing.

So it begins said his premonition.

When he found Tregar the wizard was talking to Temor and Anparas. They were going over the plans one last time. Cookson's plea for help went unspoken and all he could find to say was: 'Good morning. Is everything worked out?'

'Well, that depends,' the wizard said, 'on the weather. If we have storms or fog, or anything extreme, the mountain road will be difficult. But it's a risk we must take.'

'I'm still worried about supplies," said Lomal. "Not at my end of it: if we're lucky, the boats will have docked in Coldharbour by the time we reach the Francon road. Jemenser will have arranged carts and drivers and it's a good track. Anparas will be well fed, but I'm not so sure about Temor. You'll need more food than you have at present, Shaf, and your men'll be sick of carrying what you do have long before you reach Greteth.'

'You worry too much, Lomal. The thing about food is it's a lightening load: it gets ate. The less we have to carry on the last few thousand feet the better. When we get there we'll either walk into Greteth and find Jaspar snoozing or we'll have a fight on our hands. If we fight I can't see us being held for more than three days, so we'll have enough whatever. And don't forget we have carts for the first part and we can do some foraging on the way.'

'Well, if you've time. Hannayford's your best bet."

'If the rats haven't beaten us to it. You said the grain hadn't been harvested, Tregar?'

'Left to rot, Shaf, but Gordon said there's a dried food store near the exchange: fruit, biscuit and such. That should suit us.'

Owen stood impatiently to one side as they talked. Fruit and biscuit! The hypocrisy sickened him. But that was what generals were all about: they'd look out for their men, keep them happy, keep them fed, right up to the moment they get a sword in their guts.

'I am glad to see you before we go, Mr. Cookson. May I thank you on the King's behalf, and for all of us: we couldn't have been received more hospitably. I have spoken to your young men as you asked but I don't appear to have dissuaded them.'

'No you haven't. I've just had a word and they're as keen as ever. I won't deny them. They're good lads and dear to us, My Lord – I'll trust you to give them a good chance. For my part, though I have no great store of weapons, I can find swords for most, and packs, and provender. They'll not be wanting.'

'Thank you, Owen, but really you must keep your weapons. We brought extra gear from the armoury. I imagine we have enough swords for your twenty.'

'And will you give me a sword?'

They all turned. Seth and Cal had joined them, unnoticed till now.

'What do you mean, Seth?' Owen asked, though he understood very well. 'You don't need a sword. You've a duty to the stead.'

'But dad, I can't stay here when Tom's gone, and Gest. Even Geoff Cross has his dad's blessing and he's just sixteen. We can't be the only family to send no one. From what I can mek out, everybody'll have to do something.'

'There's plenty to do at home. War or no, people have to eat next year. Soldiers can't fight without grain for their bread. Why risk your life fighting when you can do something worthwhile back here?' It was cowardice that was talking. And panic. His son go to war? To this war? He couldn't allow it. *You'll never see him again,* said that voice in his ear, *never again, never again; he'll die horribly, never come home.*

'But the family's honour, dad. What's worthwhile and what's right, it's not the same thing. I'd be ashamed.'

'Seth, it's not that. Can't you see? It's…' he couldn't say it. How could he explain this stupid fear? Here was his son, talking like a man, telling him about honour and shame. The boy teaching the father what he should already know.

Tregar's face wore that frown he favoured. Seth and he had become friendly over these last few days and he seemed concerned about the lad. An ally, perhaps?

'Seth, what about your Rowena? It's hard to go to war without a farewell. Why don't ye go find her first? The war won't be away that quickly, I fancy.'

'No Tregar. This is my chance and my choice. Dad's got his men looking for Ro and her family. They'll likely end up in Riverport and I reckon that's as safe as anywhere.'

'And they'll be welcome!' boomed Temor. He was becoming bored with the tension, 'We've set them to preparing for a siege just in case. They'll be wanting as many recruits as possible.'

'You see, dad, everyone has to do their bit. I have to go. Can't you understand why?'

Of course he could understand why. None better. Owen was fighting a war even now: a war between cowardice and honour, their weapons fear and shame. For the moment honour gained the upper hand.

'Yes, son,' he said, though the words could have strangled him, 'Of course I understand. I wouldn't have you go without my permission and I know you'll go whatever I say. So yes, I give you leave. But remember, there's no need to be a great hero, or to risk everything. Do what you must son, but come back to us.'

It wasn't his way, but he felt the need to hold his boy, to embrace him even though this was a public place. Seth wasn't expecting the hug but he accepted it.

In the background, forgotten for now, stood Owen's middle son, Cal. He was watching the scene with a grim face. If he had wanted to spare his father he could have let it rest there. Instead he stepped forward.

'I wasn't thinking of going to war, myself,' he began, 'but I've made a vow that if Seth's to go, I won't let him go alone.'

'Cal, there's no need. You don't—'

'You might see no need, Seth, but I do. I have to go with you, and I will. Look, dad doesn't need me here. Gordon's done with his travels: he'll stay. They'll manage well enough between them. I'm coming, Seth, and that's that. I'll not let you go alone.'

Owen couldn't speak. He realized that just inside, hardly below the surface, he was already crying and he didn't know what to do about it. There were no tears as yet, but they were there, ready to consume him. None of his family had ever seen him weep, and they wouldn't see it now. The hug he gave Cal was a fleeting thing. 'I've something for you both,' he said, 'Wait here.' And then he turned and more or less ran back to the house, and barged through the nearest door.

He hated to show his feelings. It was his job to be strong and reliable. Even when Marjorie lost their fifth child at birth, or when his father had died, Owen had been the steady earth in the storm of his family's grief. So what was this? A wave of emotion was breaking over him, breaking through him. He tried to outrun it but he was weak and he was cowardly, and he loathed himself for it. In the darkened corridors of his father's house the first pricking of tears was hidden, but still he wasn't safe. Desperate for refuge he ran to the strong room: his own private room. He managed to lock the door behind him and light one of the lamps, but then, in the centre of the room, with weapons and gold, the treasures and heirlooms of the family, the safe reserve of the years all about him, Owen Cookson finally collapsed into a chair and wept as he had never allowed himself to weep before.

It was a brutal thing, a physical trauma that gripped him. Convulsions racked his body. He was in pain from trying to hold it back, each sob preceded by a battle within; he fought but failed and the tears won out, to his complete humiliation.

And what a thing to cry over! He should be proud of his sons. Happy for them. They had the chance to prove themselves, for the honour of the family. But it wasn't the thought of them going to war that had him skriking like a child. Men can die a thousand ways and there was little use in wailing over that, but that little devil on his shoulder, that nasty grinning voice murmuring filthy secrets, it threatened a fate much worse than easy death. 'Dishonour! Disgrace!' it cried; 'Damnation! Destruction!' it promised. There was no detail involved, but the knowledge was undeniable, the premonition was real. Disaster had come upon them, and he cried and he cried because there was absolutely nothing they could do to avoid it. This room, his world, the history of everything they were, was awash with his despair.

As is the way with tears, the sobbing subsided, because eventually there was nothing left in him. His thoughts became a little clearer now even though that terrible understanding remained. He began to wonder how long he had been sitting there. A long time. Everyone would be waiting for him. So he pushed himself up, dried his eyes and stepped over to a long thin box that lay alone in the middle of the floor, to the thing that had drawn him to this place. The box was padlocked but the key was in the lock and Owen didn't hesitate to turn it. Inside were two swords, one on top of the other. The topmost was an unusual weapon. It was very long and the metal was black and hard. The hilt was fashioned of the same black metal as the blade but it was decorated with a single blood red ruby. The ruby was nearly two inches wide.

Was he false-hearted? The thought that he should take the sword for himself, and take his place at Seth's side in battle, excited only his fear.

'The sword is for Seth,' he said aloud as though repeating an instruction. It was meant for Seth – how could he interfere? The idea that all of this was preordained dominated his thoughts. Cowardice, honour, shame, glory, they were all irrelevant.

And the sword? It was cold and lifeless and yet it spoke to him. It desired battle, demanding Seth's hand, requiring Owen's complicity.

'Don't be stupid!' he shouted, as if his words could deny the truth. 'It's all fancy. All of it! I've come for a sword to give my son. And that's all.'

He straightened, stood erect, lifting both the bloodstone sword and also the lesser blade that shared the box; he picked up the belts and scabbards, swagged them all in old sheet, and left the room.

He found the others where he had left them. As he approached they all stopped talking and Owen realized that the talk had been about him. His behaviour must have seemed strange. Seth stepped forward to meet him.

'It's for the best, dad,' he said, 'Can't you see?'

'It's all we can do.'

Seth grimaced at the reply. Owen was pained to see the dismay in his son's eyes. It wasn't right. That was no way to speak to him. He tried to sound more business-like. 'Look at what I've brought you both,' he said, dropping his swag to the floor, "something to trouble your enemies.'

First he took out the minor sword and gave it to Cal. 'Here's the blade your Grandfather carried. Fought for Rearden for five years and never took a wound. Let's hope it keeps you as safe. I've spent many an evening whetting it, so it's good and sharp. I kept it proper for my father's sake, and I hope you will too.'

And then he crouched to pick up the other.

'Something a bit weightier for you, Seth. Here, see what you think of this.' He passed over the sword casually, as though it was of less worth than the other, but as Seth took the hilt the sun caught in the bloodstone, flickering off its edges, enflaming its depths. Everyone saw it. It was as though the gem had come to life.

'Dad, what are you giving me?'

Death! It's Death. The noise of the thought rang in Owen's head. He struggled to not say it out loud. He pretended to cough, but Seth neither saw nor heard. His eyes were fixed on the ruby, and the sun's light poured through it, and the bloody rays bathed his face.

'That's a seemly blade, Mr. Cookson,' said Temor, and Owen heard envy in his voice, 'How did you come by it?'

Owen hadn't even considered that someone might ask or he'd have had a good lie to hand. He floundered for a few seconds before blurting out that, like the other, it was an heirloom.

'But older, much older. I don't really know how it came to us but we've had it as long as my father could remember.'

Temor's frown said he didn't believe a word of it. The Lord looked at the wizard. The wizard raised eyebrows but said nothing. Owen was afraid Tregar would interfere. He was a wizard after all, and wizards have strange powers. What if Tregar could read his mind?

Seth was still deep in his adoration of the weapon and so it was to Cal that Temor looked for confirmation of Owen's story. The farmer couldn't bring himself to look at his dark haired son, frightened of what he might say.

'Is that what you've been hiding in that trunk, Dad? All these years. You could've shown us. We guessed it were a sword, but I never thought it'd be as good as that.'

Good lad Cal! Owen could have kissed him. Honest Cal telling a lie, to save his father's honour. Again he felt ashamed.

Tregar found this whole affair disturbing. Standing aside in the present discussion he found himself contemplating the motives of their host: he was lying, surely, but why?

Temor was unwilling to let the matter go and looked all set to interrogate Owen's son until Lomal stepped in:

'Seth. May you use the sword well,' he said, 'Your father has given you a splendid gift. You should thank him.'

Seth shuddered as he drew his eyes from the sword. 'It's a *mighty* gift. I'll wield it for you and for the family, father, and we'll be remembered forever.'

'Aye you will, if only ye can get it out the scabbard afore you're clobbered.'

'It is a big'un and no mistake,' the lad replied with a grin. 'Look at it, Tregar. Have you ever seen anything like?' Seth held out the sword to the wizard's reaching hand.

'I haven't. I wonder if—'

But before he could grasp the hilt a clattering of hooves on cobbles distracted them. It was one of Cookson's men, on a horse ridden very hard. He almost fell out of the saddle he was so weary. The Master of Small Cuttings, looking pale and shaken for reasons Tregar could not even begin to guess, went over to his man and said:

'Now then, Len, what's up? You look like you've been chased by demons. Sit down there and catch your breath; I'm sure the good Lords don't need any bowing.'

Len really did need to catch his breath but he began to tell his tale at once.

'You… You'd sent us to find th'Hannayers,' he gasped, 'so we went… we went down t' Semner as you said, being t' quickest road, but we've come across sommat queer. Proper queer. And horrible. The way he were laughing…' Len's words petered out, for a moment he was lost in the memory.

'Who was laughing?' Seth demanded, 'What're you talking about, Len?'

'Just hold hard, young Seth Cookson,' said Lomal. 'This man has had a strange experience, it seems. Just give him a minute to get it straight in his head. Now then, Len is it? Good. Tell us, Len, what you found, starting with where you found it, and take your time.'

Len gulped a breath. 'As I said, we were riding along t' Semner – the river – and about thirty mile down, just on t' plain, we saw this tent, a red un', but a bit like yon,' he said pointing at a blue tent that belonged to Anparas riders.

'A staging tent?'

'Whatever. Like that except red.'

'Red'll be for Sands,' Tregar observed.

'We reckoned they were Sands. There were… I still can't believe it. There were seven dead men inside the tent. They were stinking and there was blood everywhere. And their faces, Gods above! I've never seen a face as scared looking as that. Well, there were seven dead men and there was one other still alive: a great big man, sitting on his bunk, just rocking himself. He kept like giggling and shouting, and crying and laughing. I was for running. He had a bloody sword in one hand and this scroll in t'other. Look, it's got Sands' emblem on t' seal.' Len was about to hand the scroll to Owen but Anparas said 'I'll take that!'

'What have ye done with the man?' Tregar asked, 'I'd like to question him.'

Len turned red and stammered, 'I'm… we're sorry, your worships, but I've to tell you he's dead. We couldn't help it.'

'What happened, Len?'

'He came at us, Owen, with that great bloody sword of his; and he got Arnold knocked on his back, an' he would've killed him if Bill hadn't bashed him wi' a log. Bill must've caught him wrong, a bit hard maybe, and, well, he didn't move again. Bill's right upset. We're not soldiers, we're not used to killing. I sent the lads on wi' Bill, but I thought it best to bring the letter back here.'

'A good thing ye did,' said the wizard. 'Will ye not open the letter, Lord Anparas?'

'It's addressed to the King but I'm sure he'll forgive me.' Lomal broke the seal, 'Jaspar's own hand. You'll understand if I don't read it out. It is, after all, the King's mail.'

Tregar understood well enough but he was itching to get at the letter. *Hurry up old man*, he thought, and he tried to gain some idea of its contents from Lomal's expression. The Lord Anparas, however, was a past master at keeping his feelings hidden. Eventually he said: 'I think you should read this Tregar, and you Shaf. It informs our expedition. Meanwhile, Mr. Cookson, could you or your sons find Marshals Amnal and Senca, and ask them to meet me in your parlour? If you could arrange some food and drink we'd be grateful. Before anything else though, please see to Len's comfort. He has done us all a great service.'

Tregar had only half an ear on what Lomal was saying but even so he admired the man's tact. They'd need to discuss this right away, but without too many present. Jaspar's letter began on a despairing note and got worse.

My King,

Our greetings would seem inappropriate in our present situation: this is a letter of appeal. I have this past five weeks sent out epistles telling of our progress into the North, and your replies were encouraging. For a month now that encouragement has been sorely missed. I must presume that the leaguer is complete.

It is with a heavy heart that I send you this last brief news of our position because I fear for the life of the messenger. When he is gone I shall send nothing more until there is some change.

This is how it is with us today. We are at Greteth. The fog that denies us our eyes stands unassailable, as it has stood for half a month. Deep in the mists, above in the cwm and down in the Francon, the sound of infernal drums beat on and on through the days. We are not attacked; we have had no sight of the enemy and yet we are under siege so grim that history would not comprehend it.

Each night visions come. Spectres, ghosts walk the battlements taunting us. They are not real, not unreal, their presence ineffable. My soldiers are unmanned: they fear these shades. We can do nothing to them.

But I will not move from this place: It is in my mind that I cannot. Eventually they will have done with their game and the fighting will begin. Until then we sit and wait.

I mentioned an appeal, My King, and it is necessary, as sure as I sit here. This is magic, Majesty, the fog, the ghosts, the drums. Magic, and I understand nothing of it. We need Tregar. How he will come to us I do not know, but we need him all the same.

Majesty, we await your reply,

Sands.

Tregar passed the letter to Lord Temor as they walked back to the house, anticipating his response. He wasn't disappointed.

"Good Gods. What's the man talking about? More damn fairy tales!"

Temor, it seemed, didn't believe in ghosts. Tregar was not so sceptical. He held to the common ideas that ghosts were the bodiless souls of people who had just died, or they were memories of events long past caught in the fabric of the earth. As far as Tregar knew, there was nothing to them, whatever their origin. A shade could not cut your throat. Like a projected image from a Pedersen Light-box, they existed only in dimensions of sight and sound. What perturbed Tregar most about Jaspar's letter was that it seemed to indicate the presence of many ghosts. He'd never heard of ghosts congregating before.

And what about this fog? Temor probably didn't believe that part of the letter either. It did seem unlikely. Tregar knew many wizards who could alter the weather to their own designs, but to do it for so long? Tregar wasn't particularly adept: one or two hours was all he could manage before the rule of nature regained control. Keeping the forces of the world at bay for two weeks and more would be an incredible feat. This was clearly something like the Word of Dissolution spoken on Ayer, that amazing displacement of the common order. Someone somewhere had tapped into a power far beyond the means or indeed bravery of any practitioner Tregar knew. And how could it not be the same someone in both cases? And in that case, both must be an expression of the same strategy.

Tregar had the uncomfortable feeling that they were walking into a trap.

As the Lords walked away, Seth sheathed his sword and the light that burned in its red eye was hidden. Cal laid a hand on his brother's shoulder.

'We should talk to Mum.'

'Tell her we're off to war.'

Cal nodded. 'There is that, but I was more thinking we should tell her about Dad.'

One evening during early April, when pockets of snow still lingered on the high moor, and when Owen's mind was on the lambing, he had ridden out on a two year old called Singer to inspect the flocks. He rode alone as he often did when anything troubled him, and as he climbed out of the home valley he wondered what it was that made him feel so gloomy. The sheep had no answers for him and the ride made him tired but solved nothing. A cold wind burned his ears and the dampness in the air gave him a fit of shivers. He turned for home as the sun was going down and he reached the head of the valley again in the early twilight. His mind was far away when he was hailed by a man who sat on a bank by the path.

'Your help, sir, if you please, sir.'

'What!'

'Your help. I am an old man and have walked far today. Did I startle you?'

'You did,' Owen looked the fellow up and down. He was indeed quite old, with a wizened face and a long, bright silver beard. Age had not shrunken his belly though, and his dress, outlandish to say the least, seemed to emphasize his pumpkin shape. Instead of trousers and jacket he wore a long split smock that reached nearly to his ankles, covered all over with exotic designs of animals on a bed of deep, dark blue, dotted with stars. He wore a length of black cloth wrapped intricately about his head, and on his feet he had a pair of light shoes that curled up at the toes. By his side lay a sheathed sword with a covered hilt.

'It is so cold,' he said pathetically.

'Yes. The weather could be better,' Owen agreed, but feeling that talk of the weather was somehow inappropriate. 'How can I help? If you are looking for shelter tonight you're welcome to stay at my house. It's not far.'

'So kind, dear sir, but no. No. A fair offer, very fair, but my journey is urgent and I cannot afford to stop this night.'

'Then what is it you want?'

'I was wondering, as you are so close to home, whether you would sell me your horse?' The old man's voice, behind the odd accent that made Owen think he might be from Masachea, had a wheedling tone to it. 'You see, my horse was stolen earlier this week, out in the wilds, and I have had to walk since then.'

'Stolen?'

'Yes, you know how it is these days.'

Owen had never heard of such a thing. Not in these parts, at least. But why would the old man lie?

"I can pay you well for the horse."

Owen shook his head. 'I see your need, sir,' he said. 'but I can't sell you this particular horse. Why not come down the valley with me? I've a couple of good mares you could look at.'

'But this young fellow is a very fine horse. Just exactly the horse I need, sir.'

'As I said, I cannot sell you this horse. It doesn't belong to me; I'm just borrowing it for the day.' Owen was beginning to dislike the man.

'Would not the owner be pleased with this for such a young horse?' The old man held in his open palm five golds. Owen was amazed. He was hoping to buy the two year old himself. He'd thought of offering Will Skillern twelve silver pennies for it. Here was a man prepared to pay five times the price. Owen was tempted, but it wasn't done. Will hadn't yet agreed to sell.

'He'd be pleased, that I'm sure, but the selling is his decision, not mine. Why not come down and speak to him?'

'No, no, no. Listen to me,' the old man's voice deepened, *'Listen to me!* I will give you these five pieces, and also my sword for that horse. Are you listening?'

'I'm listening.' And why shouldn't he listen? It was only fair to hear him out.

'The miles are long. Night is drawing in.'

'The miles are long, it's true, especially on two feet.'

'I cannot walk all the way.'

'And the night's drawing in. And there'll be rain later.'

'I must have the horse'

'You can't walk all the way. In the dark, and the rain.'

'Five gold pieces and this sword.' The old man picked up the sword. 'Is that not fair?'

'It is a fair price. Better than fair.'

The old man cast off the cover and drew the sword from its sheath. 'Look at the sword. Is it not a fine weapon? A thing of beauty?' The jewel in the hilt glinted in the gathering dark. The blade was black but with a sheen to it. 'You will take this sword, and take the gold. Pay the man for his horse but keep the sword. The sword is yours, take it. Take it!'

Owen slid down from the horse. He wanted to get closer to the blade – just to look. What a fine thing it was, a weapon of beauty and power. He grasped the offered hilt, ran his fingers over the smooth length of the blade. So fine, so balanced, and not a blemish. It was perfection. Victory sang from its hard edges; called out to the warrior in him. The hilts were warm in his palm. He raised the sword to the skies, a salute to its potential, imagining glory and valour and praise. With this sword he would bestride the battlefield; men would flock to his side. With this sword he would be the saviour of the world.

When he came to himself he was still standing, the sword in one hand, tip lowered to the ground, and the five pieces of gold in the other. The scabbard was propped up against a boulder. He picked it up, belted it on and sheathed the sword. The coins were thrust into his pocket and then he set off on foot down the darkling hill towards home. What choice did he have? The horse and the old man had gone. His only concern was in how he was going to handle Will Skillern.

III

THE EVIL THAT MEN DO

The Gift Of Ah'remmon

An extract from 'The Song of Ages' attributed to The Keepers of the Truth, published Astoril 3069 by Gombret and Son.

It was in opposition to the Gift of the Father that Ah'remmon gave Mankind the Blood Rite.

The King of All That Is was pleased that so many of the leaders of Mankind had bowed to his Rule and so he called to him the most powerful and most faithful of his servants. These men and women were of many sorts: some were kings by arms, some were priests in his service and yet some were men and women of considerable strength, Magi, granted knowledge and power in the making by Zurvan himself. These last, who had turned their faces away from that Bright Child of the Truth, became known as the Black Magi, whose get would live to alter every Age of the World, and never for the good.

And when they were gathered Ah'remmon asked of his own:

'Each of thee is pleasing to my sight and I would give thee a gift of my own hand. How then shall I reward thee?'

It is not wise to ask anything of a god, still less the Lord of Darkness, and many of the people there gathered had the wit to keep silent and to still the words of others.

'As it pleaseth thy Greatness,' was the only reply they could give.

Ah'remmon, whose own people were nothing but as tools to him, gave according to his design, as is the way with Gods.

'My gift is this: I choose to make thee vessels of my truth.'

And at that word he opened a vein in his arm with one talon of his right hand. The blood of Ah'remmon was black like tar. In his left hand he took up a leaden cup and filled it with that blood and presented it to his servants.

'Here is a cup of my blood,' he said, *'the blood of an everlasting covenant with my people; drink of it and know the gift of life. Do this in worship of me.'*

Some have said that the Cup of Ah'remmon survived all the destruction of the Ages but that is of no matter for the blood of Ah'remmon at once became mingled with the blood of Mankind and from that moment there could be no turning back. Those

few he had blessed soon understood the nature of the Gift of
Ah'remmon, and soon understood their curse.

ABLUTIONS

Huaresh 3057.7.27

Benito struggled to keep all the wood, the small branches, the scrap twig and cut, inside the basket. It would twist so in his grip threatening to spill the lot. A wise head might have told him to try carrying less and then he'd be more successful. He thought that through. He knew he'd always been a little slower than the other lads. It wasn't that he *couldn't* think of things: his thoughts just didn't seem to connect with what he was doing. Not quickly enough anyway, and not now with his wits scrambled. No. No, Benito would not think of *that*. All he knew and all he wanted to know was that the master had said to get firewood, and lots of it, and so that's what he was trying to do.

With his arms aching he stumbled towards the house, taking a long route that kept him away from the bad things, much as he'd been stumbling towards the house for the past week. He no longer stopped to look at the destruction. Perhaps all houses were like this now. Certainly all the houses in the village were damaged in some way. This one, their home, had lost a quarter of the roof and half the frontage on the first floor, and one side wall had somehow been exploded into splinters. Benito had no idea how that might have happened. Hidden away in Ma Bera's cellar at the time, he had no idea either how the schoolhouse had been destroyed. These things were mysteries, but he didn't need to know and he wouldn't ask. He made for the front door, which he had left ajar with the quietly pleasing idea that the scent of the honeysuckle clinging to the wall might drift inside and be a better smell for his master and the little ones. No one would have understood if he tried to explain why this would make him feel happy because his words always came out jumbled. But that didn't matter, in fact none of the awkward or mysterious things mattered anymore because something wonderful had happened to them. Now, like the rest of his new family, he knew that he was blessed.

Inside he made his way through a small parlour and into the

reeking kitchen.

'Got it!' he called out.

'Good lad. Ah aaehh, you're such a good lad Benito. What would we do without you?'

The master waved at him from his chair, every movement giving him some sort of pain that Benito could see in his face, shooing the lad and his load over towards the range and little Carla who was busy supervising the pots and pans and bubbling things. Benito liked Carla a lot because she reminded him of his little sister.

On the table the baby squalled as the Signoren fumbled with the swaddling. The baby, their blessing, had done another poo and it was time for a bath. And it was time to change the Signoren's dressings too. That was fine. Benito didn't really understand *why* that was fine and right, and made him feel like the honeysuckle: it just was and it just did. And when little Carla learned to speak again, as the Signoren had said she would, then *everything* would be fine.

Fletton-on-Marsh 3057.7.27

On the eastern edge of Gothery there were others in need of hot water. A bedraggled looking, feeling sorry for themselves sort of a crew stumbled through the salty bogs towards the small town of Fletton-on-Marsh. Covered in mud and sand and rotting weed they were unlikely to enter the town unnoticed. Seama laughed as he mulled over his battered plans. His laughter lacked humour and went un-remarked upon by his companions who understood the meaning of it only too well. Their planned detour via the marshes was intended to deliver thirty or more well equipped men and women into Middle Gothery, all capable of making their way as they pleased. Fate had dealt harshly with this plan. Without food, money, weapons or even sufficient clothing, all was in ruins. Ten of them remained to carry the burden of survival, mostly without any hope of a happy outcome. Their spirits were weary. Some bore the horrors of Tumboll better than others but all were scarred.

Seama's grim laughter was a poor disguise for his grief.

Among the fatalities of Tumboll were counted Bellus and the Mule: his 'family'. The bereavement was nearly too much to bear. Guilt dominated his thoughts. There had been too many deaths. Surely with all the power at his command he should have been able to save them. For some reason he could not comprehend, the power he had come to expect as his birthright had deserted him. He should have been aware of the imminent danger much more clearly; he should have been able to control the pangalori. The power had failed him for the first time in his life and others had suffered for it. He laughed again even more bitterly. 'Pyrotechnics! Ha!' Was it credible? The Great and Mighty Wizard Lord Seama Beltomé reduced to risky tricks with fireworks! What had happened to him? He understood well enough, better than anyone, that the power inherent was not of constant strength and it was true that other Wizards found the power unpredictable, but for this to affect Seama Beltomé was unthinkable. Seama was not as other men: he was the Sayoshant. He shook his head in bewilderment. After over one hundred years of sublime certainty the Wizard Beltomé had at last discovered doubt, the unthinkable had happened and the consequences had been severe. What if the power were to fail him altogether?

'Never! Impossible!' he spat out the words in answer. His companions, not party to the debate, questioned him with looks but he chose to ignore them and strode on ahead, his thoughts locked in a tangle and a fury. He should have been able to save them. They shouldn't have died. The guilt, that is always and everywhere the scourge of bereavement, was remorseless.

Fletton-on-Marsh could be approached by a single log causeway, the major road from the west, or by several criss-crossed tracks from the east, tracks that wove erratic paths on rush mats and pontoon bridges through a sodden land of marsh grasses, dykes and still pools. By one of the latter the company advanced. Only Seama knew what gain there was to be had from these wetlands but he was silent and no one else cared enough to ask. The air was thick with billowing clouds of insects all prepared to bite or sting and the stench of the marsh under the broiling sun was nauseating.

'And about bloody time!' burst out Sigrid. She had not spoken since they left the raft. 'Is that really the town ahead or am I delirious?'

'You're not unless I am too,' said the Captain, shading his eyes with a stubby paw. 'Lot of buildings, wood by the look of it. I reckon it must be this Fletton we're supposed to be making for. That right, Seama? Seama?'

Seama looked up. He had been concentrating his gaze on only the few yards ahead of him for far too long. Looking up at last, and seeing the town for the first time he actually managed a smile of relief. 'Thank the gods innumerable! Yes it is. Do you know I was beginning to think this path was going in circles, and the stench! It's as though it clings to you.' He surveyed his besmirched companions as if seeing the mud and filth for the first time. 'In fact it *is* clinging to you. Us. Gods but I could do with a bath.'

'Couldn't we all,' Sigrid agreed, sniffing and pulling a face, 'but are they likely to take us in? We don't look good and we don't smell good and I don't know about the rest of you but I haven't a farthing: my purse disappeared on Tumboll.'

A search of pockets produced barely enough to buy bread.

Isolde at this moment appeared to waken from a trance; she broke silence only to embarrass herself:

'What can we do? What can we do?' she said with a surprising degree of agitation in her voice. Perhaps, like Seama himself, she had been filling this strugglesome, silent, hopeless march with far too much thinking back. She moved to clutch at Seama's arm. 'What shall we say?' she begged, 'How… how *can* we carry on?' Overcome with sudden weakness she sank to her knees and wept as though everything was lost.

'Steady on girl,' said Bibron as gently as he could while levering Isolde to her feet, 'No need to fuss now is there? Now that we're safe and we've the Lord Seama with us. He'll have everything sorted, soon as you like. That's right, innit Seama?'

Once again Seama did not appear to have heard the question

but now it was because he was too busy studying Isolde's face. He was unexpectedly taken with the sheer beauty of it. The bruises she'd carried when she first joined the expedition had faded and now the smooth skin seemed radiant in the strong summer light. Her anguish didn't mar the effect: the tears rolling down her cheeks made him want to reach out and brush them away. Or kiss them away.

'Well My Lord, what *is* the plan?' Bibron tried again.

'The plan? Oh yes, of course, Captain Farber. Fletton's the answer. If we're lucky, and I'm sure we will be, we shall find a friend of mine,' the wizard reassured them. 'He'll sort us out. The only problem is he may well have given up on us and moved on. If he received my message from the Council he was asked to wait until the twenty-fifth: today's the twenty-seventh of July.'

Angren was frowning. He disliked the histrionics, of course, and he had begun to wonder what on earth this woman was all about, but more importantly than any of that he was concerned about Seama. He worried that his friend seemed distracted. It wasn't like him to be so unfocussed, so lost in thought. He worried that the distress of Tumboll might somehow have changed him. Could they still rely on him to keep them safe, to do the right thing, to always have a plan? Was Seama still in control? So far this mission had been less than a success: how long would it be before the next disaster struck?

'Who's this friend?' he asked.

'Wait and see. His name is Terrance De Vere.'

The noon bell was ringing as they walked into town. People stared at them, some amazed, others concerned, some highly amused. One or two faces were openly hostile. Angren tried to brazen it out with a haughty expression but the few jokers laughed all the louder for it and so he gave up. It would have to be lunchtime! Hundreds of people had stopped work and were sitting on shady verandas, relaxing before their noonday meal. Angren's only consolation was that they were in Gothery and not Terremark where the catcalls and laughter would have been deafening. Gotherians were legendary for their reserve.

Seama took the lead, more confident now that he knew where he was going, and they soon reached the town square. It was an uninspiring muddy place with pontoon walkways connecting the various drab buildings. And yet for most visitors it was strange to the eye: all the houses, shops, inns and halls stood on stilts with the bottom floor of each at least six feet above ground level. Though dry now the square suffered regular and severe flooding. Three hostelries competed for the variable trade but Seama didn't hesitate in his choice. Angren was pleased to see him stride off with purpose toward the cleanest and brightest of the three. The brightness came from window boxes full of colourful marsh flowers but it seemed cleaner because it was the only painted building in the square. In any other town the blue walls would have been sneered at, but here the inn was an island of taste in a mud-smeared, pitch-coated sea.

That the wizard hadn't chosen the hotel for its beauty soon became apparent. Angren saw that the owner, who stood defensively before one of the inner doors of the house, was not so very well pleased at the prospect of having this dirty crew trample mud into his floor mats. His eyes revealed dismay, disgust and doubt in equal measures. Seama forestalled anything he might have said.

'Apologies Landlord, for all the mess we're making. I insist that, when we are bathed and clean, we'll borrow your mop and bucket to make amends. Meanwhile I'd be grateful if you could tell me if—'

'Where the *devils* have you *been*?' came a cry from within as they edged through the door. A tall thin man was pacing towards them from a small parlour on their left. 'Honestly! How you can expect me to spend more than a week in a place like this, I really don't know.'

He was dressed in dapper style with flounces and baggy sleeves; he wore thin moustaches that curled at the edges and a wispy shaped beard that exaggerated his already angular chin. He was just the sort of dandy Angren habitually despised.

'This is your friend?' he asked, barely disguising the contempt. The friend to his great credit managed to ignore the tone in

Angren's voice.

'Landlord,' he said, 'these are all friends of mine. Could you find room for them, and perhaps some hot water? I shall meanwhile open up the windows!'

The Landlord was still hesitating. 'It's all very well, Mr. De Vere, but you'll forgive my asking who's going to pay for them? Would they not be better with Vick's place?'

'Mr. Severan!' De Vere was aghast. 'I must assure you that, though it may be difficult to tell at present, these guests of mine are all gentlemen and fine ladies of Pars. Obviously they have suffered some misfortune and if they find themselves robbed and poor, I will myself guarantee your fee.'

The Landlord looked these gentlemen and fine ladies up and down once more before finally shrugging his assent. 'Well if you say so: it's your money. There are five rooms up these stairs still free. Use them as you please and I'll get you some baths and get a meal started for you. I expect you're hungry.'

'Hungry?' shouted back Angren, already half way up the stairs either carelessly or deliberately dropping a trail of mud behind him, 'I'm so bloody ravenous I could eat a battered donkey. On second thoughts, better make that two.'

The Landlord shook his head in disbelief before retreating into his kitchens. As he went he was muttering to himself something about mops and buckets.

There were ten of them to share five bedrooms. Angren was happy to room with the wizard and generously awarded Seama the single bed as opposed to the couch in exchange for the first bath.

Edro and Piedoro both offered themselves as roommates for any of the ladies but didn't seem displeased to end up sharing with each other. Bibron and Garaid had become firm friends over recent days and they took a third room with no argument. There was a small problem then with the other two. Sigrid made it very clear that she wouldn't care to share with Ruspa. Berta said something like: 'I don't blame you' and neither was prepared to let Isolde out of their sight. Ruspa couldn't have been less interested. He stepped into the smallest of the rooms still on offer and closed the door behind him. The women considered what they had been left with.

'How the hell are we going to sleep three in there?' Berta wanted to know. With its single inadequate bed, no couch and precious little floor space the others had to concede she had a point.

'You don't fancy snuggling up together then,' said Sigrid with a sly wink.

'What with you and Is? Well I might, but I reckon I'd be the one ending up on the floor when things warmed up.'

Isolde blushed at the suggestion.

'Only joking,' said Sigrid.

'Perhaps I can help?' De Vere was on the stairs behind them. 'My apartment is really quite commodious. I'm sure the three of you would be happier there than here.'

Sigrid looked at him very suspiciously.

'I would of course sleep here. Quite sufficient for my needs.'

'You are kind, Mr. De Vere,' ventured Isolde timidly.

'Oh, please don't mention it.'

'Alright we won't,' snarled Sigrid, 'But thanks all the same. I did think you were about to offer one of us a bunk for a dunk. Good to be wrong for a change.'

Berta laughed out loud and Isolde turned pink once more.

De Vere smiled.

The room De Vere had gifted them had a huge bed of feather and down and a fitted bath large enough to swallow even the mighty Berta. The water arrived. Sigrid and Berta raced to be first in. Stripping off their clothes as fast as weariness would allow they were surprised to see Isolde sit on the far side of the bed and turn her face.

'We were only joking before,' said Sigrid already naked. 'No matter how pretty you are, I'd rather have a man in my bed. Or are you shy?'

'Let her alone, Sig'. She's not shy.' Berta, not known for her sympathetic nature, nodded at the quaking shoulders.

Sigrid raised eyebrows but said nothing. Berta went over to

the young woman and made to put an arm around her shoulders. Isolde jumped away startled and then burst into tears.

'I'm sorry,' she said, 'So sorry. I didn't mean… I don't know what's the matter with me. I'm not normally like this. I know I could never be as strong as you—'

'Not everyone needs muscles, little'un,' Berta said, not understanding at all.

'No, no. I mean that you don't ever cry, nor Sigrid. These horrible days don't seem to have touched you, but I… I've… It's all been… Oh Gods! Why am I so weak?' She continued to sob.

Sigrid wasn't over fond of soft women but the days on Tumboll had affected everyone. Aboard the Cottle Isolde hadn't been particularly lively but she had joined in when invited. On the island she'd seemed a little changeable, coming up with ideas one minute, silent the next. But then what was there to say? Thinking back Sigrid remembered that Isolde had been brought to the compound some time after everyone else, her clothes had been bloodied but she was apparently uninjured. She hadn't offered anything to explain. Sigrid frowned.

'What happened to you on Tumboll?' she asked.

Isolde turned white, and then pink, and hid her face and her tears.

'Bastards must have raped her,' Berta growled with an angry look on her face that would have made most men mortally afraid.

'No. Not quite that.' Isolde mastered her tears, 'But they… they touched me.'

'You can take a little pawing, love,' said Sigrid, 'You must've… you're not a virgin? Oh. So… Look some men will always do these things. Just remember, they haven't actually hurt you, not physically, and that's the main thing.' Sigrid's attempt to comfort trailed away as she realized she could think of nothing to say that was not either fatuous or insulting. Berta took a more pragmatic line:

'Come on, little 'un, let's get you bathed. You'll be feeling dirty but dirty can always be made clean.'

'It's not that!' Isolde cried, 'Not that. Not what they did to me. It was those poor men!'

She went on to tell them of how two of the sailors had done their best to protect her but had been overcome. She was stripped by two of the Halfi but not raped. They seemed content to explore her body and when they became aroused they decided to use the sailors. They were showing her what they would like to do with her, what they would do later, when they were allowed. Both men were buggered many times and then, almost as an afterthought, they were tortured to death. Isolde was forced to watch everything.

'Every time I close my eyes I see it all over again. It was my fault they suffered so much.'

'Don't be silly. All the sailors were killed. Not one had a clean death. You can't blame yourself for what the Halfi did to them.' Sigrid was furious. 'Men can be unbelievably horrid, love,' she told the girl, 'and there's no explaining it.'

Along the corridor the conversation was very different. De Vere had gone to speak with Seama and, by reason of proximity, with Angren as well.

'I can see you've been having adventures while I have been sitting here cooling my heels. I can tell you, it was most uncomfortable.'

'Uncomfortable!' Angren exploded. Luckily he had left the bath and was towelling himself dry otherwise De Vere would have suffered a dousing. 'Do you think we've been on a jolly or something? Fifty dead, Mr De Vere, that's what we're talking about. Sort of *adventure* you're looking for is it? I can tell you, us few are bloody lucky to be alive and in one piece.'

De Vere wasn't cowed by Angren's reaction. 'Now sir,' he said, 'there's no need to get angry. Perhaps I did use an unfortunate word, but all I am trying to say is that my situation was made uncomfortable by reason of those who were spying upon me.'

'Spying Terrance?' Seama asked mildly. 'And are we being watched even now? I hope not.' He was still in the tub, disinclined to hurry before the water got cold.

'As ever, my dear wizard,' Terrance reassured him, 'your timing was impeccable. I arrived here with the excuse that I had business with a bog-trotter I know.'

Angren was baffled. 'A bog-trotter?'

'Works on the marshes. This one's a dealer in bog-oaks, name of Rojo. Now the— Bog-oaks? Just what they sound like: a very hard wood they find preserved in the peat. As I was saying, the problem was he didn't turn up when he was supposed to. And that left me twiddling my thumbs and raising suspicions. I did a little trading by the by but nothing that could justify my being here so long. Someone was bound to get curious. You know how it is these days: there are at least two spies for every interest in every little mud-hole in the world. The difficulty is in working out who they're spying for.'

'So what happened with these particular spies?'

'Well, I was getting to that. Four days ago I noticed that a couple of odd-bods had come to town. And they were asking questions, wanting to know if there'd been any sign of people coming through lately – not from inland, you understand, but from Pars *across the River*. What people must have thought about that I don't know. It was hard to make out whether they were very bold or just completely incompetent and rather stupid. But now I think they must have had news of Mador's little expedition. Of course someone must have mentioned that I'd been hanging around as though waiting for something, and soon they were everywhere I went, one or the other or both. Perhaps they thought I had you hidden away somewhere and if they watched closely enough I'd lead them to you. Then after a few days of nothing happening I think they became confused and a little weary with the waiting. Eventually they decided to interrogate me. This was yesterday evening. I was at my meal when one of them, a great fat fellow, came to sit at my table, if you please. He asked me all sorts of stupid questions, in a so-called casual fashion, buffoon that he was, and I had to spend the whole meal fending him off. I tried my best—'

'Which I am sure was excellent, Terrance,' Seama said rising from the lukewarm depths, 'Pass me that towel, would you?'

'Well thank you,' Terrance smiled, a touch ironically. Angren squirmed in distaste. The dandy ignored him and continued:

'But I would have had a hard time of it if my bog-trotter hadn't turned up. Honestly this fat man was becoming quite aggressive but he backed off pretty quick when Rojo plonked himself down and started haggling. In fact he left us to it. Either he found the conversation boring or he simply thought the better of it – Rojo being six foot five both ways may have had some bearing on the matter. To end my tale, my dear wizard, we are now safe. After he had left the inn I followed. He went to meet his partner in crime, an evil looking weaselly sort, rather like that fellow Ruspa though much more ill-favoured, just outside the public stables. They had a bit of a to-do. Quite an argument in fact that ended with the fat man boxing the weasel about the ears. I couldn't get close enough to hear the substance of the quarrel but the outcome was that they both took horse, not theirs I've since discovered, and rode away like the clappers. I'd like to think I've thrown them off the scent and that they've lost interest in me but we cannot be sure.'

'Huh!' said Angren, 'What if they're just waiting on the road for us?'

Terrance smiled once more. 'Oh I'm quite sure they're not. You see it was still an hour or so before dark when they left and the land hereabouts, you may have noticed, is somewhat flat. I climbed the bell tower on the Town House and watched them all the way to Fourway Cross. They went south: not our route, I fancy.'

'Could've just said yes,' Angren muttered, put out that the dandy was obviously efficient.

'Good!' said the wizard, 'Now, if the Landlord is ready, I could do with something to eat, and over dinner we can decide on where we go from here. You have lots of money I hope, Terrance?'

'Well, I have enough, but that's no excuse to be extravagant. How much will you need?'

'Oh, a modest sum: we need horses, weapons, food, clothes—'

Terrance, paling at the thought of so great an expense, was spared for the time being by a knocking at the door. It was followed by the appearance of Ruspa's sharp face.

'A word, Seama, if you don't mind.'

'Come in Ruspa, but let's make it quick: we're all hungry.'

Ruspa was in and, not a person to bandy words, he told Seama what it was he wanted:

'I need money. I have to buy a horse and provisions, and I'll need more as well to get me to… to get me to my destination. And a sword would be useful.'

'We were about to discuss this over dinner, Ruspa. We are all in the same predicament.'

'Can't wait. I need it now. I've no time for dinner parties. I have to be away before dawn so I'll need to buy a horse immediately.'

'Your mission seems urgent?'

'As every mission, no doubt, but I have further to travel than most, I think.'

'Well Ruspa, I won't ask for an explanation. Mador has his own plans. Terrance, how can we help our friend?'

Terrance's brow wrinkled. 'It will be difficult to find a horse today. Tomorrow is market day and I was hoping to save some money by buying a dozen nags together. Now, let me see; the Landlord has a horse he might let go. I'll see what can be done. I trust Mador will be considerate in my recompense Seama? We are likely to use all I have with me and you'll need more.'

'I agree. Is Mr. De Vere's offer good enough Ruspa?'

'I'll need to see the horse.'

'Why don't you both go now. We'll meet again downstairs.'

With a look of resignation on De Vere's face and an eager light in Ruspa's eyes they went.

Their meal was, surprisingly, splendid: the presentation immaculate, the food varied and elaborate; Angren was pleased with the quality of the beer and the wine was 'remarkably good considering', according to De Vere. A pity then that most of them were so ravenous they wolfed the whole lot down in minutes. Savouring the delicacies was not on their menu. Only Isolde and De Vere achieved anything like gentility in their table manners. Seama had asked for the meal to be served in a private room so they could talk freely but the food was more important and conversation brief.

Decisions were made over dessert. Seama of course would continue his journey into the West and Angren with him. Sigrid and Berta had been heading for Eastern Aegarde on a simple mission to gather information on allegiances in Kelle, Eszola and Ciudad Valdez. They readily agreed that travelling in numbers through Gothery would be no bad thing and decided to travel with Seama's company at least as far as the border. Bibron was in a misery over the murder of his crew on Tumboll. He felt that he'd let them down. The thought of returning to Riverport and being asked to take another ship horrified him. He needed a break from the sea. The wine helped him explain his position, several times over, and he ended by asking whether he could make the company five. To the Captain's amazement and great pleasure the sailors, Edro and Piedoro, declared that if, as honourable men, they could never mutiny at sea they could never betray their Captain as he struggled with the land. They too intended to follow Seama's cause, whatever that might be. Angren grinned a wry grin and wondered whether their decision might not have been a little influenced by the prospect of keeping in with Sigrid.

Isolde nobly decided to continue her mission alone.

'I must go to Astoril,' she told them determinedly. Her shaky voice ruined the effect. The court of King Sirl II at Astoril was no dangerous place under normal circumstances but it was clear to everyone that Isolde was not up to the task. She seemed incapable of putting aside the trauma of Tumboll – how would she cope alone in a foreign court? Her given task required a degree of calm Isolde could not muster.

'I had thought,' said Seama, 'that we could ask you to undertake a more important mission.'

'But the King needs me to—'

'Mador will understand that your plans must change.'

'But what would you have me do instead?'

'We have suffered a major setback and the King knows nothing about it. Could you be our messenger to the King?

He must be told about Tumboll. We can't have Riverport or Coldharbour taken by surprise.'

'Do you really think Mador would prefer—'

'Yes of course he would,' cried De Vere, 'And I can put you in the company of a friend of mine who'll see you safe into Pars. You shall ride out with me tomorrow.'

And that was that: Isolde did not need asking twice. Angren found himself wondering whether Isolde might be sharper than she pretended to be but he concluded she was best out of it. He for one wasn't going to spend his time nurse-maiding, no matter how pretty the baby.

'Thank you,' she said, her complexion flushing easily to that delicate shade of pink once more. 'Thank you all.'

Ruspa took this exchange as his cue to leave.

'Mador needs news urgently, and not just about Tumboll. I wish you all luck and speed; it's time I started.'

They all wished him luck in return and he left them to it. Though each of them would have found it hard to say why, not one of them was sorry to see him go.

'And what about you, Garaid?' Seama asked then, 'What is your mission?'

The big man grinned. 'I'll tell you, but you won't like it.'

'Oh?'

'At the start I was to help Anparas in Gothery setting up communications, but when the new orders came I was given another job.'

'Which was?'

'Mador said: "Stay with the wizard: I want to know what he's up to."'

Angren and a few of the others burst out laughing but Seama wasn't well pleased.

'Did he now? Did he really!' he said, 'And I thought Mador trusted me.'

DOCTORING PHILOSOPHY

Astoril 3057.7.27

Dr. Bliss smiled benignly at the servant carrying the tray of boiled ham and soft bread rolls into the antechamber.

'Very thoughtful of you,' he said.

The servant raised an eyebrow. 'It is the *King's* supper.'

The smile left the doctor's face. 'The King wishes to sleep now. He will need no supper. The draught I prepared will do him more good than cold meat and breadcakes. As I have already explained. When he wakes you may serve him soup – a vegetable broth, no meat, and make sure it isn't too hot.'

The servant shrugged his assent and it was only as the man turned away that Bliss caught the look of frustration and quiet anger on his face.

'Carl,' he said softly and the servant froze, 'Do be very careful. You know that I carry the King's baton.'

The servant took a deep breath. Bliss wondered which way he would jump.

'Well Carl?'

The servant, without turning, nodded curtly. 'Yes sir, as you command it,' he said and then left the room, taking the food with him.

As I command, indeed! The doctor's habitual smile became a plump grin. *All as I command. It is so easy,* he thought, *even with the Chancellor. Not one of them has the guts to face me. Much safer this way than having Acchulpa copy him. Better to let her loose on the Partians than waste her talents here. And besides, one really cannot trust her. Especially when she's hungry!* Bliss shuddered at the thought. Her tastes were not to his liking: too much blood and too much pain were involved. Bliss was somewhat squeamish for a Doctor.

He giggled aloud this time. It was hard for him to credit how easily people could be taken in. In this country people with great minds and tremendous energy were changing the world around them as though they were demigods. Science was their byword, unravelling the mysteries of the universe their aim for the profit of all. And yet there was not one of them who could see past all the hokum. They all wanted to believe. Any crackpot philosophy, any quackery that came along, so long as it promised health and long life, was embraced like a new bride. They had to have it, they would plumb its depths and the more they had, the more they wanted, right up until the point that the medicine killed them. That was the interesting thing about these new scientists: they so needed affirmation that anything merely dressed up as science automatically gained their allegiance. Idiotically, they had a corresponding dislike of magic and magicians. As if science was something different! 'Dr. Bliss' the medical expert suited them an awful lot better than 'Tarangananda uh Bib, the Wizard Balipurum'. So be it! The Smiling One would use their preferences against them.

The King had been very welcoming when Bliss managed to get himself introduced as 'the greatest medical scientist of the age.' Keen, in fact, to beg treatment for the powerful headaches that had plagued him for a month or more. Not that Sirl was as foolish as the rest. He knew and understood the power of Errensea and would never dismiss the idea of magic. But surrounded by all these scientists and engineers, who filled his court with petitions for grants, bursaries and royal warrants for their various endeavours, there was very little chance of Sirl making the right connection. That the headaches might have been anything out of the ordinary never occurred to him. The thing about magic was that, if done properly, the victim rarely realised what was happening to him. The best magic did not show its hand: it wasn't called 'the occult' for nothing.

The Doctor took a quick look into the King's bedchamber. Sirl was motionless on the bed, his face grey with the poison he had just taken, so frail now it was no wonder that the servants were upset. Tomorrow he would have to give the King something to make it seem that he might actually be getting better at last, something to put a bit of colour in his cheeks. For today however he would have to suffer a little more.

Back in the antechamber one of Sirl's clocks clanged out

the ninth hour. Bliss closed the door and locked it. He picked up a small hand bell from the table beside the door and rang it to summon a guard. While he was waiting for the man to arrive Bliss passed his hands up over the doorjambs and lintel, humming a small tune as he did so. The guard would doubtless be very trustworthy but Doctor Bliss was not the trusting type. Nobody would be going in and nobody would be coming out. Not for a while yet.

Some time later a stout figure, silhouetted by the light of one of the new gas lights over on the Market Road, rapped on the iron-studded door of a large terrace house in the 'merchants part' close by the Stralli market, an in-between sort of place that was not quite respectable but certainly not rough. It was a suitable destination: the plump man was an in-between sort of character too. Bliss looked up and down the street. Nothing. He had been tracked along the genteel avenues surrounding the palace by two ill-disguised policemen. Their incompetence had made him sigh. He had taken them down into the Lanes, a labyrinth of small shops and studios. What chance did they have? Here were jewellers and glassmakers, painters and printers, carpenters and joiners; here were dressmakers and shoemakers, milliners and drapers, devisers and builders: craftsmen and merchants of every imaginable persuasion. Bliss was entranced by their variety, impressed by their constant endeavour and amazed by their energy. It was already past the tenth hour and yet lights still shone in all the windows, the alleys were full of comings and goings, and the calls of the bobyboys and the whirr of their wheels filled the air. Did these people never stop working? Still, this dedication to labour and enterprise proved to be most helpful. With just a little magic, in such lively surroundings, it was a simple matter to confuse any inquisitive eye. The Doctor had lost his markers in a matter of minutes. Of course, he would have preferred more of a challenge but it was just as well the Chancellor's men were such poor spies: Tys Heald was looking for anything he could use to damage the Doctor's standing with the King. Making a connection between Bliss and the extremely dubious resident of this house could be just what he needed.

The door remained unopened. Bliss reached for the knocker and the sound of it echoed through the street. There was still no reply and the Doctor was becoming quite irritated. In a sudden fit of fury he had raised a hand to force the door but at the last moment held back: inside the bolts were pulled, a mortise lock turned. His fingers curled into a fist as the door opened.

'Do you really think they are so stupid,' he hissed, 'that you may let me stand openly at your door?'

The masked man before him made the slightest of shrugs.

'You can stand where you please, uh Bib. It is no matter to me whether you are seen or unseen. Come in.'

Zaras turned stiffly and led the way into the house.

'I have not fed for some time, Doctor, and this body is suffering the consequence. Have you brought me anything?'

They entered a well-lit drawing room.

'Yes, but my supply is running low. Can you not use more traditional means?'

'It is difficult without Franner and Creel. I had thought they would be here by now. It was... inconvenient to me that they had to go.'

Bliss was in no mood to be rebuked. 'It was important at the time and I had no one else.'

'But seven days, uh Bib! See what it does: this atmosphere is ruining me.'

Zaras removed his mask. Bliss examined his host more closely. The face revealed had the pallor of death; King Sirl looked healthy by comparison. Of course Zaras had never looked anything like normal, nor any of the Exiled, but he looked better than most. Now, however, Bliss could see that if something were not done soon the damage to the skin would be irreparable.

'The Necromancer has promised me a new batch, Zaras, but it seems to me that the General is pressing his claim for all they can bleed. It may take some time.'

'I do not have time. Seven days without anything...'

'Yes, yes, I see. Words will be spoken. I would go myself but I cannot leave just now. The Chancellor is waiting for the slightest chance. Take this.'

A glass phial had appeared in Bliss's hand. It contained a thick brownish liquid. 'I am amazed that it works. The Necromancer claims it has lost none of its potency since the first drop. The Halfi were very lucky to find her. It is just a pity it does not work so well for the Exiled.'

'A pity indeed. Though I prefer the other way. There is nothing like *fresh* blood.' Zaras took the phial and moved over to a small table. An odd looking contraption stood there, a combination of leather straps, a tapering bottle with a bladder at the wide end and a spike at the other. Using the straps, Zaras attached the bottle to his left arm with the spike poised over the dark green vein at his wrist. Bliss noticed that without the need of a ligature the vein was already hugely distended. The flesh around it looked like putty. Zaras removed the bladder, tipped in the liquid from the phial, so thick that it took a minute to transfer completely, and then reattached the sump to the bottle.

'Let us make ourselves more comfortable. This will take some time.'

They sat in chairs before a cold, unmade fireplace. Bliss was already feeling queasy and had to look away when Zaras plunged the spike into the vein and tied off the top of the bladder with the one remaining strap. Over the course of the next hour he would progressively tighten the strap to maintain the pressure until the bottle was empty, and each time he did so Bliss found himself contemplating his fingernails or the pictures on the walls. Zaras, too caught up in the process, did not appear to notice the wizard's discomfort.

'Have you had word from them, my procurers?'

Bliss felt almost regretful he had thought of using the pair. They were Zaras' men, not his, but when the word came that someone or something important was expected in such a backwater as Fletton he had to know what was going on. Creel and Franner were at hand, attending to Zaras as the Kumite made his regular report. Bliss hadn't realised fully what they did for him.

'Yes. It is partly the reason I am here. They claim there was nothing, no one. It was a garbled message I had from Franner. I wish I had never given him a stone: he has no skill – not in communication at any rate.'

'He has other talents.'

'So you say.' Bliss paused to consider the innuendo. Franner's talents were certainly useful but the Doctor felt at liberty to find them distasteful. 'I have sent them on to Slaney, and that is where you should meet them. Ekstrom remains elusive but there is someone there I would like you to meet and, shall we say, engage.'

'More agents?'

'Zaras, you are hardly the perfect spy. I have a man who would sell his mother, daughter and wife to finance his ambitions and he knows our mark very well. More than that, he claims to have run into him in Pars.'

Zaras paused before replying. His hand pulled on the strap. Even on such an un-expressive face it was possible to discern a certain hunger. 'You're sure Ekstrom has the answer?'

'If anyone has. He is well motivated and has the skill. I think it is only a matter of time before this atmosphere of ours will begin to suit you better.' Bliss favoured Zaras with a pleasant smile, almost as though he liked him. 'It is difficult, sometimes, to correctly understand people, to identify their problems and needs. We are all too caught up in our own concerns. For example, I had until now surmised that the problem of the Exiled, your problem, derived from the poisonous air of that hidden land and not from the good clean air of this existence.'

'Water is death to men and air death to fish.'

'A simple matter of mechanics then.'

'There is nothing simple regarding this mechanic. According to the science I was taught, fish and men both need the same thing: a gas, you would say, called Oxygen. They exist in different mediums but Oxygen is everywhere on this Earth, this Earnor as you call it. Each has developed a means of extracting the oxygen from the fluids they travel through. But the strange thing is that as much as they, man or fish, need this oxygen that they might live, the same thing is steadily killing them. I believe that our bodies in Exile have been made to continue without Oxygen, or that they have learned to exist without it. And now this life giving gas has become a poison to us.'

'I see.' Bliss paused to reflect. He was something of an expert with poisons but he had never considered that the good air itself could be pernicious. 'And what is this poison actually doing to you?'

'Everything becomes slow for us. In exile we seem able to move and react more quickly. The blood we have is more suited to the atmosphere of eternity. Instead of bringing us energy Oxygen burns in our veins. I am no chemist and was never any sort of scientist but this seems to be the truth.'

'But you have the antidote in your... procurements. And in this drug from the Necromancer's spider woman.'

'Antidote would be too strong a word.'

'What surprises me—'

At this moment Zaras noticed that the 'antidote' was seeping out over his arm and he reached down to force the spike deeper into the vein. Bliss winced and looked away.

'Yes? You were saying?'

Bliss stared at the floor. 'Well, you are a magician of no mean ability and some power. As your body cannot cope with this atmosphere, I have wondered that you have not thought to find yourself a *new* body.'

Zaras looked up from adjusting his strap. His movements were already becoming quicker and more natural. The look he gave Uh Bib was almost understandable. Uh Bib seemed to have caught his train of thought.

'It is something alike to the questioning technique I taught you. I suspect—'

'Something alike but not the same and even that is difficult? It does not sound very promising. You should understand that when I say we become sluggish here, that also is the case with our minds. The blood helps, but live bodies, *live minds* they are so... The speed is frightening.'

'Frightening?'

'At first I was like a man caught in the sands with a tide racing in. It was unnerving. I am not sure I have the courage to go further.'

'But what is there to lose?'

'Everything. This carcass I inhabit may seem a poor thing to you but the thought of losing it and then failing to gain another… I have no wish for death, I have no wish to be a ghost. You may say that I have the ability, but if I get it wrong what would become of me then?'

Uh Bib was momentarily lost for words.

'What more can I say. I can easily explain the method and I consider it quite straightforward. I have worked on it most carefully.'

'If it is so straightforward why have you not used it yourself? Surely you too could find something better than you have?'

Uh Bib was horrified at the notion. He had worked on the technique partly because the notion intrigued him and partly because he thought that it might be useful to him some day far in the future. But not now. He liked his body. And it worked.

'I am quite happy with what I have, thank you.'

'And of course I am not at all happy with this.' Zaras indicated the contraption strapped to his arm. 'And you would think that I would jump at the chance, but I tell you: I will not do this except in the last resort. It is simply a matter of balancing risks and I consider the risk too great.'

'In that case I *will* instruct you – our business here is far from free of risk and last resorts may threaten us all. Trust me, you will come round to the idea in the end. It is an option more certain than anything I can promise your peers. With a new body you will be renewed in vigour and yet still be yourself.'

'And mortal.'

'If you can do it once…'

'So that is your plan for the future?'

'I am not sure I desire immortality just now but my opinion may well change as age begins to tell and my mind falters. I could not bear to lose the power of thought and the memory of who I am.'

'Pity then the Exiled. They are practically immortal and yet they live only for the moment. Most of them cannot remember who they are – or were. Any name they give themselves has little connection to the lives they have led; they know nothing now of their true identity.'

Bliss looked at Zaras. He was removing the phial. It was empty and Zaras was almost a different man, his glance sharp, his thoughts delivered crisply and coherently. Bliss thought it a little ironic.

'We are what we are at the time the question is asked. Sometimes that will be all to do with our past, sometimes only to do with our present. Think of a Corayan galley slave. Once he might have been a baker or a soldier, a teacher or a lord, with family, with wealth. He had memories: falling in love on a summer's night, the birth of a child, a first home, the death of a loved one – a thousand events that helped to make him what he was. And then a stroke of ill fortune puts him in the hands of the Corayans. In a very short time he is no longer the baker or the Lord. All he is, and all he will be is an oar slave –there is no escape, no hope of redemption except in death, no chance of regaining anything that has been lost. For such a man memory is a curse. If you speak to a Corayan slave, not a common experience I will grant, you will soon realize that his sanity is dependent on how well he can discard his past. His former life can mean nothing – he is a slave and that is that.'

Zaras was silent for a little while. He appeared to be mulling over what the doctor had said. Eventually he grinned, though to the average observer it might have seemed a grimace of pain.

'I am astounded Doctor Bliss, if that is what I must call you here, not only by the callous presentation of such pain, but by the fact that you seem somehow to understand something of the trauma of our exile. But we do not all lack memory and some of us haven't the least desire to discard the past, even in the extremity of our condition.'

'I do not offer the example as an exact parallel: the Exiled are not slaves, Corayan or otherwise. But that desperate need I see in their eyes is corrosive to them. And you all share that need.

Even in those who, as you say, have no recollection of who they are, the lust to reclaim life remains. And this lust governs you all, and it becomes what you are.'

'How do you know this? How can you know?'

'I do not know. I speculate. But I have had many a conversation with your fellows in misery. The General is a typical Kumite and the tale of the Exiled is written on his face and breathes in his voice. The punishment of the Exiled is easy to understand.' Bliss paused here and looked steadily into the eyes of his host. 'What I find more difficult is in trying to understand *you*. You particularly. While the General is typical you are atypical and I wonder why that is. Why are you so different?'

Bliss watched the question settle on Zaras' face. It was clear that he had an answer to give. Zaras must have long considered through all the dragging years of his existence every possible question that wit could ask. He seemed to be considering whether he should answer or not.

'This is a strange evening, Uh Bib. Perhaps it is time to talk. In Kyzylkum we have all the time there could be for such considerations and yet we have little desire for philosophy or psychology.'

'Psychology?'

'An old word. It relates to the study of the mind. An ancient word in fact. And there is your answer: I am different because of what I was before The Choosing. You see, I am *very* old.'

'Strange to talk about being old when each of the Exiled have endured for some eight thousand years.'

'I was born in the fourth age of this world.'

Bliss opened his mouth to speak but then thought better of it.

'You scarcely believe there *was* a fourth age.'

'Intellectually I must. Given all I have seen and all I have read. But my mind reels at the thought that mankind has lived so long. It is almost impossible to believe that one man—'

'Here I am. And, this may discomfort you further, I am aware that I may not be the oldest. The Blood Rite was given in the Age of the Oath.'

Bliss was indeed discomforted by the whole notion. 'The Age

of the Oath? The book makes that the second age of the world. To have memory that reaches so far must be… I don't know: godlike?'

'I am no God, just a man. I may seem to be immortal but I'm not. I have no great power. My memory does claw back through the ages but it is a feeble thing. There is much in my mind that remains from my early life, a little from the years between, and many scenes from more recent times but in all of this it is only the critical moments that survive. And most likely not all of those. I remember nothing of my daily life, the names of friends and enemies are lost to me, days of pleasure, days of loss all impossible to recall. My memory is a random collection of sudden illuminations in a world of darkness, the stilled life revealed by the lightning flash. Do not ask me to explain my life to you: too much has gone and there is little order to what is left.'

Bliss was fascinated. It had been a long time since an idea had so completely enthralled him. He needed to know more.

'Can you remember, at least, how it all began? What you were—'

'Before I became this? And how it changed? There are scenes, pictures of those times. I have never spoken of this. I am not sure I should.'

Bliss shrugged. 'What harm could it do?'

'Reviving memories may possibly revive the feelings too. But as you say, where is the harm in that?

'It started,' he said, 'with sex. I enjoyed sex with young girls. Very young girls. When was this? I wish I could remember the numbers we had for the years then but the phrase in my head is 'after the war.' I was an immigrant in a big city. My parents had a shop in somewhere called Green Lanes – though I don't remember trees and gardens. Some of the pictures of this time are vivid still – I think we must have sold vegetables and fruit, there were cars for the first time in my life – a kind of carriage – and busses, though that may have been later, red busses. Perhaps it is all so vivid because this was before my life changed. Or perhaps it's because this was *when* my life changed.

'You see I met other people who shared my interests. We

had a society and took it in turns to provide the entertainment. That was easy enough: there were lots of poor children, fathers dead or damaged by the war, lots of runaways to choose from. I was really very cruel to them. One night one of the men at the club asked if I would like to meet some other friends of his – I seemed to be the right sort for them. I didn't know then what he meant by that, but somehow I knew I would like what he had to offer.

'It was the Blood Rite. They were old, some of them, very old. I remember that one claimed to have been a general of Xerxes' Immortals. That will mean nothing to you but I was keen on the history of our people and Xerxes was one of ours. There were all sorts of men and women involved though, from many countries and races, not all of them interested in the sex but all blessed with the Blood of the God and all needing young blood to keep them fresh. I remember the Rite, I remember the feel of the Blood as it worked its way through my veins. And the fire of my first treatment – Uh Bib, it is addictive. Once tried you must have it again and again. Nothing to do with the need to thin the tar in my veins. Believe me, after the Rite there is nothing quite like young blood.'

Doctor Bliss, the squeamish Doctor Bliss, sat quietly through this exposition. His face, he hoped, was impassive but the answer he had sought so eagerly was more than he wanted to hear.

'I am sure you're right,' he said, 'But now, enough of the unpleasantries, it is time we got down to business. And there is that spell to teach you.'

Zaras glanced sharply at Bliss. A sudden eagerness transformed his features. 'Yes the spell. A new body! Perhaps I might after all. I could experience pure, untouched flesh and blood. Just like the first time.'

'The idea no longer scares you?'

'Fear never was the strongest part of me.'

Doctor Bliss had little doubt what was.

Shortly after Uh Bib had left him Zaras put on his mask and donned a dark hooded cloak. The blood of the spider woman was running in him now and his body was full of vigour for the first time in many days. His mind was full of memory. The memories drove him out of the house and onto the streets.

It was just midnight as he reached the more lively parts of the city. In many towns of this world midnight squares were deserted spaces but here at the heart of Gothery the lights were burning in taverns and halls, voices were raised in song, jest and good cheer, and men and women in various states of excitement filled the streets. Many visitors to the city were amazed and even appalled by such behaviour. They couldn't understand how anyone would be happy to work so late, party even later and rarely get out of their beds before noon. Many visitors didn't bother trying to understand and simply came to the city to participate. Zaras, refreshed, revelled in the atmosphere at least, even if real participation was not a possibility.

He liked to watch them: the fire of life burning in their faces, the fierce laughter of youth and vitality and the tease of lust shining in their eyes. He liked to watch the couples with their bodies up close to each other and hands wandering. Tonight the memory of lust made him ache.

Two girls stepped out of a tavern on the other side of the street, giggling extensively. Zaras stood still and was pleased to see them turn in his direction. They had linked arms the better to chat head to head and also the better to walk without stumbling. He could see that their faces were flushed with the heat and the drink and the possibilities of the night ahead. Lovely young women dressed to attract, blouses daringly unbuttoned to reveal something of the soft swell of their breasts. As they passed him by it was clear they knew he was watching. There was suppressed laughter as they continued on their way. Zaras was unconcerned. He was busy trying to imagine his hands on those breasts, his knees pushing their legs apart, first one and then the other, he tried to imagine their giggles turned to squeals of protest.

It didn't work. Nothing stirred. He knew that nothing would work as long as he lived in this failing body. The thought of it made him so angry that he strode off down the street so quickly and so aggressively that others had to step out of his way. He turned a corner and then stopped in his tracks. He heard the woman speak and the man laugh but Zaras had eyes only for the girl. Just up ahead they walked, a family group of mother and father and sleepy daughter, returning late perhaps from a dinner party or maybe the theatre. The girl with long blond hair and a very pretty dress was maybe ten years old.

A shudder ran through him, or perhaps it was an imagined shudder, perhaps it was only in his mind, but she looked so beautiful, so innocent and so vulnerable. There were thoughts in his head now that had not surfaced for thousands of years, brought back to him tonight because of the conversation with Uh Bib and the glimmer of a little girl's hair under the streetlights. He watched, transfixed, and was utterly bereft when the family reached a front door, the father turned a key and the child was ushered inside into the safety of their home. He was so affected by this vision and by memories of the past that he didn't know what to do, and so he did nothing but stand still and stare at the door.

After some time he came back to himself enough to look around him. This street was now quiet with only a few people visible and some way off. He took the time to survey the houses and gardens more carefully than he had before and now he noticed that from the main pavements on either side of the street many smaller paths led off down small alleyways between the houses. There was an alley next to the little girl's house, lit only by the dim light from one of the windows. When he was sure that no one was watching he slipped down the alleyway and disappeared into the darkness.

SHOPPING

Fletton-on-Marsh 3057.7.28

Angren had a headache. He sighed for a youth that was gone: a youth that could be without beer for weeks and still not have a hangover on the next morning after. What had he done to feel so bad? It was probably the very serious drinking competition that started shortly after Seama had gone to bed. Angren, Bibron and the two sailors all drank well, all four easily getting into double figures; Garaid, already drunk from too much wine over dinner, made a valiant if foolhardy attempt at a seventh pint but lost his way before he reached the bottom of the glass; Sigrid refused any suggestion of beer but managed an extraordinary and potent range of spirits and port. Berta was the clear winner. She drank faster and longer than anyone and after sixteen pints the others stopped counting and conceded victory. They became rowdy as the night wore on. It was inevitable. This was their first chance to relax fully after their ordeal, a chance to celebrate being alive and a chance to forget if only for a little while that others were not. Bibron's prodigious memory for rude, crude songs and a determination to sing them came into play towards the end of the competition and was, no doubt, appreciated by his companions. It was the singing that at last provoked some response. De Vere, on behalf of the Landlord and all the other residents, and several neighbours, was sent in to ask politely if they would please, *please* just shut up and go to bed. Angren seemed to recall an attempt to confiscate the remaining booze. Brave man. He wondered whether the attempt had succeeded. He wondered because, for the life of him, he couldn't seem to recall anything else.

'I hope Seama has something for bad heads,' he said, speaking aloud to himself to see if he still had the power of speech.

'Even if I have I don't think you deserve any.' Seama was standing by the open window. 'You all behaved abominably last night. Particularly you. I'm amazed at Terrance's patience. However, if you promise to get up and get washed *and* make your peace with Mr. Severan, I might feel more disposed to helping you.'

'What did I do?'

'Nothing that a mop and bucket couldn't cure, but not very pleasant all the same.'

'Oh.'

'Well don't dawdle. We have a lot to do this morning. It's market day, don't forget.'

The market was just outside the front door of the hotel, its multi-coloured awnings enlivening the dusty square and filling it with folk from miles around. The noise of nearly a thousand voices in contention or agreement or shouting words of greeting reverberated between the mute houses whose wide-open windows looked on amazed. Seama's party plunged into the fray with De Vere leading.

'Where to, Mr. De Vere?' asked Angren. He seemed much recovered after Seama's medicine and Terrance was pleased to note that he was apparently quite prepared to be polite and friendly. Probably delighted to be spending someone else's money.

'Does it matter?' he replied, 'I had thought we might wander and buy whatever seems necessary. While you were still sleeping I made a number of deals and the major purchases are completed. We have horses and saddlery, provisions and packs. In fact all you have to do is buy clothes.'

'And weapons.'

'I suppose so. Now look, I don't want to sound stingy but really I do think you ought to be careful with my money. We are not poor but our purses are only so big.' Terrance's face wore a worried frown as he made appraisal of this motley crew he led. After last night he could hardly expect them to exercise any form of restraint. Angren especially: there was a look in the man's eyes as he said the word 'weapons' that spoke of obsession. He hoped Seama would be able to control them. Clutching his already lightened purses more tightly than was necessary, he stood aside to allow them a clear run at the stalls.

'Don't worry, Terrance,' said Seama as he passed, 'Poverty is a salutary experience and as such, one to be relished.'

'This expedition won't be a total waste then. I'm so pleased.'

Any qualms about spending De Vere's money if they had ever surfaced were quickly and irrefloatably sunk but that didn't mean the buying was undisciplined. All experienced campaigners, wary of excess baggage, the company intended extravagance of quality rather than quantity – they didn't buy much but they bought the best they could find. The strange thing was that although everyone found more or less what they wanted the quality they looked for was not much on show. The clothes available were, in general, poorly made of poor material. And this was strange because in the normal course of events Gotherian markets and merchandise were held to be the best throughout the continent of Asteranor and beyond. Pragmatism ruled of course and apparel was bought, but not one of them was satisfied. The atmosphere in the market was poor too. All around them Flettonites and visitors alike were expressing their disapproval of 'uneven colour', 'shoddy cloth', 'slack finishing', some of them quite vigorously. Nearby, in an area of stalls selling pots and pans, a scuffle developed between an over vocal customer and an irritable marketeer. Bystanders, improperly, egged them on and the stallholder swore at them. This incident aside most vendors rode out the abusive comments with a practised calm, insisting they had simply bought the best available to them back at the Stralli market and from the manufactories of Slaney. If folk didn't like what they saw no one was forcing them to buy it. Outraged locals took the implied advice to heart and took their purses home early. The Fletton constable charged the scufflers with affray and took them off to see the magistrate.

Terrance found it all unsettling: the unease, the ill-made goods, the fractious behaviour. Everywhere he travelled in Gothery it was the same and getting worse by the day. Malcontent seemed to multiply while order retreated. Seama's arrival offered some hope at least of getting to the root of the problem but whatever they decided to do about it, Terrance had the very strong feeling that they ought to do it soon. Before it was too late.

Entering a side street, off the main square, the company was confronted by a sprawling blue and white striped tent taking up most of the thoroughfare. A small table at the open flap displayed in gruesome isolation a spiked ball of steel on a chain and handle. For effect the spikes had been painted red as though bloodied from battle. Above the entrance hung a board carrying the legend 'Weapons for Sale' also in the same lurid red.

'There you are Angren,' said Bibron, 'I reckon that'll do you, wunnit? Angren? Now where the heck's he gone?'

Angren had scuttled back around the corner as soon as he saw the familiar blue and white stripes. They found him peeking out as he hid behind a table of kitchenware. Terrance forgot his worries and chuckled.

'What on earth is the matter, dear chap?' he asked, delighted to see the hero of Tumboll cowering behind a pile of copper pots. 'Something worrying you?'

'That canvas, blue and white, I'd know it anywhere: it's Rixbur. I don't know how he got here so quick but I can't let him see me or he'll call up the constables.'

There were several blank or curious faces around him and so Angren explained for the ignorant the full history of his dealings with the sword-seller. They all had to agree that the last thing they needed was for someone to start asking tricky questions.

'Hang on a second,' said Garaid, 'If you threw away his gear he couldn't possibly have had time to set up again, never mind get himself to Fletton in time to meet us.'

'Don't know whether he could or couldn't Garra but I'm telling you, that's his canvas!'

Terrance took pity on him. 'Never you mind, Angren. You stay here. Garaid will look after you while we find out about the big bad tent.'

Angren glared but Terrance, now feeling a lot happier than before, smiled back pleasantly: 'We'll get you a knife or something, shall we?'

Ten minutes later Bibron came back to fetch them. Terrance actually wanted him to come and choose a weapon for himself.

'But what about Rixbur?'

Bibron explained: the tent was indeed Rixbur's but he'd sold his canvas to the present owner as soon as he had arrived in Banya's Harbour, intending to acquire another on leaving Riverport. Obviously Angren hadn't been paying attention on the journey. Riverport had permanent stalls made of wood, or stone warehouses for hire and the use of tents was discouraged. It would be needlessly expensive to ship the tent to Pars when a sale in Gothery and the saving on portage would easily cover the cost of new gear. This weapon dealer in Fletton knew Rixbur quite well in fact but unsurprisingly was in no way a friend – in fact he spat when the name was aired.

'There you are: mystery solved and no problems!'

'I hope so, Bibron. That Rixbur is a nasty beggar and I expect he's got a long memory.' The thought of him made Angren scowl so much that Garaid and Bibron exchanged a puzzled look.

'You really don't like him, do you?' said Garaid.

'Forget it!' said Angren.

What Angren didn't feel like explaining was the very strange intuition he had about the man. He thought it might be something to do with having robbed him, because on most nights Rixbur turned up in his dreams. Essentially it was the same dream every time: Rixbur, sweltering in his finest regalia, at a Royal Court denouncing him as a common thief. Angren found it hard to get rid of the image even on waking. Fat face red from the vigour of his attack, his whole body quivering with fury and the hat he gripped in both hands mangled as though it was Angren's throat he held, Rixbur stood up before the King to demand a warrant for Angren's arrest. Angren could never make out which court or which King it might be, nor ever did he hear the King's reply, but each time the dream ended with the ranked soldiers, lining the Throneway, all laughing and jeering uproariously. He hadn't a clue what it might all mean beyond a simple concern that Rixbur may one day get his own back. He had considered asking Seama about it but in the light of everything else that was happening to them, it really didn't seem that important.

Inside the tent were heaps of weapons jumbled together on tables or hanging from the wooden supports. Angren made it clear to everyone including the owner that he was far from being impressed by the merchandise, but his companions, still amused by the problem with the tent, decided he was just being grumpy and left him to it. Everyone but Angren soon found something that would suit them very well and all of them besieged Terrance for the means to pay. No one bought cheaply.

Seama still had his sword despite his ducking in the River. It was a blade of ancient power, of great lineage and was not easily lost by reason of certain spells. But to supplement this he bought a small dagger and a light breastplate strong enough to turn a stray arrow. His glorious suit of armour now lay at the bottom of the Hypodedicus, no doubt close by the bones of his faithful Bellus and The Mule. In their memory he vowed never to wear more than minimal arms, to enter battle as vulnerable as they had been in his service.

Sigrid was delighted to find a pair of lightweight swords as keen as razors. They were designed to be worn crossways on a woman's back for ease of carriage and access. They looked insignificant in Garaid's hands as he examined the fine chasing of the hilts, but frighteningly lethal as Sigrid gave the doubters a little show of her ambidextrous skill.

Garaid himself chose a weapon that surprised them all. Such large men were often seen with great, heavy two-handed swords and were often unassailable with them. Garaid would have settled for something of the sort but dropped the idea when he found, propped up by the entrance, a powerful Aegardean mid-bow made of quality Ridderswood. He explained that he had in his youth been archery champion for all of Misin Part on two separate occasions. He admitted that his youth was some time past but claimed that it was much like riding a horse and besides there were enough swords among them already.

The lady Titan of the company chose a more fitting battle

friend: a great mace of armour crushing weight, set all about with sharp spikes. The long knife she chose was for more delicate work; a leather sling for emergencies and a cosh completed the haul. The sword-seller looked on in amazement until Berta scowled at him so fiercely he retreated.

The sailors, including the Captain, were more used to shipboard catapults than anything else but they all claimed average ability with the sword. In fact only Bibron was average and Piedoro a braggart; Edro, however, was far too modest. The gash in his right arm had stiffened his movement, despite Seama's ministrations, but luckily he was left-handed and the whip-like blade he had chosen with great care whistled through the air quicker than sight. Angren wasn't slow to praise him. Give him a few weeks for the wound to heal, he told anyone who cared to listen, and Edro would be unbeatable. Edro shrugged.

'Do I have a few weeks?'

'Well, no.'

Piedoro laughed. 'Just go for *capable*, brother, or better still stay out of the fights and keep it for the ladies, eh?'

As the ladies weren't listening to the exchange Edro didn't bother to respond.

Isolde bought nothing. She hadn't the slightest intention of fighting with anyone, she said, and with De Vere's promise of a safe passage to Pars she had no use even for the daintiest piece. She marvelled at the skills and power of the other two women but, then again, so did the men in one way or another.

Still Angren was not impressed. He was looking for his favourite weapon: the short-sword, good weight, perfect balance with an edge hard as diamonds. He looked but he couldn't find. He clattered and pushed his way miserably through one rusty heap after another and swore throughout.

'Are you looking for anything in particular, sir?' asked the dealer, worried at the thought of losing a sale. These people were spending money like water and he wanted as much of it as he could get.

'I am. And I'm not finding it. All this is just so much rubbish. Haven't you a short-sword anywhere here?'

The dealer was put out and almost argued back but then decided against. 'There isn't much demand these days, sir. Most people would rather get behind something a little more substantial. How about—'

'Most people might, but I'm not most people. You'll be telling me next the smiths don't make them anymore. You must have something for me to look at.'

'No, I'm afraid not,' the dealer said as if it gave him great pain. He hated saying no. 'The last two went to your lady-friend.'

'What! I said a sword not a razor blade. Don't you know the difference?' Angren proceeded to explain the difference very slowly, with words of few syllables and a definite air of condescension. The sword-seller refused to get annoyed and contented himself with saying, 'Yes sir, I'm sure you're quite correct,' at every pause. Nevertheless, Angren did know what he was talking about and the dealer was listening to what he had to say, and eventually the light began to dawn on the dealer's broad face.

'Well sir,' he said, scratching his chin, 'I think I might know what you're getting at, and come to think of it, I think I might just have one. I'd thought it a broken long-sword ground up.'

'At bloody last! Let's see it then, for the Gods' sakes, or we'll be here all day.'

The dealer led Angren over to a wooden chest. 'It's not in the best of condition,' he said as he opened the lock, 'I bought it from a poor farmer and it seemed nearly as old as he was.' He scuffled about in the box for a minute or so before he found what he was after and hauled it out with a deal of grunting and puffing as it snagged and scraped through the rest of the mess.

Angren made a face as the rusty old blade came into view. 'You want me to buy that? Good joke.'

'But it's just what you wanted. Needs cleaning, I grant. I've been meaning to get it sorted myself but you know how it is, no time for anything these days. Still it's the only 'short sword' I have and I can let you have it for er… five pieces.'

'Five pieces! Look I'm not sure I even want it. It's in a rotten state. I think I'd rather have a good knife than a bad sword.'

'Four pieces.'

'Seriously my friend, we both know it's a mess. If I take it I'll only throw it away as soon as I can get something better. Maybe I could give you two and hope there isn't any hard fighting to be done with it. Or three, if you throw in that shield over there.'

The dealer was delighted but kept a straight face as he resignedly agreed to take just three little pieces for a stick of rust and a battered leather and steel arm shield. He saved the grin for later when he was counting up his takings.

Outside at last, Garaid came to talk to Angren as he examined his 'new' sword.

'I think you were conned,' he said.

'And so do I,' De Vere put in, 'and I'm the one who paid for it.'

'Conned? Really? You should take better care of me then,' Angren said, and then began to laugh aloud. The others were confused.

'What's the joke, Angren?'

'Oh, it's too much. Listen Garaid, that dealer's a fool. He thinks he's put one over but that's because he doesn't know his job. As soon as I held it I knew: this is one of the best I've ever found. It's perfect! Forget the rust, that's only surface. You wait till I've cleaned it. I bet you I find a Glavier mark on it.'

'Worth more than three pieces, then?'

'I would've paid thirty. Just you wait.'

Before noon De Vere and Isolde rode out of town while the others took a little more time over their packing. Terrance had gone ahead on a fast horse to find more funds, to set Isolde on her way back to Ayer and to start a few wheels in motion along the proposed route. Seama and the rest of the company left Fletton in the early afternoon, adopting an easy pace for the benefit of their newly shod mounts, and taking their chance to relax a little along the way. The sun shone benevolently upon them all day through into a pleasant moonlit evening. It was not until dawn that the rain found them.

PASSING THROUGH

It was a cold evening for summer. The sun was an hour gone and the cloudless sky had let all the heat of the day escape. The driftsman sat upon one of the prop timbers that held together the three mile sand bar. A chill downriver breeze made him shiver. He drew on his thin green bind, as if for warmth, and breathed out the smoke with a self-pitying sigh. His was a hard life. Oh, it could be worthwhile collecting drift, he wouldn't deny it. Like a travelling merchant, the river carried with it the wealth of all the lands it passed through. Any man willing to pay the price of honest toil might discover treasure in that flood. It could take a hundred years, for all the driftsman knew, but boulders that became pebbles would be rolled, inch by inch, down from the mysterious mountains that he had never seen, and some of them would end up on his bar. And in the Hypodedicus any stone, any lump of rock could carry a diamond, or emerald or some other precious gem. Usually it would not, but it could.

Banya's Harbour was originally a bay hollowed by the swirling currents of the river but as Gothery became established the port became busier and the limited harbourage overused. Gothery's answer was to build a dead-water. This was done by driving thirty-foot timbers into the silty flats that paralleled the coast north of the port. The sand and mud between was dragged and dredged and piled onto the wooden bar, and then the river was let in. Over the years the Hypodedicus helped scour the channel but it was constantly maintained by the harbourmasters against the possibility that the silt would build up once more. They had lately built mighty water gates at the down-river end with which they could regulate the depth of the docks, and they had plans in hand to build a similar barrage at the head of the channel.

Let them. The driftsman didn't care. The bar was his home and his business. He patrolled it, day after day, picking up anything the river would leave him, certain that sooner or later he would land a prize worth the waiting. Meanwhile, there were good times when he did well enough and times when he was starving poor, but overall he managed to scrape a living if only by selling firewood.

Today he was hungry. He was going through a bad patch where pickings were poor and so was he. When hungry he often walked out along the bar to sit and watch upriver. It didn't matter much that night had fallen as he wasn't expecting a find, but he could watch the red harbour light shine on the waters and think of what might be.

The man on his post stiffened in a heartbeat. Splashing! A commotion nearby made him consider a fish supper, or, to judge by the noise of it, seal steak! He peered out. The whinnying surprised him. 'Not seals then,' he muttered. And then his searching eyes found them. There in the red glow, floundering in the mud, in a tangle of limbs and leather straps, three poor beasts cast up by the uncaring river, and set to change his life.

'Neptis' scruffy beard!' he cried in delight, 'Horses!'

He wasted no time in rushing back to his shack where he roused the boy and grabbed the long rope. Together, man and boy a practised team, they lassoed the biggest of the three and pulled and strained, the driftsman all the while screaming at them in his excitement. The big horse kicked and pushed and grunted its way to solid ground and behind came the other two, attached to the first by a tether of sail rope, one on its knees in the mud and the other on its side and not moving. They were all exhausted, man, boy and beast, but the driftsman didn't care: he had gained such a prize for his efforts and he knew there was more to come. If it was sail rope then it must have been used on board ship to keep the horses in order. And if a ship had gone down and the horses had drifted this way... He was dizzy with the possibilities. Other flotsam was bound to follow, may already have come to ground. With any luck, and it was about time he had some, they were in for a busy few days.

He inspected his find. One horse was dead: long drowned. He wondered, fleetingly, whether the meat would still be fresh but then turned up his nose and forgot about it. On dry land the biggest of the three seemed gigantic and weird in the red light, but stranger by far was the other odd creature that now stood, shakily, between the living and the dead. The driftsman had never seen a mule before. Both survivors were sick with the cold and fatigue, but the driftsman rubbed his hands in glee: the sickness would soon wear off and fit and well the pair would be worth a fortune.

Over the next two days he rudely nursed the two beasts back to something like health, and the boy helped him without being asked. The lad was quite taken with the poor animals and spent every spare moment he could with them, grooming and stroking and communicating, without words, kindnesses the driftsman would never have thought to offer. The boy was a deaf-mute but somehow the animals spoke to him and he spoke back. His gentle touch became more persuasive than the driftsman and his stick, and saved them many a blow.

Because now the work began. The man had already located most of the booty. He had found good ship timbers, smashed in places but still useful; an assortment of clothes and packs; a barrel of salt beef; a water-tight and buoyant chart box, with the charts intact; and perhaps thirty more pieces well worth the salvage. The horse and mule did hard labour hauling out and transporting, the boy helped with the cleaning and the driftsman began to count up in his head the value of his hoard. He could not have been happier.

Beasts of burden were a luxury but he began to wonder how much it would cost, in food and lost profit, to hold on to the mule after their current work was done. The charger was a tremendous worker too but the driftsman couldn't keep that one. In a few days he would take his wares to market and she'd undoubtedly be the most profitable part of the haul. Of course, all horses were expensive but this creature was special. They'd go to Astoril and the Stralli market. That was the way: it was a long haul to the capital, and he had not made the journey more than a handful of times in his life, but the situation demanded it. Prices there were bound to be better than in Banya's Harbour. The charger would pay his way for years to come, and with the mule to pack and a fine horse to ride upon the journey wouldn't be so bad. Not so bad at all.

But on the fifth evening the driftsman had only just tied up his charger alongside the mule for the night, a mind full of the plans for the trip and plans for a wealthy future, when his chances of a good price simply upped and left him. The huge beast lifted her head as though listening to something and then reared up snapping the ancient leather strap that held her. Free, she paused to bite into the rope that restrained the mule and tugged it loose, and then, without any sort of farewell, the pair of them cantered away.

The driftsman was stunned by this unlooked for display of independence but after a moment the enormity of his imminent loss shocked him into action. He gave chase, his panic giving him strength, and with lungs straining and the effort making his head swim he launched himself at the trailing rope. The attempt was useless. The animals increased speed and, with a yelp, he had to let go. The rope had burned his palms and he fell to his knees in pain and despair. A week past he would have been happy with a bit of good meat and some bush baccy but now, with a hoard still in hand that would keep him in means for more than a year, he felt that he had lost the world. His dream of another life had slipped through his fingers and nothing would be any good ever again.

The Lyndons, Makerfield 3057.7.30

Roddy dipped his brush into a bucket of water. Sally, Isolde's old pony, had taken to rolling around on the rough ground under the poplars that lined the long lane, and unfortunately the wood pigeons had taken to using these same poplars as their preferred place to rest and to drop. As a result the old girl was covered in hardened pigeon crap and it was Roddy's job to do something to get it all softened enough to brush out.

He didn't mind. Roddy liked straightforward jobs that didn't need too much thinking about: he found it satisfying to see what was needed, to get his tools together, to set to and then keep going until the job was done. And he couldn't help thinking that was what life was really about. Some people, though, just didn't see it in the same way. No matter how much he respected his employers in a formal way, he couldn't understand them at all. Old Mr Robarn was mostly at home these days, to be sure, writing his poetry and drinking too much beer, but Roddy couldn't help remembering all the stories his mam used to tell him about the Master's adventures. She seemed to think all the intrigues and the politicking exciting somehow. Roddy just looked upon it as *toff's* work: nothing at all to do with him or his family or his kind. Sometimes it made him angry to think about it. They were dangerous folk, the Robarns, anyone could see that, but somehow Roddy had convinced himself that, so long as he kept his head down and put in his hours, all the *stuff* they got involved in would just pass him by. Roddy the handy man, that's all, and happy to be it. Or he had been.

But now look at it: some sort of demon woman attacks and kills an honest mother and her daughter and straightaway the Miss is mixed up in it, and then, wouldn't you know, Old Master Gerald steps in to take it on. And all this not five miles from where he now stood. It wasn't common goings on. Not this monster and not the way the Robarns just seemed to attract trouble. The Lyndons wasn't a normal place, the Robarns weren't normal people, and yes, without a doubt they gave him the creeps.

Jeb was used to it, he guessed. When they came back from Riverport Jeb was up with the Master straightaway. Then they all took off to the place where it had happened. Of course they wouldn't let Roddy come in with them. Told him off to wait for the militia. So he did that: hung about in the road till the soldiers turned up and then sent them down towards the cottage where Jeb and the Master were doing whatever they were doing. They were all grim when they came back, the Master included, but it was only the soldiers who said anything. It gave Roddy the screaming heebie-jeebies whenever he thought about what they'd told him. Roddy thought of his girl, Jilly, and the wedding they had planned for next year. He didn't want her anywhere near all this. Enough was enough: he needed another job. He brushed vigorously at Sally's withers and the poor old pony snickered in complaint. *Never mind that*, he thought at her, *there's some of us here have real problems in this life.*

At that moment the clattering of hooves made old Sally buck in surprise. Charging into the yard on a hired nag came the Miss herself. She bore down on him, reined in hard, leapt from the saddle and already she was talking.

'Right Roddy, where's my father?'

As if it was his fault!

'Well?'

Roddy struggled to hold onto Sally.

'She's only a pony! Just let her go!'

He did and the pony shied away, escaping onto the lane.

'Now, where is my father?'

Roddy panicked for no reason he knew.

'He's g… gone,' he said, 'he's gone.'

'Where?'

'Ayer,' he said.

'Ayer?'

'Well that's what he said.' Roddy had never seen her like this: she pushed up close to him, her face right in his. What was happening to them all? First Jeb, and then the Master, and now Isolde – all acting like mad things. It was worse than ever it was.

'To court? You're saying he went to court?'

Roddy nodded.

'Right then: get me the best horse we have left. Get it saddled and get it now!'

'Yes. Rightaway. Yes Miss,' he said and ran off to do as he was told.

The horse Isolde had been riding, a rangy old thing, looked half dead from running. Shame to do that to a horse, Roddy thought, as he clattered into the tack room. He grabbed the Miss's best saddle, a good bridle and reins, barged through a door to the first stable and threw the saddle onto Black Whisperer's back so suddenly the gelding jumped two feet in the air in surprise.

'Now don't you give me any trouble,' he said as he struggled with the bridle. But Whisperer, roused from a pleasant afternoon nap, was in no mood to be helpful and Roddy had to lead him out into the yard with the straps still loose. The Mistress was tying up the hireling to a rail but when she turned to face them Black Whisperer began to kick and twist and turn and Roddy was pulled this way and that.

'For the Gods' sakes, Roddy, get a grip.'

She stepped up to help him and, whether because the horse was done with his protest or because Isolde had more skill than Roddy, the gelding calmed enough for the lad to sort out and tighten the straps ready for her journey. In the few minutes this took, the Miss looked about her at the spilled bucket of water and the brushes kicked into the mud and, it seemed, she viewed the scene with dissatisfaction.

'This'll need cleaning up,' she stated, 'And the rest of the yard. It's a mess. And get that horse taken to Morton's in Makerfield – they'll have it sent back to Riverport. The bill's paid.'

Roddy pulled at the saddle strap furiously and over-tightened it.

'Oh come on, Roddy. I haven't all day.'

He was glad when he finally got her up and she turned the horse to go, but she caught his stare as she did so.

'What are you looking at?'

Roddy was glaring at her with a feeling of utter contempt building in his heart. But he said nothing.

'Oh, never mind,' she said, 'I've no time for it. I'm off. Get this yard sorted.'

And with that she kicked up Whisperer and started for the drive. Roddy watched her for no more than ten seconds before he turned and grabbed his pack from a peg by the nearest stable door.

'That's it!' he spat out, 'I'm done with this.'

He pushed his dirty old work jacket into the pack with his fist, pounding at it as though he would have liked to pound something else entirely.

'I am not,' he yelled at the empty yard, 'staying here to be pushed around by those weird bastards *anymore*!'

He hadn't noticed that Isolde had pulled up at the gate to the yard, but when he looked up and saw her approach once more he decided that wasn't too bad a thing after all.

'Did you want to say something to me, Roddy?' she asked dangerously sweetly.

Well she could stuff it.

'Too right I do!' he said.

Moreda 3057.7.30

Trant made a half feint, spun to the left and then swung the blade high in a killing arc aimed at the back of Chaldonie's unprotected head. It stopped inches before steel met flesh and bone.

'Now that is what you *call* a well-balanced sword,' he said.

Chaldonie, who was busy examining a cabinet of short knives, had failed to notice that Trant was anywhere near him.

'What are you talking about, Trant?'

'Oh, nothing much.' Trant grinned to himself. 'There's a lot of good stuff here and even more to bring in from the field. I'm going to re-arm the lads. You'd better take what you fancy before I let them in.'

Morgan Trant had given his lads free rein in the house and grounds apart from a few chambers for himself and the sorcerers, and this magnificent armoury. The Masters of Beltez were very rich and very keen on the quality of their weapons. '*Were*' being the correct tense. To a man, the Masters of Beltez were by now either lying in the mud in the fields around the house or already burning on the pyre Trant had set his men to building, out by the forest's edge. If they wanted Moreda to be their base for even a few days Trant wanted the place to be free of the stench of rotting meat. Of course the lads weren't happy about it, more used to cut and run tactics, but Trant told them there'd be no fun until they'd finished. Amazingly they'd accepted his rule on this. He could see they were getting weary. Murder and mayhem took it out of you. And so did surprise attacks. For once Trant had agreed with Semmento on the best next move. It didn't matter that they'd pretty much taken care of the two wizards and the town was open and ripe for the taking, they both decided that putting some distance between the Black Company and Altiparedo would definitely be a good thing. The eagle had unnerved them both. And it was still out there somewhere.

'Very proud of themselves, these Beltesians,' said Chaldonie, now looking at the pictures on the wall in front of him, 'Just look at this: the gentlemanly sport of fox hunting. The caption reads 'Giorgio Beltez explains his Superiority to the Pretender.' He's dangling the poor creature by its tail, draining its blood into a cup. Very noble.'

'They were well known for it. Hunting was as important to them as the quality of their weapons and their skill in arms.'

'Skill in arms? Look how far that got them.'

Trant swung the long-sword into a practice dummy with more force than he intended and the thud of it made Chaldonie look up at last. He wore a smirk on his face.

'Is something bothering you, bodymaster?'

'I manage the men. We need the men and they need managing. I can't see what you find so amusing about that.'

Chaldonie's face was scornful. 'We do not need them. Just as the Beltesians did not need their weapons or their skill at arms. They should have hired a sorcerer.

'Or a wizard, perhaps?'

'It is much the same thing.'

'Never went to Errensea, did you? Or did I get that wrong: you went there and they wouldn't have you. That it?'

Chaldonie drew himself up like a snake preparing to strike but then apparently thought the better of it and relaxed. Though he wouldn't like to admit it, Trant was relieved. He could have had the sorcerer's head off in a stroke but what could Chaldonie do in *half* a stroke? That young red-headed wizard had certainly found out.

'You really wouldn't be wise, Morgan, to provoke me. You may feel safe with your foul little army around you—'

'Foul? That's rich coming from you. You're so foul even the rats run when you turn up.'

Chaldonie actually laughed at that one. 'The rats, yes they do! But the interesting thing is that you don't know why.'

'There's a reason?'

Chaldonie smiled but did not offer anything. It was an unpleasant smile. Trant decided he'd rather not know and Chaldonie appeared to consider the exchange finished.

'In fact I do have work for a couple of your men, Trant,' he said. 'Whatever these Beltesians thought they were, I will admit that their taste in art was not wholly self-obsessed. Look at this hanging.' He indicated a large tapestry that occupied a portion of the south wall of the chamber. The theme was military, in keeping with the suits of armour that flanked it, but it told an episodic tale of the progression of an ill-made youth, through many trials on the way to knighthood and glory. 'The Trials of Alsiphar. The craft of the makers would suggest Apian school but the real clue is in the composition of the scenes: the presentation of only the key characters with no chorus or audience, the absence of captions, the sparing treatment of architectural elements so that the action is unhampered by detail.'

Trant was surprised and a little suspicious. 'I had no idea you had an interest in such things, but where do my men figure in this?'

'I want them to take it back to Bulidzhan for me. I have a house there.'

Trant considered the size of the tapestry. It would need a large room to accommodate it, and would take strong men to shift it. Though it billowed slightly as it hung, seemingly delicate enough to catch the slightest draft, when rolled he was sure the weight would be considerable.

'And are we to start stripping every manse we take? I wasn't aware that finding decorations for your country seat was part of the job in hand.'

'Your men get what they want, Trant. Have they started on the women yet? No, but they soon will. We all need incentive. I see no reason why I may not collect a little along the way. Semmento can have no objections… *Is* there a problem?'

Chaldonie had realised that Trant had stopped listening to

him. The Captain was in fact studying the tapestry. As Chaldonie spoke it had billowed again. Perhaps there was a door behind it, Trant thought, an open door. He was about to investigate when a commotion at the entrance to the armoury distracted him.

'And I say leave now. What do we have to gain by staying? It's not as though it pays well. Semmento gives most of the money to Trant here. That right, Morgan: the pair of you splitting the proceeds between you?'

More trouble. Trant took a deep breath before answering. 'Look Kelsly, you know I have an army to feed and to pay when we're done. On your side of the equation it's just the four of you. If you have a problem with the rewards of your work your argument is with Semmento, not me. And if you fancy leaving before the job's finished then that's something else you'll need to discuss with him. If you dare.'

The two new arrivals exchanged glances. Kelsly, a wrinkle faced, skinny limbed individual of indeterminate old age, carelessly dressed in dirty black trousers and an ancient brown leather jerkin, and Malbur, a corpulent man in loose robes, with a neat turban of purple silk and an immaculately groomed black beard but oddly no form of moustache at all; together they made such a contrast that Trant sometimes laughed to see them. But today he just found them annoying.

Malbur smiled widely, making his fat cheeks even rounder and his deep-set eyes narrower. 'Have we, perhaps, been having a little... ah... disagreement, shall we say? You seem a little tense, Morgan.' His voice was deep but rounded and full of the rich wine he drank in preference to water.

'How could I be tense in such relaxing company?'

'Ha ha! Always a response. That's why I like you so much Trant. Semmento said I would. What do you think Kelsly: will he favour me one of these days?'

Kelsly's dry laugh was almost as irritating as the fat man's chuckle.

'Not on your life, Malbur,' Trant said, meaning just that, 'Remember it. Where's Semmento?'

'He has another conference to attend first,' said Kelsly, 'He's talking with his betters.'

'Talking? With this Bliss person, you mean – and how is he doing that?'

'Well not talking exactly. We have a connection, a clever little item—'

'And quite, quite secret!' Malbur put in quickly.

Chaldonie was scornful. 'What difference does it make if he knows? He hasn't the wit to use it.'

Trant sucked his teeth rather than reply. He was becoming bored with all this and considered the notion of taking his men and leaving these sorcerers to get on without them. They would be hanging by their necks before the month was out.

'You can keep your secrets,' he said, 'but we were supposed to be having a meeting. A little difficult without—'

'I will speak for Semmento if there is need,' Chaldonie cut in, 'We have had some discussion already.'

'Right then. Let's get started. Look at this, will you.'

Trant had liberated a map from the chart case and spread it out on a table, weighted down at the corners with spiked catapult shot.

'As you can see this map covers the Seno del Bosca, the length of the Haçen Cordillera, from there through the feoffments of the Huecca and beyond that down into northern Matagorda, River Hathen in the west and River's Twist in the East. What interests me is the Huecca.' He indicated an area of many small rivers trailing away from the mountains to join the Hathen on its way to a confluence with the Fugagrande, the start of it not more than fifty miles from where they stood. 'I've been through the area. These valleys are deep but very fertile. The villages are well separated, mostly undefended and, best of all, wealthy.'

'Oh not more villages! Really! Couldn't we find something a little more interesting? I've heard that River's Twist has quite the most liberal atmosphere.'

'Malbur, we're in the business of stirring up trouble for Gothery, not for ourselves. Even with the four of you working together, taking on the City Militia might just be too much for us.'

'Oh how wrong you are. River's Twist isn't a problem. Niplock Sterrett has seen to that.'

'Niplock Sterrett?'

'An old friend of ours from Garassa. Don't you remember him: he was supposed to be the elected councillor for the Sinks but he was the biggest crook in the place. Not surprising Athoff took a fancy to him. Apparently he's been sent to River's Twist to act as King's Legate. Just peach isn't it! Last I heard he'd already bankrupted the City Treasury.'

'Bankrupted?'

'Well, shall we say that Athoff and Niplock are a good sight better off now than they were three months ago. Of course he's worked out some plan to blame it all on the Gotherian trading community.'

'Which means that we'd be completely mad to march openly into River's Twist.'

'I wasn't thinking of doing anything openly.'

'What do you think of all this Chaldonie? What will Semmento say?'

Chaldonie had been standing back from the table watching and listening. He regarded Malbur now with a look of deep distaste that was plain to see.

'We will not go to River's Twist, openly or otherwise. Our task is straightforward and our plan unaltered. And if you are thinking of leaving, Malbur, or you Kelsly, then you had better think again.' He stepped up to the table to stand between the two of them, resting his palms on the edges of its polished surface. 'Trust me,' he said twisting his neck to look venomously into Malbur's eyes, 'you would be unwise to try it.' He favoured Kelsly with the same look and then stepped away. Trant watched him walk to the end of the table where he turned and regarded them all without speaking. The Captain had never seen him threaten any of the others before and he wondered how the pair would react. As it was, they were each motionless, both staring at the table before them. Curious, Trant followed their gaze. Deeply impressed or etched into the surface of the table were the prints of Chaldonie's thin hands, the dark wood blanched, the polish around the outline turned green as though an acid had been applied.

'You were saying, Captain Trant.'

'I was… Yes, as I was trying to point out,' Trant decided to move on. 'We'd be best to make our next moves in the Huecca rather than travel any further west from here. Better to attack good-sized villages than small towns: they attract too much attention. As we've already learned. Last thing I want is to lose any more men – there were twenty killed in Altiparedo before you lot managed a response. I'm not having that again.'

'At least we managed a response,' huffed Kelsly, 'Just shows how well you'd do without us, don't you think?'

'Gentleman! Enough of this.' Chaldonie gave Kelsly another of those warning looks and the thin man subsided. 'Captain Trant is right: we must keep wastage to a minimum. I was harsh before, Captain. We each have our roles. Your men play their part in the terror we create and news of them diminished will lessen the effect. Do we know much about the journey through the mountains?'

Trant was astonished. He looked at the map. 'By this I'd say it's fifteen miles to the Blancagua Pass, and then some rough travel for another ten. After that another thirty to get into villages of any significant size. A couple of days. But I'd want to scout ahead before we go anywhere. And besides the men need a break.'

'We all need a break,' grumbled Kelsly. 'Whatever anyone says I'm not getting on a horse again for a week at least.'

Malbur chuckled but the amusement seemed a little forced. 'So you need a rest? Then you won't, perhaps, be finding a use for those five children you had locked up earlier?'

Kelsly smirked. 'Oh well, you know: a little exercise every day—'

It wasn't a loud noise but very clear and Trant recognised it at once.

He screamed out 'Get down!' just as another voice yelled 'Catarina, NO!' and a young woman stepped out from behind the tapestry loosing her crossbow as she came. The bolt fizzed over his shoulder and nicked Kelsly's cheek.

It was a foolish attempt. There was only ever the chance of hurting one of them and leaving the rest to reply. A grizzled old man emerging after her, short sword in hand, barged the girl aside and sent the crossbow clattering across the floor. Trant launched one of the catapult balls at him and the two inches of steel glancing off the old man's collar-bone made him falter. Trant drew his own sword intent on putting an end to it but he wasn't quick enough. With a look of unimaginable terror upon his face the old man, against his will, reversed his sword and slowly pushed the point into his own belly, shuddering horribly at every inch. Trant looked behind him to see Chaldonie mimicking the old man's actions and then realised that he was in fact directing those actions. The sorcerer made a twisting motion with his hands and the old man turned the blade in his vitals.

'No!' The young woman screamed in anger at the unnecessary cruelty. 'How dare you—' Trant grabbed at her arms, forcing them behind her back where he tied them at the elbow with a buckled leather strap. He wasn't gentle but she didn't struggle much. The sight of all the blood pooling around her feet took the fight out of her.

Chaldonie stooped to pick up the crossbow.

'What a *silly* girl you are. You should have stayed hidden. What shall we do with her, Trant? Kelsly, I think, will want her to make amends for his wounds.'

Kelsly, dabbing at his cheek with a handkerchief and examining the bloody cloth with unusual interest, was magnanimous. 'The old man paid for this. Why don't you keep her safe for me?' He turned to leave the armoury but continued as he walked: 'After all, I will have devotions to make very soon. Of course Azrazal does seem to prefer the pretty ones but I'm sure he'll forgive me in the circumstances.'

He went and Chaldonie, without a glance at those remaining, followed him.

'Seems to have recovered his sense of humour,' said Malbur, the wide grin returning to his features now that Chaldonie had left the room.

'Yes,' agreed Trant, 'I suppose he has something to look forward to. He'll be sharpening his razors. I'd better have Hoggy put her in the cellars with the rest of the catch.'

The girl was too stunned to respond in any way.

THE EMPIRE OF WHOJIT

Slaney, Gothery 3057.7.30

'When you are fighting a war, Angren,' said Seama, impatiently, 'the greatest advantage is to know the strength of your enemy and how it is deployed. It's possible then to make a strategy based on certainty rather than guesswork.'

Angren, slightly drunk, pondered a while before trusting himself to reply. With metal cloth and oil, he had been working on 'the Mighty Stick of Rust', as Sigrid had taken to calling his new sword, but now he laid the cloth aside and, out of habit, reached for his jar of ale. Seama cleared his throat. Angren thought the better of it and picked up his tools once more. Seama was not in a good mood so beer would have to wait.

'But I thought we didn't know anything about them,' he said finally.

'Oh, we know a little already and we'll find out more soon enough but actually I was talking about *them* wanting to know more about *us*. It seems clear they already know a great deal about Gothery, the politics, the industry and so on. That's easy enough. But what do they know about the rest of it: Mador's reaction, Athoff's warmongering? What about the Council's plans, what about my mission?'

Angren guffawed exaggeratedly. 'Well they couldn't know much, could they? I mean, let's face it, you haven't even told *me* what we're up to. I thought we were supposed to be heading out west not piddling around up here.'

'Up here' was a small room in a second-class public house in a major town of Gothery's industrial midlands. They had struggled through two solid days of dreary rain and muddy roads to get there and to Angren's eyes the place didn't seem to warrant the effort: it was all manufactories and noise. In fact Slaney was not far off the obvious route into Aegarde and so not much of a diversion but to Angren the stop felt like an unwelcome interlude, an interruption he could do without.

'We are here, Angren, because I have more information than

you may think and even some clue as to what is actually going on. We need to be here.'

'Fine. So tell me: what is *actually going on* then?'

'I suppose I should explain.'

'You suppose right.' Angren was beginning to feel put upon. Normally he would have followed Seama to the ends of the earth and never asked a question but that was when Seama was determined, decisive, invincible. But for now Seama seemed to have lost some of that air of certainty they'd all come to rely on. If he wanted to keep Angren's support then, at the very least, he'd better start talking. The whole situation was beginning to feel very uncomfortable.

'Very well. Firstly, you have to understand that something of great importance is taking place in this country. It's what you see all around you: all this industry and imagination. You mightn't think it but these mills and tool shops and weaving sheds don't just affect the type of clothes you wear and the goods you buy at market and the roads you travel, but they will inevitably alter the way we protect ourselves and the way we make war.'

Angren nearly asked what had clothes to do with war but he realised, despite the alcohol, that deeper questions needed answering. Seama wouldn't wait for him to catch up.

'No you must try to work it out for yourself. Secondly, I have solid information that some unidentified interest has a number of spies infiltrating the region. They're mostly involved in questioning the people in charge of the manufactories but they're far too obvious and as a result are more often than not fed the wrong answers. More recently, perhaps because of their lack of success, they've adopted a new strategy. Several important people have gone missing—'

'Now hang on,' Angren had to butt in, 'If it's so flamin' obvious these spies are out kidnapping people, why hasn't the King's wonderful bloody Public Guard nabbed 'em?' Gothery's 'wonderful bloody Public Guard', a cross-national innovation of Sirl's reign, had put Angren before the magistrates three times already for certain minor misdeeds usually involving drink and once, in fact, a spot of smuggling. Abduction seemed a little more serious.

'An important question for which I have no answer. Nothing is as normal in this country, Angren. What do you suppose these spies are looking for?'

Angren had no idea. 'Looking for someone or something? Lost treasure, secret weapons? What do spies normally look for?'

'Information. But what information? It could be weapons. Some of the people missing are alchemists; some are engineers. On the Isles we do a lot with explosives but in Gothery, what with all the iron and steel workings, who knows what they could produce? What if these spies are looking to steal secrets to help their attack; what if they're trying to find out how to sabotage our defence? I wonder.'

'What I wonder is who the bloody hell 'they' are?'

'If you're talking about the spies, they're paid men and women, in this case from ar'Andala and Masachea. But it doesn't mean that either the ar'Andalan Emperor or the Celebrant of Masachea is involved in what's going on. In fact I'm sure they're not. The Council has its own spies: we're so deeply embedded in Masachea we could monitor the incidence of the Chief Sirdar's bowel movements. And we do. The Emp Radis, on the other hand has enough troubles in the far West for him to be bothered in the least about Asteranor. His Empire is collapsing and just about all of his armies are engaged. We keep a very good eye on what's happening on Sullinor, have done these thirty years.'

'So what then? We're about to be invaded by the Spurlese, are we? Fed up with raising sheep on a couple of rocks, they've decided to conquer the world.'

Seama smiled. 'You remind me of Tregar, and not because he's Spurl*adian*. The last time I attempted anything like this conversation he seemed to think I'd lost my wits. And here we are again. There is another Empire, Angren, we must consider. One more ancient and probably much more powerful than ar'Andala, and it's close enough to pose a deadly threat.'

Angren's brow wrinkled as he tried to place any such alternative, presuming that the beer had fatally affected his ability to think.

'I speak of the Empire of Kyzylkum.'

'The Empire of Whojit? Don't think I've heard of that one, Seama.'

'Of course you haven't. Few people have.'

'So where is it then, this empire thingy? It's not another fairy tale is it? I didn't much like the last one.'

'You'll like this one even less than the tale of the Halfi, I assure you. But no, this Empire is not the sort of place your mother could have told you about. Tell me, Angren, what do you think lies north of the Dedicae?'

'What?'

'You heard me.'

'Nothing. More mountains; the sea. How should I know?'

'Kyzylkum lies beyond the mountains. A vast country – at least I think it is; an oddity, a strange place that shouldn't even exist. It is home to an ancient race, parted from the rest of us back in the beginnings of history. And they're not a nice race, Angren. They worship their ruler, The Face of Darkness, who apparently just happens to be extremely proud and utterly malicious and immensely powerful. Kyzylkum, Angren, is not a happy realm.'

'So, not worth a visit, then?' Angren's drunkenness was becoming a thing of the past. A fact he regretted. But he still didn't quite understand. 'This something to do with that smelly heap of papers you've been reading?'

'You know full well they got a soaking. But that 'smelly heap of papers', as you put it, Angren, is the key to everything that's going on and it's where I learned what little I know about Kyzylkum, and about the Raising of the Dedicae, and the Empire of the Exiles.'

Angren shrugged. 'No offence intended, but you know it really does sound like just a story. I mean what's this 'Raising of the Dedicae' stuff? You don't raise mountains, Seama, they're just there, aren't they?'

Seama shook his head in that annoying way he had whenever Angren said something stupid. 'Nothing is 'just there' without a reason, Angren and that includes mountains. Did you learn no science when you were young?'

'Couldn't be bothered with it, Seama. You don't get to be as good at fighting as I am, messing around with schoolbooks.'

'Didn't your mother make you go to school?'

'Oh she made me go alright – just couldn't keep me there. Look, why not just tell me about it, if it's important.'

Seama sighed deeply. 'It's a good job some of us pay attention to our lessons. Oh, very well. Back in the antiquities section of the Collegium Library there's a manuscript nearly four thousand years old. It's well known – they use the text as a primer in Medean Studies; it's a sort of compendium of what it calls 'histories.' Now one of those histories gives a dramatic description of an awful upheaval, deep in the past of the continent, an earthquake that shook Asteranor to its foundations and changed the shape of the land, and piled up the mountains so high the continent was cut in two: divided north and south with no chance of passage between one side and the other. Well, Angren, let me tell you that familiarity really does breed contempt. Most historians and linguists are convinced, like you, that it's just a story, an entertainment, a parable about life and death and the sundering of souls. So you're in good company. But my smelly heap of papers, Angren, insists that it is all true. Haslem, the person who wrote the smelly papers, the book itself being The Song of Ages of which I have only a partial copy, he was very sure that this tale of the past was nothing less than a factual account of a division of mankind. At some point, so long ago it's impossible to put a date on it, the Dedicae were raised to impassable heights and Kyzylkum was set apart.

'Think of it, Angren: through all the long years since the time of the Wandering, Kyzylkum has been sitting up there, all alone, unknown and unconsidered by the rest of humanity, it's people quietly getting on with their lives, but hemmed in by the mountains, imprisoned if you will, and, for all that time, wanting to escape. Imagine that!'

Angren did his best. He dropped his cloth, leaned over to one side, elbow on the arm of the chair, cheek resting on his fist, face in a frown and he thought as hard as he could. Imagination was something of a challenge.

'So who… what was it raised up the mountains, again?'

'Oh yes, I didn't say. It was Ohr'mazd, to protect us. To banish the others.'

'Ah, I see. And erm… why exactly do these 'others' want to escape then? I mean what's in it for them?'

'Perhaps 'escape' is the wrong word.'

'What's the right one?'

'Well, Haslem more or less says that what they want, more than anything else, and they've wanted this from the start, is to claim back all they have lost; to take back everything we've denied them. They mean to attack and they want to destroy us, I guess.'

'Bugger me, but what a cheery soul you are, Seama. Many of them, these 'others'?'

'No idea. But do you see, Angren, to get back to your original question, what I'm doing 'piddling around up here' when I could, and maybe should be out in the west taking on this Black Company, is grabbing at a chance to find out the truth behind all this ancient history.'

'And how are you going to do that?'

'I'm going to ask someone.'

Angren snorted. 'Ask someone? And they'll tell you the truth will they? Well good luck. What I don't understand is how come you don't know all about the place already. I mean it's been thousands of years, you say. Surely someone must have discovered the place in all that time.'

Seama took few moments, before he replied. He seemed unnecessarily tense. Angren counted that as a bad sign.

'Have you ever tried to cross the mountains?'

'Well no.'

'You never will. The sierras of the Dedicae are so high the air runs out before you can top them. And you can't go by sea either – there's too much ice in the way. And unless, Angren *'I never listened in school'* Nielderson, you've secretly invented some machine for flying, or you've figured out how to grow wings for yourself, then *clearly* Kyzylkum is beyond exploration!'

'Well pardon me for being ignorant.'

'I'll think about it.'

Angren had nearly had enough of this. He eyed his glass of ale longingly. Being drunk just now seemed a much better option than being barked at by Seama. And all of this Kizzil stuff: there didn't seem any point to it. 'Tell me,' he said at last, 'being as we can't get over the mountains to look, doesn't that mean they can't either? Why don't we just leave them to it; leave them where they are?'

'Because, Angren, they're not thinking of staying at home! You haven't got it have you? The power behind all the trouble here in Gothery and Aegarde, and everywhere else for that matter, is the power of Kyzylkum. They've found a way out. *That's* what I'm trying to tell you. Do you get it now?'

'Alright, alright, keep your hair on. So I asked a stupid question.' With Seama in this mood, he should have known better than to have asked questions at all. This time instead of looking at his glass, Angren scooped it up and took a long pull. He was getting dangerously close to the bottom before he stopped.

'Look, Angren, I'm worried, more worried than I've ever been. We may be facing something terrible, something incredibly powerful, and I just don't know if we'll have the strength to resist. Since Tumboll… well, something's changed Angren, and I don't know if I have the power left in me. It makes me nervous.'

'And bad tempered.'

'Yes it does.' Seama sighed and then bowed his head as if ashamed of what he was about to say. 'I'm going to need help, Angren.'

'There's no doubt about that bit, Seama. And you'll get it, 'smuch as you like, but not just now.' He picked up his jar and sank the remaining mouthful. 'You see, just now, and this is very important, I'm off to get another pint. I'll bring you one too, if you like: calm you down a bit.'

It was past midnight and the beer was easing Angren into a cosy sleep when he felt Seama's hand on his shoulder.

'Wake up! Wake up, Angren!'

Angren rolled over, his body reluctant to comply but he rubbed at his eyes and rolled back again. The look he gave the wizard was grumblesome.

'So what's happening now?'

'I have him! Almost. He's coming to meet me in the stables. The joke is he thinks I have information for him!'

'Forgive my asking and all, but who the bloody hell are we talking about? And, more importantly, what do you want me for? I was having a really good kip then, first time in ages. Can't we go and see this bloke sometime in the morning, or better still mid-afternoon?'

'Don't whinge, Angren. If I didn't need you I wouldn't wake you. Somehow, I can't see him turning up without friends, can you?'

'I wouldn't know, you haven't told me anything about him yet.'

'If you'd stop being so bloody minded and stirred yourself you'd find out, wouldn't you?'

Disgruntled but by now fully awake Angren threw off the shoddy blankets he had been curled in.

'Farewell Bed,' he said as he dragged on the few clothes he had discarded before sleep, 'I knew it was too good to last, but that's life. I do hope I meet another like you but it'll never be the same.'

'Cut the prattling, you idiot. People are supposed to be asleep but I wouldn't count on it.'

'I certainly don't qualify. Back to your normal self then?'

'Maybe. Look, if you are very good, I'll let you come back to your precious bed in an hour or two but for now will you please hurry up.'

Within minutes they were down in the stables but others were there before them. The stable was unlit: a place of sounds and smells. And it was a stable poorly managed where the smells were stronger than they should have been, where the horses were restless and where a clutter of unseen, kneecapping objects were scattered liberally between the stalls. Though they were in hand Seama was reluctant to let Angren light the lanterns they had brought with them. He didn't want their presence noted too soon.

'That's all very well,' Angren complained as he stumbled around among the pales and horse-dung, 'problem is they'll have heard me by now, won't they. Damn! I hope you're going to clean my boots for me.'

'They *will* hear you if you don't shut up!' The predictable buffoonery was rankling. 'Are you *trying* to ruin all our good work so far? Just get that head of yours out of sight and quick.'

'Well that's nice, I must say. Get me out of bed and then— Ahhh!' Uttering a yelp, Angren dived away from his intended hiding place, drawing a knife as he came out of a roll.

'Dear Gods!' cried Seama, 'Couldn't you possibly make a little more noise: the King in Astoril mayn't have heard you.'

'There's someone behind that stall, Seama.'

With a word, rather than a match, Seama lit one of the lanterns and stepped forward to where Angren crouched ready to spring. Seama was unconcerned and unsurprised when Bibron rose, grinning a little sheepishly.

'I'm sorry Seama. Didn't see him coming, so's I couldn't warn him.' Looking at Angren he laughed more confidently. 'I'd be happy if you didn't sit next to me for a while, Angren. I'm not sure I like what you're wearing.'

Angren's clothes had been dirtied from his roll on the floor; he wasn't pleased. Seama had suffered enough distraction and he spoke up before Angren could make any further comment.

'We'll be caught gabbling if this carries on. Both of you get hidden, and quick. Is everybody here now?'

Various positive grunts came from all around them and Seama was satisfied. 'Good. Now be quiet and wait. It could be sometime before our visitor arrives.'

Seama up-ended a stray bushel box and sat down. He had a lot to think about. The lamp yellowed his face, his features grew waxy. A change occurred. Anyone who knew the wizard, and there were a great many who did, would have had difficulty recognizing him. The overall countenance was there but it was subtly obscured; the nose slightly bent, the eyes oddly askew. His youthful face developed the wrinkles of age. It was an art he had practised so much that he now could change his face without having to concentrate. The irregularities of this new face needed firming up before his 'guest' arrived but Seama was more concerned with firming up his ideas on what he needed to know: what were the questions he needed answering? It was normal to begin with questions like 'Who are you?' or 'Who sent you?' but he was more immediately interested in what the spy wanted to know about Gothery. What was his mission? It would reveal a great deal about them, whoever they were, if he could only find out what they were after. He didn't really think that weapons were the root of their interest, for surely they already held all the cards worth holding. It would be better and easier for them to win the war first and ask questions after. Maybe they needed to know who to keep alive.

Speculation was getting him nowhere. There was only one way to find out and simple interrogation was not it. A more devious technique was called for. It was possible, in theory, for a skilled wizard to read the minds of all animals including man, but where for most animals there was no opposition to overcome – for a horse thinks of no more than food, safety and allegiance and that is no secret anyway – man is a creature full of privacies, secrets, real or imagined. It was an exhausting job to delve into the minds of men. Seama knew the problems better than most. He knew, from countless repetition, that 'preparation is everything or action is nothing' and so he withdrew his mind from the turmoil of speculation to ready himself for the struggle to come. Such was his concentration on inner disciplines that for Seama the passage of time seemed slight; for the others who shared this vigil an hour of silent apprehension stiffened their muscles.

There was a muffled exchange of voices outside the stable door and instantly Seama was alert. He stood up and taking on a nervous attitude began to pace up and down, shoulders stooped, muttering and never straying far from the lantern's arc of yellow light.

The door swung open but the moon beyond betrayed no silhouette of whoever had moved it.

'Who's there, eh?' Seama whispered, his speech a convincing copy of an uncouth local style. 'Eh? Issit you, then?'

For a few silent moments there was no reply but suddenly two men burst in. Rushing forward they grabbed at Seama, one thrusting a knife to menace the wizard's unprotected throat. Seama refrained from struggling: he knew these were just the bully boys sent in first to soften him up and he didn't want to frighten off the real quarry. Instead of struggling he preferred to whimper and grovel to make the spy feel more secure.

'Alrigh', alrigh' lads. No need t'be hasty, eh. You've got me. You don't need no knife. Whatever you want.'

The men laughed.

'You're right, my son,' said one with a leering grin that made him look demonic in the lantern glare, 'You'll do anything we want or I'll cut-off your balls.' He was big and fat but obviously strong. 'You're all alone then. Mates gone and left you.'

'He does'n' have any mates, d..d..do you, rat-face?' The second man stuttered and drooled, he had a nervous twitch, a spasm that contracted the left side of his face whenever he spoke. Seama thought this man looked more dangerous than the other.

'I'm talking t..t'you, shit head.'

'Nah! Nah, don't have no mates. They don't like me, no one does. Nah, they don't.' Seama was happy to capitulate, his voice cracking with fear.

'Good job too, o…o…or I'd have to see to you properly. Undersssstand?' The twitcher hit Seama a backhander.

'Yes! Yes. My nose. I think you've broken it.' Blood appeared behind his hand.

'That is enough, for now. Leave him.'

Seama was a little shaken by this new voice. He hadn't seen anyone else enter the stable and he couldn't see anyone now: the owner of the voice stayed beyond the lantern's reach.

'You, wretch: are you Leire?'

'Yes, your honour, that's me.' Seama contrived a bubbling,

nasal admission.

'You have an unfortunate name, Leire. You will tell me the truth.' The voice was odd: constricted and flat. 'What is the information you have for me?'

'Ah now,' said Seama in a conniving tone, 'Ah now, that all depends, don't it. Firstly, what did you want to know? And second, right, saying I know about something you want, how much will it pay me to tell?'

'You know what I seek. This powerful man, this wizard. I need to know where he is. As to payment, there will be great reward. I will give you your life.'

'Leave it. Don't own me, can't kill me so long as I got what you want. I've news for you that you can't afford to miss, 'portant news.'

'You are a fool. I have no time to waste words with you. Hold him.'

Though Seama struggled the thugs held him steady, twisting his arms behind him. A small figure came into the lantern light. He wore black clothes and displayed an unusual passion for jewellery. On each of his black-gloved hands he had at least five rings, all yellow gold and rubies and jet, and on his arms he wore bracelets. He looked like a Partian mummer dressed for pantomime except that here the jewels were real. To complete this dramatic appearance, covering his entire head he wore a black and silver mask. No flesh at all was visible.

Seama nearly relaxed his disguise in surprise. According to his sources, the spies had been seen only in Gotherian dress. Such conspicuous garb as this was unlikely to win confidences.

'Now fool,' came the voice through the slit in the mask, 'speak! Tell me what you know of this wizard and his interest here. Tell me or I will take what I need by force.'

'What d'you mean 'by force'?' Seama pretended fear but he was only moderately concerned. He hadn't expected any use of *power* but he knew what would happen next and was prepared for it. The jewelled hands reached up to grip Seama's face, the fingers pressing in so hard that the nails inside the gloves cut into his flesh. Seama recoiled in pain but the fingers pressed in even tighter. The thugs laughed as blood trickled down his cheek. The spy, or whatever he was, became still as if readying himself.

For those watching in the shadows this was an incomprehensible scene. More than one of them thought that Seama was in deep trouble and the only reason they didn't move was that he had given them specific instruction to intervene only when he signalled. For Franner and Creel however this simply seemed more of what they had grown accustomed to. They couldn't understand what it was Zaras did to his victims but they knew it was terrifying and damaging. They'd seen the looks of sheer terror and pain in their eyes as he began, and witnessed the total lack of any emotion in them after he'd finished. As though his victims' minds had ceased to function. That he sometimes went on to drain the life blood from them was something like dismemberment after death: gruesome for the onlooker, agonising for the loved one but of no concern at all to the recently departed. The two torturers were used to his habits but Creel still found himself horrified. *Any second now*, he thought, and winced in anticipation, *any second now he'll do it...*
Creel could never have seen the look of terror in Zaras' face because the muscles in that face did not respond as normal muscles do, because the eyes were slower than the eyes of a dead fish and anyway the mask obscured everything. Creel could not tell that this scene was in any way different from any other interrogation. *Any second now*, he thought once more, *the old man will turn to jelly and Franner'll have to hold tight*. But that second and that chance had gone. The old man had raised a hand as if to defend himself and, as quick as blinking, Berta had dinned both Creel and his partner about the head with her new heavy cosh, and both fell to the floor unconscious.

The stroke of mind against mind had been reversed – Zaras himself was the victim. This giver of pain, this sufferer of a pain constant through many thousands of years, had never been subject to the agony that comes from possession or invasion.

This was rape. During his first centuries he had raped others without compunction, had revelled in the powerlessness of his young victims. Now, for the first time in his horribly extended life, there was a chance to understand the impact of his crimes. But Zaras did not have the calm within even to say to himself: 'So this is how they feel, those I destroy.' Because fear ruled him.

No will had he. No matter how his mind turned and twisted he was bound, every second tighter, his tongue frozen, his muscles paralysed, killing every attempt to break free. There was no avoiding the needle of his captor's probing. He had learned to use his own mind as a surgeon's lancet, but taking what he needed and fatally discarding the rest. Zaras couldn't know that Seama's skill was so much greater. Zaras didn't know that he could survive this.

He would have screamed if he could.

'Thank you Berta. I have the other. Someone had better restrain those two: I don't want them running off to tell tales.'

It was hard work holding this strange man to heel. The body was frozen but the captive mind was squirming to be free. The pinching fingers were still tight on his face and the pain threatened to distract him. He asked Berta to hold the spy and she locked him in a grip that could break his neck if required. Garaid, to emphasize the point, pushed a knife up against the throat.

'Gentlemen and ladies,' Seama said, 'I believe we have captured the spymaster. This is better than I could have hoped for. Keep him still now as I release the body: he'll try to escape.' Sure enough the spy started to buck and kick. Berta had a hard time holding on but after only a minute or so the man relaxed, his limbs became limp and the hands fell away from Seama's poor face. Seama didn't need the contact anymore: the body was now free but the mind was his. The problem would be in exploring what was there. This would not be a normal interrogation: not simply a matter of questions and answers. The brain is a vast library. To get information Seama would have to find his way through a catalogue of events and memories.

It began.

The most vivid, immediate pictures, hovering on the surface of awareness, were to do with the last few hours. A message, met with a sense of satisfaction, eagerness, a feeling that everything would now work as it should, but then in parallel a vision sprang up. It was a parade, a march of people. The colours were all wrong, not triumphant as they should be but then, they *were* deep in the tunnel. Seama couldn't help it: the questions sprang up unbidden. *Who are they, who are you?* but the spymaster's thoughts went spinning off incomprehensibly. Deprived, denied, bereft, banished; Billi Zarassi, Zarascha, Zaras. *Where are they going?* Satisfaction again: coming not going, determination. *Why are they coming?* Return, reclaim, the New Kingdom, the Final Kingdom. Revenge. *But who's Kingdom?*

The chain of these thoughts snapped, or slipped, and Seama's mind was flying back through darkness at sickening speed until he became a God. Or there was a God. A God whose eye surveyed, the vast plain become small in his mighty sight. And His! His to behold; His to rule; His to destroy if He willed. *And what is this place?* Home, my home, before I knew this, and my fate. A great desert, Kyzylkum, once, and now, and then, and always and on forever. The Wastes of Time. Seama's vision swirled making him feel giddy and abruptly they plunged, his captive and he, plunged hurtling down towards the plain, and the City of the Plain.

It was a dreadful place.

Images of buildings and streets flew by so quickly that Seama had no time to think about them. He stored them away for later.

As the vision spiralled down and in, however, the overall vista made an immediate and terrible impression upon him. Decay. It was all decay. Seama remembered the blight in Ayer but that was a matter for a good spring clean compared with this disaster of time piled on time. Dust made soft the streets, made grey the dead gardens, made silent the footfalls, choked all voices. It was a city of dust. What had they from the palsied fields to eat; what had they from the poisoned river to drink? Nothing but dust and ashes. It was a horrible place: a country of the dead.

And the people of the city could not have known love. No honest gaiety marred faces of studied hate; the hate was tempered only by griping melancholy, enflamed only by denied lust.

Seama strove to remind himself that this was a nation and not just some waxwork of horror or an asylum. In it were ranks and tasks, rules and relations, duties and obeisance. There was a king perhaps, or an Emperor, but certainly a God.

Seama's vision took him back to an urgent summons delivered by a deformed serf to a fearing servant: Zaras. Running through ancient corridors, older than old, sadder than sad, the vision became blurred – the incumbent of this summons, disinterested in everyday surroundings, was infinitely more concerned with what awaited at the journey's end. Seama himself became apprehensive about what would happen, about the identity of the summoner. Perhaps this was when Zaras was given his mission. He would soon know: Zaras approached unguarded doors. They were doors of hell. Unmentionable scenes adorned them – of war, mutilation, torture and all that Seama thought evil. They promised worse revelation to come.

Zaras stopped. The doors swung outwards... and then darkness descended like death.

Seama staggered, struggling to pull himself back to reality, his eyes on a frozen tableau of Garaid, stooped, staring in terror at his bloodless knife; of Zaras' sliced and gaping throat; of Berta's revulsion as the head lolled back obscenely into her face.

'You, you... *imbecile*,' is what he said, 'Garaid, I had him, I had it all. There was so much to be learned. So much!' He turned away to hide his anger, and counted up to many more than ten before he spoke again. 'What made you do this Garaid? Why, by all the Gods in heaven, did you kill him?'

Angren stepped forward. 'The Gods had more to do with it than Garaid, Seama. It was all so quick but I reckon the spy pushed himself onto the blade—'

'And cut off his own head? Ridiculous!' Seama couldn't believe it. The weapons-man always looked after friends in a tight spot and even though he was in no way their leader, the others always expected his support. But, whatever Angren said, Garaid had done the deed. He need only look at the man's face to see that: he was wide-eyed and babbling. What was he saying?

'Blood… the blood, where is it?'

As one the company stared at the corpse. Not a single drop of blood issued from the grey flesh of the neck. No fluid at all. Instead the veins were filled with a noisome jelly, atrophied by time.

'We've been talking to a dead man,' said Sigrid. Despite her normally offhand approach to the death of her enemies she made a sign in the air before her to ward off evil. Some of the others looked as pale as the death before them. Stifling Bibron's oaths and Berta's slow questions Seama launched into an explanation:

'It wasn't a dead man. It was a simulacrum: an imitation man, an image that carried the thoughts of someone far away.' He wanted to calm their fears and dared not admit to being as horrified as the rest. They would all be happier if the wizard seemed unimpressed. In truth, if it was a simulacrum then it was the best ever made. 'What you see has been conjured by someone too cowardly to risk his own body. It's not even worth burying. Leave it. We should consider our next move.'

'But what was he… it showing you, Seama?' Bibron demanded, 'I heard you say something 'bout – I don't know – Kizalkum was it? And somethin' about a new kingdom?'

'Did I speak?' Seama had no recollection. Did he really say Kyzylkum? But what if he did. Perhaps he was responding to what he saw with words he already knew? This wasn't helpful. 'Captain, if I knew all the answers I wouldn't have needed to ask questions. I'll have to think deeply about what little I heard and saw before I'll be able to understand what it all means. Now's not the time. We have a lot to do before morning. This lot'll take some sorting.'

As they turned to consider their task Edro let out an angry cry.

'Bastard! The little rat!' He pointed to where Angren and the brothers had tied the two unconscious thugs. Now there was only one: the twitcher had calmly slipped his ropes and gone.

Furious, Edro kicked the other man as though it was his fault.

'Your pal's left you, eh? He's a nice bloke, no?'

The fat man didn't answer but toppled forward revealing the knife that was embedded in the base of his skull. The twitcher had ensured that no tales would be told and an old score had been settled.

'That's all we need,' Angren looked at Seama, 'Were these the two De Vere met in Fletton, do you think? He said they were arguing then.'

'They fit his description. Pity he's not here to confirm it, but I hope to meet him tomorrow in Dreffield.'

'Is that far? It had better be. That twitcher will be trying to set us up by now. This is a mess. I think we ought to leave straightaway. We need to be twenty miles from here before morning. That's what I think.'

'The beer must be wearing off then, Angren,' said the wizard, 'because that's what I think myself.'

LANDMARKS

Dreffield 3057.7.31

Terrance was surprised to see them. Angren, tired from the night ride, took great pleasure in rousing him before daybreak: why should the dandy be allowed to sleep-in while others worked? And in such a bed! Angren gazed with naked envy at the pile of soft pillows and the crisp white sheets. Why was it, he wondered, that men like De Vere could always find and afford the best rooms and the best food?

As Terrance washed the sleep from his eyes Seama and Angren slumped on his sofas. Even the wizard was weary. Angren filched some port for his breakfast. A look of reproach from Seama irritated him.

'You'd begrudge me a drink now?'

'At this time of the day? I just don't know how you can stomach it.'

Angren sneered. 'Guts of cast iron is how.' He had long forgotten his shameful behaviour in Fletton. 'I'll take this with me: I know Sigrid wouldn't mind a drop.' The others were waiting outside the Westgate.

'Did he turn up then?' Terrance asked, confident enough to shave and talk at the same time. Angren snorted.

'You could say so,' he said, 'that's if you're talking about some spy or other?'

Angren looked to Seama for some sort of explanation. He wanted to know how Terrance already knew all about it.

Seama nodded and said: 'Terrance set up the meeting in the first place. He's good at that sort of thing.'

'I'll bet he is. You'd better tell him what happened then.'

Seama told the tale briefly and without referring to any of the information the spy had provided. Terrance was curious about the mask and the lack of blood but didn't seem much impressed. Angren supposed that being there had made all the difference.

'It doesn't sound much like the fellow I tried for, Seama. I've never heard of this mask before. Someone obviously thought the information about you very important: too important for subordinates to handle. It's interesting those two louts turned up again seeing as they weren't the intermediaries I'd spoken to. We ought to keep our eyes open for the skinny one. He must know more than we thought he did.'

'If he was more than your average bod what was he doing in Fletton?' Angren voiced a thought common to them all: 'I don't like the idea that someone knew you were coming, Seama.'

Seama didn't like the idea either but he wasn't convinced. 'What if,' he suggested, stretching himself out on the sofa, 'what if this twitcher was waiting for someone else? Someone from Tumboll, maybe, one of theirs. I'd like to have questioned him.'

'Well,' Terrance offered, 'there is another of their spies in Dreffield. The twitcher may well come on here to bring him the news. So far my messages haven't been returned: this one seems more cautious, but I daresay if I try again we might get some response.'

'No. Time's running out. I cannot wait here another day. We go west. I intend to be in Aegarde by tomorrow, which means we must leave now.'

Angren groaned theatrically. 'No rest for the wicked,' he said.

Terrance raised his eyebrows at that. 'Perhaps you should say: 'No rest for the *hunted*,' Angren. Did you know that someone is looking for you?'

'What?'

'Word on the street has it there's a lot of money riding on you being found.'

'What?'

'Have you upset someone, perhaps? Oh yes, there was that Rixbur person wasn't there?'

'Now just a minute. Are you telling me someone's paying for information about me?'

'Someone, yes. Can't tell who just now, or why. I've only heard about it at third or fourth hand. I think the money on offer must be keeping those in the know quiet about the detail – of course they wouldn't want anyone else claiming the reward.'

Angren was stunned by this news. And a little confused.

'There's a bounty on my head? What did you tell them?'

'Now Angren, calm down. I haven't told anyone anything. If I'm going to be travelling with you I really don't want bounty hunters on our tail.'

'And *I* don't want them on *mine*! The quicker we're out of here the better… Did you just say you were coming with us?'

'I did. My dear Angren, I would not miss this for the world. I'm ready now if you are. Let's just pick up the supplies I've prepared and then we can be off. We'll be out of Gothery in no time at—'

The arched window behind him exploded into rainbow crystals of glass and spinning leads. Both Terrance and Angren flung themselves to the floor, arms shielding their eyes. Luckily the speed of the explosion was slower than the sound of it. Because it wasn't an explosion as such, it was the result of a sudden, brutal impact.

Seama, who had chosen to stay where he was, using a pulse of *push* to protect his face from the flying debris, shook his head in profound annoyance.

'You always have to do something over the top, don't you,' he said.

Cuahtemoc made no reply. He was perched on the chair back nearest the destruction that had been the window. But his look was unfriendly. He shifted his position and dropped from one claw a crumpled envelope of paper onto the chair seat and turned his gaze upon the two men still lying on the floor. Angren peered out from under his arm.

'Gods, but you're a big bird.'

Cuahtemoc gave a cry and a beat of wings that rattled the shutters and upended Angren's glass of port.

'Steady on,' the sword-master said pulling himself to his feet, 'That's a drink you owe me. He a friend of yours, Seama?'

Seama looked cross. 'And I just had to be here when he turned up. Terrance, there's a message for you.'

Terrance was brushing the glass out of his flouncy shirt sleeves.

'The post is not what it was,' he breathed but then, as he

looked up at the eagle he changed his attitude. 'My apologies, sir Cuahtemoc. It was the shock that made me flippant. We thank you for your efforts. Our friend Roar has such great trust in you and we know that trust is well placed. May I take the message?'

Cuahtemoc looked at him carefully, seemed to come to a conclusion and flew to the back of Seama's sofa to allow Terrance more comfortable access. Seama eased himself away a few feet.

'If he decides to go for you, Seama, a yard isn't going to help.'

'Thanks Angren.'

'It's well timed this letter,' said Terrance, as he opened and smoothed out the sheet, 'Let's see. It says the Black Company were last in a place called Altiparedo and… Oh. Wait a moment while I… ah…'

Cuahtemoc, listening, made a trilling, croaking noise that somehow seemed wrong even to Seama.

Terrance had stopped reading. He crumpled the letter in his hands and turned his face away from them for a moment. When he looked around there were tears in his eyes.

It took a long hard day's ride in fact to reach the border. Angren who had seen no sight of the bed he had been promised twenty hours earlier was feeling more than jaded by the time they stopped for the night. They avoided the smoother, easier main roads in favour of back-lanes and fields: a less public route. Gothery's constables had an excellent communications system and Seama wouldn't be delayed by a murder enquiry. Angren was missing his comforts, however. He would have given anything for an alehouse, an easy chair and a good meal. There were no alehouses on the roads they travelled. Alehouses were, for the time being at least, off limits. He was tired, his mood was already fractious, and so when Seama suggested that a cooking fire wasn't necessary he was not so much disappointed as livid.

'No fire?' He made the question an accusation but the wizard was undaunted.

'Do we need one? It's not a cold night.'

Angren swore under his breath.

'We are allowed to eat, I take it. I thought a little venison might be nice, rabbit even, but obviously I'm out of order.'

'You are. We have no rabbit or venison and we're certainly not going to start hunting now just to keep your belly happy. Grow up man. We're probably wanted for murder; we're hunting a vicious band of cutthroats. Do you really think we should light a fire and go charging through the fields creating hue and cry? Who knows what'll be waiting for us round the bend or in the next field? No, I'm sorry Angren but you'll have to put up with bully beef and biscuit from now on. What's the matter with you anyway?'

'What's the matter with me? What's the matter with you, more like. Look I know he was a friend of yours. But you don't even know he's dead – the letter didn't say that. Whoever wrote it out must've talked to him to get the story straight, to know where to send it. I guess he—'

'He said it was the end. He said there'd be no fixing him. You *know* what he meant.' Seama spoke quietly but with passion and everyone could see his frustration and anger. 'I told them it would happen. I told them! Waldin and Peveril got it all wrong. *I* should have been there not Roar McAndre, and definitely not Colm. And now it's too late.' Seama bowed his head. 'Cuahtemoc would never have left him injured.'

'You reckon, do you? So where's the bird gone now then? Eh? Hasn't he just gone back to him?'

'Maybe. To sit on his grave a while.'

Angren shrugged. He didn't believe it but what did that matter. He was either dead or not dead and there was bugger all they could do about it one way or the other. He'd never met Roar McAndre.

'Well, whatever!' he said.

'I thank you for your concern.'

Angren found it hard to leave it alone. Seama had walked off for twenty minutes or so after the last spat and had come back just that little bit calmer, but Angren had continued his grumbles throughout to anyone who couldn't avoid listening. Seama had the benefit of his thoughts all over again as he struggled with his saddle.

'Look Seama, you think I'm in a bad mood? Well I am. You've got Terrance here telling me I'm a hunted man, that Rixbur's after doing me in. Not a new situation exactly, I know that, but how would you like it? And you've got all this secrecy crap going on that we're having to put up with. You've got us chasing about the country – countries I should say – getting our arses kicked from pillar to post, madmen and ghouls all over the place. And then you ask me what's wrong! Okay, you tell me there's plenty of fighting to be done, which'd suit me fine, and alright there's been a few set-tos and whatever, but where are we now? Far as I can tell, all we're doing is running away. You know what, I wish this Black Company was in the next field, then at least I could get *stuck in*. But there's one thing, one thing that really does get to me, Seama. I tell you honest, I hated Rixbur heart and soul but at least he had half-decent camp beds!'

Angren could see that the others were watching. De Vere and Bibron had wry grins on their faces, both familiar with this sort of behaviour at this sort of time in any expedition, both aware there was nothing much to do about it. Berta, Sigrid and the brothers were dismayed, or even annoyed, to judge by their sour looks. Angren was the last person they expected to gripe. Garaid, Angren found the time to notice, simply looked sick.

Seama gave him a withering look.

'Have you finished now?'

Angren hated that look.

'Oh, forget it!' he snarled, 'do what you like, as always.' And then he stumped away as noisily as he could.

But Angren's display of anger was little more than an attempt at disguise. A useless attempt because he knew that Seama wasn't fooled. They both knew what the matter was: Angren was 'depressed'. Again. It was that Gwydion who told him about it. Gwydion Hebog, the Foreigner. According to him, not that he should be listening to someone like that, according to Hebog, Hebog meaning Hawk in their language and that should have warned him, Angren was prone to 'depression'. He didn't offer any medical cure. Hebog didn't like pills and potions, and besides, as he explained it, Angren's depressions though real enough were not very severe. All he had done for Angren was to quietly describe the problem, laying a cool hand upon Angren's brow as he did so, and then sent him away to think about it. That particular depression had lifted almost immediately. Angren supposed that being made to think it through distracted him in some way from the illness itself. Hebog had told him to remember what he'd said anytime the depression returned and it usually worked. A fine man the Foreigner whatever Angren's father thought.

The depressions usually hit in when life was dull. Angren smiled at that. After the past month – Rixbur's thugs, the sea-monsters, the battles on Tumboll – perhaps all this plodding through Gothery's backyard really was terribly dull. And while he found it easy enough to accept discomfort when the situation was life-threatening, he was in no mood to accept it now. Where were they going? What next? What if this Black Company had all packed up and gone home now they knew the Council was on to them. And the other stuff. Kyzylkum. What if that was just a just another fairy tale after all? Certainly sounded like it. So, it'd all be down to politics again, and what use was he at politics? No use. If it wasn't for Seama, Angren could have been wenching in some Aegardean brothel by now. Or making money somehow in Pullonia or Polz, something, anything but not this. It was all down to Seama, of course. He owed Seama a debt: the Wizard had saved his life. Again! Twice in just the past two weeks! And that was a problem because Angren was from Terremark where an honourable man wouldn't rest until his debts were settled.

Angren paced recklessly, stubbed his toe on a rock, yelped.

'You alright?' the Captain asked, wondering why Angren was hobbling round and cursing like the fool at a Morris.

Berta laughed. 'Stubbed his toe,' she advised and added somewhat needlessly: 'Should watch where he's going.'

Angren gave her a quick, tight smile before flopping down by his pack. He sat with his back to the others and eased off his boot. Behind him he heard Edro say something he didn't quite catch and Sigrid chuckled. Getting a bit pally those two, he thought. And then he had to ask himself what was wrong with that.

Women! And there was another grievance. It was months since his last encounter, and weeks even since his last crude thought about Sorella, Rixbur's young and compliant wife. There hadn't been anything between them no matter how much Angren had wished there had. It was a mystery to him why, but throughout his life he'd repeatedly fallen for inaccessible women and invariably ended up in bed with those he didn't much care for. He refused to analyse this behaviour but it continued to make him miserable every time it happened.

Oddly enough, by the time Seama came to speak to him again Angren's depression had begun to lift. It didn't mean he was ready to chatter. A lonely man despite his scattered battle friends he had never found anyone he could really talk to and even Seama was no exception. The Wizard had nothing original to say and Angren couldn't bring himself to speak his mind. He was a little cheered at least by Seama's show of concern and he made the effort to apologize and the Wizard apologized in return but all in all his mood remained on the edge of gloomy. Conversation in the camp was subdued and so he turned his attention to his new blade. He found solace in routine.

After half an hour or so Sigrid came and sat next to him and together they talked about weapons and technique well into the first watch.

The night wasn't long and the sun dawned red behind them as the companions packed their gear. Ahead lay The Saddle, a section of the border country where the cliffs and rough land that marched along the western edge of the Gotherian plateau, for ten miles or so, dipped towards the Valdesian plain offering a more gentle descent than any of the many other, more direct but often precipitous routes into Aegarde. Traders travelling from the Gotherian midlands and northern territories with heavy loads and high hopes preferred this gateway: it was kind on their horses, and their backsides. Western Street, a good metalled road, joined the great Middle-Way at the Wykeford Turnpike, just before the border, and this led them on west into the Hundred Kingdoms or south by the Rine-Way eventually as far as the capital, Garassa, and the many populous towns of the Western seaboard. The land between was mostly barren or undeveloped but well maintained posting stages every thirty miles along the way, offered the weary traveller, at a price, both rest and relative safety. Seama's company, however, wouldn't be going that way. They travelled north of Western Street, and would keep to the high ground on the right of the Middle-Way, and then set off north and west. Roar's letter had placed the Black Company in the villages and towns of the 'Skirt', a group of settlements clustered in a scooped out spoon of land nestling under the sharp cliffs to the north of the Saddle. Terrance wasn't so sure. His contacts claimed that the Black Company had left the Skirt, southwards they thought, but none were certain; nothing of any current atrocity was being voiced abroad in the inns or market places of Gothery but perhaps they would learn more in Altiparedo itself. Seama decided it would be best to find the last place they had been seen and then track them from there.

Before mid-morning they had crossed the border. The green pastures of Gothery lay behind them and ahead lay a broad country of rolling grassland. They would need to travel some miles out before making north in order to avoid a deep scar in the land. They could see it away on their right whenever they climbed high enough and an unhelpful feature it looked too. Seama's knowledge of the area was limited but at least he knew that the cut was known as Hammerhand's Anger, named after the supposed fury of the great storm god Syre, that some of the local population still believed in. Seama had made a study of all the Gods known on Asteranor – he was not sure he believed in all of them, of course, but he didn't like the idea of ever being caught off his guard – and he recalled that while Syre's power was supposedly immense his temper was indiscriminate and his aim, with that mighty hammer of his, less than accurate. The gouge in the earth was deep and steep and impossible for horses.

The swelling plains filled their sight. This land lay below the Gotherian plateau but after leaving that homely, rich country of enterprise and wealth this new terrain seemed to them both vast and unforgiving. Its dull green face had nothing cheerful about it even in the noonday light. Nothing much was visible. The rolling land revealed the occasional small pond or mere and, with the water, clusters of wiry trees and brushwood, but there seemed no evidence of mankind: not a house, nor a fence nor even a track to follow.

'Not much about, Mr Wizard,' said Bibron, 'Can't see this place being worth a robber's labour.'

'This is just a step along the way, Captain Farber. The villages north of here are quite populous apparently. That right, Angren?'

They all looked at Angren whose horse was now ambling along in the rear.

He shrugged. 'They were,' he said, 'some of them.'

The others waited for him to expand upon this but he didn't offer anything more.

'Ciudad Valdez is supposed to be quite big, I believe,' said Terrance, 'Over thirty thousand people, a standing militia of two thousand and the biggest horse market on the continent.'

'Yes, but *where* is it?'

'As Seama said, North and West of here, Captain. Thereabouts. I think.'

'Nice to know you're so sure, Terrance. Let's hope we don't get lost then. By the look of it there's not much chance of asking for directions. This place is as good as deserted.'

Bibron was not completely wrong. This land they travelled was populated but opportunities to meet people were few. At this end of the plain it was a population on the move, with only a few steady settlements between them. This was horse country and the Valdanas managed the herds. Further North were studs devoted to breeding the best hunters and racing horses known the world over, but on the lower plain the wild herds were maintained as a live bloodstock against the day that the breeds weakened. The Valdanas sold their bred stock the length and breadth of the continent and beyond but, as a matter of honour, they kept the wild horses for themselves. Anyone could see that even though their days might be filled with the regular toil and daily trials that filled lives the world over, the heart and soul of the Valdana was ever at a gallop with the wind in his hair, the raw power of the beast thundering on beneath him and only the stars above to look down.

Technically these people toiled in the name of Agwis, or whomever the current King in Garassa might be. Horses were supplied by long standing agreements to the court and to any the court favoured, and indeed the profit from all this labour was held to be property of the crown. In return Valdez had become recognized as a Dukedom of Aegarde. This had been the situation for many hundreds of years. This arrangement however couldn't be taken at face value: the Valdanas were an independent people, scornful of interference. It would go ill with any King in Garassa if he ever thought to demand any of the money due.

'Don't worry, Captain,' said Terrance with a smile, 'I daresay that somewhere here we'll find a road heading north and then we just need to make sure we take something easterly after ten miles or so.'

And so they set off across the rolling plain, plodding up the hills and cantering down into the shallows between. And at every crest most of them expected the sudden sight of some road or track but at every crest they were disappointed. Even trying to keep to their route was difficult though the sun rode high in the sky, as the ascents and descents repeatedly skewed their direction from the true, and the sameness of everything around them offered no clues at all. Two hours had passed before Seama's patience finally snapped.

'Angren,' he called, 'You've got to know this country pretty well over the years, haven't you?'

'I have,' the swordsman conceded with no evident enthusiasm. He was slumped in his saddle, hands on the pommel, letting the horse decide where to go.

'Then perhaps you could give us some advice. Are there no decent roads in any of this?'

'None you'd really call roads.'

'Oh?'

'Nope. Not proper roads.'

'Trails then?'

'Not so much trails. More like… routes, if you must know: straight lines from one place to another but not definite trails that anyone could follow. Well maybe a few. Not easy to find. Valdez likes it that way.'

'So how do we know which direction to go in with no landmarks and no roads?'

'We don't.'

Seama threw up his arms in despair. Angren's attitude was infuriating. He knew that Angren was being deliberately unhelpful – he knew exactly what they needed to get on.

'Angren,' the wizard said, trying for a conciliatory tone but failing, 'we need information; we need people to give us that information; we need to find a road to find the people. For The Many Gods' Sakes *will you tell me how to do it?*'

Angren chuckled: it had been a long time since Seama was anywhere near shouting mad. 'It's so easy, I thought you'd have seen,' he said. 'Look, over there.'

They all looked in the direction Angren had pointed.

'Where?' demanded Berta.

'As far as you can see.'

There seemed to be nothing but the green plain and the clouds above. Then Sigrid laughed. She had a quick brain as well as sharp eyes.

'Of course! I've got it now. You can all see it, you just haven't realised what it means. Shall I explain, Old Angren?'

'Why not,' Angren agreed, grinning broadly. Seama had no idea what they were supposed to be looking at and it was clear that Angren knew it.

'Well,' Sigrid began, 'What you can see is the land and the sky. In the sky there are clouds. The sun is nearly behind us and I'd guess, by the time of day, that we're looking north west. What counts is the colour of the clouds at that point as compared with the rest.'

They all looked again and saw now an easily definable though wavering column of yellowing smoke or steam amid the overall greyness.

'And look,' she continued, 'Away to the right of that, more northerly, another pillar of yellow like the first. Guessed yet? You can't see them from here but I think we all know what's at the foot of those clouds.'

Indeed most of them knew. Seama was annoyed with himself for not having guessed sooner but Bibron, man of the River and the Sea, had not an inkling.

'Well? Someone bloody *tell* me then, you're all so clever. Volcanoes or something is it?'

'Not quite, Captain,' Angren told him amiably, 'We're talking about dragons. It's on all the maps. The dragons have two main lairs that're connected by tunnels even though they're a good hundred miles apart. They say the dragon-fire has something to do with sulphur and that's why all those yellow fumes rise from the entrances to the pits. Whether that's the truth or not, I don't know. Doesn't matter really. You just have to know that the sky there and over there is always yellow and that you can see it from anywhere on the plain. The Valdanas have been taking their bearings from it as long as they can remember. I'm surprised you didn't know about that Seama.'

The wizard shrugged. 'It's impossible for one man to know and understand everything, even one as old as I am. No, I knew about the pits and the fumes of course but I'd never thought of them as landmarks.'

'Nice to know you're not perfect.'

'Isn't it!' Seama laughed at himself. 'Well then, how does direction finding help us at all, given we don't know where we are to start with?'

Angren grinned again. 'Actually, when we were in Slaney I did a bit of shopping. Got myself this compass, which I hope works better than Bibron's, and I got myself a map to go with it. I've been keeping track seeing as no one else seemed bothered. Another two miles and we come to the end of the Hammerhand. *That* do you?'

MIRACLE

In a lighter mood the day's journey continued. They found no trails at all but Angren led them confidently, looking to reach some form of habitation by mid-afternoon.

Angren was absurdly pleased to have got the better of Seama for once and this not only cheered him up but somehow it managed to restore his fondness for the wizard. He also found himself pleased to be leader of the company for a while, though he'd never really thought of himself as a master of men, whatever his birthright. He preferred to portray himself as a free agent, a sturdy soldier without any responsibility greater than that of obeying the orders of whoever was paying, and that only when he had a mind to. But he would have to admit that whenever the situation became serious and things needed to be done, Angren had a habit of just getting on and doing them, and if that meant telling other people what to do to get those things done then so be it – but it didn't make him some sort of general or anything like it.

Maintaining their direction was easy and so he lent an ear to the conversation around him.

The brothers were telling a raucous tale of their early military careers, much of which seemed to revolve around the outwitting of an ogre of a drill-sergeant. All armies had them, Angren reflected, both the sergeants who might mean well but were bred into petty cruelties, and the young buffoons who played practical jokes and broke the rules just for fun. Looking at Edro and Piedoro, quick-witted, lithe and rakish, he doubted they'd changed much over the years.

They were telling their story to anyone who wanted to listen but their attention was centred upon Sigrid. She was a fighter like the rest of them and yet she was a good-looking woman, small and dark, with all the curves necessary to attract any man. The brothers considered themselves to be in friendly rivalry for her affections and she was flattered by the attention, though she gave neither any promise. As he watched, Sigrid gave Angren a wink and he smiled in return. He was pleased that Sig' and Berta were still with them and he wasn't looking forward to the inevitable parting of the ways.

Given the obvious direction of the brothers' interest others started conversations among themselves. De Vere was in a wide debate with Seama about the politics of the world through the ages. He appeared to be quite a scholar and knew much about Partain history in particular. He was eager to learn more about Aegarde and Gothery and Seama seemed happy to help him. Angren was still suspicious of the dandy: he asked too many questions altogether. It was clear Seama trusted the man, and that should have been enough for him, but Angren decided to remain wary. Meanwhile, as history bored him, he left them to it.

Garaid was quiet and thoughtful and content to bring up the rear. Angren couldn't remember him speaking at all since the incident at the stables, or certainly nothing at length. Obviously it had affected him more than anyone else, but that wasn't surprising since he'd held the blade that ended it. Angren decided there was nothing to be done, the kingsman just needed time to think it through.

Bibron laughed his parrot laugh at one of Edro's jokes and tried his best to get Berta involved in the talk but she seemed distracted and ill-at-ease. Every few seconds, she'd peer ahead as if she expected something of dubious nature to crawl over the horizon. Berta had her moods, more perhaps than Angren, but generally she was always ready for a good joke. Something was bothering her.

Angren managed to steer his horse to walk alongside hers while still keeping them all on the correct course and as he did so Bibron tactfully drew back to talk with Sigrid and the brothers.

'Well, Berta, what do you think of this chase of ours?'

She didn't look around to face Angren but said, still searching the sky ahead: 'What should I think?'

'I don't know. Maybe that we're running about in the dark

looking for invisible enemies while other people are fighting proper battles.'

'No Angren. That's what you think. Or maybe you only partly think it.' She turned to him now with a half-smile on her lips. Angren said nothing. 'No, I don't think that at all,' she said. 'I know that me and Sig' have a job to do and we'll be heading on northwards without you sooner or later, but I can't help thinking that just now I'm in the right place. Oh, I know he can't tell us everything, and that's fair enough 'cause I haven't the brains for strategy and politics, but Angren, whatever my orders, I'm here because of Seama. And so is Sig, and so are you. And if he wants us to fight dark sorcerers, whatever the risk, well, fight dark sorcerers is what I'd like to do.'

'I'm glad to hear it. So, the problem is you don't want to do what Mador wants? I wondered: you haven't seemed happy this couple of days.' Angren said this quietly so that the others couldn't hear.

Berta forced a laugh. 'Think you're clever, do you? Orders, orders, always orders? No Angren, these things can't be helped. You take the commission, you do the duty. If that was all that was wrong, well... But it isn't. What it is... it's...' Berta was struggling to spit it out and Angren wondered why. 'It's... well it's stupid. I'd feel daft telling you.'

'What's stupid?' Angren had the sudden, uncomfortable feeling that Berta was going to reveal something that would embarrass them both. Surely she didn't...

'Just think where we are,' she said. 'Doesn't it worry you?'

Angren was confused. 'Not sure what you mean, Berta. I've travelled round these parts quite a bit.'

'But the dragons!'

'Oh, I see,' said Angren, immensely relieved, *the dragons.* Great vicious beasties just over the next hill and we may be attacked any moment. You don't fancy ending up in a dragon's belly?'

'It's all very well for you to scoff, isn't it,' Berta snapped in response, 'I've never been here before, and I've never seen a dragon, and all the tales we were told about them when I was a kid were not very nice at all. Dragons eat people! I never thought I'd ever end up on these plains but here I am, ready to be eat. What I don't understand is why nobody else seems bothered about it. Makes me feel like a coward.'

Angren laughed but made up for it by explaining.

'I guess no one else is worried because they've been up here before, or if not maybe they've heard more than children's stories. It's pretty well-known the dragons hardly ever come out at all. Well, not when you compare it to the number of times men cross the Plains. How do you think people manage to live and work here? Apparently the dragons live in a different sort of time to us, they sleep longer and when they fly they use up so much energy chasing their food that they only ever stay out for a few hours.'

'But I thought I'd heard Seama say something about the dragons being on the increase.'

'Ah, now you have something there: according to some of the old folk, you see more dragons now than they did say twenty years ago. More fly together. You might see ten in a wing where before they flew in pairs. Instead of two flights a year now you could see two a month. But if you think about it, Berta, even twice a month is nothing. Not on plains as broad as these. So long as men travel in small groups the dragons tend to overlook them. It's the herds they're after, horse and wild cattle: easy meat. There is a small chance we could see dragons in flight, depends on how long we stay, but they won't be close at hand and they'll be absolutely no danger to us.'

Berta tried to look as if she believed him.

'But,' she persisted, 'why are there more sightings now than before?'

'Some people say the dragons are taking less sleep and so they fly more often but, of course, that doesn't explain why they sleep less. I think that there are just more dragons than there were. There's bound to be young coming along every so often, but meanwhile the older dragons just carry on. Unless he's killed, a dragon never dies.'

'Well, I suppose you're right.' The frown returned. 'But how come it was only twenty years ago there were so few? I mean after all these hundreds of years, have they just learned how to have baby dragons? And another thing, if they carry on increasing at the same rate, how long are the herds going to last? And what happens if they don't last? I suppose the dragons'll have to take what they can get.'

Angren shrugged: his hearsay didn't give him an answer. 'I was trying to cheer you up. Can't we forget about them for now? Until we see one at least. We're not in any danger from them, you know, not now, not ever.'

'Ever's a long time, Angren.'

'It is. Stupid trying to predict the future, I know that. But put it this way, if a dragon flew up this minute we'd still be safe. So long as Seama's with us it wouldn't have a prayer.'

He tried to sound confident. His knowledge, his experience, his common sense all told him to be so, but even as he spoke the seed of doubt was sown. It was a ridiculous notion, of course, but were dragons now something else they had to worry about?

'Hang on you two,' yelled Bibron to the brothers. Edro had shouted: 'Race you!' and charged off towards the small wood down in the valley bottom knowing that Piedoro would have to follow. It was a measure of the power in the Captain's voice that they both reined in hard and came about.

'What's the problem boss?' Edro asked, shrugging his broad shoulders, 'Seama said there were only four of them.'

'Perhaps you didn't hear but he also said that three of them were children. Now I don't know how he knows these things, being able to see through the trees an all, but I know he'll be right about that. So how do you think three kids'll feel with armed men galloping into their camp?'

Piedoro thumped his brother on the arm. 'Captain's right, Edronio. Why don't you think, eh? You always rush in.'

'*Me? Rush in?* Hah! We both know, brother of mine, that if any man is reckless then *you* are that man.'

Piedoro grinned. 'Only in love, Edro, only in love. Otherwise I am cautious, sensible, wise: a man of discretion and—'

'An idiot?'

'Will you two stop your yammering? Now look, I say we send the ladies in first so the kids aren't scared – don't forget the Black Company have been in these parts and everyone'll have heard about them, even the children. What do you think, Seama?'

Seama glanced up at the titanic form of Berta as she sat in the saddle absent-mindedly swinging her cosh. 'I'm sure you're right Captain,' he said, 'But perhaps Sigrid and *Terrance* might do best. We are trying to reassure them, after all.'

'Yes,' agreed Terrance, 'We wouldn't want to frighten anyone.'

Berta frowned. 'What does he mean?'

'Well, er, just that perhaps I'm more used to—'

Sigrid laughed. 'Forget it, Terrance. She likes being scary.'

Berta chuckled. 'And just you remember it.'

'Don't worry, I will. Well then, let's be getting down there, the afternoon's getting on.'

As they cantered into the dark paths through the trees Sigrid had no worries or expectations or any real notion of what they might find down at the mere's edge.

They had seen from a distance a thin spiral of blue smoke rising above the trees. The smoke had given Seama something to focus on. Sigrid didn't pretend to understand. Typically, the wizard had been modest about his abilities, claiming that the power of far-seeing was not one of his better skills. All things were relative of course. Compared with that member of the Council known only as Sight, back on Errensea, Seama might well be considered a lowly apprentice but to most of his companions, Sigrid included, his being able to discern not only how many people were in the wood but their age and their sex too was amazing. That he couldn't tell them anything more seemed unimportant. They were just people. An odd group perhaps, but there was nothing much in that.

And yet, as their horses broke cover, it took only a moment for Sigrid to see what there was to see and understand what there was to understand, and the knowledge she gained in those few moments blistered through her heart like nothing she had ever seen or understood before. Details were not knowable but that brave lad, with acres of confusion and hurt in his eyes, trying his best to seem bold, and the silent girl clutching the baby to her breast, just as a mother should, but already beginning to shake in terror as they approached, and that ruined man dragging himself erect in an attempt to face them standing, the pain cutting through his every movement, all of this was enough. It was too much.

Sigrid burst into tears. 'Who has done this?' she cried, 'Oh who has done this to you? It's not... they couldn't have...'

'Sigrid, what are you saying?' Terrance was behind, unsighted at first.

'Don't you see what they've done?'

Sigrid slid down from her horse, trying to stop her own tears, wanting to comfort the girl, but the little one shrank away and then ran to the broken man, holding the baby more tightly than ever. She hid in the man's arms, sobbing in fear. And the look of anguish on her protector's face had nothing to do with his own pain.

Sigrid realized that the man's eyes were fixed on Terrance, who was still in his saddle, immobilized by what he saw.

'Get down,' Sigrid hissed, 'Get down Terrance. Can't you see she's seen enough of men on horses.'

Her sharp words stung him into motion. Dismounted he took off his sword-belt, cast both sword and scabbard behind him and then sat upon the ground a good distance from the man and the girl.

'There,' he said to them, 'Gone. And I will stay here, and you can talk to the Lady Sigrid.'

The broken man nodded slightly.

'Thank you sir,' the man said. His voice was naturally warm but pinched now by emotion and trauma. 'She has not... this is the first time since... You see, I have had to keep her hidden from others – until she is a little stronger. The boy manages better.' He paused. By turn he looked into their eyes. What they saw, looking back, was not the middle-aged man who stood swaying before them, the mangled torso barely disguised by a loose cassock and a face pale from suffering; they saw only the penetrating grey eyes that held them until released. He sighed. 'I think I am glad to see you. For Carla this may be a beginning.' He stroked the girl's hair, causing her to look up. 'Do you see, Pica, this nice lady would like to talk to us. Perhaps you can show to her our lovely little one.'

The girl shook her head fiercely.

'Not yet, then. Well what if you leave him with me. See, I'll sit here, and then you and Benito can make us some tea. Is that a good idea?'

Sigrid could see that the girl was unwilling to let go. Scared for herself and scared for her precious charge.

'Come Carlita,' he persisted, 'We will all be safe now.'

As though summoned by her need, the boy who had stood quietly, unmoving until now, came to stand with the girl and he stooped to touch her hand. It was the slightest of contacts.

'I'll get the water,' he said, with his slow lips. And it was enough.

The man lowered himself to sit with his back up against a pile of soft bolsters that lay by the cart. Carla watched him. It was plain she could see every spike of pain the movement cost him and distress was now mixed with anger on her face. She surrendered the baby to him, laying the infant so gently in his lap that the tears slipped down Sigrid's cheeks once more.

Sigrid wondered that the infant had not made the slightest noise so far and momentarily had the horrible thought that perhaps the child was no longer alive, and hadn't been for some time.

'Is the baby... uninjured?'

The man smiled. 'Yes, yes. Remarkably he finds it easy to sleep through any disturbance – it may be that I am responsible for that. But see he is waking now.'

Sigrid moved closer to them and Carla retreated a little.

'Carla, why don't you go to find the cups and rinse the pot. Benito, the water you promised?'

'Yes Signoren. I'll get it now. There's a *good fire going* so it won't take long.'

The boy was off with a bucket to the water's edge and Carla hesitated only a moment longer before she went into action, climbing into the back of the cart and searching through boxes. Sigrid was amazed.

'She always was a strong child, always liked to take charge. What you saw before was not the real Carla. In this small family she is the mistress her mother always taught her to be. But here, come and see our little miracle.'

Sigrid crouched by him while he pulled the swaddling aside.

'She does look after him so well but I think she keeps him too wrapped up. He needs the air in his face and the sun on his limbs.'

Oh but he was a well-made baby. As beautiful and ugly as he should be with well-proportioned limbs and skin rather golden, or maybe that was something to do with the warm late-afternoon sun that smiled down upon them. He stretched with his tiny hands clenched in the ecstasy of the movement. And then he smiled and Sigrid's heart melted.

'We have a lot to be thankful for.'

'Yes,' she breathed, 'I see.'

They were silent for a few minutes. It took Terrance coughing to break Sigrid out of the spell that held her.

'Well,' she said, dragging her eyes away from the baby's face, 'We must begin. My name is—'

'Sigrid. Yes, I heard, and your friend is Terrance. The children know me as The Signoren but Oswaldo Bassalo is my name. I was their teacher. They have known me for all of their short lives, and they trust me because their mothers and fathers trusted me. Benito and Carla are not related but Bene looks after her, as well as he can, as though she were his own sister.' He paused to look at each of the children. Benito was pouring water into the copper kettle from the bucket and Carla was watching him to make sure he wasn't overfilling it. 'We are one family now. We are all that is left. We have no one and we have nothing but ourselves.'

Sigrid was not ready for the tale and she certainly wouldn't prompt it. Not yet.

'Terrance and I came first,' she said, 'because we didn't want to worry the children.'

'Came first? There are more of you… Of course there are.' His grey eyes narrowed. 'You *knew* there were children?'

'Well… er.' Sigrid realized she shouldn't blurt out Seama's name.

'So one of your companions is a magician.'

'I… well…'

'No point, Sigrid,' said Terrance, 'He knows. Signoren, we do have a man of *power* with us but he is a wizard and not a sorcerer, and we are a small company indeed and most assuredly will be no harm to you. But then I thought you already knew that. I had thought that perhaps you may have a certain power of your own.'

'Forgive me, yes, I did know, but…' he sighed, 'It is not just the children who need to learn how to trust again. And yes I have a little *power*. Too little. Would to the Gods I had more.' Though he didn't cry, it was plain that fierce emotions racked his body quite as much as his many injuries. He mastered himself after a minute or two and then continued matter-of-factly. 'So, how shall we proceed? You have how many companions?'

'Seven.'

'Too many. I cannot have them all here. The children could not—'

'Forgive me,' Terrance put in, 'but it is a certainty that eventually the children will have to meet other people, for you cannot live in the wild forever. Now, I admit we are a warlike looking party but what if I have our friends put aside their weapons, and if they walk in, a few at a time to give us a chance to introduce them to the children? Forgive me but I cannot help thinking this would be a good thing for all of you. An opportunity to—'

'An opportunity for us to begin to learn to cope?'

'A safe opportunity. I think you know I am not lying to you.'

Bassalo relented. 'Yes. Yes I do know that, and yes I can see you are right.' He looked over at the children. The girl had stopped to listen but the boy, with his job in hand, paid no heed to anything but the kettle. 'Now Carla, what do you think? Can these friends come to see us? You can sit with me when they come. One of them is a wizard and he may be able to help us. What do you say?'

Sigrid tried to smile warmly at the girl but she found herself wanting to cry again. The resolve in the girl's face as she studied the Signoren was almost too much to bear. She was clearly assessing his disability and his weakness. If a wizard could make the Signoren well… She nodded and then, with her mind made up, briskly took herself off to the cart once again in search of more cups.

'She's so brave,' said Sigrid quietly to the Signoren.

'She is just seven years old. After everything they did, I think she is extraordinary. Well, you have your permission. Go and get your friends but, please, no weapons, no horses.'

It was done. Sigrid stayed with Bassalo and the children while Terrance went off to arrange things. As they began to arrive, Terrance first with Seama, Sigrid introduced them, speaking mostly to Carla and making sure she told her something nice about each of them. Seama was described as 'a very good man who always helps people, and famous throughout the world,' while Edro and Piedoro 'were two brothers who have loved each other and played and lived with each other all their lives – and they are very funny.' She struggled a little with Angren and had to settle for 'he's my good friend and someone I trust to always keep me safe.' She made sure Angren didn't hear this, but when she realised what she'd said she found herself blushing. Angren failed to notice.

All of the companions were very quiet according to their instructions but also because it was hard to know what to say. Every one of them was affected to some degree by what they saw.

'She's *so* like our little sister when she was young,' Piedoro whispered to Berta and Bibron. He was trying to explain the tears in his brother's eyes.

Carla poured the tea into the six cups she'd found and sent

the lad off to hand them out. Benito was pleased to be trusted with the job. They could all see that look of concentration in his face as he determined not to spill a drop. With each cup he gave them an uncertain smile inviting a response. Angren made sure he was not disappointed.

'Good lad,' he said, 'that's just what I need.'

Benito's smile broadened.

'*Always make it hot and sweet*, that's what my dad says. Oh, but we haven't any sugar.' His smile disappeared and he looked cross with himself as though he had done something wrong.

'Don't you worry, it's fine the way it is,' said Angren, 'But your dad was right. He sounds like he knew a thing or two. Look, you just sit here and tell me all about him – we can let Garaid here hand out the rest of these, give him something to do.'

Garaid was sitting at the edge of the group fidgeting and looking very unsettled.

'Garaid!'

He looked up at Angren and at the three cups in Benito's left hand and then nodded. Benito gave up his commission reluctantly and frowned when Garaid managed to spill some of the tea as he took the cups.

'So Benito, your Dad. What job did he do?'

'My dad was a carpenter, *the best in the county*. He let me help him sometimes. I did planing, what I was best at.'

'A good trade carpentry,' put in Bibron, 'My brother went for a carpenter before he got taken on as a shipwright. Do you think you could take to it?'

'Well... I'm not so good at some of the other jobs.'

'Well neither were he before he learned. But if you like handling the wood it comes to you eventually.'

Benito smiled again. Perhaps it was an unusual thing for him to talk about what he might be able to do rather than what he could not. So it went. The companions, Sigrid and Bibron in particular, took up an interest in anything Benito wanted to talk about. Carla watched for a few minutes before making up her mind about whether she wanted to go over to them. The

Signoren lifted the baby a little and Carla was quick to take him into her slight arms.

'Yes Carla. I think you should take our little wonder to see them. Benito will look after you. I need to talk with the Lord Seama.'

She nodded gravely at this idea and without any more hesitation she went to sit with them, putting herself between her adopted brother and the kind lady who seemed so gentle. And although Carla could not speak to contribute anything of her own she seemed happy enough to listen to the conversation around her.

Now that the children were well distracted Seama and Terrance sat down with the Signoren, and a quick glance from the wizard was enough to bring Angren over to join them. It was time for talk. Bassalo's story needed telling and they needed to listen however uncomfortable that story might prove to be. Anything they could find out about the Black Company would help them decide what to do next.

'So Signoren,' Seama said, as Angren settled himself, 'as Angren is the only one of us who knows the area at all, I thought that maybe you could start by giving us a picture of what life is like here and in the Skirt, and an idea of the different settlements and so on.'

In truth Seama knew enough about the region but he thought it might be better to work their way into the Signoren's story one step at a time. Bassalo seemed pleased to have some sort of structure to adhere to and so he began with a geography lesson that would have credited any classroom. Seama let him talk for a good while without any interruption. It was as the Signoren began to focus in on the village of Huaresh and his schoolhouse and the children he'd taught there that Seama looked over at the rest of the company. It was a quiet but happy scene: already Sigrid held Carla in her arms as together they cradled the baby. Sigrid found a lullaby from somewhere deep inside, and the little girl leaned her head back against Sigrid's shoulder and closed her eyes.

'Never knew she had such a lovely voice,' said Angren thickly.

'The little 'un won't like it when we have to go.'

'She will not,' Seama agreed, 'but at least she has begun to recover because of this moment, whatever pain may come later. Signoren, you know I have the ability to speak to her more deeply than with words, and she'll be able to reply. Do you want me to try? It may help bring her voice back.'

Bassalo had been watching Sigrid and the child. He shook his head slowly. 'I don't know. I think it will come back when she is ready. There is a reason she cannot speak: if her tongue cannot form the words then she cannot say it, and if she cannot say it then she does not need to think it.'

Seama pursed his lips. 'Yes I see, but I'm not sure that's a good thing. There must come a point—'

'Must there?'

'Yes. It's always better to confront the bad things in your life, because if you don't those bad things begin to control you.'

Angren wouldn't have that. 'For Gods sakes, Seama, she's a child. What she needs is time not confrontation. She'll start to feel better when she's got a long way away from here!'

Angren's voice was louder and the tones harder than necessary. The lullaby faltered as all eyes turned towards him and the look in Benito's eyes was fearful.

'Please do not shout.' Bassalo said this quietly but it was plain that he was annoyed. 'What Carla needs in fact is her mother and her father and her baby sister, she needs her home and certainty, she needs the knowledge that she can go to sleep without fear and that she will wake up to a normal day.'

They all looked at him. The words were sharp in meaning if not in delivery.

'You may wonder that I do not weep as I speak. I have lost the ability.'

It was all so desperate. Seama made up his mind to get down to it: there was no point in delaying anymore. He asked the Signoren to describe what had happened when the Black Company came to Huaresh and then both he and Terrance listened motionless as Bassalo revealed to them the full horror of that day. Not so the weapon-master – Angren couldn't sit still, rocking slightly, clenching his fists as he struggled with the deadly rage that was building in him. Seama hoped the tale wouldn't take too long.

Bassalo to give him due could see that drawing the story out wasn't necessary. He didn't dwell on the violence, and avoided offering any detail on what the Company had done to Carla and her parents. But perhaps like Carla he couldn't bring himself to speak about things he would rather forget. He gave them the mechanics: the organization of the defence and his attempt to save his people, the formation of the attack and the numbers involved, the calling of the demon. He attempted to skate through the rape of the village.

'There was murder and violation and mutilation all around. Everywhere. They left none untouched…' Bassalo was shaking and the shaking brought him fresh pain. Seama thought that weeping long and hard might have been better for the Signoren. Terrance laid a hand upon the teacher's shoulder.

'But you survived Oswaldo. You survived and you saved these children—'

'I saved no one! I was fixed at the top of the bell-tower – struck through by one of the uprights. I could not move. I just had to watch as those monsters destroyed everyone and everything that I loved, and I could do nothing.'

'But the baby?'

'*He* saved *me*! You must understand: I was ready to die – I *wanted* to die. But then I saw him, down in the wreckage of the schoolhouse. He was nestled in his mother's arms. She was hidden between a turned over trestle and the stage. I could see them only because I was so high up. For some time I couldn't tell whether they were dead or alive, but then the baby moved and his mother's arm fell away. Such a tiny chap, I could see that, but full of life. He was trying to get his lips back on the nipple, trying so hard, and then I realised he was going to cry. He was going to cry and those animals would hear him and find him. And it didn't matter that he was an infant: they had murdered at least five babes in arms already, and worse. But that was when he saved me. You see I could not let them take him – I would not let them take him.

'So I had to stay alive. And I had to cover his cries, and I had to make him sleep and do this until they had gone. You will understand what I did, Seama?'

'You drew in your strength and gave it over to those two tasks, whatever it might cost you for the future. You have my deepest respect Signoren. I used the spell to conceal quite recently. For you to have made him sleep is nothing less than a marvel.'

'The circumstance demanded I succeed. But yes it was hard and I was nearly dead, whatever my intent, by the time the Company moved on.'

'I'm surprised they left,' said Angren, 'You said there was an inn?'

'There was some complaint among the men but I think they had news of some resistance building. A group of our men had escaped into the forest; I know the plan was to meet up with others from some of the neighbouring villages.' Bassalo paused to think. He took a great lungful of air despite the pain the movement cost him. The memory of it all seemed to be taking his breath away. 'I'm not sure which would have been better,' he said, shaking his head, 'They might have carried on with their games and perhaps some of my people would have survived somehow, but before they left they were ordered to... to 'tidy up.' Yes that's what they called it: *tidying up.*'

'How did the children survive?'

'The lad was in a cellar hiding. I don't know for how long and I don't know how much of the carnage he had to listen to, but I know that he lay there waiting for them to find him. It is hard for Benito to know what to do most of the time. The boys in the village would always mock him so for being slow. They'd most likely have called him a yellow-belly for staying put. Yes they would. But they would have been wrong. He may be slow but Benito knew what he had to do for once, and I am so glad he did.

'He came out only when all the screams had long finished. It was the sound of the baby crying that called him – called both of them. I was so tired by then, passing out every few minutes.

It gave me a shock to see the pair of them climbing through the schoolhouse. Gave them a shock too when I spoke out. Poor Bene! We made him cut me down. He knew it would be bad and bad it was. I think I got most of my injuries then, and Bene thought he'd done wrong. Again. He thinks that everything he does is wrong. He's had to live with criticism all his life. Well not any more. We would have died without Benito. My Benito. He is… he is… oh such a good boy.' The Signoren had to be quiet for a few minutes before he could continue. He may not have been able to shed tears but a man can cry without them.

Edro brought over some fresh tea just then and Bassalo took the cup he was offered in the palm of his hand. Perhaps the heat of the cup was a more bearable sort of pain.

Terrance it seemed had decided the Signoren had pain enough.

'Here, let me put some milk in that. Now, let's get this tale done and then we can decide what to do next. Little Carla. She survived too and it seems to me that small though she is, she has played her part in keeping you all alive. You have become a good team.'

'Well yes. Yes we are. Benito was in a terrible state after – he didn't know what to do. The worst damage was the spar forced right through, just below my right shoulder. Carla was incredible. She could see it had to come out. Made the lad draw it a bit at a time while she staunched the bleeding. It was a bad moment. I passed out completely. When I came round I had to ask them to stitch my wounds. Benito fetched his mother's sewing box but it was Carla who did the job. She had Benito pushing the flesh together while she stitched. Imagine that: a seven year old girl! Just like her mother… so strong.

'I was lucky she hadn't been killed. That captain of theirs had taken quite an interest in them, in what they did to her parents – what they made her watch, in what they did to her. No doubt the idea of leaving her alive in all the carnage amused him somehow. Maybe they just forgot her. We may never know. If ever we meet again I'll ask him.'

'Ask him?' Angren was reaching boiling point. 'If *I* ever catch up with the bastard, I'll do more than ask him questions. Look, did you find out who they were, did you hear any names?'

Bassalo seemed surprised or perhaps confused by Angren's reaction. 'What does it matter? They did what they did and now they have gone.'

'It matters,' Angren growled, 'because when I find them, the scum are going to suffer for what they did. I'm going to make them pay.'

Terrance shook his head. 'It matters,' he said more reasonably, 'because they'll do this again, and again, until they are stopped. Any information you can give us may help us find them. We'll put an end to it.'

Bassalo was still studying Angren. 'So you are intent upon avenging Huaresh?'

Seama was irritated by the question. 'It is not, Signoren, a matter of vengeance.'

'It bloody is with me!' Angren insisted, 'I'm not going to let that lot get away with it. You were saying, Signoren: names?'

Bassalo frowned. Seama gave up.

'There were so many of them, all calling out to each other. So much movement. I can't remember. The only one was the captain. He sat upon his horse the whole time, watching everything. They'd call to him to draw his attention to whatever they were doing. It was almost a competition between them and he was the judge. I remember his name. Trant it was, Morgan Trant.'

It was at this point that Angren finally exploded into a rage that scared the children half to death before Bibron and Terrance and Edro managed to frogmarch him, swearing and frothing in sheer fury, out of the camp and into the trees.

NEW PATHS, ANCIENT LANDSCAPES

South Valdesian Plain 3057.8.1

'Morgan Trant crippled my brother. I swore if I ever found him I'd kill him.'

'So you said.'

'Crippled him! Sliced right through the back of his legs not once but *three times*. And just because he stood up to him. Told him what a traitor he was, and a murderer and a thief. Then Trant had his men chop-up Dag's school-mates, and he made Dag watch. For god's sakes, those kids were twelve years old! Killed because they wouldn't stand back, wouldn't let Trant and his gang just walk in and take what they wanted. Killed because that bastard is pure evil! If I ever find him, and I will, I'm going to kill him. Nice and slow.'

Seama sighed. Angren had been ranting in much the same vein ever since they had left Bassalo and the children and he didn't seem inclined to stop. Now it was hours later and they were supposed to be settling for the night but still the red rage ran hot in him. No more boredom, no more thinking it was just a job. Now it was personal. Seama wondered if that might not be a good thing. The blind fury would soon abate no doubt, overnight maybe, but it would leave Angren implacable, determined and deadly. And such an Angren could be a very powerful weapon indeed.

'Do you want me to help you get some sleep, Angren?'

'What? Sleep? Oh I see. You mean you want to go to sleep and I should just shut up. That's nice.' He got to his feet. 'Well I'm off for a walk so you lot can do what you like.' And off he stumped.

Sleep would be welcome, Seama thought. It had been a traumatic day and he wanted to bring an end to it. The leaving of Bassalo and the children had been awful. Little Carla had clung on to Sigrid and wailed. It was the first noise she had made in three weeks but there was no comfort in that. Sigrid had sat with her and talked to her and hugged her. Seama stood by and listened as Sig explained that she had a job to do now: to stop those bad men, to make the world a safe place for children. But she promised that when the job was done she'd find Carla again and things would be better. And she explained that Carla had her job to do too: she must look after Benito and their miracle baby and the Signoren because she could do that better than anyone.

It was this last that stopped the wailing and caused the child to straighten her face, and dry her eyes and set herself to the task. There were tears pouring down Sigrid's cheeks but, mind made up, little Carla wriggled free of Sigrid's arms and in a very determined fashion she stepped up to face Seama.

Seama didn't need words for him to understand what she wanted. She pulled him by the sleeve and made him walk over to where Bassalo sat by the cart. She laid his hand on the Signoren's back and with only the fierce look in her dark eyes she demanded his help. She wanted him to cure the Signoren.

Seama shook his head. If only he could. There was something in Seama that pushed in one way and not in another. Tregar could have helped Bassalo. He could have eased the pain certainly. He could have made the mending faster. But not Seama. It was true that he'd surprised himself by mending his own arm when it was burned, without even having to think about it, but he knew this wasn't the same. He'd often tried and always failed to use his power to heal. Most recently the best he had managed with Edro's gashed arm was to bind it and staunch the bleeding, and to speak a protection to stop infection. The raw power he had poured into his own wounds didn't seem to flow into others, or rather he seemed incapable of directing that power. It was a skill he'd failed to master, a talent denied him but one he envied.

But Carla didn't understand that. She could not and would not. Even though he tried to find the right words, words to explain, words that said he was not being selfish, her gaze remained insistent. Seama was a wizard, a real wizard. Well wasn't he? Signoren Bassalo was not, but even he could heal people. The Signoren would always help anyone in need. Seama didn't need to hear the words spoken.

Bassalo came to his rescue.

'Lord Seama, I see your problem here: we can only do what we can do, but it's hard for Carla to understand these things. She doesn't want to understand. She wants that we will all be well and safe. I keep telling them we are blessed, have been blessed. I try to tell them we could have died, and yet here we are alive, and better than that because we have our miracle too.' Bassalo paused here to reach out and touch the infant, lying in a bundle of soft blankets by his side. 'Yes, our miracle.' He looked sharply at the wizard. 'You will wonder at me talking of miracles, Seama. You may think it just a word to match the emotion. But no. I tell you it is nothing but the truth.

'This child was born in the middle of the maelstrom. All around was violence and death and yet he survived. His mother was dead and yet she gave him suck. There were no arms to hold him close and yet he found the strength to feed. There was something else looking after him, Seama, some power that was looking after us all. I will say it: the name of Ohr'mazd was in my mind. I did not know why then, but I do know now. There is something important about this child, Seama. His birth was some sort of redemption for that terrible day. I only hope I can survive long enough to see what it all means. The gods have a plan for him, I know it. They wanted him to live and they want us to live, just to protect him.

'And to protect him I need to become well. I know that, and the little one knows it too. When we left the village – as leave we must because we could not bury the dead – I had to choose a direction. For all I knew the Black Company were still in the region. I guessed that they would have gone on to attack more of the villages in the North of the Skirt. My plan, poor though it may now seem, was to make for Gothery. Ciudad Valdez seemed too far, given the state we were in. I was wrong. We found one of the Valdana field camps yesterday – that's where we found provision – and they were very kind, but all were men. I couldn't let Carla see them. I made her stay in the wagon and we left as soon as we could. But, of course, that was when I heard that the Company had actually gone south, and that the Morredans were arming for battle with them. They say the Morredans are very strong, impossible to fight. Maybe this time the Black Company and their demons will have not done so well.

'So my choice of where to go, Gothery or Valdez, would seem to have been irrelevant. We all make decisions and act upon them. Or that is what I would have said before the baby came. My actions are my own for good or bad. That is what I would have said. But now it seems to me I was *meant* to come this way; that we, you and me, were *meant* to meet, and there is deep purpose behind all the events that surround this child. What would you say to that?'

Seama raised his eyebrows. 'Predestination isn't taught on Errensea as you know, but we have documented the manipulation of men and women by greater powers for purposes entirely their own. Rarely is such contact to the benefit of mankind. I would be wary of anything that seemed orchestrated in the events of my life. But that is the Collegium in me and we are a sceptical lot. Travel to Lindis and you'll get a different interpretation. Many different interpretations. Perhaps you should follow your own instincts whatever anyone else might say.'

Bassalo looked neither pleased nor annoyed by Seama's speech. He knew the Collegium's position on this.

'My own instinct,' said Bassalo, 'tells me I am right and that I have a task. There is a reason I am still alive and that reason is the baby. But in order to perform my task I need healing.'

'Signoren, as I said, I have no ability to direct my *power*—'

'You need not direct it, only supply it.'

'You want me to lend you—'

'Give me. We both know I could not return what I take. My own *power* is very limited and less now than it was, but I can use the *power* to heal. Can we not try?'

Seama was taken aback by this request. In all his long life no one had asked such a thing. He had never considered the idea. But Healers did this all the time didn't they? Was his *power* so precious, his need for strength so crucial that he couldn't afford to give any of it away? He looked at Carla. The child was tired from her weeping and her care for the baby and her efforts for the Signoren and the boy, and so her eyelids kept dropping as the adults talked and talked, as she allowed the adults to speak. But she wouldn't let them close entirely, and she wouldn't let the wizard leave until she had what she wanted.

Seama had made his decision. If that small child could offer so much, at such cost to herself, then how could he even think about refusing her anything?

'It was well done, Seama,' said Sigrid as she handed him his portion of ham on black bread.

'How did you know what I was thinking?'

'How could you be thinking of anything else? Was it unpleasant? You seemed to be in pain.'

'Unpleasant? Well no, not unpleasant or even painful, but odd. It was like being bled. I had a thought that it wouldn't stop.'

'Blood comes back after a loss. Is it the same with your magic?'

'Well the magic is not finite. The healing left me tired as Tumboll left me tired but I expect that by tomorrow I will hardly remember it. So, yes, I suppose it is a little like blood. And given that, I find it strange that I ever even considered saying no to him. She shamed me into it.'

Sigrid looked cross. 'There's no need to go talking about shame. You could see their need and you agreed to help. If shame is involved anywhere it's the shame of mankind that such brutality could happen in the first place. That it could be *enjoyed*. Where do we get this from?'

'We? We're not anything like the Black Company. Nonsense. They are evil. Most of us are not.'

'But I like *fighting*, Seama. And not because I can make everything right by fighting but because I'm good at it. I like to win. And when you use a sword winning means hurting someone.'

'But you wouldn't attack an innocent child, an unarmed man. You wouldn't enjoy the suffering of others. We should just stick to what we know, Sig, and what we understand and how we understand it. I recognize evil whenever I see it, and my job is to deal with it.'

Sigrid grimaced in reply. 'Don't you sometimes think that a really good job would be spending your time looking after children, watching them grow and keeping them safe. Like Bassalo.'

'I sometimes think nearly anything and everything it is possible to think. And yes there have been moments. But I know myself. Raising children, teaching children, both so important, but not what I was made for. So.' He bit into his black bread and chewed. Sigrid did the same. After a minute or so Seama said: 'I note that you and Berta are still with us. No sign of you wanting to leave the company. Weren't you supposed to be travelling north into Drafas and Kellestan?'

Sigrid grimaced once more. 'Let's just say, Seama, that there are things that you should do as a matter of duty and things that you have to do. I promised Carla those men would be stopped. Berta agrees. So I think Mador's mission will have to wait. Do you object?'

'No Sigrid. Some tasks are more important than others. I would have been sorry to lose you, but I do wonder if the consequences will be all good. You won't be going north and so the north will make up its mind without Mador's influence. However, I've spoken to Bassalo at some length about the situation and he's agreed that Ciudad Valdez would be his best destination. I know that Valdez has a very good healer wizard in Rudolfo and Angren has mentioned someone called Hebog in Terremark if necessary. Bassalo has promised that on his way he'll speak with Valdez in my stead.'

'Does Bassalo still need a healer after what you did?'

'Very much. He has managed the first steps on a long path, there is far to go. At least the journey is now possible.'

Next morning they set off before dawn had fully taken hold. The first part of their journey would take them across the Middle-Way, a busy thoroughfare by the standards of the day. They hoped that an early start and a route taking them halfway between two of the regular way-stops would give them a chance of crossing unseen. And it was a good chance too: with the way-stops a measured thirty miles apart, any merchant's team setting off after breakfast would reach the halfway point by eleven at the earliest. The real trick would be in trying to avoid the fast post riders. They were frequent travellers and their journeys were not governed by set schedules but by need. A rider could pass through at any time and it was certain that any party he saw journeying off the main road would be a matter of report to someone, somewhere down the line.

It was a risk they must take. They were making for the Eastern Forest and the Beltesian Estate of Moreda to see how the Black Company had fared in their latest venture. Badly, they hoped. The road to Moreda should normally have found them back in Gothery, travelling south along the Edge Road and then down from the plateau at Hocha's Knife, a cut in the precipice of the southern plateau made by a forceful stream in a dyke of soft rock. That was the easy route. Even the descent at the Knife was better than it might sound, but Seama wouldn't go that way: it added-in both miles of extra travel and a great deal of unavoidable exposure. Instead they would travel due south, cross the Middle-way, cut through the edge of the Eastern Waste and enter the forest some thirty miles north of the Estate. An inhospitable and uncomfortable route, without doubt, but direct and almost certainly deserted.

It was not yet midmorning when they reached the highway. They might have hoped for some form of cover but their luck wasn't in. The terrain here was wide and flat and largely treeless. The company decided that nothing could help them more than speed and hope, but as they neared the road their hope proved rootless. A cohort of Gotherian soldiers came charging down on them from the east. This was the last thing Seama had expected. Quickly leading the company onto the highway and pointing their noses towards Gothery and the approaching troop, he hoped to give the impression they were a company re-joining the highway after a brief rest by the roadside.

For all the attention given them they needn't have bothered. The sweating horses pounded past in single file, kicking up a great cloud of choking dust, and without ever altering speed they galloped on into the West and were soon small in their sight once more.

Between coughs Angren cursed them.

'What d'you suppose those bastards are up to, Seama?'

'I really don't know, Angren, but I wish I did. If it was a mission to Garassa from Astoril then I must wonder who sent them and why. By all accounts, Sirl is far too ill to be doing anything. But we don't have the time or means to find out. So, let's get off this road before anyone else turns up.'

The even, green South Valdesian plain stretched before them under a grey sky. Gradually the few trees that provided focus and contrast became even fewer and grew stunted. Camp that night was a quiet affair. They had stopped by a small river that wriggled a path down from the distant edge of the Gotherian plateau and out onto the plain to finally disappear into nothing on the northern edge of the Waste. The company knew nothing of its source or its eventual fate but the river was a welcome find. The horses were unburdened, rubbed down and well watered; rolls were laid out, some food was eaten and they quickly got down to sleep.

In the morning there was discussion about their forward route. Angren told them that finding water along the way was unlikely and he worried the horses might not cope.

'It's not just the dry lands, and there's three days of that, but even when we get to the forest there's no telling how long we'll go without finding a stream.'

He was amazed then, and almost impressed, when Terrance announced that water would not be a problem, producing from his bags a clutch of cleaned and cured pigs' bladders.

'Here we are, one for each of you. I'd thought we might end up coming this way so I bought these in Dreffield. It'll be extra weight for the horses but worth it I think.'

'Good idea that,' Angren admitted.

'Thank you. The nomads do it except they use ox bladders.'

'But you preferred pig.'

'Just a matter of what I could get. They use them for footballs.'

'The nomads?'

'No, fool: back in Dreffield. An energetic sort of game but a bit brutal. I think the Spurladians invented the rules but they play it all over Gothery now and in some of the northern Parts. A hundred people a side, five balls and scant regard for anyone who gets in the way. Quite an event to witness providing you can keep yourself out of the ruck. You should try it sometime. I think it'd suit you.'

'You could be right. Let's hope I get the chance one day.'

Within a few hours of diligent plodding by the doubly burdened horses they found themselves under a blazing sun in a country where nothing but yellow grasses could survive. The transition seemed sudden. It was as though the Waste had sneaked up on them as they rode. Facing the company now a drying, salt choked prairie whose scarce energy was withdrawing from the fierce summer heat – a prairie desperately awaiting that first cloud, those first pattering drops of the season's close. They were all glad of Terrance's forward planning.

And they were thirsty after only a few hours. The heat was bearable but a wind, dry as bones, scoured the plain, filling the air with dust. It stung their eyes and clogged their throats. The constant rush deafened them and stifled conversation. They covered as much of their faces as possible with scarves and kerchiefs but the dust was fine and invasive.

This was not a settled part of Aegarde, for obvious reasons, but there were several groups of nomads – ancient cousins to the Drafasians – who made a living following the vast herds of bison that roamed the plain. They killed the beasts for food and for hide to trade in kinder settlements farther west. They had no name for this land other than 'le plan-visent', the plain of bison, but it was all things to them: home, nurture, succour; it was to them the greater part of the world and anything beyond le plan-visent was quite insignificant; it was to them the spiritual source of everything they were: when they prayed they prayed to the mothering sky and the father earth. They knew themselves as 'the children of the sky' while those who met them named them 'the plan-visents'. Maps in Garassa marked off this land as The Eastern Waste. To the Aegardean court the Waste, Eastern and Central, was as unconsidered a space as ever could be.

According to plan, the companions saw no one. Their route was so lonely it was hard to believe that men ever travelled there. Even the scavengers of the air, the petty vultures of the plan-visent, were few and far off: they would come closer only if the party stopped for too long in the heat of the day. That evening Angren spied a dust cloud against the setting sun and everyone was excited at the prospect of seeing something more than grass or sky, but as they watched it dwindled in the distance. If it was one of the great herds then it was moving away from them. Closer to hand, a solitary gopher, sniffing the air, unaware of their presence for a few seconds before disappearing into its burrow, seemed to emphasise the desolation. It was the one land creature they had seen all day. Of course there was life aplenty if they had taken the time to look, hidden from them by the grass and the dust and their need to stay on the move. If there were gophers then there must be spiders and snakes, beetles and ants, lizards and scorpions and a hundred other creatures they knew nothing of.

The waste, however, had one overriding, overarching and unmissable glory. The clouds that had dogged their Gotherian miles had no power to intrude upon this plain, and so the night – a sudden night – came on like a celebration. Crowded in the clear sky were the jewelled millions of infinity to lift their souls: stars in strings and spirals, clusters and solitaires, achingly bright and beckoning. What made the stars seem more imminent it was hard to say. The lack of trees, the lack of all moisture in the air, scoured by the wind, the contrast with the un-forgiving dreary daylight hours, all must have made their contribution, but actually none of that mattered. Why question what it is that creates beauty and majesty and glory? What matters is the beauty itself. Angren had experienced the prairie sky a number of times but now somehow it seemed greater than ever before. He lay on his back and drowned at once in the sky's bottomless ocean. All thoughts of the world left him; the never-ending susurration of the wind released him; the self-consuming distance drew him. He was not sure how much sleep he managed on that first night, but dawn was an unpleasant shock, and the day of toil ahead was not a happy prospect.

Their journey dragged on through the barren land. Nothing of interest happened, no one spoke more than a few words all day. It was a journey to be suffered not enjoyed.

But snuggled in the tall grass, at the end of that second day, after food and water had eased dry throats, conversations started and stopped and started again, shaped by the gusty wind. Sigrid listened-in but she wasn't really in the mood for idle chatter. All day long she'd been thinking of little Carla and the evening rest changed nothing. She found herself wavering between anger and tears and… and something else she couldn't identify. Excusing herself she took a walk away from the camp, seeking solitude, hoping to think it all through, wanting to get it straight. It wasn't to be. The noise and power of the wind muddled her thoughts, she paid no heed to where she wandered, her intentions slipped away. She became confounded and entranced by a world of the senses: buffeted by the wind, cooler now than in the curse of the day, the fresh, stinging air making her eyes weep again, a caress almost bruising her cheeks; the grass stems all around, tangling her legs, impertinent, familiar ghost fingers barely seen in the starlight; and above everything the stars. The prairie claimed her. Consumed her. Became all there was. War, desire, tragedy became words without meaning. Could good or evil alter this moment, this feeling? Any of it? The question had no answer. Questions and answers had no coherence in the face of raw creation. Time was lost to her, there was only motion, her limbs working in the flow, and sight! Again and again she gazed into the monstrous depths above, below, beyond.

'Magnificent,' she breathed, staring into infinity hardly aware she spoke.

'Well thank you very much. I am quite impressive, I'd agree.'

It was a shock. She felt dizzy. And annoyed.

'The stars, idiot!' Trust Angren to spoil the moment.

'Oh those,' he said.

'What d'you mean: 'oh those'? I've seen you star-gazing like the rest of us. Even you're not that insensitive, for all your stupid bragging.'

'Me? Brag? You've got me all wrong, Sigrid, I'm just honest.'

'As a judge, no doubt. Oh no, that's supposed to be sober, isn't it? Not really something you could lay claim to.'

'Sober now, aren't I?'

'Only because you've no choice, or did you find a hip flask back in Slaney?'

'Come off it girl, you can knock it back with the best of them.'

'You'd notice that, wouldn't you? Well, let me tell you, red-nose, drinking is a skill I've learned. For you it's a matter of pure need. Why did you have to follow me anyway?'

'I didn't. You just happened to wander back into camp,' Angren pointed down to his gear already laid out for the night. 'Daydreaming were we?'

Sigrid hadn't wanted any of this conversation, this stupid arguing. It was astonishing that the pettiest things could get in the way of what was really important, could wipe out the grandeur of existence in just a few ill-chosen words. She felt sad and angry but most of all rather foolish. Damn man!

'Oh just go to sleep will you!' she said and turned away, not wanting him to look at her. As she stumbled over packs and saddles, searching for her own gear, she heard him mutter: 'Bloody woman!' and looking back was pleased to see him pummelling at his bag of clothes, ostensibly to make it a better shape for his head.

'It'll need to be bigger than that,' she thought and grinned to herself as she got ready for sleep.

At last they reached the trees. It was early morning on the fourth day after their meeting with Bassalo. The trees were twisted, scattered things at first but soon they became tall and rampant, fighting each other for light and space. The wind could not follow them and stirred only the canopy leaving the forest floor to calm and relative silence. Seama allowed them a long halt and they revelled in the stillness. The change was better than a rest: good humour was very nearly restored and a meal made the prospect of having to move on almost bearable. But when they did move on, the fledgling mood did not survive. Within only an hour of resuming their journey there was not a man or woman among them not desperate to be out in the open once more. The forest was a mixture of competing stands of conifers and deciduous trees and was, at this point, completely untended. The undergrowth was a clawing tangle, the air dead and stifling and the constant noise of their thrashing progress no less wearing than the wind. Each yard was a struggle to be hacked out or forced or trampled. At least on the plain they had made good time.

There was no way round it: this forest stretched all the way to the foothills of Mount Hathen, or Mulhacen as the people of that area would say, and Moreda was deep in the centre of it. As they worked their way southward the travellers hoped to find the forest steadily easier, with decent trails and tidy glades, for clustered around the various streams and rivers that tumbled down from the Hathen range to become tributaries of the Rine, Asteranor's second River, were many villages of foresters and even a few large towns. Their industry was in pollarding and felling, shredding and coppicing the incredible variety of hard and softwoods available to them; their commerce in supplying the timber needs for much of Southern Gothery, Matagorda, Garassia and the Fat Thousands. Everyday construction in those regions was much more reliant on wood than on bricks-and-mortar or stone and even the faraway capital city, the sprawling Garassa, made accessible by the Rine, was more than half built of timber from the Eastern Forest.

Angren knew quite a bit about the Beltez family and Estate, and the great manse: la Casa Moreda. They were among the chiefs of the foresters and their Lord ruled a substantial part of the central area, el Seno del Bosque. They were a noble family, well regarded by Kings and Governments, scrupulously fair and unquestionably honourable. They were the sort of good people

Angren could not possibly get on with. Agonizingly formal in everything they did, as much between themselves as in dealing with outsiders, Angren could never feel comfortable in their company. How could he live with people who thought eating a duty not an entertainment; who thought that drinking alcohol to excess not only unwise but unseemly? All of this was bad enough but it was their strict marital code that caused Angren the most difficulty. Many of their women were beautiful: dark haired, brown eyed, fair skinned and wasp-waisted. All of them were also out of bounds. Angren's various employments in the region had all been short-lived. He had only to show the slightest interest in any of these fine ladies and someone's sense of family honour was outraged, and the Weapon-master was thrown out on his ear. He was not, after all, considered to be anything like a suitable partner for any daughter of Beltez.

The villains of the Black Company were not suitable partners!

The thought of what might be happening at La Casa Moreda made the muscles in his stomach tighten as anger fed his imagination. He may have been uncomfortable among the Beltezians, but it didn't mean he disliked them. He admired their discipline, their forthright attitude. He knew that the men would fight to the death to preserve the dignity of their wives, sisters and daughters. But what if they'd been defeated and the Company were even now enjoying the spoils of a new victory? Angren made himself remember what the Black Company had done in Huaresh, and he thought of what Trant had once done to his own family. The anger frothed inside him. But anger was good and revenge a necessity. Both would drive him on. If the Black Company had taken Moreda, there would be savage retribution – the red rage would see to that.

Already his own companions felt the impact of Angren's fierce dedication: whenever they wavered he pushed them on; whenever the way ahead seemed hopeless he got them through by making them work harder. As they fought and struggled through this nigh impossible forest they were beginning to lose patience, but Angren allowed no respite. There were no stories now, no jokes, only curses and moans and Angren's best sergeant's voice booming out to bully, to cajole and encourage. The normally unquenchable brothers were tetchy and didn't much like being told what to do but they got on with it; their good natured captain became more and more grumpy and said more than once that he wished he'd never left the River. Only Berta seemed more cheerful than before and Angren supposed that was because every step took her a little further away from the dragons.

Seama, as often since Tumboll and the loss of Bellus, was completely withdrawn from the company. Angren wondered if it was grief that kept him quiet. Or perhaps he was thinking things through. He'd been spending a lot of time with those papers of his, admittedly with a frown on his face, but wasn't that a good sign? If he was busy planning ahead then all the better. The wizard didn't offer any help in beating a path, and Angren decided to let him get on with it. Whatever it might be.

The dandy too was quiet. With no possibility of conversation with Seama, and little prospect of intelligent conversation with the rest of them, Terrance seemed content to suffer the journey in contemplation of his surroundings. Time and again he paused in his labours to study leaves or flowers; he seemed to find fascination in the soil beneath his feet and the insects and birds among the trees. Such an interest, such behaviour left Angren baffled.

They travelled in single file, with the horses trailing behind, the better to weave their way through the trees and, excepting Seama, they took turn-about in taking the lead. It was a tough, exhausting job and fresh arms were needed every twenty minutes or so. Angren and Berta did more than their fair share but it was Garaid, the King's spy, who put in most of the work. He chopped and pulled and ripped and pressed, driven by something far more potent it seemed than Angren's barking. Perhaps it was an attempt to make up for the debacle back at the stable. Clearly, the affair had unnerved the man. They had all come to accept Garaid's long silences and the few words he spoke between them. He seemed lost in a world of his own making and now in the trial of the forest it seemed to be getting worse. Pleased that Garaid was doing so much to push them through the tangle, Angren tried to ignore the contortions that wracked the man's face but he couldn't help wondering what was happening. It was as if the King's spy was engaged in some sort of internal struggle; the grimaces and grunts a part of some frightening argument only he participated in, that only he could hear. Angren dismissed the idea as fanciful and put it all down to the severe exertion. Angren's fancy was closer to the truth.

'Keep still! Not such easy meat. Trying to say something? Well you can keep that face of yours sweet and straight. I'll wear you down, Garaid Barbossa. You cannot win. That's it: swing your arms, chop it down; the exercise is good for us. And it'll keep you busy; keep you in your place. Down in the Pons and Medulla, down in the spinal column. House-keeping: that's your province now. Reticular Activating Circuits? Ha! It's all coming back. It's amazing what fresh blood can do. Somatic Functions, that's it, that's your end of it. The Cortex is mine. I'll keep the communications: the mouth, the eyes, the ears. And I'll enjoy them. I've not had sensation like this for ten thousand years. So just you keep quiet!'

Without warning, so dense was the undergrowth, they came onto a massive clearing. At its edges there were stumps of trees, whole trunks lying flat and a continuous scrap heap of branches, twigs and leaves stretching away to left and right. Ten yards beyond that there was no evidence of trees at all. The far edge of the cleared circle was almost half a mile away and crossing the middle of it was the line of a small brook bridged with logs and mud. A road ran roughly east to west. An earthen road. Above them the late afternoon sky was cloudy once more – there would be no more stars. They decided to rest awhile.

Angren tied the reins of his horse to a hewn branch and took out his sword for a little practice. After a week of cleaning and sharpening it was bright and deadly and all he needed now was to get used to the weight and the balance. The others were delving into their packs for food while Angren stood, legs planted two feet apart, hefting the blade all about him.

'Must you do that?' Berta demanded after she had nearly

stepped into the arc of one of Angren's backswings.

'Got to put in the hours, girl.'

'Girl?'

Angren grinned. His mood was improving by the minute.

'It won't be long now,' he said meaning to cheer her up, 'and I need to get the feel of this beauty. Reckon I'll be using her soon enough.'

'I hope so,' Berta said, 'but until then just you watch who you're using it on.'

'Hey, Angren. Why not teach Piedi a few strokes while you're at it.'

Piedoro gave his brother a push. 'Just because you can play with that needle you call a sword, don't make you more useful in a fight, not with only one arm anyway. Tell you what, big brother, how about a duel? You can use your sword, I'll use Garra's bow.'

'Oh, very fair! What do you think Angren? Could you teach him?'

There was an edge to Edro's voice that seemed to suggest he was worried about his brother. Among these fine warriors it seemed all the more obvious that Piedoro was actually a very good sailor.

'Oh pretty easily, given a year or two. Still, he'd be better off with a bow: it'd keep him out of the man to man stuff. *Can* you use a bow, Piedi?'

'Can *I* use a *bow*? Is he a fool? Eh, Edronio tell the man.'

Edro laughed. 'You want me to do your bragging for you now? Why not? It hurts me to say, Angren, but he's not too bad.'

'Not bad? I am an artist!'

'Now let's not get carried away. Is he always like this?'

Piedoro was strutting around with Garaid's bow and spying a rabbit thirty yards off, he let fly. And he missed by no more than a whisker. Angren was impressed.

'If you're so good,' he asked, 'why didn't you buy a bow in Fletton?'

'I felt that a sword would better suit my character.'

'So what character's that?' Bibron asked with a grin, 'Sado's

Clown?'

Piedoro was most offended or pretended to be. He was not very good at pretending. The banter continued until it was time to go. Angren was pleased to hear them all laughing again.

After a good break, they were beginning to remount when Terrance De Vere, who was first in the saddle said:

'Well my friends, I believe we have company.'

They all looked. To their alarm, at least fifty knights were breaking the cover of the trees where the road led east. Someone among the brigade had quick eyes, and the knights immediately turned to charge towards them, leaping the brook in an instant. As they approached the attack took on a formation like an inverted vee or arrow. Familiar with the pattern, Angren knew that the arms of the vee were to catch anyone attempting to escape, and that the inside of the vee would be lined with spikes.

'Not just messengers this time then,' he said.

ABDUCTION

'This doesn't promise to be all that comfortable, Seama,' said Terrance, 'Will we sit here and wait for them?'

'I think we shall. Angren, can you tell who they are? I don't think they can be Black Company. Isn't that an Aegardean banner?'

Angren looked at the banner flying in the wind of their approach. It was important for a travelling Aegardean to have a good grasp of heraldry. Some nobles were altogether too easy to offend.

'Yes, Seama. I think we've the company of Baron, The Lord Gumb by his colours, or his soldiery at least. I can't say I've ever met him and I'm buggered if I can remember anything more than the name.'

'Some guide you are,' snorted Bibron. 'Don't you know whether he's friendly or not? Some sort of idiot to go by his name, but then Aegarde's full of queer names.'

Angren raised his eyebrows. 'I don't know, *Bibron Farber*, Aegarde's a big place.'

'We'll find out more soon enough, I should say', Terrance said, 'Here they come and still charging. If they don't slow down soon we shall all be stuck like pigs.' He pulled a large white handkerchief from his pocket and waved it vigorously above his head. Being mounted the message he gave was unhindered and the approaching knights slowed to a canter and then to a trot, though they kept the same formation.

They were lightly armoured with breast plates, light helmets and gauntlets of heavy leather. Each carried a levelled spear and, buckled on their saddles, heavy swords. At least twenty wore short bows across their backs, and quivers to match. All of their livery was adorned with the same motif as on the banner: a boar's head with red eyes and round it a crown of oak leaves.

The knights came to a halt only when they had enclosed Seama and his friends between the arms of the vee. They didn't lower their weapons. One man at the head of one of the arms made himself spokesman.

'Name your business and name yourselves,' he commanded.

'Despite your obvious superiority of main strength, sir, I would still remind you of courtesy, and I reserve tale of our business to one more worthy of it than you, Sergeant.'

Angren turned. It wasn't Seama who spoke but Terrance De Vere. Surprise was a part of what he felt. Angren looked at Seama but the wizard made no sign. He decided to say nothing.

'You are not speaking to a sergeant,' bellowed a red faced, bewhiskered man who rode out from the point of the vee. 'You'll tell *me* who the devil you are and what you might be doing on my land, and you'll be sharp about it!'

Terrance was unmoved and with an impressive display of confident calm continued as if the man had merely passed the time of day.

'You, sir, I must take it, are the Lord of this demesne?'

'You can count on it!'

'Then I must suppose, as my servant and guide here tells me,' Terrance pointed a finger at Angren, 'that you are the Lord Gumb.'

'Gumb! Are you *trying* to insult me?'

'Certainly not, My Lord. How can it be that I have upset you?'

At this point a pleasant faced young man rode forward to his Lord's side.

'May I explain,' said he 'your servant's knowledge seems inadequate, unless he has deliberately led you astray. My Lord's name is Gumb, without the pronunciation of the 'b'. Sounding the 'b' is considered impolite. I am sure you meant nothing by it. Uncle, I'm sure there was no intent. Being *Gotherian*, how could they know?'

The smile did not leave the young man's face, but there was something unpleasant in the way he stressed 'Gotherian'. Angren scowled, but Terrance spoke up undaunted, 'In all honesty, My Lord, we had seen your name in script only and so the mistake was made. May I apologise?

'Permission granted! Now, who the blethering hell are you?'

'My name is Terrance De Vere'

'From?'

A pained look crossed Terrance's face. 'Why, from the town of Vere.'

'In Gothery?'

'Well no, it is in the east of Pars. Though I am often in Gothery on business.'

'And that is?'

'I am a boat builder, or rather my men build the boats while I provide the money and materials. I am presently wanting to buy Keeler's wood.'

'What, you take wood from Aegarde to the east of Pars to build boats where there's hardly a decent stretch of water to navigate? What kind of a fool do you take me for?'

'Nay My Lord, my business is on the Hypodedicus. I left Vere a long time ago. I am here on a journey to visit the Masters of Beltez in order to arrange supplies of certain hard woods, particularly Keeler's wood as I said. These, my companions, are my guards for fear of brigands. Just now we appear to be lost, and yonder road is the first we've seen since we went astray.'

The Lord and his nephew exchanged meaningful glances.

'You say you have business at Moreda,' questioned the nephew, 'Then you may be able to tell me who exactly you intend to meet there?'

'What an odd question,' Terrance decided in an incredible display of naievity, 'I would speak, as seems sensible to the Beltez responsible for contracting business. Who else would I need to speak to?'

'You have had no news of Moreda, then?'

'None since I left Gothery and then it was that Morredan prices were high and getting higher because of transportation costs in the face of the new banditry. Am I ill informed?'

Instead of replying the Lord Gumb took his nephew by the arm and led him aside. They spoke in lowered voices. It was obvious that Terrance's story was being questioned and the companions were relieved when the two returned to offer assistance and advice. They told them of the defeat of the Morredans and explained that the Black Company had taken up residence at the manse. Terrance was suitably amazed. The others, less used to such impromptu acting, said as little as possible.

'I'll tell you this for nothing,' said the red faced Lord, almost smiling now, 'when we saw you, all dressed in Gotherian clothes, well, we thought you might be something to do with this Black Company but I'll give you the benefit of the doubt for now.'

'For now,' said the nephew, and he gave a short laugh, 'it seems obvious that you cannot continue your journey, and it would be a shame if your venture should show no reward.'

'It is more than a shame,?' said Terrance despairingly, 'it's a tragedy. My people are relying on me. Commerce is cruel and no work means no food. What am I to do?'

'I was about to say, Sir, if you could do us the honour of keeping our company for a while, we will shortly be turning homeward and there you would learn that Beltez is not the only name in forestry. I am certain that Gumb will be able to supply your needs.'

It was quickly arranged after that, and half an hour saw them all heading westward. Angren was confused, to say the least, by the whole chain of events. He didn't understand why their true quest was such a secret here whilst back in Valdez territory it was no secret at all, and he didn't understand why Seama had let De Vere get them held up with this Gumb person when they should be making for Moreda, but most of all he didn't understand De Vere's role in this. Obviously Seama and Terrance hadn't simply discussed history on their journey. He wanted to ask Seama about these things but realized that now was not the time. Instead he decided to learn some more about the knights and their business in the forest. He rode a little forward of their group to come up alongside the sergeant who had first spoken to them. He seemed friendly enough.

'Now then. Come up for a word, have you? Me name's Arthur: Arthur Thackray,' he offered a hand over his saddle as Angren was on his left and Angren took it in his firm swordsman's grip.

'My name's Angren Nielderson.'

'You're from Terremark then? How come's th'art in Gothery rags?'

They laughed at the sarcasm.

'I've been working here and there for a long while now; as a matter of fact, I can't remember when I was home last. Such is life.'

'It's not for me. A've never been further than River's Twist, and even then a were workin'.'

'Well, I'm not exactly on holiday myself. Mind you, I can't really call this work, can I? I don't think he needs a guide just at the minute. Where are we off to, by the way?'.

'Well, tha'll know soon enough even if a don't tell thee. Milord Gumb,' and as he said the name he couldn't suppress a chuckle, "is face were a picture when tha called him Gum*b*. Anyways we're off to pick up 'is niece from Stoneybrook. That's about thirty miles west of 'ere.'

'Thirty miles? We're not going thirty miles to turn around again, are we?'

'No, never fret. 'We'll meet her and her father's escort about ten miles on.'

'It's a lot of effort for just one girl.'

'We don't think so,' the sergeant said, 'It's a matter of tradition. For as long as any can mind, the families of Gumb and Travers have given their children a home whenever they come of age. It's sort of a way of showing we trust each other; that we'll help if the other's in need. Now Alan Travers is the young man you're boss were speaking to and its his sister as we're picking up. She's just eighteen and we're not going t'allow this Black lot to mess up our ways. There's not usually so many to guard a lass, but then there's usually no need. You've landed lucky anyway: we've a big do planned. There'll be a party and a feast.'

Angren and the sergeant talked of this and that and got on together like old comrades. They were both soldiers of complimentary dispositions. Angren liked to tell people about the places he had been and Arthur liked to listen. He didn't disapprove of Angren's womanizing ways but he did warn him to keep his leery grin well disguised, particularly where Helen Travers was concerned. Angren was free with his assurances but then he hadn't seen her yet.

They travelled without haste as the meeting was intended for early evening. Though the clouds didn't lift the late afternoon was uncomfortably hot and everyone was expecting a storm. They weren't expecting that lone, wounded rider.

They'd made a pause at a stream to water the horses. The path wove on ahead through the forest. It was a wide path but the twists and turns prevented much of a view ahead and so the horseman was heard long before he was seen. The cloddering hooves echoed along the green halls of the forest. Gumb called for quiet and they all sat still. The three or four minutes they waited, listening to the erratic advance, seemed like an hour and it was almost a surprise when man and horse rounded the final turn. The man was slumped over the horse's neck holding on to her mane. The horse was a wonder of patience: when the man slipped a little the horse voluntarily slowed her pace to allow the man time to drag himself up again, and then ran on as fast as possible. She stopped abruptly in front of Gumb and with quivering legs waited for her master to dismount. The poor thing had a great streaming cut on her flank, her eyes were glazed from her mortal effort and still she wouldn't let her master drop.

Two of Gumb's knights helped the man to the ground. He was bleeding from several cuts to his back and legs. It was a tragic sight. Seama dismounted as they arrived and ran to the horse. She was beginning to waver as she stood. Laying hands on the horse's forelock he blessed her and thanked her for her master's sake and in this extremity he managed to take away much of her pain. 'Sleep now, faithful Sorrel; sleep: you have won,' he said and slowly she sank to her knees. Her breathing was laboured and her muscles locked in spasms and gradually she fell over to one side and died.

Lord Gumb and his men barely noticed the horse but crowded around the wounded man: they were not Valdanas.

The wounded knight was given whisky from Lord Gumb's

hip flask and the sharpness of it brought him to life. At first he stared wildly about him, terrified, but upon seeing the colours and the boar's head on the coats of those around him he calmed down. He began to speak slowly but deliberately, concentrating on each word in turn. He wanted no mistakes. Volume was the problem.

'Speak up, man. We can't hear you. What's happened?'

A cough brought blood from his mouth. His teeth were broken. He tried again.

'Lady Travers' guard. We were… attacked, black sorcerers. All killed – no, no, Lady and maids taken. Travers killed. Bastards called a demon. All dead.'

'Where? When? Come on man. C'mon. Damn it!'

The knight had told all he could and then collapsed. It would be days before he recovered enough to tell more. Gumb sprang to his feet and stalked off back to the horses. His anger was frightening.

'Nephew! Alan Travers come here!' he bawled at the young man. Alan was standing dumbstruck as he tried to comprehend the immensity of the knight's news. He was too shocked to cry. His sister was taken; his father murdered.

'Come on, lad. Get up on your horse. You can't help her by gawping like that. Sergeant Thackray! Take that man back home. De Vere will help you. Him and his people.'

At last it was time for Seama to speak. Things were moving; Angren was ready. The wizard stepped up to stop Lord Gumb moving off.

'My Lord Gumb, may we ride with you instead? My friends and I are not what we seem. No, do not mistake my meaning. I am charged with a task by the High Council of Errensea and by King Mador of Pars to bring an end to this evil, to challenge and defeat the Black Company for the good of all. I had considered stealth my best ally but now I understand the need for armed strength. I was intending, over the next few days, to sound you out on the possibility of action at Moreda but if you're ready to go now, then so are we.'

'Errensea, eh? So who the devil are you, and who's he, that

deveerey fellow? And why on earth should I believe you?'

'Are we to leave at once?'

'That's my aim.'

'And will we have cause to stop at a town or village on the way?'

'Shouldn't think so. Why do you ask?'

'I would prefer to come to Moreda unannounced, My Lord Gumb. It is certain that if I'm recognized too soon then words will travel quicker than we can. However, it seems there's no chance of that.'

The Lord Gumb wore a sarcastic, doubting face but his manner changed when the wizard said:

'My name is Seama, I am sometimes known as the Wizard Beltomé. You may have heard of me.'

After an unguarded sagging of the chin, Gumb's eyes narrowed. He was suspicious and had a right to be so.

'And how would I know if you are telling the truth or not. I've heard a deal about the Lord Seama but he's never been to Rippon. You could be anyone.'

'True. There's no way I can prove my identity beyond doubt. My friends could vouch for me but they're suspect too. We could be spies for the Black Company, though I'd hope—'

'If you'll forgive me, My Lords?' It was Sergeant Thackray, 'I can vouch for the Lord Seama.'

'You? What the hell would you know about it?' Gumb was rarely polite to his men. 'How could you know anything?'

'Well Milord, you'll remember a was wi'thee father's guard afore he died. Once a was part of his escort when he went to meet the king at River's Twist. It were a big do: the King was having Mador of Pars to a hunt. All the local gentry went to a banquet in their honour.'

'That's right, that's right! Just a year before the old boy passed on. Had quite a time as I remember. Left me to look after the shop while he went off enjoying himself. Canny old beggar he was: came back with a deal or two I can tell you.' Clearly Gumb had been fond of his father but he didn't let the nostalgia distract him: 'But I still don't see... Ah yes: now I remember. He complained that some damned wizard had been there and he didn't like it. Had a notion this 'Lord Wizard' was a troublemaker; something always happened whenever the chap was around… Ah, no offence intended of course. So, Thackray, we have a wizard here and a wizard there and you reckon they're the same? Can you be sure of his face after all these years?'

'No question, milord. You see he'd a way about him: a habit of talking to us lot, commoners as well as nobs… er our betters. Spoke to 'im myself a few times. A don't forget that sort. That there is the Lord Wizard Seama o'Belto, but a doubt a'd have placed him if he hadn't spoken up.'

Seama nodded a couple of times as if counting. 'Of course, Arthur isn't it? I'd been trying to place your face. You weren't a sergeant then, were you?'

'No sir, made up last year.'

Gumb cleared his throat. He was convinced and now the question was cleared up he was impatient to get started.

'Shall we get on then?' he said.

Seama nodded briefly. 'Arthur, when you get home I'd appreciate you keeping quiet about me being here.'

'No problem, Lord Seama.'

'Good. Now before we rush off, Lord Gumb, couldn't we have a brief word about what exactly you are planning to do?'

'DIE, FOUL SEED OF DEMONS!'

El Seño 3037.8.5

It was Gumb's plan to catch the villains and attack them before they could gain safe refuge. He didn't want any discussion about it. To this effect they were soon travelling a diagonal route through the forest, abandoning the dog leg of the main road, in the hope of crossing the villains' path some six miles northwest of Moreda. The problem with the scheme was that the wounded man hadn't told them where or when Travers' caravan had been attacked

Angren hoped they'd be too late to catch up with the Company. Sudden battle was not a problem for him, but there would be confusion on both sides and that was the last thing they needed: the Travers girl was more likely to end up dead than rescued. As far as Angren was concerned she'd have to suffer a little while longer if she wanted to escape.

Not that he'd evolved any specific means of rescue as yet. He knew next to nothing about Moreda, and he needed to know more about the Black Company. In the absence of Sergeant Thackray he moved up the line to speak with the nephew. Given the circumstances the lad had regained his composure well and Angren thought him an easier prospect than Lord Gumb.

Alan Travers was taken aback when a man who had been introduced as a servant had the temerity to approach the Heir of Hartest unbidden. Angren bridled at the condescension in his eyes and the tone of his voice.

'Yes sirrah, what do you want?'

'My name is Angren Nielderson, sir.'

'Well Nielderson, again, what is it you want to say?'

Angren decided to be polite.

'I was looking for information. My friend Seama and I have only old news about this Black Company. I thought you might be able to tell us something new.'

Travers' eyes widened. Angren had been right to use his familiarity with Seama as a lever. Putting aside his first impressions the young man was now willing to talk. In fact his tongue was loosened too much.

It was quickly apparent that he couldn't provide anything more than rumours they'd already heard. He described how the Black Company had ravaged the land of the Valdesians before coming south to the Forest. He dwelled on the atrocities. 'Rape, torture and murder their stock in trade' he said, 'Their victims, often as not, children. Imagine that!' How many were there? 'Oh about twenty, or fifty, or a hundred.' The figure changed with every attack but the number wasn't important: they won each battle with the help of sorcery. Demons sided with them, striking terror into everyone in their path.

And how do we know all this? Apparently news of their villainy came from this habit of letting some few live to tell the tale – 'My father's man: that's what he was for. These monsters delight in killing and they want the world to know about it.' Angren asked about the Gothery connection. 'They're from Gothery. No doubt about it. Everyone says so. Their clothes, their speech. The people they spare always say so. That's what I heard.'

Angren wasn't impressed. 'Gothery cloth' was a phrase that implied a quality of material, that and a tendency to use subdued greys and blacks rather than the bright blues and greens and reds common in rural Aegarde. But you could buy Gothery clothes in markets all the way from the border to Garassa. And the question of their tongue was hardly any more useful. In Angren's experience, in this confused continent, every five miles travelled threw up another accent but Gothery, famously, had three main styles of speech. You could easily tell a bayman from a northerner, from a plainsman by his accent. But accents can be copied. Angren could do a northerner better than he could do a bayman but he'd be confident that he could pass himself off as either, providing he was outside Gothery that is. It didn't take much to fool people. No, he didn't believe any of it. He already had his clue from Bassalo: if Trant was in charge then these people were most likely from somewhere in western Aegarde. The problem, when it came down to it, was that misinformation was easy to seed and difficult to overcome.

But there was no shifting Alan Travers from his view that Gothery was at the root of this villainy. He had no notion as to why the Black Company did what it did, but political manipulation, he was sure, had nothing to do with it. 'It's simple, they're murderers, and they come from Gothery.' He told Angren that the whole forest region was up in arms, 'or would be if they dared' and, as far as he was concerned, 'If there's blood to be spilled, and children butchered, and women attacked, then better it was over the border than over here. If I had my way, we'd drive these 'demons' back to where they were spawned, and teach Gothery a lesson it wouldn't forget.'

The Heir of Hartest was surprised by the look of distaste on Angren's face. He matched it with a snarl.

'Traitor!' he accused.

Angren took a deep breath and somehow managed to keep in his seat.

'Now let's calm down a little shall we?' he said, aware that he was in need of a little calm himself. 'I'm sure, when you think about it you'll realise where you might be going wrong. I keep my likes and dislikes to myself, and I'd advise you to do the same, particularly in front of Lord Seama. Like you, he's sometimes quick to judge. Difference between you and him is that he knows what he's talking about.'

A short while later Angren went to give Seama the gist of his conversation with young Travers. The wizard agreed that the situation could be better: it seemed obvious that even if the Black Company was defeated, peace between Gothery and Aegarde was not guarunteed. Without the sorcerers to restrain their ambitions, these foresters seemed likely to start some raiding of their own. If Athoff was recruiting in the region he was probably doing very well.

'Still,' said Angren, 'Let's get rid of that bastard Trant anyway, shall we?'

'Let's. The more I hear about him and his Black Company the less I want to hear. Time for a bit of direct action.'

'Can't come soon enough. Erm… You won't mind my asking,

but, given we're here to do a job and we won't exactly be quiet about it, what was the point of the charade back then?'

'Terrance's little deceit?'

'Well yes. I mean, what was the point of being so secretive down here when up in Valdesia we were so free and easy?'

'Were we? We didn't meet anyone but Bassalo and I didn't much consider him a threat. Even if he'd said something about us, I doubt if it would have mattered. If these sorcerers heard there were people in the Saddle who wanted them dead, it'd hardly be news to them. But if the same story was told about a similar group, this time in the Forest not far from their base, I think they'd be more concerned. I think they'd be preparing a little reception party for us.'

'I suppose, but how come Terrance knew what to do back there?'

'He is very astute. And besides we'd already discussed the possibilities. I always intended to recruit some aggrieved party along the way. Stealth might get shot of the sorcerers themselves, but it'd be a tall order for our little band to take on a hundred or so armed men. We needed help, but you have to be careful who you ask. Until I was sure of their allegiance I wasn't prepared to give anything away. Terrance has been planning our cover for most of the journey from Gothery; that's why he was so interested in the trees as we travelled: he had to remind himself about things he'd forgotten. Naturally, the charade, as you put it, became pointless when Gumb heard of the abduction. Gumb and Travers were already planning to raise the forest against the Company. They know that their own people and lands are under threat. These men are spoiling for a fight. With us to encourage them, I think they'll ride all the way to Moreda without even stopping to think about the danger.'

'Yes, it'll be the house where we'll find them. We're not going to catch them before they're home. Have you any sort of a plan yet, Seama?'

'No. None at all, nor will have 'til we get there. Tell the others how it stands. I'm going to have a word with Gumb. I can promise him a battle that'll be to his liking. If only we didn't have the girl to rescue it would all be a lot easier.'

'We could leave her if it was too risky.'

'Shame on you, Angren. Though I know you're not being serious. This is about good people bringing the bad people to book. I won't give her up lightly, nor anyone else if I can help it. Besides, it'd do us no good if the Company was defeated but Gumb was still after revenge. There's a war to fight not just a battle, and we want as many on our side as possible. Anyway, you can tell Bibron and the others to relax for now: there'll be no fighting for another day yet—'

'*Die! Foul seed of Demons!*'

'What the bloody hell—'

Charging pelmel at the cluster of Seama's companions just ahead, was a heavily armoured knight, shouldering a lance. He looked dangerous and set to kill someone before they could stop him. The wizard was quick to react. He wheeled around and, with just a word and a push at the air in front of him, he bounced the knight out of his saddle to thump with a clang and clatter into the compacted earth. As the man fell his lance broke under him and he lay still.

In moments he was surrounded by men of Gumb's company as well as by Seama and his friends. Seama bent to unbuckle the man's armour and Angren helped him.

'Ay ay,' Angren said, 'breast plate's a bit bent. Probably bruised a few ribs. Hurt does it?'

The knight whimpered as the armour came off. Seama was having difficulty with the helmet.

'What sort of knight are you then if you don't know how to fasten your helmet properly?'

Gumb was peering over Angren's shoulder.

'Taking that gold and black plume,' he said, 'and that gold crossed shield into account, I'd say he's a knight of Beltez. I couldn't tell which one obviously. What's the blasted fellow up to, though, attacking like that?'

'I imagine,' said the wizard as he finally got one of the straps free, 'that he took us for the sorcerer's crew because of our clothes.'

'It's a damn good thing he fell off his horse then, ain't it? Funny that: he looked a good rider. Lucky for him he's with friends.'

Angren said nothing about Seama's actions but pursued a more important topic.

'Did you say he was Morredan? He may be able to help us then; tell us about the house.'

The wizard frowned, 'But Angren, I thought you already knew the house. You said you'd worked for them once.'

'Twice actually, but Beltez have property all over the forest. Moreda's not the sort of place I'd be invited to. I met a man once who wore these arms. I wonder if it's him?'

'There are thirty of them, don't you know.'

'Sorry, Lord Gumb, thirty of what?'

'Oh, the elite guard who wear all that gear. Always thought it a bit over the top myself. Still, they know how to use it. Rumour had it they were all killed.'

Seama who had continued to struggle with the man's helmet all the while at last managed to pull it free.

'Well, well,' he said, 'Angren, do you know this 'man'?'

The face was not that of an experienced warrior. Here was an ignorant youth of some fifteen years. He was barely conscious.

'By blazes, he held the saddle well for a young 'un. I tell you, he had me worried.'

Gumb was right, he had looked a doughty knight with years of experience, until Seama intervened. They were all surprised. Many of the older soldiers smiled at the lad's bravery.

'Gumb, we all need a rest and I doubt we'll catch up with the Black Company now. So let's stop and eat and rest the horses – we may see a long battle tomorrow. It'll give the lad time to come round and tell his story.'

'But Seama we… Oh, I don't see why not. Right lads, get the tucker out!'

The boy was resilient and soon regained his senses, with a little help from Seama. Seeing the Gotherian style clothes before he saw Gumb and his men, he was belligerent and obviously frightened. The fact that Seama had thrown him from his horse by magic didn't encourage any sense of security. He calmed down when Gumb spoke to him. The baron introduced Seama and the others, emphasizing that they were not from Gothery at all. The boy was much relieved.

A short while later, Angren went with Seama to speak to the lad. He sat up against a tree just off the path, crumbs all around him from the loaf and cheese he'd demolished. Angren thought he looked lot less shaky now that he had some food inside him.

Seama sat down close by and began by asking the boy his name.

'Guy Banco, at your service, your honour.' As he spoke he somehow managed an idiotic grin. His eyes were pale blue and set wide apart and his nose was a tiny bump on his face, his mouth wide as a china saucer.

'Three questions, Guy, spring to mind. Where are you from; how did you get that armour; and what are you doing charging around the forest single-handedly attacking full companies of men? You may answer them all at once: we cannot dawdle long.'

'I'm from Moreda, your honour.'

'Just Seama will do.'

'Oh, right, Seama then. Well, I've lived all my life at the House… until… just before. I'm, well, I'm not anyone special. I worked in the kitchens.' He smiled as he spoke but it was a little strained and then he remembered his apparrel. 'I didn't steal this!'

'Don't worry. Tell us your story. How did a kitchen boy become a knight? We wouldn't punish you even if you had stolen the armour.'

'Well I didn't!' The boy seemed more concerned that someone might think him dishonest than anything else. It made Angren smile. *Just like a Beltezian*, he thought, *kitchen boy or lord: as honouable and as brave as they come.*

'Right, well, I can't remember how many days ago since they came but we were expecting them. I didn't think they'd ever stand against us. Thought they'd be mad to. The Elite Guard were ready. Rode out to meet them with another fifty horse after them, and another hundred on foot – men had come in from all over the Estate. This… Black Company d'you call them? They didn't even seem to know what to do – all in a jumble they were and then when the charge started and this lot took off into the trees rather than face it, well, we all thought they were nought but cowards. And maybe they were. But it was all a cheat. Soon as they'd left the field, and the Guard come to a stop with none there to fight, the monsters came.

'There was a terrible black hairy thing came out of the wood… it was horrible… like a… a great fat spider, bigger than four horses together. And it was so fast. The guard had hardly managed to set themselves before it was on them. They hadn't a chance no matter how hard they fought. We all saw, from up by the house, it was so strong, it's legs were everywhere, and every move it made was another man dead. And then there was the other – just appeared like it'd come out of the air – all scales, and solid, not as big as the first and it had only the four legs, and a head like a boar, but it was like a great hammer, smashing into everything it met, man or horse, throwing them up in the air, and trampling any on the ground. The horses were panicking, riders were thrown off. Swords were no use to them, spears just sprang away. Nought and no one could touch it. They did so much damage the two of them.

'Soon there were none of our cavalry left standing and the spider thing had starting eating as well as killing – eating whether the men were dead or alive – but then, somehow, both of them were just disappeared. Just gone and none knew where. What was left of the foot started to run for the home field – I thought they were scared the monsters'd come back but maybe they were just looking for a better place to defend. Us up at the house we took up whatever we could find, swords or axes, some were carrying nought better than a spade, and we ran out to join them. There was nought else to do was there? We're Beltez. We attack, and if we can't attack we stand.

'Well that was when the black men came again, all swagger, just walking their horses up towards the house like they'd already won the fight. Every one of us, all the foot that were left and every man left in Moreda, we set ourselves up to face them.

'Well, it didn't last long. Not long at all. They smashed into us, broke us in the one attack, and then they started to hunt us down just as they liked. I don't really remember any more of the battle. Maybe I was knocked out… maybe I just fainted. Don't know why, I'm not normally so soft.

'They must have missed me, lying there. When I came-to I was in a pile of bodies. Had a struggle to get free. Bloody crows were everywhere, pecking at whatever they could get at. I didn't want them flying up – it'd give me away, I thought – so I lay there a while. It was a good way to the house from where I fell but I could still hear the screaming. My sister was in there.

"Course I wanted to fight them, wanted to rescue her, but I knew I was too weak. So I just lay there. A good while. Night was coming on before I got myself moving. I had to crawl through all the bodies in case any of the black men were looking out. Moved off towards the trees – what else had I to do? But that was how I found him: that was how I found my dad. If I'd gone another way…'

Guy came to a stop. Angren was all for calling a halt to this but Seama shook his head. The lad stared ahead at nothing, his eyes seeing before him only the horror of that night.

The wizard spoke firmly:

'Tell us Guy. And then it will be done.'

Guy set his chin hard and continued.

'His body was all twisted and I couldn't understand how, but then I saw they'd hacked him, chopped him all over. All… just blood and bones. He was only a pikeman, with no armour. They didn't need to do that, did they? Not chop at him when he was down… so many cuts… and his eyes were still open… There was nothing I could do… He was my dad…'

It was too much for him. Guy Banco wept and shook and Seama took him into his arms. Angren had never seen Seama so gentle with anyone.

'If your father could see you now, Guy Banco,' the wizard said a little while later, finally letting the boy lean back against his tree, the tremors now fading away, 'Your courage would make him very proud.'

Guy scrunched up his shoulders and took a breath and he pushed away the memory. 'And I am proud of him, your honour. He fought for Moreda.'

'And he fought for you, and for your sister and mother too. Come, let's make an end of the tale. How did you get the armour?'

'Aye, there's still that. After I left my father, after I'd straightened him best I could, and closed his eyes, though I couldn't do more, well I moved off closer to the wood. Then I heard a noise. Something was moving up in front of me. A man in full armour, trying to sit up. One of the Guard. His armour was covered in blood. I think he'd heard me with my dad. He called me over, not more than whisper really, he was so hurt, and when I came up to him he says: "Take it, these arms, my sword, I need them no more," and then he falls back. I thought he was dead there and then but when I leaned over to see he grabbed my arm. "Avenge our people," he says and that was it, nought else. Avenge our people? Me, Guy Banco, by myself? I don't think he realised I was only a lad.

'But I sat there for a bit and I thought, well, what else have I to do? Just as well take the gear as leave it. Just as well find some way of fighting as crawling into a hole to die. So, I took it. We were close up to the trees so I knew I'd not likely be seen, but it took me ages to even roll him over so I could get at the straps. And it was all slippery with the blood and... Well anyway, I managed. Dragged it all off into the trees a good way, a bit at a time and then... well, that was that.'

Guy's wide grin brightened his face. He'd done it: the ordeal of his tale was over.

Angren shook his head in wonder.

'You're a good lad, Guy Banco,' he said, 'you deserve a medal.'

Guy pulled a face.

'For that? But I'd done nothing yet. I wanted to do as he said: 'Avenge our people.' Not much point stopping there, was there?

'I really thought I could attack them a few at a time, if I could handle the sword – it's much bigger than I thought it could be. You have to be strong to be a knight, don't you! And the armour's so heavy too. Well, there were a lot of horses in the woods, run away from the battle, and I found that big one there.'

'And how does a kitchen boy know how to ride a horse like that?'

'Oh,' Guy grinned again, 'My grandfather, he retired with a bit of land and The Master made him a gift of his old charger as thanks for service – to help him with the plough and pulling the cart, that kind of thing. I thought it was great. There was a proper saddle and reins so I used to take off on rides through the forest every summer whenever my gramps would let me. So I wasn't new to a horse. Besides I've been practising since – with the lance and all.'

'Now explain why you attacked us,' Seama interrupted.

'Well, like I said, Seama, I thought I could take a few at a time. What're you laughing for? I bet I could beat a few.'

'This company isn't exactly a few, is it?'

'No, but I've seen loads of the enemy over the last week, in twos and threes, and I've... well I haven't had the courage to attack until today.'

'And no one could blame you, but don't you think it was a little rash to attack so many at once?' Seama was all seriousness unlike the other soldiers gathered around.

'It's that bloody silly helmet.'

'The helmet?'

'You can hardly see out of it and all the armour clanking means you can't hear what's happening. I came past some trees and all I could see was two of you in Gothery cloth and and then... well, I couldn't hold back any longer.' The boy paused, his face reddening. 'Pretty stupid, wasn't I?'

'Maybe,' Seama replied, 'but courageous. You looked a fine knight when you charged. You had us all worried.'

The boy grinned. 'I am better than I thought I would be. Must have looked dopy the way I came off. Was that you, Sir Wizard?'

Seama nodded.

'I'm glad. I've never come off before. Besides, I might have hurt someone and got myself killed if you hadn't.'

'And I'm glad you realize it. Now then, after all that talk I think you need a hot drink inside you. Go with Angren here, he'll sort you out. In an hour or so I'll need to ask you some questions about Moreda, the house itself. We need a quiet way in before the fighting starts, so you have a think about it. Get us in there, Guy, without us being seen, and your people will be avenged. That I promise.'

MOREDA

Seama was worried. About all sorts of things, rash promises not being the least. And he couldn't help mulling them through as they tracked through the forests towards their inevitable conflict with the Black Company and their mysterious masters.

They were called sorcerers by men who didn't know the difference between a shaman and a wizard. What if, beneath the trappings of arcane knowledge, they were not natural men at all? The creature in Gothery had surprised him. It was not a simulacrum. Seama had thought it through: there was too much individuality there, too much self expression, too much real fear. Whatever that thing had been it was no mannikin or puppet dancing to the pull of a string. Blood or no, it had a life and will of its own. What if these 'sorcerers' were more of the same? Would that make any difference? Would that mean they had greater powers than he could cope with? The creature in the stable in Slaney had been dispatched easily enough but perhaps they'd been lucky.

No. That wasn't helpful. Seama made himself step away from the question: if it couldn't be answered what was the point in asking? He was drifting back into speculation again, except this time he was inclined to come down on the side of the doubters. A more logical place to be. He remembered his argument with Tregar now in a new light. Had it been Tregar *blæthering* on and Seama doing the listening instead, how would he have responded? Probably not well. But there was a difference between that speculation and this speculation: the Song of Ages had been behind the first argument, but it wasn't behind this one. What he needed to do now, Seama decided, in the absence of that gut feeling that had driven him before, was keep to the facts and not the fears.

The fact was Athoff Ringsøyr was using the Black Company as an incitement to war. He was using their atrocities to promote a muster. If he succeeded in mobilizing the nation then war would become inevitable whatever might happen here at Moreda. Once gathered his army would have a momentum that would be hard to stop.

Thankfully, Athoff was hampered in his efforts by the Aegardean political system, and his mustering might take a long and wearisome time. In Aegarde there were many hundreds of districts whose chiefs or Lords ruled as though they were kings. In all the North Eastern district of the forest, for example, Lord Gumb was the final authority in matters of law, business and social organization. If any man disagreed with his decisions there was still a possible court of appeal: the court in the Aegardean capital where the King was the final arbiter. But it was many years since the crown had gone against any of the regional plenipotentiaries: why would a king upset the people who organized the collection and payment of taxes.

The consequence of that was not helpfull to Athoff. The crown couldn't force all or any to raise armies for the nations sake. They could be persuaded by oratory or convinced by payment that taking up arms would be a good thing but they couldn't be coerced. To raise a substantial army Athoff would need time and a lot of money. Seama's problem was that they didn't know how far the King's son had progressed his cause. Seama feared it was his own cause that was running out of time. Somewhere in the Partian northlands Tregar, with the Houses of Anparas and Temor, was confronting the real enemy. Seama was certain of it, whatever logic or reason had to say, and he knew that if this real enemy was ever to be repulsed, all four nations had to be brought together. As yet they were fighting amongst themselves. In a way Seama'a work was similar to Athoff's: he needed to muster the support of as many men and women as possible and he needed to do it quickly. The first step in the process was to remove the cause of dispute between Aegarde and Gothery and hence Pars. He needed to defeat the Black Company and prove Gothery's innocence and he needed to stop Athoff.

And all of this in double quick time.

They had a trouble-free passage through to Moreda and that was something of a surprise. Gumb had chosen a minor route that wove through the glades and avoided the main road, but even so, Seama thought, any army worth its salt would have contrived some form of early warning. The forest Lord had sent out his most experienced woodsmen to scout ahead as a precaution against ambush but even as they covered the last few miles there hadn't been a single sighting of the enemy to report.

Seama talked it through with Angren and Terrance. Angren was convinced they were already expected and that the lack of guard patrols meant the enemy had other means of protecting itself. The Company had sorcerers after all. Terrance disagreed. He preferred to think that they were just arrogant. After months of repeated and poorly opposed victories they believed that no one would dare seek them out. Seama decided to keep an open mind.

It was nearly midnight when they came upon the home clearing. Skirting the perimeter towards the main road they found a wooden hut lurking beneath the dark edge of the forest. It was a guard post and yellow light shone through the open shutters – the enemy at last. Laughter and yelps of pain came from within and it was soon apparent that the guards had decided to make their duty lighter by bringing beer and a young boy out with them.

Gumb's best archers were detailed to take care of it; three of them moved up to the two slightly open windows, another two waited to kick-in through the door.

'I want one of them alive,' Seama had told them.

Within the hut, the guards were engrossed. When the door burst open they had no time to save themselves. Bowstrings thrummed eight times and it was done. Seama, Angren and Gumb followed the archers inside.

A sobbing boy of maybe eleven or twelve years was bent over a table with a dead man slumped over him. The boy was covered in bruises. Three other men lay dead amidst the spilled beer, arrows sprouting from chests or backs, but the last man, the one 'spared' by the archers, had been sitting on a bench with his back to the wall and now he sat with four arrows piercing his arms and groin. One arrow had been fired with such power that it had passed through his fleshy right arm and pinned the man to the wall behind him.

The first thought was to free their victim and Seama took off his cloak to cover the child's nakedness. Cold and pale and now silent the boy confronted the pinned man who had been the first to abuse him. The abuser, distracted by pain, didn't even acknowledge his presence. The boy spat in his face and turned to leave on his own two feet. They carried him when he collapsed at the door and took him to a camp that Alan was setting up among the trees.

The Wizard Beltomé looked at the man nailed to the wall. He was in a piteous state with blood oozing through his clothes and agony engraved on his drool smeared face. Every slight movement he made, every breath he took, caused the muscles to tear a little more; the torment stiffened his arms in premature rigor. Piteous but unpitied. Seama had seen blood and bruises on a boy of twelve. It was evil that faced him and he could spare no compassion for it. He stooped to examine the white contorted face, quite prepared to twist the arrows if he must in order to gain information.

The man, however, was ready to talk. He wasn't concerned with honour or bravery, but thought he might bargain for his freedom. He told Seama that ninety men remained in the main house with another ten out scavenging amongst the corpses in villages thereabout. Their weapons were swords, spears and arrows, and all were mounted. Prisoners, nearly all women and some children, were locked in the cellars unless they were required upstairs. He couldn't tell Seama where the new girl was being kept and couldn't say how many prisoners there were as some didn't last very long.

It was probably because of his pain that he couldn't control his features: an habitual leer came over his face as he spoke. Gumb had been standing just behind Seama, and now, bristling with rage, he pushed past the wizard and dealt the man a mighty backhander with his gauntleted fist.

'I'll knock that grin off your face, you piece of slime!' he yelled, and hit him again. Everyone heard the sickening crack.

Gumb was a very strong man. The piece of slime could tell them nothing more. The baron stepped back, muttering an apology to the wizard.

Seama had been hoping for some description of the sorcerers, the name of their leader, an idea of their powers, anything that might give him a clue as to how to deal with them, but although that hope was now gone, it wasn't in him to criticise Gumb's action.

'No apologies,' he said, 'the man was bad. We'll act quietly tonight, My Lord, and tomorrow we will battle – nothing is changed for the lack of knowledge. Leave the guard house with its full compliment and a few more people in the wood nearby, in case those scavengers return. I'll not have them raising the alarm at the last minute. How many men have you?'

'You'd better ask Alan,' he said, indicating his nephew who had just walked into the hut, 'He picked the guard of honour.'

'How many? Well we started with sixty-six, Uncle, before Thackray and his two left us.'

'Sixty-three then,' said Gumb. 'That makes us well outnumbered, never mind any sorcery.'

'If you can cope with the numbers, I will deal with the sorcery. You'll have my people, don't forget.'

'And worth their weight by the look of them.'

'They are. But there's a lot to do before morning so let's get on. I don't believe in fate but it was lucky we found Guy. Just a little more luck and we'll be in and out by dawn. Whatever happens inside, Gumb, you have to be in place or we'll be caught.'

'Never fear, My Lord Wizard. My fella's are looking forward to it.'

Whether or not that was true, Seama didn't doubt they would be ready.

The house was set on a mound surrounded by a moat but although it had castellated rooves it was in no way a castle. It was a manor house and as such separated from the surrounding villages by a few sacred miles. Here, as elsewhere, the rich were jealous of their privacy. There were some outbuildings beyond the protection of the moat: housing for labourers, storage for tools. Stabling covered an acre beyond the moat to the left of the house but Guy warned that normally half a dozen horses were kept close by the main doors for the convenience of the Lords. Seama didn't want to risk a reconnaisance of the main entrance but he hoped the practice had not been discontinued. They would need horses from somewhere and they could hardly picket their own mounts near the causeway.

The unabated clouds grew heavy over the leaded rooves of La Casa Moreda. Ten, eleven, twelve miles away sheet-lightning flashed in the sky and the lazy growl rumbled through the night. Three men, a woman and a boy, crept and stumbled through the dark pastures to the rear of the building, hoping as one that the rain would hold off until they reached shelter. There would be no main door for these five but a safer, less exalted way in. Guy's help had proved invaluable. He told them that he often wandered out after dark, though he failed to say why, and to avoid the disapproval of elders or betters he'd made himself a secret entrance. There were several decorative trees in the park and one of them, a cedar with drooping limbs, grew very close to the moat opposite the new pantry. Its branches reached low over the water and Guy had discovered that, with just a bit of a jump, he could get across without a ducking. Only Angren miscalculated his leap, slipping at the edge of the water. It made him curse when water ran into his boots.

Low on one side of the pantry was a sizeable hole. Its function was to ventilate the store and, in order to keep out the rats and mice, an iron grille and screen of wire mesh had been installed to cover the gap. 'They seemed to have come loose sometime,' Guy told them. It had taken him hours.

From the pantry there was a door into the kitchen and the house proper. The cellars were close at hand.

It all seemed too easy. Some movement, drunken sounds, could be heard in the depths of the house but sodden with fulfilled lusts, jaded through lack of useful activity, most of the barbarous army was most likely fast asleep.

So conceited an enemy Seama had never known. They hadn't bothered with guards on the house perimeter or on the rooves, or at least any sentries so posted had been too indisciplined to forego their little pleasures and had casually abandoned their duty. Terrance had it right: these villains felt themselves invulnerable.

And so the fields were behind our infiltrators, the tree climbed and the moat crossed. Easing out the grille Guy made a little noise but drew no response from within. The pantry was lit by a single candle that was nearly burnt out: a forgotten stub. A brighter light outlined the door to the kitchen and Terrance was first to it. He motioned for their silence while he listened at a gap between the door and frame.

'We may go on, but quietly,' he whispered, 'I can hear snoring.'

He took the door handle and turned it, and tutted when it refused to turn far enough. Without a word he removed three slivers of metal from a jacket pocket and began to pick the lock.

Guy pushed forward and when he saw what Terrance was doing he tried to attract his attention.

'Mr. De Vere, sir—'

'Quiet youth, while I am working, if you please.'

'But—'

'Oh damn.' He had bent his picks to no effect. 'The lock is stuck.'

'That's just what I was trying to tell you. It's been stuck for as long as I can remember.' Guy grinned.

'So how come it's locked? Do they not eat in Moreda?'

'Well clever cloggs, if you were a bit stronger youd've found it wasn't locked at all.'

'Impudent little rascal," said Terrance. 'Perhaps Angren would do the honours then?'

Guy was enjoying himself. This was a much better way of getting his revenge. Full of confidence he reached out.

'No need, I'll do it.' He twisted the handle with all his might and the catch snapped open with a loud clack. Even Guy froze in his tracks.

Terrance had his ear at the door again, a frown on his face as he strained to listen. Then he relaxed: the snoring had continued.

He turned to Guy.

'Now youth, when you have a leader you will do as he says and nothing more, is that clear? We all know you had the strength but Angren has more and wouldn't have had to jerk at it. What if you'd raised the alarm? What chance would we have had? It's been easy so far, but when we're inside mistakes may cost lives.'

All of this was said in a whisper, but Guy heard every word and his blushes were loud. He dropped back to let Angren and Sigrid get past.

Terrance pushed gently at the door and then peered round it, quiet as a mouse wary of cats. The room he saw was a disaster area. Yet another night of ribaldry had passed through and left broken dishes, spilled pans and a liberal scattering of food refuse: chicken bones, gravy pools, rotting cabbage, crusts and crumbs everywhere.

Left behind amidst the rubbish were two men. They were sitting at the greasy kitchen table, empty mugs at their sides, playing cards scattered around them. Their celebration had taken its toll. One man, fat as a pregnant cow, wearing what was once a white vest that was too small for him, slumped forward unconscious, his sweaty, hairy belly flabbing out for all to see and feel nauseated by. His companion was the snorer. Though physically neater and dressed in good Gothery shirt and trousers, he was as grotesque as his partner. He slept in his chair, head tipped backward and mouth open wide, oblivious to the mess around him.

Terrance signalled that Sigrid should enter first and by the time Guy was allowed to follow, there were two dead men at the table. One had nearly lost his head while the fat one had blood spreading over the back of his vest. Sigrid stood to one side wiping her twin swords on a rag.

"Guy,' said Terrance, ignoring the gruesome tableau, 'which way is the cellar from here? We must hurry while everything is going so well.'

Guy took Terrance to the cellar door, saying nothing. He had never known people like Seama and his friends: people who would kill without thinking about it and yet, obviously, good people. In the Eastern forest fighting was a gentlemanly occupation rather than a means to an end. Bravery and chivalry forbade the killing of a sleeping man, and yet these good people didn't give it a moment's thought. He didn't know what to think let alone what to say.

When he'd shown the others the entrance to the cellar, he hung back, trying to sort out his thoughts and occasionally looking through the open kitchen door to where Angren was disposing of the corpses. The weapon-master was bloodied by the time he'd forced them down behind the old black range. How many times had Guy hidden just there as a boy? The scene and the memory made him queasy and sad in a way he'd never known before.

Angren came out and taking Guy firmly by one arm led him away.

'Come on, young'un. We've done with the kitchen now. There's no time to dawdle.'

They were waiting for Terrance to pick another lock when Guy remembered the spare key on the ledge over the door. Terrance gave him a withering look as he took the key and Guy grinned in spite of his gloomy thoughts.

MISS TRAVERS AND THE SORCERER

Moreda 3057.8.6

Helen Travers was not on the other side of that door but in proof of her passing something of what she was remained. At eighteen years of age, and born of a noble family, she had little experience of men and what motivates them. Her parents had made sure that she knew something about the physical love they shared and that she might look forward to, and of course she had seen the kissing and caressing of lovers in the parks of Ripon, so she was not wholly naive. But it hadn't yet occurred to her that a man could enjoy forcing himself upon a woman. When she was captured by men without limits, who let their hands wander, who made lewd comments and told her baldly that later she would be providing the entertainment, she was confused and scared. But when her maids were raped on the way to Moreda and left naked and battered and bleeding in the forest, she was outraged.

She was consigned, after a great deal of trouble with Helen causing most of it, to the cellars of Moreda. She was amazed at the women she met there and by the stories they told. They ended irrevocably her ignorance of violent men, but rather than terrifying the girl with these tales of horror, travail and brutallity, their words stoked her fury. 'How dare they?' she demanded. By what right could these men treat women and young children so cruelly? And why, in the name of the gods, with the children to protect, and in the face of such apparent evil, why did the women allow it? Helen was surprised by their bitter laughter.

One young woman, hardly older than Helen, explained, as though she was talking to an impetuous child, that soon she would have her own answer to that last question. Her fighting spirit would no doubt be an addition to the excitements in the hall and in the bedroom. What would she do then? What could any here do to refuse these men their pleasures?

The young woman seemed to take grim delight in her warning, but if she expected her prognostication to humble

Helen Travers she was mistaken. Helen took up her cause over and again, railling at them all for being defeatist, for being cowards and for being stupid. If they would act together, they could achieve something. She bullied, she cajoled, she argued, loudly and continually until the men came for her. Silence fell upon the room as they entered but Helen Travers broke it: 'Can't you see?' she cried, 'There are just five of them. Why won't you fight?'

But the only resistance was from Helen herself and she was dragged away kicking and shouting, twisting and biting, willing to try anything to fight back and get free.

The key turned easily in the lock and the door opened. A black hole faced them where they had expected some small light at least, and so taking a torch from a bracket in the corridor, lit from a constant lantern fixed to the wall, Terrance led the way cautiously down the cellar steps. All that could be seen was an aisle lined by vast barrels.

As he set his foot upon the last step chaos was let loose. Terrance was set upon by a dozen screaming women brandishing staves of wood with murder in their hearts. Helen Travers' words had set a fire that was now blazing.

Seama moved quickly. A sudden gust of wind tumbled the victim and his attackers into a jumble of limbs and skirts on the stone floor and doused the torch.

'STOP!' he commanded. 'Ladies, we are come to rescue you. I am Seama,' and as he spoke, white light flared up to brighten the farthest recesses of the chamber. The light blazed from his upraised sword. He picked up the torch De Vere had dropped and relit it with the tip of the blade.

Guy was not the only one to gasp. If the sword was hot enough to light the torch then surely it was too hot to hold. The white light went out.

'Please relight any lanterns or candles you have, ladies, then you can see us properly.'

From all around came sighs and exclamations and the sound of weeping. One woman who had been attacking De Vere dropped her stave, flung arms around his neck and clung to him sobbing all the while. Though patently embarrassed at this, he held her tenderly, muttering reassurances.

Other women hugged each other or sat or stood confused, not knowing what to do, but there were a few stronger than the rest who had their wits about them. They gathered together away from the infiltrators and after a hasty conference they came to face their rescuer.

'It is him,' said one.

'Are you sure, Estella?'

'Yes, I saw him in Garassa,'

'Lord Seama, I am Catarina Beltez, granddaughter of The Master.' Her bearing was regal; she seemed an able leader. 'We are no doubt in your debt if you have indeed come to rescue us but how on Ea' will you do that? We are but women here. *We* cannot fight and you are five only, and one female at that. Upstairs there are hundred men and all of them armed, and all of them cruel – or perhaps you have already defeated them?'

'No, we have not, but our plan is moving on smoothly. If everything goes well you will all be free by tomorrow. If it does not then nobody will be free tomorrow.'

'And I suppose until then we must continue to pleasure those devils above?'

'No, Miss Beltez, we would not allow you to suffer one minute more. Please listen everybody. I doubt we have much time to spare and we need your help. First of all, have you seen Helen Travers?'

She had been dragged most of the way because she refused to walk. They didn't beat her for it: that was the prerogative of their sorcerer chief. The men would take recompense later. Dumping her on the floor of the Master's appartment they retreated, one or two of them sniggering; one or two sporting bruises, bite marks and scowls.

She sat there, as they slammed the doors behind them, skirts in a tangle, wondering what would happen next.

'So you are here at last, young lady.'

The voice, unexpectedly urbane, came from her left. In that side of the room she saw a fireplace. The mantlepiece was a huge affair of heavy oak standing six feet high and nailed to this mantle were a pair of manacles at least five feet apart. The fire was not lit because of the oppressive heat.

Before the fireplace a man of formidable size lounged in a large brocaded chair, the back of his red-necked head towards her, his black hair greased and combed back, his shoulders nearly too large for the chairback.

'Come and sit here,' he commanded, indicating a footstool with a kick.

'Why should I?'

There was a pause before the sorcerer spoke again. Could it be that he was surprised by her defiant tone. He changed tack and in a softer voice said:

'Because I ask you to, My Lady. Only that I can see you better by the light of these candles.'

The room was indeed brighter where candles clustered on candelabra by the fireplace. Helen considered her choices and concluding there was little point in trying to run away she decided to comply with this modest request. Even so she hesitated before seating herself at his feet. Was this the first of his many victories over her? Unsure she looked up at his face and nearly knocked over the stool in surprise. He wore a black mask and though there were holes for his eyes she gained a disturbing impression that nothing stared out of them.

He seemed pleased by the effect but that was not all his desire.

'You are very beautiful,' he said. She had been told this before but from this man of power the flattery was something to be blushed at.

She was beginning to experience an unfamiliar feeling of inferiority and she didn't like it. She glared at him to disguise her doubts.

'Well done. I am bored with the gutless women of this petty house. Where is your home? It sounds like more of a challenge than Moreda! No don't bother: there'll be plenty of time for questions later. I am pleased that your resentment is not veiled like those other bitches.'

'They have a cause for resentment, sir, and reason to be cautious with wicked men like you ruling their lives. You have them all wrong. The women here are not gutless. They demonstrate the true meaning of bravery, though I doubt you know the word.'

'I do not. What does it mean?' His tone was sarcstic. Not wishing to be a foil for his enjoyment she held her tongue. He reached out a calloused hand to stroke beneath her chin, as though she were his lap cat. Helen recoiled at the touch.

'Do you hate me so much?' he asked. Her reply was the contempt in her eyes. 'You see, it's very wearing to meet only frightened people: people who hate me without knowing me. I had thought, perhaps, that such a fierce will could forget fear. They said you were a fighter. It would be good to talk to someone who could listen and respond as normal people do. Do you understand?'

Helen was sure she did, but wouldn't admit it. Was he a lonely man? Because of the power he wielded, because of his mask and because of his cruelty he had become loathsome and loathed. But eventually even evil men must tire of their games of violence and yearn for some less fraught relationship. Perhaps this evil man was looking for a friend.

'No!' she said firmly. 'I will give you nothing of my self. You are repugnant: a murderer, a torturer of children, a violator of all things proper, and I should be worse than you if I—'

'If you what? Let me save you, Miss Travers, from your conscience,'

Helen shuddered. The sorcerer bent over her, his mask inches from her face.

'Whatever you wish to deny me I will demand; whatever you seek to refuse me I will take. You have no free will in this place. I will take what I want from you. Grubb! You see, Helen Travers, I have complete power while you have none. My pleasure is to exercise that power and your role is to suffer it. Grubb, get in here!' A hard looking man followed by two other leering thugs entered the room. 'See here: this pretty maiden wants to dance for me. The fireplace, if you please.'

When Helen Travers had been taken away an hour before, she had left the women in a state of turmoil. The cowardly and unnerved women, those weak at the start and those who had suffered most had been beyond her power to move in any way – they were too much in shock. As for the stronger willed or less tortured there had been two opposite reactions to Helen's arguments. The older women had lived their lives honoured by men who acted always with the utmost chivalry; and chivalry is a fine system for protecting the weak from the excesses of the strong. The problem is that those honoured by such a system may become little more than worshipped possessions. Within such a code women can lose the power of self-determination. In the whole of El Seno men had come to rule everything. They had the power to be generous and fair minded, while women had the honour and duty of accepting the kindnesses of men. Men owned the houses and lands, the wealth of the forest; they allowed their women the pleasure of managing the domestic necessities. The women of Beltez counted themselves lucky, and were happy to defer to their lords and masters. All was well. But in time this happiness promoted an inability to do anything else but defer. Now, no matter that the 'masters' were no longer kind, decent or generous, a perverse sense of dignity and honour demanded that they continue in their allotted role, that they followed the 'normal' rules of life. There had been suicides already among some of the older women not prepared to accept the dishonour forced upon them, but there was in the cellar, their prison, a majority who could do nothing other than meekly accept whatever happened to them. Their sex had become their fate.

Miss Travers had spared little time on these women, but for their part they were quick to condemn her arguments. They considered her shameless and dishonourable. Helen was angry with them. 'You've got to fight for your damned honour' she told them, "You can't *submit* for it.' Her words carried no weight with these women. They assured her she was wrong and returned to their prayers, praying for the strength to survive their travail first, and for deliverance second.

There was a younger group who prayed less and less as their incarceration continued and Catarina Beltez was their leader. Catarina was a proud woman, she was after all granddaughter to the Master of Beltez, and the idea of her ancient and noble family murdered by cut-throats roused more fury than tears. She'd not been cowed by her experience in the armoury. She was inflamed by the needless butchery, outraged by the continuing abuse of the women and children, and she was enraged by the timidity of her peers. And yet she could do nothing about it. Catarina had tried her best to stir them up but she found it impossible: too respectful of her elders her upbringing had left her without the language or forcefulness that came naturally to Helen Travers. As one hideous day succeeded another, however, without any chance of relief from the excesses of the Black Company, that respect diminished. Catarina and others like her were ready for something to change.

One evening the men had come for Catarina herself, as they had come for other women on other nights. Sometimes the women were returned to the cellar in a terrible state but sometimes they did not come back at all. Catarina feared the worst. Kelsly's threat of offering her up as sacrifice was ever present in her thoughts, and utterly terrifying to her, and she expected now a quite horrible death.

They took her to the Hall. The Company was at feast and they were very drunk. Catarina breathed a little more easily when she realised that none of the sorcerers were present and the men were in a mood for jest rather than spilled blood. She was surprised at the indiscipline in the hall – that man Trant seemed to have the whip hand over this pack but, by rumour, he was now travelling south in search of more victims. With no one to keep them in check these man might do anything and Catarina wondered what indignities awaited her.

An auction was what they had in mind. Aware of her pedigree it amused the men this evening to put her virginity up for sale. As they continued with their feast she was stripped and then forced to parade naked along the tables. The prospective buyers took their opportunity to inspect the merchandise before they made an offer. Though Catarina was twenty years old she had yet to develop a womanly figure and her face might have been described as homely, but her hair was the typical lustrous black of her family and she was, overall, far from ugly. The brutes at their trough, however, decided to insult her bluntness of feature, to cast doubt on her status, and in the end she was dismissed unsold. They had better looking pigs in the yard, they said. Her ordeal lasted just half an hour and although she was roughly handled and lewdly displayed, she suffered no hurt so great as her battered pride. As she was bundled out of the hall and back down to the cellar, clutching her clothes to her, there was one thought in Catarina's mind. She wasn't scared by them any more, and she didn't care what they might do, her only desire was to pay them back. All she needed was support as she planned her revenge.

Miss Travers' arrival had gained her that support. Helen's speeches had raised the temperature as Catarina could not. Helen made them feel ashamed by their lack of courage; they were resentful of the new girl's jeering (and none more so than Catarina); they were left desperate to prove that they too could be brave, and actually do something to save themselves.

It was Catarina who started the hasty plotting after Helen had been carried-off, and she who attempted the first blow. That her attack on De Vere was a failure was a great annoyance. When Seama asked about Helen's whereabouts she was livid. Why was this uncouth Travers girl thought to be so important? What about the women of Beltez, the slaves of Moreda who had suffered so much?

'Helen Travers is undoubtedly lost to you,' she said. 'She has been taken to the chief of those monsters upstairs.'

To her dismay, Seama didn't seem very concerned.

'It seems that I will need to see to this man earlier than I intended. Do you think we can rescue her, Angren?'

'Why not? We need something to do before daybreak. They stay up late in this house, don't they?'

'Nothing is as it should be in Moreda.' Catarina was not only talking about her captors. 'And what are *we* to do until dawn?' she asked. 'Don't you think we need rescuing as well? Are we to sit here praying we'll be forgotten? Many have died already, many are so ruined they want to die. We have had enough. There are over fifty of us here. Are we not more important than that single girl? Why do you risk your lives for her instead of us?'

'Lady Catarina, we intend to save you all. Outside is an army whose sole reason for braving these deadly sorcerers rests with the safety of that one girl. I must show them a minor victory: I must bring her from the house in order to give them the courage and the confidence to complete the task. We have planned that Mr. De Vere and young Guy here will stay with you to help organize your defence. Now, if that is clear, will you please tell me how I can find this sorcerer?'

The scene in the Master's rooms was not much changed except that the manacles nailed to the chimney breast were now occupied. Helen Travers hung there, arms spread, toes just touching the floor, with her back to the room. Thankfully they had not lit the fire. It seemed to her that she could smell the burnt flesh of earlier victims. They had stripped her down to her shift and she shivered now as the first gust of cold wind rushed down the chimney. Outside lightning seared the night and thunder battered the rooftops as the storm attacked the house, smashing a tumult of rain against the rattling windows.

'Cold?' asked the devil's voice from not far away. 'Well I'm sure I can warm you up.'

Oh Gods, she prayed silently, *not the fire, please not the fire!*

He made no movement. She hated not being able to see him. The words of the women downstairs came back to her. She realized that fear was clutching at her heart just as they said it would. But she was determined not to show it.

'So kind. Why am I chained like this?' There was no reply. 'Do you want to take off that mask? Is that it? You are ashamed to show your face. Is it so vile? It's said that evil shows a fair face; are you pleased to be the exception?'

'Wit from such an unfortunate position is a novelty. It all

adds to the amusement. I wonder if it will save you any pain at all.'

He came up close behind her. She could feel his breath on her neck. 'You are all questions, Lady. You mistake your role once more. I like to cause pain. I like to see a fine young body quiver in anticipation of pain.' Without warning he tore off her last garment, burning her skin in the process. For the first time in her life she was naked in the presence of a man but she barely thought about it: she was more concerned with her aching arms and the promised torment to come.

'Ha! And what a fine body you have,' he said, 'still young but shapely all the same. What shall we do with it?'

'I don't suppose you would know what to do with a woman, being more used to pigs and cows.'

He sniggered. 'Such crude insults from an innocent. Delightful. Well you can be my pig. I'm going to make you squeal.'

Before she understood his meaning she heard a sudden rush of air and received a cutting lash that curled round her back and flicked at her left breast. She screamed. For perhaps four seconds the pain was excruciating.

'I am glad you appreciate this whip. I had it specially made. The steel tip is particularly effective. And these bands of wire make for a nice pattern.'

Helen bit her lip as the afterpain rolled across her back.

'Why are you doing this?' she gasped.

'Do you not know?'

'Would I ask if I knew?'

'You might. You may think that if you keep me talking I will forget to do this.'

The whip cut through the air but the stroke made no contact.

'I suppose you think that was amusing.'

The sorcerer chuckled softly.

'You really have no idea.' He ran a finger down her spine and then followed the line of his first stroke with his fingernail making her jump. 'The last stroke was to do with conditioning. My pleasure lies in both hurting you, and in mastering you. Let me explain. You will begin this adventure feeling that you can control your response to the whip. You will believe that you can deny me in some way. But there will be a process of change. You will reach a point when you think that I will *need* no more. But I will continue. Stroke after stroke will fall. That beautiful skin of yours will be striped red and white: a delicious sight. And then you will think that you can *take* no more. But I will continue, perhaps more strongly, laying one stoke over another. And soon you won't be thinking at all as your body simply responds to the pain. And still I will continue. When your body is shaking, when your hands are numb and the muscles in your legs can no longer support your weight, I will feel that I am getting somewhere. Then I'll have them take you down and if it pleases me I shall use you in another way. And after that, then maybe we will start again.

'Do you understand now?'

Helen listened to this hideous monologue completely appalled.

'I don't understand. I don't understand why you find pleasure in this. Are you insane? Normal people do not, cannot think like this; they *should* not—'

'Is that what you think? Do you know, Miss Travers, there are women I have met who would envy you. The thought of being used and abused and so helpless truly excites them.'

'Not true. It is not true, just what you choose to believe.'

'Really? And the opposite is merely what *you* choose to believe. Trust me: down there in the cellar of Moreda, waiting for my men to come calling, are at least four or five women who—'

'And that makes it right?'

'I am unconcerned by what is right and proper. Actually I prefer women who do not want this at all. Much more fun: the chances are that this will be their first time, for the whip and for—'

'You are despicable!'

'Yes I am, thank you.'

This time the lash made contact. And this time she screamed in terror as much as in pain.

'But at least I am the pick of a bad bunch. You're lucky. Kelsly would have bled you from thousands of cuts – he pretends it's to do with religious observance but he is merely fascinated by blood. Trant's crew are utterly brutal. They would ravish you and batter you and break you. They are savages. But if you please me, then maybe I'll keep you for a while. If you do not then I will pass you on. Your challenge will be in trying to determine what it is that I find pleasing.'

Helen struggled to master herself once more. That second lash had drawn blood, she could feel it trickling down her side. Somehow the thought of the damage helped. She had hardly known fear in all her young life never mind the terror the sorcerer sought to induce with his words, but anger was something she could use. As the buzz of pain subsided she forced herself to react, she put at the front of her mind her loathing for this man, her contempt for all he was, her rage at his foul deeds. Anger would be her saviour.

'You foul creature! You foul cowardly excuse for a man! I pity the mother that gave you birth. And yet you think you are special. You think yourself better than your disgusting company: that your pleasures are more refined, that the others are animals, that you are civilized. Oh, I can hear the arrogance in your voice. But you're wrong! You are worse than an animal. There's nothing refined about hurting other people. There is nothing clever in controlling them. You are a rapist just like the rest, taking what you want by force, treating everything and everyone in the world as objects for your use. How you have managed to banish any thought of sympathy and understanding— Aaaah! Oh Gods!'

For a third time the whip found her and this time even more powerfully, the tip snaking round to lick at her stomach. The bolt of pain it provoked closed off Helen to the world about her, lost in the agony of the moment, and so she didn't hear the sudden noise of someone banging on the door of the chamber.

But at that noise the sorcerer himself flew into a rage. He had left specific instructions he was not to be interrupted for anything. Those damn guards never listened to anything he said. In a mood to match the fury that raged around the house he stormed to the door and flung it wide.

'What do you want, fools?' he demanded of the figures in the corridor. 'I told you not to dis—'

His word's stopped dead as one of Sigrid's blades thrust deep into his chest. She was so quick that she was already wiping her blade before she realized that, incredibly, impossibly, she had not killed the man.

Crushing hands wrenched the sword from her grasp and threw her against the wall. Angren's short sword bit into the sorcerer's sword-arm before he could advance but finally, barging the weapon master aside, Seama swung his nameless blade in a deadly arc, almost severing the sorcerer's head and body. Blood spewed from the corpse as it tumbled to the ground.

Angren picked himself up, looking a little shaken. 'Real blood then. When I saw that mask, I thought—'

'And so did I, Angren. Especially when he didn't fall at Sigrid's strike. Garaid stopped that thing in Gothery by going for the throat so I went for the head. But anyway, it was just a man.'

Sigrid had recovered from her fall and she reached for the stolen sword. 'Not just a man. He was a sorcerer and he should have died the first time.'

'A sorcerer is nothing more than a man who has learned several formulae. He had no power to protect himself from a blade. No time to summon sorcerous help. I think you must have missed his vitals, Sigrid.'

'Never, I always—'

They heard a groan from within the chamber.

Angren jumped over the corpse and ran into the room. There he was halted by a vision of beauty itself. Perhaps it was the extremity of the situation, the fact that she looked so vulnerable, the long blonde hair, the lack of clothes, but in that moment Angren thought he had chanced upon a goddess. She was without compare. He scowled noticing the weals caused by the whip and was at once angry and full of pity, but when she heard him, an unseen menace, and began to swear royally at him, he was dumbstruck.

Sigrid came in but he failed to notice until she elbowed him in the side. 'Don't you think, Old Angren,' she said, 'that you should be helping the young lady down from there instead of gawping at her backside.'

Angren flushed red. Sigrid's sarcasm always made him feel uncomfortable but this time he was affronted. This was not lust: he was in awe of the girl. Nevertheless, stung into action, he rushed to help. Mumbling an apology, he released the manacles and then busied himself with gathering her clothes. He was blushing even more deeply as he offered them up, and he quickly turned his back upon her bold nudity.

'Why such courtesy?' she said, 'Haven't you already seen all I have to show?'

QUEEN OF TEMPEST

Moreda 3057.8.6

Sigrid had experienced fear before but never so much as when
the sorcerer attacked. He should have been dead. Could she have
missed his heart? Admittedly, she'd been ill at ease creeping
through the darkened corridors, expecting every minute that
lights would bloom to reveal a trap. She had dismissed the two
guards without a flicker of emotion but knew deep down she
was on edge. Killing the guards, who were engrossed in peeping
through the keyhole, was the last step before their meeting with
the sorcerer. When Seama had suggested *she* should strike their
Chief she'd thought him mad. Surely it was a job for the wizard?
It was, of course, beneath her dignity to refuse. Perhaps with
so much depending upon speed and accuracy, and with her
uncertainty about what would happen if she dared the strike,
perhaps she had missed her mark after all. But, gods above, she
had been scared when he grabbed her.

The lady warrior was rubbing witch hazel ointment, recovered
from the Masters bathroom, into the young woman's back.

'Ouch' the girl yelped as Sigrid pressed a little too hard.

Sigrid smiled. It was the first complaint Miss Travers had
made. She was a tough little cuss. Pretty too. That damned
Angren had not missed any of that. Sigrid was almost beginning
to like the man until she saw him goggling at the girl's backside
like he'd never seen one before.

'Angren,' she'd said sharply, 'hadn't you better go and help
Seama?' And he would have gone straight away but that little
minx had to put in her two-granath first.

'He needn't bother on my account. It's a little too late for him
to think of sparing my blushes.'

And the fool almost ran for the door. A grown man acting
like a fumbling youth. Hey ho! Sigrid worked in the last of the
cream with much more vigour than was necessary.

Just outside the door the wizard was searching the body of the dead sorcerer rather gingerly.

Angren took a deep breath and tried to look normal.

'Is he dangerous still even without his head?' he asked.

'Ah! I wondered where you'd got to. You took your time in there.' He looked up. 'Angren, have you been drinking too much lately? You're all red in the face. Out of condition, perhaps?'

Angren winced. Seama was laughing at him: he'd heard. It had always been one of Seama's more regular jokes to tease him about his troubles with women. – a fatal attraction that invariably brought chaos into his life. But at least he had affairs! All Seama had was his magic. Why should he worry about what Seama thought, or Sigrid for that matter? All he knew was that Helen Travers was the most lovely woman he had ever seen. The image of her hanging from the cuffs was burned in his mind: the slender arms and legs, the blonde hair cascading over smooth shoulders to reach the small of her back, and... It was not lechery that made him feel weak at the knees, he was fairly sure. But Seama had already dismissed the issue, and so Angren decided to try and pay attention.

'Dangerous?' the wizard was saying, 'Not at all. There's not much power in these sorcerers. I just don't want blood all over my clothes. We made a mess of him. Come on, let's get these bodies out of sight. We'll have to hope no one wants to speak with their Chief until we're gone.'

'What were you looking for?'

'Whatever I could find.'

'And what was that?'

'Absolutely nothing. I thought there might be some clue about his superiors, but maybe there's something in the room. Do you think that linen cupboard is big enough for all three of them?'

Angren stepped forward to size it up. He was quite an expert in the disposal of corpses.

Ten minutes later they rejoined the ladies who were relaxing with glasses in their hands. Both were silent in each other's company, both had enough thoughts to occupy them.

Seama took in much of the situation at a glance but decided that at least half of it was nothing to do with him.

'Have you explained our position, Sigrid?' he asked.

'No. I thought I'd leave that pleasure to you.' Sigrid smiled her sarcastic smile but then added in a more friendly manner: 'Would you like a drink, My Lord? This port is exquisite and there's sherry as well.'

'Thank you. One small port wouldn't hurt.'

'And what can I offer Mr. Nielderson?'

Angren was oblivious to any innuendo it seemed and he charged in with: 'Is there nothing stronger, Sigrid? Ah now, that looks like brandy. It is!'

Seama, accepting his drink, raised his eyebrows slightly and Sigrid grimaced in reply. He considered the idea of taking Angren to one side. It seemed that Angren had never noticed the wistful look in Sigrid's eye in all these days they had travelled together. Perhaps he'd be doing his friend a favour by pointing it out. Of course, much of the fault was with Sigrid: Angren was not the sort of man to realize that all the sharp words were simply a means of engagement. That they might mean something more than dislike hadn't occurred to him. If she wanted to get somewhere with Angren she'd have to be less ambiguous. Seama had no time for these emotional quandaries.

'Angren,' he said, 'You won't forget where we are will you? There'll be no time to sleep off a heavy session, you know.'

'It's just a small one, Seama,' Angren sounded aggrieved. 'Well sort of.'

Seama ignored him.

'Miss Travers,' the wizard said. 'You may have guessed that we are not yet safe. Not by any means. There are only the four of us against a whole house full of cut-throats.'

'Four? Are you mad? How can we hope to get the women and children out with just the four of us?' Seama was startled by her vehemence. These were the first words she had spoken to him – they weren't the polite thanks he had expected. 'I hope you weren't proposing to sneak out without them?'

'I am afraid that's exactly what we must do. However, it's not as bad as it seems. Two of our companions are with them now preparing a barricade. It won't be possible to get into the cellars and if any want to try it then at least it'll keep them busy until we're ready. But it's already halfway through the night so I doubt they'll be bothered at all. We will face these thugs on the field at dawn.'

'What, four against a hundred?' she said scornfully. 'Isn't that just a little bit steep, even for the mighty Lord Wizard?'

Seama gave a slight nod in answer to her sly greeting. She was not slow. Seama was beginning to understand Angren's difficulty with the girl.

'I take it you haven't yet bothered with a full introduction, Sigrid?'

'The circumstances never brought us to the finer points of courtesy. She's heard our names.'

'Apart from yours,' Helen said.

'I think you heard Seama call me Sigrid?'

'That's hardly your full name. I know of the Lord Seama by common report and this person is Angren Nielderson from all I have heard, though where he comes from and why I cannot guess.'

'Let me tell you: he's a countryman of yours. Is he typical?'

Seama saw Sigrid wink at Helen Travers. She was trying to relieve the tension, albeit at Angren's expense.

'A countryman of mine? I'm surprised. Certainly his manners would be described as lacking if he were a man of Southern Aegarde.'

'Well thank you very much.' Angren was unaware of the collusion between the two women. He was having a hard time of it. 'I'm from Terremark, if you must know.'

'That would explain it. Terremark is a long way away, isn't it? Up in the Northern wilds.'

'Wilds! You cheeky young… I'll have you know…'

Seama couldn't restrain a chuckle, Sigrid and Helen were both grinning and Angren realized he was being baited.

'Let it drop, Angren' the wizard said. 'We're not getting our story told here. You asked, Miss Travers, about the three of us fighting a hundred. Actually our task is a little easier. We have sixty of the best waiting for us to draw these villains out. We've a good chance of winning, do you not think, Angren?'

'I'd say so, so long as Gumb's men are as good as they look.'

'Angren!' Sigrid said, but it was too late.

'My uncle? My uncle is here?' The smile had fallen from her face. She paled. 'How did you know who I was? I didn't tell you.' She worked it out all too quickly now that she considered it. 'And my father? Is my father with him? Tell me!' she demanded, daring them. The look on Seama's face must have been answer enough but she wanted it saying.

Sigrid was never one to drag things out.

'We met Gumb,' she explained, 'and rode with him to meet your procession. A wounded man reached us first. He said that you'd been abducted and everyone else murdered.'

Such a blunt recitation, Seama was annoyed, but there was never an easy way to tell anyone that someone they loved was dead. What a pity she had to find out so soon. Seama looked accusingly at Angren but the weapon-master was too concerned with Helen's reaction to notice.

Her face had frozen as the words were spoken, frozen as her thoughts sought desperately for an interpretation less dreadfull. But it wasn't possible. She gathered herself up and then let out such a scream that all three rescuers took a step back. They took another when she burst into action and grabbed at the poker by the fireplace.

'He's dead now, love,' said Sigrid, 'He's paid. He's dead and can't hurt—'

She wasn't listening. 'I'll kill them kill him kill them,' she screamed and with each 'kill' she battered the sorcerer's chair. And then she laid in without words, only screams, and the force of her blows broke off one of the wings and splintered the legs and ripped the fabric apart.

Angren in a panic rushed up to try and stop her but Sigrid pushed him away.

'What are you doing, Sig?'

'Just thank me for saving your life and let her get on with it.'

'But they'll all hear her.'

'What if they do? They'll think she's being beaten – not an unusual event in this house.'

Something of their exchange must have permeated Helen's wall of rage because she was suddenly still and quiet. As they turned to see, all the colour of her emotion fled her face, and all the furious strength left her limbs. She sank to her knees and by degrees curled up on the floor, clutching her stomach as though she had lost a baby. And then she began to wail, low and wordless and awful to hear. It was the cry of a lost girl knowing that her greatest source of constant and deep love was gone forever; the cry of a child alone in a terrible world with no comprehension in her heart of how she might possibly continue. It was the cry that all mankind must make over and over again.

Sigrid and Angren and Seama exchanged looks. Sigrid shook her head. How much more harm would these monsters do, how many more hearts would they break?

'It's time we were done with this Black Company,' she said, 'Time to end it.'

It would have been impossible to comfort Helen so no one tried. They just let her work through the pain and after a long ten minutes the sobbing congealed into silence. Without saying a word to them, she got up, walked over to the heavy curtains and drew them back. Seama watched as she stood silhouetted by lightning, staring out at the forgotten storm. When she opened the window the wind snatched it from her grasp and slammed it against the outside wall, cracking the glass; the gale blasted into the room, billowing the curtains, spattering rain onto her face. The sky boomed in the repeated stabbing light but Helen Travers was unmoved. As she faced the elements, hair flying, Seama had a fancy that it was she who ordered the storm, that her emotion had taken mighty force and the tempest of her anger was punishing the earth for its crime. Was there synchronicity in nature? Could it be that the emotion of one tiny part could be played out on a wider stage? Perhaps every cataclysmic event Earnor had suffered was as much dependent on the actions and feelings of normal men and women as on the cruel whims of gods.

Helen closed the window and pulled the drapes and came back into the room. Rain had washed the tears from her pale face. Gone was the Queen of Tempest and now a bedraggled, upset young woman stood before them.

'Must we stay in this room?' she asked desolately.

'I am afraid we must,' Seama told her, 'till nearly dawn.'

She tightened her lips and flopped down into a chair. 'Let it come quickly then.'

Angren picked up the decanter of brandy, shook off the marble stopper and poured himself another drink. Seama wasn't happy about it and glared at the Aegardean.

'Alright, alright. I'll pour half of it back. It's just a night cap.' He tipped nearly half of the amber liquid back into the decanter and then made himself comfortable on the settee. 'I think we should all get some rest, don't you Seama?'

'I think you should, and you too, ladies. I'll keep watch.'

'But we can take turn about,' Sigrid said.

'No. We haven't that much time so it's hardly worth it,' Seama assured her, 'besides I want a good look around this room before we leave. You carry on but I'll need the candles lit.'

Angren and Sigrid were quick to make themselves comfortable. Angren kept to his sofa and Sigrid took the bed. Helen Travers made no move to attempt sleep. Seama briefly considered making her sleep but after his own recent bereavement he understood the need for silent thought. He left her to it and began his cautious search.

He searched cupboards, drawers, the desk, the Sorcerer's spare clothes and even the garderobe. After an hour, with the night in its second half and the storm far away, Seama had found precisely nothing of interest. There were weapons of course, a hidden cache of precious gems – stolen no doubt from the strong rooms of much of Eastern Aegarde – a locked money box that when opened revealed only a booty of gold, and several items of arcane significance such as pure chalk for marking out pentacles, tannis root incense and almost fifty talismans. But there was nothing peculiar, nothing that indicated any connection with a paymaster or superior. By all the evidence, bar his intuition, this Black Company was working for itself. Seama was tired by now and very frustrated.

He decided to try a different technique. Instead of trying to find the object, whatever it might be, he would force the object to reveal itself. The only problem was that the spell he intended to use normally demanded a most vital piece of information: the Name of the item sought. Seama was looking for anything that might give him a clue but that wasn't specific enough. And so his first request was for 'a letter of instruction'. The spell he used was not complicated and required Seama to say: 'Any letter of instruction given to the Chief Sorcerer, who but lately dwelled here, come to me', but he had to say it in the Language of Command taught in the Books of Lore, using the True Name given to objects of such description. Seama had no difficulty in remembering the True Name of a 'letter of instruction' – *a'levella* – and within seconds of him speaking the spell he heard a rustling, though nothing appeared. He traced the sound to a jerkin that lay in the bottom of a cloak cupboard. From a pocket he'd previously missed he extracted a fold of official looking paper. It was a summons 'to appear for the King's pleasure in the Court at Garassa'. Not what he was looking for but what he had asked for. It was an interesting document though in that it named the sorcerer as 'Gaspar Semmento, an alien to the country of Aegarde.' He would never now appear before Agwis and Seama would never know where exactly he came from.

At least the spell had worked. This time he would try another Name. If there was a connection with someone else, he reasoned, and they were sorcerers after all, then there may be some means of communication. Again he spoke strange words, speaking the name inherent to a material means of communication – *kozeg i kozloma*. He spoke quietly, the power was all in the language. Nothing happened. Seama looked around the room for any sign of movement but was dissapointed.

'Damn' he muttered. Despondent he returned to his port but before the glass reached his lips he heard a sharp crack. It was the sound of something very hard hitting the varnished parquet floor. He looked towards Angren and saw, rolling on the floor, the stopper that had been used to keep the dust off the brandy. Seama snatched it up and examined it. It was a marble. A dobber as he would have called it when he was young: an inch and a half wide piece of white brushed, black marble that had been smoothed into a ball.

He tutted rather loudly.

More or less at the same moment Sigrid sat up in her bed cursing softly about something. The noises were enough to rouse Helen from her reverie.

'What's the matter?' she asked. Both Seama and Sigrid answered at the same time. Seama apologised.

'After you.'

'Just trying to get comfortable – lying on something hard.'

'What?'

''m trying to fish it out – what about you?'

'Oh, nothing really. I thought I'd found what I was looking for but it turns out to be a child's best dobber.' He explained his spell to Helen as Sigrid struggled with her clothes. He was pleased that at least the girl was taking an interest.

'Why did it appear then, if it's not what you named?'

'Good, old fashioned coincidence, I expect. Angren must have been playing with it as he fell asleep, and dropped it as he relaxed. I'll make sure when he wakes.'

'Aah. Got you.'

'What is it, Sigrid?'

'Oh, something I picked up on Tumboll – down in the passage when I was with Ruspa. Had it in my trouser pocket ever since. Funny I haven't noticed it till now.'

Seama looked up sharply. 'Can I see that?'

Sigrid shrugged and tossed it across the room for Seama to catch. It was made of a stone similar to Angren's marble though much darker. The shape was peculiar: a little like an hour glass but thicker in the middle and flat at each end. Seama studied it minutely but after a few minutes he sighed and said:

'Nothing. Just a piece of stone, something from a game

perhaps, like the marble. I'll keep hold of it for now though if you don't mind?'

'Keep it. I'm off to sleep.'

Seama put the marble and the Tumboll stone in his pocket and went over to the window as Sigrid snuggled down. It was inky black outside. 'There's still over an hour to go,' he said, 'Aren't you sleepy, Helen?'

'No, not now.'

'Then let's talk. Tell me about your home and about your family if you can.'

SWORDS AND SORCERY

Moreda 3057.8.6

SWORDS

They talked through till the eager rooks began their black clamour. The night had slipped away and far in the east a crimson glow preceded the rising sun.

'The day breaks red.' Helen announced as she drew the curtains.

'And will continue so,' Seama said. 'It's time to be doing.'

They woke the others. Sigrid needed a quick wash before she was fully awake, but Angren was alert immediately.

'This is it then, Seama. We've been through a lot to get here, let's hope we can finish it.'

'We must if we're to go on to the next task.'

'There's more?'

'As we discussed, Angren, but there'll be time to talk some more about the options when we've rid the country of these particular devils. Ah, Sigrid. If you're ready we'll go.'

His plan was to leave the house by the front door. If there were horses close-by then they would raise the alarm themselves. Seama wanted to be chased across the fields by men groggy with sleep and hangovers. If there were no horses in the yard the rumpus would have to wait until they reached the stables beyond the moat. What he didn't want was to be discovered before they could leave the house.

Seama led the way with Sigrid and the girl following closely and Angren taking the rear. All had weapons in hand, even Helen who carried a knife taken from one of the guards. One of Sigrid's twin swords was sheathed for now: instead she partnered the other with a jewelled dagger she had taken from the bedroom. She counted this as recompense for the scare the sorcerer had given her. Seama had insisted on examining the blade, but it was simple metal and he had passed it safe.

They crept along darksome corridors to the head of the main

stairs. Snores, giggles and moans echoed in rooms to left and right but no one challenged them. Seama was aware of a slight feeling of disappointment. Though he didn't want to be caught, he would have liked to lessen enemy numbers a little as he went.

The opportunity presented itself in the great hall at the foot of the stairs. Six men sat or lay on the wide steps, all asleep with their tankards all around. There was no way to get past without waking them or killing them. Whatever happened it was going to be risky. Dreading the inevitable creaks and groans from the ancient timbers they descended the stair and were lucky a enough to reach their prey without raising either a grunt or a grumble.

Seama signalled Angren and Sigrid to dispatch the men as quickly as possible while he held back. He had no scruples about killing sleeping men, but he'd be more likely to save the girl if anything went wrong. It should have taken just the two of them anyway. In the gloom of the hall he watched as they began their clinical task.

One: a stab through the side of the throat; two: a knife between the ribs. A gurgle, a shuddering breath quieter than snoring, and two were dead. Angren's second was a disaster. He again went for the throat but in the half-light didn't see the iron collar. It rang with a dull note and jarred Angren's arm. He'd killed his man but the other three were awake in a second and ready to fight. Angren would have been in trouble if Seama hadn't leapt down to help. In a short flurry of blades, arms and legs, Seama dealt decisively with his quota while Sigrid got her second with the sorcerer's knife. They were clear but they'd made too much noise.

Shouts came from behind as they ran pell-mell across the marble floor to the doorway. Two men running in from outside to see what the trouble was found trouble for themselves. Again Sigrid's speed was frightening, downing both in the one slash and stab movement. Pushing Helen before him, Seama made for the horses picketed in a corner of the gravel drive. There were no guards: they lay inside the door, bleeding on the white marble. The sound of many footsteps on that marble clattered in their ears as they tried to mount. The horses were confused and made life difficult but need fired Seama's efforts and he calmed them with a single, powerful word. As the enemy burst from the house the four thundered across the bridge, chasing the remaining horses before them.

The fields were sodden. Great clods of earth were thrown up by the horses' hooves and the escapees were caked in mud very quickly. Angren was surprised to note, as they crossed ditches and fences in their race to the woods, that he was, by many a teeter, easily the worst horseman. Helen was masterly and Sigrid little less so. They had cleared over a quarter of a mile before the first pursuit was mounted but looking back over his shoulder, Angren was amazed to see that the entire house was out already. Despite their debauchery these men were quick off the mark. Angren urged his mount onward and they pounded on through the puddles, and the spray marked their passage.

They kept no order in their flight and Angren was thrilled to see Helen forging ahead. She looked good in the saddle but her face was grim with concentration. What a fine girl she was, he thought: what a pity they'd started off on the wrong foot. He decided, reasonably, that it would be interesting getting to know her. The reflection that she was under twenty and he was over forty didn't linger for more than a second. She was so beautiful and… and now was hardly the time for any such thoughts. Angren was angry with himself. He had a job to do, there were wrongs to right, payments to be exacted. Yes for Helen's sake and her murdered father but what about all the others: Bassalo and his children, the villages these men had destroyed, the lives they had taken or ruined? And what about his own brother Dag? Was it six years now since Morgan Trant had blighted his life? Angren had spent much of the time since trying to catch up with the renegade but to no effect. Trant and his men had always given him the slip. But Angren wasn't the sort of man to forget an injustice, nor the sort of man to forgive one either. Of late other ventures may have put the weapon-master off the scent but Angren knew that sooner or later they'd meet, and there would be a reckoning. Perhaps today would be that day.

The smouldering embers of Angren's fury were blown into a flame by that thought. Never mind Terrance and Seama lecturing him about revenge and how it was a bad idea, Angren had no time for such a notion. Revenge was right and necessary and to be relished. Or at least the thought of it was to be relished. It was an odd thing but Angren had noticed that when the moment came the sense of satisfaction rarely lived up to the anticipation. Though that never put him off finishing the job.

There would be little time to draw out either the agony or the ecstasy of revenge in this fight. Angren knew it would be fast and furious, and all the better for it. Looking back, precariously keeping his saddle, he was alarmed to see that about twenty of the fastest, first horsed riders were gaining fast. He wondered if Trant was one of them.

'Ride on,' he yelled, 'Ride on! They're catching us.'

The trees were in sight but where was Gumb and his men? Angren could see no one ahead and his suspicious thoughts became uncharitable.

'Pull right,' Seama was yelling, 'Pull right. We've come too far over. There they are!'

So they were. Angren and the others followed Seama's lead by wheeling sharply towards Gumb's cavalry and as they did so their pursuers gained more ground. Angren realized that the enemy couldn't see past the spray and were unaware of their peril.

A horn sounded its clarion note: a brave, clear, beautiful sound voiced loud over the fields. Lesser horns broke out to support it and Gumb's battle made the ground shake as they began their advance.

The twenty in close pursuit, an ample force to retrieve four, found themselves outnumbered three to one and didn't like the look of it. They pulled up and tried to turn away from the onslaught and might have saved themselves but for Gumb's mounted archers. Adept at shooting from horseback the confusion they caused with their arrows was enough to delay the attempted retreat. With several killed outright and many unhorsed, they were easy pickings. Five escaped, saved only by

Gumb' s order to withdraw. The baron had seen, half-a-mile distant, the larger force of the Black Company ordering their reply and he had to be ready for them.

His nephew, with an exultant look upon his face rode back to him. He had killed a man and was proud of the deed.

'That's twenty less to worry about, Uncle.' he cried, 'and look: there she is! Helen, Helen!' He leapt from his horse and ran to meet his sister as she approached. Seama, Angren and Sigrid meanwhile went to speak with the Captain and Berta.

'You managed then,' said Bibron. 'Quite a beauty isn't she?'

'Yes and yes,' Seama responded. 'But more importantly she's unharmed, more or less. Terrance and Guy are in place; in the house, the Chief Sorcerer is dead and also another twelve of his men. With that twenty on the field our enemy is reduced. Are we ready for the fight, Bibron?'

'I am if you've already killed the sorcerer but I don't look forward to fightin' on horseback.'

'Nor me', said Berta. 'What about you and me waiting while a few have been knocked off, eh?'

'I'm with you there. How about you, Angren?'

'No. I'm not the best horseman in the world but I'll stick with it. Where are the others, Captain?'

'Well Garaid and Piedoro are with the bowmen comin' in from the West, unmarked I hope. His brother should be with that group comin' in from the guard post, see 'em? They'd best hurry and so'ad we: they've started movin'.'

The enemy, in regimented precision had begun to walk their horses towards them.

'Come on; come on!' yelled Lord Gumb, 'Let's get it together. One man to take Miss Travers back to the trees. Good man! Off you go Helen, and quick about it.'

'Yes, yes. Good luck uncle. Make them pay, won't you.'

'Oh they'll pay alright, don't you worry. Now go! Seama, will you join us? Can you follow the formation?'

'We'll work it out, Gumb.'

'Right lads. Double Phalanx,' the baron screamed, his face redder than ever, 'and move on!'

Fifty horses rode out to meet seventy. And to meet whatever the three remaining sorcerers could conjure up. It was a daunting task but Gumb and his men were brimful of confidence. Their enemy's chief was dead, they had yet to suffer a casualty, the woman they championed had been freed unharmed and they had the legendary wizard Seama Beltomé to give them victory. Why should they fear?

It was a matter of minutes between Gumb's order and the conflict. Twenty riders formed a loose wide spread vee-shape with the point faced to attack and in the arms of that formation the remainder formed a second and much more compact vee. The first line was a screen and a decoy which would split into two halves and compress just before impact while the main body, suddenly revealed would charge heavily through the centre and smash into their opponents with their lances thick before them. From head on the array may have looked like a disordered rabble: it was anything but.

Their opponents, though, were not only well-disciplined when it came to fighting, they were also well-schooled. They'd not be caught like novices, and with alarming speed they altered their battle stance just before the critical moment and in two columns they charged thunderously outwards on either side of the phalanx and quickly began to curl in behind Gumb's cavalry. It was the obvious reply. Without a pair of swords meeting, or blood on a single spear, the Black Company had gained a brief advantage.

But Gumb could box clever too. As the brigand army circled in to attack the rear, Angren was amazed to find himself the only one of his company charging towards the house. Everyone else had managed an about turn that brought about a mighty clash of steel. Blades at last rose and fell, blood spewed from gaping wounds on men and beasts and conflict finally took its toll.

The two cavalries rode through each other and left the dead and dying trampled behind them.

Angren found himself on the wrong side and in some danger but he was saved by his Gotherian clothes. The Black Company in the confusion had no time to realize he wasn't one of their own. The antagonists wheeled again and Angren followed after his enemy wondering how he could avoid being skewered by his own side.

There was a pause as the opponents took a moment to size-up the challenge before them and then set out for a collision.

An arrow whistled through the air barely an inch in front of Angren's nose. Gumb's archers were taking their chance and added to his problems. He hoped that Garaid and Piedi would recognize him.

On a slight rise to the left of the dispute Piedoro and the eight other archers waited for their chance to let fly. Piedoro was glad to be out of the melee. He was no coward but sword fights were not for him. Now give him a catapult and he'd show them all. A bow was a reasonable alternative, and he'd scavenged a good one from the guard house. Though he would never admit it, he was more than happy for Edro to grab all the glory with his swordplay.

They'd been too far away to cause any damage at the start, but after the first feint and clash the archers found a closer shooting point. Piedoro was so startled to see Angren cantering along behind his enemies that he dropped his first arrow, but all around him the bows of his partners strummed a deadly tune.

'Garaid, it's Angren. Be careful', he shouted to Mador's spy. Though the rest had been aiming at the centre of the pack, Garaid had picked the straggler as his target. 'No Garaid, it's Angren!'

Piedoro barged into Garaid's shoulders a second after the arrow was loosed.

'What are you doing, you fool?' Piedoro demanded, 'you could have killed him.'

Garaid stared at the sailor with fear in his eyes. His face twisted into a scowl but the fear remained. Piedoro realized that Garaid had not mistaken Angren for one of the Black Company at all. The shot had been deliberate.

'Who are you?' he said, clutching at Garaid's arm as he

turned to rise, pulling him back face to face. 'What are you?'

The rest of the archers had run forward following the fight heedless of the two of them picking themselves up off the ground, and the sailor was suddenly frightened to be alone with this man, this traitor.

Piedoro moved to draw his knife but he was too slow. Garaid picked up Piedi's arrow and sprang at him. The King's spy was a heavy man and the sailor was flattened and winded before he could attempt anything. Garaid sat on top of him, knees pinioning flailing arms, and Piedoro could barely catch his breath and had no strength to move–he knew his life was finished. The mad man above him raised the arrow but then stopped. That strange expression of fear and guilt intensified on the face and the hands trembled as though they held back a great weight, and the lips moved to deny.

'No' was all the whisper said, but then the big man grabbed Piedoro by the hair, yanking back his head, and savagely rammed the arrow up his nostril and into his brain. Piedoro's last thought was that he could hear his murderer screaming 'No, No, No, No.'

The sailor shuddered and was dead. The narrow-head arrow had ripped his brains apart, but when it was pulled out left no sign of violence beyond a bloodied nose.

The man who was not Garaid picked up his bow and quiver and went to join the fight once more.

Yelling and screaming the two sides clashed for the second time. It was the once and for all moment of the battle. Men died on shivering spears, horses died or threw their masters and fled. The mounted struggle became disordered and individual battles spread over the field. They left behind a death struggle of grounded men.

Angren landed with a thump but luckily the fall was into soft muddy earth. He was up in an instant, sword whirling. This was more like it: up to his ankles in miry ground with the enemy all around him. He put himself about with a vengeance and killed three or four men before he had some breathing space. Looking around he saw that the balance of the fight had shifted slightly to his own side. Bibron and Berta were not far away. Although the Captain was competent enough to take on any one man at a time, Berta wreaked havoc on a grand scale. Things were looking up.

As his gaze shifted, Angren became aware of three well attired men, sitting on fine horses, on a hummock well away from the melee. The sorcerers at last. They were watching the battle with interest but showed no sign of wanting to join in. That was not their role. Where in all of this fix, Angren wondered, was Seama?

He turned to look just as a huge curved scimitar swung toward his head. Remarkably it changed direction and nicked his left thigh. The wielder of the blade, a man seven feet tall, lurched towards the weapon master but his scarred face had turned white and he fell heavily into the soggy earth. His helmet was crushed and his head stove in.

'You'd better wake up, Old Angren,' said Sigrid. "Me and Berta won't always be around.'

Berta grinned wickedly, swinging her mace, while Sigrid bent to look at Angren's bloodied thigh.

'I'm alright, Sig', Angren said, squirming away from her like a child avoiding a blackheading session.

'Keep still, you. baby. You're right though, only a scratch.'

'There's no need to sound so disappointed.'

'How's the rustic rust stick, Angren?' Berta asked.

'The what?'

'Your new sword! You know: that heap of junk you've been cleaning-up.'

'Oh Yeah.'

Angren held up the sword for them all to see. The rust was long gone but the blood of his last opponent still ran along the blade. He frowned. 'Do you know, I've barely noticed it. Not sure whether that's good or bad.'

Berta laughed. 'I'd say good, judging by all the bodies round here.'

'Could be right,' Angren nodded, 'but I'll give it another go before I decide.'

'Well, lets get to it then.'

SORCERY

Seama was not in the fix at all. He had joined the original charge but after a few private and purely physical conflicts, he'd retired from the fray to prepare for his real work. He quickly marked the position of the three remaining sorcerers and as he approached he was careful to keep hedgerows or hayricks between them. They'd know of his presence soon enough, but the longer they were kept guessing and the longer they were unsure about their plan of action in the absence of their chief, the better it would be for the men in the field.

The battle had settled down to the heavy blood letting that always occurred when opponents were well matched. Here strategy had been met by counter strategy and all the cleverness of war would have brought no conclusion. The antagonists knew it and squared up to each other quite early. It became clear to Seama as the hour progressed that Gumb was gaining the upper hand, a feat due in no small part to the mighty efforts of Angren, Sigrid, Berta and even Edro despite his wounded arm. Gumb led those still mounted against their counterparts and with him his nephew Alan Travers, who had taken his sister's exhortation to heart and laid about him like a fury though rarely to any conclusion. Seama couldn't see Piedoro or Garaid, or Bibron for that matter, but that was hardly surprising in the confusion.

He was in the middle of wondering about his friends when he was staggered by a sudden exhalence of power. He was so close to the centre of whatever it was that he was nearly thrown from his horse. He was hiding behind a haystack previously misshapen by the storm, but now it had been demolished. For a moment all Seama could see was a turmoil of straw and dust hanging in a thick, filthy yellow smoke that loomed above him. Then rising into the air came a juddering, angry yeowl, so loud it almost pierced his ear drums. It sounded like some gigantic and furious cat.

In a wind that did not belong to Asteranor, the smoke cleared to reveal the horrific sight of a many-taloned demon. It crouched as would a cat, but this beast was as large as a young dragon, smooth skinned and jade in colour, and the flat long-toothed face displayed a flat hatred for all things living. But then the features contorted in pain and Seama understood the nature of the invocation.

There was much said about demons in Errensea, some of it correct, but speculation was the basis of most of the teachings – who would be mad enough to research the subject? Now, by adding the wisdom of Errensea to the history contained in the Song of Ages, Seama was sure he had it right at last. A demon was not a god: it was a creature made in the beginning of time by the Lord Evil, and everything he made was brutal and foul. It was not a creature of magical power but of conspicuous physical strength far exceeding the ability of any man or group of men to conquer. Magic alone could withstand an onslaught of demons. During the first age of the world, according to the Song, demons wandered the Earth killing and maiming as they pleased, and it pleased them to kill. The Earth then was a terrible place. But the rule of the Dark God did not last and a new age dawned when Orh'mazd, the Bright God, brother of Ah'remmon, came to power. His greatest act, at the end of a mighty war with all the forces of Ah'remmon, was to banish the demons from the world of men. They were exiled to a place set apart from this existence leaving the Earth free of their predation. In the Hell they made of their exile the Demons continued as before, except that now they must rend their own kind.

Many sorcerers became demon-callers to make up for their lack of natural power but there were some who became expert in the art – mainly those who somehow managed to survive their early attempts. There were books, foul books of black lore that gave a name for each of the demons. Once learned the names could be used time and again to drag these creatures back into the real world. But they would not come willingly or uncalled. And because Ahura would not suffer the breaking of his rule without sanction, a visit to Earth would bring a fiery pain to the demon, an inner burning that tore through them for as long as they remained. It was important for a sorcerer to keep that fact in mind. A demon would like nothing better than to pass on some of that terrible pain to the summoner. A wise man – no, not a wise man as the wise would not dream of calling demons into torture – a clever summoner would place himself in a protected space, a pentacle or triangle, but most sorcerers relied on the simple fact that the demon's only chance of returning to Daemonia, of escaping torment, lay with the invoker breaking his spell. Demons had occasionally (and catastrophically for anyone nearby at the time) found themselves trapped forever because they'd killed the fool who had called them. Enough to say that seeking to use a demon without disastrous consequence required a very astute and strong mind.

The cat-demon was in agony plain to see but this was not a new experience. It knew very well what was required before the spell would be broken. It faced the sorcerers on the hill with a glare of contempt and then stalked the battle.

Quickly it came close and panic hit the men of both camps like a blow. The Company was unused to a demon being called when it was so closely engaged – there was no time to draw off and the men were unsure about what the beast might do. The forresters were plain terrified. They'd never seen a demon before and weren't keen to see one any closer.

'Don't run,' Seama yelled, thinking that it wouldn't attack indiscriminately. But it was no use: Gumbs men ran as fast as they could. With an incredible leap, the cat-demon was among them. In the first attack it killed three men, ripping them to shreds. This was no creature of illusion, the claws were very real.

Seama could wait no longer. It wasn't possible to break into the spell; all he could do was face the creature. His horse screamed in fear but, trembling and sweating, obeyed his command. He charged. The demon was by now devouring a second batch of victims. Seama's sword flamed angry red and the beast saw him. It became enraged: nothing had ever dared an attack before – at least, nothing of this world. It prepared to pounce.

A bolt of flame sprang from Seama's sword and sizzled the

earth before the monster's bloody feet. The monster stepped back. Another bolt scorched the air around it, and again the demon retreated a little. Seama didn't want to hurt the creature. Demons, had little enough ability to reason and it was probable that more pain would make matters worse. He was playing for time while his mind ran through lists and descriptions. Eventually he would find it. The demon saw Seama lose concentration and leapt, but the terrified horse moved just as quick and dipped away from the ravening claws. Another bolt of flame. This use of pure energy would become too tiring to keep up. If the name couldn't be found he'd have to attack in earnest.

And then he had it: 'Angraa Bast', Seama shouted the name and the effect was instantaneous. The cat-demon leaped high and landed right in front of him. It crouched like the mountainous sphinx, and Seama was no more than a mouse between cats' paws. The demon was so close he could see the veins that overlaid the muscular limbs throbbing powerfully, could feel the rumbling growl that came from deep in its chest, could smell the nauseous odour of its ensanguined breath. Bast regarded him with obsidian eyes.

It couldn't speak in any tongue but had the force to project and recieve mental images. A mishmash of dreadful scenes crowded into Seama's mind, and their meaning was hard to decipher at first. It was some form of query. The confusion, Seama guessed, was the result of the pain. Whatever the query might have been, Seama had only one answer: a sharp reply warning of his power. The beast was unmoved. Seama reminded the demon of the pain, and with an image of the three sorcerers clear in his mind, reminded Bast of the cause of that pain. The beast sent a kaleidoscope of scenes in response and Seama understood the fear of being stranded upon Earnor forever.

The wizard was strangely piteous of the creature. His plan would help them both. He knew the hardest part would be to explain the idea, but he had to try. The face of the beast loomed over him, blood dripped from its jaws. The horse backed off but Seama wouldn't be distracted. He pictured a succession of incidents beginning with the demon attacking the sorcerers in a slow, deliberate action; he showed the sorcerers in fear as they were injured but not killed. Seama wanted them so frightened for their lives that they would end the ensorcelment and send the beast back to the nether world, to Daemonia where it belonged.

The demon growled so loudly that the trauma of it vibrated through Seama's chest. It stooped to inhale, to make some sense of this thing that had called its name. The poor horse was now shaking in terror, staying its ground only because Seama held it by strength of will. Seama went through the sequence again, projecting the images as clearly as he could, but still the beast seemed more interested in deciding which part of this horse-man thing to eat first. One last time he tried. The horse was ready to run, he wouldn't be able to hold it much longer. The demon eased closer, the blood and saliva from its jaws now spattered on the horse's mane, but still Seama refused to yield. He forced his thoughts upon the demon. He pictured those bloody jaws closing on the leg of one of the sorcerers, ripping it from his body, he pictured a broken thigh bone, the twisting of gristle... And then there was understanding. Immediately Bast turned away from them, turned away from the remnants of the battle and growling low and steady, slinked up the hill to confront its so-called masters.

Seama, partner to a strange alliance, was too far away to see the looks on their faces as the sorcerers realized their peril. He saw one of them leap from his horse to attempt the making of a pentacle. The man scraped at the ground with his sword but it was hopeless. Before he had half-completed the first passage, Bast had him on one claw. The other two tried shouting spells but in their panic they must have misspoken because nothing happened. Bast tore a limb from the man it had captured and the two unhurt sorcerers decided that was enough.

'Go, Go! We release you!' one of them cried. The other didn't speak at all but made a gesture with his hand, and it was the gesture that worked.

Seama could never be sure about the process behind what happened then but he was grateful for it. Not only did Bast depart as quickly as if it had fallen down a hole, but with claws still sunk into his flesh, the creature somehow managed to drag the maimed sorcerer along for the ride. Only the severed leg remained. Seama supposed that this first visit to Daemonia by man would be very short lived.

Seama breathed a sigh of true relief. While the demon had stalked the battle there was no hope, but now the situation was much improved. Of the four sorcerers, two were finished but two remained. He went to meet them.

There was no move to attack as Seama rode up the hill. Instead they wanted to parley. A fat man with a beard, but no moustache, made himself the spokesman, while his gaunt companion, an albino with bloodshot eyes, kept back and seemed hardly aware of the conversation.

'Hail friend', said the fat man.

'I am no friend of yours. Why the talk? Do you need rest?'

The man laughed. 'Well said, well said. A man of wit, and asperity perhaps? Don't be angry with us. We are of similar nature, are we not?'

'Are we?'

'Why yes, of course. We have the Power, and the Knowledge.' He smiled a quivering-smile. His jowels were so heavy that it must have been an effort. 'Should not brothers in art work together?'

'What work?'

'Now then, you're interested I can tell. Well, my partner and I have a commission; a well paid commission, my friend. I tell you, it's money for nothing.'

'Demon calling.'

'You have it plum, sir. Just so. And with the wages there are the extras: girls if you like them, as many as you like, as young as you like – or perhaps boys are your preference? What do you say? You would make a welcome addition to our party, so powerful, so bright and if I may say, handsome too.'

Seama was at once disgusted and amazed. It was difficult to imagine why the fat man thought Seama would be impressed by such an offer but maybe it was worth his while playing along. The fat man continued.

'Now, it seems to me, seeing as you have so cleverly rid us of that bully Semmento and boring old Kelsly too, that we find ourselves shorthanded. I dare say our employer would be more than happy to take on such a sturdy replacement. We can come to some arrangement perhaps?'

'An arrangement? I am sometimes open to offers if the conditions are right. But I need to know more before agreeing to anything. For example: who would be paying the bill?'

'Now then, don't be silly. A little disappointing. Please do not take me for a fool. When you have proved yourself—'

'Enough!'

The red-eyed man was awake and his single word made the fat man's flesh quiver.

'But Chaldonie, dear fellow, this here is a friend, or he would be if you let him. He could be useful. Now Semmento is gone we lack—'

'No.'

The fat man sighed theatrically. 'Oh well. As you please. It seems, Sir, that you have missed your chance and we will have to part company. My friend Chaldonie is very clever and very determined and not at all to be argued with. I quite like him for that – sometimes.'

Seama had heard enough too. 'It isn't going to be as simple as saying goodbye, fat man,' he said, but his eyes were on the other. This Chaldonie was the one in command here.

'Now sir, there is no need to be impolite. We shall not say goodbye just yet anyway. We still have work to do. But you will not interfere again?'

'And what if I do?'

'Then I expect Chaldonie will have something to say. Were I you, sir, I would not cross him a second time.'

"Thanks for the warning, but I think I might test him.' This was ridiculous. Why couldn't they just get on with it?

He backed off a little to encourage some response, and in the next second he was thrown and at risk of being trampled. His horse had finally gone mad and with good reason. It was flayed as it stood. Gone was the sweating coat, the mane, the tail all in an instant and what remained was a mass of dripping flesh and bone. Of course it was an illusion, but it was very deep. The horse didn't merely see the weeping flesh, but suffered intense pain. Seama couldn't easily cancel such a spell when inflicted on another. The horse screamed and screamed. Struggling to keep out of the way, Seama had no choice. Reaching out with both hands he grasped the air in front of him and broke the horse's neck with a twist. He rolled to one side as it collapsed nearly on top of him.

Chaldonie was not impressed at all by Seama's evident power. He gestured at the earth where the wizard had fallen and issued a command. The mud and grass swarmed up around Seama's body and buried him as he lay. The wizard was smothered.

Again it was illusion, but such a fine one that Seama almost admired it. He wasn't simply buried. His chest seemed incapable of movement because of the weight of the earth; there was soil in his nostrils. And the illusion reached deeper, slipping beneath Seama's conscious thought, speaking it's message of death to his organs, to the nerves and the arteries. If the nerves told his brain that his lungs could not inspire, then soon it would become true. Seama had to take command. He plunged into his deepest concentration cycle. He forced his body to react. It was a mighty struggle to overcome the inertia, but finally he broke through; finally even in the dark recesses of his nervous system ran the knowledge that he was free and clear. His lungs sucked in clean air.

And just in time. The sorcerers were not averse to using metal where magic had failed. The fat man had dismounted and was swinging his sword inexpertly at the wizard's neck. Seama rolled again, drawing his own sword in the one fluid movement, and then attacked. But this was no time for the niceties of swordsmanship: the sword raged fire and made a torch of his opponent. Blazing, the fat man dived headlong into a ditch and Seama left him to it.

The battle had rejoined after the departure of Bast. Gumb's men had the upper hand again and many was the villain that looked back desperately to where the sorcerers stood chatting while they were losing their lives. They had no time to curse their employers.

Angren too looked often towards Seama. For him the fight was less furious and he found the time to wonder what on earth was going on. Seama and the sorcerers seemed to be talking. Talking! He waited impatiently for the fireworks, but when they came he didn't like it at all. Seama was grounded and his horse looked likely to kick him to death. Angren was up and running. He had no idea what he could do to help, but his friend was in trouble and he wouldn't desert him. As he ran he saw the maddened horse crumple and die. Seama lay on the ground as if stunned.

'Look out,' Angren screamed as the fat sorcerer raised his sword, but the wizard seemed to have matters in hand and Angren's heart leapt as Seama's power was revealed. Fireworks were not a match for Seama's sword. The fat one burned and fell out of sight but the second sorcerer rode in at great advantage as Seama, now on his feet, stumbled over the fallen horse.

Just then a commotion louder than before burst out afresh behind Angren. Turning he was amazed to see a whirlwind of action in the middle of the melee. A sound of raucous braying shouted from the centre of it. Braying? Braying! It was the Mule. The Mule, spinning and kicking foe and occasionally friend alike. He was tempestuous in his rage, like a storm in the grass. Angren couldn't believe it. How on Ea'… And then, glory be, trumpeting her approach with deep-throated neighing ran a bay charger. She looked thinner and her coat was filthy but there could be no doubt it was Bellus. Angren called out in amazement but nothing would distract her. She had seen that her master was in need, and hurtled through the crowd to save him.

Seama's need had lessened despite his disadvantage of being on foot. His blazing sword met the other's icy blade in showers of sparks, and a second blow dented the sorcerer's shield. Chaldonie drove his horse at Seama but the wizard stepped aside, and then leapt. Sorcerer and wizard fell jarringly to the ground. Seama was up first but the sorcerer blocked his opening cut. With the handguards locked together, he dragged Seama to his knees. Chaldonie wrenched away his sword, scrambled to his feet, and rushed at Seama, hacking with two-handed swipes.

Angren couldn't reach them quickly enough – the air was heavy with a bitter odour that made him gasp and slowed him down – but with hooves tearing through the claggy earth, Bellus charged past him and set herself for a collision. Chaldonie was fatally distracted by her neighing. His wide, red eyes understood her intent to run him down. They completely missed Seama's thrust. The wizard's fiery blade bit deep into the sorcerer's chest and Chaldonie shook with the impact. His desperate hands clawed at the hilts but his black robe began to smoulder. He writhed as he collapsed. The sword burned inside him, his flesh hissed and sputtered, his blood boiled.

Seama payed him no more attention. Abandoning his sword he ran to greet her.

'Bellus, Bellus!' he cried, dancing in his excitement and his grief and his joy. 'Oh Greatheart!' He threw his arms around her proud neck. 'You're alive, alive, alive! Oh, by all that's good, you're alive.'

She butted her nose at his shoulder and whinnied gently. He kept his nose buried in the rough of her mane for more than a minute.

Angren trudged up to them through the mud.

'Well there's a turn-up,' he said. 'How did you manage that?'

'I may be a great wizard, my friend, but this isn't my doing. I could never have managed so great a magic as this.'

'How did they get here then?'

'I haven't a clue and I don't care, I'm just so glad they did.'

'Glad?' Angren raised his brows, a mocking expression on his face. 'Quite happy, eh? You great soft fool.'

Seama grinned. 'I don't have the words for how I feel, Angren. This is the best moment... the greatest... Oh you know well enough.' He turned back to his beautiful Bellus and spoke to her in silence for a minute more. Angren, keen to find something to do, walked over to Chaldonie's corpse and busied himself with extracting Seama's sword. As he wiped it clean on Chaldonie's robe the wizard appeared at his side and held out his hand for the blade.

'Thank you Angren. You're right, this is joyous. And incredible. I thought they were… well…"

"Yes I know. But they escaped the slaughter. The gods know how."

"Well they might but I don't. There isn't time now, but when this battle's over I'll spare the strength to ask Bellus for their story. She'll tell me.' He looked down at the remains of the battle. 'Mule's doing some damage down there. I hope he's kicking the right people. Come on, let's go and make sure— Hush!' He stopped speaking and put a finger to his lips.

They heard a whimpering moan. It came from a ditch behind them.

'The fat man!' Seama rushed to find him. 'This time he'll tell me.'

Malbur was in a pitiable state with almost all of his body charred and blistered from Seama's angry fire. The ditch was full from the night's storm and the water had quenched the vicious flames but it was red from his bleeding. Seama stepped into the ditch to get close and reached out to touch the fat man's forehead as he writhed torturously in the water – from his throat came a horrible, fizzing gurgle. Bending to look closer Angren realized the man wasn't only burned on the outside: there was a red flame beneath the flesh, a flame that devoured him one layer at a time. It made Angren feel queasy. He'd never seen Seama do anything like this before. The fat man's pain must have been terrible. For his own part Angren spared him no pity: he was one of the bad men and the punishment seemed reasonable, but he wondered what Seama was thinking. The wizard stood motionless and silent and it suddenly occurred to Angren that some sort of communication was taking place.

'Ask him about Trant, Seama, ask him! I've looked everywhere for the bastard.'

'Quiet Angren! That can wait. Now, listen to me, fat man.' Seama's voice lowered to a murmer. 'I asked you before, now

I ask again. Tell me his name and I'll release you. It will be quick—'

Seama froze. He had the answer. 'I should have known!' he spat out in fury, 'What was I thinking?' The look on Seama's face was terrifying. It carried such anger. He looked down upon his enemy, his victim. 'My promise.' The wizard raised an empty hand. The fingers curled as though they held a staff and tightened into a fist. There was a sharp twist of the wrist, and the snapping noise told Angren all he needed to know.

The wizard was silent for a moment, the snarling expression fixed, but after that pause he was all action. He launched himself out of the ditch and straightaway leapt onto Bellus' saddleless back.

'Angren! Follow me when this is finished. Bring Gumb with you.'

'And the others?'

'Yes, yes, of course.'

'But where to?'

'Astoril, where else? Where else would he be! Uh Bib is in Astoril and I will have him!'

Angren was astonished at the wizard's temper.

'Steady on Seama,' he said, 'You don't do revenge: that's my job.'

'Not this time. Look Angren, I have to go. Will you make a fuss of the Mule for me? Tell him I had to leave – I think he'll understand.'

'Understand? More than I do. I don't exactly speak Muleish.'

'And follow after – Gumb with you. You must make him come. Now Bellus, now! Faster than the wind or I'll lose him.'

Bellus reared and turned and ran. The pair splattered down to the road through a marsh of puddles, and left Angren gaping.

'I think,' he said to the air around him, 'that our wizard is in a bit of a hurry. Poor old Bellus.'

And then, as he watched their incredible progress, he began to feel peculiar. He became weak and found it hard to breath. 'What the hell!' It was as though he'd been working hard for days without rest. He was dizzy with fatigue and had to sit down. When he looked towards the last vestige of the fighting he was amazed to see men everywhere sinking to the ground exhausted. Several badly wounded men had been screaming in agony, but they became silent as their lives seeped away into the mud.

'Seama', Angren shouted as loud as he could, 'Seama, don't leave us. Help us.'

But his shout was more like a whisper and Bellus galloped on unchecked.

LOOSE ENDS

Astoril 3057.8.6

In the small sunbathed courtyard exotic fronds crowded the formal edges of a tiered pond; a cool green lawn, perfectly edged, softened the footfalls of a departing servant and a stone seated arbour set between two scented jasmines proved to be exactly the right place for cool wine and dainty cakes. How charming it all was: the breezy rustle of leaves, the verdant shade and sun-dappled green.

Tarangananda uh-Bib heaved a fat and contented sigh. What a shame, he thought, that the King was not well enough to brave the elements. This was, after all, his favourite place in all the palace. He had told uh-Bib all about it: his favourite seat, his favourite vista. Now he must lie in bed and dream only of past pleasure. Such a shame.

Uh-Bib decided he must remember to compliment King Sirl on the depth and quality of his cellar: this white wine of southern Apia was exquisite, so light, so fresh. The King, sadly, had been persuaded by his doctor to abstain from alcoholic dalliance. Uh-Bib allowed himself an evil giggle. He was astounded that such a wise old man as Sirl could be taken in by all of this medical hokum. At first uh-Bib had used hypnotism but now all he needed to keep the King under control were his 'restoratives'. Sirl II may not have been ill before uh-Bib had arrived, but he was certainly ill now.

What a delightful situation it all was!

It had taken uh-Bib less than six months to bring enlightened Gothery to the brink of disaster. He was proud of his achievement. The King was sickening towards death; power had been transferred to his doctor (ha, ha!) in all but name; a simple spell kept the chief ministers docile, and out in the country paid agents sabotaged manufactories, spread discontent in the work places and generally increased confusion among the authorities.

Semmento and Chaldonie were his key men of course. They had done a marvellous job on the borders: the Aegardeans were screaming for war. It amused Tarangananda uh-Bib to speculate upon which of the two powers would invade this tiny country first. He had a small wager running with Semmento on the outcome. What a pity the others were too po-faced to appreciate the joys of gaming: the Necromancer seemed to think that gambling was beneath him.

That outcome would depend on Mador, of course, as Athoff had been given precise instructions on what to do and when, but uh-Bib expected the result within days rather than weeks now that Mador was under pressure at home. At the moment Mador was following the path Uh Bib had laid out for him but it would be foolish to think the King of Pars dim-witted and there was always the chance he might do something unpredictable. Unlikely though. No, all in all, the plans were proceeding nicely.

Well almost. There was that inexplicable mix-up on Tumboll to account for. The Necromancer hadn't explained himself. Surely the plan was to keep Tumboll a secret for as long as possible, so why bring Partians to the island in the first place? And then to let them escape! For all his airs of nobility and wisdom the man was a fool – but at least he did his job.

But what about Zaras? No great loss of course – he was hardly the most successful of spies – and yet he was their Master's favourite. He would soon be wanting an account of what had happened and why, and he would want to know who was responsible. Someone powerful, certainly. Zaras was no easy target, and he wouldn't have jumped unless he was under severe pressure. If there hadn't been firm news that Seama Beltomé was hiding-up in his rooms on Errensea then... *Hmm, Not satisfactory!* Firm news that someone is hiding unseen is not as good as a sighting. Uh Bib frowned. The affair in the stable was a little on the brutal side for the great wizard but perhaps he ought to speak to his people in the College, just to be sure.

They'd brought Zaras' body down to Astoril only yesterday, and Franner with him. Both had taken a blade to the neck and the other, Creel, had been seen running away some time before they'd been discovered. Uh Bib wondered momentarily whether Creel might not have done the deed himself but then spurned

the idea. Creel taking on Zaras? Ridiculous. But then again…
Well why not? The irony of the matter had been playing on his
mind: one corpse with not a flicker of a soul left in it and the
other with a personality blazing and screaming for life despite
the deadly blade and the fact that he'd already started to decay.
It would have been no surprise if Zaras had been the latter, but
intead it was Franner. Uh Bib used a form of Nepenthe to see
if he could reanimate the torturer but so far there had been no
sign. Still, Nepenthe and the Blood were ever slow to act.

So the question remained: where was Zaras? Not in his old,
cold body, that was plain. Perhaps it was with Creel that Zaras
had escaped. Uh Bib giggled. *Fancy*, he thought, *vain Zaras, with
a whole world to choose from, ending up with that scrawny, twitchy,
smelly little specimen. The justice of it is too sweet.* Sometimes uh
Bib found life extremely entertaining. Zaras would have to be
found, he decided, but perhaps there was no real hurry. Other
matters were pressing. He looked down at the glass in his hand,
admiring the way the crystal captured the light and made the
wine seem as golden as the sun.

'Well Sirl, my dear King,' he said, 'time for your medicinal
draught, I think.' He savoured one last drop of nectar, and then
placed the glass on a silver tray. Before rising he slipped-on his
discarded shoes, the ones with the curly toes, and dusted the
crumbs from his star-signed black robe.

He walked over to where the pool was still and looked at
his reflection. Hair black, complexion healthy, whiskers exact.
Satisfied with his demeanour he left the garden smiling. He
began to whistle a gay tune as he went. Yes, everything in the
garden was fine.

Southern Gothery 3057.8.6

Her mind was open to him: the full trauma of the past two
weeks indelibly printed there, ready to read. The failure to land
on Tumboll; the agony of the icy water and the panic and death
of Bayling; the mysterious appearance of the seals. They were a
miracle. He had never heard of anything like it. It seemed clear
that both horse and mule would have drowned too, hampered as

they were by the corpse of the other, except that the river-seals had come to buoy them up and push them at last onto the sand bar. Through Bellus's eyes he saw but could hardly believe. And there was more to come. For Seama the most incredible part of their adventure came after the escape from the driftsman. The two had first made their way north while Seama was in northern Gothery, then west as the wizard rode into Aegarde, and then veered south-west to meet him at the battle of Moreda. What Seama could not picture or understand was how Bellus had known where to go. Her Master, a wizard of the highest repute hadn't even known his family was still alive! Bellus had no magic, that was certain, and the Mule was, well, the Mule. Someone or something must have helped them.

Now, joyously reunited, Bellus and her master hurtled through a countryside vibrant before them but sickening after. Reading Bellus' mind as they rode was a minor work of magic, but the incessant one word chant, following the pattern of his breathing, was decidely major and far reaching in its effects. Bellus had arrived at the battle willing but exhausted and now Seama asked her, commanded her to ride harder and longer than ever a horse had ridden. She used a borrowed strength. Seama provided the energy by taking a little of the life-force of everything they passed. It was a dangerous thing to do, lethal even for those whose life was nearly spent anyway, but what else could he do? If he stole a few hours from a dying man to save a country from dying, wasn't that right? Seama had no doubts. The emergency demanded drastic measures. He needed the energy to get to Astoril and he would need more, much more, to do battle when he got there. While the smallest advantage might win the day, he had to prepare for fireworks. At least uh-Bib wouldn't be expecting him.

At least Seama *presumed* uh-Bib was not expecting him. The fat man said that the spechan stone was on a chain hanging from Chaldonie's burnt neck, now likely to have been cracked by the heat. Would Chaldonie have realized his danger early enough to have made contact. It was unlikely: Seama was sure the sorcerer had expected to win the fight.

Seama cursed himself as a fool. He should have guessed. Tarangananda uh-Bib, the *Blissful* One. There was a time, thirty years gone, when those smiling features were well respected in Errensea. So well respected, in fact, that uh-Bib had almost come to rule the Council. Taken in by his foreign charm, eight of the ten members of the High Council were preparing to make the 'Randalan Tap Rod. Seama had been travelling at the time of the intended coup, and if it hadn't been for the True Sight of Holander, who could never be fooled by any type of deceit, the deed would have been done before Seama knew anything about it. They realized afterwards that uh Bib's attempt had been planned from the first day he set foot on Errensea, and at that time even Seama considered him a friendly and talented student eager for knowledge to take back to Sullinor. How he'd managed to provoke the dispute between two Aegardean wizards, renowned for their commonsense, Seama never really found out, but it was a perfect ruse to draw the strongest wizard of the continent to the remote Bulidzhan Peninsula, a thousand miles from Errensea. But such a machination was trivial in comparison with the present debacle.

Knowing that uh-Bib was responsible for the actions of the Black Company, and for the state of disorder in Gothery, raised more questions than it answered. They flooded into Seama's mind. What was the connection with Zaras? Was uh-Bib the source of the spell that blighted Ayer? How did the episode on Tumboll fit in? Was he also co-ordinating the strange events in the Norberry Part? Questions with no answers unless he could squeeze them from those maddening, grinning lips. And that wasn't going to be at all easy. But one question concerned him above over all others. He knew that uh-Bib was a mercenary – even the attempt to subdue the Council was apparently the first move in a planned invasion by the Emp Radis, the ar'Andalan tyrant; an invasion that could not happen after uh-Bib had to flee the Islands harried by the whole council with Seama in the lead – so the question that hung over Seama's thoughts was simple: who was paying the Blissful One this time? If it was, as Seama had already decided, the 'Evil beyond the Mountains', how on Ea' had this contract begun.

Astoril 3057.8.6

Seama's quarry wriggled his large backside into a more comfortable position on the Gotherian throne. He had so confounded the court that the desecration went largely unnoticed, and certainly without challenge. The country was his. He had no special reason for choosing to sit there: he had no decrees to make, no petitioners to impress. He did it because he could, and revelled in his wickedness.

Tarangananda uh-Bib examined his pudgy hands, cleaned his fingernails with a sliver of a knife. An observer could be forgiven for thinking that the man on the throne was idle, but like many men and women of intelligence the outward display of indolence masked an industrious mind. His calculating brain was presently revisting all the areas of concern that he'd been through earlier in the day. Something, he was sure, wasn't exactly right.

Perhaps it was the affair on the island. Ever since the message saying that the Necromancer had lost his prisoners and Tumboll was on fire he had been suspicious. The news had come from his witch, of course, but since then there had been nothing on the matter from any of them. The Necromancer was most likely sulking, but what if there was more to it. There'd not been a word from the General either since he'd returned to the Partian mainland. They were all busy, he knew that, busy following his plans, but it just wasn't good enough.

Uh Bib assumed that the prisoners had been something to do with Anparas. He had to admit it had been a worrying few days when he thought that Mador was sending troops into Gothery, but in the end they actually went north from Riverport, mostly by land with a lot of supplies shipped to Coldharbour. A Partian army in Gothery too soon could have been risky. Of course he had contingency plans. Three of General Alling's marshalls, much against their will, and without reference to their commander, had been preparing for an invasion, their divisions marching across the plateau toward Banya's Harbour. He called them all back when he got news of Mador's change of heart. And back they came. Marching them here, marching them there.

A giggle burst from uh-Bib's fat lips. They all had to do his bidding whatever they thought of him. He found that most amusing. And not only these Gotherian fools. Even among his allies his was the whip hand.

The Kumites had been jealous of his authority from the first. That their Master favoured him, a powerful outsider who knew nothing of their suffering, came close to rousing their fury, except they couldn't quite manage fury. The Necromancer, on the other hand, simply thought himself above it all: dragged into the conflict only by Uh Bib's machinations and by fear of The God. He was desperate for a way out. As he had been these five hundred years. And Zaras, so self-confident, so powerful in his own right and so proud of his finery and intelligence, well Zaras hated him for his virility. Like all the rest he was just dead and stinking meat. But no matter their disdain or hatred, obey they must. Or they could choose to argue the case with their Master. And He wasn't too keen on dissent.

There was, of course Acchulpa, in the mix. He'd be foolish to think she was in the least concerned with following orders: she had her own agenda. He expected no reports of progress, no interest in his plans. Manipulation was the key to Acchulpa. She was greed incarnate. Acchulpa wanted to eat the world. In her philosophy whatever she consumed made her stronger. Her desire was to take up the power of all the souls she destroyed. Uh Bib had simply suggested that Kings must have very great souls indeed. He didn't know exactly where she was just now, but he had no doubt that she was making her way, one bloody mile after another, across the Partian heartlands.

Uh-Bib tapped his fingers arhythmically on the arm of the throne, and he nibbled at the thin end of his thin moustache. What was it? His review of the situation revealed irritations but overall everything was working well. So what was it that made him feel so uneasy? Perhaps it was because the agent he'd been expecting from Garassa was late. He hated impunctuality: it was impolite, it was sloppy and it caused problems.

The wizard watched silently as the late afternoon shadows tracked across the floor of the hall. An hour had passed since he had come to sit on the throne and his backside was numb. If the agent didn't arrive soon, Tarangananda decided, he would go for his dinner. The thought of food usually cheered him and he scratched his belly as he contemplated roast beef. But as he scratched, his hand tagged on the green stone that hung by a fine chain on his breast.

'And that's another thing,' he said out loud to the empty hall, 'it's about time Chaldonie made his report.' He slapped, rather weakly, at his chair arm, somewhat annoyed. Things seemed to be coming unstuck.

The Lyndons 3057.8.5

'It's come loose, Evie, just a rope and no bucket.'

'Never!' Evie shook her head in despair. 'Is there nothing right with this place now? Things just get from bad to worse.'

'That's life for you,' agreed Daisy happily, 'Some of the time you think everything's come alright and you've got everything sorted and then next day it's all gone bad again. We're here to suffer Evie, that's all I know.'

Evie frowned. She wasn't sure she was as pessimistic as all that but she did know that expecting things to stay the same was daft. Look at the Lyndons.

Ten years ago with the mistress still alive and old Gerald still a force to be reckoned with, and Isolde running them all ragged but filling the place with her friends and with their laughter, life had been just about as perfect as it could be. Evie had taken over as cook when old Hebe had retired and Jeb, her lovely Jeb, was made up too and given responsibility for managing the estate. They ran the house and the farm with pride and pleasure and they ran them well. She couldn't have been happier. All gone now. Nothing, whether good or bad, lasts forever.

But she'd never expected it to turn out like this; for things to change so quickly. Of course nothing had been perfect since Louise Robarn had died but they'd managed alright. But then with Isolde taking herself off on adventures here, there and everywhere, leaving the Master moping around by himself, well, it had put a gloom on the place. And now look at it. First 'our Izzy' getting attacked and then Jeb and the Master acting so strange when they'd been up to the place it happened, and all those militia men tramping about as though they knew what they were doing. She'd more or less begged Jeb to stay with her, what with some monster on the loose, but he wouldn't have it. Said it was all to do with duty; said he had to go off to Ayer with the Master and that was that. And that's all he'd said. Her eyes filled with the memory of it.

'Never you mind, Evie. Don't you listen to me and my daft notions. Me mam's always telling me I need to be a bit more cheerful, and I know she's right.'

Evie blinked the tears away. 'Nay, it's not you lass. It's just everything's getting on top of me.'

'Well it's a big house and no mistake if you're on your own. You want to get someone in to help you. Roddy's left, you say?'

'Without a by-your-leave. Run out on his girl too, or so I'm told.'

'I'd never have believed it. But you never can tell with people.'

Evie smiled. 'You never can tell. But anyway, I'm glad I can rely on you. It's been a few years since I last pulled water. Here, let's get another bucket on it.'

She was a good lass, young Daisy, even if she did have an odd view of the world.

'Honestly Evie, you want to get Arthur from the Rose to send someone over. You want that pump looking at if something's blocked it up. You can't come out to this well everytime you need water.'

'That I can't, not with my back. That's why I waited for you to come. Knew you'd be early.'

'Course I would: I'll not have you waiting for the milk all day before you get a cuppa.'

The cook sighed. 'Time was when we sorted our own milk, Daze. You don't mind giving me a hand do you, lass?'

'Mind? Me? No love, I draw water every day at home – there's no pump in our kitchen. Now then, let's see. That knot should do it.'

Daisy, the milk lass, lifted the catch on the handle, let the bucket drop into the well and waited for the splash.

'Getting a bit rusty that catch,' she said, but then leaned over to look down the well.

The splash hadn't been right. Daisy gave the rope a wiggle to make sure the bucket wasn't caught on anything. She grinned and nodded to Evie when she felt it pull a bit tighter as it filled with water. She took hold of the handle and, with a practiced motion, began to wind it up.

'You going to swing it out for me, Evie, when it comes?'

'That I will lass, if you'll carry the bucket back to the kitchen with me.'

Up it came. Evie pulled the bucket over to the edge of the well and as she did so it caught on the lip and tipped a little.

'Steady Evie, I don't want t'have to draw it again. Evie?'

Evie had started to scream. The bucket fell from the wall and a swollen, maggoty head rolled onto the grass at their feet.

Evie clutched at her chest, her breath taken by shock and sudden grief.

'It can't be,' she gasped, 'It can't be!' They were all the words she could manage as Daisy dragged her away.

LIBERATION

Moreda 3057.8.6

Getting up from the mushy ground, Angren shook his body like a wet dog but with less effect: he remained unpleasantly soggy. His muscles felt leaden, but most likely from lying still in cold mud for thirty minutes than for any more mysterious reason. His energy had returned and he was as bemused by its return as by its previous departure. Looking about he saw more signs of life amid the dreadful scene of death. Angren tried to ignore for now the scores of corpses and went to speak with the living.

Lord Gumb, rehorsed after the strange weakness they had all suffered, cantered his steed to Angren's side as he walked towards the largest group of survivors.

'Good to see you well, Lord Gumb,' Angren told the forester, 'that was a hard fight.'

'And a strange ending don't you think? Felled like a young pine I was. Horse too. What did you make of it?'

'Haven't a clue,' Angren replied while trying to suppress a smile: Gumb was no young pine. 'I'm just glad whatever it was has gone. I thought I was dying.'

'It's not the only thing that's gone, is it? Did I not see the Lord Wizard bolt from the field as though all the fiends of the underworld were after him?'

'I think the fiends were fleeing before him. I've never seen him in such a temper. He's gone to Astoril and he wants us to follow straight away.'

'Straight away' proved to be impossible, there was too much to do. First of all Angren helped Gumb organize care for the wounded. A fast rider was despatched to Lavenda, the nearest unravaged town, to pass on the news that the Black Company had been defeated, and to beg for surgeons to treat the most severely injured. Limbs would be lost, men blinded or maimed or witless as a result of the battle. The field was a pitiful sight.

The conflict had spread wide and there was no meadow

without its reddening earth; no hedgerow without a corpse beneath; hardly a tree not shivering to the laboured breathing of a man nearly dead. Seeing such a quantity of gore, Angren found it hard to believe that there were survivors. Eighty or ninety dead seemed as bad as a thousand. Who would think they had so much blood in them?

As Angren overlooked the sad fields his eyes were ever searching for his friends. Where was Bibron and the twins, and Berta and Sigrid? The thought of them hacked like the man just in front of him made him flinch from the sight.

'Terrible to see, Angren.'

'Yes.'

'Blood is too precious to be wasted.'

Angren turned. The voice was right, but the words seemed off key. Garaid was staring at his open palm. Blood was pooled there as though he'd just scooped it up from the chest of the cadaver that lay on the ground before him.

'Garaid are you—'

'Look! Bibron.'

Sure enough, a few hundred yards away was the worthy captain and two more friends. Angren was overjoyed and ran to meet them. Berta and Bibron, supporting Edro between them, raised a cheer to greet him. The sailor had a slashed thigh, not deeply cut but too painful for walking, and his companions were taking him to the camp in the forest to have the wound cauterized and bound.

'Leg this time then?'

'Angren! It's only a scratch. The filthy dog was pretending to be dead. I trod on him, and this is what he does. Pah! He pretends no more.'

'Good. We don't want any of that sort left to bother us. How's your brother?'

The swarthy Partian looked troubled. 'I haven't seen him. No one has. I fear for him you know. It's very strange, but I think he's… I don't know if I'll see him again.'

'Less of that. He could be anywhere. He was with the bowmen wasn't he? Garaid'll have seen him. Garaid…'

But Garaid hadn't joined them, and in fact he was nowhere in sight.

'That's odd,' Angren muttered. 'Look Bibron, take Edro over to the camp and see if you can catch up with some of the archers. They might have news. I'll keep my eyes open but I have to help Gumb over at the house.'

'And what about Sigrid?' Berta spoke up, 'I haven't seen her since that bit of trouble you were in. She can't be hurt: there was no one to match her in that crowd.'

'I was hoping she'd be with you. But you're right, the way she was fighting today, well, she'll be fine. Glad she was on our side! Don't worry, I'll have everyone that's fit looking out for the pair of them. See you later. Don't give up, Edro, we'll find him.'

'We'll take care of the lad,' said the captain, 'Oh, Angren… er…'

'Yes?'

'If you should happen to find any rum in the house, you couldn't—'

'Purely medicinal, of course, Bibron?'

'What else? Being thirsty's unhealthy. Serious though, some spirit'd help with the pain for quite a few.'

'I'll see to it.'

Gumb had packed off his nephew with a handful of men to scour the edge of the forest for any survivors, whether friend or enemy – his instructions about the enemy were brief – when Angren caught up with him again.

'How many have we left, Lord Gumb?'

'Well, there's you, and there's me. Enough to storm a castle, what!'

'Probably. At least one without defenders. Let's hope they all came out.'

'We'll see. Come on, we must find out whether the ladies are still alive. I won't have them locked up any longer.'

Angren took the reins of the horse Gumb had found for him, and they wasted no time in making for Moreda. But they'd not gone far when Angren pulled up short.

'Hang on a minute. I think I see a lady in distress.'

Sitting in an untidy heap in the muddy ground, hair half-loose and eyes glazed, was Sigrid. She wasn't bleeding but she looked as though the wind had been knocked out of her. Thinking she wasn't much hurt, Angren chuckled: she looked just like one of his sister's rag dolls.

'Now then my little warrior-woman, you look a bit sick.'

Sigrid didn't respond immediately, and when she did it was to shake her head, and then peer unfocussed at the pair of them.

'Angren?'

'Yes Sig, no one worse or better.'

They dismounted and Gumb fished out his hip flask. The spirit helped a little and though she was bleary-eyed and dizzy, she managed to explain that a horse she'd found had stumbled and thrown her. She must have whacked her head on the nearby fence as she fell. Angren was relieved it was nothing more serious. His understanding of medicine was limited to field action, but he believed that, after a whack on the head, as long as you came round fairly quick you were generally alright.

'What say we take her to the house, Angren? With any luck we'll find someone there to look after her.'

Angren nodded agreement and picking up his rag doll very carefully he managed to lift her onto his saddle. He was climbing up behind when they all heard the hoofbeats of a horse cantering towards them. Hair rippling gold in the clear sun, the vermillion cloak borrowed from one of Gumb's men streaming behind her, Helen Travers looked like a goddess of war, a queen at the very least. To Angren she was an uplifting sight, but to Sigrid the dizzy flashing of bright colour was the final discomfort that pushed her over the edge. She leaned over and retched and retched and retched. Spew splattered over Angren's arm as he supported her.

'Poor Sigrid,' said Helen, all concern. 'You're unwell. Let's get you up to Moreda. You need looking after.'

'It's a bit risky, niece. I think you should wait until we've found out—'

'I am coming with you Uncle! I want to see those women

safe.'

Lord Gumb regarded his niece with an appraising eye. He refrained from asking questions. 'We'll go then. I haven't time to argue.'

Catarina Beltez had been the worst. She so obviously resented Helen getting all the attention, that she refused to listen to what was only common sense. Helen wasn't surprised. The Beltezians had always turned up their noses at the people of the northern divisions, though Helen couldn't understand what they had to be so proud of. And here they were again, denying sense because it was spoken by an uncouth Northerner. Helen wanted her revenge. Not the violent revenge of the field, but a gentle teasing revenge to pay them for allowing the sorcerer's men to carry her off undefended. Walking in to greet them like a victorious queen would do it. She couldn't wait to see their faces.

The relief force of the two men, one woman and another but very sick woman, threw caution to the wind on their approach to Moreda. They were certain it was unguarded and luckily they were right.

For the second time that day Helen galloped over the moat bridge and clattered through the gravel yard. Angren was first to dismount but by the time he had helped Sigrid down, Helen had beaten him to the door.

'They're still here,' she called, and then laughed at the alarm on the men's faces. 'Don't panic. I mean those two Sigrid cut-up this morning. They must have left them dying. You would have thought they'd be good to their own.'

'There was no good in any of them, niece.'

Gumb squeezed past Helen and looked into the hall. 'There seem to be more dead by the stairs. Sigrid again?'

'As I remember, uncle, she had only two of those. Angren and Seama shared the others, but she is amazing, isn't she?'

'Yes, and it would be good to keep her that way. Let's see if there's somewhere she can rest.'

A very short search found them a small parlour, and they were helping Sigrid onto the couch when they were surprised by a polite cough. Rising nervously from behind the couch was a girl of about fourteen years, hair tousled and cheeks red. She didn't say anything to explain her presence but after a few moments she managed a smile.

'Hello,' Angren offered, but the girl merely smiled more broadly. 'What's your name?'

'Giselda, your honour; Giselda Banco.'

'By heaven, Angren. I know someone who's going to be happy. What were you doing here, lass? Did they hurt you?'

She dropped her head in answer and Gumb decided to question her no more. She seemed grateful.

'Is the lady hurt, my Lord?' she asked, seeing Sigrid so close to fainting. 'I could get some medicine. There's a chest-full in the kitchen, I'll—'

She had been striding to the door but stopped, suddenly frightened to leave the room.

"Are they all gone now Sir? Are they?'

'Yes, yes. Fear not, lass,' Gumb took her gently by an arm and made her sit down. 'You just sit here. Did you not see the battle?'

'I watched until the monster came and I... I could't watch anymore. Not again.'

'Well then. The demon is gone, and those that called the beast are dead. What do you say to that, Giselda?'

'It's good.'

'Good? No more than that? It's a time for rejoicing, young lady! A time to be happy.'

'Forgive me, My Lord, but I can't... My father and mother are dead. My brother too. He was so brave, he...' She began to weep softly and Helen, hiding her own grief, found it painful to see the girl's misery.

'Hush little one, hush.' she said and took her in motherly arms. 'They died nobly, I'm sure. We've all suffered by these evil men but now they've paid for their crime. Hush now.'

'Gumb! Will you not tell her?' Angren burst out.

'I was about to, Angren. Given a man chance. My dear, all is not so terrible. I cannot do more than console you about your parents, but as to your brother...'

'Guy?'

'Yes, the lad himself. He is, as far as we know, alive and well, and what's more, he's somewhere in this house.'

Giselda didn't know where to put herself.

'Where is he, where is he? I've got to find him.'

'All in good time. Now then, first of all we have Sigrid to care for. We cannot leave her like this. I'd thought, perhaps, you could look after her, while we release the others.'

'Oh. But… Yes, of course, my Lord.'

Helen looked on. The girl must have suffered so much, and said not a word about it. Her only tears were for her family and now, despite the desperation to find her brother, she still had the goodness to think about poor, injured Sigrid.

And there she lay, the woman who had done so much to save Helen's life, pale as death. She deserved all the care Helen could provide.

'It won't do,' she said aloud, 'No, Uncle, you must take Giselda to her brother, and release those poor women from that awful cellar. I'll stay here to look after our friend. Well? Go on then: they've waited long enough.'

And so it was that despite her more ignoble yearnings, Helen Travers settled for the inglorious task of nursemaiding and she found herself satisfied with the role.

The night in the cellar had not passed without incident. After Seama had left, De Vere assessed the situation and decided how they would last the night. He knew that barricading the door would be a mistake, would risk raising the alarm too soon should any of the men upstairs decide to come down. The answer was to marshall the women into a force willing and capable of trapping or killing anyone that entered the cellar. Terrance De Vere had no problem in motivating the ladies of Beltez. He was not a strip of a girl, he was a man and they were used to taking orders from men.

Guy tried to help at first, but he wasn't much use. He was more concerned with trying to find his sister and mother. When it was established that his mother had been among the first to die, he was inconsolable, but when he learned that his sister had been taken away a few hours before they arrived, he was blazing. Guy ran for the cellar steps, all set to rampage through the house and prepared to kill the lot of them, if only he could save her. But Terrance blocked his path.

'You'll spoil everything if you start trouble now,' Terrance told him.'It's hard Guy, I know, but that's the way it has to be. If you cannot help us here, I suggest you keep out of the way. But mark this: if you attempt to leave the cellar, I'll have you bound to a rack. Do you understand?'

Guy was too angry to speak, but understood the look in Terrance's eyes and backed off. Attempting to bottle his rage he flung himself down in a corner and spoke to no one.

It was with Catarina Beltez that Terrance arranged things: a simple trap that would require only a little confident dissembling. He suggested that two women might begin a fight at the first sign of company. The men would almost certainly want a closer look.

He could hardly believe their luck when he found a tarpaulin so close at hand, and wasn't slow to think of a use for it. They strung the canvas between wine racks, too high to be noticed in the dim light. The ladies, with their wooden staves ready for more worthy targets than earlier, waited all-innocent, weapons hidden in the folds of their skirts.

It must have been nearly four o'clock when they were called upon to use those weapons, and they used them with all the vengeful strength they could muster. Three men came to amuse themselves and were delighted at the spectacle of a fight. Sure enough, they descended the steps to see better, the tarpaulin fell, and the blows rained down on them as they struggled to get free. It was a horrible death. A death in confusion. The women didn't stop beating for some time after all movement had ceased.

Shortly before dawn, De Vere allowed them to erect the barricade knowing the real trouble was about to begin. None of them had slept much. Terrance was worried that if they had to fight, fatigue would count against them. In the end it didn't matter. Some women screamed when the uproar began, but most took it calmly. They heard yells, the clash of steel, and the sound of people running.

Some men ran down to the cellar door and hammered on it when it wouldn't open. They shouted orders and threats, but before they could work at forcing the door other voices were heard.

'Mart Scarik wants us on the field. Leave 'em. We'll see to the bitches later. Come on! You'll miss the game.'

A sort of silence fell. There were dim noises far off, but it was impossible to understand what was happening. All they could do was wait.

After what seemed an age there was more hammering on the cellar door.

'Open up! Open up! Terrance, it's me, Angren. Let us in. I've Gumb with me. Hello! Is anybody there?'

It took a while to dismantle the barricade but eventually the door was opened. Instantly a small figure flew through it, surprising everyone except Guy, who didn't notice because he was skulking around at the back of the crowd. He didn't see her coming. Giselda launched into his arms before he even had the chance to understand who it was. But then he knew her, and then he laughed and then he cried, and he clung to her as though he would never let her go.

Over a bite to eat they decided who was to come, and who would stay, and who would follow later. Of Seama's company De Vere, Garaid – who had reappeared when the house was explored for any more survivors – Berta, Bibron and a now much recovered Sigrid, would all accompany Angren and Lord Gumb on the road to Astoril. The baron would bring with him four regular soldiers and, on Terrance's advice, young Alan Travers.

Terrance had said: 'That boy is stirring trouble, my Lord; trouble we can all do without. Why not invite him to take the journey? Why not insist? I want to keep an eye on him.' Gumb hesitated only to observe the bragging youth exhulting with the younger surviving soldiers, before nodding and saying: 'So do I.' Helen would stay, of course, to help with the wounded, and she was apparently happy to do so.

Edro wasn't fit to travel. His leg was heavily bound and very stiff, but the discomfort was nothing to him. Piedoro's body had been found, dead, seemingly without a wound. Angren understood well enough the young sailor's need to see his brother given a decent and proper funeral. Sigrid offered to stay with him, but Edro declined saying that the journey alone to Astoril would be good for him.

'Don't worry about me,' he said, 'When I'm finished here, I'll come. Tell Seama. I know they're all dead, this Black Company, but… I don't know: it doesn't feel as though it's over. I need an enemy and I think Seama will find him for me. I need to make someone pay.'

The company rode briskly, though not recklessly, having a care for horses hard worked in battle only hours before. The road was well made and direct and they hoped to make good time. Angren pushed them on, sure that Seama would need them sooner rather than later. They'd done nearly twenty-five miles before he let them stop. With forty more to go he planned on reaching the Gotherian capital by late afternoon on the next day. It would be a hard ride for animal and human alike. What they all needed first was a good night's rest and no one would argue about that.

They had wearily begun to set up their camp for the night when Sigrid, who'd been resting up while others worked, jumped to her feet and raised a cry.

'Look, look over there!' She was pointing north-east, and everyone stopped what they were doing when they saw it.

It wasn't yet dark, being not quite nine, but more brilliant than lightning on a winter's night, piercing bolts of fire burst into the sky. They were a long way off, perhaps even as far as Astoril itself, but the green and red and silver flames were clear for all to see. And then as they watched, rolling like a slow wave beneath their feet came a tremor that made the trees quiver and tipped over a kettle of water.

'Gods above!' Gumb cried, 'What the blue blazes is that?'

MISSING

Seama reached the outskirts of Gothery's capital by five o'clock. The sixty-five miles from Moreda had taken only ten hours riding and not surprisingly, despite magical assistance, both horse and rider were exhausted and sore. The magic had given them the energy to make the journey, but acting as a channel for that energy had been almost torture. The road behind them was littered with wagons and traps halted by the sudden feebleness of horses and drivers. The people were amazed by the passing of a couple so ragged and yet so brisk, but they were too tired to wonder what it might mean.

Seama finally reined-in a mile from the city gates. He dismounted stiffly and, after resting for a few minutes to catch his breath, he walked Bellus thankfully to a place she could rest.

'You're my greatest friend, Bellus, bonny Bellus. I couldn't manage without you. But you know that, don't you?

He ruffled her mane as they walked but the horse was too tired to respond.

'Yes, I know,' said the wizard, 'You've worked harder and acted more nobly than you ever you should have to. Taking up with me was a mistake, Bellus. One day I'll ask too much of you but you'll try anyway and suffer for the trying. You'll be gone and I'll be desolate. It will happen, Greatheart, and there's no way of avoiding it.'

Seama talked to his horse regardless of the scornful gazes and bemused glances of those wayfarers he passed by, and he chattered and rambled all the way to Burgil's gate.

Burgil was an old friend of the Wizard Beltomé and he lived half a mile from the now mostly dismantled city walls. Burgil – 'Burgil what' or 'what Burgil' no one knew, least of all Burgil – was a sort of wizard himself, and, until his retirement four years ago, he was one of the most respected teachers on Errensea. He was a particularist rather than a true wizard: a person with power that could be used in only one direction. In Burgil it was a most unlikely, and, to the uninitiated, a most terrifying direction. He was a changer. He could, for example, transform himself at will into any number of birds or beasts; more subtly, he could become someone else. It was not an illusion he created, not a trick. What was in one minute a human male would be a scabby dog in the next: a real scabby dog, though minus the fleas as he could manage only one entity at a time. He claimed to have achieved the feat of once becoming an ant, but it was an attempt he would never repeat. Apparently, ants lack the important factor of individuality and without self-awareness it was impossible to empathize properly with any other individual. Changing back had taxed Burgil severely.

For students, shape-changing was hellishly difficult. Very few ever managed to achieve success in the extreme form of the art: changing from one animal into another. It wasn't unknown for students to achieve the first step but then have such difficulty changing back again that Burgil had a job to rescue them. It was a dangerous art to learn. In all the years he had taught his most succesful student was a young man called Stey Asinus, and it seemed that he, like Burgil, had been born with the ability. From his early years the boy had shifted from one form to another quite naturally, according to his needs. Like Burgil he'd suffered the prejudices of others who suggested he was not entirely human: that he had been born in a form not true to his nature. Neighbours, at their home in Pullonia, began to suggest that his parents were also not quite what they seemed. People are easily frightened. Seama had seen it happen many times. The neighbours didn't disguise the fact they wanted rid of Stey and his family, but Stey's father was a stubborn and brave man. For many uncomfortable years he stayed where he was, refusing to be intimidated, refusing to retreat. Nobody ever was going to tell Stey's father what he should or should not do. Except his wife, of course. A patient and intelligent woman, she realized that Stey's gift should be trained not suppressed and eventually she persuaded her husband to move the family to Errensea. The wizard's school was quick to accept the boy.

Seama thought it strange that the story should crowd in on

him so. Intuition or coincidence? The story of Stey Asinus and his mysterious disappearance was Burgil's one obsession. It preyed on the changer's mind. The move to Errensea, of course, had not been the end of it.

It was two years ago at the Stralli Horse Fair that Seama heard the tale. Burgil, not long retired to Astoril, was looking for livestock and Seama had his eyes open for a pack donkey. They had a successful day: Burgil laid out for a stately plough horse and some goats and Seama found The Mule. Celebrations in order, they stopped at an inn for a drink, or two, or three, or more but the alcohol had a depressive effect on the changer and the story poured out without preamble.

Apparently from the start Burgil realized that at last he had an apt pupil and within a few weeks he made Stey his apprentice. The boy had raw talent and over the years Burgil managed to add to it the theory, the knowledge, the finesse. He was surprised but delighted that the boy wanted to stay on at the College to teach. Everyone presumed he would take over when Burgil finally retired. Stey seemed happy to be considered for the position and Burgil's recommendation to the Council was readily accepted.

Why then did Stey Asinus leave without a word? Why disappear so effectively that he was never heard of again? One evening he had said: 'Goodnight, see you tomorrow,' and that was the last Burgil saw of him. He failed to turn up the next morning, the morning became a day, the day a week. His room remained empty. Sure that Stey had not simply gone away and believing he was too astute to get into trouble of someone else's making, Burgil made his way to Stey's parents' home looking for answers. There the tale took another twist: the house was deserted, left open. The chickens roamed the kitchen, the donkey and the horse chewed lettuce unhindered in the kitchen garden, the starving dogs prowled the rooms, too well trained to take the chickens. Another mystery. There was no sign of violence, nothing to suggest that Stey's parents had gone unwillingly to wherever fate had led them.

Burgil's only clue was something Stey had said the day

before his disappearance. He was involved in some new work on identifying *essential nature*: an important point of study for any magician. Burgil had found him in his workroom, a book open in his lap, staring into space.

'You know, master,' he said when he noticed Burgil had entered, 'You can live with people for many, many years: all your life in fact, and think that you know them well. All their history, their likes, their dislikes, their loves, their fears, their hopes. But the fact is, all of those things are secondary, they come after. What comes before is what we call true nature. Most people know nothing about their own true nature – they just guess at it. And if they can't understand their true nature, then how could anyone else really know them? Unless there's a *testing* of course. And you'd not think of testing your own family, would you? The tricky thing is, master, unless you can understand your family, your antecedents, you never will be able to understand yourself. I know this to be true.'

Burgil started to ask what he meant but Stey distractedly closed his book and left the room. Obviously it had bearing on the disappearance. Burgil suspected that all three had shape-changed: shifted back perhaps to a form that better suited their essential nature? Stey's studies, he guessed, had led them to some sort of revelation. Perhaps. But it was all speculation. Stey never returned, nor his parents, and Burgil retired a disappointed man.

Master and apprentice both were missed in Errensea. Shape-changing had not been the most important part of their work, but the basic techniques involved had other adaptations. Interrogation was only another step beyond testing essential nature and many wizards desired the skill. Burgil disliked the whole idea of interrogation and taught the subject reluctantly. He preferred to spend his time teaching the more regularly used art of disguise – an art that had nothing to do with make-up. There were other teachers but none so good as Burgil or Stey. The wizard's school was depleted by their absence.

Seama swung open the unlatched gate and led Bellus into Burgil's front yard. The flowers were bright in neatly laid beds but the grass was overgrown. The front door of the single storey cottage was slightly ajar. Seama knocked and shouted a hallo and was dismayed to hear no reply. Rather than enter unbidden he decided to explore outside. The stables were at the rear of the cottage alongside the kitchen garden. Burgil was nowhere in sight. The back garden led into a twenty acre wood and Seama supposed that his friend might be out gathering firewood or herbs. With the stable so close at hand, Seama decided to get Bellus settled before he did anything else.

'Old Burgil must be out, Bellus. Not too bad an evening for walking or visiting. We'll wait a while, I think.'

Soon Bellus was drifting into a well deserved sleep in the clean, cool stable and Seama was free to investigate further and perhaps find something to eat. The back door was unlocked and it led straight into the kitchen. He filled the kettle, put it on the stove and lit the fire with matches rather than a spell. There was tea in a stone jar and honey in another. Seeing a tall jug in the cold pantry he expected to find milk but it was all mould. The bacon was smelly, the butter rancid. Burgil had been gone for some time: a week at least.

In the front parlour the furniture was in disarray as if there'd been a struggle. Seama was alarmed and confused. Had his friend been abducted? Who would want to kidnap Burgil? And why? Uh-Bib was an obvious candidate. Perhaps Burgil had recognized him. But how? Burgil, a recluse by inclination, was not a likely guest at court, so how could they have met? That was another question the Randalan could answer. He had a lot of explaining to do. But not just yet.

Whatever had happened Seama still needed rest. He made his tea, found biscuits in a tin box that were still crisp, eat them, and then threw himself down on a sofa to sleep. He could afford two hours and no more.

TUMULTUOUS FLIGHT

Astoril 3057.8.6

Two hours were as good as ten for a wizard; well, that was what
Holander always said. Ten would have been better but Seama
shook off his lethargy well enough and, after bathing his head
in cold water, he was more or less ready for the trial ahead. The
same was not true of his horse. Bellus could not be roused. She
didn't hear Seama's farewell.

The wizard stepped onto the main road and began to walk
the last half-mile to the city gates. He hadn't gone far when
a lumbering cart filled with cabbages rolled past him and the
driver shouted for him to jump up.

'Come up here, sir. We can't have you walking when you
could just as easy ride. Lost your horse, then?'

Seama settled himself onto the bench seat and said: 'That's
very kind. Thank you. My horse? Well, she was tired out, so I've
put her to stable not far back. Horse or not, I have to reach the
City soon.'

'An appointment, then?'

Seama knew Gotherians were an inquisitive race and the
questions didn't worry him, but he wasn't sure yet how he was
going to find uh-Bib. Naming him didn't seem a safe option.
Instead he lied.

'I have a message for the King, Mr. Farmer, and it'll not wait.'

'The King you say?'

'The same. A message for him and no one else.'

'Well you're out of luck then. You'll never see him; anyone
could tell you that. Nobody sees the King except his doctor, and
the Prime Minister, maybe.'

'No one else? How can he run the country if he see's no one?'

'Worked through that doctor of his. You know Sirl's ill, of
course? Well, the doctor holds any meetings the King should
attend and then he reports back in private. I reckon your best bet
would be to go as a petitioner at his evening session. My brother
had to go up over his son being in the army and promoted to the

King's Guard and… well you won't want to know that, will you, but anyway, he says Dr. Tubby—'

'Dr. Tubby?' Seama couldn't help laughing, and the farmer grinned as well.

'Well, it's Bliss actually but everyone calls him Tubby now on account of him being so fat. I know we shouldn't. What was I going to say? Oh yes, this Doctor holds an 'audience' at about eight. After his dinner, I suppose. He'll take your message to the King and no doubt your reply'll come the same way. I'd best whip-up the horses a bit, you've only half an hour.'

At ten minutes after eight a limping but respectable blacksmith arrived at the Palace. He carried his tools in a bag hung over his shoulder. The guards grumbled at him for not being on time but after a little argument they relented and led the smith into an antechamber. He seemed worried and out of breath, but when he saw there were still people in the room waiting for admittance he relaxed. He managed a smile, even, when he recognized, lurking in the shadows, the small sharp featured type with the nervous tic. Seama was glad he'd decided against using his 'old man' disguise.

Soon they were all ushered into the audience chamber and Seama gasped. The man had no shame. Dr. Bliss was sitting on the throne itself, at his ease and smiling! The petitioners were allowed close by order and Uh Bib dispensed the law like medicine. Seama followed two men involved in a half-hearted dispute about the tenancy of some crown land in the city centre. The debate between them had been going on for over five months and at this rate there would never be a settlement. Dr Bliss listened, grinning all the while, and then told them their message would be forwarded. He suggested they might both benefit by taking a sleeping draught whenever they were likely to meet in order to avoid bad temper and conflict. Disgruntled and still sniping at each other, the two were led out. Seama glanced at the twitcher but the man held back, wanting to keep his news for a private audience no doubt, and so it was Seama's turn to step up to the throne.

'And now Mr. Smith, what had you to tell our ailing King. No problem too taxing, I hope. Indeed, nothing about taxes, if you please. They're such a bore. Well, speak up then. I don't bite, not after dinner at any rate.' Bliss giggled.

'Dr. Bliss is it?' said the smith and the fat man smiled, 'Or is it Tubby, I get confused?'

The smile disappeared.

'Sounds like a bit of a joke, you being so fat. Bliss is a bit of a joke too, isn't it? For those in the know.'

'Those in the know?' Dr. Bliss's smile had returned, but it was of the order of a cobra smiling at the thought of closer acquaintance.

'About your real name, I mean: Tarangananda uh-Bib, the Blissful One. The grinning Hippopotamus!'

Uh-Bib was not the sort of man to fly off the handle but Seama could see that the wizard was annoyed.

'Congratulations, Mr. Smith. Or is there another name I should be using. Come now, you have me at a disadvantage. You do indeed.' The punctuating giggle had an edge in it now. Could it be nervousness?

'You are too easy a mark in your curly shoes," Seama advised. "Enough of this nonsense! You were not pleased at your last sight of me, and I'd wager you won't be pleased to see me now.'

Seama's disguise came apart: the smith was gone apart from his clothes. The bag of tools was a cloak and its contents were revealed as a sword and a knife.

Tarangananda uh-Bib did not quite gasp and the look of dismay was fleeting. He now smiled broadly.

'Congratulations once more, Lord Seama, Wizard Beltomé, Ambassador to the High Council, etcetera, etcetera. It will be an entertainment to receive you.'

'A little surprised, uh-Bib? Spies not performing as well as they should; not even Rat Face back there?'

They both looked to where the twitcher had been but there was no sign of him.

'Ah, Creel seems to have found the prospect of your company unattractive, Seama. I shall teach him manners some day soon.'

'I wouldn't count on that, Tubby.'

'You persist with the name. Do you not think the insult a little childish. I expect better from you.'

'You expect better from me?'

'Indeed I do. I wonder, are you feeling yourself today? You seem both exhausted and excitable. I have a potion you might consider.'

Seama laughed. 'Oh I'm sure you have. Something that has been helping the King also, no doubt.' Seama spoke lightly but uh-Bib's observation did have some truth in it: he wasn't exactly dizzy but he felt most peculiar. It was as though something was rising up inside him, something that might be hard to control. 'No, good Doctor, exhausted or excitable, I think I can manage without your drugs. I wouldn't want to be made *too* comfortable. Shall we begin?'

'Begin?'

'With the questions and with the answers.'

'Ask away, Seama. I am sure your questions will be diverting at the least.'

'What are you up to, uh-Bib? Who are you working for? And why?'

'My dear Seama! You are too much,' the giggle was genuine this time. 'What am I up to, you ask? Well let us say I am organizing a party, an event, an entertainment – but let's not spoil the surprise. And as to who is paying the bill, well you wouldn't expect a good doctor to compromise his client's confidentiality?'

'I expect nothing of good from you, uh-Bib, and everything of bad.'

'Now then, you are being uncharitable, and I impolite. If we are to talk let's be more comfortable. Take some supper with me, and perhaps some wine. Carl,' he called out, 'A light meal for two, if you please, and a bottle of Furide, in the garden, at once. Lord Seama? An honest meal, I promise – we might as well be civil about this.'

Seama agreed. A glass of cool wine might just calm that tingle in his gut. Of course Seama didn't trust him an inch but it wouldn't be poison in the wine: uh-Bib would count that unsubtle. Seama needed information. He'd have to play the game but keep up his guard. There was chance that uh-Bib would let something slip. No doubt uh-Bib was waiting for a chance too.

Tarangananda uh-Bib walked casually, calmly along the corridor towards the garden. He found time to enquire about the health of various members of the Council, and to reminisce about his time in Errensea. It was likely that Seama was taken in, to some small extent, by this splendid display of unconcern. He was certainly not aware that deep inside the 'Randalan was a turmoil of emotion and calculation not far removed from panic.

Uh-Bib was amazed at his own reaction. Years ago, though powerful enough to sway most enemies, he was a weakling as compared with now. He would count himself the strongest wizard on the five continents if only he didn't have this persistent fear of the Wizard Beltomé. How had he come by this new strength? Uh-Bib had no time for the naive explanations doled out by the Collegium. Their theories were tortuous, their Texts of Power nothing more than conjecture. In reality the source was obvious. Once he had bowed to the ar'Andalan Emperor and his reward had been great, in both wealth and influence. Now he bowed before another and far greater Emperor, and the raw *power* he had gained was a reward beyond measure. For six months now it had grown in him and around him, its source was infinite, and the reserve he could draw upon was limitless. It made him feel that he could defeat whole armies single-handed, that he could challenge the combined strength of Errensea and win. It had given him great confidence.

And yet it took only one glimpse of Seama's annoying face for all that mighty confidence to drain away, for his fears to return and mock him. Of course he feared Seama and with good reason when he remembered his abrupt exit from Asteranor thirty years past. Seama had nearly destroyed him. He had no doubt that Seama now intended to finish the job. What should he do? He could run, and he would run if necessary, but that was not his plan. Things had changed. He had changed. It was time to face his fears.

Uh-Bib was about five paces in front of Seama, mildly denying any part in Burgil's disappearance, when they reached the garden. A servant was arriving with the food through another doorway and the sight of food reminded Seama that he had hardly eaten since the previous night. As he scanned the platter to see what was on offer, he was picked up, as if by a huge hand, and slammed against a wall that cracked with the impact. He slumped to the floor and lay face down in the grass. Uh-Bib stood over him, grinning.

'I've thought about it, My Lord Wizard, but for the life of me I cannot think of anything I need to say to a dying man.' Seama groaned and blood trickled down his neck. Uh-Bib stooped over him, pushing his delighted grin into Seama's face.

'What would be the point in telling you about the Necromancer and the General? Why burden you with knowledge of the Angra Mainyu? But then, just to make sure your dying moments are as painful as possible, perhaps I could just explain how awful the situation is.' Uh-Bib tapped Seama's arm with his foot. 'Would you like that?'

Seama managed another groan.

'Well then, I don't know how much you have already guessed, and it would take too long to give you detail – I wouldn't want you dying before I've finished now, would I? But Old Harry has a vocation, you see, a mission, we could say, to cause you and yours as much suffering as possible; and most importantly, he wants his old kingdom back. Did you know this was once his domain? I'll bet you've never even heard of him, have you? Not that it matters. It's been a long long time since this world was taken from him – the fact is, he's done enough waiting. Forces are mobilized, Seama, undefeatable forces. All of Kyzylkum is ready to win it back for him, and for themselves; all his people, all with one aim! And at last they are ready while your paltry few are not. *How did this happen*, you cry, *why now? Who has done this to us?* It is because of me. Me! Tarangananda uh-Bib, Hand of Ah-remmon. You should never have treated me so badly, My

Lord Wizard. I am not a good loser. I have been plotting your downfall for thirty years. And your precious Asteranor? Well, I'm having it destroyed. I'll give your petty kings, your arrogant Council, your good citizens a few months of freedom, and then it will end. And as for you, Lord Wizard, your time is up!'

Uh-Bib stepped back and raised a clenched fist. The look on his face was ecstatic as he poured energy into that containing hand. In seconds the hand began to glow with a red-gold radiance. He need only release the power and his enemy would be torn asunder.

Seama rolled, staggered to his feet and drew his sword.

Uh-Bib angrily loosed his bolt but too late: Seama found the time to smile as his raised sword flared before him, deflecting the energy and destroying the stone bench beside him. The exchange left them both unharmed but uh-Bib was furious.

'Don't think to play games with me, petty conjurer. Before I was little more than a student at your feet, now I am Emmissary of the Dark King, and my power is great. Much greater than you can know.'

'What should I do then, Tubby, lie down and die for you? I— aah!'

A vice clamped Seama's chest and gradually closed. The breath was squeezed out of him; a rib snapped. Unless he could respond, they would all go, crushing his heart. Seama gave a soft push at the air and uh-Bib, standing beside the pool, intent on Seama's destruction, was caught off balance and fell backwards into the water. If only Seama could have pressed his advantage, but though the pressure disappeared as uh-Bib struggled to get his head clear of the water lilies, the pain brought Seama to his knees still gasping for air.

Uh-Bib emerged from the pool by levitation, his robes half smothering him. He was retching pond water as he ran from the garden. A door took him out into the city at a place called Haslem's Bright Field: a place of festival and fireworks.

Meanwhile, Seama had begun a healing cycle. He uttered a chant that plunged his mind into deep concentration. He searched along the paths of his veins, as he had been taught, to find those damaged and bleeding. And when they were found his cells seemed to explode inside him. The blue nimbus that had bloomed to regenerate his damaged arm after the fire in the library bathed him once more. A million points of energy, it seemed, or one great source of heat – it was impossible to tell. What could be cleaned and cauterized was taken in hand, what was gone was made anew. The bleeding stopped, the wound receded. His ribs, though seriously damaged, knitted and eased and the pain flew away. He couldn't believe it. The tingle in his gut had swollen, it crept out into his limbs but it was no longer an unpleasant sensation. It was a promise. His whole body was throbbing with potential. And then he was himself again. The whole cycle had taken hardly a minute and yet he was ready: ready to pursue uh-Bib to the home of winds, ready to attack, ready to conquer whatever he had to face, be it man or demon or God. He burst into action.

Seama rushed out onto the Bright Field and found Tarangananda uh-Bib waiting for him. The old people who had been enjoying an evening stroll, the children playing, the lovers quarreling all stopped to look at the two men squaring up, thinking that perhaps this would be some sort of performance or debate. The bobyboys passing by, who all knew the makings of a fight when they saw one, skidded their twoers to a halt, calling out to their pals to come and see; a city constable, sniffing trouble, ambled towards the pair, confident in his authority.

Uh-Bib screamed words of a tongue none of them could understand and raised an arm to point at a tall house nearest the green. It erupted into flame in an instant, incinerating all within. The pointing arm then swung in an arc and a plume of flame, thirty feet wide, roared from the house in a rainbow of fire to descend as damnation upon his enemy.

Seama stood motionless. The onlookers, staggered or felled by the horror, shocked by the inhumanity, covered their eyes as the flames enveloped him and all about him. But as the flames hit the earth they died immediately in a whoosh of steam for the ground water had risen at Seama's command: the field had become a marsh and Seama walked unsinged out of the sudden fog.

Uh-Bib was not expecting an easy victory. Already he was at work on another spell. This time he required a greater, more frightening power than fire. His arms moved as if gathering-in invisible ropes. His ululation screamed into the air. His robes whipped about him as winds from the four quarters crashed in upon the field, buffeting all those still standing to their knees. And on those winds came together the biggest, blackest storm they'd ever seen. Day killing clouds met in battle over the innocent houses. The whole of Astoril quivered uncertainly in the charged air of it. Across the city people ran for cover or stood paralysed by fear. No rain fell but the electrical power in the clouds snapped and crackled, seeking an opportunity to discharge.

So far, Seama had been forced to defend but his intentions upon surviving the Randalan's onslaught were ambiguous even to himself. Uh-Bib had more to tell him about Ah'remmon and the war to come, if only he could subdue the man. But now here was a chance to destroy his enemy once and for all. It was a chance that might not come again.

Uh-Bib had called the storm with little more than words. It would be much more difficult to harness and direct the power it held. Few could attempt it and fewer would succeed. Power harnessed power, strength grappled the elements. The forces encompassed by the black clouds surged and hummed back and forth as uh-Bib struggled to bring them together, and to deny them easy passage to the earth. With the whole city throbbing under the pressure of it, uh-Bib smacked his palms together above his head, and the rending, annihilating energy blasted in a single stroke targetted upon his foe. The noise of that lightning flash toppled buildings, broke men's ears; the light of it blinded them for days to come.

And when it had blasted, when it had burned the air it tore through, and when the boom and flare had passed, seeming to glow blue in the gloom, there stood Seama. He had restored his spell of ingathering but it was subtly altered. He had taken in the power and essence of the earth beneath his feet. It was as though Seama was himself the plateau upon which the capital stood; he was the rock and the soil. He was earth itself, unmoved by tempest and violence. He had not been destroyed. Though his clothes smoked eerily, his body was unharmed. The power had flooded into him, into the extended him, and he held it: dispersed and yet still present. The extended Seama was a sump, a reservoir for all the destructive energy of the storm. And he had control. He raised his nameless sword as a conductor of that energy. His baton was a terrible weapon.

Uh-Bib was aghast and almost failed to react in time; he grabbed at whatever was nearest. Seama struck and in the next second uh-Bib was tumbling over and over as a translocated wooden pavilion appeared for a fraction of a moment before exploding, disintegrating, vapourizing between them.

The Randalan was no sooner down than he was up. He was a pitiful sight, blackened and ragged, but he had survived. If Seama's arrival had made the fat man nervous, now he was scared. He couldn't believe that Seama could control such power.

Running fast with borrowed strength, but completely out of breath, Tarangananda uh-Bib gained a few seconds. He was well hidden by the fire and the smoke and the fog that lingered about the field. Mingling with a crowd of injured people he gained again, knowing that Seama couldn't attack for fear of hurting them. He ran through the gates of the public stables, and clambered onto the back of the first saddled horse he found. As he swung into the street again a bolt of fire destroyed the hanging sign above the gates. The Lord Wizard was only yards behind him, but he was hampered and unsighted by crowds of terrified pedestrians. The reins hurt uh-Bib's badly burned hands but he held on tight and kicked the horse to gallop, knowing that death was at his heels.

The two wizards were separated by innocents and Seama's choices were limited by an ethic. He too mounted up as quickly as he could and gave chase, hoping for one clear chance. That was all he would need. Uh-Bib was obviously drained or he wouldn't be running, while Seama had lost only the energy of the storm.

The power inherent grew within him with every exchange, and from without his ingathering continued and grew.

Uh-Bib had to gain time, gain distance, and he needed help. Without hesitation he begged his master for aid, but it was no prayer he made. He didn't call out in the dark to some remote God unpricked by the needs of mortal men. He spoke to the Dark One directly using the spechanstone he'd been given, and he asked for the strength to survive. The answer came instantly, and the weight of *power* that fell upon him then crushed the horse beneath him. Rising from that wreck of a life he paused only to send out another call, a summons which would cost him some of that God–given power, but essential if he was ever to get free, and then set himself to working easy magic until he felt ready to face Seama again.

His first ploy was to create an illusion but not something to fool Seama. It was a deceit designed to induce panic.

Seama was impressed. As the pursuit clattered down a cobbled road, walled by tall buildings, a river, a wave of prodigious proportions spewed out of the clear air and swamped the street. People screamed; they thought they were drowning as the wave flooded to a depth of fifteen feet; they tried to swim. Seama was thankful the illusion was not as deep as those Chaldonie had made. No one would really drown. But fearfully confused men, women and children couldn't understand why their swimming didn't work. Their only achievement was to delay a madman trying to ride through the flood as if it wasn't there.

Uh-Bib had made ground before Seama could fight his way through the madness. He'd taken another horse – from a man stripping off his clothes that he might swim better – cleared the vision from its mind and ridden on. At the end of the street the illusion abated and both horses were unhindered. Tarangananda uh-Bib now produced another surprise. Sorcery filled the air with fire drakes: demon arsonists not longer than six inches but winged like dragons. Translocated they were in pain but their discomfort was soon forgotten. Cutting through the agony was the realization that all about them was a city: houses, wooden doors and frames, curtains of the most flammable cloth, carpets that would make such a smoke, tar that would catch the breath. They went to their work with delight and soon fire was blooming in every house within a half-mile. The drakes circled gleefully in the smoke of it as people ran onto the streets in fear of the flames.

The 'Randalan assumed that Seama would stop to take on the fire-drakes before they caused more destruction, but no, the Lord Wizard galloped on regardless, gaining on him by the yard. It was only when a child ran in front of Seama's horse, her skirts ablaze, that he pulled up. Looking back uh-Bib saw him douse her clothes with a command and then, to his relief, slip from the saddle to make sure she was safe. Uh-Bib rode on, turning one corner and then the next as he made for the Northgate Road.

Seama was in a rage. He wanted to leap back into his saddle and get after his quarry; the urge to continue the fight was almost uncontrollable. But something inside held him back. Because this mad rage was not the real Seama Beltomé. The little girl was screaming and shaking with the pain. Her mother ran over to scoop her up, but then she stopped in despair – there was nowhere to go not ringed by the flying demons. It was too much. The real Seama could never leave these people in danger. The drakes had to be stopped. But how?

Seama searched for an answer. He wanted to send them back where they belonged: to Deamonia, but only uh-Bib could do that. He couldn't reason with them as he had with Bast. They were everywhere, hundreds of them, and each had its own Name. He couldn't command them without using those Names. How uh-Bib had managed to call them all was beyond him. There was one solution: they must be destroyed. Then he had it. Power answers power, so why shouldn't he likewise answer one invocation with another. They had an enemy, these drakes, one that hated them as a mother hates the murderer of her children. Bor'eth. A god of the third order, a nature god, sometimes named God of Dreaming Trees because of his affinity with alder and willow, but his province was the forest, his people the trees, his enemy the axe wielder or fire raiser. Seama had no paraphernalia or ritual with him, and it was decidedly an improper way to proceed, but such was the power he held in that hour that he didn't hesitate for a second. He called out to Bor'eth by focussing upon the trees that lined the avenue, many of them already aflame. Bor'eth was a god dwelling in the fabric of Ea', he was, in a way, ever present, but never in his life had Seama been able to make such a strong connection so quickly. The negotiation was brief, the offer a feast of fire drakes and the God of Dreaming Trees was pleased with that. The answer was immediate. With a droning of woodland insects and a smell of rotting leaves Bor'eth invested the city, keen to start the killing.

Seama shuddered as the god's presence became manifest but he refrained from looking. His work was done, and he could leave Bor'eth to his part certain the god would prevail. Seama had more pressing problems: uh-Bib was now out of sight. The Wizard Beltomé galloped on towards the North Gate, the nearest exit from the city. Actually by the time Seama took up the chase again uh-Bib had already passed through, but not without leaving behind one more surprise to harrass his pursuer.

The gate and wall had been erected by Banya with the aid of the master builder Arvis Bo'wouderner, and they were daunting works. Tarangananda uh-Bib had no respect for that or for their history. He had no qualms about bringing them down. He began in a single grain of rock and with his power to force movement, he started a vibration that would grow to its neighbours, and to the neighbours of the neighbours and further on until…

The gate burst asunder and the walls buckled in sudden ruin just as Seama drove through. Rubble bounced on and about them, his horse was raving at the noise, but uh-Bib had done his job too well and the grain was so fine it caused only bruises. Seama left the collapsed gateway behind and the chase continued.

The wide highway bolted through open fields, and the fields were full of harvesters. Seama's one clear chance continued to elude him but he found it more and more difficult to restrain himself. Somehow the energy he held in check demanded use, regardless of consequence. Seama forced himself to keep control.

He must not endanger innocents.

Uh-Bib couldn't care less about their welfare. He had put over a quarter of a mile between them, and he was growing in confidence as well as in power. He pulled up and turned his horse quickly to face his enemy once more. If he'd waited until the horse stopped moving he might have been more accurate, but when he flung out his arms before him, as though throwing a football, a great gouge of earth to the left of the road was torn up and piled in a fold twenty feet high. It buried three farmhands but not the Wizard Beltomé. Other field workers, in terror, began to run back towards the city.

Seama's anger flared. He was torn between the urge to kill the man, and a strange desire to scare and to embarrass him. The power he held back made him tremble. It needed release. He gave an expressive push and behind uh-Bib as they faced each other, soil and stone was scooped and piled into an impassable wall two hundred yards wide. The plateau beneath them trembled.

Uh-Bib was trapped. Staring wildly at the wall Seama had made he knew that he was outmatched once more. But he wouldn't surrender. Escape was only minutes from his grasp. He reached deep inside for every vestige of the strength that remained to him. He concentrated all his power into one movement.

Seama saw what was coming. He too marshalled his forces. This time he would bury the 'Randalan.

The combined effect was catastrophic. They had both dug deeper, cutting into the bedrock and the two thrusts met each other with a dreadful shock. The earth boomed and plumed. A shock wave, a quake not of Ea's making, rolled under the fields of Gothery and down through the Aegardean plains and forests. Both wizards were tumbled to roll down opposite slopes of a huge mound they had made between them, and both were battered by a rain of stony earth. Seama's horse was killed.

Pulling himself into a crouching position, he wiped mud from his eyes and then fell again in the trauma of the aftershock. Seama was truly dizzy now. He found it difficult to focus properly on the chaos about him and his head was full of a terrible ringing noise. No, not a ringing, more of a whirring, pulsing noise. He shook his head to rid himself of the unpleasant sound but failed. As he finally regained sight and raised his eyes to look for uh-Bib he understood why. The noise was not in his head at all, it was in the sky above him.

In a blaze of gold and emeralds and green scales, a dragon hung in the air. It's long sinuous body would have stretched to fifty feet if it could stop its curling and twisting. Its translucent wings, seeming frail as the evening sun shone through the green membrane, throbbed in short bursts which raised clouds of dust eighty feet below. Seama had never seen a dragon so close and though this one was on the smaller side of medium, he was dumbfounded by its size. The short legs were held close to the body as it flew, but even so he could see the sharp talons glinting as they extended then retracted. Radiant eyes and pearly teeth made the long head seem beautiful, but a gust of the warm, fetid air of dragon-breath reminded Seama of his peril. This beauty was more dangerous than even the 'Randalan.

A glowing green dragon against a darkling sky: it was a sight of horror, and one totally alien to Gothery. Dragons had been forbidden entry to Gothery by the Great Oath and by Haslem's spells. How could it be here? And why? Seama was confused and didn't know what to do next.

He stood to face the worm, wondering why it didn't attack immediately. The wings whirred again and again as the dragon maintained height, snaking its neck back and forth as though searching. Seama was about to attempt conversation with the dragon when it swooped.

A mighty wizard he was, and brave as a man could be, but when the green monster came hurtling towards him he ran for cover. Cringing behind a displaced boulder he waited for the searing blast or poisoned ichor. But the dragon had other intentions. It was not concerned about the puny individual performing acrobatics below. It had swooped to pick up a current of air and was already soaring over the mound before Seama realized it was gone.

Crawling around bedazed amidst the rubble on the other

side of the hill was a fat, bedraggled man with curly-toed shoes. The dragon dipped towards him and extending a deft claw, he gently dragged the gasping wizard into the air. Seama got to his feet in time to see them rise beyond the new horizon. His enemy was borne into the clouds and out of his reach.

Blind fury took hold of him as he saw uh-Bib escape once again; a fury so profound it consumed all other motives or considerations. Still unbelievably powerful, with energy sparking at his fingertips, he threw bolt after fiery bolt at them. The weapons of his anger rose a thousand feet into the sky in dazzling colours. There was no point to it, it was too late, the dragon too fast, but Seama raged and raged until he was utterly spent.

IV

LESSONS IN CONFLICT

Jaganatha

(An extract [with footnotes] from MALIN, Jøram; Errensea 2999 'A Commentary on the Texts of Power'; chap 2 'Duality as the Source' pgs 28 – 29)

'And to each creature He made, Ohrmazd[1] gave of his own Power in various measure, and to the best children of Gayomard, the Just Men, he gave Great Power, and to the least none.

'And to each creature of Ah'remmon, all crooked and vile, the dark god gave of his own power according to his design. To the Just Men he could give nothing for they were unmoved by his glamour; but to the least of Ohrmazd, Ah'remmon gave Power in various measure, that he might lure them to his purpose.'

Thus to this day, men and gods and creatures of the earth have all different degrees of power, and that power may derive either from the dark god or the bright. This is the power we call the Power Inherent as contrary to that power which may be assumed from others.

Some philosophers have questioned the origin of the Power that resides in the two brothers. The obvious answer is that all power comes from the Creator, their Father, but that does not explain the variability of the Power. It is well documented that the Power waxes and wanes even in the strongest and in the general course of events it is hard to discern any reason for this.

There is some confusion here: are we to believe that Ohrmazd is the creator of Mankind? Probably not. This quotation in the Texts is an unsupported fragment. Extant texts of the same period without exception describe Zurvan as the creator with Ohrmazd as his son and, by proxy, ruler of the creation. It is likely that the passage preceding that given here described Zurvan's creation of both Earnor and of Mankind. The clue is in the capital H. Texts of the First Period never allocate that honour to either of the sons, only the Father. It would not be in the nature of Ohrmazd to seek a role as creator, instead he awards power to his best servants as would a king to his favourites. See appendix 2 Syntactical norms and anomalies of the 1st Period.

However there is one circumstance which will ever lead to the increase of Power, providing the individuals involved show no weakness of intent. It is the view of this school that all Power derives from the tension that exists between Good and Evil, Ohrmazd and Ah'remmon, as created by Time or Zurvan. It is in the constant clash between these two forces that Power is released and in the Immediacy of the Struggle that the Power may grow.

On the continent of Sullinor which lies to the West of Asteranor, in the central states of the ar'Andalan Empire, there has survived the incredible practise of Jagantha. Colossal statues of ancient gods are made and mounted upon gigantic wheels. These great vehicles, the Jagana, are built in pairs: the actual form and name of the Gods involved would depend upon local beliefs, but one would be made as a representation of the Spirit of Evil, and the other would be a representation of the Spirit of Good. Each of these Gods would have supporters among the population and these gather by the thousand to watch as their idols are charged at one another from opposing hills. Many devotees are so inflamed by religious zeal that they throw themselves beneath the wheels of their god's chariot, believing that they are adding the power of their lives to the forthcoming clash. When the Jagana meet of course there is a tremendous crash but it is reported that upon the point of impact the Power of the two gods is released and many people present are endowed with immense strength as a result.

Whatever truth, or indeed idiocy, lies at the root of this behaviour, it should be noted that often great battles ensue between the opposing groups and there occurs mighty destruction and much death before the event is deemed to be finished.[2]

Reader please note: By Order of the High Council of Errensea, any student of the Collegium found to be engaged in the construction of the above described Jagana is liable to immediate suspension. The practice to conclusion of this rite of Jaganatha will, if the practitioners be yet living, lead to their expulsion from this school without appeal.

MANOEUVRES

Segyllin Part 3057.8.1

From, the diary of Lomal, Lord Anparas:

1st August – 'We started out before dawn. Night, these dark hours, must not disturb our determination, but I have to admit, if only to myself, that everything about the present circumstance disturbs me. Three thousand we are. Actually at last count three thousand, four hundred and seventy-nine. Under my command two thousand and forty-five; the rest with Shaf. I know it exactly: my clerk has just asked me to sign for their pay. What men will do for pay!

'No, that is unfair. They do what they do for their house and their nation, not knowing what they face, but unmoved by ill rumour. Brave men. Braver than I. You're no warrior, Lomal; a general, that's all.

'We passed the Sands' staging post at noon; the tent was still there open to the wind, and the fresh cairn walked over by crows. There were dark stains on the canvas.

'Our route was that taken by Cookson's men, but thankfully we had a less troubled passage of it. The days are shortening, and heavy clouds left us lacking light earlier than I had wanted. We have stopped on the edge of the River Plain, the Dales are behind us, and we are one day closer to conflict.

2nd August – 'We caught up with the advanced foot brigades before noon. Callin and some of the others charged off up to the head of the column to take command. As I required, of course. But there's a bit of swagger in the way he does things. A sort of arrogance. Able man though.

I sometimes wonder if they resent it: forever marching while we ride. I gave the horses an extra day in Cookson's fields. Did them good but from the foot end of things it must look like me favouring the cavalry again, giving them time off while everone else is working. And then up we come, laughing and joking, letting the horses run as though we're out for a day's hunting. Must be irritating.

No matter: time to be on my rounds, talk to the men, see how they're doing. I'll put the cavalry on watch duty tonight and let the foot get a good rest.

3rd August – 'The more time one has to write, the less there is to write about. I hate days like these. We are like lost souls plodding unknowing through eternity. As though we have made no progress we seem to halt where we started. This plain, that sky, grey as the cold sea, stretch on and on.

'Good grief! What do I sound like? Surely I'm not as depressed as the words I've written. We've done some useful miles today, Lomal. And no trouble at all, not so much as a lame donkey. The men are in reasonable spirits. They set up camp as quick as ever and the captains are among them talking battle and swordplay. We'll do!

4th August – 'What was wrong with me yesterday? Today was good. We've now done most of the journey to Glenogwen. In the morning I'll have the march swinging north onto the Francon Road, but I've work to do meanwhile. Jemenser will ride to meet me on the road ahead and soon I'll be making tracks towards him: no point in taking the army any closer to Coldharbour just so that I can talk with the Admiral.

'Nothing of note today other than good progress.

5th August (morning) – 'I will never be able to say that I was let down by lack of supplies or incompetent support. Jemenser had it all under control. He's done the requisition of transport, brought everything up from Riverport, and even recruited another three hundred for us back in Coldharbour. They're all on a path that will meet ours some time around noon. Pity Jemenser couldn't have fitted us on those boats of his, still I'd rather be tired than seasick.

'Must be getting old. The ride to meet the Admiral has ruined me. I don't get saddle sore but riding when I should be sleeping has made all my bones ache; I can barely keep my eyes open. Stubson's making my breakfast while the army takes a breather and the captains sort out the new marching order – I don't like having the same troop lead each day: they seem to get bigheaded and feel put upon at the same time.

(evening) – 'Well that's it. We're on the Francon Road now, and there's no reconsidering, and no way of avoiding the thought that soon we'll be at war. Of course, I don't even know that for sure, though I cannot believe Jaspar is silent for no reason. This is no good for a thinking man. Shaf has the edge on me in this one. You can't make strategy when you know nothing – well not very well. Shaf's a warrior. He'll just charge in headlong while I'm still fretting over it. He should have been an Anparas: we have a history of reckless Lords. Most people have forgotten. Not surprising given it was more than a thousand years ago, long before the founding of Gothery. Whenever there was a fight there was always an Anparas in the thick of it, whirling away with that mighty sword they were so proud of. Whenever there wasn't a fight there was always an Anparas to stir one up.

'All gone now. No magic sword, no warrior Lords. They say Haslem put a stop to it. Tregar was telling me it's all in the Chronicle. Just before he disapeared for good, the story is that Haslem turned up at the Palace on Tumboll, gave the family a good talking-to about honour and nobility, used a spell to send everyone to sleep (though that was maybe down to the speech!) and then helped himself to the Bloodstone. Apparently he was never seen again. The Lord Hibron – my ancester –missed the blade whenever he came-to, told all and sundry that he would kill the perfidious wizard with the very blade he had stolen and then rode off in pursuit. Of course, no one saw him again either. My line was never quite so bad after. Hibron's sister, our Noble Marion, was head of the new line and she married a man of Re'arden.

'All old history, but as the poet says, our present is our past. It has not escaped my notice that the young farmer's sword bears more than a passing resemblance to The Anparite Bloodstone. Of course it couldn't be that particular sword, not after so many years, but there's certainly something about the blade. Had it the same properties as the other it would be a weapon indeed; but I would worry about the hand that held it: some of my ancestors were little better than berserkers.

'Perhaps I could do with some of that old recklessness. The

valley of war is not far away and, so far, our plans are vague enough to give me the jitters.

6th August (noon) – 'We are all weary. The land continues to rise, as we knew it would. Being forewarned of labour never made the labour any easier. We cannot complain though, our rate of ascent is gradual: a thousand feet a day. I pity the House of Temor. Their road is all mountains. Tregar will have a hard time of it after all that soft living at court.

'Amongst the men earlier I was surprised and pleased to learn that their tails were up. They are actually looking forward to a battle. Cannot think what the captains have been telling them. Don't care as long as they're in good spirits.

'We have reached the town of Thesda – empty and silent as a tomb, but we expected that: Jemenser had told us of the refugees he found in Coldharbour. I am a little worried by their claim, like Jaspar, to have seen ghosts. Would we suffer the same visitations? So far not. I have not told the men about it, much that Lieutenant Marish argued the case. The other commanders made no complaint but Marish said I was not being fair to the regulars. 'After all,' he said, 'they'll be the ones who have to fight.' I could not follow his logic but again I find myself wishing I was a warrior, not a general.

(late) – 'Dark as the grave outside but still no ghosts: they must be busy elsewhere. We have made progress today even though the road was harder. Everyone is fitter than me, but I'm worried we will all be exhausted by the time we reach the Francon. There's not much point in getting there if we're too tired to fight. I've had the Captains trying to slow them down but there is no holding them back. Apparently the men are all fired up with the idea of rescuing the Lady Xandra. Looking for the King's favour, no doubt. Or hers.

We have passed through more villages, emptied by the threat of war, and they have given rise to an unpleasant development in our progress. I will be sorry to report the unfortunate increase in the incidence of looting among the ranks. It's minor and casual, of course: the odd trinket left behind, a fine knife, good clothing. There has been no ransacking but it's theft whichever way you look at it. The culprits have been tried and found guilty. They know it's due but their punishment will have to wait.

7th August (morning) – 'A day and a night and we will be there. Sometimes I am eager for it, but I confess that at others I am dreading this confrontation. I have lived fifty-six years, good years, and although I am not old, I believe that death now would not be too great a disappointment. I've done all I wanted to do, seen all I wanted to see. My children are grown, my wife has gone ahead of me and the prospect of moving on, without her, into sadness and dotage and infirmity does not seem so good.

'These lines make it seem that I seek death. Let me be clear: I do not. But death does not scare me.

'So, what is it then that I dread? Mutilation? The destruction of my army, my people? Certainly not the ghosts! It is the unknown, Lomal. Our blinkered advance. I cannot stand this uncertainty.

(evening) – 'Morale was high, but morale is a delicate thing and it takes very little to damage it. On this occasion, fog. I don't care if I never see another, if I never hear the word. I'm reminded of Jaspar's letter. This fog is a horrible thing. It's blinding; it's drowning in cotton wool; it stuffs up your head like a cold, makes you shiver and makes you lost. At least it came on only as we made camp – perhaps it will be gone by morning. We will have to get ahead whatever happens. Five miles to the mouth of the valley. The outriders should have been back by now but the fog will have delayed them.

8th August (morning) – 'No outriders, and no sun. The fog hides them both.

'We can see twenty or thirty yards, we can see the road. Camp will be left behind, left to stand for the event of our return: my army is girding its loins, loosening its limbs, we will not carry tents into battle! I ride at the head of my army. It's breaking my rule but there are plenty of commanders to sit back and watch.

– 'I have made a halt. We must be close to the valley. We must, and yet there is nothing but twenty yards of road, the fog and a dreadful silence. I have ordered a ration and a nip for the chill, and take up my journal to occupy my thoughts. I will not allow myself needless speculation. When the time comes…

'That's the shout, here we go: the fog is lifting!'

Hannaydale 3057.8.2

Tregar was sweating and out of breath. His earlier journey to Hannayford had been leisurely compared with this steeplechase. If he'd found time to think of the infantry footslogging he would have pitied them, but he had thought for his own discomfort only. The small horsed contingent of Temor's army were not an elite by any means; the horses were not for comfort but for speed. Temor wanted to reach Hannayford as quickly as possible even if it meant leaving the army a day behind, and so the hundred horse ran fast with little regard for safety. Temor himself led them and beside him rode Owen Cookson's son, Seth, to act as guide. Seth's brother Cal was with them even though his assistance seemed superfluous – Tregar presumed he had been invited out of courtesy to the other. Naturally, Tregar had to go with them. 'You never know when you might need a wizard,' he was told.

Temor's purpose in striking on for the Hannay with such haste was ostensibly to make the foraging easier. The advance group would pinpoint the supplies and anything else that might be useful for those who came after. With Temor, however, it was impossible not to suspect another reason for haste: plain impatience. If he could have reached the Francon in a day he would have done it and damn the plans.

Tregar wasn't at all sure that keeping Temor's company would be good for him. The wizard was himself hot tempered and certainly not fight-shy but compared with Shaf, the Lord Temor, Tregar was a wonder of reserve and good common sense.

Hannayford gave him a decent rest. He wasn't needed by Lord or soldier and so he parked himself in a rich man's house and sipped port because he could find no beer. That was the limit of his foraging. He was on his second glass when Cal found him.

'Hello Cal, I suppose someone's found me a job, eh?'

'Not that I know about,' Cal frowned and then said, 'Oh, I see. No, I've not come to fetch you. I wanted a word.'

'Well sit ye down. Port?'

'No thanks.'

'How can I help ye?'

Cal looked at the wizard with his good eye and Tregar at once found himself looking at the wayward one.

'Have ye ever been to a healer with that eye of yourn?'

'No point, it can't be fixed.'

'Who told ye that? I could have a good try if we ever get a day's peace.'

'Then you'll never try, will you. There won't be any peace anymore. Not for my family anyway.'

Tregar was ready to rebuff the boy's pessimism but something in his look held him back. The gaze from the one good eye was so intense, so implacable. Tregar couldn't help thinking there was something strange about the lad that went beyond the physical. As if to prove him right Cal continued provocatively:

'I've seen it, seen it all. No peace ever again.'

Tregar took a slow, deliberate sip of his port and placed the glass on the table before him. He was playing for time. He wanted a few moments of cool thought before he committed himself.

'Cal,' he said, 'I don't quite know how to put this. Think about it before giving me your answer. Are ye saying you are prescient?'

'I don't know.'

'Well think about it for—'

'I mean I don't know because I don't know what that word means.'

'Oh. Well there's no real reason ye should. What I mean is, do ye think ye have the ability to see into the future? Known when someone was going to get pregnant, that a storm will come weeks before it happens, a stranger will turn up; that sort of thing?'

'No. None of those. I only know when someone's going to die.'

The lad didn't mince his words.

'How, er, when did ye—'

'The first time? My mam was about to have her fifth. There was nowt wrong with the labour, that's what they said after, but I knew. I'd dreamt it dead at birth. I saw the birthing and all, and I knew it must be true because I were only seven and I'd never seen a baby born. How could it have been a normal dream if I could see things I knew nowt about. Then when I were eleven me best friend's eldest brother were on a trip to Coldharbour and I dreamt his horse had thrown him and he'd broken his neck. He came back on a bier.'

'And ye've dreamed recently?'

'Aye, a shameful dream.'

'Are ye going to tell me?'

'Can't. But it's our Seth,' Tregar nodded. He thought he understood: the pair were close. 'Can't you send him back, Tregar? You must send him back. For his sake and for mine. It won't happen if he doesn't go.'

'Now then Cal, just you calm yoursel'. Let me tell ye what I do know. We were taught all about this sort of dream on Errensea. Think about this: ye say ye've dreamed that ye've seen deaths before they happen. Well my guess is that ye've also dreamt of deaths that didn't. You're sensitive, Cal, ye realize the danger where no one else can see it. Sometimes that danger, that threat becomes real and has the effect ye feared, but most times nothing at all happens and then ye forget that ye've had the dream. Now, take that riding accident. I'll bet ye knew the horse, knew it was in a funny mood before the man took it. You realized it was dangerous to ride but who'd ever listen to an eleven year old? There was a risk he would be thrown and ye knew it. D'ye understand me?'

Cal said nothing for a minute and then said, 'You don't understand me. Going on wi'all that rubbish! I'm telling thee, Seth 'as to go back or we've all had it. Speak to the Lord, mek him see. My brother can't come wi' us.'

Statement made the boy spun on his heel and strode out of the room leaving Tregar amazed.

Before nightfall Tregar did try to speak with Lord Temor about Cal's fears but found the lad had beaten him to it. Temor was still swearing.

'So that blasted boy has been on at you as well. He must be slow in the head if he thinks I'll send warriors away before the battle. Mark me, young Seth is an asset. Him and his sword will do more damage than I will.'

'By the sound of things,' Tregar agreed, 'he undoubtedly will.'

From then on Tregar kept a close eye on Seth Cookson. Certainly the lad seemed different but that wasn't unusual. He was a soldier now, heading for his first battle, ready and willing to prove himself or die in the act. But the boy's words were brash and reckless, gone the reserve and modesty Tregar remembered from their previous journey, gone the gentle manners. The wizard was convinced that it was mostly down to Temor. Any impressionable young man was bound to become infected by Shaf's impetuous style. The Lord and the farmer's lad had fast become friends. They rode together, walked together, ate together. It was no surprise that Seth's manner had changed.

As he watched Seth, Tregar found himself watching Cal too. The boy was always there dogging his brother's footsteps and looking as though he carried the burdens of the world on his young shoulders. Tregar wished he knew what the boy had dreamed.

When Tregar reached the point on the road where he had, days before, cast ahead with his Sight, he took a moment to try again. The army was putting up tents and starting fires after a third day of toil; there was shouting and joking, there was clatter and turmoil all about. Tregar decided to ride out a little to get away from the noise. This was not his best skill and he needed to be able to focus on the job without distraction. After quarter of a mile or so the path turned and put a hill between him and the camp.

'Right then,' he said to Sirrah, 'Which way first, d'ye reckon?' The horse didn't reply of course but he did begin to graze with his head pointing southerly. 'Back the way we came? Aye, why not: back's better than forward. It'll help me work my way into it.'

So he settled himself and then cast back along the route they had travelled. Five miles back, just the trampling of the grass to mark the army's passage; ten miles, more of the same, some deserted villages. He was beginning to feel pleased with himself. He wondered how far he could get. Small Cuttings was, of course, out of range but Hannayford now, that might just be... Yes! There it was: the empty High Street, clear in his mind's eye, the Town Hall with a great padlock on the doors, the tall houses, Mr Richard's pottery and... and, wandering aimlessly, forlornly, among the cracked pots of the pottery yard, the Master of Small Cuttings, Owen Cookson, haunting the ruins.

Tregar was so surprised he lost concentration and the image disappeared. Owen Cookson in Hannayford. Why? He'd been adamant his place was at home. Was he now set on following them into battle? Did he think perhaps that his sons might have lagged behind? Was he set on bringing them home? The questions were getting in Tregar's way. Try as he might Hannayford and Owen were lost to him.

He took a deep breath and tried to think of something else. He pulled Sirrah about and put everything he could muster into looking out westaway. Could he see the River Plain? Could he find the Anparas army? No: too far. The end of the dales were perhaps forty miles from where he now stood. The only point to note was that some of the most westerly villages were still populated – it cheered him to see men and women going about their business.

Ahead then. The North and the seat of all the trouble. As before his view surged along the way ahead; as before the country opened up before him. It was pointless. Nothing had changed: empty moorland, gaining in height, rocky scars above a path often less defined than a sheep track, twisting and turning up into the mountains. He saw nor men, nor sheep, nor carrion.

Disappointed once again but resigned to it, the wizard kicked up Sirrah from his grazing intending to amble back down to the camp just in time for supper. But Sirrah wasn't happy. The grass he'd found was sweet and despite his master's insistence he was inclined to stay put. It was as Tregar tugged and struggled with the reins that something flew past his head. He lurched to one side and very nearly fell out of his saddle. With a rustle of creaky wings a large raven landed on a rock beside them: a large, dishevelled raven whose midnight black feathers were in places dusty brown and crumpled. The raven tutted and the look it gave him from its one good eye was steely with disapproval.

'Yes Ravn, can I help ye?' Tregar said.

The raven tutted some more and shifted from foot to foot as though it was standing in tar. It croaked a filthy word that Tregar did not know but could understand perfectly well, and then flew away over the hill. Tregar watched it go and afterward sat bemused in his saddle for a long ten minutes.

'Well Sirrah,' he said to his horse. 'if a ravn can talk there's hope for ye yet. I hope ye pick up a fairer vocabulary.'

Sirrah made no comment but continued to chew while he could.

It came to Tregar's ears, on the following day, that the men were unsettled, not just because of the hard toil of walking through the hills, but because of mysterious portents that littered their way: a two-headed sheep dead on the path; one shooting star too many; a snake choked upon its own tail and, significantly, a raven that circled the advancing army three times the wrong way, and then three times the right way. Self-professed prognosticators argued between themselves about the meaning of the doubtful signs and the army was ablaze with their speculations. Tregar refused to be drawn on the subject.

After twenty-four hours of this doom-mongering it was widely accepted that a war of the Gods, at the very least, was in the offing. Lord Temor had had enough. He took Seth with him and toured the army as it marched. Wherever he went the soothsayers fled, forewarned no doubt of the coming of his wrath. Tregar was impressed by Temor's skill in turning the falling morale on its head. By ridiculing the astrologers and augurors he had the men laughing and with Seth supporting him he went on to talk of battle glory and victory. It was a clever work of manipulation. The day ended with an extra ration or two of the diminishing supply of beer. Temor wanted to keep the good mood going.

It was late on the next rather more subdued evening that the raven turned up again, though few saw him as he flew directly to Tregar's small tent.

"'Tis a poor tent for a mage,' it crowed and cackled at its own wit.

Tregar decided to pretend that talking ravens were nothing out of the ordinary. 'Enjoyed confusing the army, I take it? A portent of doom are ye, or a vagabond god with one eye for mischief and none for anything else?'

'You seem a wee bit more confident at our second meeting, wiezart. Cheeky even, though no doubt I deserve it.'

'Are ye here to discuss your sins then, or is there something you want to tell me this time?'

'There is a limit, Tregar, croak, to the lip I am prepared to take, croak. Don't forget who it is I am.'

The raven wandered around the tent examining Tregar's bits and pieces: pulling out a bright red kerchief from the wizard's pack, meddling with the charms in his jacket pocket.

'How could I forget? But ye're right, I'm not in a position to be bladdie rude even if you seemingly are.'

'Shall I, croak, Shall I start again Tregar? I am not here for the exercise. I want to speak to you of peace and persuasion.'

'Last time it was war and magic.'

'Yes...'

'And the fact that all who are so called evil are not all evil, and all who are so called good are certainly not all good.'

'Well done, cr..craw.'

'Bless you.'

'I wasn't coughing! Don't, croak, don't think I made the throat quite right, ah well.'

The raven stretched its wings and tried to rearrange a few feathers with its beak. It was not very effective.

'You're going to have to practise that if ye want to fool

anybody.'

The raven glared at him.

'So, peace and persuasion?'

'Yes, that's it craw. I'll go now.'

'What! I thought ye were going to tell me about peace and persuasion!'

'Cannot you understand anything? Do, croaw, do I have to spell it out? In order to achieve lasting peace, that is to craaa stop the basis of, croak croak, the basis of war, the only way is persuasion. That's all. You just have to know what you're persuading them to do.'

'And that is?'

'I cannot tell you.'

'Spurl's tits! So, I'm supposed to get to the Francon and persuade the enemy, whoever they are, to be peaceful and they'll listen?'

'Croak, no, crak, don't be ridiculous. It won't work this time I don't, croak. Damn, croak. No this will be when you need to, craa, use m… croak croak croak, magic damn, croak, oh, croak!'

Temor appeared at the doorway.

'Tregar, would… Get out, out stupid creature! Go on, out and begone!'

The Lord Temor ran about Tregar's tent, bowling the wizard over in his attempt to chase the raven away. He finally succeeded and with a few more rude creaks and croaks the ancient flapped off.

'You shouldn't encourage that bird, Tregar. What will the men think!'

'Who knows, Temor, who knows?'

Tregar slept badly. The words of Uovin, brief and seemingly trivial were obviously important but Tregar couldn't see it. Use persuasion rather than force of arms, but not this time? Again the god told him to use magic, but surely it wasn't right to attack common soldiers with a weapon they couldn't resist, no matter where they came from. Was Uovin implying that his enemy would use magic? He'd soon find out: they were due to reach the

Francon by afternoon on the very next day, the 8th of August. Just what they would find there he wondered again and again as he lay in the dark, wishing it was dawn.

A WELCOME OF SORTS

Astoril 3057.8.7

When Terrance saw the hill he was speechless. He had visited Astoril at least twice a year for longer than he cared to remember. He knew it as well as a visitor could: things would change between times, there would be new buildings, new roads but always the underlying structure remained. Astoril was ever lovely, a city of spires and steeples, columns and arches. Structures of strength balanced frames of delicate poise; wide avenues circled bustles of narrowness. Glass was everywhere. Crystal sparkled in the most modest of houses, glittering cascades carried waterfalls in the Garden of Fountains, music was bright in fluted glass pipe organs and frosted sculptures adorned roadsides and grottos, villas and halls throughout.

All of this was built on a plateau that rose a thousand feet above the level of the Aegardean plain: a slab of the earth forced upwards in the calamity that had dammed the Hypodedicus, and filled out with liquid rock till this reach of the plateau was as flat as a screed floor. Whatever vantage chosen there was nothing to hinder a view of that fair city, nothing to distract the eye from its glittering towers. That was Astoril, capital of Gothery, as Terrance knew it.

Not as it was now.

The plateau was flat as a screed floor no longer.

Gumb's company approached the city along Western Way but their eyes hardly strayed from that abomination on the fields to the north and east. As De Vere saw it, that obscene pile must have been over three hundred feet high, and uglier than the barrens of the Dedicae. Distance blurred the detail but De Vere's imagination was quick to fill in. It was unnatural: made of naked earth and broken rock yes, but tragically bits of roof, garden gates sticking out of the surface like tombstones, chimney pots, animals perhaps, human corpses perhaps, all acted as mortar to the brick. The sheer scale of the mound threatened worse to come. What must the hand of destruction have done to his beloved Astoril?

As they rode into the city Terrance's fears became horribly real. At the outer reaches farm buildings were shaken and damaged, the scattered homes were sometimes missing walls, their doorways were collapsed, roofs had fallen in. The familial lives of common people were exposed to the view of passing strangers. Windows were now gaping holes. There was glass everywhere – shattered.

And it became worse with each and every furlong they progressed. The Garden of Fountains, that favourite resting place, was broken down, the waters awash with splinters and blades. Terrance's stomach churned in his distress. Half the sculpture was gone: a nose, a claw, a glass feather lay beneath pedestals as the only clue to identity. His nausea grew at each new desecration. Up ahead lay the centre of the city. It was a changed horizon where everything delicate and fine had gone and only the bulky remained. The towers had fallen, the steeples were topped, the spires toppled. Weighty buildings, survivors of the chaos appeared gross and in some strange way responsible.

And everywhere as they travelled through Astoril to its heart, sitting or standing or wandering aimlessly, the people of this once fair city seemed witless and lost. For Terrance this was the worst of all. He thought he knew them: ever resourceful, unfailingly hopeful men and women and children who enjoyed the challenge of life. To see them now in this extremity was awful. It was as though the shock-wave that had flattened much of the fabric of the city had battered at their spirit and ground their innate courage into the mangled earth.

Near at hand, the piteous sight of grubby two year old girl holding up her empty cup to a father staring hopelessly at the ruins of their home, unresponsive to her needs, finally tipped Terrance over the edge.

He leapt from his saddle, grabbed at his water bottle and marched over to confront the man.

'She needs water, can't you see? And she needs you to be her father! Give her this.'

He thrust the bottle out to him, but the man just pushed it

away, and then sank to his knees, and began to cry.

Someone clutched at Terrance's shoulders and pulled him back. It was no man Terrance knew: a neighbour of the other.

'Leave 'im, will yer. We only got his wife out an hour past. There was none to help him yesterday. And now… well, she's gone; died in the night we reckon.'

Terrance held his hand to his mouth.

'Look mister, why don't you and your friends just get on to wherever you've a mind. I'll look after these two. Thanks for the water, though — none too clean round here.'

Terrance nodded because he couldn't speak and then spun away. The nausea had won. He threw up there and then, in full view of all.

They continued in an even more sombre mood than before. Here and there were men and women digging still at the rubble of lost houses but it was a forlorn task. A cold night had taken away the urgency of the previous day. The company had almost reached the palace before they saw any sign of proper, official organization and activity. Here sergeants were putting together work parties of soldier and citizen alike. The hopeless shook off their inertia to join in with something, anything that might prove worthwhile; the bereaved came forward wanting help to do their duty to the lost. But there was more than that. Here at the centre of the city a new feeling was spreading, born of despair but transformed by need into a sense of purpose. These work parties would soon march to the outer limits of the city and they would carry a new mood with them.

At the centre of activity, the palace itself, someone had found the time to post guards and the guards were bright enough to question strangers. Angren spoke up at their challenge and no one was surprised when, at the mere mention of their names, they were provided with a guide and encouraged to proceed. The horses were taken to stabling where the Mule met an old friend and was fed carrots by instruction of his owner.

The Palace of Astoril had not escaped the destruction caused by that terrible shaking of the earth but the damage done was mainly to ornament rather than the walls of thick sandstone. Dozens of servants ran to and fro sweeping up shards and fragments, resettling upended furniture and generally tidying up the worst of the mess.

Lord Gumb peered about him as they were guided towards the throne room, and occasionally stopped to examine the furniture, doors and carvings.

'There's some good wood here, nephew; good crafting too.'

'Uncle! Must you?'

'Must I what?'

'Anyone would think we were in another part of Aegarde. We're in the heart of Gothery and all you can see is wood!' Alan Travers' face reddened as he spoke and Gumb found himself wondering whether the lad was angry or blushing.

'I don't understand you, boy. Never have, come to think of it.'

Angren and Terrance had taken the lead in following their guide but they had no words to say to each other. It was another's voice they wanted, a voice that would put it all right, a voice to explain and reassure. They led the company because they were desperate for it.

A corridor they came upon was so crowded with people that the company had to barge their way through. The people were all waiting for admittance to the room ahead but there was no impatience, no ill-feeling among them. Whatever they waited for was important and inevitable. At five tables inside the hall names were taken, occupation and abilities listed and direction given. Builders were in demand, architects and doctors. Teams were being put together. Further on the team leaders were allocated sectors and told where to find their volunteer labourers among the groups forming outside the palace.

Twelve men sat on one side of the hall, each commanding an area of responsibility: food, water, mechanicals, hospitals, and so on, and they were attended by a constant stream of clerks seeking authority to proceed in one way or another.

Beyond that hall was the throne room. There the activity was no less, but the focus of all enquiry was one man. Seama sat on a small chair below the throne and the King's Ministers were gathered around him as the needs of the emergency were discussed and decisions made. Seama held a red baton that signified his appointed stewardship, and he wielded authority to no obvious dissent.

Their guide went forward to give Seama news of their arrival. Seama looked up, acknowledged their presence with a nod, spoke a few words to the guide and then returned his attention to the Ministers.

'My Lord Seama, Steward of King Sirl II, asks me to welcome you to Astoril. He sends apologies for not being free to greet you personally as the emergency requires his immediate attention; however he will be able to see you all in an hour. Until then he has bid me find you some accommodation.'

Angren and Terrance looked at him in disbelief but said nothing. Neither had realized that their friendship with the Wizard could possibly take second place to matters of state. They were being selfish and uncharitable; it was Lord Gumb who accepted both Seama's priorities and his welcome.

'We are grateful for any hospitality in this difficult time,' he replied for all of them, 'A room is more than enough, beyond that we will make do: there are many others in need of attention.'

'Thank you, Lord Gumb, but we have matters in hand, and your comfort will not affect them. If you will follow me?'

Though bare of ornament, their apartments were pleasing and well equipped with wonderfully soft beds, comfortable couches and basins, with ewers of warmed water quick to arrive. After their long journey the beds looked very inviting, but there was only enough time to wash and change and eat a few sandwiches before they were asked to meet Seama in the garden.

Seama was sitting alone in the same arbour uh-Bib had used only the day before. He sprang up to greet them.

'You cannot imagine how happy I am to see you! Angren, Terrance, all of you.'

'You could have fooled me,' Angren said huffily. 'We've been here two hours already.'

'Angren, really. You mayn't have noticed but Astoril is in

chaos. There are people injured and dying. I really think they have first right to our attention, don't you?'

'So we've been on a jolly, have we?'

'No, of course not, and that's why I forgive you. Don't be ungenerous. I know you're tired, but you're fit and healthy – others are not so well off.'

'Yes, I suppose so. Sorry, but, well you ask us to come here all urgent, leaving Moreda in a pretty bad state itself, leaving Edro to bury his brother. You ask as if the world depended on it, and when we arrive you tell us to take a bath. What's going on Seama? What's it all about?'

'Piedoro's dead? How? In battle?'

'Yes. Edro's taken it bad.'

'Of course. How did the rest of it turn out?'

So far only Angren had spoken to Seama but as the Wizard looked at each in turn, appraising their private losses by the weariness in their stance, in their eyes, Lord Gumb took it upon himself to describe the outcome of the battle and their work after it. He too wanted to know why they'd been asked to come to Gothery: he'd thought the trouble in Moreda more or less a private matter for the Forest Lords to deal with, and there was a lot yet to sort out in the aftermath.

'The trouble was not so private, Gumb. Not simply an Aegardean affair and what you see in Astoril is part of the aftermath, as you put it.'

'I see. The Black Company is defeated and Astoril is in ruins and those two events are not unrelated. What happened here, Seama?'

Then it was Seama's turn to tell a tale, but he was brief and left many questions unanswered. It was obvious that Gumb and the others were not satisfied.

'So the fat man told you this uh-Bib was their paymaster, and you'd met him before?' Terrance asked.

'Yes and yes. And I knew I had to get to him before news of our victory could reach Astoril.'

'Why?'

'To make sure that he was on the back foot. Can you imagine

the damage he could have done if I had given him time? I did think I might even capture the man, but it was beyond me. He was too powerful.'

It was not only Angren who raised his eyebrows at the notion that Seama had met his match.

'Nevertheless,' said Gumb, 'He's gone and you're still here.'

'He is and I am, and that's just as well. Now look, all of you have questions and I do intend to answer them, but this piecemeal fashion is pointless. There'll be a council meeting first thing tomorrow. You can have the full tale then and ask as many questions as you like. I brought you here because you deserve an explanation, and because there's a job to be done. I am particularly grateful to you, Lord Gumb, for making the journey: your role will be very important.'

'And what role is that?

'Tomorrow, Gumb, tomorrow. I cannot make decisions without the backing of you all, and I cannot explain a part without explaining everything. It must be in council. I want you to get some rest – I desperately need sleep myself. We must all be fresh and ready for work in the morning. You've been given rooms?'

'We have,' said Angren, still rather stiffly, 'I suppose by that you mean we should go and use them?'

'I do. Maybe when you wake you'll be in a better temper. Sigrid, wait a while. You are not well, I think.'

'Oh, I'll survive.'

'I'm sure you will but a little attention wouldn't hurt. Sirl has a new doctor, a good man and true. I'll take you to see him while I visit the King. Sleep well, all of you, but don't sleep late: we begin at nine.'

Castle Ayer 3057.8.7

Two hundred and sixty miles away in the Castle of Ayer King Mador sat on the edge of his throne, looking as if he were about to jump up from it and run away. He had just had news. Not the dispatches from the North: Anparas riders turned up like clockwork every day at noon though they had little to say other than report progress towards the Francon. There was a time delay of course but Lomal had managed to get it down to three days, a feat of organization and forward planning, and surely a display of tremendous effort by the couriers. Yesterday's dispatch said that Anparas was three days out from the Francon and four to the head of the valley. So, actually they would be thereabouts by the end of this day. Tomorrow they would find what there was to find.

But the news that had spoiled his breakfast was closer to home. It had started with Robarn turning up. 'Riana had come to him saying she'd arranged for his former chief spy to take up the grace and favour house Mador kept in the town, and that he was asking for audience. Typical of Gerald to work through the King's butler rather than the Chamberlain who determinedly handled formal requests with a measured lack of enthusiasm. 'Riana of course would not be bound by such formalities. This was five days back. The odd thing was that Mador hadn't been too keen on seeing his old friend and wished the Chamberlain *had* been involved. Nonetheless he awarded Gerald fifteen minutes in the Presence during the next morning's petitions.

It was fairly clear that a meeting in a public place with guardsmen and ministers all around them was not the sort of meeting Robarn was after. In fact he was quite grumpy about it. Mador was amazed at the change in the man. He seemed thin, haggard in the extreme and more brusque than he could ever remember. Robarn excused himself on the grounds that he was suffering from a summer cold and from the exhausting journey.

'I am not so young any more, Mador, and I make journeys only when truly necessary. There is much we could be talking about if we had more privacy but never mind that now. I have come to warn you: there is a terror abroad in your country and we need to do something about it. And quick.'

Mador had listened uncomfortably to Robarn's tale of the murders in the cottage and the attack on Isolde. Robarn had been quick to reassure the King that his favourite survived the attack and had continued on her mission, but then he went on to explain how several other mutilated bodies had been found in villages along the road to Riverport.

'They're heading for Riverport?'

'No Mador, it *came* from Riverport. The militia told me that three people were murdered in the city during the previous week.'

'It?'

'I believe it is some sort of animal. But an intelligent animal, with a purpose.'

'Did Isolde not describe the creature?'

'Apparently not. My man, Jeffers, was with her but not close enough to see what happened. He asked, of course, she was so battered and shaken, but she wouldn't talk about it. Just told him to get me on the case when he got back to the Lyndons. Said he'd pressed her on what it looked like but she just shook her head and clammed up.'

'That's not like Isolde – to leave us without a clue.'

'No. But then she had just been through a fight for her life. Make no mistake Mador, whatever it is, this thing is vicious and powerful and deadly. How Isolde got free I don't know.'

Mador didn't want this news. It was more trouble. More evidence that they were not safe, not even here in the heart of Pars.

Robarn was quick to his point. He wanted Mador to give him the job of flushing out this creature and he wanted the manpower to do it.

'And where do you think I can find the men to spare? And how many men do you think it would take anyway? It's one small problem, Gerald, brutal and terrible for those affected of course, but we have a war to fight. We'll send word to the Constables. You should go and rest until that cold is done.'

Gerald Robarn, while remaining outwardly civil, had marched off in a temper plain to see. The King's ministers had shaken their heads. Mador wasn't sure quite whose behaviour it was that distressed them.

And then only the day before yesterday Isolde herself had turned up. According to the cook, who was also a spy in permanent residence at the grace house, Isolde had hammered on the door sometime after nightfall, barked at Jeffers when he came to see what was happening, demanded that she must see her father at once and then stormed off into his rooms. The cook said there was a tense atmosphere in the house, as though they were all wary of each other. Isolde's arrival was so unexpected. He presumed she must have important news, from Sirl perhaps, or possibly of Seama from whom he had heard nothing so far. And of course he would have seen her at once but for the spell trouble breaking out yet again.

Just the thought of it put him in a fury. The words *damned magic* charged around in his head so much he was beginning to wonder whether he was still safe from the spell. And when would it all be done? He was thoroughly sick of it. Ever since the two wizards had set out their own cantrip against the atrocious spell that was ripping apart the fabric of Ayer, and then ridden off as though they had done a good job, Castle Ayer had become a terrible place. Mador kept to his presence. He had his servants and the guard and his ministers all organized to do their work and then to leave the castle as quickly as possible. The burgers of the town had lodgers from the court, marquees and tents had been set up in the meadows. He would not have his people exposed to this chaos any more than was absolutely necessary. The spells had gone mad.

It was like living in a whirlwind. The wizards' intent had been to slow the decay; they'd presumed their counter spell would take precedence over the other. Well for some of the time and in some places that was indeed what happened, but in others the reverse was true and instead it was the spell of dissolution that won out. And then, just as the changing pressures of air force the winds of the world into storms, so these two spells began to contest their ground. They chased each other through the castle first one way and then another. In one moment there would be calm and in the next plaster was cascading from the walls only to be spun into columns of dust and then pasted back into place again. You could hear the progress down the corridors and through the halls as weapons fell off the walls and suits of armour first collapsed, and then crashed about and then found themselves mended and ready to be put up again by servants run completely ragged by the effort. For several days balance might be achieved and calm descended like a blessing but then the pressure changed and another explosion of activity would break out and bring turmoil to their lives once more.

Yesterday the upheaval had been so bad that Mador had everyone leave the castle except for those who could be housed in the Presence and his apartments above. There were no meetings that day.

By the morning the worst of it had passed and there had been no movement for several hours. Time enough for them to bring in reports of the damage, time enough to bring in news from outside. And it was the news from outside that had him on edge.

From out in the Heartland came stories of horror. A publican walking home from a dinner with a friend had been found with his heart torn out. A teacher working late after concert practice had been ripped to pieces in his schoolhouse. In each case parts of the bodies were missing. Just off the road at Three-Ways Cross an Errensea trained doctor had been found savaged and decapitated. The crossroads were on the Misium Way only twenty miles west of Ayer, and this attack must have happened in broad daylight: the woman's corpse had been discovered only a few hours after she'd been served lunch at a nearby inn.

And then from down in the town, a town spilling over with refugees from the Castle, came the terrible news that had Mador sweating. Where the River brushed up against the edge of the town there were small quays for shallow draft barges. Cargoes of flour or wood or any bulky item went up and down the River Misium to spread the wealth of the land through the countryside and down to the City of Pilgrim's Bay. This morning the bargees woke to find the gruesome remains of a mutilated man bleeding onto grain sacks that had been loaded up only the night before. His head had been speared onto a gaff thrust into the soft earth at the river's edge. Despite the rigor of pain that fixed his features the face remained recognizable. When the militia men arrived, all wondering what the bargees could be babbling about and unprepared for the horror that awaited them, they knew him instantly. The murdered man was well known throughout the town: it was Alaric Goss, Captain of the King's Guard.

He should have listened to Robarn. Mador knew that now. Should have had everyone searching, everyone on their guard. He got to his feet.

'Sergeant,' he said to his Man at Arms, the man himself reeling from the news he had just heard, 'I want you to double the guard. Now. No man is to do duty alone. The palace is the priority. Take men from the curtain wall if necessary. I want the portcullis down and double duty on the gate. Chamberlain! Get a message to Robarn and to Isolde. She is to come to me at noon tomorrow – tell her I will want a full report. Robarn is to join us after one half hour. Tell him to have his plans for the hunt begun. Until then I'll be in my apartments. Send the librarian. Beyond that I will see no one.'

What else was there to do? His captain's head on a post was as clear a warning as there could be: the beast had come to Ayer and it had come for the King.

Astoril 3057.8.8

As functionaries busied themselves with furniture for the meeting to come, Seama took up a position by the doorway to greet each person as they entered the chamber. Like the groom at a wedding, he shook their hands in turn and thanked them for coming.

Seama had invited thirteen people to attend the council: a meeting, had they known it, that could affect the fate of millions. Only one failed to appear. The King's ministers were first to arrive. Keth Hardie was Sirl's Prime Minister, an astute man of sound judgement. Seama expected no less of a man appointed by Sirl before his illness. After uh-Bib's departure, Hardie was deeply embarrassed about the 'nonsense' he had been responsible for in the previous months, and offered his resignation. 'I never liked Bliss, of course, but I didn't really understand,' he told Seama, 'I was blind. How can a blind man expect to govern?' The wizard had taken great pains in persuading him to continue his work 'at least until the King is well enough to cope.' Hardie's arrival at the council was the answer Seama expected.

His colleagues were Tys Heald, the Chancellor, Gurdy Younger, Minister for Defence, and Fel Awdry, the man responsible for industrial development. Arts, Science, Transport, and Health Ministers were busy elsewhere and not invited anyway. Of the three, Seama knew Fel Awdry well as a friend, the others more formally. Fel had held various offices, at Sirl's direct request, for more than thirty years and Seama sought him out whenever he visited Gothery: he was not only deep in the governance of the country but also excellent company. Now seventy three years old, his beard was very white and his stoop more pronounced but his eyes hadn't lost their sparkle.

'Seama, it's good to see you!' he cried as he crossed the threshhold. 'Where've you been these twelve months, you rascal? Oh, I know Asteranor's a damn big place, and work and all that, but you should visit your friends more often and save me from boredom!'

'You're not saying you lack company.'

'Company! They're all children to me now. I can't abide this deferring and polite attention they all go in for. Do you know, someone introduced me at a dinner, some blasted young crawler, as 'the Venerable Minister Awdry'. I ask you! Makes me sound like an old monk, ancient and not much use. Oh they reckon I'm good for a joke or a story or two, but I've no pretentions: my tales are small beer. What we need is somethin' a bit more vital.'

'Well I shall be here for some weeks I expect, though there won't be much time for tall-tales. Where have you been yourself? I missed you yesterday.'

'Well there's a thing. It seems I was off up to Slaney when you and Dr. Tubby had that to-do, but for the life of me I can't remember why. The earth trembled so I stopped the coach and looked out the window. Were those lights in the sky really made by you? Amazin'. When I saw 'em, I decided to come back, and I'm glad I did. What's it all about Seama?'

'Yes, My Lord Seama, what is this chaos and destruction *all about?*' Tys Heald had been standing to one side as Awdry monopolized the wizard, and Seama had seen his face wrinkle with distaste as the old man bantered on. His words were imperiously delivered; the polite 'My Lord' a matter of form. Seama and the Minister for Industry both looked him up and down and exchanged a comical glance. The man was thin, too thin for his round, chubby face but the pomposity in the set of his chin and the nose in the air demanded ridicule.

'Ahem,' Seama coughed to avoid grinning. 'Well, that's what the meeting's about, Chancellor. So, if you will excuse me, I'll just welcome the others and then we can begin.'

Next to arrive were Seama's companions of battle. Angren and Terrance were arguing while Bibron, Sigrid and Lord Gumb walked a few paces behind, unwilling to get drawn into the dispute. As soon as they saw Seama the two quarrelers shut up.

'Angren, Terrance,' Seama nodded to each, his eyebrows raised. Neither wanted to look him in the eye but they both said hello as shortly as possible. 'Something wrong, Terrance?'

Terrance clenched his jaw so that the muscles stood out. 'It can wait till later, Seama,' he said at last.

'Very well,' the wizard assented and then gave his attention to the group as a whole. 'I hope you slept well, friends, because we've a lot to do and not much time to do it. I'm sorry if I seem a bit brief and cool to you all: bit of a formal do this one, but we'll get together after. Oh, but where's Berta?'

'She's decided to stay away.' Bibron told him.

'Why?'

'I don't know. Something about her being a fighter not a talker. Don't think she's the sort for long explanations but you'll have to ask her about it.'

'I will. Now shall we get on?'

Lord Gumb nodded and led the group to the long table now placed below the dais. Angren lingered until they were out of hearing and then said, 'While we're on the 'where isses', where's Garaid?'

'He may be along later.'

'I noticed he had the privilege of your company last night.'

'A half-hour or so, yes. I had my reasons, Angren.'

'Which were? Come on Seama. I'm not going to spread it around am I. Don't you trust me?' Angren was obviously upset at Seama's lack of openness, and the wizard felt guilty for neglecting him.

'I'm sorry, Angren. Of course I trust you, but this business has put me on edge. I've had no time to stop and think about what happened here but… well, there were things I don't understand at all. I've changed. I don't think I'm the same person I was three weeks ago. As strong as that – but now's not the time. It'd be good to talk – if we could? Really it would.'

Angren's voice was thick as he said, 'You only have to ask. Anything. You know that.'

'I do. And I rely on it, Angren. Anyway, about Garaid now. Have you noticed anything different about him?'

'I haven't really known him long enough to say he's acting differently. It's not even two weeks since I first met him. But he is acting a bit odd. Tried to talk to him this morning, but he was twitchy as a bag of cats. What do you suppose it is?'

'I don't know, but I think it must be the strain. We've had a hard time and that ruckus in Slaney seemed to upset him.'

'Upset us all, Seama.'

'Surely. Anyway, I thought he'd be better if I gave him some work. He's quite the communications expert, you know. I've got him recruiting for a link to Ayer.'

'Is he up to it?'

'If he isn't someone else will be. At least it keeps him away from the Council for a while. I don't want him thinking about Zaras.'

'Probably a good idea. Look out: who're these two? The short one looks a real charmer.'

Seama gave Angren a look that said 'Be quiet, he might hear you', stepped towards the newcomers and extended a business-like hand.

'General Alling; Admiral Alveson. I'm pleased you've come.'

General Alling, 'the short one', dispensed with Seama's hand as soon as he touched it and said coldly, 'I didn't see how I could avoid it. You carry the baton.' His face was as cold as his words and the neatly trimmed moustache barely moved as he spoke. Seama had never liked him and the General apparently liked no one.

Admiral Jom Alveson was no cold fish though, his handshake was warm and his manner even. 'I was happy to receive your invitation, My Lord, but would have come along anyway. It was quite a show you put on for us the other day.'

'Yes, a show,' interrupted the General, 'that has cost Gothery dear. You will no doubt have your reasons. So, let's get it started.'

'If you could find your seats, gentlemen, I'd be grateful, but we can't begin just yet: one more to come.'

Alling scowled but made his way to the table. Seama was glad Alling wasn't last to arrive: the man already had an inflated sense of his own importance.

The last to arrive came along a few minutes later. He was a thick-set, dark featured man, sporting a huge black moustache. He gave the wizard a curt nod but said nothing. Seama smiled broadly in return. This arrival would save them a lot of valuable time.

'Welcome. Now we are complete.'

As Seama and the stranger took their seats at the head and tail of the table respectively, he saw Angren look at Gumb and raise his eyebrows. Gumb looked flabbergasted. They recognized the man easily enough but had no idea why he was there, or how.

Scribes, discreetly positioned at desks set-back from the table, rustled their papers and inked their pens and the council was set to begin.

CURRENT AFFAIRS

Astoril 3057.8.8

Angren settled back in his chair. It was going to be a hard morning, he might as well get comfortable. Though his was the easy part: listener not speaker. The heavy duty lay with Seama. And he certainly had some talking to do if he wanted these people to follow him – only two days ago he'd made half the Astorians homeless.

When he had silence the wizard began.

'Ladies and gentlemen, what I have to say will take time and may stretch your belief, but you must hear me out. A terrible threat hangs over our heads, a threat more dangerous than anything you have known or could have known. We here are charged with answering that threat.'

'A rather enigmatic beginning, Seama.'

'Yes Fel, but if you give me space I will explain. The matter is complex and you'll all need to do a lot of listening before it comes clear. There'll be a time for questions after I am done. Now, I have pondered how best to begin the tale—'

'Forgive me, Lord Seama,' it was Gurdy Younger, 'before we have your speech couldn't we begin with introductions? I'd be happier if I knew my peers.'

'No please forgive *me*, Minister. It's becoming a fault of mine to presume that everyone of my acquaintance knows every other. I must be getting old.'

Angren snorted loudly at that. Running both hands through his thinning blond hair he leant back extravagantly, ending with his fingers linked behind his neck. 'Old are you?' he said, 'Well if it's a drug you're using, can I have some?' Fel Awdry was the only one who smiled. Seama gave Angren a sharp look and shook his head slightly. Angren shrugged. He didn't think it such a bad idea to remind the councillors they were in the presence of someone remarkable. The wizard obviously didn't agree.

Seama began the introductions.

'On the left of the table: Tys Heald, Chancellor to King Sirl II; Fel Awdry, Minister for Industry and King's Counsellor; Lord Harald Gumb, Baron of Rippon; Terrance De Vere, Freeman of Pars; Senior Captain Bibron Farber of the Partain Fleet; Angren Nielderson, Marquess of Hallingdale and heir apparent to the Dukedom of Terremark.

'On my right are Gurdy Younger, Minister for Defence, King's Counsellor; General Mart Alling, His Majesty's Commander of Land Forces; Keth Hardie, Prime Minister of the State of Gothery, Doctor of Philosophy and King's Counsellor; Admiral Jom Alveson, His Majesty's Commander of the Navy; and Lady Sigrid Althoné, third heir presumptive to the Royal Partain House Althoné.

'Sitting opposite me is Duke Enric Valdez, Liege Commander of Agwis III.'

There was a brief pause before anyone could think of something to say that would not reveal their astonishment. For most the appearance of the Duke Valdez was the biggest surprise; for Bibron it was Angren's pedigree, but for Angren himself the revelation that Sigrid was a Partian noble was unexpected. He realised that she was looking at him looking at her and was suddenly embarrassed, as though she'd caught him with his flies undone.

'Is everyone satisfied? I thank Mistress Younger for drawing my attention to such an important factor of this meeting. There are here invited representatives of the three countries of Gothery, Pars and Aegarde. I am only sorry that at present we include no Masacheans. No, don't be surprised at that. No matter what you may presently believe to be the case, we are all under attack and share a common enemy.

'Already battles have been fought, lives have been lost; we have witnessed destruction and cruelty and pain; but these are merely the opening forays in what will be a long and considered campaign. In recent weeks my companions and I have cut a path through the heart of this continent and everywhere we found peril and mystery and wicked intent. Most of you have had the tale of our adventure in one way or another so I'll not cover the ground again. Mador's problems at Ayer, the affair on Tumboll, our encounter with the spy in Slaney, the Battle of Moreda and the dispute in Astoril were all critical moments for those involved but these events were only symptoms of a greater malaise. Today I want to explain to you the nature of the disease we face. Yes, General Alling?'

Angren had noticed that Alling seemed distracted as though something was preying on his mind. Now he'd half risen from his chair as if to make some pronouncement. All eyes were upon him and the wizard's were steely with disapproval as though he knew what the General would say. Alling at first bridled at that look but then thought the better of it. 'I suppose it can wait until you are done,' he said frostily, 'but mark my word, I *will* have my say.'

Faces around the table displayed astonishment at the General's lack of good grace but the wizard was unmoved.

'I look forward to your comments but, for now, perhaps I can continue? Good. As I was saying, we are all under attack but it is Pars that currently bears the brunt. King Mador is beleaguered. In the East, five months gone, Masachea made a massive and unprecedented attack upon Mador's border garrison at Aristeth. I offer condolence to Lady Althoné: her family and house were decimated by that attack. Mador's reply was as swift and potent as could be and now his armies police the Masachean border. But it is no easy job. The Masacheans continue to press against them as though driven to it and there seems little chance of respite.

'In the North, six or seven weeks back, rumours were voiced talking of brigands or a rogue army destroying towns and villages. Mador sent the army of the Royal House of Sands to investigate. Their commander, Lord Jaspar, made several uncomfortable reports. He found no brigands and no army but only a land emptied of people. The garrison of Castle Greteth in the Francon Valley was deserted. Jaspar has made the castle his base but how he's doing there we don't know. His last report was received in Ayer on the twenty-fourth of July, almost a month ago. Anparas and Temor have been sent north to face whatever there is to face and to rescue Sands.

'And then there is the West. It was back in March that Athoff first moved to usurp the authority of his father. He was clever. I don't know what poison was used to make his father seem confused and incapable, but it took very little persuasion to convince the senate that Agwis was unfit to hold office. At present the King is held under house arrest and Athoff is free to do whatsoever he likes. Apparently what he likes is to cause trouble. He is raising an army, and it's heading this way.

'Mador takes this as a direct threat to Pars. He argues that Athoff's plan cannot end with the annexation of Gothery. He may be right: Athoff is ambitious. Possibly he sees himself as some Asteranorean Emperor: a potentate set to rival the Emp Radis on Sullinor. Whatever Athoff's intention, for the defence of Pars, Mador knew that he must do something and do it quickly. If I hadn't spoken to him, Anparas and Temor would have crossed the River and marched on the capital. They would have placed Astoril under martial law.'

'Utter rot!' Gothery's ministers were all shocked at the thought of a Partian invasion but Alling was furious. 'I bow not to invaders, east or west. Four thousand to take Gothery? Not while I stand. Do you think my forces tame?'

'Well there is the point General: I think them *tamed*.'

'Then you're a fool.'

'Am I? Think about it. How is the State of Gothery? Mador was very sure the force he sent would be sufficient to the task. His spies tell him that nothing in Gothery is as it should be. Do you disagree? Any of you? Fel?'

Awdrey nodded vigorously. 'We all know it, Seama. My end of things is terrible. The manufactories all seem in trouble at once: managers gone missing, machines breaking down, all sorts of bother with payments going astray, materials not coming through. It's a mess. Come on Mart, it's the same with the army. You were only saying the other day that you hadn't a single captain you could trust to be in the right place at the right time. And Gurdy, what about all that trouble with the defence budget? Soldiers not getting their pay, no money for upkeep, be it property or weapons. And what about that damn stupidity when the launderers refused to clean the Royals' uniforms unless they got cash in hand? What a sight eh, the King's Elite washing their own smalls! Where's the dignity in that? Seama's right, my friends, and we know it. It's all gone to pot.'

Fel Awdrey's colleagues looked as though they were sucking lemons, even Mart Alling, but the old man hadn't finished.

'And I'm surprised we haven't had more trouble. Have you read the papers lately? Have you seen the cartoons? Headless chickens, that's what they call us. People on the street think we're a joke and some are saying it's about time something was done about it. Two small armies take Gothery? I tell you, a party of pensioners could do the job!'

There was some nodding of heads but not everyone agreed with him. 'Theatrical as ever, Fel,' said the Chancellor, 'but off the mark as usual. I am completely on top of what the papers are saying. Let me assure you of that.'

'Theatrical am I? Well I'm not sure whether I'm in a farce or a tragedy but it's easy to see the villain of the piece. I've heard you had Gombret's son arrested—'

'Enough!' The Marquess of Hollingdale nearly toppled over in his chair. Seama's voice had a paralysing quality to it. *Shame*, Angren thought, *I was beginning to enjoy that.*

'I didn't ask you here to argue the toss about the Chancellor's methods – though I am sure words might be said at some point in the near future. For now, Fel, we have issues more pressing.'

Awdrey bowed slightly and gave Seama a quick grin. Chancellor-baiting was obviously one of his favourite pastimes. Angren thought he could get to like the old boy. The wizard continued.

'The Chancellor, whatever his actions, really is not the villain of this piece. You all know where that title lies but at this point you don't know why.' He looked from one face to another and then settled his gaze upon the Prime Minister.

Keth Hardie nodded. He seemed embarrassed.

'Yes. Yes, we all know who. Everyday we sat in conference debating what we should do about him, and everyday we did nothing. How could we have been so weak?'

The question brought out sighs of agreement from his colleagues. Angren wasn't impressed: the Gotherians had such an air of defeat about them, slumped in their chairs or leaning on the table, heads in hands. Even the arrogant Chancellor seemed at a loss. Where was the fight? Where was the pride? This pathetic bunch was supposed to be running the country and all they could do was mope. Angren pulled a face in disgust and Seama noticed.

'No Angren, you don't understand; you shouldn't blame them. These are good, strong people in the normal way of things, but this time they faced an adversary completely beyond them. He was very nearly too strong even for me.'

Angren didn't believe that for a minute and thought the wizard was just trying to make the Gotherians feel better. Not too bad an idea, he supposed.

'So,' he said, 'Tell us about this Dr Bliss then. Sounds like he's in the thick of it.'

'He *is* the thick of it. Tarangananda uh-Bib, that's his real name, Dr. Bliss only here in Astoril. A part of his name actually translates as *bliss*; why he should want to be so obvious I don't know. He arrived in Gothery at just about the same time the Masacheans attacked Aristeth. Within a month he'd manoeuvered himself into a position in the King's household. It was easy for him to manipulate the situation here because he's not really a Doctor. He is, as you now understand, an extremely powerful wizard. He used magic to confuse you all – even now when you think of him you become compliant because the magic lingers. He used potions to control Sirl, he corrupted loyal servants to gain control of the Court, and he set saboteurs and spies to bring Gothery's industry to wrack and ruin. Dr Bliss is the greatest of villains.

'Much of his activity was designed with the purpose of softening you up. He wanted to make Gothery an easy target for that hot-head in Garassa. What Athoff needed then was an excuse to invade and a cause to help bring his forces together. You see, raising an army in Aegarde is a convoluted process.

Pars of course has professional armies all pledged to the crown; they obey orders, they fight whoever their King tells them to and they do it without question. In Aegarde there's a system of allegiance, certainly, but it's far from regular. Valdez can tell you that the four Dukedoms are each a law unto themselves; the Fat Thousands, the Hundred Kingdoms and the biggest part of Matagorda a hotch potch of local powers and private armies. None of these jump at the King's command. What they all need is something to get their gander up: a common threat, a wrong to right. And so Dr Bliss gave Athoff some help.

'The Black Company made its first appearance barely a month after the good doctor arrived in Gothery. I can tell you, beyond any doubt, that Uh Bib was their paymaster. Of course there is no independent evidence linking the Company with Athoff, nor even any physical proof that Athoff was in communication with the wizard—'

'On that I beg to differ.'

'Chancellor?'

'I never trusted Bliss. Keth may say we stood by and did nothing but he should speak for himself. It was plain to me that he had some hold over the King less wholesome than the office of Doctor would suggest. It was easy to understand the career he'd mapped out for himself but it wasn't in my mind to give him a free hand.'

'And yet, Tys, that is exactly what he had.'

Heald was rarely daunted by criticism.

'That may be true, Prime Minister, but at least I sought evidence against him. It fell to me to have him watched very closely—'

'Apparently not close enough,' Fel threw in with a grin, 'You don't normally require so much evidence before arrestin' people.'

'No easy task arresting Tarangananda uh Bib,' said Seama, 'I tried it myself and failed. Not exactly easy to have him watched either.'

'As I found,' agreed Heald, 'My agents never seemed able to keep up with him. We did however manage to identify his familiars and functionaries – not all, of course – and so we watched them instead. Even some members of the Royal Troop seemed all too ready to jump at his command. Captain Cardre was always at his door. Cardre is master of the King's despatches, a critical commission in the circumstances, and so I had a man in there. According to his report, every few days a party would leave before dawn on fast horses bound westerly. My man never got in on any of the missions but he did get to see the direction on one of the papers sent: it was addressed to Athoff Ringsøyr. Clear evidence of collusion, don't you think?'

Many around the table murmured agreement but Admiral Alveson piped up in protest.

'Well, it's not clear to me,' he said. The Admiral had a high pitched whine in his voice that Angren found irritating. 'At a time of dispute between nations, surely this is simply some official communication, a step in negotiation?' He looked to his friend Mart Alling for support but the general shook his head.

'Not official – I'd have known about it.'

'I agree,' said Gurdy Younger, 'the protocol is that we agree communiques in cabinet. You must know, Admiral, that we sanctioned nothing of the sort.'

'But still, without knowing what was written…'

'Does this matter, Admiral Alveson?' Seama was clearly annoyed that his argument was heading off on the wrong fork. 'The fact remains that a connection exists between Uh Bib and the Black Company and with Athoff. Otherwise none of this makes sense. The threat to your borders from Aegarde has been constructed by uh Bib. What I am trying to get you to understand is that your Dr Bliss has more than Gothery in his sights.

'I'm convinced that Uh Bib is the author of Mador's problems also. It's true that I can't place him in Masachea; nor could I swear it was his spell-making that threatened Ayer; and there is no evidence that he's connected with the Halfi on Tumboll. Yet still I'd wager anything that he's the prime mover in the East as in the West.'

'A busy man then. You have to admire his energy.'

'There is nothing I admire about the Randálan, Fel.'

'No,' Fel admitted, 'perhaps not.' He scratched at his beard. 'What I don't see, Seama, is why he's doing all this. No doubt it keeps him entertained but where's he going with it?'

Gurdy Younger was with him on that one. 'You called him the Randálan Are we to assume he's in the pay of the Emperor?'

'A worrying thought isn't it, that the Emp Radis is casting his gaze once more upon the green fields of Asteranor? But no. The Emperor has too many troubles at home. The city states on Oxitor have become a thorn in his side since he tried to annexe them; and the Scorpion Men in the south-east become ever more radical – some elements are threatening open rebellion. If you add to that a thousand miles of ocean to cross, the problem with the Corayan pirates and throw in, if you like, the Emperor's own personal discomforts, the chance of his attacking us seems increasingly remote. A different story in his youth of course. Thirty years ago he set his best agent to prepare the ground for an all-out invasion, and that agent very nearly succeeded.'

Fel Awdrey was quickest on the uptake. 'Thirty years ago?'

'Yes Fel.'

'Then it's all the more likely, aint it? Thirty years ago was when that fellow... damnation! I knew I'd heard the name before. Uh Bib, the Randálan, Dr Bliss. It's the same man. Same man, same task.'

'But a different paymaster.'

'You've lost me,' said Gurdy Younger, slightly exasperated, 'Are you saying that Bliss has tried this before?'

'Yes. His strategy then was not the same. He tried to take control of Errensea. As Taprod he could have created mayhem. Fortunately we managed to oust him before he could complete the spell.'

'He has great power, this wizard, if he could attempt to subdue the Council?'

'Yes, Mistress Younger – and more now than previously.'

'But you say he has a new paymaster. If Bliss is so powerful I cannot see him bowing to the odious Athoff.'

'It's not Athoff, Gurdy.'

'Not the Masacheans surely,' said the Chancellor, plainly

outraged at the thought, 'they can hardly walk in a straight line!'

'No, Tys, it is not the Masacheans. They are a part of this but they wouldn't have the capacity to drive it. Bliss is our designer, the drive comes from somewhere else entirely.'

Angren knew where all this was leading but around the table was a sea of confused faces. Seama needed to get on with it, he thought, or he'd lose them. Apparently the wizard had reached the same conclusion.

'Ladies and Gentlemen,' he said. "The time has come to complete the circle, to reveal the missing link in the chain. The answer lies here.'

Seama had reached into the leather satchel at his feet. He threw a bundle of manuscript pages onto the table before him.

'This is a copy of The Song of Ages. It is the answer to the mystery.'

Angren looked over at Alling and wasn't disappointed. The general rolled his eyes to the ceiling. 'Pieces of paper!' he said, 'And foul looking pieces at that. Where on Ea' are we going this time?'

Seama shrugged. 'Yes, it's a little discoloured and tattered. Luckily I managed to recover it from my saddle bags before the Cottle went down, but it got a soaking and I haven't Grek's ability with scrip: I spoiled some of the pages trying to dry it out, yellowed the rest. But never mind the condition, the text remains. Within these pages is a tale of the past and, more importantly, a warning for the future. These are the revelations of Haslem the Great and we'd do well to consider them.'

'Haslem the Great?'

'Yes Gurdy.'

The Minister's voice was edged with reverence. An essential study at the Collegium but elswhere Haslem's texts were relatively innaccessible. The common people of Gothery rarely had the honour of reading them.

'Oh, this goes from silly to stupid!'

'That, Mart Alling, is hardly respectful to one of the Founders,' said Fel Awdrey, his voice was mild in tone but there was a glitter in his eyes, 'and most certainly not respectful to the

Lord Seama.'

'Control of His Majesty's forces is my office. My remit does not extend to finding soft words for interloping conjurors!'

'You little pipsqueak! You'll apologize for that and now!'

Awdrey was out of his chair, the better to press his point, but Seama intervened.

'Forget it, Fel. His comment is fair. The fact is it's up to me to show that my argument is neither silly nor stupid. General, may I ask, *once again*, will you allow me to continue? Perhaps I'll be able to persuade you?'

Alling seemed taken-aback at being called a pipsqueak: it didn't tally with the very serious picture he had of himself. He looked around the table in search of allies but found none. Even his co-conspirator Jom Alveson avoided meeting his eyes.

'Continue if you must, but don't expect me to fall for all of this… claptrap.'

Seama shook his head in bewilderment. 'Thank you for your kind and gracious permission. If only I could remember where I was—'

'Haslem. Song of Ages.'

'Yes, yes. Thank you, Angren. Let me tell you all about the burning book.'

Seama didn't dwell upon his own discomforts when he gave them the tale. Plunging his arms into the liquid flames became 'we managed to get the book off the shelf and put out the fire'. The actions were not what mattered, he told them. What mattered was, in no particular order, that someone had tried to destroy the book, that somehow the book had summoned him, and that this was the second time it had done so. Fel Awdrey was curious about the earlier incident in the Collegium Library.

'It's all of a piece then: Uh Bib taking the Mayoris, and this Song of Ages calling out to you?'

'Yes Fel. Uh Bib first discovered The Song thirty years ago but at the time all he took from the library was the Mayoris. That is clear. What's not so clear is the how or the why The Song called out to me. My thought is that when Uh Bib woke the Mayoris—'

'Woke it?'

'Well yes. Because of the spells that surround the making of grimoires of this level of power it's almost as if such books actually have a life of their own; when they're not in use they close down, fall asleep if you will, and become active again only when they receive the correct stimulus. The reality is they are less like living creatures and more like machines reacting to the press of a button, the pulling of lever. I guess that when the Mayoris was woken, one of it's first tasks was to send out a seeker that would in turn awaken the Song. On one of these pages there's a passage where Haslem states that *The Song will bring itself to The Man of Power*. There were certainly other people upon Errensea at that time with great power but I was the only one summoned.'

'Except for this Uh Bib chap.'

'Well, I don't know about that, Fel. Certainly he *found* the book. Perhaps it was simply that he was nearby when it began to call or perhaps it was something to do with the fact that he'd been the one to wake the Mayoris. The books are undeniably linked. I suspect Haslem presumed that whoever held the Mayoris would likely be a member of the Council rather than an enemy or he wouldn't have bound one to the other. You see the Song contains information that should never be in the wrong hands. Unfortunately it looks like Uh Bib found himself another copy of The Song, and something in it led him towards a plan of action and, on top of that, it gave him the means to carry it out.'

'Well that's just peach!' said Angren, 'The only reason Bliss can do what he's doing is because Haslem told him how to do it? Fine bloody idea that! Better if he'd never written the book in the first place.'

'The irony hasn't escaped me, Angren, but I'm not going to stray down the path of 'If only…' The fact is we have a problem now and the Song may be the one clue we have that can help us solve it.

'This bundle of scruffy looking papers contains a secret: a secret beyond the imagining of most people alive today. We all look at the world from the perspective of our own time and everything that's in the past, even though we might know it to be true, is emotionally little more than a story to us. Nontheless we do have a sense of history and its importance, and throughout the generations we've worked hard to keep a record of all that has gone before. But each generation has a different view of that history. Tys Heald, you're an intelligent and well-educated man. Tell me, what is the oldest historical event we know?'

Heald actually smiled, unused to compliments of any sort.

'I… well it depends on what you mean. The first specific event was surely the Battle of Grammary Field. But obviously that event presupposes the existence of the Medes and the Parisi and acknowledges that there was a cause of dispute between them. And this dispute takes place in a landscape inhabited by a number of tribes that collectively we call The Wandering People. And this all depends on the viewpoint we share on this continent of Asteranor. The people of Sullinor would certainly point to some event that was local to them: a coronation perhaps, the birth of a prophet – they have quite a number of those – or maybe even some natural disaster. And each of these must undoubtedly mark an end to something just as much as it might mark a beginning.'

Seama was pleased by the reply.

'You warm to my theme, Chancellor. But let me pick up on that 'natural disaster' idea. There are stories in some ancient texts that describe a terrible, cataclysmic event that occurred during the early years of The Wandering. You won't know about this. It's the considered opinion of our scholars that this 'cataclysmic event' is merely some garbled memory of a less impressive, local disaster; of no more significance say than the 3051 Pulonian earthquake.'

'Fairly significant for the people caught up in it, Seama.'

'Yes Angren, I know. People died—'

'And some good friends of mine too!'

'Yes, of course. But let's not get sidetracked. I'm talking about something that was much more ah… momentous… and… Look this isn't helping. You must keep up.'

'I think,' put in Jom Alveson, 'the Lord Wizard is trying

to explain that small people always make more of events than they deserve. A flood that destroys a few villages becomes an inundation that destroys all life as we know it. Primitive people had not and have not the enlightened perspective of modern times.'

'No Admiral,' said Seama, 'I am not trying to say that at all. Other people might but I believe them to be wrong. *That* is what I am trying to say. The problem with the perspective of the present is that too often we look at the past and presume that earlier generations were primitive, innocent or ignorant, and yet in a thousand years from now people may look at our own civilisation and shake their heads in wonder at our stupidity. An *enlightened* viewpoint should recognize that human intelligence and endeavour are eternal traits and that the advances and views of each generation are of equal standing and importance.

'And so, what I am trying to say in my roundabout way is that we would be foolish to dismiss out of hand the knowledge of generations past. What I am trying to tell you is that the perspective of our age is blinkered. We have a picture of history that goes only so far and anything that may have come before that history is left to the priests and their Gods. With the help of the Song I have taken off the blinkers: the cataclysm I mentioned was a real event and beyond that cataclysm lies the deep past of gods and men and this earth beneath our feet. The Song of Ages reveals the hidden history of our world.'

He cast his eyes around the table expecting some comment, some sign of impatience or exasperation but none was forthcoming. He had their full attention at last.

THE AGES OF THE EARTH

Astoril 3057.8.8

'There have been six ages of our world and everything we know, our lives, our history and even our geography belong only to the last of those. That is a remarkable thought. Our written history takes us back four thousand or more years, our understanding of the unrecorded time before that is vague. But you must understand that I say 'unrecorded' because I speak only of Medean History. As Tys mentioned these things depend upon perspective. It's perhaps not widely known that long before the first words were written of the history we count our own, there was a civilisation of men upon Asteranor that, Gothery apart, would rival any of the nations of our present day. They made their cities on the peninsula we call the Captofinxus, the finger of Masachean land that points towards the eastern oceans. Their history was certainly recorded, and in many ways, but most of what they were and what they did and thought and said has been lost. It is such a waste of time away, we guess at eight thousand years, and so the more fragile methods of keeping record haven't survived. But there are tablets of hard stone kept in the vaults of the faculty house on Errensea, recovered from the ancient remains of those cities, and they're covered in characters and figures that dance with intelligence and knowledge. Undeniably they represent a script of some sort but it's beyond our understanding.'

'What happened to them? If they were so clever?'

'Being a match to the nations of today, Angren, does not necessarily make them 'so clever.' But actually we know little enough about them or what happened to stop them in their tracks, or even if they really were stopped in their tracks. History is full of accidents and catastrophes. How many civilisations have come and gone? How many do we remember, how many are lost to us? Though I may easily tell you that this Sunrise Civilisation is the oldest known, that's not the same as saying it was the first. Wherever we stop there was a before.

'But we want our history to be finite: to have a beginning, a middle and an end, just like the most comforting stories. We want to be able to comprehend the whole structure. The scholars of our day believe that all of human history can be compassed by eight and a half thousand years. Beyond that they seem content to say nothing.

'Well I can tell you, friends, that it is not so. The world is not eight thousand years old. Those wastes of time I mentioned stretch on and on unimaginably. They go back so far that there is no sense in even trying to make a count of years. They go back past thousands of beginnings and middles and ends, the civilisations of man are legion, each rising through the ruins of what has gone before and each ultimately doomed to fall in their turn. Nothing we men have made can be held onto; nothing remains what it was. What stands today fair and proud will one day lie beneath the sands leaving only fragments to make passing strangers pause and wonder. And yet there is so much; and always we continue. The full tale of life is truly awesome. What is *frightening*, ladies and gentlemen, is that this deep past, this great weight and burden of year on year on year now bears down upon our present lives and lays siege to our very existence.

'The Song of Ages is a complete history of Earnor. Or at least it would be if I had the entire text to hand. Unfortunately I have here only the introduction and parts of the main text that describe the first two Ages of the world. The Introduction is brief, and actually that may help: often too much detail clouds the truth. Haslem gives us what he believes to be the important issues of each Age and after that a conclusion. But the approach is thematic: he follows one train of thought at a time; he pays scant attention to any idea of chronology. It has taken me all of these weeks since the fire in the library to get even the order of the ages clear in my mind.

'There was a creation: an Age of Creation. We're used to regarding such talk as conjecture at best or at worst plain fantasy. We may choose to take the story as a metaphor of a more prosaic truth, or an attempt to make simple a reality unimaginably complicated, but it is important to realize that in the Song of

Ages the history of even this first age is given as though it were fact. Zurvan is the great creator god. His name actually means Time. For reasons not stated he decides to create The Earth – yes that's the name given, as if the soil beneath our feet is all it is – and he makes the growing things and the animals of Earth and the weather of the world so that the key to his creation, mankind itself, can find food and shelter. But also he makes the world a dangerous place. From him come all the convulsions of the earth, the winds, the tides, the floodwaters, the lightning. The idea is that man will learn to deal with these things and so become stronger and more wise. At the same time Zurvan creates also *the gods of Earth*, the nature gods as we would say, and their role is in part to govern the forces of nature and in part to help mankind through its earliest years.

'You'd have thought all that enough for any decent sort of creation, but Zurvan knew that one thing more was needed. For some reason we cannot know, it was not to Zurvan's purpose that he should impose himself upon the Earth. Having created he wished to remain beyond his creation. Like the man with an ant colony he has set in glass, he chooses to withdraw his influence and merely observe the dramas that unfold before him. And yet Zurvan could see that the progress of his creation would need governance, mankind would need a father to look up to, would need a source of just authority to give order to life on Earth. With such a need plain to see, Zurvan got himself a son.

'Here we come to the great problem of the Age of Creation. Instead of one son Zurvan actually got himself twins. One of the twins turned out to be entirely good and we know him even in our own age as Ohr'mazd, God of the Just. The other is also worshipped today, though most likely you won't recognise the name. Ah'remmon he was then and now but he has had other names throughout the ages. He is in fact the source for the great God of Masachea presently known as the Rightful King or Father of Mankind. A worrying description if what Haslem says is correct. You see Ah'remmon is the exact opposite of his brother and he is entirely evil.

'Yes, I see that some of you, *Angren*, are finding this all a little too fanciful—

'Not so much that it's *fanciful*, Seama: it's just that it's like a bloody history lesson.'

Seama's reply was frosty. 'I make no apology: if you want the knowledge you suffer the lecture. If you don't there must be something else you could be doing outside? I believe they're still looking for extra labourers?'

'Ah. Well, if you put it that way, I guess I'll sit it through.'

'I'll get on then, shall I?'

'Fire away.'

'The second age of the world is called The Age of the Oath. At the time of the birth of his sons, before he understood anything about them, Zurvan made an oath that whichever came first then he should have rule of the Earth for 9000 years. Ah'remmon, lusting after power, as was always likely, ripped himself from the womb, before he was due, to make sure that the Kingdom of the Earth would be his. And so the second age is the time of Ah'remmon's dominion. This was a terrible time. Imagine all the foul and cruel rulers there have ever been all rolled into one. Mankind had no choice but to accept his Kingship, and such is human nature that while most of mankind abhorred Ah'remmon's rule, there were always some who were more than happy to bow to him. One of the more confusing passages in the introduction is to do with *The Gift of Ah'remmon*. It's an idea that affects all of the Ages of the Earth and seems all bound up with *The Gift of the Father*, with an *Act of Communion*, with *Life Eternal* and *The Bounty of Death* – Haslem's a little over fond of these phrases. The way I read it the gift is a tithe of the God's own blood – very gory – and given in *The Age of the Oath* as a reward to the followers of Ah'remmon; and it was most certainly given contrary to his Father's design. You see, Ah'remmon was not content merely to rule: his desire was to challenge and supplant his Father. In all things he considered himself his father's equal and in that mind he took up the role of creator. He made for himself all manner of demons and monsters, all filled with his own insatiable urge to subvert or destroy the work of Zurvan; and he set them free upon the Earth, and mankind, the pinnacle of his Father's creation, could do nothing against them.

'In his pride, Ah'remmon presumed that his rule would have no ending, but he was wrong. Zurvan wasn't weakened at all by anything Ah'remmon had done and his will could not be set aside. The nine thousand years he had promised were soon done and a new age of the Earth was begun. This was supposed to be the *Age of Long Dominion* when good Ohr'mazd would take the crown and rule the earth, according to the Father's purpose, until the ending. Instead Haslem names this time *The Age of Chaos*.

'The third Age was in some ways better and in some ways worse than the long years of Ah'remmon's rule. It was better because Ohr'mazd could at last order the world to the defence of mankind. It was worse because Ah'remmon was unceasing in his attack upon his brother and his brother's people. Even for Haslem not everything is clear about this age. It's undeniable that a portion of mankind kept Ah'remmon as their God despite the goodness of Ohr'mazd. Chief among these were his acolytes: those who had *taken the god's blood*. There is a suggestion that because of this the Bright God commanded a flood to wash away all the filth of Ah'remmon and in this flood a great part of mankind was lost. But this may be a corruption of the real story: a lie put about by the servants of the Dark God himself.

'The significant advance made in the Age of Chaos was in the joining together of Ohr'mazd with the Kings of Men, and with those gods of the Earth as yet un-swayed by Ah'remmon. It was only in this alliance that enough strength and will and power of magic could be raised for a decisive victory. The demons and monsters of Ah'remmon were already hugely reduced by the great flood and now, assailed by new generations of men, in company with the Gods of the Earth, they had little strength to resist. Many of Ah'remmon's creatures were killed outright but then, with a great act of will, Ohr'mazd managed to end their threat entirely: he cast out the survivors from this existence to *another place* and they had no power to return. The demons of

Ah'remmon should never have been a part of this world and it is a great shame upon mankind that some among us have since sought to bring them back.

'From the beginning, whatever he believed to be the truth of the matter, Ah'remmon was the weaker of the twins. Now, without the protection of his creatures, the Foul God was defenceless in the face of the wrath of Ohr'mazd. Ah'remmon accepted his banishment from the world but said at his leaving, and this is a direct quote from the Song, *I will live on the edges of this World you call now your own, for the peoples of the Earth still hold me in their hearts as Lord. I would not have them call upon me and I could not hear. And my people will do my work even though I dwell beyond and they cannot see me, for so I have taught them. And for every man of yours there will be three of mine. And how will you know, Brother, which is yours and which is not? You name me the Father of Lies but man is an apt pupil and his thoughts are his own according to your law and by our Father's design.'*

'And that was that: the end of the *Age of Chaos*. Ah'remmon was gone from the Earth, his demons just a bad memory, and at last Mankind was free to act and do according to his own designs without fear of divine retribution. The glorious *Age of Man* was begun.'

'I say 'glorious' only because that's the description given in the Song but I do wonder if the word is being used ironically. It's an incomprehensible age in many ways, partly because the history is so complex, partly because the development of mankind seems to far outstrip anything we have managed since. It's frightening to think of all we have once discovered but have now lost.

'This Age of Man as a passage of time seems to have been as long as the history we claim for ourselves: eight thousand years; and yet, whatever the great achievements and mighty dramas and extraordinary characters of all those many generations of mankind's growth, Haslem's attention is fixed upon the final two centuries of the Age.

'We don't share the words to explain or understand his description of those years. It's a time of, of...' Seama pulled out a page from the pile, 'of *global information systems*, of *mass media*, *solid state*, of *genetiks* and *byoinformatiks*, and all of these things together somehow give mankind incredible powers; knowledge of… *cloning* and *stemcells* that can bring an end to all the illness, frailty and decay we'd come to expect from life. There's probably no point in dwelling upon the meaning of these words and phrases – we could never understand them; the significance of what was achieved is all that matters.

'As Haslem has written it, this new understanding of what life is, and can be, these new powers mankind had gained through his own labour and intelligence, this ability and desire to deny what might have been thought of as the very laws of creation: all of this was *abhorrent* in the eyes of The Creator. Zurvan was outraged. None of this was part of Time's Purpose. Mankind had gone too far. Yes, Fel?'

'If I understand you rightly, you're saying that mankind had learned how to make new life and figured out how to put off death. Well that all sounds fair enough to me. I mean we've been having babies a good long while now and how many of us here wouldn't want to live a little longer. That's why we have doctors ain't it?'

'I suppose it is, and I don't entirely disagree with you, but you must understand that I'm trying to shorten the argument. There were other words and ideas all bound up with the reason for Zurvan's anger: *consumerism*, *packaging*, *marketing*, all seemingly to do with *world trade*.'

'So they were *selling* medicines. What's the problem with that?'

'Perhaps I haven't made this strong enough: it wasn't just medicine to help people live a little longer. I think that at the end of the 4th Age there was the very real chance that man might learn how to live *forever* and that most of mankind was eager to lay down money on the outcome.'

Seama looked around the table, expecting a reaction but most everyone was looking up at him, waiting for him to say more. Seama wasn't sure he wanted to. The whole idea of living forever made him feel uncomfortable, as though it was a crime for him to address, something so wrong that it was his duty to prevent it. And yet he himself could hold onto life far beyond the span of normal men. Was it guilt he felt? He noticed that Sigrid was staring fiercely at her own clenched fists.

'Do you have something to say, Sigrid?' he asked, 'What do you think about the idea of life eternal?'

She looked up with a face like thunder. 'What do I think?' she said, 'I think that nothing ever changes. So damned clever these people, so caught up in what they can do instead of what they should do. What's the point in cheating death if you don't understand the real importance of life? This world is so full of people dealing out horror and misery, all for the sake of their own amusement. Everywhere you look people are irredeemably self-centred, and some of them unutterably cruel, and the only respite we have from these evil men and women is that either they die or we die. The thought of these people living forever makes me feel sick.

'And what will happen, anyway, if no one ever dies? What will happen to normal people? Will they still want children or will they be so happy with themselves they won't be willing to bring new life into the world? Nothing but selfishness, that's what it is. But perhaps some women won't be able to stop having children – that's what we're here for isn't it? Perhaps the world will become so full there'll be no space left to live in; and not anything like enough food or water to go round. What do you think the *eternals* will do then? Put up with it? Or put a stop to it? There you are: selfish! That's half of mankind for you in a single damnable word. And you think we should live forever? Do you? For me, give me one good day of true happiness, of peace, of love. And that will be enough. That's what I think.'

She stood abruptly and walked away from the table. There was not really anywhere to go to be out of sight except to leave through the doors of the chamber and so she walked over to where some jugs of water had been placed on a trestle and poured herself a drink.

Seama almost regretted asking her to speak but only because he would have spared her the pain of it. The Gotherians present didn't know Sigrid. They seemed embarrassed or even resentful at the outburst. There was silence until she regained her seat.

'Ladies and gentlemen, I am sure you'll think kindly of Lady Althoné. She has seen more pain and terror and loss in recent months than you can imagine. And what's more she is right. The thought that men or women could concern themselves with the prospect of eternal life when all around are poor, oppressed people, desperate only for a few hours of comfort and escape from suffering, seems to me obscene. I don't know how it was in this last century of the Age of Man. It may be they had achieved a reality of just, peaceful and productive lives for every man, woman and child on the Earth. Maybe they had banished disease and famine, war and cruelty. Perhaps this search for eternal life was the logical next step for them.

'But I think it was this endeavour that put mankind beyond the favour of God and was the root of what was to follow. The next and fifth Age of this Earth is named The Intercession.

'The Intercession was an Age more like the Age of Creation than the others: it is difficult to say how long it lasted, it seems there are no records of the deeds of mankind. And so again we have a passage you might take as metaphor if it weren't for Haslem's insistence that it is all true. If it is true then it is truly terrifying.

'In his fury over the *Apostasy of Mankind* Zurvan literally rips the Earth apart. It seems an improper description but Haslem suggests that Zurvan is like a child in a rage destroying the castle he has built on the shore because it isn't the perfect thing he had imagined. We spoke earlier of a cataclysm remembered by our ancestors: that was an appalling event but it was insignificant in comparison to this. Here the fabric of the Earth was mangled, great rents were made in the bed of the oceans, torrents of molten rock ran free, the air was filled with poison. Mankind and the Earth were finished, an end had come to the Creation. That was supposed to be that.'

'And yet still here we are.'

'Yes Keth, we are still here. Our saviour was Ohr'mazd,

the Bright God, Zurvan's better son.' Seama flipped through the pile of pages before him until he found the right reference. 'You'll forgive me if I keep to Haslem's styling of the story – this is how he describes it:

'From the moment Zurvan raised his hand Ohr'mazd stood before the Father to hinder his intent. He took many blows that might have destroyed all that is and yet stood firm. And many blows passed him and smote the Earth and still Ohr'mazd would not yield. 'Do you have no memory of mercy?' he cried, 'Do you have no memory of love for your children?' but the Father closed his ears. Ohr'mazd fell to his knees and destruction rained down upon the Earth. The brightness of Ohr'mazd was in that moment dimmed. 'Do these tears for my people mean nothing to you?' he begged. The Father refused to look upon his son and continued with his task. But then Ohr'mazd reached down into the ruins before him and took up in his hand that which was most precious to him, and he held it safe from the fury all around. But the Father saw this and said: 'What is that thing you seek to withhold from my justice?' and Mazda said, 'I withhold nothing from your justice only from your temper.' 'Whether it is justice or temper,' said the Father, 'It is not for you to withhold from me anything that is mine.' Ohr'mazd now stood proud to face the Father. 'There is nothing that is not yours and yet there is much that is precious to me though I seek to own it not. And here is a thing that is most precious.' And Mazda held forth that which lay in his palm and said to the Father 'Is it not precious to you also?' And in that palm, warmed and calmed by the heat of the God lay an infant of no more than five hours. 'Here, Father, is what you made in the beginning; here is the greatest part of your creation: it is potential, it is hope, it is future, it knows not of evil. This surely is the key to all you have made. Will you not look upon this child and see in her the beauty of your thought?'

Seama paused, he was quivering from the intensity of his recitation, but it was the image that filled his mind of Bassalo's miracle child, struggling to stay alive in the ruins of the schoolhouse that brought the sudden tears to his eyes. He looked over at Sigrid. Her head was bowed, her hands covered her face. He wouldn't let it stop him. He took a good breath and continued.

'*Zurvan was stilled then but not chastened. 'I see the beauty of my Creation but did all the infants of man come to my hands I might find in one hand a potential for goodness and humility and in the other a promise of arrogance and evil. Why then should I save the beauty of my Creation if it will become corrupt?'*

Seama turned more pages of the text before him, it made him feel more business-like, less emotional. 'The answer seems obvious to Ohr'mazd, but Haslem takes another two pages to get through to it. Yes here we are: the Bright God comes up with a plan. He knows the pain that will be caused among mankind by it, and yet for that one chance of survival for at least that one child he holds safe, Ohr'mazd knows what he must do.

'*And what if, Father,*' he says, '*you found that in the one hand was the goodness of which you speak and you made for it a place of sanctuary on what remains of this Earth, but, as with that other Son of your making, for that which is in the other hand, and is less pleasing to your sight, might there not be found another place?*'

'Again Haslem gives us a great deal more dialogue than you will need but the upshot of all this is something I consider to be a truly infernal decision, *the* infernal decision. Zurvan says:

'*If this your plan will succeed then all that remains of mankind on this Earth will know a debt to your Goodness; if it comes to failure then all will come to ruin, and you and I and your brother too will know it. If this is your judgement and your intent then I will ordain one more Age for this Earth when there might have been nothing. It will be The Age of Last Hope for, know you now: it is my intent that there will be an ending. Is this your wish?*'

'*Ohr'mazd then gave assent, knowing that he must, and yet bowed his head in shame. Zurvan, the Father, released his grip upon the world.*'

'This is the moment and the act that made our world and made our chance of life, and it gave us too the constant threat that hangs over our heads. *The Age of Last Hope* was dependent upon *The Choosing*.

'Firstly Zurvan recovers nearly a half of our world from the forces of destruction he has unleashed, and brings it back to the state of the first creation. He separates this from Vastos, the great sea that encompasses the rest of the globe that is the Earth. The men that survive the trauma of the Intercession name their new home Earnor for in it is saved all that was the best of the old Earth. There is no comment in the Song to indicate how long this work might have taken. Clearly the Age of Intercession must span many thousands of years and what happened to mankind throughout this time is simply unknowable. It is my thought that maybe all of mankind was put in a place beyond time until all was ready. But when the land became settled and calm and mankind had been restored to Earnor, then Zurvan demanded the price he had been promised. Zurvan had not made this world for the benefit of that part of mankind he considered evil, the part of mankind that had taken Ah'remmon as their Lord, that part of mankind who had taken Ah'remmon's Gift over his own. *So that there could be no mistaking of his intent, The Father brought back to the Earth the First Son to stand in opposition to his Bright Twin. Now, together with the Father, they made, for the Judgement of Mankind, the Place of the Choosing.*

Seama paused here. He had come to it at last: the point of connection between The Song and everything he considered his life to have become. The memory of the trauma rushed through him, the finality of that day, the terrible reality of that place filled his thoughts. He shuddered but found the strength to continue.

'It is still there,' he told them, '*The Place of the Choosing.* Up in the Norberry Part, a pass in the mountains close by the source of the Deiva. We call it Kentreth's Grave. As the last act in *The Age of Intercession* all of mankind was brought to that place: every man or woman or child that yet drew breath. They were brought to stand and be judged; they were examined by those three mighty forces of existence right down to the last vestige of their free will. And a choice was made. *'Ohr'mazd called to him all of those he deemed to be of good heart and right mind and who went freely and happily into his embrace. But Ah'remmon called to him whomsoever bowed before his feet, whomsoever rejected the peace of Ohr'mazd.'* I am sorry to say that for those who made no choice at all, of their own free will, it was left for The Father to decide, and his decision was harsh. The Father reached down into the waste and took up a great desert of the old Earth in the palm of his hand and with the mighty power that is in him he set it *'in a place beyond'* that it would be free of the corrosive waste and yet distant from Earnor. That new land was named Kyzylkum after the name of the desert and Ah'remmon was to be its King. *Banished from this Earth, cast into the desert, were all the people of Ah'remmon, and banished too were those who could not freely stand in the presence of Ohr'mazd. And so Earnor was cleansed and Mankind was made new as it was in the beginning.'*

'And so began The Age of Last Hope.'

'This is all very religious, Seama. You don't normally go in for this stuff.'

'No, Fel, I don't, but I'm learning that perhaps I ought to pay a bit more attention to some of the people on Lindis.'

'It's those ones and twos they were on about on Tumboll!' Captain Farber had enjoyed a moment of revelation. 'You know those fellers who reckoned Earnor was a second creation – well, sumthin' o'the sort.'

Seama was confused. 'I don't remember.'

Sigrid, looking a little less emotional now that Seama had moved on, spoke up to help him out. 'It was while we were captive on Tumboll. The place we were held was similar to a Oncers' temple. Garaid gave Angren a quick lesson on the difference between Oncers and Twoers.'

'Well then the Captain is right. What is written in the Song matches pretty closely the standard Twoer creation story.'

'Well that isn't surprising is it?" put in Tys Heald. 'Didn't Haslem line up with the Twoers early on in his career? Saved a whole cabal of them from that temple fire on Lindis; had the culprits put in prison.'

'I hardly think that made him a Twoer, Chancellor. Had the situation been reversed, with Twoers trying to burn *their* rivals off the face of Earnor instead, I think Haslem would have been with the Oncers. He was tasked by the Council to bring the dispute to a close. That's what we do. However, it's certainly in a last chance world that we now live and according to The Song that last chance could have been very short lived indeed. There is one more event to describe.'

'Yes, as I recall,' Tys reminded them, 'You promised us a cataclysm.'

'Haslem has no notion of how it might have come about, but in the remaking of Earnor and the creation of Kyzylkum the two places were not *completely* set apart. Perhaps it is against the day of a further *Choosing* that Kentreth's Grave endures and will ever be a connection between our world and the Land of Exile. That path was, of course, made for passage in one direction only but what if it could be altered? What if it has become a route of escape from Kyzylkum?'

Alveson let out a sharp laugh: 'Escape? Oh, surely not. Hadn't these people had spent their lives worshipping the foul god? Finally they're in his company for good: isn't that what they wanted? They should be grateful they weren't all obliterated.'

Seama grimaced. 'This is no straightforward thing, Admiral. First of all, I'm not entirely certain that all of those exiled deserved their fate – many were children with little enough experience of life. How could they have the perspective to understand the question put to them? And what of the offspring of those banished, those born in exile? Are we to hold children responsible for the crimes and choices of their parents? And good or bad, why shouldn't they all want to escape their exile, and return to this beautiful world of ours? I have seen it, ladies and gentlemen, I have seen Kyzylkum through the mind of the spy in Slaney and it is a very hell. No soul that was ever made could wish to stay there.

'And so yes, in the first years of exile there were many who looked for a way to be free of it. And they were supported in this by their King, their God. The Song explains that Ah'remmon had long sought return to the Earth, had long worked to cast out his brother and create a New Kingdom for himself. The Song suggests that if a way could be found for the Exiles to return to Earnor, then surely the Dark God could follow. The tragedy is, of course, that there was indeed a way to be found. There were weaknesses in the earth that worsened with time. It needed only the use of *power* and the labour of man to widen and mine these weaknesses for any who wished to pass. The introduction to the Song doesn't say how many lives of men were used in the making of this escape, and little enough about the Black Wizards in exile who made it possible, but it is a certainty that one or more passages were eventually opened. We're told that while the wandering peoples of Earnor were still few in number and scattered, the armies of Kyzylkum, *in their multitude*, broke through the last barriers between our worlds and bore down upon the virgin lands of Asteranor.

'If only the Introduction were not so brief. The next section mentions almost glibly that Ohr'mazd would not, could not permit this *'Incursion'*. *'With his left hand'* it says, *'the Bright God reached beyond the world, opening the Gates of Time; he released for the succour of mankind the Fierce Guardians of the Earth.'* There's no name given for these creatures but they must have had a fearsome strength. They *'fell upon and utterly consumed'* all of the exiled already come onto the plains. And then: *'With his right hand,'* we're told, *'and with the strength of The Father running in him'* Ohr'mazd *'put a force upon the Earth that raised up the mountains, rank on rank, to deny all passage and so banish the servants of Ah'remmon once more. The Heights then stood between, and the whole land of Kyzylkum was sundered from the free earth, for the days of the ending were not yet come.'*

'A few words only to describe something that must have been terrible, incredible to behold. Tremendous forces piled up the mountains to dizzying heights and crushed the hope of escape for all the Exiled that remained in Kyzylkum. *That* is the cataclysm remembered by the Wandering People but denied by the scholars of our age: the making of the Dedicae at the hand of Ohr'mazd.'

Seama paused for a moment to collect his thoughts, took a sip of water and then gathered together the pages of the Song. 'Well there you have it, fellow councillors, a complete history of this world right up to the date of the history you already know.

Does anyone have questions?'

'Well, just the one, Seama,' said Lord Gumb who had listened in silence all morning with something of a glazed look in his eyes, 'It's nice to get a clear picture and all that, and I daresay it makes quite a tale, but, you'll forgive me for asking, *what the bletherin' hell does it all mean?*'

Seama almost laughed. He thought he'd made it as plain as a pikestaff. 'It all *means*, Lord Gumb, that we are in trouble. Tarangananda Uh Bib has had a full thirty years to open up a way into Kyzylkum and to engineer passage out again. It means that Uh Bib's paymaster and the source of his new power is the Dark God himself. What it means is that, even as we sit here talking, the Exiled are coming again to recover what they have lost, and I do not think they will be coming in friendship.

'And yes, if *they* can make the crossing…'

MONSTERS

Castle Ayer 3057.8.8

Goggalog – Human in form though of diminutive stature, male reaching a maximum of fourteen palms, with attenuated arms and long digits. The face is narrow, the seat of the eyes hollow. A skin pallor much like red veined white marble. Without the advantage of any sense of society, feral and solitary and naked to the elements, it commonly haunts the northern reaches of Oxitor Ulta, occasionally found to have crossed the land bridge to threaten the nether lands of the Tetra Ka. Seemingly weak in limb and mind, the goggalog yet carries a fearsome reputation. Avoid contact. Deceptively quick to attack, the grip, sufficient to kill in its own right, carries a deadly shock that will stop the heart of a grown man. As like to prey upon its own kind as any other, but an inefficient carnivore: with a small mouth the goggalog might need several weeks to consume any large prey, apparently unconcerned by fouling of the meat through time. A lazy predator, hunting only when there is need, confident in its power and without natural enemies unless it were mankind. In this regard it has become wary of archery and is quick to flee when pressed.'

Mador pushed the book away, upsetting a glass of water all over the table in the process.

'Majesty!'

The librarian rushed to the table desperate to rescue his precious texts. Mador reached for the napkin that had accompanied his breakfast and started to mop at the mess.

'No need, sire. Let me.'

Mador gave up the napkin readily enough. He got out of his chair to give the librarian more room.

'Why have we nothing with an index?'

'Ahm, there *is* an index of names, sire.' The librarian with his books now safe from the water, carefully turned the heavy pages of the bestiary Mador had just abandoned. 'As you can see each entry lists page numbers, there is a guide to pronunciation—'

'Where's the use in that? What I want to do is look up 'eats human hearts' and get a list of likely candidates.'

'A concordance.'

'A what?'

'Concordance, sire: a different sort of index that lists themes common to diverse entries.'

'That's more like it. Bring me one like that.'

'Ahm, to my knowledge, sire, there is no such bestiary outside Errensea.' The librarian looked most uncomfortable. 'I could spend some time researching the topic if you gave me more detail or perhaps speak to my sister Grek. She—'

Mador shook his head. 'I need answers now, Philemon, not in a year's time.'

'No doubt, sire, many of your predecessors have said as much.'

Mador could not help smiling at that one. 'A just rebuke, Philemon, and neatly delivered. I'll write the order of commission. Get me a concordance even if it does take a year.'

Philemon also allowed himself a smile. 'Thank you, sire. Was ahm, was there anything else?'

'You mean anything else I want you to look up?'

'Or indeed commission. There are any number of serious gaps in our armoury of knowledge.'

'Are there? I thought we had the best library on the mainland.'

'One of the best, sire. However there is always room for improvement.'

'Indeed there is. So, why don't you write me a list and I will consider the costs. But meanwhile find me something with claws and teeth that eats only major organs and find out how to kill it.'

'I will have the clerks look into the matter at once, Your Majesty.'

"Come to me as soon as you have news, wherever I am."

As the Librarian prepared to leave, the door to the snug opened and the Chamberlain came in with his ledger. The two servants nodded as they passed but, of course, said nothing to each other.

'Sire, it is time for your morning meetings. The Committee of the Guard will be first – you called them to discuss the appointment of a new captain. Then there is the Captain of the Watch – you wished to review the day's arrangements. After that I have scheduled-in Isolde Robarn with her report and after that Gerald Robarn with the options for—'

'Yes, yes, yes, Abram. I am not so scatter-brained that I forget my own plans for the day. But the order is wrong. Get me the Captain of the Watch first and then the Committee. As for the Robarns, the elder should have precedence: ask him to attend me at 11.00 hours; Isolde's excuses can wait. Now, where are we?'

'I've had a table set up in The Presence, Sire, and the room placed off-limits to everyone other than the delegates. The guard on both doors has been doubled.'

'Treble it. And what of the spells: any sign of them today? I don't want the guards made useless.'

'Well, we could move the guards *into* The Presence, Sire.'

'No, no. The meetings will be in private. No guards, no servants. Just make sure everyone is awake and ready for anything.'

'The doorward, Anders Belori, will have duty but I will myself have the point forcibly made. Are you sure, Sire, about the servants? There is food and drink ordered. Will it not be a distraction to be concerning yourself—'

'I can pour my own water, Abram. But perhaps you're right. Very well, ask 'Rian to attend us – apologize to her for me, but I must have people I can trust. Today of all days.'

'Yes, sire, I'm sure she'll understand.' The Chamberlain paused a moment and Mador wondered what was coming. 'And what of messengers, sire?'

'Well have them report to you. Anything personal, if written, claim and pass on to me at luncheon; if oral then hear it – I'll give you a sealed order. Any general news can wait until the end of the day. Unless it has bearing of course.'

The Chamberlain cleared his throat.

'There was some news, just before I came up.'

Mador took a deep breath. He just knew it wouldn't be good news.

'Tell me then.'

'It was another killing. In his own bedroom, sire, an horrific scene.'

'Who?'

'Robben Marque, your Chief Constable. His wife was killed also.'

'In his bedroom?' Mador's words came out rather weakly.

'Yes, sire.'

The Chief Constable had a suite of rooms in the North West Tower of the Curtain. The monster, it seemed, had penetrated the castle.

Mador stood motionless for just a moment before marching to the door. He was not dithering. He was pulling himself together. If there was to be a fight he would be ready for it, whoever, or whatever the opponent.

'Presence!' he threw over his shoulder as he went, 'Now!'

Astoril 3057.8.8

The smile worn on the face of Garaid Barbossa was not pleasant, reminding all who saw it of the rictus of death, and the dark staring eyes spoke of some terrible and haunted grief, but the intelligence behind that smile and those eyes was mostly unaware of anything amiss. Admittedly he had found that his dealings today, as he struggled to organise an efficient line of communication between Astoril and Ayer, had been hampered by a certain reserve displayed by the Astorian guardsmen allocated to the mission. Hampered too by his inability to completely control Garaid's thoughts or wantonly plunder Garaid's memory. It was as if the man had somehow managed to lock down anything he thought useful. Most useful would have been a list of the Partian contacts Zaras would need to complete his task. There had been surprise that this man, appointed by Lord Seama at King Sirl's behest, seemed so unprepared for his duties. But Zaras was not too put out by his failings. He was intelligent enough to find a way through and quick to access the knowledge of those under his command. The only part of it that disturbed him was that he hadn't expected any resistance at all from his victim. That Garaid could, by a deliberate act of will, control even the smallest part of his own mind was not acceptable and was not safe.

The big man navigated the avenues of Astoril oblivious to the crowds that parted in panic before him; he failed to hear the muttered concerns in his wake. He strode on with more vigour than could possibly be normal, he seemed unconcerned by the notion of direction or of destination or of time, he might wheel face about at the end of a street and march back the way he had come, and scatter the people once more, or he might not.

Zaras was in two minds. It was surely important for him to get to this meeting of Seama's, to find out what they knew and what they did not. Old Harry would expect it. But the urge to do his Master's bidding was not nearly as strong as other urges and one in particular. The power of life was thrilling through him. The *virility* of life!

For the first week after he had made the leap from his old carcass into Garaid's fine strong body Zaras had been so completely caught up in the struggle for supremacy that he'd found precious little peace in which to enjoy the change. It was only as they journeyed to Astoril after the battle at Moreda that he found his eyes and his thoughts resting upon the dark hair and tight body of Sigrid jogging along just ahead, only then that he felt the first stirrings of something long missed. And the mental urge became married to something entirely more satisfying: physical ability.

That Sigrid was the object of his attention was no surprise, but he knew he ought to be careful as far as that one was concerned. From what he'd seen so far she would be a troublesome target, far too fast with those swords of hers. *Tied-down* she might be more amenable even if possibly a little less fun. Just a matter of making sure the Aegardean wasn't around. He'd considered the matter at some length, lingered on the details, but the opportunity hadn't come.

What did that matter now! He was back in Astoril and here he'd find opportunities aplenty and maybe even a few closer to his preference. And that was what he was doing pacing the rubble strewn streets: looking for a chance.

Tumboll 3057.8.8

They were egging each other on to do the deed. The two biggest boys homed in on the girl. It was a strange language they used but Hadradag could understand the meaning. She was telling the boys that they were cowards and the boys were saying to her 'Do it. You think you're hard. Go on. You want to stay in our gang, you have to.' The interesting thing was that the girl was clearly the bravest of the lot of them. It was often the case. The smallest have to risk more to prove themselves. And that was why he was here.

Hadradag lay quite still watching them through his closed eyelids. He was happy for them to think he was asleep. Happy to observe these children of men. It was a new experience. The girl stooped and looked for a good stone: not too heavy, not too light, and when she found it she smiled. It was an *'I'll show you'* smile. Her gang fell silent as she moved a couple of paces closer weighing the stone in her hand, judging the distance. It was a pity this scene was coming to an end. They were so small and yet all the emotions, the rivalries, the bravado, the courage he might expect from his own kind were clearly present. Perhaps there was more to mankind than he had thought.

The girl paused. She was right to do so. There was a difference between deciding to venture something and actually doing it. The decision might acknowledge there may be danger, the deed itself will bring the danger full on. But she set her chin. She raised her arm. She threw.

Hadradag's head moved so fast that he had caught the stone on his tongue and spat it out a hundred feet into the air before any of the children began to run. But they ran fast enough when his head swung round to face them. All except the girl who was frozen to the spot. He wondered at that. Was it fear? Amazement? Acceptance of defeat? Her hands curled into fists. *Defiance.* He flattened his long neck so that his head came down to her level ten feet from where she stood. And then opened his eyes.

The girl gasped. It was probably the incandescence that surprised her though he had been told many times that his eyes were particularly beautiful. He thought to her: *you are a fine cub, you have great courage and I am proud to have met you* and then he breathed gently upon her, taking great care to make that breath just warm. The girl shivered in pleasure and she smiled. It was an excited smile. It was a thank-you smile. Hadradag smiled too but probably she could not tell.

'Playing with your food, Hadradag? She's hardly more than a mouthful.'

The girl's smile disappeared and fear overcame her at last.

Run little one, Hadradag thought, *you are not safe here. Run!*

She ran.

'Not hungry, then?'

Hadradag favoured his questioner with that wondrous gaze but the man seemed unaffected by it.

You are not amusing, Uh Bib. You are insolent. And yet still I do your bidding. This is a great mystery to me.

He could not decide what to do with the wizard. Some of the time he wanted to kill him quickly but there were many moments when he contemplated something much more lingering.

'Let us not say you do my bidding: there is reward to be gained from our collaboration. If you can assist me to my ends then I will help you achieve yours.'

So you say. Who is that, skulking by the castle wall?

The wizard glanced over his shoulder.

'I asked him to wait until you consented to see him. He is known as the Necromancer, Lord of this island. May he approach?'

To what end?

'A matter of courtesy to you, that is all.'

Then no. I have already had the pleasure of more worthy acquaintance: it is sufficient that he can witness my glory from the shadows.

'I can never tell when you are joking.'

I care nothing for your entertainment, wizard, only for my own. When will we leave this place?

'That is why I have come. We are needed in Aegarde. Athoff is losing his way; his army is wavering. I need to stir them up.'

Hadradag sprang to his feet, arched his long back, shook out his wings and belched a great gout of flame up into the sky. The fallout from it set fire to several trees.

A live dragon settling in their camp might stir them up more than you need.

'That I am prepared to risk.'

Astoril 3057.8.8

She sat on a crumbled wall, tears rolling down her cheeks.

'Are you lost?' the man asked gently but the girl didn't look up at him. Her bare slender legs were grubby and the long black hair tumbling over her shoulders was in a tangle from inattention but she was a pretty little thing. And upset.

'Was this your home?'

The girl nodded.

'And where are your parents?'

She hid her face.

There didn't appear to be anyone else in sight.

Five minutes later on an elderly woman came out of a house in the opposite terrace, drying her hands on a towel.

'Elsa, Elsa,' she called out, 'Where are you, my darlin'? Elsa?'

She looked up and down the street, eyed the still standing front door of her daughter's house, shivered a little as she did so but saw nothing.

'Where is that girl? Elsa! Elsa, where are you?'

'Anything the matter, Mrs Fornum?'

Mrs Fornum scowled at the neighbour who'd come out to see what the trouble was.

'Well everything's the matter, isn't it? What's right about any of this?'

'Nothing m'love. But some have it harder than others.'

'Ay, well.' Mrs Fornum nodded. 'It all comes one thing on another. That's the problem. First our Tom with the cancer and Jess having to work so hard to keep them; then all that trouble with the bailiffs when he died. But she never gave up. Always had a smile for you. She'd just got herself straight and… and now this happens. It's not right…'

Her face crumpled.

'Now then. C'mon m'love.' The neighbour reached out but the old woman pulled away.

'They got her up to hospital quickly enough though, didn't they? They'll know how to look after her. They will.' The neighbour didn't sound all that convincing or convinced. 'It was her legs, wasn't it?'

'Ay lass, lintel stone fell on her. I tried to shift it myself but it was so damned heavy. Lom Tanner got some lads… and when they lifted it… Oh Mary, she's such a good woman. It's not right for this to happen. It's not right!'

Her neighbour reached out once more but the old woman still wouldn't have it. She stood stiff and alone with her arms fiercely folded. 'Our Elsa's taken it bad. Cries all the time whenever she's not shouting. I'm too old to be looking after a child, Mary. I tell her to sit and she stands, I tell her to hush and she screams at me, I try to give her a hug and she runs. What am I to do with her?'

'She'll come round.'

'Not that I blame her: she was such a little love.'

'Ay, and she still is.'

'But where's she gone this time? I've told her over and over to keep out of that house.'

'She won't be in there, surely.' The neighbour stepped up to the door of the ruin. 'Elsa? Elsa, are you in there? Elsa, come on out, your gran's that worried about you.' She listened. There was nothing except maybe the noise of the mice skittering through the fallen bricks and timbers. 'She's not here, Annie. She's like to have gone up to the hospital, ha'n't she?'

'Oh I suppose so. She will keep going up there, though we're not long back. I'd better get my walking stick – why everything you need has to be uphill I don't know.'

'Now then, m'love, let me go up for her.'

'No, her mother's trusting me to keep her safe: I'll get her.'

'Right then, I'll walk with you. Just let me tell our Will and I'll be ready.'

'You're very kind Mary. You'll forgive me my sharp tongue?'

'You can be as sharp wi' me as you like, Annie Fornum. Just you go and get your stick.'

THE BEST OF MEN

Astoril 3057.8.8

'Crossings? Dark Gods? Exiles? What are you talking about? Are you mad?' Alling was scathing. 'It's all very simple isn't it? Bliss is a villain trying to make trouble – whether for gain, or revenge or sheer delight in malice I can't say. Athoff is a warmonger trying to build an empire. It's as straightforward as this meeting is overlong.'

Seama sighed audibly. He looked down at the papers on the table and said nothing. What could he say? Unexpectedly Keth Hardie came to his aid.

'It would be comforting, Mart, to believe this all a straightforward matter of greed and common malice; comforting for all of us, the Lord Seama included. There he sits with his tales of the past spread before him and an unshakeable conviction that they are true. But why should we believe him? Of course he has always been seen as a bastion of the truth, but perhaps on this occasion he is misguided; perhaps the trials of the past months have affected him more than he knows. And you may be right to say that the villains we already know are more than capable of causing all this misery by their own deeds and designs without any need to speculate upon monsters from another world. The problem I have, Mart, is that I *do* believe what Seama has to say and I am not comforted.

'Already monsters from another world have been seen: the demons of the Black Company bringing ruin to the people of Eastern Aegarde; a real live dragon that hung in the skies over this city while its smaller brethren brought fire to our streets. We live our lives in Gothery struggling to alter the world around us according to the dictates of science and engineering and rarely do we give real credence to the other powers that affect us. But we are alone on this continent in thinking this way. Elsewhere wizards and sorcerers are woven through the fabric of society; though we choose to think of the Wizard's Council of Errensea in merely political terms, its influence is respected the world

"

over. It seems that magic is all around us. Seama's battle with Bliss was ample proof of that. And if magic *is* present why can we not go further than that? I have heard from witnesses on the day of the battle who speak of a strange presence investing the streets, a presence that deeply shocked all who felt it. Why should I not believe Seama when he tells me that this presence was nothing less than the essence of the nature god Bor'eth? He knows more about these things than I do. And if we can talk of nature gods then surely it takes little imagination to take one step futher.'

'Take as many steps as you like, Prime Minister,' said Alling with a sneer, 'But you will not convince me that this is anything more or less than the nonsense we had from the other conjuror. Where is the evidence? Where is the proof? I cannot be the only one to doubt him?'

Gurdy Younger took him up on that. She didn't seem best pleased by the General's attitude.

'General Alling! Your argument is reasonable and must be heard, doubt must be given breath, but your lack of respect, sir, is something that must not be continued. Our Prime Minister was appointed by the King as your superior and you would do well to remember it.'

Alling's sneer didn't disappear but he said. 'I will remember it, Minister, just as I remember that the defence of this nation lies primarily in your hands rather than mine. But it is *my* duty as master of his majesty's forces to make sure that our actions are based upon truth and good sense. And so I ask again without apology, where is the proof?'

He glared provocatively at Seama but the wizard merely smiled.

'You seem determined to pick a fight, General, but I have no problem at all in providing proof.

'Some people might think my interview with Uh Bib when he thought I lay dying, or the interrogation of the spy was evidence enough. But of course villains have been known to lie. Some people might think all the events of recent months indicative of something quite extraordinary happening in this pleasant world of ours, but of course coincidence has made fools of mankind through the ages. Luckily we need not rely on these things at all. Ladies and gentlemen, it is quite simple: *I* am the proof. I just need to tell you why.

'As we have explained, Haslem wanted to leave the book as a warning but there's a problem in doing that. Haslem was ancient when he died, more than eight hundred years old. His great age gave him a perspective on the future that few of us can match. We tend to live in the present, we remember little of the past beyond a few generations and rarely think more than twenty years into the future, one generation or two. Of course thinking in that way it is no wonder that the power of warnings fades. Haslem knew that his fears may not come to pass in a thousand years and yet still represent to every year between a clear and present danger. Think of those who live in the shadow of sleeping volcanoes: the danger is evident but through years and years of inactivity people forget to be scared or even watchful. It is worse with this threat of the Exiled because all knowledge of the true past has been lost. So what to do? The Song of Ages is Haslem's answer to the problem.'

'Hardly a matter for deep thought,' Alveson again, 'To put it in a book!'

'Perhaps a few of us would see that as the answer, Admiral. But Haslem knew he had to do more. A book is a fine thing and might easily keep the truth alive for a thousand years but not if it is lost in an overgrown library, and not if the language no longer makes sense, and not if the legend therein begins to sound like the insane babblings of a fantasist. That is why Haslem made *this* book.'

Fel Awdrey nodded at the bundle of papers in Seama's hand. 'Not much left of it, Seama. Looks like fire and water has scuppered us whatever Haslem intended.'

'But that's where you're wrong, Fel. The book was a success. It did its job before it was destroyed. What Haslem did was to make the book call out to one particular type of person.'

'Someone with Power, you said.'

'Yes, I did, but I could say more. Actually Haslem is quite

specific about who will be called, which is why I consider it merely coincidence that Uh Bib came to know about the book. According to the Introduction the book is designed to call out only to The Sayoshant. The Sayoshant is quite specifically a person who will know the danger and will know when the threat is imminent. If he couldn't *know* that, then the book couldn't call him. It is a matter of logic. The book will call only to someone who can recognize whether or not the Exiled are at hand. That person is always the Sayoshant of his age. If there is no Sayoshant then the book will remain unfound.

'So you see, ladies and gentlemen, the proof that what the Song says is true, and the proof that what I say is true is remarkably easy to find. I *am* the proof because I am The Sayoshant.'

Gurdy Younger squirmed, very obviously, in her chair. Seama was aware that the meeting was taking up such a length of time that it was bound to be hard on the flesh, but he realised that it was not physical discomfort that moved the defence minister.

'I am not, Seama, utterly convinced by your logic – it all rests rather precariously upon the notion that everything you say is truth – but even were I convinced by your honesty, I would still have a problem.'

This wasn't very promising. He hadn't necessarily expected them to swallow it just like that but he thought Gurdy at least might be on his side. 'Yes, Gurdy?'

'Yes. You've used the word a number of times now. Tell me, what exactly is The Sayoshant.'

Seama more or less collapsed into his chair; he was shaking.

'Lord Seama!' Gurdy struggled to get up to go to his aid.

Angren snorted and shook his head. 'I wouldn't bother, girl,' he said, 'he's just laughing. Wake me when he's finished, won't you.'

And he was right.

'I'm so sorry,' Seama gasped, trying to suppress the tremors, 'Sorry.' He breathed deeply a few times but giggled a little more; he bit on his sleeve, buried his head in the folds of his gown. Eventually it stopped.

'Ah, yes. Sorry. Ha! Ridiculous. Me, I mean.'

All around the table were faces of outrage, annoyance or just plain astonishment. Angren and Fel aside, they all looked so serious it made him want to laugh all the more. He put that thought from his mind and tried to think more sensible thoughts. He needed to control himself: that was one; and then he asked himself why he had reacted so extravagantly: and that was another; and then he wondered if he was completely himself: and that did it. First the battle and now this. Very odd.

'Yes Gurdy, once again I ask you to forgive me. Having the whole story in your head is a good thing but it's so easy to forget what you have told and what you have not: difficult to remember what is known and what is not known. *Sayoshant.* A strange sounding name. It is one of the most ancient Medean names known – indeed now I think that it may extend through many ages of the world. We translate the word as a phrase: 'The Best of Men.' A grand title! Not one for a modest man, but you must understand that it's not merely some vague description that could apply to many an honest soul. *The Sayoshant* is a title gained by a person who has completed a specific task. That I have done and so the title is mine.'

'And the task was?'

'Well Gurdy, I did think I might be able to get through this meeting without troubling you with that particular detail, but I now see that you'll have to know something about it. I've already told you about the existence of Kentreth's Grave, or The Place of the Choosing. My knowledge of it is not book-learned but born of experience. I have walked the path through the vale, I have undergone The Choosing and been returned to Earnor with The Greater Power.'

A clamour of comment and question burst out on both sides of the table and went on for some minutes, with Seama struggling to answer each and all coherently. He insisted this was not the time for detail. The plain truth, he told them, was that he, Seama Beltomé, was The Sayoshant, and therefore the book had called to him and to him alone, and these two facts together should be proof enough. He was beginning to feel weary of it all.

'So you are The Best of Men?'

The voice rose through the babble. Seama cast his eyes down the table to see his friend, Terrance De Vere, leaning forward the better to be seen.

'Terrance?'

'So you are *the Best of Men?*'

'I… well only as I explained.'

Angren had been waiting for this. Ever since they had arrived in the ruins of Astoril and heard of the battle, De Vere had been hopping mad about it.

'The *best* of men?'

'Look Terrance,' Angren said, 'Can't we do this later?' If ever a discussion needed to be in private this was it. The people around this table really didn't need reminding of all the death and destruction. 'We've more important things to talk about than Seama's er… qualities, and I'm sure everyone agrees with me. So…'

Seama sat back in his chair, a thumb stroking his chin, eyes alert, both hilarity and weariness forgotten. Terrance would not be stopped.

'I think not, or rather, I happen to think this point at least as important as the rest. Our leader, for that's what he is, should be our example in all that may follow, should *be* the best of men. I want to know why the best of men has wantonly destroyed the most beautiful city of our age. A city of art and science unrivalled on the continent. Perhaps he can tell us? Perhaps he can ask himself why this should have happened?'

'But it wasn't Seama destroyed Astoril,' Angren protested. They had been through this already and Angren was exasperated with Terrance's continued refusal to see things the right way. 'It was that other wizard, that uh-Bib; everyone knows that.'

'Do they indeed?' Angren hated the way Terrance's words needed no shouting to aid them. 'Do they, Seama?'

Angren threw up his arms in disgust and turned away from the argument. It was up to Seama now; Angren understood none of it. He knew that Terrance was one of those sensitive types, a man for high culture, but surely even he realized that war had its casualties: didn't care whether it spoiled a pig-sty or a temple. For all De Vere's dandy dress, Angren had at least come to expect common sense.

Seama leaned forward, frowning. 'What are you saying, Terrance?'

'Don't you know? Simply, it seems to me, you cannot wholly pass-on all the blame to your enemy, can you? From what I heard, this uh-Bib was fleeing the city, and had left quite some time before it was flattened.'

'Yes, and so?'

'So why was the city destroyed?'

'We were engaged in conflict. He challenged and I responded. I needed to stop him. Just because he escaped me doesn't mean the attempt was wrong. In our conflict we each released so much energy in such a way as to cause the earth to move.'

'And in so doing destroyed the totem of every thinking man. You say you responded, but was it necessary? It seems to me that you fell prey to pride. You wanted to prove your power over all others. It was Seama Beltomé and no one else who allowed the conflict to escalate. If you had simply allowed the wizard to go, none of this would have happened.'

'It was my duty to prevent his escape, or to try. He is a formidable enemy and may still cause us great harm.'

'So why didn't you pick an easier way of killing him instead of showing off, throwing the earth about. Why not shoot him with an arrow or something.'

Seama looked annoyed and Angren expected strong words, but then the wizard's countenance took on a thoughtful look.

'He is a Wizard of immense *power* – at least he was in that moment. Translocation and movement is the most draining use of *power* and I sought to tire him, to break his defence. He should not have had the strength to respond... and maybe I should not have had that degree of *power* to attack.'

'It seems to me,' said De Vere less sternly, 'that the power went to your head, and I think you should try to understand why. I would have spoken before, Seama, but never had the chance, or after, but when you spoke lightly of being the best of men, how could I stay silent? People have been killed through no fault of their own; thousands are homeless as a consequence of your actions. You are supposed to be our beacon, you're the source of all we know in this war, you *are* the best of men and yet so you acted, a slave to the power you wield. And you thought you had done nothing wrong? How does that leave us?'

Seama looked desolate. Angren didn't like it: there was muttering between several parties around the table.

'Look,' he said, 'Can't we move on? I don't know about you but I think we all need a bit of a break. Why not—'

General Alling got to his feet.

'Finally we come to the point. Fellow councillors, I take this opportunity to advise you all that Seama Beltomé is, until his trial, under arrest at my command.'

Angren's response was predictable to some. He stood abruptly, unbalancing, and his leap covered the breadth of the table before the chair clattered to the floor. Almost between breaths, Angren had left his seat and tumbled his opponent to the floor. A knife appeared in his hand and it pressed close-in to Alling's throat.

Everyone else scrambled to their feet in alarm, but Seama's voice rose over the many words of surprise.

'Angren! Leave the General alone.'

'But he has us by the balls, Seama. His troops are all over the palace. We won't get out without him.'

'We don't need to get out, Angren. Leave him. Now! I'm sure we're in no danger, though I'll admit I'm a little confused by this. General?'

Angren grudgingly let the General get up, but he kept his knife in hand and loosened the sheath of his sword.

'It would seem that I have made a mistake,' the General said coolly, and Angren harumphed, 'in allowing you people to enter the chamber without confiscation of arms. Still no harm is done. You cannot leave: the exits are well guarded. Like your friend De Vere, Lord Wizard, I hold you solely responsible for our problems and you will answer a charge of murder by negligence.'

Terrance was appalled. 'But General, you have missed my point. We need this man. You cannot charge Seama with—'

'I can, and have, Sir, and were the King well, I am sure he would support the charge.'

Gurdy Younger was the first of Sirl's ministers to speak: two others wanted time to consider, and the third, Fel Awdry, was so furious he couldn't get the words out. Admiral Jom Alveson was pasty faced in the guilt of having discussed the move with Alling before breakfast. Mistress Younger said:

'General Alling, need I remind you that the Lord Seama himself holds the King's baton?'

'No minister, but I wonder how he obtained it. The King is a sick man, if you take my meaning.'

'I do, and I resent it, General.'

They were not Gurdy's words. She looked to the doorway where an elderly man had entered quietly. He was small, hunched at the shoulders and almost drowned in a mane and beard of wispy silver-grey hair. He looked so much older than his sixty years but his words were as clear and strong as ever.

'I do not give up that rod lightly, Mart Alling,' he continued, 'Uh Bib took it without my consent and yet you and all my ministers appeared eager to accept his word and his authority. All that time I was held prisoner by his drugs and hypnotism. Now I understand that your actions too were proscribed by Dr Bliss. Let me say it this once: whatever Seama did to rid us of that leech was unimpeachable. Now, Alling, do you accept my unfettered word as law?'

Alling's cold face went red as he realized his position but then said with supplication rather than the innuendo his words might have suggested: 'Gladly, majesty, providing you are again the King I knew and respected.'

'Seama has healed me, Mart. Properly, not like Bliss's so called healing. Friends all, take this moment not so ill. Mr. Nielderson blame him not so entirely and put away that blade. Mart has struggled to do the right thing in impossible circumstance these five months, with no help from me. That we are all confused is no surprise when we consider the wiles of our enemy. In ousting

the usurper, saboteur, in destroying his minions, the Black
Company, Seama has had a great victory. He has cured us all to
fight better our next battle. We owe him thanks, General, not
false retribution.'

'It is a sad cure that ruins us, My King.'

'It is sad indeed, but what have we lost? There have been
casualties and that cannot be mended and for those brothers and
sisters we mourn. The transitory works of our race, artifacts of
art, of our science, the physical expression of what we are, have
been ravaged, obliterated. For that I do not mourn in the least.
Because Seama has rescued something far more important: he
has given us back freedom, he has broken the spell, released the
bonds that held us. What makes us who we are was under threat
but, thanks to Seama's intervention, we live again, not just to
fight another day, but to build anew, to create a world around us
with more urgency, with more vitality than ever before.

'Now hard times are coming but at least we face those times
as we should: free, dynamic, determined. If we survive the
coming war all of this must enrich our understanding. We shall
miss our past glories, of course we will, but we are the makers
of our own world; we cannot sit still with minds siezed with the
memory of what is gone; we stride on, seeking out the future.
That is the Gothery I know, that is the true nature of our people.

'Mr Nielderson, will you not return to your seat? We are all
friends here.'

Angren jumped at his name. The King had spoken with
such authority and such vision that Angren was lost in thought.
'Your Majesty, at once,' he said promptly, and with a respectful
bow. He returned to his place and righted his chair. The King
continued:

'And so, friends, in this new mood, shall we now carry on?
There's much to be done. The enemy is at our door and we need
to start making plans.'

THE END TO A BUSY MORNING

Astoril 3057.8.8

During the ensuing pause King Sirl took up Berta's unused seat, refusing the chair at the head of the table. Angren was impressed.

Keth Hardy, the Prime Minister, greeted his King formally, as the occasion demanded, but then continued more naturally.

'Glad as I am to see you,' he said, 'I wonder if you should be out of your bed so soon. Seama said the poison was still in you. We don't want to risk losing you again.'

'I hope you're not going to start nagging me before I'm completely recovered, Keth. I'm tired, I'll admit, but I can sit here quiet and listen. Tell him, Seama.'

'I'm no true doctor, Sirl,' the wizard said. He had regained his composure during Sirl's speech and now looked as confident as ever. 'However, if I'm not mistaken, you suffered the worst of it yesterday with the antidote, so I suppose it will be alright.'

'Right then, let's get on with it.'

'Lord Seama, could you give the King a resumé,' said Hardy, falling into his regular role of chairman, 'or is the King already familiar with our situation?'

'Oh, I know quite a bit about what Seama has been up to, and about his reading of the situation. I'd already heard of The Song of Ages, so I'm sure it's all less of a surprise for me than for you. When Bliss first came to us he simply came straight out with it and asked to see Banya's copy. I was intrigued and he was impatient but we were both frustrated: as hard as we looked it remained unfound. Of course the fact that he asked for the text adds considerable weight to Seama's theory, wouldn't you think?'

'But you couldn't find it? Doesn't that mean it's not there?'

'Hard to say, Mr Nielderson, it's a big library. But I've had my Librarian looking all this time, and there's still no trace.'

'Good,' said Seama. 'That's very encouraging.'

Angren was confused.

'How's that good?'

'Well, in the preface to the copy I have,' he explained, 'Haslem made the point that the book would actively lose itself. He asked Banya to keep a secret record of where it was placed. That means that if the book is still in the library there's likely to be information somewhere telling us approximately where we should look. There's a fair chance I'll find it. And that's good because we need the full text. If we had the section covering The Incursion I think we'd find a detailed description of the passage the exiles made through the mountains. It's my guess that Uh Bib did something to open up that passage. That's how he came to Kyzylkum, how he gained his new master and undertook his commission.'

'To prepare the way for a conquering army?'

'Yes, General Alling.'

Alling had looked a changed man since his King had arrived. Angren wondered whether he ought to rethink his opinion of the him. He was certainly single minded in his devotion to king and country and that wasn't such a bad thing. Now that he wasn't trying to get them all locked up, Angren decided that his professionalism at least was actually something to be admired.

'Then, how long do we have before this army arrives?'

'A part of it has arrived already. Tregar with Anparas and Temor must face them soon, if they haven't already done so.'

'What makes you think it only the vanguard?'

'I don't think it, I just hope. But would Uh Bib want the major force here before this damaging war with Athoff was done? The scheme is to deplete us before they make their move. What Tregar faces is the first foray, a trial run.'

'Then that is our chance.'

'Just so, General Alling. Providing we can engineer some sort of reply to those already here, my effort must be given to finding the passage and somehow blocking the entry of the greater force. That's why you are here, ladies and gentlemen. Our agreement and commitment must be the first step that will bring the nations together to face this menace of the deep past. The time has come, for decisions. King Sirl has given me his answer, but if we decide to act, we must act as one. How do you decide?'

Angren wasn't surprised that no one wanted to be first. He *was* surprised that it was Valdez who broke the silence. So far he'd opened his mouth only to yawn. He cleared his throat and began in a rough deep voice:

'Lord Seama, you knew my answer at the moment of my arrival in Astoril. You people need a lot of talk to come to the obvious, I do not. Let me tell you why I say yes.'

'This is how it was,' said the Duke. 'Fourteen days past, heralds came to me. They were Athoff's men. It is our custom to make strangers welcome and they were honoured. At meat they spoke Athoff's words for him, asking for my support. 'In what', I asked. 'In the war with Gothery', they said and began to make their case. I let them continue without saying yes or no. They told me that Athoff's army was nearly complete. Aside from Valdez and two others, every Lord north and west of the forests, and south of the lights had already sworn allegiance to the King's son. Soon, they said, the tally would be filled. Counting chickens, I think.'

'Excuse me, Duke Valdez.'

'Angren Nielderson. I said we would meet again, but I did not expect it to be in Astoril.'

'Same here. But did I hear you say 'every Lord *south of the lights*'?'

'Yes, Angren. Terremark is unmoved. Your father, I'm told, threatened to have Athoff's herald tarred and feathered if he returned. The others are Drafas and Kelle, and I know the Drafasians have no time for Athoff.'

Tys Heald voiced a question that all wanted to ask. 'Are we to understand by your presence, that you too have no time for Athoff and propose to come in on our side?'

'That is the sum.'

'May I ask why?'

'*Five* days ago I met with an extraordinary man: Oswaldo Bassalo. He carried a message from Lord Seama, but more than that he carried witness to a crime that I cannot and will not see rewarded. Already my people were seeking out that foul crew. There is a distance between Ciudad Valdez and The Saddle and often tales grow with the miles but I do not seek an excuse: we were slow to respond to the needs of our people, slow to understand the horror of their bloody career, slow to count this Black Company the enemy of all good men. It is shame to me to admit this much.

'We have heard Seama draw together the elements of this plot of war. Ringsøyr, the Black Company: they are the same enemy. The decision is easy to make. My loyalty is given to Agwis King, not to his so-called regent. Agwis could never want war with Pars or with Gothery. It is easy to believe Athoff a traitor to us all. So, I have chosen my side and I accept Seama's word as command.'

'Now hang on: you said the *heralds* turned up two weeks ago. If they call themselves *heralds* doesn't it suggest that there's an army not far behind them?'

'Mr Nielderson, that thought came to me also, and so I had scouts sent out to see what was truth and what not. Do not worry about the words he uses. Athoff is too grand to have *messengers* but the fact remains that the scouts found nothing of Athoff's army within one hundred miles of my borders. The rumour is that the force he has gathered sits on the Langeland Street seventy miles shy of the Turnpike. Rumour says he's finding it hard work keeping all those gathered watered and fed. Meanwhile Athoff besets the Hundred Kingdoms making speeches. He is far from ready.'

'Well that sounds all very well but, call me a pessimist if you like, Athoff could still be knocking on our door in two weeks flat.'

'I don't think so, Nielderson. I think he will wait some time for news of the other Dukedoms. It is a long journey to Kellestan and he could not expect their reply for some days. His route must be determined by their decision. Together, the three of us, Valdez, Drafas, Kelle, we span Gothery's northern border. With Drafas and Kelle to support him he will feel he can cross my borders with impunity. Without them... well he would have to be mad to try it. All is changed for him if he has to come at Gothery from the south.'

'What is your guess?'

'At the very worst we will see their swords in three weeks. I think not before.'

'Lord Seama,' Alling cleared his throat and Angren thought he looked embarrassed to speak, 'You say we can get no help from Pars, or implied it, but surely we must at least co-ordinate our defence. We must act as one force, and yet we have not so far considered our long allegiance or had any word from Mador or his people.'

'His representative here is the Lady Sigrid Althoné, and I'm sure that shortly we'll have her thoughts on the matter, but remember the real problem: out there, somewhere in the Norberry Part, my friend, Tregar MacNabaer with two of the King's finest armies are facing already an enemy beyond the imagining of Athoff Ringsøyr. I know this in my heart. Do not expect help from the east. Mador of Pars has enough troubles of his own. However news must travel between us – we must share whatever knowledge we gain. And so I have given thought to that already. You may think we've had something of a busy morning ourselves but, believe me, others toil also on our behalf.

'But councillors, before we continue, I am still waiting for answers! I want nothing taken for granted. This is a business far too serious for us to presume allegiance where there is none. General Alling?'

'My allegiance is to King Sirl who I think has given you his backing, but I do offer my personal support.'

'And I', said Jom Alveson, seemingly eager to be thought keen and ready, and then one by one each member of the council said aye without retraction, and when they had done Sirl yawned and stretched.

'Well Seama,' he said, 'what now?'

'For us, lunch. For you, bed for a few hours. Then we will get down to the real business. Look, here's Garaid, just in time to fill his belly.' Over by the doorway officials were checking the big man's name against the description Seama had given them.

'Gentlemen, and ladies,' the wizard said by way of introduction as he was let in, 'here is the man set to spy on me.'

The effect was remarkable. The strangely smiling features showed surprise before the 'spy's' face turned a choking red, and he collapsed, gasping and writhing as though his body was fighting itself.

They were quickly to his side and something Seama did quieted him. When the wizard was satisfied Garaid was not dying he allowed attendants to stretcher him to the hospital.

Angren was perhaps less astonished than everyone else, but not much.

'The strain got to him at last,' he explained to anyone who cared to listen.

Bibron nodded agreement, saying: 'Shame to see a good man suffering like that. Let's hope they can do something for him.'

'Well, Captain,' Angren assured him, 'The Garra I've got to know is a fighter. You saw him on Tumboll. There's no way a man like that'll just lie down and give up. Trust me, he'll be back on his own two feet in no time.'

BRINK OF WAR

Francon Valley 3057.8.8

'You're being totally ridiculous, Shaf.' Tregar had lost his temper at last. He had been doing well to ignore the impetuosity that was exhausting the army, the mad rush that Temor lead, regardless of the hard terrain, heedless of the grunts and groans. He could excuse that. It was the duty of the leader to extract as much effort as possible; his job to get them to the Francon in good time. Even if the man did rant and rave like a blood-crazed berserker about the glories of war and the gruesome things he was going to do to his enemy, so what? Tregar had always thought that men should be judged by their actions, not their words.

But today, today of all days, he had gone too far! The wizard and the Lord had argued once already and Tregar was still seething from it. Shaf, not content with cursing his enemy, had started in on his allies as well. The subject of his abuse was a man Tregar admired: Jaspar, the Lord Sands. There was some rivalry between these Lords. They were the two youngest men ever to hold such high office, though Shaf was by fourteen years Jaspar's senior. They had met in the lists on a number of occasions and, as far as Tregar could remember, Jaspar had always won. That a slip of a boy, in Temor's words, should have been elevated to Shaf's own status, as Lord of a Royal House, had not improved relations between them; it took little provocation for the elder to snipe at the younger.

'Our biggest problem,' Shaf had said seriously over breakfast, 'is Sands, We'll see no help from that quarter.'

'I don't follow.'

'Tregar, the idiot's got himself stuck, hasn't he? And we all know he's too cowardly to risk coming out of his shell. That's if he's still there.'

'Ye do yoursel' no honour by slandering Jaspar.'

'Slander is it? I say the man's a fool and his house no better for having accepted him. He's holed up like a rat and the ferrets are closing in. Any Lord worth his salt would have settled the matter a month ago. Of course he's a fool!'

Tregar had bottled his rage, but only just, managing to leave the table before he could say something he would regret. He had avoided Shaf all morning until now. Just ahead was the final ridge that barred access to the back wall of Cwm Francon. There was a path but not a pass: a steep rocky path that needed hands and feet to ascend. And Shaf wanted to take the horses with him! He saw his cavallry riding down the valley like a battle of the Gods casting all before him.

His protégé, Seth, shared the vision.

'He's right, Tregar. We've got t'ave 'em. We've got to mek'em scared. Horses'll mek us too fast for 'em.'

'Make *who* scared? Just at the minute, young Cookson, we know bugger all about what's waiting for us over that ridge. We think Jaspar's under siege but by how many? How are they arranged? We don't have a clue. What if they've horses of their own? The only real advantage we have just now is they don't know we're coming. I hope. Our best chance is to get as close as possible before we're seen. We don't want to give 'em the time to sort out a defence. So, bearing all that in mind, tell me how one hundred whinnying horses are going t'help us? Not at all! But the fact is, it hardly matters anyway: look at that path.' He turned the lad by his shoulders to face the ridge; Temor followed suit. 'Com'on Shaf, they'll never get over it. What's the good of laming the beasts?'

'They give us flexibility, Tregar.'

'No Shaf, they're a handicap, a distraction. That path'd be the death of them. Can ye not see that?'

Temor looked at the path and his face grew dark with frustration.

'I see it, Tregar, and I don't like it. Come on Seth let's get sorted out before the wizard says the path is too hard for the rest of us.'

'Aye, let's get going. Wi'luck, job'll be done before dark.'

Tregar, watching them go, was sickened by the obvious relish in Seth's words; sickened at the way Temor had corrupted this farmer's boy with the promise of heroism and fame. Cal layed a hand on his arm and made him jump.

'It's too late now, Tregar. You should have listened in Hannayford.'

The wizard wished he knew how to fly. The climb was killing him, though he suffered more from embarrassment than from the physical hardship. It was only three thousand feet but he was sweating and panting long before they reached the summit. Stopping for the twentieth time to catch his breath, he looked behind and saw that he was not alone in his suffering. All tents and camp paraphenalia had been left behind but each man carried still a pack with food, extra clothing and bandages, and also his weapons. It was all extra weight and it bore on them as they advanced. To Tregar it felt as though the more he tried to climb the more the earth clawed him back.

There was no other way save retracing their steps for ten miles and that with the new route would add a day to their journey, but Tregar wondered again whether it was sense or stupidity to insist on speed. Typically, Temor, Seth, Cal and the elite force had forged ahead and were by now out of sight, and yet the army of Temor was strung out along the path for a mile behind them. Tregar spat out the phlegm that hindered his breath and grunting with the exertion dragged himself onwards. What else could he do?

It was an hour short of noon before the last weary soldier reached the broad, windwept saddle that curved around the southern part of the cwm. With just a short march ahead of them the Lord Temor had called a halt and Tregar was not the only man grateful for the chance to rest. Temor was gathering his army before the final effort and the high moor was full of it, shivering as sweaty bodies suffered the impact of a cold north wind. Those first to reach the top of the ridge had wormed themselves into the fern-brakes to escape it, and the laggards rumaged in their packs for woolens. Everyone took their chance to eat, all understanding that for some it would be their last meal.

When the tally was complete their Lord found himself

a suitable boulder and stood upon it. Upwind of his army he reckoned that most of the men could hear him.

'Bit of a struggle wasn't it?' he yelled and the men responded in good humour despite their exhaustion. 'Well the good news is you've done your climbing for now. From here on in it's downhill all the way.'

'What's the bad news,' a voice yelled against the wind.

'What's that? The bad news? We're moving out in ten minutes.'

'That's good news!'

'Good man! Yes lads, we've a job to do and it won't be any easier for putting it off. And it won't be easy. Not at all. I'll tell you now, the scouts have not returned, but I'll not wait for them. We go to break a siege and bring death to our enemies for their boldness. Aegardean scum have dared to make war in Pars, behind our backs. They've trapped the House of Sands and with it Mador's heir, the Princess Xandra. They've driven good Partians from their homes. What do they deserve, these murderers?'

'Death!' It wasn't a roar, but several voices raised the cry. The well-placed captains knew their business.

'What are we going to give them?'

'Death!' The cry came stronger.

'Death to the invader. We'll teach 'em. No one brings war to Pars while Temor stands fast. What the enemy has started, be sure that we will finish it. Get your gear ready men, loosen your muscles. We're going to war! On the other side of this ridge the rabble are waiting. They think they're waiting for Jaspar to give up. What are they really waiting for?'

'Death!'

'Death to the invader! Death! Death! Death!'

Now the soldiers were roaring, forgetting their aching limbs. This was what they lived for: the honour of their nation, the power of their arms. But as the crowd yelled, another sound was blown in on the wind. It came as if in answer to their own cries, and it served only to make them more impatient. It was a sound they knew: a ragged pulsing of human voices in their thousands and a dreadful clash and clatter of swords uncounted. It was the sound of battle joined.

'Do you hear it, men. Do you hear? Anparas has beaten us to it. Do we allow him all the glory? Captains, to me!'

Tregar watched distastefully as Temor made his speech. War was bad enough without all this. He wasn't squeamish and he'd enjoy the fight when he got going, but he couldn't abide this business of setting nation against nation – as though each of them was made of people who all thought the same! Still, whoever it was, waiting for them in the valley, they *were* the enemy and Tregar wouldn't be chary of treating them as such.

Tregar put himself at the front of the army. He wanted to see the enemy as quickly as possible but that wasn't his only reason. Lord Temor and Seth were there too and the wizard wanted to keep an eye on them. The army was Shaf's to command but Tregar was determined to have his say. Tregar had a bad feeling about this battle and his lack of confidence in the commander made it worse.

They made a slow start with Temor concerned to keep his army in some sort of formation as they struggled over the broken terrain. Twenty minutes of effort brought them to the lip of the cwm but the low clouds whipped up by the wind swirling in the valley hid it from view. Tregar was suspicious of the cloud at first but however hard he concentrated he couldn't discern any magical property in it. It was just cloud and soon they'd get under it.

There were four paths downwards according to the maps they'd made in Small Cuttings, and though they couldn't see them all at once, they were quickly found. Lord Temor had the army divided up in a few words and the descent began. It was not easy. Tregar's route, the one chosen by Temor himself, was well defined by many cairns but it traversed a wide scree slope. At every step Tregar expected the scree to start moving with the weight of five hundred men, but surprisingly it held firm. They had not long crossed the worst of it when the cloud lifted giving them a clear view of the scene below.

The din of battle assaulted them. A wide circle of grass, half a mile across pinned to the mountains by a round tarn glinting like a bright thumb nail at its centre. At the open end of the cwm peering out at the majestic Francon valley stood old Greteth, quaking and hard pressed by a sea of dun-clothed people who beat at the castle in waves of steel. Desperate defenders fought on the walls to push back the grey tide swarming up long ladders.

In the conflict dozens of swords met each few seconds, but that clash was diminished by the sound of a greater, unseen battle that raged below and beyond the castle.

'Do you see them lads?' Temor yelled to his men as they stepped free of the cloud. 'Do you hear the cries of Anparas in the Francon? It's bloody battle and we'll be in it. No fancy plans now. Come on, let's break 'em.' And so saying he led a reckless charge down the last few hundred feet, and his men followed.

All but Tregar, who was jumping up and down flapping his arms and yelling in fury. He snarled as he yelled, like a great bear.

'Come back, come back. Stop ye bladdie fools. Aargh! For the god's sakes can't ye wait? Stop, stop! Ye can't run all the way! Temor, Shaf! Stop!'

His cries were in vain. Sprinting away at the head of the charge were two figures. They were already too far away to be recognized by feature, but one of them raised his sword before him as he ran, a sword with an eye in it that burned a hungry red. At this remove it almost seemed as though the sword was dragging the man.

Tregar's frustration silenced him. They had done exactly what he feared they would and it was no way to enter a battle. Shaf should have known it but lately he'd been a man possessed and there was no reason left in him. Tregar searched out the other three parts of the army and in despair saw that they were following their Lord as their duty and their battle lust demanded. The wizard grunted his disgust.

'Well, not me!' he said out loud.

Tregar would approach cautiously. He'd see what there was to be seen, and decide what needed to be done. And *then* he'd draw his sword.

He continued his descent at a brisk pace but was surprised before long to see two Partians ascending the wall towards him. They were running up faster, if that were possible, than Temor was coming down. As they drew nearer Tregar recognized them as two of the missing scouts. They were screaming like mad men.

'No, no. Go back! We can do nothing. Gods help us! They've risen. They can't be killed.'

'Wait up. Stop! Stop, I said!' Tregar grabbed one of them by an arm as he tried to run past. The man struggled in panic and they both fell onto the stony earth, wrestling for mastery. Tregar was far the stronger and he managed to pin the man by his shoulders.

'What's happening? What are ye talking about man?'

'They can't be killed, can't be killed.'

'What do ye mean? Why can't they be killed.' Tregar shook him, just hoping the man would come to his senses. He was rewarded only by grim laughter.

'Why?' he said as he laughed, 'Because they're already dead. You can't kill a dead man. I tried, I hit him, chopped him, cut him. But he just kept coming. They're all dead. The dead have risen.'

What was the man babbling about. The dead risen? The *dead risen!* The man was confused, insane, but… 'My enemies are men, what are yours, I wonder?' That's what Seama had said. Did he know? And Uovin, his so called advisor, had he known? Tregar was suddenly very, very angry.

'Come on, One Eye,' he yelled to the skies, 'Tell me whit to do now. All this bladdie nonsense about Good and Evil, and faecken' *Persuasion*! All that crap! Couldn't ye just have told me the *one useful thing*! The faecken' dead have risen and ye couldn't even tell me that!' He shook his fist at the clouds above him as though he thought Uovin was hiding there. 'Well come on, ye useless old cripple. Are ye too scared to show your face?'

Beneath him the scout squirmed violently and managed to push him off. With no one to hold him back the man pelted off up into the mountains but Tregar never spared him a glance nor saw him ever again. Instead he charged down the slope, all caution forgotten, and yelling as he ran:

'I *told* ye, I told ye to wait. Ye bladdie fools!'

FIRST BLOOD

Francon valley 3057.8.8

Lomal, the Lord Anparas, responsible for an army of two thousand men and their families, was never reckless. In any confrontation there was a time for caution and a time for total commitment, and in Lomal's mind the former invariably preceded the latter. There were generals who happily charged into battle believing the sudden onslaught a valid tactic, but for Lomal, winning was not a general's only purpose. Men were not just numbers. They had a right to the chance of surviving and Lomal considered it his duty to provide that chance. He would never sacrifice a platoon as a mere diversionary tactic; he would never advance infantry before he knew whether they faced cavalry or not. This consideration for his soldiers' lives may have been a fault in him.

Faced with the unknown his instinct was to hold his ground and see what there was to see. The army had advanced into the mouth of the Francon. Black Greteth dominated the view. The end wall upon which she stood seemed close though a league separated the general from his target. What stood between claimed all of Lomal's attention. A milling, churning mass of grey shapes, indistinguishable in their multitude, filled the valley floor and swarmed the slope like so many ants in search of a new nest. The enemy at last.

Lomal considered the scene. The valley end was defined by a massive dyke of hard granite, sheer and almost impassable. Upon this dyke, at centre, Castle Greteth stood proud and cold and forbidding. Truly a daunting prospect, but she hadn't been raised at this point for dramatic effect: her gate opened upon the only point of weakness in that great bulwark. There in aeons past the retreating glacier had spewed out the refuse of earth and broken rock that now lapped against the dyke and, weathered by the years, this moraine formed a level thirty acres fifteen feet below the base of the castle bailey.

A winding road climbed the easier gradient on the northern

slopes of the mound, a road currently thick with activity. Lomal took out his glass and trained it upon the raised meadow. From what he could see every minute that passed swelled the ranks of those before the castle, but perspective and distance and the haziness of the air denied him worthwhile detail. There were no siege towers in sight but surely there would be ladders at least, and rams of course and perhaps catapults yet to be assembled. It was a worry that he could see nothing clearly.

A commotion behind him caused his horse to turn. It was Callin Senca, his second in command, returning from a tour down the line, with all the senior officers trailing in his wake.

Lomal gestured ahead with a flick of his chin.

'Looks as if we've a fight on after all,' he called to them.

Senca shrugged: a show for his captains.

'What? That lot? Look at it. They're a shower.'

Lomal grinned mirthlessly. Callin could see them no better than he could.

'At least now we know Jaspar wasn't just having nightmares. Let's get a better look,' he said.

What Lomal desperately wanted was some idea of numbers. With the opposing army a thick grey line of indeterminate depth stretched wall to wall across the Francon he needed height and he needed his scouts. A knoll, shouldered against the southern side, some seventy feet higher than the road, solved his first problem and, by the time they had climbed it, approaching horses solved the second. Lomal smiled a proper smile.

'Well Callin,' he said, 'A bit of luck to give us heart.'

'Nothing lucky about old Udsal, he's just so good at it.'

'The best, Callin. I'd hate to lose him.'

'Aye to that.'

Senca nodded to a sergeant who promptly sent a man off to fetch Udsal up onto the promontory, but when they looked the tracker was already on his way up, puffing and blowing and grumbling as he came.

'Why you can't wait down there?' he wanted to know, 'I tell you two hours – here I am.' He gestured at the eyeglass in Lomal's hand and shook his head. 'Glass, tin: no use eh? I tell you, then you see with my eyes – all is clear.'

Lomal grinned. 'Had I your eyes in the first place, Uz, I wouldn't need the glass. I hope you've good news for me?'

'I have news. You must say good or bad.'

He was a rounded, hairy man. At court he would have been considered uncouth, loutish. His shabby fur parka, a companion of all seasons, was hardly more weathered than the man himself. The voice he produced in fits and starts, deep and rasping, seemed more suited to swearing than polite conversation though, as far as Lomal knew, swearing was something the tracker never did. Nomads were very religious. How a Plan Visent nomad had found his way across the Hypodedicus to become Chief Scout of the Anparas army Lomal couldn't guess. Udsal was impenetrably silent about his early life whoever asked the questions and Lomal suspected that some dark secret bound his tongue, some shame.

The captains were now gathered in a loose circle waiting for Udsal's news. His first move was to attack one of them. After a short flurry of arms and legs Udsal stepped back into the centre of the circle with the captain's sword in his hand.

'Could've just asked, Uz,' said the captain seemingly unconcerned by the incident.

Udsal grinned. 'I just wake you up, Mister Honry – you all lazy, sleepy.' Some of the younger officers, men not familiar with Udsal's antics, were affronted by the suggestion but nonetheless pulled themselves erect. The tracker prowled the circle challenging them all with his eyes. 'Who next, eh? Who next? Mister Burstan?'

'Enough, enough,' cried the senior captain, with a laugh, 'I'm too old for horseplay. Here,' he said surrendering his sword, 'What do you want them for anyway?'

Udsal, clutching the swords under one arm, gestured with the other asking them to gather round an area of flat, smooth rock. Here he lay the swords in parallel. 'Uh, valley sides.' He pulled a coiled whip from somewhere inside his parka and arranged it in a circle at one end with the stiff end representing the dyke. He used Captain Honry's gauntlet for the castle and found himself a large flat stone to show the position of the raised meadow.

'Yes, yes. There is huh baby valley, huh castle and yes, high aaah *pasture*,' Udsal used his hands widely to make up for his uncertain language: a language he had maintained in its uncertain state with some difficulty over the years. 'Big trouble for you bossman. Listen,' he said and raised a finger, meaning that they should wait for a moment. Rather theatrically he chose a fern frond from the brake nearby and wrestled it away with a great deal of gasping and grunting as though he was too old for such exertions. Returning wearily to the centre of the group he began to pull the frond apart, each segment the length of a thumb. When he had enough he turned to Lomal and said:

'Each ten by ten.'

Scooping up two handfulls he walked about his diagram pouring the pieces thickly or thinly according to what he and the other scouts had seen.

On the flat stone, and before the belt dyke, thirty pieces of fern fell; another twenty were tight up against the cwm-side of the gauntlet castle. Between the sword arms a scattering, ten or more, fell by the side of the flat stone and then half-way to the open end of the sword valley was a block, five deep and five across, holding the centre ground.

For a few moments the gathered captains stared incomprehendingly at the diagram. It was not too difficult for them to understand but the small pieces of fern seemed so insignificant and it was hard at first for their imaginations to make the necessary substitution. Lomal was quicker than most and even he was momentarily lost for words. In this age of the world the combined army of Anparas and Temor was considered a large force, sufficient for most eventualities short of total war. Was this total war? Callin Senca was the first to speak.

'Each piece a hundred, Udsal?'

'Yes, yes! I *say* ten, ten times.'

'Lomal, we are three thousand facing more than eight.'

'I've counted it Callin, though it's not quite as bad as you paint it. Our army is three thousand, eight hundred and Jaspar has another twelve hundred. Even so, I share your concern. Let's hope they're poor fighters. Any more to tell Udsal?'

'Yes, Uz, some good news this time or you get no supper,' prompted Dom Honry.

Udsal laughed fiercely. 'No Mister Honry. No good news, no supper. Not today. Not ever again.' He fixed the captain with a compelling gaze and it was with some strange delight that he added: 'This is the day for the killing. The day for death!'

A silence fell. Honry's grin faltered. Prognostications of doom, however gleefully given, were not well received by even the most levelheaded soldiers. They were certainly not what Lomal wanted and he was angry. 'I asked for information, tracker, not fancy. Speak your news and have done!'

Udsal was contrite: 'Yes, boss; sorry boss. But they fight no good.'

'You rogue,' Honry burst in, 'I almost believed you. No good news, a day for death. Udsal you're a fraud. So they can't fight, eh?'

'Wait, wait! They fight no good; they *die* no good. I stab, yes; I cut, yes; die?' He shook his head.

'Whatever's that supposed to mean,' asked Senca, 'They fight when they're wounded? We face a dedicated crew then…'

'No, no. Not that. You'll see.'

Senca and his Lord exchanged puzzled glances. 'The sooner we see the better,' said Lomal. 'Udsal, do they have horses? I see none from here.'

'No horses.'

'And the force in the valley, how is it deployed?'

'Like I show you: they stand in rank, like parade. But in group, ten times ten. That's why so easy to count. But yes, in valley aswell, three tens to scout, and listen,' Udsal paused, looked around at all of them and wagged his finger in the silence, 'They have seen,' he chuckled evilly, 'they come close.'

'Three different platoons?'

'Of ten. Now you see, eh?'

Lomal didn't need prompting.

'Well, who's going to fetch me ten enemy scouts,' he asked,

and immediately grey haired Captain Burstan spoke up:

'My horse are closest, Lord Lomal.'

'Thank you, Burstan. Take Udsal with you.'

Udsal snorted at that: 'No, no, no,' he said,' *I* will take *him* with *me*.'

Over an hour later, Lomal and his commanders were still discussing the possible tactics of the engagement when Burstan returned.

Lomal turned to chide him for taking his time but the words died on his lips. The Senior Captain of Horse looked as though he had aged another twenty years, and borne many a wound and many a grief in that time. The haggard, drawn face had lost all colour.

'What happened?'

'Udsal was quite correct, My Lord. Well almost. May I sit?'

'Stubson, fetch the Captain some brandy. Take your time, Burstan, but we must have it.'

Burstan tipped off his helmet and sat for a moment massaging his forehead with whitened fingertips. 'My Lord, ' he began, 'I will tell it in order, but... well, it's hard.' His eyes, as he spoke, had a disturbing, absent look about them. 'We found the group,' he said, 'with Udsal's help, of course. Two of their platoons had come together. I had forty horse, they were twenty on foot. Thought they'd yield easy enough. Damned if they didn't just ignore us. They were pale men, Lomal. No, it was more than that. They were white: they had the look of the grave about them. Their eyes, I swear it, were dry like on a bad fish. They never spoke or screamed or anything. I told them to drop their weapons. The swords they had, all sorts, all fashioned as I've never seen, and pitted as though ages old. They didn't lower their weapons; didn't even try to run. Well, there was no command I heard but of a sudden they advanced on us, not quickly but as though they were walking through jelly.

'I dismounted, and half my men. We wanted to drop a few of them and take the rest. I thought it'd be easy. Dear Gods! Easy enough to pass their strokes at first. Worse than farmboys. I stabbed my man high on his left breast, stood back to watch him fall. Lucky that Erol was at my side. I'd dropped my guard. The man hadn't fallen at all. He wasn't even bleeding. Erol swiped at his guts but that still didn't stop him. All I could think was to hack at the sword arm. Thank the gods I managed to sever it. Ordered my men to fall back then, and we stood facing each other. I'd lost three, they'd lost none.

'It was madness after that. Arrows were useless; spears didn't stop them. They just pulled them out – like it was an inconvenience. Somehow they got quicker at their job, as if they'd remembered how to do it. Came in among the horses, cut 'em up as we tried to beat them off. The horses were in a panic, six got killed; I lost another three men.' The Captain punched his gauntleted fist into the earth where he sat. 'We bled alright! We died! What could we do? Hacked at them but it was no use. Some were still walking, still fighting with great rents in their sides, injuries that'd have stopped any one of us. It was horrible. My men couldn't live with it so I ordered another withdrawal.' He looked at the faces of his peers daring them to judge him. They stood in silence, all wanting to disbelieve what they heard. 'Don't you worry,' he said, 'you'll understand soon enough. We didn't retreat fully – still had a job to do, orders to obey. I sent back for reinforcement. Decided the only way was to face them on foot with sword and knife, and so we set-to again. That was a terrible hour. My men are as brave as you can find, you know that Lomal. Some of 'em were gibbering by the end of it.'

Lomal blew out a long breath. 'Yes, Burstan. They're some of the best.' *What sort of challenge is this?* he was thinking. *Who are these people, these devils?* Tregar had told them about Seama's land of evil. By their very bodies these were evil. 'But you returned Burstan, you're unmarked. Give us the end of it. They cannot be indestructible, can they?'

'It's a moot point my lord.' The Captain looked again at the faces surrounding him, everyone intent and frowning at what he had to say, all shocked by the tale he told. Dom Honry. Callin. Young Solan Cole. They were worried faces, every one, but at least there was the spark of life in their eyes, the flush of good honest blood in their cheeks.

'By Tammaz, but it's good to be among common folk.' He sighed. 'Is that brandy you have there?' Stubson passed him the flask. 'A bit of warmth is just what I need.' He took a pull at it and then clutched the flask to his chest. It seemed to buoy him up. 'The end was a long time coming. It took three of mine for every one of theirs, but eventually we managed to dismember the lot of 'em. Arms, legs, heads. One of them, I'd chopped off its head but it just kept coming at me, waving its sword as though the head didn't matter. Like a bloody chicken! When the arms and legs were gone I quartered it myself – had to make sure, you see. And, you know, when I left, all the bits were still twitching.'

The senior captain shook his head as if to deny the image in his mind. He took another pull at the flask.

'And are they dead now?' cried out one man for all of them.

Burstan looked at them, a half-smile on his face.

'Were they ever not dead?' he said.

'What are we going to do, Lomal?' Callin's voice had an edge to it. 'With Udsal's numbers on top of Burstan's story we don't stand a chance, not a hope. With Temor and Jaspar it's still two to one and we need two for every one of theirs. So what are we going to do?'

Lomal's look was cool and steady. 'We cannot leave them unfought, Callin. Our course is set. Jaspar is holed up but without us he'll be destroyed. Temor has less than we have. What could he do without us? And, anyway, how would we fare with our backs to them?'

'But it's suicide, Lomal!'

'No Callin. We may find a way to defeat them. Tregar will soon be at hand. This is work for wizards if ever there was. He may find an answer, but even if we're heading for a defeat, this will be no suicide. I hope you're all listening. This will be no suicide! A sacrifice maybe. You all know me. I will not waste lives. But everyone here must remember that nothing stands between this horror and the green fields of Pars: the mothers and children, our brothers and sisters. We cannot let it pass unfought. We have to give Pars time to muster.'

'But who are they, Lord? What are they?' Solan, the youngest man present was clearly moved by Lomal's words of the threat to his homeland – his family lived in Coldharbour – and he knew where his duty lay, but still he was confused. 'Why have they come to attack us?'

'Why indeed? What they are I can say no more than we have heard from Captain Burstan. The great wizard Seama Beltomé gave Tregar some warning of this, though even he could never have expected such a terrible crew.' Lomal gave them a brief account of Seama's guess about the evil that lay beyond the mountains, past the mighty Dedicae where the Sea of Ice attacked the land. Before Burstan's tale the men would have scoffed at such foolish ideas but now every word seemed reasonable. Lomal told them the names Seama had given them: Ah'remmon and Kyzyl Kum and Ohr'mazd. The last they all knew as the great god still worshipped by many as Lord of the Just, but Ah'remmon was little more than a footnote even in Lomal's mind: a god of evil, the king of an evil country. The captains hung on his words. Lomal was embarrassed that he could tell them nothing more.

Callin Senca was an imaginative man, more information was not necessary. 'Do you mean we are to fight a god?' He was prepared to believe it.

'I shouldn't think so. I'm sure Seama used the name only as a symbol which, awful though that may be, cannot be quite so invincible. We fight for Ohr'mazd in this war, but I doubt our enemy expects to fight the Lord of the Just himself. Now Solan, does that half answer your question?'

'If we'd not heard Burstan's tale… I hardly know what to think.'

'I hardly think it matters', said Honry, 'I mean, who cares where they're from, what they are? They're here to raise war and we've a duty to oppose them. Whether we're capable or not. But it'll be hard killing dead people, don't you think? Perhaps we should ask Ohr'mazd if he can arrange for us to rise from the dead aswell.'

'A little too blasphemous, don't you think, Honry?' said Callin, 'Especially for a man about to meet his maker.'

'Enough!' said Lomal. The thought of death filled his own mind, but he refused to admit it. Maudlin thoughts were not going to help any of them. 'The battle will be hard enough without us trembling at the words of a misplaced nomad, no matter how good a tracker he might be. I suggest we proceed as previously discussed. In fact, I command it. The task will be more difficult given Burstan's report, but the form of our battle must remain the same. What we must do is make sure every man hears the tale before we begin. I don't want them too shocked to respond. Shall we get on with it?'

POINTS OF VIEW

The tactics of engagement seem so obvious when they are planned, arrows on paper, pieces on a table, but in the inferno of battle the paper is burned, the pieces are scattered. A footsoldier has too hard a time saving his skin to be bothered whether he is in the right place or not. And yet, as Lomal looked down upon the opening moves he had ordered, somehow the men and the pieces followed the same pattern. *We begin well*, he thought.

A squirm of guilt caught him by surprise. The general was not at the head of the army as he had promised himself. So much for resolutions. Of course it was his duty to stay out of it, his lot to watch and to control. Romantic gestures, he reminded himself, were Shaf's province, good sense his own. The guilt abated but didn't disappear.

His soldiers were now comfortably small in his sight. He looked down from a vantage point high-up on the southern wall of the Francon upon what seemed no more than toys of brass and clay. His view was bloodless, distanced from the flesh and the bones and the guts of war. Up here the screams of agony were nothing in the anonymous, frantic din.

Five hundred perfect mannikins hurled ferociously into the centre of the enemy line. The momentum carried them deep, toppling all before them. If there was hesitation, a sudden shock as the opponents met, Lomal did not see it and he certainly didn't feel it. 'Now!' he whispered and, as though his word had carried half a mile, a second assault crashed down upon the field from the northern wall: a sudden flood, a dam-burst that nothing could stand against. What a power they were. An army working as one. A raised hand released the cavalry. His signal would bring ruin.

A large part of the enemy on the southern flank had turned to assist their comrades in the centre and north. Lomal's cavalry, charging in a scything loop from the south, made them turn again. A simple manoeuvre, but sure. Lomal admired the graceful arc: in, cut and away; admired the straightforward hammer and anvil of the combined foot brigades. He was watching for the reply. He expected the deployment of the still ranked rear lines of the enemy this way or that. His tactics depended upon that reply, but in watching the enemy Lomal missed the moment when his own army faltered.

The cavalry were already looping back for their second pass and his third wave of foot was running in behind them before Lomal saw his hammer broken. The advance had been illusion. The trampled and scythed had not been harvested by the final reaper, the enemy sprang up like prairie grass after the storm and they attacked again. In the fury of the initial movement Lomal's soldiers had forgotten Burstan's tale, ignored their instruction. A slash, a stab, enough for mortal men, was not enough. Only now did they understand.

'Callin,' Lomal screamed, 'Sound a retreat. Now! They must all withdraw.' And under his breath he prayed: 'Gods, let them have the legs.'

That was how Anparas opened the Battle of the Francon.

Solan stumbled as a headless corpse piled into him, arms spread and clutching. He had cut into one of those arms and flinched as it curled around his neck, expecting to be covered in blood and nothing worse. And then he was gasping as the cold fingers pressed into his throat, the black nails ripping his flesh. Solan tore at the hand, desperate to shift it. He was on the verge of passing out when the grip slackened and he was free, free to breath again. He pulled the hand away, and just a hand was all it was, chopped off at the wrist by a swing that must nearly have shaved-off his nose. His saviour, rolling about under the rest of the thing, was screaming.

Solan hardly hesitated. He hacked at the remaining arm as best he could and then kicked and kicked and kicked until his comrade could roll away. The thought of having to touch the creature with his hands made his stomach heave. He swung his sword in a protective arc as his comrade got to his feet, but the fight had left them a few safe yards.

'I owe you, Deller.'

'And I you, Captain, so the debt's even. Look out!'

Solan lurched aside as Deller swung and hacked at another of the walking dead. This one was unmarked so far, and quicker with its sword, parrying and attacking in turn. Deller alone would have been in trouble but Solan cut at the legs from behind and as it toppled they both waded in to dismember the thing. Deller was quick to strike, taking off the sword arm at the shoulder, but young Captain Solan stopped in midswing and could only watch, frozen-faced, as Deller completed the job.

Deller looked up when he had done. Forty years old he was, a seasoned campaigner, his Captain his junior. 'You'll get used to it, Captain. Think how much harder it would have been if it had been a real live woman.'

'She looked so much like my wife. I couldn't do it.' Solan had seen her face and, though now hideous because of the death that gripped her, he realized she had once been beautiful.

'With respect, Captain Solan, you're going to have to do it again and again. Or we won't survive.'

Solan shook himself mentally and physically. There was no time for this. To prove himself he thrust his sword hard into the eyes that still watched them, still watched even though the head and body were almost severed. With that stroke he destroyed all memory of her beauty. He felt the better for it. Lying before him now was just another rotten corpse.

The retreat came soon after and Solan lost sight of Deller in the chaos. The cavalry were amongst them and the horses heaving about threw up a rain of mud that covered hair, eyes and noses and clogged the wits of those on foot. It was hard to say whether the retreat was being punished by the enemy or not but after ten minutes the order to regroup was blown. To Solan's surprise, he saw that the enemy lines had not moved a yard. Neither to pursue nor to gain ground. They had refused the advantage.

'Warfare exceeding strange, Captain.'

Burstan sat on the ground not ten yards away, the reins of his horse curled loosely around his gauntlet.

'Never more so, Senior Captain. A strange enemy and stranger tactics. Why don't they take ground? They could have it for nothing. Is it fear that holds them?'

Burstan snorted in contempt.

'The Dead fear the Living? The priests are always telling us that evil must fear the good, but I don't see that either'

'You think them evil then? Is it so clear, Burstan?'

'I do; it is. The wizard's story spoke of a kingdom of evil and we laughed at that, but is this not far worse than anything he could have imagined? There stands the proof. Their lives are long past. They don't bleed, they don't breathe. Have you heard one of them speak? Or shout, or scream? I doubt it. And their clothes and weapons: so many different styles. Who are they? What sort of place do they come from? A kingdom of evil, surely, and a land of the dead. You have to wonder how long they've been there, and where they were before?'

Solan shivered, perhaps from the cold. His eyes beheld the carnage beyond their line but more present to his mind was the image of the once beautiful woman he had killed for a second time, and he was full of his own questions. Was she once some man's wife, some baby girl's mother? Had she sung as she worked; had she a house near a river, with sweet peas in her garden?

'What are you thinking, Solan? It's not a good day for thinking.'

'I was remembering my wife and my home.'

'Don't do it. Today all is duty: a hard thing when you have something to lose. Today it is everything.' Burstan's voice was matter-of-fact but there was a far-off look of loss in his eyes. Solan remembered that the captain's wife had died several years ago in some sort of accident. Burstan caught his glance.

'That was too hard. I'm sorry. For me the House is all I have left.' He looked away, then suddenly, furiously, he demanded: 'What are you doing here? You have a wife, children, a home. How can you desert them? Life is short enough without seeking death like this.'

Solan was surprised and had no ready reply. Why was he

here? It was simple: 'It's my job,' he said.

'A hard job for a young husband.'

Solan shrugged. Looking forward and trying not to think about anything difficult, he saw movement in the enemy ranks. 'Look: the line's thicker. They've advanced more of their centuries.'

Fifteen minutes later they had new orders and made to follow them. Burstan began to lead his mounted troop away to the right of Solan's foot brigade, but he had moved only a few yards when his mount stumbled in a foxhole and fell. The attack sounded as Burstan was struggling to his feet.

'Ride on, Marrin,' he shouted to his second, 'There's no time to wait. Ride on. Take the command, I'm for the foot now.'

His horse was lame and with tender regret he patted and stroked the poor beast before leaving it to its fate. 'Well, young Captain,' he said as he fell in beside Solan, 'it seems I'm to fight by you awhile.'

'That pleases me.'

'We fight in pairs, I take it?'

'That's the order. We won't go as fast but we'll make less mistakes.'

'I wonder, Solan, whether they'll let us take our time. So far they've done nothing but hold their ground, but I'm hesitant to think it shows lack of imagination. They'll do something.'

'Yes, but should it affect us? It's no use trying to contemplate tactics so close to the action. Lomal is looking for their answer. We can only cut and thrust; use our experience to stay alive. Win our own personal battles.'

Burstan turned a mocking eye toward the younger man. 'Your pragmatism does you credit,' he said, and not wholly ironically, 'I hope that at his remove, Lomal doesn't miss the answer, that he'll know what to do about it, and that he won't abandon us to our experience: an uncertain ally at the best of times. Look around you. A hundred experienced men lie dead already.'

'Does age always make men cynical, Burstan?'

'Not age, but war certainly. I've seen more of it than you. Quite honestly, I'm surprised I've lived this long.'

Solan, forging ahead, wouldn't believe it. Burstan was a soldier, a Captain, a swordsman many aspired to emulate. Raising his eyes to the black line they advanced upon he said: 'You must admit that getting through so many battles is a fair proof of skill.'

Just behind him Burstan chuckled, perhaps at the thought of his apparent fame. 'Proof?' he asked. It was his last word. Solan heard rather than saw the javelin. He heard the sickening thump as it sank into metal flesh and bone; heard Burstan gasp his final breath as it smote him full in the chest.

There was no time for grieving: the two armies charged at each other. It was the third file of centuries that brought the javelins, a weapon unfamiliar to the Partians, and their deadly shafts filled the air and hurt Anparas severely before swords could answer. Captain Solan, in his anger, danced through the hail uncaring and was first to meet the enemy once more. His sword raked back and forth, biting and hacking. With a two-handed backward sweep he almost bisected the first creature before him. Pulling back to finish the job he yelled like a savage, voicing his anger in one long, unintelligible cry. It was a cry for Burstan, and a cry for himself, and for his wife and child. A sword had pierced his side and his life so soon was gushing out of him. He sank to the miry ground and though the air was full of the sound of trumpets he heard only the weeping of children, and saw only loving faces that quickly grew dim.

Xandra was in a frenzy of excitement; there was no holding her. Oh, it was certainly Jaspar who ordered the sortie, but what choice did he have in deciding who would lead it? None. He'd tried to remind her of the earlier disaster but somehow she managed to see that incident as some sort of personal success. He'd tried to suggest caution and she had told him to hang his caution. 'So be it,' he'd said, 'If you choose to forget that you're Mador's heir, and your responsibility is to the whole of Pars, then go on. Take your own way as usual, but make sure, make very sure that you lead my people either to victory or safety. This is no time for heroic sacrifice.' And she'd gone, a scornful glance his only answer.

Jaspar raised a hand. The trumpets blew a more wholesome note than had foredoomed the previous sortie and the gate opened. He stood on the wall above the gate and watched as she emerged at the head of the four hundred, her red hair blazing as it fanned out from beneath her helm. In some ways he envied her. He'd always envied her though there was no jealousy over her position – the title 'Heir' was not at all attractive. What he admired and coveted was the heedless resolve, the unthinking bravery, the ungovernable recklessness: in short, all of those things in her he most criticised.

Battle suited Xandra. It made him sad to realize that it would eventually destroy her. It needed no soothsayer to foretell that.

Below him the cavalry thundered onto the high field that lay before the gates and, predictably enough, was led to attack the largest part of the enemy that remained, despite his order that they should deal first with the smaller contingent on the right. 'Damn woman!' he muttered, well aware that those nearby could hear him. Needing something else to think about he called for reports from the cwm-side of the castle.

The fog had lifted at or about the tenth hour or rather, it had disappeared as though it was no longer required. Below the Francon Gate they were ranked, grey on green, a huge army of at least three thousand. But three thousand what? They were people of sorts but so pale. They had with them ladders and rams, they carried swords and some sort of spear. Not one of them brandished a bow; there were no siege engines or catapults. Jaspar thanked his gods for that mercy but found himself uneasy about it: why were they lacking? Because they weren't needed?

Seconds before the first assault from the valley, runners from the rear walls had brought news of another army massing in the cwm. From that moment until the arrival of Anparas in the valley, all that the defenders of Greteth knew was frantic, desperate action.

It was only the numbers in opposition that daunted him. The front of the castle was not wide, nor the rear. Only a fraction of the enemy could attack at any one time and the defenders found it surprisingly easy to dislodge ladders and climbers. The ram carriers were halted time and again by hails of boulders. But the Partians grew weary as the hours passed and their store of boulders ran low. It was true that the constantly renewed front rank of the enemy could gain little momentum as they stumbled over the boulders that had already fallen, but neither their numbers nor their enthusiasm for the attack diminished.

It had been quite some time before the defenders realized the implication of that fact. Their opponents were not dying. Save for those few with massively broken limbs, each of them simply got up and walked away from sure fatality. Eventually a few managed to mount the walls and the truth was discovered.

The situation was beginning to seem impossible but then Lomal and his army arrived. The attack on the castle front was halted as the enemy commanders began to reorganize. Shortly ten centuries turned away from Greteth to make their way down the valley. Anparas would not be made welcome.

Jaspar, Xandra and the Commanders of the House of Sands all ran to the highest tower to view the battle and to discuss their next move. It was then that they saw the failure of Anparas' first-attack, then that they watched the enemy reinforcements swelling the ranks of Lomal's opposition. It was Jaspar, anticipating what Xandra might say, who decided upon a major sortie. Anparas was disengaged but would soon advance once more against heavier odds. The Lord of Sands hoped that by initiating an attack of his own he might draw off some of the weight of bodies that Lomal faced. If they timed it right, retreating as soon as the reinforcements returned to the castle, he might keep the enemy commanders vacillating between the two fronts.

And so it was that, as Solan Cole lay dying in the valley, Jaspar let blow the trumpets and his cavalry burst forth to smite a blow at the heart of the enemy. If such an enemy could be said to have a heart.

Jaspar listened to the reports from the cwm. They were not

good: the supplies of arrows and stones were running out; the wall had been topped several times, the creatures that attacked them barely repulsed. Jaspar looked out at the cavalry. Xandra was in her element, losses seemed few.

'Stimson,' he said, 'keep me in touch. I'm for the east wall. If the battle turns don't wait for me, sound a retreat – and don't hesitate or we'll suffer for it.'

The fight for the east wall was hectic. Selby was commanding. Jaspar was happy to give the man full responsibility. Arguments in council didn't alter the fact that Selby was a fine leader. By sending the commander to control the rear defences, Jaspar was not simply keeping him out of the way. The dispute and the bad feeling between them had not been settled, however, and Jaspar was apprehensive about the commander's mood.

'Come to check up on me, have you?' Selby sneered as soon as his Lord approached. 'Making sure I play it your way?'

'You're in command here, Selby.' Jaspar refused to be drawn, but there was no warmth in his voice. 'What's your report?'

'They attack, as you see, and we defend. They'll win unless something miraculous happens. I heard Anparas had arrived.'

'Two thousand, at a guess.'

'Not enough.'

'I'd say not, Commander.'

'We agree on something then.' Selby didn't smile but pulled a face as though he'd just bitten on something unpleasant. 'Do you think Anparas a fool, Lord Jaspar?' he asked.

'I have not left the valley front to check up on *you*. Anparas is no fool and it's worth remembering that Temor's army has yet to be accounted for.'

'That was my thought. Let's hope we're right and that they come sooner rather than later.'

'It's obviously a day for agreement, Commander Selby. A shame it needs impending doom to force it.'

Jaspar and Selby had a hard hour to wait before their guess proved good, and in that time Xandra's glorious attack had turned to predictable retreat and out in the valley Lomal's soldiers weakened and died, the green Francon turned red and the living slipped and stumbled and struggled on.

THE CONQUEROR

Francon valley 3057.8.8

Tregar entered the nightmare. Lord Temor's initial and seemingly successful dash had been clawed to a halt. Now each of his men was engaged in a dance of death, hacking and writhing and screaming, desperate to get away from throttling hands or a crushing embrace. The first walking cadaver Tregar encountered wore gleefully its badge of arrogance: a Partian knife that skewered its heart and emerged bloodless between spine and shoulder blade. Despite the horror of what he saw, Tregar didn't delay and hefted his sword with all his considerable might at the creature's neck. The leering face was smashed away and the head rattled round, dangling from a strip of yellowed flesh and skin. The body came on and only tumbled to the ground when Tregar chopped at its legs. That was the first of many as the wizard threw himself body and soul into the conflict.

Through the clatter and screams he heard Lord Temor's voice booming out: 'Arms and legs, lads! Top and tail 'em!' Tregar glimpsed him through the press and he was cutting up rough around him. 'Arms and legs,' he yelled again, 'Can't do anything without 'em!' He was an inspiring performer and the men who heard and saw him shook themselves, shook off the terror, and got down to work. There was one soldier, however, who needed no encouragement. There was one young man who was like a bull in the pottery, a stampede through corn, a tornado through a village of straw: he demolished, destroyed, razed all before him. Seth Cookson was unstoppable. The long, black sword swung and whirled faster than the eye could follow. The lad was possessed of a battle lust, and a power to indulge it, that Tregar had never seen in his life. It was breathtaking to behold, and also very frightening. Tregar was relieved the enemy had nothing like him.

Following this example, Temor's men flung themselves into the carnage with renewed vigour. As Seth sang and yelled, they sang and yelled, and perhaps it was only Tregar who thought the singing somewhat hysterical.

But there was one who was silent. One who stood a little out of it and watched as the black sword rose and fell. The ruby eye seemed to wink at him. Cal's face wore tragedy for a mask as he witnessed a more horrifying sight than all the walking dead could ever be: as he saw his gentle brother turned into a bloodthirsty monster. Tears fought for release on that face and won and Cal Cookson turned away from the battle.

Tregar MacNabaer had no time to study or wonder and hardly noticed as Cal walked back into the cwm. He had more pressing problems.

Distracted by Seth's awesome career the wizard suddenly found himself surrounded. Four of the enemy, inadequately dispatched, had risen again and he was soon struggling to fend-off too many blows at once. He discovered that his weapon-skills had grown rusty through disuse. He should have practiced more regularly. Two more enemy soldiers joined in the attack and it occurred to a certain detached part of his brain that, unless he was lucky, very lucky, he'd never get the chance to practice ever again. A sword fizzed at his face and Tregar threw himself backwards, crashed into patch of fern and struggled to right himself in the tangle of it, all the while expecting the sting of a blade.

Temor himself came to the wizard's rescue. With two other Partians at his side he had waded in, swaggering, enjoying his power, and after a few minutes he gained them a little space. He chuckled as Tregar finally got to his feet.

'Well, wizard, what do you think?'

Tregar was disgusted to see Temor so happy in his work, but also slightly embarrassed he'd needed rescuing. 'What do I think?' he said, his frown fiercer than usual, 'I think we're lucky to still be in it, that's what I think.'

'You are, anyway.' The soldiers nearby grinned like lunatics as though Temor had made a truly witty comment – at least that was how Tregar saw it. Incredibly his frown deepened.

'That's not the point, Shaf, and ye know it. If ye hadn't charged in like a mad bull this situation might never have come about.'

'Rubbish. They'd still need fighting whatever I'd done. Come on Tregar, we haven't done so badly, have we? Haven't you seen Seth?'

'I've seen him, but that doesn't help us decide how we can possibly beat them. In case you hadn't noticed, there are hundreds more of them than us, and they're not that easy to kill.'

Temor stopped grinning. Tregar counted that small concession a victory. The Lord's forehead wrinkled as he remembered his opponents. 'They're a rum lot, Tregar.' he said, shaking his head, 'What the devil are they?'

'I don't know, Lord Temor. Not devils. Devils are more like demons. These seem to be simply dead men and women. Dead men that walk. I don't know how— Aaadh! Wee bugger!'

Tregar was hopping around clutching at his ankle. A head partially divorced from its shoulders had taken it in mind to bite whatever was closest. The wizard shook it free, hacked at the neck, and then began to kick the head around the field, screaming curses. He lost control. In temporary madness he imagined himself playing his native game of soccer, the head a grotesque and rather inefficient football. He kicked it over to Temor and yelled for the return.

'One-two! One-two!'

Temor complied, laughing at the desecration, and Tregar scored a goal between imaginary posts. The exercise left him with a sore foot, panting and laughing idiotically. He was lucky the battle was not close. Gradually the madness like the panting subsided. It was the pain that brought him back. Standing, he tried to examine his ankle and ended up holding his foot in both hands, hopping wildly backwards, very much to Shaf's amusement.

'Bit clean through the leather,' he said, ignoring the laughter, 'Clean through!'

'You need better boots.'

'Very bladdie helpful.'

'Well, if you're going to be like that, Sir Wizard, we'll leave you to it. I told you they were a rum lot. Perhaps you could think of something useful whilst you're nursing your foot."

Tregar growled in reply and Temor returned to the battle.

Incapacitated as he was, he thought it prudent to put some distance between himself and the fighting. Picking up his fallen sword he used it as a walking stick as he stumbled his way to a cluster of rocks well away from immediate danger.

He soon discovered that Cal had beaten him to it but Owen Cookson's second son seemed unaware of Tregar's approach. He sat motionless, staring unseeing at the battle for Greteth. Tregar noticed at once that Cal's normally wayward left eye was held as steady as the right by the power of the trance that bound him.

'What d'ye see, Cal Cookson?' he called out, hoping to break the trance, but Cal's voice was as faraway as his eyes when he said:

'The blood stone, blood on the blade, a crime to put men to shame.'

'Say what?'

The staring eyes faltered and swung apart and the young man looked about him in some surprise, fighting to control a sudden, violent shivering. He turned his face away from the wizard for a moment and then with a forced smile looked back.

'Lord Tregar,' he said and dipped his head.

"Just plain Tregar will do. Are ye alright? Not hurt, I hope?'

'Oh no. No, thanks for asking, but… I'm just…' he shrugged and seemed embarrassed.

'Is there anything you want to tell me? I thought ye might have been dreaming again?'

Cal's features twisted into a pained grimace. His wayward eye twitched as it tried to match the good one and Tregar could see tears forming in the corners of both.

'Aye. I've dreamt and dreamt and dreamt and its allus the same. Have you seen him? He can't stop, he loves it: all the fighting and the killing. What's this war going to do to him? What's it doing to us?'

Tregar shook his head slowly, 'War is war, Cal. There's nothing good in war, even if your cause is just. It changes everyone. What's your dream, Cal? Perhaps I can help. Cal… Cal! Cal, come back. Come back. Damn!'

The young man had barely listened to the wizard's little homily and walked away, this time back into battle, clutching his grandfather's sword in both hands. Tregar let him go, wondering whether both of Owen Cookson's sons would survive the day.

For some few minutes Tregar busied himself with his wound and, being a master healer, he managed the cut without the use of medicines or bandages. What little *power inherent* Tregar had was virtually all directed towards healing. It was his major talent. Not every wizard could be like the great Lord Seama whose *power* could adopt almost any mode of expression he required. Why else would others study for years the arts of magic: the making of spells the naming of names, the lore of the elements? Why else, other than to supplement their lack?

Tregar rubbed his ankle and, satisfied he'd done a good job, he replaced his sock and boot. He was half-risen to get back to the fight before he caught himself.

'Now just hold on, my laddie!' he said aloud. 'By the Gods but it takes a lot to get through that thick skull of yourn.'

He plumped himself back down again and looked to the battle for inspiration. He'd remembered not only Temor's request that he should think of something to help them win, but also something a god had said a week or so before. 'Let the warriors fight: you must use your skill,' he'd said, and 'if you're a wizard, behave like one.' A *god*. Uovin himself wanted Tregar to use whatever magic he possessed. And what had he done so far? Gotten himself bit in the ankle. Not very impressive. But where should he begin? He couldn't blast people with sheer power as Seama could, and even Seama would have had some trouble with an entire army. Could he call a spell to send everyone to sleep? Then, perhaps, keeping some of Temor's army out of it... *Don't be ridiculous*, he told himself, *a spell to send three thousand to sleep? Ha! And two thousand of them dead men at that.* A dozen other stupid ideas wriggled through his brain as he watched Temor's army grind to a halt once more and the enemy inexorably gain the advantage.

And then he was looking at the castle itself and his heart

lurched in fear for those within. He had seen no archers amongst the crowd of their opponents, and hadn't seen any other means of delivering flaming shot, but, sure enough, within the walls a black smoke swelled up and spilled over the battlements. He saw flames. Perhaps there were siege engines, ballistas in the Francon? He saw flames on the walls, flames that fell ragged over the sides. Tregar blinked rapidly to clear his eyes and looked again. Again the flames fell.

'Jaspar, you're the man himself!' Tregar yelled and gave a jig for joy as he watched the burning oil fall on the enemy and beyond all expectation *set them afire!* Apparently, dead men burned. Burned like fat from a pan! And as easy as speaking Tregar's answer burst from his lips.

If his spell had been an arrow and he a master bowman it could have flown no straighter, nor plunged with more ferocity into the target. Tregar's spell to another wizard would have had visible form, a blur of light erupting from his mouth and crossing the quarter mile to the castle walls in half a second. It exploded the falling oil like a huge firework over the main body of the enemy. A million drops of deadly rain showered them. Each drop found a mark, landing on flesh or cloth, it made no difference, each drop ignited and the fire spread. In minutes a quarter of the enemy were ablaze and the House of Temor was singing for joy. Their Lord led another foray and his men, with a new hope in their hearts, followed him.

The wizard looked for another opportunity to use the spell as he ran closer to the castle. Another large part of the enemy ranks held the ground to the left but Jaspar's men were not close enough with their buckets of oil. The last thing Tregar wanted was to use the spell indiscriminately and end up wounding their own, but the men on the walls seemed bemused by the explosion and hardly knew what to do next. As he ran Tregar flapped his arms and yelled to draw their attention but even when he had it they didn't seem to understand his extravagant sign language. He stopped, frustrated, scowled at his allies and yelled:

'Can't ye hear me, ye stupet beggars?' and of course, despite Tregar's mighty voice, they could not. He gave up yelling. He thought instead; and thought; and again it worked. The answer just slipped into his mind: a picture of Seama back in the Old Dog jumping at the bodiless voice in his ear. There was a similar technique he could use now. Instead of shouting he whispered and he gestured with his hands at the same time, as though he was waving. The words he spoke took wing and up on the walls of the castle a tall man heard his name spoken.

'Jaspar, Lord Sands! Look beyond the crowd below, over to your right. It's me, Tregar.' The man nearly stepped off the inside wall in surprise. When the message repeated, he looked out and saw the wizard waving.

Tregar's grin was now fixed on his face. Magic, he decided could be quite enjoyable. Jaspar was returning his wave. Tregar quickly gave him directions and soon men were scurrying toward the left hand walls carrying buckets of flaming oil on long poles. While they got themselves ready Tregar checked on the battle once more. At first it was difficult to make out what was happening in the central, seething mass but shortly, and to his dismay, everything became clear. Lord Temor's spearhead attack had cut too deeply and despite the heroic efforts of Seth Cookson to force a way through to him, Shaf was in trouble. The enemy had closed around and only ten men stood with him – another thirty had been killed already. Some enemy commander was quick to realize the possible gain and hundreds of the walking dead swarmed around the desperate struggle, cutting off any hope of a rescue. Lord Temor, a mere ten minutes earlier, had victory in his heart and now, because of the rashness that ruled him he was doomed.

Tregar saw red. Not just the red in Seth's sword, but the red of Lord Temor's men dying to defend him. The rage that sometimes consumed him took hold of his every thought.

On the walls Jaspar's defenders signalled their readiness. Tregar made up his mind. He spoke, cold and furious, into Lord Sands' ear:

'Altogether in the same place. The whole bladdie lot and do it now!'

The order was passed and on count of three, thirty buckets

of oil swung into the air to converge above enemy heads. Tregar spoke.

The blast and roar deafened every man on the field. White hot oil, the molten metal of the buckets ripped apart, both fell as a second damnation upon the unfortunates beneath. The first deadly rain had been a shower, this was a deluge. The destruction was spread over so much of the field that many of the Partians felt the pain of it. Some suffered severe burns wherever the oil landed, many lost much of their hair. But the living did not ignite so easily as their enemy. The dead men burned and burned and Tregar with only a word, had won the cwm.

The enemy survivors, those fortunate enough to be standing in the lee of some angle in the walls, were only a few hundred. At first they milled about, as bewildered as the Partians, but even as the disgusting stench of burnt flesh crawled into the air, obeying some unspoken command, they formed themselves into an ordered squadron. Using the cover of smoke, fire and confusion they made a retreat. By the time Temor's men caught up with them they'd almost reached the difficult path over the dyke. Tregar wasn't surprised to see Seth Cookson leading the pursuit. Less than half of the escapees made a safe descent into the Francon, while the majority made the journey much more quickly.

Back in the cwm, battle won, the victors were silent. It was a tainted victory. Who could cheer? Who would dare? Lord Temor was dead.

They lifted his body high above his vanquished foes and bore him in all honour to the opening gates of Castle Greteth.

Lomal stood upon his hill and watched his men die. He felt sick. An anger swelled in him that he fought to keep down. What good would anger do? In the valley the battle was deteriorating. The enemy commander, wherever he might be, had put most of his resources into demolishing Anparas' impertinent attack, eager to have his victory. Under increased pressure Lomal's line of command broke down, plans and stratagems were forgotten and his soldiers were fighting for their lives. The cavalry were a shabby band now that so many horses had been chopped to the ground; platoons of foot, separated from the main battle groups, were systematically destroyed and the main groups found themselves surrounded and each under siege.

This was the first time in his life that Lomal had been at such a loss and not known what to do to retrieve the situation. All he could think was that somehow Temor must rescue them. He wasn't aware that Temor was also hard pressed. When the first smokes rose from Greteth he presumed that the castle was on fire, and that Temor had not arrived in time. The two explosions were diminished by distance but were loud enough to scare him. He now feared a more wizardly attack. When a young sergeant nearby shouted and pointed toward the nick in the dyke where the cwm path traced a treacherous route, and at the sudden rush of the enemy coming onto that path, he resigned himself to their eventual defeat. It was by chance that he caught a glint of red above the dyke and yet, in that lone flicker understanding came flooding through him like a healing balm. He could hold the bile within, he could keep anger in check but he couldn't restrain his shout of relief and joy.

'See! See there, over on the dyke,' he yelled, 'Can't you see him? That red. That's Cookson's boy! That's Seth Cookson or I'm the wizard's monkey!'

His men weren't so sure, only a few of them had seen the sword that Seth carried, but, almost as if to reassure them, it wasn't long before every trumpet on Greteth's black walls was blowing a brave fanfare of a tune, a stirring song to get the blood pulsing: they were blowing *The Conqueror*, a song of victory!

THE FAREWELL

Temor's men had wanted the *Farewell* blown for their Lord and said so in no uncertain terms as they carried him bloody from the field. They were incensed by Jaspar's refusal but he wouldn't be swayed.

'I will not allow it for Anparas' sake,' he told them, 'They'll think we have lost.' His argument failed to impress. These soldiers had no good opinion of Jaspar to start with and now that their grief ruled them they did not and would not understand. When they spoke of dishonour Jaspar grew angry and an ugly scene would have developed if Tregar hadn't stepped in. It was a delicate situation. From now until they all returned to Ayer it was likely that Jaspar would take command of Shaf's army. Beginning with bad feeling was not a good idea. Clearly, Jaspar was in the right. *The Farewell* would give the wrong message, but Tregar had an alternative for them that seemed so obvious he was surprised Sands hadn't thought of it.

'He has conquered against the odds,' he told them. 'We *all* count him a great man, a great leader, a great warrior. We'll honour him best if we keep our farewells in our hearts and shout about his victory. Blow *The Conqueror!*'

Tregar's true opinion he kept to himself but the suggestion was met with favour on both sides and so the trumpets sang out in Temor's praise, and gave hope to those toiling below. The circumstance would not allow for ceremony, even his most loyal supporters would agree to that, but Jaspar detailed a small company to clean the Lord's wounds and to dress him ready for the long sleep. And so as the battle raged on they laid Shaf, the Lord Temor, in the castle crypt with all honour. It was not the most noble resting place nor was it the least.

Up in the Hall Tregar was relieved to find Xandra still alive and uninjured. It was perhaps a cynical viewpoint but Tregar was certain that the safety of the Heir was crucial if King Mador was to be of any use in this war. They needed to keep her safe at all costs. The Lord Sands had called a meeting of all his commanders and Tregar supposed she was there as a matter of courtesy. They were all gathered around a map table over by the great fireplace. Though the fire was not lit, there was plenty of fire in the room. Xandra and Jaspar were going at it tooth and nail.

'We've got to keep them rocking,' she exclaimed with ferocious delight in her voice, 'Got to press them until they give! Get them on the run. That's what Shaf would have done and he was a General *worth* his ribbon.'

'Meaning I'm not?' Jaspar, fresh from his dispute with Temor's men, was in no mood to take anything. 'Let me remind you that it's Shaf they're wrapping down in the crypt right now. And even if we did play *The Conqueror* for him, it's very obvious to me that his victory belongs to others yet walking.'

'How dare you! You're nothing but an old woman. Don't risk this, don't try that. You're scared of shadows. Don't you dare talk about the Lord Temor. You malign him to disguise your own weakness. Shaf was a hero!'

Tregar realized he'd already had enough of all this.

'*With respect*' he yelled at the pair of them, 'This is not the time for stupet arguments! I'm surprised at ye, Jaspar.'

'But you're not surprised at her, are you.'

Tregar thought about that for a few seconds.

'Well, no I'm not.'

Xandra looked as though she might burst for a moment or two but then she subsided into something that sounded almost like a chuckle.

'Thought you might fold that time, Tregar,' she teased.

'The day I won't stand up to you, little Xan, is the day I pack it all in.'

'Good. Let's hope that's a day far off. So, was that explosion all your own work?'

'Let's say I provided the spark. Others did the hard work. And Shaf amongst them. We fight this fight together, we have all a part to play.'

'Just what I was telling Jaspar. That's why I'll be leading

another sortie—'

'You'll… what?'

'We've got to get out there now before they hem us in again. Last time it was different—'

'*Last time?* Good Gods, Jaspar, ye haven't been letting her fight?'

'*Letting* her?'

'*Letting* me?'

This time she was furious. 'I am not a teenager still, Tregar, I'm twenty-nine years old, though you never seem to realize it. What did you expect me to do? We've been fighting for our lives you know. Wouldn't it have been just fine and dandy if Mador's Heir had sat on her backside and done nothing! Do you want me kept hid like some pretty, precious girl? How fine, how noble; a splendid tale for my children.'

'Well that's just the point isn't it, Xandra: I want ye to survive long enough to *have* some children. What your father would… Whit the divilment's that?'

It seemed that the stones beneath their feet quivered, swords propped against a wall clattered to the floor. Below, and they stood in a chamber directly two floors above the Francon Gate, a powerful, measured thumping sound set in. They could feel it through their feet; they'd soon have headaches. The respite gained by the victory in the cwm was over and Tregar was let off the hook.

'Rams,' explained Selby, 'Sounds like they've brought that big one in at last. Damn great, ugly-looking iron thing. It'll have that gate down if we're not quick. You ready for some more fireworks, Tregar?'

'I'm sure we can manage something suitable. Let's get the oil fired.'

'Oil?'

'Yeees, Jaspar, oil. Black, sticky stuff; use it in lanterns. Oh don't say it.'

Jaspar looked sick and Selby swore.

'We've used it all,' Xandra said. 'One of the reasons I wanted to get out of the gates.'

'You said all together,' Jasper explained, 'so I used all we had left.'

'Fine, just fine! How do ye suppose I can make fireworks without something to burn? Eh? I'm just a simple, idiot wizard, you know, not a bladdie *god*!'

'I thought the oil was just for effect.'

'Great Spurl's tits, Selby. Do ye think I've time to worry about effect when I'm up to my balls in blood? And ye can stop that grinning, Xandra. This is hardly the time for humour.'

'There's plenty of peat,' Jaspar offered cautiously.

'Whit can I do with bladdie peat? Clod it at them?' Exasperated, he turned away and found himself facing the mantlepiece. Almost growling in frustration Tregar thumped the stone in time with the thumping on the gates. It was satisfying somehow to react so badly. And when he realized that fact, he stopped both the growling and the thumping. Nobody dared speak. After a tense moment he turned back to face them rubbing his knuckles and said: 'I'm sorry. Sorry about that. A wee bit disappointed, ye know how it is. Peat now, ahem. Well peat would work, probably. If we could figure some way of throwing it over the walls. Though I doubt it'd spread the same, whatever I do to it. I think it'll take too long to sort out, far too long.'

Jaspar looked a little sheepish. 'Well let's forget the peat. Stupid idea. But we have to do something quick. My people have more or less run out of everything and that gate'll not hold much longer.'

'Never mind the gate. That hammering's got te stop before my brain rattles loose. Now what's occurring?'

Distracting them from their problems for a few seconds, there was a commotion along the hallway. They all looked to see what was happening. Soldiers from Temor's army were trying to push past the guards. Tregar was surprised to find himself with something to grin at after all: he had recognized a face.

'Just the man. Jaspar, Your highness, Commander Selby, meet Seth Cookson. He's the young man who won quarter of our battle all by himself.'

The risk of opening the gates was more than made up for by the vigour of Seth's attack. He led five hundred foot into the ram carriers and the ladder men, and the suddenness of the attack pushed the enemy back several hundred yards. Then on came the cavalry with Xandra at the head, despite Tregar's protests, and the thrust won them quarter of the high meadow. And there they stopped. Jaspar wanted to consolidate his gains, wanted to make sure that there were no surprises. To that end he set the cavalry to cutting up any of the enemy still walking in their part of the field and the foot soldiers to even more gruesome work.

It couldn't last of course. After thirty minutes or so of this less than glorious task, Xandra, with Seth at her stirrup, became bored and impatient. The Heir peered to the fore rather than the rear. The ranks of the enemy, she determined, seemed fearful. Wherever Seth had come they'd fallen back almost in a panic. Scared by his great skill perhaps; they'd certainly learned to respect that sword of his. Retreating they'd gathered witless and dithering in the last third of the field apparently unable to initiate any sort of reply to the Partian advance. Xandra spoke a few well chosen words to Seth and to the commanders in his group, all exclusively Temorians. Just as exhilarated as she was by the charge, just as annoyed by the delay, they had revenge in their hearts and were more than ready to get on with the next move.

She looked around to see that Jaspar was ordering his own battle group into a sensible defensive array some way back towards the castle. She laughed.

'Old woman,' she called. 'Let's show you how it's supposed to be done.'

Jaspar obviously heard her call and raised his head, but couldn't make out what she'd said. He rode a few yards towards her looking puzzled. Xandra grinned and called out again:

'See if you can keep up! Right lads! For Temor, for Sands, for Pars! Let's break them!'

And with that she went, the cavalry too fast and the foot struggling to catch up. Selby over on Xandra's left must have presumed that the attack had been ordered by Jaspar. He shouted up his hundred and led them into the fray at a tremendous pace oblivious to Jaspar raging and swearing and shouting at them:

'Not there, not there! Remember the map.'

They couldn't hear him. Selby had come too late to the briefing anyway, and Xandra hadn't been paying attention, and so a large part of Sands' cavalry, and half of the Temor foot went bowling along, heedless of their peril, into a huge morass.

Because of the angle of his approach, Selby's horse were first to reach the enemy lines with the commander running at the head of his command. He dealt savagely with the creatures he ploughed through and in numbers they fell back before him. But it was all deceit. Within moments his mount floundered into a bog, his command piled in after, and their fate was sealed. Trap sprung, hundreds of the pale warriors returned, seeming somehow native to such an environment, and very carefully they began their awful work. The javelins flew and when those had done enough damage they waded in to finish their task with blades. As Xandra, faring better on more solid ground, considered the chances of rescue, Commander Selby was encircled by ten axe wielders. He understood their intent but could do nothing to escape. Selby screamed and screamed as, stroke by bloody stroke, they took off his legs and arms and only stopped when they'd hacked off his head. This commander of the living would not be rising again from the mire, they made sure of that. Abandoned to death, his men themselves either dead or hideously dying, Eduard Selby found no better grave.

The next hour was desperate. Jaspar led the charge himself in the attempt to get Xandra out of the action but once again it was only the energy and threat of Seth Cookson that gave them their chance. This was the most wasteful hour of Sands' battle. Hundreds were slaughtered, hundreds more were wounded, but eventually, with that great bloody sword still guarding their backs, Jaspar dragged them back platoon by platoon into the safe shadow of the castle, and there he found the space to count his losses.

Tregar had kept thirty of Jaspar's people with him and had them transferring the huge pile of peat turves out on to the narrow gorge of the road east. It was hard labour; Tregar took off his jacket and mucked in with the rest. He noticed that the men, much more than the women, were discontented with their ignominious role. Typically they wanted to be out there among the blood and guts of the fight. Men were ever perverse creatures.

'What are we doing here anyway?' one of them demanded loudly so that the wizard could hear. He threw down the stack of turves he carried with contempt. 'If we're meant to be building some sort of wall, there isn't enough of the stuff; and even if there was, it wouldn't be much to hide behind.'

Tregar could only smile grimly. Sword work would have been more to his own taste but this had to be done.

'Ye must realize' he said when they had a few yards to themselves, 'we cannot prevail today. I don't believe it, anyway. But with the gods' favour, we might just survive. That's what this is for. Once we're throught it, and the gap closed, this'll become a wall of fire.'

A biased observer might have seen enough evidence to say the honours were even, that the battle was stalemate. Incredibly, the numbers on each side were now not so very different after Tregar's fireworks and the relentless attacks led, on the one front by Xandra and Jaspar for Sands, and on the other by Honry and Senca for Anparas. The enemy held the central ground but it was effectively surrounded. Jaspar still had a cavalry to speak of, even if it was rendered ineffective by the marshy ground. They still had Tregar and the chance that he might discover some new weapon they could use; and they still had the farmer's boy and the fear he seemed to generate.

An observer might even be tempted to say that Pars had the upper hand. Unfortunately there was one factor in this conflict which inevitably upset the scales. While the Partians were dead on their feet with weariness, the 'walking dead' they fought seemed tireless and only *died* after extreme duress: duress that became harder and harder to apply.

To Lomal it seemed that the enemy, sitting unconcerned in the centre of the valley or guarding the path from meadow to valley floor, were inviting attack. Well, why shouldn't they? The earlier desire and rush for victory had been replaced, he presumed, by the quiet knowledge that victory was assured. Lord Anparas knew that the time had come to consider retreat. They had done all they could: the enemy was much reduced. If the two Partian forces took opposite routes from the valley he thought it unlikely that the enemy would pursue both or either.

To that end he turned his gaze upon the Western road, the road that had brought them to this place. Tired, at first his eyes couldn't focus properly, and then when they did he thought he was mistaken. He turned to his aide.

'Stubson, look out there. Where we came. What do you see?'

'Yes, my lord.' His eyes traced the road out to the end of the Francon. 'Is it… is it reinforcement? Jemenser, perhaps?'

'I think not, Stubson.'

'Then it is our death. The tracker was right.'

It wasn't a huge force: he guessed at two thousand. But two thousand were as good as ten in the circumstance. Lomal realized he was trapped. The Anparas army was locked in and all they could do now was fight to the finish. How much of all this had gone according to some wretched plan? He understood the arrogance of the army in the valley. He began to realize why the siege of Greteth had lasted so long: it had been a trap from the start. Instead of destroying the House of Sands and marching on to meet whatever Pars could stand against them, they had enticed three eighths of Pars' standing army into one confined place with the simple intention of destroying it. The anger took him at last.

'Death for us in the valley, Stubson, but not for everyone! I'll not have it! Find me eight horses. Quickly man! Four trumpeters and three guards to give them a chance. If the cwm is clear Jaspar can escape, but he must go now.' And then he stopped, and he sighed. 'And perhaps, just perhaps, some of our own may find a way too.'

Stubson was quick to his task. 'I've sent Sergeant Colham,

my lord. They'll be here soon. Ah... Lomal?'

'Yes, Charles?'

'You asked for *three* guards and four heralds.'

'I did. I'll go with them. Let me say goodbye now, before they come. You know I've counted you as my friend these many years? I want to thank you for putting up with me so long.'

'Never mind that, Lomal. Friends don't have to say thanks and sorry – not at a time like this. I never thought... It's a bad way for a friendship to end.'

'There are worse.'

'Yes. Yes there are. You don't expect to get through to Jaspar then?'

'Hardly. Those devils are not that lax. But we must get close enough to blow the retreat so they can hear it.'

'Then I'll come with you. As well die there as here, my lord.'

They didn't embrace, it was never Lomal's way. It *was* his way to be fair. He made sure each of the seven with him understood the situation, understood they would almost certainly die. Lomal wanted none to go unwilling: they did not; he expected none to back out: nor did they.

They rode the southern wall of the valley as far as they could but shortly came to a stream too rocky and deep to cross. Pushed down so quickly onto the edge of the conflict, it seemed as if the valley walls themselves were against them. The delay set Lomal cursing, his rage no longer held in check. They plunged through groups of the enemy with such reckless speed that they were through before weapons could be aimed. Inevitably, however, their progress was observed and their charge became a desperate scramble to twist and turn their way. Lomal and the three guards each rode just ahead of their chosen partner, and now each pair took a different route. After they had parted so Lomal never saw the others again.

They were more than half-way to the eastern front of the battle before Lomal screamed back to the herald with him:

'Blow it now! Blow till your lungs burst, man. Blow!'

Looking over his shoulder Lomal saw the brave man cast aside his sword and raise the instrument to his lips. And Lomal saw the black blade that caught him in the midriff as he galloped through. The trumpet spat away and he was hurled backwards over his saddle, feet still caught in the stirrups.

'No!' Lomal screamed and 'No!' again as he looked away. He caught the full force of the javelin in his face.

Two hundred yards away another soldier was blowing the retreat: blowing madly, blowing wildly, dodging blows, ducking behind his comrade, his protector, one Charles Stubson, who fought and cried and fought some more. They had lost their horses and soon they would lose their lives.

Jaspar understood at once. He had returned to the walls of Greteth to see how the battle progressed and was searching for some chance, some advantage that might turn things in their favour. It was only a blur in the distance but from that trumpet call he knew what was coming. With a heart cramped by the grief of the situation, he added his own trumpets to that sad, desperate voice. Below, he could see Xandra halt at the sound. It was not an order to please her, but one even she would obey. Up on the walls questioning faces turned to him but he was looking out over the Francon. He imagined he could see that lonely trumpeter and imagined that he heard the dying note.

The retreat was close fought at first but once Jaspar's army was within the castle or in the cwm the enemy seemed to lose interest. Jaspar presumed it was a matter of priorities.

Within a half-hour the retreat was complete. The Francon gate was closed once more and barricaded. The gap in Tregar's wall beckoned but the army of Sands and Temor did not leave immediately. Jaspar had a duty to perform, the saddest duty of his life.

He ordered a silence. The fifteen hundred survivors of the battle stood to attention, hands clenched, chins somehow set. They listened, with the tears blinding them, to the horrible sound of defeat: the brave shouts, the clash of arms, the screams of agony, screams of despair.

And then Jaspar let the trumpets blow one last time over the weary walls of Greteth, over the Francon Deep. They blew the lament at last, the honour of honours.

Farewell, comrade, in whatever life you go to;
Farewell, your deeds live after you.
Farewell.

The peat wall burned, would burn for more than a day because of Tregar's magic. The flames stood in bright relief against a darkening sky. Over in the Francon no eyes picked out the red glow of it, no mind wondered what it might mean. Already Udsal had found his death day while Dom Honry struggled on over the ruined body of Marshall Callin; and forgotten, left behind by the storm of bloody war, the cold, cold corpse that was Lomal, the Lord Anparas, was trampled into the mud by cold, cold, heedless warriors from another land and time.

EPILOGUE

AUDIENCE

Anders Belori, Mador's number three door-ward, was not in the best of moods. In fact he rarely was. In a way it came with the job: door-wards were meant to be solid, unflappable, adamant and judiciously grumpy. The King most certainly did not want people thinking the Presence an open invitation for them to come along and bother him. This was not Astoril where by all accounts King Sirl kept his door open to anyone. Such freedom of access would not be encouraged here. No appointment meant no entrance.

A skirl of laughter from the duty guard made him frown but he didn't say anything. The past few weeks had been, well, problematic, and it was actually something of a relief to see them relaxed enough to stand easy whenever they were not needed.

Anders double-checked the doors. In the regular way of things he wouldn't have needed to lock them at all, but for some reason today the message had come down that the King wanted extra security. And that was partly what had niggled him. It was almost as if the King didn't trust them to do the job properly. In all his years as number three door-ward Anders had never once let anyone get past who shouldn't. Abram, the Chamberlain, knew that, but still along he comes with his instructions, given directly to the guards without ever a nod in his direction, with no respect for the hierarchy of command, without even having the decency to speak to him first.

Anders gave the door handles a rigorous tug but they didn't move a quarter of an inch. Door locked and secure. And now he stepped over to the left-hand side of the doors and his high desk. With an air of ceremony he inked his pen and carefully began to fill in the names of Mador's current visitors.

Isolde Robarn, The Lyndons, Makerfield.

Normally he would have made the visitors wait until the names had been properly entered before letting them through, but, well, it was not an easy task trying to gainsay young Miss

Robarn when her dander was up. Something of a favourite that one.

Gerald Robarn, The Lyndons, Makerfield.

Of course they were out of order. First the Miss all in a bother, insisting she was due as arranged – and yes she had been, before the schedule was changed. The fact was, on the rosta Abram had given him, what with crossings out and the scribblings-in, it wasn't at all clear. Well, not clear enough and if the chamberlain had to apologize about the mix-up to the king, well, Anders was not going to be too upset. Then the *father* turns up two minutes later, acting as though the world was about to end, and demands to be let in *'or there'll be trouble!'* Trouble indeed, what nonsense.

Mark Jeffers, Secretary to Gerald Robarn, The Lyn—

What was that? The guards heard it too. A crashing noise, screaming…

Anders swore as he struggled with the key in the lock. The guards had their swords out.

'C'mon boss, get it open!'

The screams, male and female, continued as they pushed through the doors. There was the sound of metal clattering on the stone floor. As they ran towards the throne the conflict came into view. Anders tried hard to understand what he saw.

On the floor two people lay sprawled in a tangle, blood blooming on the white marble beside them; above them two other figures fought hand to hand. There was metal in there, and… claws, but the figures twisted so quickly it was hard to see what belonged where. But…

As one, Anders and the three guardsmen stopped in their tracks, completely at a loss, for what could they do? The man they were there to protect, King Mador of Pars, was fighting ferociously, tooth and nail, fighting to the death… with himself!

For more information on Wilf Jones'

<u>A SONG OF AGES</u>

The Best of Men
The Twist Inside
The Last Exile

please visit:

www.wilfkelleherjones.co.uk